A FORTRESS OF
GREY ICE

By *J.V. Jones*

A FORTRESS OF GREY ICE

Book Two of Sword of Shadows

J.V. Jones

www.orbitbooks.co.uk

An *Orbit* Book

First published in Great Britain by Orbit 2002
This edition published by Orbit 2002
Reprinted 2003

A CIP catalogue record for this book is available from the
British Library.

ISBN 1 85723 996 2

Typeset by Palimpsest Book Production Limited,
Polmont, Stirlingshire
Printed in Great Britain by
Clays Ltd, St Ives plc

Orbit
An imprint of
Time Warner Books UK
Brettenham House
Lancaster Place
London WC2E 7EN

For Russ

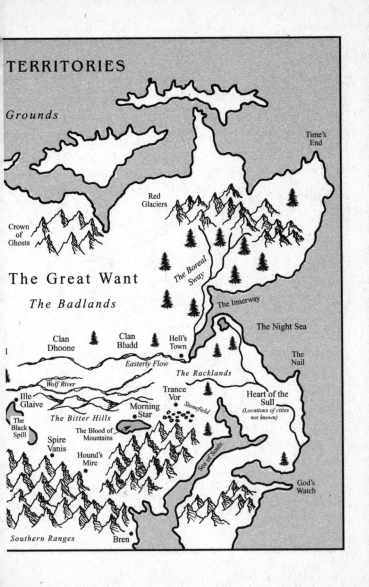

TERRITORIES

Grounds

Time's
End

Red
Glaciers

Crown
of
Ghosts

The Great Want

The Badlands

The Boreal Sway

The Innerway

The Night Sea

Clan
Dhoone

Clan
Bludd

Hell's
Town

The Nail

Easterly Flow

The Racklands

Wolf River

Ille
Glaive

Trance
Vor

Stonefield

Heart of the
Sull
(Locations of cities
not known)

The
Black
Spill

The Bitter Hills

Morning
Star

Spire
Vanis

The Blood of
Mountains

Hound's
Mire

Sea of Souls

God's
Watch

Southern Ranges

Bren

CONTENTS

SWORD OF SHADOWS:

The Story So Far

Raif Sevrance of Clan Blackhail was ravenborn, chosen to wear the raven lore by Blackhail's clan guide. One morning, while he and his older brother Drey were away from the clan's winter camp, shooting ice hares, their father Tem and their Chief Dagro were slain by agents of the surlord Penthero Iss. Dagro's son Mace Blackhail was also present, but survived and went on to claim the chiefship of Clan Blackhail. From the very beginning, Raif questioned Mace's story of how he escaped the raiders, accusing the new chief of having foreknowledge of the attack. A few weeks later, during a savage ambush on the Bluddroad where Mace ordered the slaying of innocent women and children, Raif realized he had no choice but to leave his clan. Mace had turned Clan Blackhail into something Raif no longer recognized.

When Angus Lok, Raif's uncle and a member of the mysterious and secretive Phage, offered to take Raif with him on a journey to Spire Vanis, Raif accepted with a heavy heart. On the way they visited Duff's Stovehouse, where Raif admitted being present on the Bluddroad the day women and children from Clan Bludd were murdered in cold blood. A fight broke out between Blackhail and Bludd, and Raif slew three Bluddsmen defending the actions of his clan. Yet no one ever thanked him for it. By speaking out in his clan's defence, Raif had not only confirmed the details of the massacre but also admitted to being part of it. There was no going back for him now.

When Raif and Angus arrived at the little-used southern gate of Spire Vanis, they spotted a girl being chased down by red cloaks. For reasons Angus Lok refused to divulge, he immediately set about saving the girl. Raif saw no choice but to aid his uncle, and when the gate was dropped, trapping Angus inside the city, Raif shot his uncle's attackers through the grille.

Raif heart-killed four men that day, his arrows expertly sighted on their hearts. Ever since the morning his father died, Raif had realized he had a talent for shooting game. And now, following the events at Duff's and at Spire Vanis's southern gate, he learned that same talent extended to the shooting of men. For Raif it was as much a burden as it was a gift, this ability to kill so surely, and he became increasingly uncertain how to live with it.

The girl he and Angus had saved was Ash March, a foundling fostered by the surlord Penthero Iss. Ash had run away from Mask Fortress, fearing that her foster-father wanted to use her in ways she barely understood. Some kind of power was awakening within her – a darkness that demanded release – and she had begun to suspect that this was the only reason Iss had fostered her. He never called her daughter without using the word *almost* first.

Angus, Raif and Ash headed north toward Ille Glaive, pursued by the surlord's men. By the time they arrived at the city, Ash's health had begun to deteriorate. The darkness inside her had grown more powerful, causing her to lapse into unconsciousness. Heritas Cant, a toll collector in Ille Glaive and Angus Lok's contact in the Phage, explained the nature of Ash's illness. She was being overtaken by forces of evil that had been sealed away for a thousand years. Ash March was the Reach, born to release the Unmade from their dark, hellish prison known as the Blind. Heritas Cant warded Ash against the darkness, but warned that he could only do so much and that she must not overreach herself. The dread beasts of the Blind and the Endlords that ruled them craved freedom, and Ash March was their sole means to secure it. Ash must release her power or die, and the only way she could do this, without causing a break in the Blindwall, was to find the Cavern of Black Ice and release her power there.

Sobered, Ash, Raif and Angus travelled east to Angus Lok's farm, where Ash met Angus's wife Darra and their three daughters. Darra Lok could not hide her disquiet at seeing Ash, and Ash was left wondering why her presence upset Angus's wife so deeply.

On the journey north from Angus's farm, the small party of three was captured by Cluff Drybannock, the Dog Lord's right-hand man. The Dog Lord was chief of Clan Bludd, and it was his grandchildren and daughters-in-law who had been slain by Blackhail forces on the Bluddroad. The Dog Lord had seven sons and loved none of them, but he loved his grandchildren with all his heart. Upon learning that Raif Sevrance was present that day on the Bluddroad, the Dog Lord had become obsessed with capturing Raif – someone must pay for the Dog Lord's losses. Raif was taken to the Ganmiddich Tower and tortured. When he came within a hair's breadth of losing his life, Death refused to take him. *Kill an army for me, Raif Sevrance* she had whispered, *any less and I just might call you back*.

The Dog Lord had sought to make himself Lord of the Clans. With Penthero Iss's aid he had taken the Dhoonehouse, and had then gone on to annex Ganmiddich and Withy. He was a man who had always prided himself in his jaw, and the methods he'd employed for capturing the Dhoonehouse had begun to worry him. There was no jaw in taking a roundhouse by underhand dealings and foul magic, and he had come to regret his actions. When Ash March fell into his hands, he saw a way of ending his association with Penthero Iss by sending the girl back to her foster-father: payment in full for Iss's aid with the taking of the Dhoonehouse. So the Dog Lord released the girl into the custody of two of Penthero Iss's men; Marafice Eye, Protector General of Spire Vanis, and Sarga Veys, magic-user.

By this time the wards set by Heritas Cant had grown thin, and when Marafice Eye and his men attempted to rape Ash March in the Bitter Hills, Ash lost control and lashed out with her power. Too late she realized her mistake and tried to pull the power back. But the damage had already been done; a hairline crack had opened in the Blindwall.

As a weary and frightened Ash March headed west from the Bitter Hills, the magic-user Sarga Veys killed the man who he believed to be his only fellow survivor. Veys had glimpsed the darkness called forth by Ash, and immediately recognized it was his destiny to serve it. Leaving his old life behind, Sarga Veys went in search of a dark and glorious future.

Back at the Ganmiddich Tower, Raif awaited his execution at the hands of the Dog Lord. The night before he was due to die, Ganmiddich was attacked by Blackhail. The Dog Lord and his forces were forced to flee north to the Dhoonehouse, taking the prisoner Angus Lok with them. Raif was saved by his brother Drey. When Raif had taken his yearman's oath at Blackhail, it was Drey who had acted as Raif's second; Drey who kept Raif's swearstone safe until that day. Both brothers knew that Raif could no longer return to his clan – Raif Sevrance had been branded an oathbreaker and a traitor – and Drey let his brother go, wounding himself in the process so that it looked as if Raif had overpowered him. It was a hard parting for the sons of Tem Sevrance: both knew they would never see each other again.

A day later, Raif met up with Ash on the banks of the Wolf, and they headed west toward the Storm Margin and the Cavern of Black Ice.

Blackhail's storming of Ganmiddich had plunged the clanholds into deeper conflict. The three northern giants – Blackhail, Dhoone and Bludd – were now engaged in a messy and unclear war. Bludd vowed vengeance on Blackhail for the slaughter on the Bluddroad; Blackhail blamed Bludd for the murder of its chief; and dispossessed Dhoone desperately needed to retake their roundhouse. The architect of all this unrest was the surlord, Penthero Iss, who had been working to destabilize the clanholds for many months. Iss planned to invade the clanholds, and to this end had offered Marafice Eye a mutually beneficial deal. In return for Marafice Eye raising an army and leading it north to crush the clans, Iss would name Eye as his successor.

Meanwhile, Mace Blackhail was working to consolidate his position as Blackhail's chief. To strengthen his hold on the chiefship, Mace had coerced his father's widow into marrying him by raping her and then claiming the union had been consensual. Raina Blackhail was a proud woman, and rather than admit she had been raped by Mace, she preferred to keep her silence and retain her standing in the clan. Only one other person besides Raina and Mace knew the truth of what had happened that day in the Oldwood. Effie Sevrance, Raif's and Drey's younger sister, had witnessed the rape, and for that reason Mace Blackhail determined he must be rid of her.

Effie Sevrance was bearer of the stone lore: the little chunk of rock she wore around her neck warned her of dangers by moving against her skin. When it went missing one day, she knew to be afraid: without it she felt naked and exposed. A few xvi † J. V. JONES

days later Effie was attacked outside the roundhouse by the lunt-woman Nellie Moss and her son. It was the shankshounds – the dogs belonging to the wealthy clan overlord Orwin Shank – that saved Effie, by breaking free from their kennel and ripping her attackers to shreds. The rescue only served to isolate Effie Sevrance, for now people began whispering that she had enchanted the shankshounds and was a witch. Mace Blackhail, sensing an advantage, let the rumors go unchecked. The next time he moved to rid himself of Effie Sevrance, fewer people would speak up in her defence.

On the journey along the Storm Margin, Ash's condition had grown worse. The bone-chilling cold pierced her and the wards set by Heritas Cant had been blasted away, leaving her vulnerable to the creatures of the Blind. When she lapsed into a coma at the end of a long, freezing day, Raif picked her up in his arms and carried her. Raif had forsaken his clan, his year-man's oath, and his family: Ash March was all he had. When wolves attacked he was forced to set Ash down to defend himself. Although he heart-killed the pack leader and scattered the other wolves, Raif could not save Ash. She had begun to hemorrhage during the attack, and he did not possess the power to help her. Drawing a guide circle in the snow, he had called upon the clan gods.

Raif's cry was heard leagues away by two Sull Far Riders, Ark Veinsplitter and Mal Naysayer. The Far Riders had been called north to a parley with Sadaluk, the Listener of the Ice Trapper Tribe. The Listener could hear things that other men could not, and he knew that a Reach had been born and that the Blindwall was in danger of collapsing. The Far Riders saved Ash's life, and later escorted Ash and Raif onto the ice of the Hollow River, beneath which lay the Cavern of Black Ice.

Ash March discharged her Reach-power in the cavern lined with black, ensorcelled ice. But it was too late. The hairpin crack she'd caused earlier could not be mended, and even as she and Raif left the cavern, someone, somewhere, was working upon the flaw.

Penthero Iss's bound sorcerer, the Nameless One, had made a deal with the Endlords. *Push against the crack*, they had said, *and in return we will give you your name*. And so the Nameless One had pushed and the Blindwall was breached, and the first Unmade rode through.

PROLOGUE

Diamonds and Ice

The diamond pipe was hot and stinking, and when the water hit the walls the rock exploded, spraying the diggers with a cloud of dust and steam. Scurvy Pine swore with venom. Fierce blisters of sweat rose on his forehead and he wiped them away with a greasy rag. "Fires have only been out an hour. What do those bastards think we are? Crabs to be steamed for the pot?"

Crope made no reply. He and Scurvy had been working the pipes together for eight years, and they'd been scalded worse in their times. A lot worse. Besides, speaking took up space for remembering, and Crope had important things to remember today. *"Don't you go forgetting, giant man. You be ready when I give the word."*

Placing the empty bucket down on the blue mud of the pipe floor, Crope watched the rock wall as it continued to crack and pop. The fire set by the free miners heated the rock, making it split and break. Water hauled up from the Drowned Lake cooled the walls so quickly, boulders the size of war carts shattered to dust. "Softening", the free miners called it, making the pipe ready for the diggers' picks. Crope could see nothing soft about it. Mannie Dun had broken his back pickaxing a seam last spring. Crope remembered carrying the old digger away, Mannie's legs jerking against his belly as the free miners called Red Watch and sealed the area off. The sealing wasn't for safety's sake—Crope didn't know much but he knew that. The sealing was to keep the diggers away. Before Mannie's spine had twisted and popped, the tip of his ax had lodged in a rock wall speckled with flecks of red stone. Red Eyes, the miners called them. Red Eyes meant diamonds . . . and diamonds were the business of free men, not slaves.

"Pick to the wall, giant man. Don't go giving me good reason to spread my whip."

Crope knew better than to look at the man who spoke. The guards in the pipe were known as Bull Hands, on account of their oiled and flame-hardened whips. Scurvy said they could take the hands off a man before he even heard the sound of bullhide moving through air. Crope dreamed of that sometimes; of hands not attached to any living man, clutching his neck and face.

Diamond rock split and crumbled to nothing as Crope took his pick to the wall. Water still warm from contact with the heated stone ran through the cracks at his feet. Above, the pipe twisted up and up, its walls gashed by stairs and pathways hewn from the live rock. Tunnels and caves pitted the sides, marking seams long run dry or walls overmined to the point of collapse. The entrances to the older tunnels had been plugged with a makeshift mortar of horsehair and clay, for there were some in the pipe who feared shadow things rising from the depths.

Rope bridges spanned the pipe's breadth, their wooden treads warped by steam, their fibers ticking as the wind moved a thousand feet above. The sky seemed far away, and the sun farther still, and even on a clear day in midwinter, little light found its way into the pipe.

Down below, in the lowest tier of the pipe, where a ring of pitch lamps burned with white-hot flames, the hags were at work with their baskets and claws. *Scratch, scratch, scratch*, as they raked the new-broke ground for the hard clear stone that was valued above gold. The hags were slaves too, but they were old and weak, bent-backed and stiff-fingered, and the Bull Hands did not fear to let them near the lode.

Crope thought he spied Hadda the Crone, in line with the other hags, her black wool cap bobbing up and down as she raked and clawed and sorted. Hadda scared Crope. She had long, sunken breasts shaped like spades that she bared to any digger who looked her way. Scurvy, Bitterbean and the rest looked her way often, but Crope did not like Hadda, and he would not look at her breasts.

When the lash came he was half expecting it. The sting was cold, *cold*, and it took the breath from him like a punch to the gut. The tip of the whip curled around his ear, licking flesh hard with scars. Tears of blood welled in a line around his neck, and he felt their hotness trickle down his shoulders to his back. The salt burn would come later, when the gray crystals of sea-salt that the Bull Hands soaked into their whips worked their way into the wound.

"It's not enough that they whip us," Scurvy always said. "They have to make us burn."

"I can smell you, giant man." The Bull Hand pulled back the whip with practiced slowness, drawing the leather through his half-closed fist. He was a big man, hard-mouthed and fair-skinned, with broken veins in the whites of his eyes and the shineless teeth of a diamond miner. Although Crope had seen him many times, he couldn't remember his name. That was Scurvy's job, the remembering. Scurvy knew the names of every man in Pipe Town; knew what they were called and what they *were*.

The Bull Hand thrust the whip into his belt. "You stink like the slop pots when your mind's not on the wall."

Crope kept his head down and continued to break rock. He was aware of many eyes upon him, of Bitterbean and Iron Toe and Soft Aggie down the line. And of Scurvy Pine beyond them, watching the Bull Hand, yet not seeming to, his eyes so cold and hard they might have been mined in the pipe.

Scurvy's gaze flicked to the chains at Crope's feet. Iron they were, black with tar and dead skin, and they ran from ankle to ankle, from digger to digger, joining every man in the line. "Don't you go forgetting, giant man. You be ready when I give the word."

Crope felt Scurvy's will working upon him, warning him to keep swinging his ax. Eight years ago they'd met, in the tin pits west of Trance Vor. Crope never wanted to go back there again. He hated the low ceilings of the tin caves, the darkness, the stench of bad eggs, and the drip, drip, drip of the walls. Spineless, that was what everyone had called him, before Scurvy had made them stop. Scurvy had picked no fight nor raised a weapon; he had simply told the other tin men how it was going to be. "He carved the eyes out of an ice master who cheated him at dice," Bitterbean had once told Crope. "But that's not the reason they 'prisoned him."

Out of the corner of his eye, Crope thought he saw Scurvy nod minutely to Hadda the Crone.

Time passed. The diggers continued breaking the wall and the hags kept sifting through the dust. Crope's lash wound began to burn with the hot sting of salt. Softly, so softly that he wasn't even sure when the sound began, Hadda the Crone began to sing. It was like no song Crope had ever heard, high and wavering and strange to the ear. It made the hairs around his wound stand upright. Other diggers felt it too. At Crope's side, Soft Aggie's chains rattled as he stamped his feet in the mud.

Bitterbean and the others slowed their strikes, and the sound of breaking rock lessened as Hadda's song began to rise.

If she sang in words Crope did not recognize them, yet fear entered him all the same. High and higher, her song rose, keening and wailing, her voice disappearing for brief moments as she reached pitches that only dogs could hear. Other hags joined in, chanting low where Hadda soared high, rough where she was as clear as glass.

Crope felt a queer coldness steal into the pipe. He watched as the shadow cast by his ax lengthened and darkened, until the shadow seemed more real than the ax. One of the pitch lamps blew out, and then another. And then one of the Bull Hands cracked his whip and shouted, "Stop that fucking wailing, bitch."

Crope risked a glance at Scurvy. *Wait*, his eyes said. *Be ready when I give the word.*

Hadda's song turned shrill. The diamond drilled into her front tooth was the only thing that glinted in the darkening pipe. Crope felt sweat slide along his fingers as he raised his ax for another strike. A memory of a time long ago possessed him, a night roaring with flames. People burning alive; precious stones popping from their jewelry in the heat, smoke curling from their mouths as they screamed. Bad memories, and Crope did not want to think of them. Driving his ax deep into diamond rock, he sent them smashing against the wall.

Two Bull Hands jumped down into the lower tier, where the hags squatted as they sifted dust. A tongue of black leather came down upon a thigh, opening skin stained blue with mud. A woman screamed. A basket full of rubble dropped to the floor, sending stones the size of rat skulls bouncing into the hole at the center of the pipe. "That's where the diamonds come from, that hole," Scurvy had once told Crope. "Leads right down to the center of the earth. And the gods that live there shit them."

Fear quieted the hags. Hadda's song rose alone and defiant, beating against the walls like a sparrow trapped in the pipe. As the Bull Hand moved toward her, the Crone set down her basket, straightened her back and looked into the blackness at the bottom of the pipe.

"*Rath Maer!*" she murmured, and although Crope had no book learning or knowledge of foreign tongues, he felt the words pull on the fluid in his eyes and groin, and he knew she was calling something forth. "*Rath Maer!*"

"*RATH MAER!*"

One by one the pitch lamps blew out. Crope smelled the dark, wet odor of night, caught a glimpse of something rising from the center of the pipe . . . and then Scurvy Pine gave the word.

"*To the wall!*"

Men moved in the shadows with a great rattling of chains. Quickly, and with perfect violence, Scurvy sent the tip of his pickax smashing into the nearest Bull Hand's face. The guard jerked fiercely as he dropped to the floor, his jaw muscles clenching and unclenching as he worked on a scream that would never be heard. Bitterbean moved quickly to finish the job off, the pale flesh on his arms and many chins quivering as he stamped the life from the Bull Hand's lungs.

In the lower tier of the pipe all was chaos. The Bull Hands were lashing the hags, sending up sprays of blood and pipe-water to spatter against the wall. Hadda was still standing, but as Crope looked on, a hard leather edge snapped against her temple, pulling off her cap and revealing her scarred and shaven scalp. A second edge found her robe, and another found her legs, and the Bull Hands stripped her bare, and lashed her sagging flesh.

All around, diggers were attacking Bull Hands and the few free miners who remained in the pipe. Iron Toe had gotten hold of a whip and was forcing the leather butt down a Bull Hand's throat. The tiny cragsman was speaking to the Bull Hand as he choked him, asking him, quite softly, how it felt to eat the whip. Soft Aggie was sitting propped against a wall, blood sheeting down his chest from a lash wound so deep that Crope could see the bones at the back of Aggie's throat. Jesiah Mump was kneeling at his side, his mud-caked fingers sliding in his pipe-brother's blood as he struggled to close the wound. Down the line, Sully Straw was frozen in place, unable to move because of the tension in the chain that connected him to Jesiah Mump.

"Giant man!"

Crope swung his head when he heard Scurvy's call.

A single tooth was embedded in the gore on Scurvy Pine's ax, and he drove it deep into the spine of a free miner as he screamed, "The chains! Break the damn chains!"

Crope felt heat come to his face. *"Don't you go forgetting, giant man. When we start attacking the Bull Hands it's your job to break the chains."*

Putting all his weight behind the drop of his ax, Crope severed the links that connected him to Old Bone. *Half-wit*, the bad voice said. *Can't even remember to break the chains.* His was the only ax crowned with a blade broad enough to chop metal; and his were the only shoulders capable of delivering such a blow. Scurvy had made him practice on the iron staves that bound the water buckets. "Chop, chop, chop," he'd say. "Like you did when you cut the leg-irons from Mannie Dun."

Crope didn't remember cutting any iron the day that Mannie broke his back. He remembered only that Mannie was hurt and his body was twitching and all the Bull Hands cared about was sealing the lode. It was later, when Scurvy pulled him aside and told him that he, Crope, had broken Mannie's chains with his ax, that he realized what he had done. "Say nothing, giant

man," Scurvy had warned. "The Hands are so busy pissing themselves over the Red Eyes that they don't know who did what."

Crope brought his ax down on another chain, splitting the
iron as if it were wood. Mannie was dead now. One of the free
miners had given him some of the black. The black was poison,
Bitterbean said, and the free miner had given it to Mannie as
a mercy, for everyone knew that a digger with a broken back
was as good as dead.

Shaking off his leg-irons, Crope crossed to where Jesiah
Mump was speaking last words to his pipe-brother. Soft Aggie
was already gone—Crope had been around death often enough
to read it on any man's face—but Jesiah spoke to him all the
same, telling him how they'd raft up the Innerway in high
summer and gorge themselves stupid on raw leeks and fried
trout. Crope severed the chains that connected them, though
he did not expect them to pull apart.

He knew what it was to love someone wholly.

"Here, giant man! Cut me free!"

Responding to Bitterbean's voice, the giant digger moved
along the ranks, chopping metal. A blackness lay upon the pipe,
and men fought in the near-darkness, grunting and cursing,
killing in violent spurts, then leaning against the wall to catch
their breath and hack up dust. Crope watched as some diggers
continued to beat the Bull Hands even after they were dead.
He understood little of their need, for dead was dead to him,
yet he made no effort to stay them. Men did what men would
do, and he'd learned long and hard that nothing good ever
came from interference.

*Keep your eyes and hands to yourself, half-wit, for looks start
fights and touches set women to screaming rape.* The old words
could raise the fear in him even now. He was big and he was
dangerous, and so he must make himself small and unassuming in other ways.

He was careful as he stepped around the corpses.

As he raised his ax to break Scurvy Pine's chains, the last glimmers of light faded. The cold deepened, and the air began to move. Crope felt it swelling against his back like icy water. Men ceased fighting. Scurvy rattled his leg and hissed, "Cut the chains," but Crope could no longer see Scurvy and he feared to drop the ax.

A sound rose from the center of the pipe. Crope had heard the cries of many beasts, of lambs torn apart by dogs and mares split open during foaling, yet he'd never heard a call like this: cold and wanting and alive with pain. The urge came upon him to flee, for he had lived long and seen many things, and knew something of the darkness that lived within the night. Not all things that cast man-shadows were men.

One of the hags screamed. A great *whumf* of air shook the pipe, sending the rope bridges creaking and lifting the hair on Crope's scalp. Men began running; he couldn't see them, but he heard the clatter of their chains against the rock.

Scurvy pressed something sharp against Crope's leg. "Cut me free, giant man. I won't be taken alive in this pipe."

Crope heard the urgency in Scurvy's voice. The Bull Hands had ways of killing ringleaders. John Dram had been fed a meal of diamonds—chips and splinters and gray and cloudy stones—and then he'd been thrown alive into the crowd at Frozen Square. They'd torn him apart, Bitterbean said, their hands steaming with blood as they plunged into John Dram's guts.

Crope dropped the ax on Scurvy's chains. The digger grunted as he pulled his ankle free. "You bled me, giant man," he murmured. "Sweet blood, and I'll hold no grudges for it. Take my arm and let's begone from this pipe."

"But—"

"But what? There are others still in chains? Would you stay and free their corpses once they're dead?" A random gleam of light caught Scurvy's pale gray eyes. "Nine of us came from the tin pits, that winter when the Drowned Lake froze. Who's left, giant man? Mannie's gone. Will's gone. All gone. All dead, except you and me."

Crope remembered Will. He knew all the words to the old songs, and could sleep standing up. It was hard to think of him as dead. He said stubbornly, "I'm going to fetch Hadda."

Scurvy seized Crope's arm. "Forget her. She's just a hag. There's nothing left to save."

With gentle firmness, Crope broke free of Scurvy's grip. He didn't like Hadda, but she had sung, the song that brought the darkness. And without darkness they'd still be in chains.

Scurvy cursed with disgust. He went to turn away, but something stopped him. Reaching into his torn and ragged tunic, he muttered, "Let no man say Scurvy Pine doesn't pay his debts. Here. Take this." He held out a small round object. "Show it in any thieves' den north of the mountains and you'll find protection in my name."

Crope's big fingers closed around a metal band: a ring, light and very fine. Not a man's ring, not even a woman's, something made for a child. He looked up to find Scurvy watching him.

"Take care of yourself, giant man. I'll not forget who broke my chains." With that Scurvy was gone, slipping through the darkness and the snarl of panicking men, a shadow amongst the shadows, moving swiftly toward the light.

Crope carefully tucked the ring into the seam of his boot, and then went looking for Hadda the Crone.

It was cold and gloomy in the diamond well, and not one human was moving. The rock was sticky underfoot and the smell of blood rose from it. Crope went unchallenged as he walked amongst the bodies. It was hard to tell the hags apart. All their hair had been shaved so they'd have one less place to conceal stones. He wouldn't have recognized Hadda if it hadn't been for the diamond in her tooth. Bitterbean said the pipe lord himself had given it to her the day she found a stone as big as a wren.

Hadda was barely breathing, but he picked her up all the same. There were wounds across her legs and belly, lash marks that ran straight and deep. She was so light it was like carrying twigs for the fire, and he was overcome with a sense of shame. Everyone who helped him ended up hurt. *You're good for nothing, you misshapen monster. Should have been drowned at birth.*

Crope shook the bad voice away. Something dark and full of shadow was moving at the corner of his vision, and he knew it was time to leave. He heard the blistering crackle of charged air, the swift *snick* of something with an edge severing limbs. And screams: screams of diggers he knew. It was hard to hear them, and harder still to turn his back. But he had Hadda, and his chains were gone, and it was time to find the man who owned his soul.

Sixteen years without his lord was too long.

Bearing the dying woman up through the pipe, Crope began to plan his search.

The ice on the lake creaked and rumbled as it cooled, its surface growing colder and drier as the quarter-moon passed overhead. There was no wind, yet the ancient hemlocks surrounding the lake moved, their limbs rising and falling in air that was perfectly still. Meeda Longwalker had made camp on a plate of shore-fast ice, three feet thick and hard as iron. It was the coldest night she could remember, so cold the shale oil in her lamp had frozen to thick yellow grease and she had been forced to burn a candle for light. Smoke rising from the candle's flame cooled so quickly it floated back down to the ice, and Meeda had to keep pushing it away with her gloved and mitted hands so it wouldn't cumulate and kill the light.

She should have returned to the Heart. It wasn't a night to be out alone on the ice, yet she had something in her that had always rebelled against good sense. She was a Heartborn Daughter of the Sull, mother to He Who Leads, and it seemed to her that any wisdom she had a claim to had come on nights such as this.

Besides, she had her dogs; they would warn her of any danger. Warn, but not protect. Meeda Longwalker was no fool. She wasn't like some trappers who drank themselves stupid on green elk milk turned sour and then passed out around their dark-fires, sure in the knowledge that their dogs would save them if . . .

If what? Meeda pulled her lynx cloak closer, wishing for a moment she had bare hands so she could feel the sweet soft-ness of the fur beneath her fingers. Almost it was like touching a living thing, and Meeda Longwalker knew some men who claimed it was better. Trappers knew little of women and a lot about whores, and a scraped and combed lynx fur had a warmth to it that couldn't be bought in Hell's Town for any amount of gold.

As she watched the fur ripple beneath her horsehair mitts a cry sounded in the forest beyond the ice. Low and hollow, like the wind moving down a well shaft, it made the skin on Meeda's shoulders pucker and shrink. The flame above the candle dimmed from yellow to red, and then twitched upon its wick as the sound passed into the ice. Meeda felt its vibrations in her old and rotted bones . . . and knew then that the creature who made it was no living thing.

"*Raaks!*" she called. Dogs!

A hand shot onto the ice to feel for her stick as she waited for her terriers to heel. Damn dogs. She should never have let them go after that elk cow. Yet they had smelled age and weak-ness and the festering of a wolf-made wound, and such scents were irresistible to any animal trained to hunt. It was either let them go or drive a stake into the ice and leash them to it. And much though Meeda Longwalker hated to admit it, her hands had trouble forming the shape needed to hold a hammer this night.

As her fingers groped for her stick a new sound rose from the edge of the ice. Fifty years she had coursed these headlands, fifty years of setting traps, snapping necks and peeling skin, and not a day without a dog at her heels. She had heard her terriers moan and yelp in childbirth and pain, heard them scrap amongst themselves over the weeping remains of a skinned fox. Yet never until now had she heard them scream.

High it was, high and terrible and so close to human that it might have been children instead. Meeda's fist closed around the three feet of icewood that had been her walking stick for a hundred seasons. The wood was pale as milk, and so smooth it ran with moonlight like live steel. Icewood, from the heart of the tree; no earthly cold could warp it, and none but master Sull craftsmen could shape it to their will. It dulled saws, people said. Made bows so powerful that they defied air and wind. Only the Sull King and his *mordreth*, the twelve sworn men who guarded him and were known as the Walking Dead, were allowed to carry bows of its making. A single tree had to grow for a thousand years and its timber aged for fifty more before a master bowyer would dare cut a stave from the *dann*, the latewood that was laid down in the sacred months of summer and late spring.

Meeda hefted the stick across her chest, taking comfort from its familiar weight and hand. It was a hard life she had lived and chosen, and she had not reached such an age by being easily cowed. The night was alive with noises, with black lynx and horned owls, moon snakes and old ghosts, and she had long since realized that none of them liked the smell of living men. Rising to her feet, she called once more to her dogs.

As she waited for them to respond, something crunched softly on the frozen snow beyond the shoreline. Water swelled beneath the ice. The dogs fell silent one by one.

Meeda bit off her outer mitts, and spat them onto the ice. The sky was dark, darker than it ought to be when quarter of the moon hung there for all to see. There were no stars, or if there were they shone black like volcanic glass. Moon and night sky. No Sull prayer was complete without those words, and Meeda found herself mouthing them as she stepped toward the shore.

Damn her eyes! Why couldn't she *see* anything? Her hard old corneas were slow to focus in the biting air, and she felt the anger come to her as quick as if it had been hiding beneath her fear all along. She hated her old woman's body with its humps and slack pouches and dry bloodless bones. Some nights she dreamed Thay Blackdragon, the Night King, came to her, offering youth in return for her soul. Sometimes she dreamed she said *yes*.

Frost smoke steamed above the ice margin, switching colors from blue to gray. Meeda felt its coldness in her mouth, stinging her gums and numbing her tongue until it felt like a piece of meat against her teeth. Underfoot the ice was black and transparent, swept clean of snow by northern winds. It ticked as Meeda's weight came down upon it. As she stepped beyond the candle's light, something red broke through the trees, something broken and limping and not *right*. Meeda braced her stick with both hands, and then recognized the bloody shape of one of her dogs. Marrow. Its rear left leg was gone, and the skin on its rump and belly had been torn away, revealing glistening muscle and coils of gut.

Meeda feared to call to it. She knew the look of wolf- and lynx-made wounds. She knew what wolverines could do to creatures twice their size and what a coven of moon snakes was capable of when they hadn't fed in a week. Yet this didn't smell like wolf or cat or snake. This smelled like night.

The dog had caught its mistress's scent, and it dragged its lower torso across the ice to reach her, trailing blood and viscera from its great black wound. Meeda barely breathed as she waited for the creature to heel. She did not think, knew better than to think, just raised her stick to the height she needed, waited to feel the push of the dog's snout against her leg, then drove the butt through its heart.

"Good dog," she said quietly, as she pulled the stick free of its ribs.

Blood and bits of bone were already freezing to the wood by the time she turned to face the shore. "Come for me, shadows," she said, "for I stand ready in the light of the moon." The words were old and she did not know where they came from, yet they were Sull words and she felt something fill her as she spoke them. She thought at first it was courage, for her heart quickened and her grip tightened and something hard and excited came alive in her chest.

Then the ice around the shore began to crack. White splinters shot up from the surface in a footstep pattern toward where she stood. *Crack! Crack! Crack!* The air rippled like water, and suddenly it was cold enough to turn her breath to grains of ice. Meeda's hands ached as she adjusted her grip on her stick. Her eyes burned as she tried to *see*. Something glinted. Moonlight caught an edge and ran along its length. A man-shape shimmered into existence, dark and silvered, like no man at all. Its eyes were two holes that held no soul. Its hand gripped a blade that drank the light. Meeda watched as the cutting edge came up and up, saw how moonlight outlined the thing's arm and mailed fist, yet found no purchase in the black and voided steel. It was like looking at a distilled piece of night.

Meeda knew then that what she felt wasn't courage. The fear was in her, twisting her bowels, speaking to her in a voice that sounded like her own, warning her to run for the thin ice at the lake's center and find for herself an easy painless death. Yet something older stopped her.

Not courage, she told herself; she would not lie about that. Remembrance. The old memories were coming back.

Ice shattered and exploded as the thing came for her. Fracture lines raced along the lake's surface like lightning branching in a storm. Meeda saw shadows and gleaming edges of light, smelled the dark odor of another world. Eyes that held nothing met her own. She braced her stick to meet that cold black blade. And then, as the sword hummed toward her, burning a mark in the air that hung there long after the blade had passed, she noticed the shadow man's chest. Rising and falling like a living thing.

A heart lay somewhere within the darkly weighted substance of its flesh. It was beating. And it made Meeda's mouth water like a meal of ham and wine.

Icewood and voided steel met with a *crack* that sounded the beginning of an Age. White pain shot up Meeda's arms, and it took all she had to hold her ground. Three feet of ice bowed under the mass of the shadowed thing. Yet still Meeda did not lose her footing. She was Sull. Every hair on her body and drop of blood in her veins demanded that she should fight.

ONE

The Ice Fog Rises

They found blood on the trail on the seventh day, five spots, red against the gray of old snow. It wasn't new-spilt, but it might have looked like it to someone who was unfamiliar with killing game in midwinter. Blood began darkening to black the moment it left the body, thickening and distilling until there was nothing but copper and iron left. It was different when the air crackled with ice. Blood could freeze in perfect red drops in the time it took to drip from an elk's collarbone to the tundra below. Raif remembered how he and Drey would scoop up frozen beads of elk blood after a kill and let them melt upon their tongues; sweet as fresh grass and salty as sweat. The taste of winter and clan.

But this wasn't elk's blood before them.

Raif glanced ahead to the top of the rise where towers of white smoke rose straight in the still air. The trail had been rising all day and they still hadn't found the source of the smoke. The ground was hard and brittle here, formed from basalt and black chert. Cliffs soared to the east, high and straight as fortress walls, guarding knife-edged mountains beyond. To the west lay the farthermost tip of the Storm Margin, its rocky draws and moraines disguised as rolling hills by a thick layer of snow.

Beyond there lay the sea ice, and beyond that lay the sea. Stormheads gathering on the westernmost horizon had begun to silver the floes.

"What happened here?" asked Ash, who was standing above Raif as he crouched over the blood. Her voice was clear, but there was too much space between her words.

"One of the Sull breathed a vein."

"How can you be sure?"

Raif faked a shrug. "Even a clean kill leaves more blood." He fingered the red spots, remembering frozen carcasses, ice-bent blades, Tem Sevrance laughing at his sons as they strained to push an elk kill down a slope only to have it crash into the lake ice at the bottom and sink. When Raif continued speaking his voice was low. "And the blood wasn't sprayed. It dripped."

"How do you know it's human?"

Abruptly, Raif stood. He felt an irrational anger toward Ash and her questions. They both knew the answer here. Why did she force him to speak it?

"Listen," he said.

Standing side by side on the headland, their breath whitening in the freezing air, Raif Sevrance and Ash March listened to the sound they had been heading toward all day. A crackling hiss, as if lightning was touching down upon water.

Raif counted the columns of smoke as he said, "They were here: Mal Naysayer and Ark Veinsplitter, they heard what we hear. They saw the smoke." *And knew it was something to be feared, so they let blood to still their gods.*

Ash nodded, as if she had heard what he had not spoken. "Should we make payment too?"

Raif shook his head and started forward. "This is not our land and not our business. There are no debts here for us to pay."

He hoped it was the truth.

They had been following the Sull warriors' trail for nine days. It had led them north and west from the Hollow River, across land Raif would never have dared to cross if it hadn't been for the telltale markings in the snow. Horse casts buried shallow, human hair snagged on the bark of a dead pine, a footprint stamped on new ice. The Sull had left *"Such a trail as can be followed by a clansman"*. Raif's shoulders stiffened as he walked, aware of the insult in Ark Veinsplitter's words. *"We travel without leaving any trail,"* they boasted, *"but will make effort to leave one for you."* Even as Raif had resented the Sull's arrogance, he knew to be thankful for their skills. No clansman would cross a green-froze lake, nor scale an unknown ice sheet in the hope of finding a pass.

The journey had not been easy. The days had been short and the nights long and full of silence. What could he and Ash say to each other? Raif wondered as he stripped bark for the watch fire each night. They could not talk about the Cavern of Black Ice, nor what had happened later, when they emerged from the river and something, *something*, came with them. All Raif had seen was a shadow, but shadows don't make pine needles crack beneath them . . . and shadows can't scream.

Raif shivered. Whatever it was, it was gone now. Fled. And even though they had seen nothing since, it had changed everything.

Ten days ago, in the cavern beneath the frozen river, he and Ash had spoken of returning to the clanholds, of finding Angus and journeying with him to Ille Glaive and visiting the Broken Man one last time. Heritas Cant had a promise to keep. *"Return safely from the Cavern of Black Ice and I will tell you the names of the beasts,"* he had said. But now the word *safely* seemed an impossibly high standard to keep. They were not safe. Raif did not count himself a clansman anymore, but the old instincts had not left him. He knew when to fear. A deep unease had settled upon him, making him watchful and ready. The ice pick he counted as his only weapon lay cooling the skin at his waist.

He could not say whose decision it had been to follow the Sull north. It was something else he and Ash didn't speak of, the need to learn more. The two Sull warriors knew what Ash was. They could provide proof that it was all over. And it was safe to return home.

It took them an hour to top the rise. Ash pushed ahead, and Raif was content to follow the shadow she cast against the full moon. Neither spoke as they surveyed the valley below. Twelve geysers of steam erupted from the ice and rubble of a dry glacier bed. A ring of blue fire blazed at the base of each column, leaping up from a crater of ash and melted stone that had formed around the burn. The roar was deafening: the crack of exploding rocks, the hiss of melting snow, and the constant *rip* of igniting gas.

The quickening wind brought the stench of char and lightning to Raif. He had no words for what he saw. To find fire and smoke here, at the frozen edge of the Storm Margin, seemed as impossible as finding breath in a corpse.

"Is this where the trail leads?" Ash asked, turning her face toward him.

He found he could not look into her eyes. Once they had been the gray of silver and hailstones. Now they were the color of the sky at midnight. A perfect Sull blue. "The trail cuts through the valley, toward the coast."

"So we must cross here?" As Ash spoke the ground moved beneath them, and rocks and snow spewed forth as a new column of smoke rent the valley floor.

Thirteen, Raif counted, feeling the heat of the explosion puff against his face. He remembered the tale of Murdo Blackhail, the Warrior Chief, who had led his men to war across the

Stairlands. On the final day of their descent, the mountain had erupted above them, and a spray of molten rock had burst forth. Murdo had been riding at the head of the party, high atop his stallion, Black Burr. His breastplate had burst into flame with the heat, and later, when his armsman pulled it from him, Murdo's skin and muscle came with it. In the two days it took him to die, Murdo Blackhail directed his men to victory over Clan Thrall and took his wife to his bed, fathering their only son. Bessa, his wife, was led to her husband blindfold and with plugs of wax within each nostril, for the sight and stench of his burned flesh was said to be terrible to behold.

Raif grimaced. "We travel through the valley," he said.

The gas vents glowed blue in the failing light. Ash had little fear of them and picked a path through their center, once drawing close enough to a crater to drink water from its moat of melted snow. Raif spoke no word of warning, though he saw the danger clear enough. The entire valley floor was under pressure, its ancient rock buckled and twisted by whatever forces lay below. It might have been beautiful, this corridor of burning gas and rising smoke, but all the tales of hell he had listened to as a child had begun with an approach such as this.

They walked well into the night, Raif postponing making camp until the gas vents were far behind them. The next day the sun barely rose above the horizon, and what light it gave could hardly be called daylight at all. The following day was darker still, and the trail left by the Sull became more difficult to follow. As the afternoon wore on Raif began to spot signs of other men. Ice-bleached bones and sled tracks, dog fur and slicks of green whale-oil pitted the path. The snow itself was hard and frozen, the air so dry and clear that even the finest specks of dust were revealed.

They came across the Whale Gate at some time during the long night. Formed from the jawbone of a massive bow whale, the ancient archway rose as high as two men and as wide as four. It stood alone on a headland of frost-cracked rocks and graying weeds, marking entrance into the territory beyond. Raif bit off his mitts and touched it with bare hands. The ivory was stained and scaling, its edges jagged with the stumps of baleen combs. Designs had been burned into the bone. Dolphins chasing stars had been seared atop an older, darker design of beasts slaying men.

Raif took his hands away. In the sheltered valley below the gate, the faintest discernible lights twinkled, and above them a white haze of exhaled breaths shifted in the air like sleeping ghosts.

"The trail ends here." Raif couldn't remember the last time he had spoken, and his voice sounded strange and rough. He looked down upon the village, if village it was. Stone mounds, rising mere feet above the ground, formed a circle around a smoking firepit. The mounds were built of obsidian and basalt and other black things, and their edges glowed faintly in the starlight. They reminded Raif of the barrows of Dhoone's Core. Twelve thousand clansmen dead, each corpse interred in a stone tomb of its own. For three thousand years they'd lain there, rotting to bone dust and hollow teeth. Withy and Wellhouse kept no history of the massacre. Raif had once heard Inigar Stoop name it "the Price of Settlement" but warriors and chiefs gave it another name, whispered around campfires in the deep of night. The Field of Stone.

Suddenly Raif wanted very much to turn back, to grab Ash's hand and take her . . . *where?* No land that he knew of was safe.

Abruptly, Ash stepped through the gate, leaving Raif no choice but to follow her into the village below.

Dogs began barking as they approached. Yet even before the first growl of warning caused lights to brighten and stir, a figure stood waiting at the first of the stone mounds. Raif recognized the pale bulk of Mal Naysayer, his cloak of wolverine fur stirring in the wind, the haft of his great two-handed longsword rising above his back. The warrior stood unmoving as they approached, silent and terrible against a field of burning stars.

"The Sull are not our people and they do not fear us." The old clan words came to Raif as he raised a hand in greeting, yet they were old words and often said and men who knew nothing about the Sull spoke them, and they fell from his mind when the warrior began to kneel.

Mal Naysayer, Son of the Sull and chosen Far Rider, dropped to his knees as they approached. He held his position until Ash and Raif passed within speaking distance and then laid himself down upon the snow.

Oh gods. So it begins.

Muscles in the warrior's back moved beneath his cloak as he spread his arms wide to form a cross. Raif could see dozens of white letting scars on his knuckles as he dug bare fingers into ice. *Not for me*, Raif knew with certainty. *No Sull would prostrate himself before a clansman without a clan.*

Ash stood silent above the Sull, wrapped in lynx fur and boiled wool, her hair lifting and falling in the changing air. Nothing showed on her face, not exhaustion or fear . . . or surprise. "Rise, Mal Naysayer of the Sull, for we are old friends met in far lands and I would speak to your face, not your back."

Raif felt a tremor pass through him as she spoke. *How could he have come so far with her and not realize she had been leading the way all along?*

In silence, Mal Naysayer pulled himself to his feet. The silver chains and brain hooks at his waist chimed softly as he brushed snow from his mouth. Raif watched his eyes. Pale as ice and colder still, they spared no glance for the clansman. The warrior looked only at Ash.

"Snow burns," he said.

A chill went through Raif . . . and for one brief instant he almost knew why. He saw thirteen columns of smoke rising from a valley thick with snow, heard the old guide chanting a fragment of a cradle song, long forgot: *Snow burns, the Age turns, and Lost Men shall walk the earth.*

Ash breathed deeply and did not speak.

Raif spotted a line of men coming toward them, bearing spears pointed with volcanic glass and torches that burned with white-hot flames. Small and dark-skinned, they moved in the fluid and soundless manner of men accustomed to stalking large prey. Ribcages of walrus and seal were bound to their chests in armored plates, riding over layer upon layer of skins and strange furs. Forming a defensive half-circle behind the Naysayer, they thrust their spear butts deep into the snow.

Raif watched them watch him. He supposed he should be grateful that *they* at least considered him more of a threat than Ash, but the Sull's words had stirred a fear within him, and he found little satisfaction in the wariness of other men.

Their rank parted, and a tiny old man stepped forward. His skin was the color and texture of cured wood, and his eyes were milky with snow blindness. On either side of his face, aligned with cheekbones as sharp as crab claws, two deep black scars bored into his skull in place of ears. A ruff of vulture feathers warmed the broken flesh, their quills rising upright from a collar of rolled bronze. Over his shoulders and across his back lay a coat of fur so dark and lustrous it was as if the soul of the slain beast still lived there.

"*Inuku sana hanlik,*" he said in a voice thin with age.

"The Listener of the Ice Trappers welcomes you to this place."

Ark Veinsplitter came to stand at the old man's back, his face grim and his eyes narrowing, as he translated the Listener's words. He wore scale armor over padded silk, with a heavy fur mantle thrown back over his shoulders. His left arm was bared to the elbow, and a trickle of blood circled his wrist. *He could have stanched the letting wound before he came to meet us, yet he wanted us to see the blood.* Raif suddenly felt weary enough to lie down in the snow and fall asleep. He didn't want to greet this old man, didn't want to know who he was.

The Listener spoke again, and Raif realized that some shadow of sight still survived behind his eyes, for he looked directly at Raif as he said, "*Mor Drakka.*"

The wind rose, and the old man turned and walked away. Gritty bits of ice flew into Raif's face, stinging the raw flesh beneath his nostrils where his breath continually froze and thawed. Without thought, his hand rose to his throat, searching for the hard piece of raven that was his lore. Nothing but cold skin and raw wool met his touch. He had forgotten he had given it to Ash.

"The Listener bids you follow him." Ark Veinsplitter stepped aside to make a path. Raif watched the dark-haired warrior for a moment, noticing how the skin at the base of his neck was the only part of him that was untouched by the letting knife; and wondering why the Sull had chosen to translate the Listener's gesture, not his words. Raif did not know what tongue the old man spoke in, but he knew his last words had been meant for him. And they were not some soft-spoken request to follow him home.

Ark Veinsplitter glowered at Raif as the two drew eye-to-eye. Something in Raif made him slow his pace and exhale in the warrior's face. Something else made him lay a hand on Ash's shoulder as they passed.

Almost, Ark Veinsplitter managed to hide his alarm at seeing the color of Ash's eyes. Muscles tensed beneath the uncut skin on his neck, and his gaze sought and found his *hass*. Mal

Naysayer's shoulders bowed once in acknowledgment . . . and Raif knew that the blue in Ash's eyes meant something to them.

He tightened his hold on her as they made their way to the farthest of the stone mounds. Men in walrus-bone armor lined the route, naked thumbs pressing against the kill notches on their spear shafts, faces dark with mistrust. They were not young, these men, Raif noticed, recognizing a careful show of force when he saw one. Briefly, he glanced westward to the sea ice, wondering if the younger warriors were out upon it, hunting seal.

Light spilled from the entrance to the Listener's mound, shining on pits of ashen tar and frozen blood. The Listener stood in the shadows behind the light, beckoning Raif forward with the curled black fingers of a corpse.

Raif had lived so long without warmth that the heat of the chamber burned him. His vision dimmed as he raised his head after passing through the opening. A liquid queasiness in his stomach reminded him he had not eaten in two days. The piglike smell of walrus meat made him retch.

The Listener unclasped his fur and laid it upon a bench of plain black stone. He gestured that Ash and Raif should sit upon it, close to a little soapstone lamp that was the only source of light. The walls glittered weirdly. Plugs of hair and skin had been used to shore the chinks. Raif realized he must be experiencing what clansmen called "coming in from the cold madness" when he found himself wondering if the Listener's missing earlobes had been stuffed between the cracks.

They waited in silence as Ark Veinsplitter entered, and closed the door. A raven swung upside down on a whalebone perch, making the soft chuffing noises of a bird whose vocal cords had felt the heat of a throat-iron upon hatching. Spying Raif, it righted itself and fixed him with its sharp black gaze. Unnerved, Raif found himself speaking when he had not planned to.

"We'll be on our way in the morning. We need to head east while the calm still holds."

"You do not know the way east, Clansman." Ark Veinsplitter poured a line of water under the door, sealing the chamber with ice.

Blood rose in Raif's cheeks. The Sull warrior was right. No clansmen knew this territory or the ways to and from it. He hardly knew what had made him say such a thing. Neither he nor Ash had spoken of what they would do once they arrived here, and both of them needed time to rest.

Now all he wanted to do was be gone.

"You could share knowledge of the eastern trails, Far Rider," Ash said, and even though he was aware she had spoken to support him, Raif was not glad to hear her speak. Some insane, heat-fevered part of him wanted to believe that if she were quiet, barely moved, barely spoke, they would not notice her. Or want her.

The Sull warrior rose heavily, revealing the brace of knives strapped to his back. "Knowledge of Sull paths comes at great cost. Would you have me give them freely, as if they were nothing more than deer tracks through a wood?"

"I would have you tell me what's happening here," Raif fired back. "Why did the Naysayer drop to the ground when he saw us? And why is there blood on your wrists?"

"My blood is mine to spill, Clansman. Would you tell me when to piss and shit?"

Raif sucked in air to reply, but the little man with no ears hissed a word that could only mean *Silence!*

In the quiet that followed the Listener of the Ice Trappers poured steaming liquid into three horn bowls. Raif nodded thanks when the first was handed to him. He smelled the sharpness of sea salt and fermented flesh, watched as Ark Veinsplitter and Ash held bowl rims to their lips and sipped. The old man arranged himself on the chamber floor and waited for Raif to drink.

The liquid scalded Raif's tongue. It was thick with invisible threads of sinew that floated between his teeth and then slid back into the bowl when he was done. Strangely, the heat seemed to null the taste, and although he had been expecting something acrid, he was left with only a vague sense of fishiness and a whiff of lead.

The Listener refilled Raif's bowl. "*Oolak.*"

"Fermented shark skin," explained Ark Veinsplitter. "The Listener brews it himself."

Raif nodded. Bad home-brew was something he was familiar with. Tem's brew had been so bad that no one but blood kin would drink it. It had been a point of honor with Raif and Drey, the enjoying of it, the laughing, the one-upmanship as each tried to outdo the other in lavishing the foul brew with praise. Tem would cuff them for their cockiness, then walk away grumbling about how a father could have too many sons.

Smiling, Raif drank deeply. When the Listener filled his cup a third time he drank more. He was hungry for its magic; the way it let him think of the things he had lost without the pain of losing them.

"Raif. Open the door and let out the smoke." Ash's voice seemed to come from a very great distance. As Raif lifted his head to look at her, he caught a glance passing between the Listener and the Far Rider. Dimly, he realized many things— that Ark Veinsplitter had not answered any of his questions, that it was the old man, not the Far Rider, who held power here, and that it would serve a clansman well to be cautious in this place—but there was a heaviness settling within him. The fermented shark skin and the lamp smoke and the heat had slowed his thinking, along with his blood. He knew things yet could not act.

Slowly, he rose to his feet. A rim of ice had formed around the driftwood door, weeping where it touched the chamber's heat. As he reached for the pull ring, Ark's hand came down upon his arm.

"*Mora irith.* The ice fog rises this night."

Raif pulled back. He knew about the ice fog, of how it had risen the night Cormac HalfBludd, first son of the River Chief, had been standing vigil on the banks of the Ebb, and how the old Croserman who found his body the next morning thought he was looking at a river wraith's corpse, so inhumanly blue was Cormac's skin.

Raif reclaimed his seat. The Listener refilled his bowl. As he accepted the steaming liquid, Raif felt Ash's hand touch his thigh.

"Guard yourself," she murmured.

He watched her face, saw her desire to say more stifled by the nearness of other men. Unable to name the emotion behind her eyes, Raif raised the cup to his lips and drank. Who was she to warn him? The ice fog was rising and the door was sealed against it, and a man could do worse than sit in the warmth and drink.

So that was what he did. Hours passed and the lamp smoke thickened and sea ice beyond the chamber boomed and cracked. No one spoke. The Listener paid attention to the lamp, tamping the wick ever lower into whale oil. Raif's shoulders sought the hard comfort of the chamber wall as his head grew heavy with sleep. Soon it became increasingly hard to stay awake. And as his eyes closed and he drifted toward oblivion, he saw the Far Rider watching him with cold and knowing eyes.

"*The Sull are not our people and they do not fear us.*"

Raif heard the voice of his clan and knew to be afraid . . . but the alcohol was in him and sleep pulled hard upon him.

And when he woke two days later Ash was gone.

TWO

The Widows' Wall

The only way to drink mares' urine was quickly, so Raina closed her eyes, scrunched her face and downed it in one. It really was quite dreadful—sweet and pungent, still steaming from the horse's bladder—yet she'd sampled worse in her time. Tem Sevrance's home-brew, for one. And the taste of her own fear.

Besides, it had to be better than sheep dung . . . that and ground-up beetle parts set to stand in curdled milk. Anwyn Bird swore by sheep dung, but she was a ewe farmer's daughter and heavily biased toward sheep. No. Better to be safe in this. The old family remedies were the best; the ones whispered by sisters and cousins and mother and aunts. How best to prevent conception of a child.

Letting the ladle drop to the bucket, Raina rose to her feet. She needed to be gone from here. A pale dawn was breaking, and Eadie Callow and the other dyers would be taking their places soon enough. A chief's wife could not be seen here, not alone, not with the newly delivered mares stale from the horse-block. Eadie Callow might have the slow eyes and stained hands of a dyer, but a sharpness lived behind her dull gaze, and the black ink on her fingers concealed the pale white flesh of a

Scarpe. All the dyers and fullers were Scarpemen. They had ways with potash and urine and fuller's earth that other men lacked. It was said that no other clan in the clanholds could dye such a perfect shade of black.

Mace had brought Scarpemen by the hundred to the Hailhold. Every day more arrived: warriors mounted on Spire-bred horses, women pulled behind them in poison-pine carts. The Scarpehold had been torched. The silent white-winter warriors of Clan Orrl had sent a message of fire in the night, and flames from the Scarpehold's sod-and-timber roof had been seen throughout the North. By many accounts only the stonework still stood, but even that had been cracked and blackened, and returning Hailsmen whispered that sleeping there was like spending a night in a scorched field. Stangs from the Scarpe Tree, the poison pine that grew nowhere else in the Clanholds except the hills surrounding Scarpe, had been used in construction of the roof. Many of them were still whole, but the deadly smoke given off during their charring caused more deaths than the most fiercely burning oak.

Raina's mouth tightened as she closed the dyehouse door. She could find little sympathy for Scarpe.

Mace Blackhail's birthclan was not her own. Yelma Scarpe, the Weasel chief, had brought the torching upon herself. She had unleashed her sharp little tongue upon Orrl, claiming land and strongwalls and hunting rights, and then, never short of clever talk and clever schemes, she had set the might of Blackhail upon them. Five warriors murdered in the frost-broken lands to the west, one the Orrl chief's grandson; a dozen more Orrl warriors slain during a border skirmish when both Blackhail and Scarpe rode against them.

And then there was the killing of the Orrl chief himself.

Corbie Meese and his crew found the bodies, on the Old Dregg Trail, two days west of Dhoone. Eleven white-winter warriors and Spynie Orrl, their bodies clad in the strangely shifting cloth Orrl was known for, their heads forced so far down into their chest cavities that the scout who first came upon them thought the bodies beheaded. Corbie Meese knew the truth of it. Only a score of hammermen in the North, himself included, were capable of striking such a blow.

Shivering, Raina made her way toward the widow's hearth that formed the uppermost chamber of the roundhouse.

No one knew who had ordered the Orrl chief's slaying. Spynie and his men had been traveling a dangerous path between warring clans, and there were some who whispered that the Orrl chief had been returning from a secret parley with the Dog Lord at Dhoone. Raina set no store by that. She *knew* Spynie Orrl, had spent a summer at the Orrlhouse in her youth, and even though he had no liking for the Hail Wolf, he would not turn his back on his oath.

Old words and old loyalties ran deep here, in the westernmost reaches of the clanholds. Clans were older, the living was harder, and for a thousand winters the Hail chief had looked upon the Orrl chief as his man.

"Lady."

Raina turned on the stair to see Lansa Tanner on the landing below. The young girl bobbed her head, setting golden curls dancing.

"The chief awaits you in his chamber."

Raina could still see the blush on her cheeks. *Foolish child, to let a conversation with Mace impress her so.* "Tell my husband I will join him when my business with the widows is done."

The girl waited for more, lips prettily parted, bars of light from the arrow slits slicing across her throat. No one dismissed a chief's request out of hand; there had to be an apology or explanation. When none came the girl's mouth closed and something less pretty happened to her face. Without another word she turned and descended the stair.

Oh gods. What is happening here? Resting her weight against the sandstone wall, Raina watched the girl go. She had woven birth cloths for all the Tanner girls, washed their soiled linens and combed their tangled hair. How had Mace managed to steal their loyalty from her?

The sounds and smells of early morning followed Raina as she climbed the little stair to the widows' hearth. The crackle of newly lit fires and the sizzle of ham upon them competed with the clangor from the forge. Once her mouth would have watered at the aroma of blackening fat, and her pace would have quickened to meet the day, but here and now she felt nothing but the hard sense of duty that had become her life.

She was chief's wife, first woman of the clan, and Mace Blackhail could not take that from her.

The door to the widows' hearth was old and deeply carved, the wood a silvery gray. The lightest touch of Raina's hand was all it took to set the quarter-ton of rootwood in motion. The steady clack of looms greeted her as she stepped into the room.

Merritt Ganlow, Biddie Byce and Moira Lull were at their frames, weaving. Old Bessie Flapp, whose great dislike of her husband made her a widow by choosing if not fact, was carding raw wool with her liver-spotted hands. Others were at tables, sewing and embroidering, spinning, and stretching the warps. The light was good here, and all the heat generated by the countless hearths burning throughout the roundhouse rose through the timbers on its journey toward the roof. The ceiling was low and barrel-vaulted, the bloodwood stangs made bright by a wash of yellow ochre. As always upon entering the chamber, Raina's gaze fell upon the hearthstone.

The Widows' Wall, it was called, and the brown stain upon it was said to be Flora Blackhail's blood. Wife to the Mole

Chief, Mordrag Blackhail, Flora had gone mad with grief upon receiving word of her husband's death. A messenger had arrived at the roundhouse in the dark of night, telling how Mordrag had been crushed by a collapsing cave wall in the Iron Caves to the south. Frantic and inconsolable, Flora had fled to the uppermost chamber of the roundhouse and stabbed herself with her carding shears.

Stupid woman, Raina thought. For the messenger who brought word was a stranger to the clan, and Mordrag still lived, though he had lost half a leg to gangrene. When news of his wife's death reached him, Mordrag mourned for thirty days, and then took himself a new bride. And the chamber in which Flora had died became a home for the widows of the clan.

"Raina!" Merritt Ganlow spoke from behind her loom, her hands never losing contact with shuttle and thread. "Are you here as widow or wife?"

Raina nodded at the stout woolwife. "I'm here as friend, I hope."

Merritt grunted. "Then as a friend I trust no words will find their way back to the Wolf."

The widows had little love for Mace Blackhail. No Scarpewoman ever found her way to the Widows' Wall, though there were plenty of widows amongst them. They knew they were not welcome, could see that their tattooed widows' weals set them apart. Scarpe widows did not cut themselves, as Blackhail widows did, claiming the pain of loss was enough. Why should they cut their flesh and pain themselves more?

Pushing back her sleeves so the raised skin around her wrists showed, Raina said, "You and I both lost husbands in the badlands, Merritt Ganlow. Would that their deaths had generated kinship, not distrust."

"You found yourself a new husband quick enough."

Other women looked up at Merritt's words and nodded. Someone at the back whispered, *"Quick as a bitch in heat."*

Oh Dagro. Why did you leave me alone to bear this? Steeling herself against emotion, Raina said, "Life goes on, Merritt, and the clan needs strong women to guide it. Perhaps your place is here, with the widows weaving cloth, but mine is not. I have been too long at the fore of things to retire to a life of wool and stitching. Losing a husband does not change who I am. And it's not within me to claim the widow's privilege of sitting near the fire and growing old."

The shuttle in Merritt's hand slowed. "Aye, you always were a hard one, Raina Blackhail."

"Hardness in a man is called strength."

"Aye, and *strength*, as you would have it, isn't solely the preserve of those who lead. There's strength to be found here, in the act of weaving quietly and carrying on."

"I know it, Merritt. That is why I have come."

For the first time since she had entered the widows' hearth, Raina felt a lessening of the tension. Slender and lovely Moira Lull cleared the space beside Merritt on the bench. The women at the back returned to their tasks as Merritt took both hands from her loom and turned to face Raina full on. "You're looking thin," she said.

Raina sat. "Food is scarce."

"Not for a chief's wife."

"I'm busy." Raina shrugged. "There's little time to stop and eat."

"Anwyn says you're wearing yourself out."

"Anwyn should look to herself."

That got a smile from Merritt. No one worked harder or longer than Anwyn Bird. When the grand matron of the roundhouse wasn't cooking or butchering, she was down in the armory, tilling bows.

Merritt pushed a flagon of sheep's-milk ale Raina's way. "So, what brings you here this early?"

Raina drank from the jug, savoring the milky coolness and the bite of malt liquor buried deep beneath the cream. As she wiped the froth from her lips, she wondered how best to approach this. Guile failed her so she came straight to the point. "You have kin at the Orrlhouse?" Merritt's nod was guarded. "And your son travels back and forth, trading skins and winter meat?"

"Only Orrlsmen can bring home fresh meat from a deep-winter hunt."

"Aye." There wasn't a Hailsman in the roundhouse who wasn't in awe of Orrl's white-winter hunters. No one could track game across snow and ice like the men of Orrl. "So your son must have knowledge of what's happening at the Orrlhouse?"

This time Merritt's nod was slow in coming. Her clever hands tied off a length of thread. "What's it to you what my son knows, Raina Blackhail? Don't you learn enough of Orrl's business abed with your husband at night?"

Careful, Raina cautioned herself. *Think what Dagro would have done here.* "I learn only what Mace chooses to tell me."

Merritt sucked air between her teeth. "So you come here seeking what he will not?"

"I come here seeking the truth." Raina met and held Merritt's gaze. "We go back a long time, you and I. You and Meth danced swords at my first wedding, and when Dagro went hunting that last time it was Meth who shared his tent. I might be married to Mace Blackhail but my loyalty lies with this clan. You might think I gained much upon marrying him, but you cannot know all I have lost. What I'm asking for is information when you have it. I know the steadfastness of this hearth. None here will go running to my husband with tales of his wife's deeds."

"He watches you." Ancient turkey-necked Bessie Flapp did

not look up from her carding as she spoke. Skeletal fingers combed and stretched, combed and stretched, as a chill crept upon Raina. "Eyes everywhere. Little mice and little telltales. Meetings by the dog cotes and the stoke holes. Squeak, squeak, squeak. Who goes where? Who does what? Little mice with weasels' tails."

Raina took a breath. She had not known it was as bad as this.

"Biddie. Fetch Raina some of the griddle cakes from the hearth. And bring honey to sweeten the ale." There was mothering in Merritt's voice and Raina wondered what was showing on her face to change the woolwife so.

Biddie Byce's long blond braids whipped the air as she went about Merritt's bidding. She was too young to be a widow, barely nineteen winters old. Cull had wed her the spring before he was slain on Bannen field. Now Cull's twin, Arlec, had begun to pay her court in small and unassuming ways. After the taking of Ganmiddich he had returned home with a necklace strung with green marble beads. Shyly, he had pressed it into Raina's hands. "See Biddie gets it. She need not know it's from me."

Raina smiled as Biddie returned with cakes and honey. She didn't want the girl to see the envy stabbing softly in her chest.

"Here. Pull this round you. Your skin's as blue as Dhoone." Merritt arranged a fine wool shawl across Raina's shoulders, pulling it here and there until it covered all the bare skin. "Hatty. Bring one of the pieces you and your sisters are working on—Raina needs to see it."

Silent and big-boned Hatty Hare snapped a thread with her teeth. Slowly she rose from her embroiderer's stool to place a fist-sized panel in Raina's hand.

The Hail Wolf, worked in silver against a black ground. The Blackhail badge; only no clansman since Ayan Blackhail had worn it.

"All the needlewomen have been set to work on them, under order of the chief himself." Merritt poured honey into the milk ale. "We were warned to sew in silence and let none but the silversmiths know it, as they're needed to stretch the wire."

Raina's fingers traced the line of the wolf's jaw, expertly worked in silver wire so fine it moved as if it were thread. Almost she knew Merritt's next words before she spoke them, for it took a fool not to see what this meant.

"This is how he keeps them loyal, this man whom it pleases you to call husband. He gives our clansmen back their pride. Five hundred years ago in the Tomb of the Dhoone Princes, all the chiefs in the clanholds met to strip Blackhail of its badge. *Ayan Blackhail slew a king*, they said. *A coward's shot to the throat.* No Hail chief has challenged that judgment since; not Ornfel, or Mordrag, or Uthan . . . not even Dagro himself. Yet along comes a Scarpe-born fosterling, winning wars and gaining territory, daring to wear the Hail Wolf at his breast. And that's not all. He wants every warrior in the clan to wear it; a whole army of Hailsmen bearing their badges with pride.

"He's a subtle man, Mace Blackhail, I'll give him that. And he knows the value of small things. For five hundred years our warriors have ridden into battle without badge or banner. We are women, and we cannot know the shame they endured."

Raina hung her head. She felt Mace's cunning as a weight upon her. Was there nothing he could not arrange? A chiefship. Loyalty.

Marriage.

Do not think of it, a hard voice inside her warned. *Put the day in the Oldwood behind you. Hate is all it will bring, and hate is like acid; it only burns the vessel that holds it.* Raina raised her head. She would not be burned.

"I'll be on my way now, but I thank you for your straight words. I'd like to visit you from time to time, to talk and exchange news." She waited for Merritt to nod before standing. "It's good to find a hearth free of my husband's sway."

"Squeak, squeak, squeak," croaked Bessie Flapp. "Little mice with weasels' tails."

Merritt frowned at the old battleax. "Come." She beckoned Raina. "I'll walk with you to the stair." When they were out of earshot, she said, "What is it you sought to know about Orrl?"

"Who is chief now? How are they coping with our hostilities?"

"Stallis stood Chief Watch ten days since. By all accounts he's a sharp one, Spynie's sixth grandson, the white-winter warrior with the most kills."

"Does he hold Blackhail in favor?"

Merritt made an odd sound, almost a laugh. "Come now, Raina. Do you honestly think Stallis will forgive Mace for ordering his grandfather's slaying?"

"But—"

"But what? No one can say for certain who sent the hammer into Spynie Orrl's brain? 'Tis said in the Orrlhouse that the Scarpe hammerman Mansal Stygo did the killing, and that the marks of Mansal's hammer were stamped on Spynie's skull." Raina made to speak, but Merritt forestalled her again. "And it is also said that a burned-out campfire was found east of where the bodies lay, and amidst the campfire's ashes lay tokens of Blackhail and Scarpe."

"Stone Gods." Raina touched the horn of powdered guidestone at her waist. She wanted to deny it, but it sounded like the truth. Orrlsmen were not given to wild stories and swift conclusions. They were stoic men, preferring to save their energies for hunting, not loose talk.

"None of this looks good, Raina. Orrl against Blackhail. War on more war." Merritt Ganlow's ice-green eyes studied her. "Best be gone now. Keep the shawl about you. It's cold in this roundhouse . . . and days darker than night lie ahead."

Tiny hairs on Raina's arms lifted. Merritt's words were old and she did not know where they came from, but they stirred something within her. Unnerved, she turned to go.

Merritt caught her wrist. "You are welcome at this hearth, Raina Blackhail. Remember that when you return to your world of husbands and wives."

Raina nodded. She could not speak to thank her.

The journey down through the roundhouse was long and tiring, and she found herself making stops along the way. She saw the casual glances from charwomen and alewives differently now. Were they watching her for him?

Lost in thought, she almost missed the broad and misshapen form of Corbie Meese, crossing the entrance hall with enough firewood strapped to his back to build or burn a house.

"Corbie."

The soft word made the hammerman turn. A frown had started upon his face, but upon seeing Raina he grinned. "Are ye mad, woman? To halt a man whilst he's toting a ton of logs?" Bending his back as he spoke, he resettled the load. Leather straps whitened with the strain.

Raina grinned back at him. "That old load? Why, there's more air in there than wood."

Corbie laughed. "By the Stones, woman! You'd drive a man hard if ye could."

Now he had Raina laughing along with him, and it felt good. *Good.* It was suddenly difficult to talk of other things. "Corbie. Can I ask something of you?"

"Aye. If I can ask something of you."

"You can."

Serious now, the hammerman put a hand against the stair-wall to brace the weight of his load. The great dint in his head where a training hammer had clipped him as a boy showed up

starkly in the torchlight. "It's Sarolyn. She's near her time now
. . . and . . ." His gaze dropped to his feet.

Raina nodded quickly, knowing full well what he meant to
say and knowing also that mannish reticence kept him from it.
"I'll watch her day and night, Corbie. And both me and Anwyn
will be there during her confinement."

Relief showed itself plainly on Corbie's face. "I thank you
for that, Raina Blackhail. It does a man's heart good to know
that his wife will be well cared for whilst he's riding far from
home."

*Such a good man. He does not speak of his own death, but
the thought is there inside him.*

"Name what ye would have of me."

She met the gaze from Corbie's light brown eyes, feeling as
if she had trapped him. "It's said that only a dozen hammermen in the North are capable of the blow that killed Spynie
Orrl. Is Mansal Stygo one of them?"

Corbie's whole body stiffened at the question. To ask a
hammerman to speak against a fellow hammerman, even one
from a foreign clan, was calling for blood. There was a close
honor amongst them. Hammer and ax had been wielded in
the clanholds before the first sword-blade was forged, before
even there was metal, just stone and wood and bone. And
neither Corbie nor Raina could pretend this was a casual question about a man's skill.

The chief's wife asked much of the hammerman, but the
hammerman had given his word and he was bound by honor
to answer her . . . even though he knew he named a murderer
as he spoke. "Mansal trained for a season with the Griefbringer,
here in this house."

Naznarri Drac. The Griefbringer. Exiled from the Far South,
granted asylum by Ewan Blackhail, victor of Middlegorge,
trainer of Corbie Meese. Six years dead now, the last man he'd

trained was Bullhammer, the strongest hammerman in the North.

Knowing she had her answer, Raina bowed her head.

Corbie watched Raina for a moment, then shouldered his burden of quartered logs, turned and walked away.

Raina stared at the great slate tiles that formed the entrance-hall floor, letting the knowledge settle inside her. Two meetings, both good and bad. Would that somehow she could avoid the third. There was nothing for it, though. Mace Blackhail had summoned her and she would be a fool to defy him. Gathering Merritt's cloak about her, she made for the Hail chief's chamber.

The crooked stairway was narrow and poorly lit. Once Raina had rushed down the steps, eager to be with Dagro to talk about her day. Now she moved slowly, noticing the mold on the walls and the defensive capstones overhead. Too soon she was there. The tar coating the chief's door seemed to ooze from the wood in the torchlight, and she did not want to put a hand upon it. Mace saved her the trouble by pushing from the other side.

"Wife," he greeted her, a smile flashing oddly upon his face. "I had expected you sooner."

He did not make way to let her enter and she was forced to reply while standing at the door like a child. "Did the girl not tell you I had business elsewhere?"

"She was sent to fetch *you*, not your excuses."

"Then that's her failing, not mine."

Almost she thought that he would hit her. The anger was there in his eyes, but it shifted as quickly as it was born, leaving nothing but the hardness around his mouth. Turning, he bade her enter with a crook of his wrist.

She watched him move. The leathers he wore were as fluid as cloth and they curved to his spine as he walked. Wolves' eyeteeth had been mounted around the hem of his greatcloak to weight it, and the fist-size brooch that held it to his throat was fashioned as a wolf pup, carved and silvered and packed with lead. Coming to stand behind the block of sandstone known as the Chief's Cairn, he bade her seal the door.

Even now, after fourteen weeks of marriage, she feared to be alone with him. But she could not let him know that so she closed the door and drew the bolt.

"I see you have discovered one of my schemes." He nodded toward her left hand. "I take it you approve?"

Feeling like a fool, Raina glanced down at her hand. *The badge*. She had not realized she had brought it with her. Feigning casualness, she tossed it onto the Chief's Cairn. "A pretty plan."

Mace's strong, blade-bitten fingers closed around the badge. "I thought so." He observed her coolly, and she knew he had seen through her bluff.

She spoke to dampen the gleam of knowing in his yellow-black eyes. "So, what would you have of me?"

"A wife."

His words seemed to stop the air itself. Dust and heat and lamp smoke ceased rising. Mace's gaze held hers, and for the first time since he had returned from the badlands she saw the man behind the wolf.

"You were a partner to Dagro," he murmured, reaching for her hand. "Be one to me."

Raina closed her eyes. *Sweet gods, how can he say this to me? Does he not remember what happened in the Oldwood?* Yet she saw in his eyes that he did, and that, given a chance, he would speak soft words to reverse it. *I was desperate, I acted rashly, I thought you wanted it too.* She shuddered, unable to find her voice.

Mace watched her closely. Minutes passed as he held her hand. And then, at last, he released it. "I have my answer, then."

She drew in breath. There was no anger in her, just sickness. She thought that she might faint. "I've done my duty by you."

A hard sound issued from his throat, and suddenly he was beside her, his hands on the small of her back. "Do you think I am grateful for your *duties*?" Sliding his fingers across her breast he turned the word into something obscene. "Don't flatter yourself, Raina. There's more warmth to be had in the heart of the Want than in your bed." Abruptly, he let her go. "Have no fear, I shall make no call upon your *duty* again."

Blood burned in her cheeks. She turned to leave.

But he had not done with her. Returning to his place behind the Chief's Cairn, he said, "We have matters yet to discuss."

She kept moving toward the door. "Such as?"

"Such as what's to be done with the Sevrance girl. All who saw her that night by the dog cotes swear she's witched."

He knew he had her. She had to turn and face him.

Casually, Mace rested his hand upon the Clansword that was pegged low upon the wall. Wielded by Murdo Blackhail and Mad Gregor before him, forged from the crown of the Dhoone Kings, and symbol of Blackhail power, the unsheathed sword shone blackly in the torchlight.

"I've protected the girl as best I can, but tempers show little sign of cooling. You know how superstitious the old clansmen are. Turby Flapp would see her stoned. Gat Murdock thinks she should walk the coals. All seek her gone." Mace shrugged. "I cannot set aside the will of the clan."

You bring Scarpemen into this house, she wanted to say. *No Hailsman wills that*. She said, "Not all in the clan condemn her. Orwin says the Moss woman deserved what she got, and that his dogs attacked her of their own free will."

"It's hardly surprising that Orwin defends the girl. All know he does so out of love and loyalty for Drey."

Raina felt the net closing. He was too clever, this husband of hers; she didn't have the words to best him. Still, she could not let Effie go undefended. "Cutty Moss was trying to kill her. No one can deny that. You've seen her wounds."

Mace sighed. "Yes, but there are those who whisper that Cutty only sought to bring an end to her witching."

"He stole her lore."

"And look what she did to get it back." Mace shook his head sadly. "Come now, Raina, don't let your love for the girl blind you. Even if she didn't witch those dogs into attacking the lunt-woman and her son, most *believe* she did. I would change that if I could, but I'm chief, not shaman. And as chief it is my duty to becalm the clan."

He wanted Effie harmed, she could hear it in the softness of his voice. Effie knew what he had done in the Oldwood . . . and possibly more. There was no telling what the girl could learn through her lore.

Mace spread his fingers wide across the pocked surface of the Chief's Cairn. "She must be tried."

Raina held herself still. She knew how such trials had ways of getting out of hand, how supposedly sane and rational clans-men could flash to anger in an instant, stoked by nothing more than their own ignorance and fears. Effie Sevrance, with her watching eyes and silent ways, wouldn't have a hope against them. Delay, that was the only thing to be done now. Delay.

"It would be wise to save your decision until her brother returns from Gnash. Drey would not thank you for trying his sister in haste."

She saw she had made him think. Drey Sevrance was a chief's man. When the Ganmiddich roundhouse needed to be held for the returning Crab chief, Mace had chosen Drey to watch its high green walls. And when the Dhoone chief-in-exile had called the Hail Wolf to a parley, it had been Drey whom

Mace had sent in his stead. Indeed, Drey hadn't set foot in the roundhouse for five weeks, and Raina found herself wondering if his absence wasn't what Mace had wanted all along.

Mace said, "Wait, and I risk the possibility that clansmen will take matters into their own hands, and that's something we both might regret." He favored Raina with a husband's smile. "But I'll see what I can do."

It was no answer, and they both knew it. He would see Effie harmed either by trial or delay. And that meant she was no longer safe in this roundhouse. Raina pulled Merritt Ganlow's shawl about her. Suddenly she wanted very much to be gone.

"Be about your business," he said, dismissing her. "And take comfort in the fact that I'll be keeping Effie close."

His voice was so soft and reassuring it barely sounded like a threat.

THREE

In the Tomb of the Dhoone Princes

The Tomb of the Dhoone Princes was located a hundred yards north of the Dhoonehouse, sunk to a depth of eighty feet. A single passageway, cut out of the hard blue sandstone that Dhoone was built on, connected the tomb to the great barrel-vaulted guidehouse where kings and princes had once lain in state. Vaylo Bludd walked that passageway now, his bulk heavy upon him, his sword sheathed in dogskin at his thigh.

He told himself he was old and jaded and hard to impress, yet he couldn't help but marvel at the blue-gray light that shone upon him, filtered down through man-size blocks of cyanide quartz sunk deep into the earth. Only light the color of the Dhoone Kings' eyes was allowed entry into their grave.

A *nice fancy*, Vaylo thought. But it was probably just as well no one had ever thought to do such a thing for Bludd, for the Bludd chiefs were a hard-drinking, hard-fighting lot and their eyes always burned red. Vaylo grinned. Stone Gods! But the Bludd chiefs were ugly! No one would have raised fancy tombs for *them*, that was for sure. Old Gullit's nose had been split so many times by brawling and hammer blows that it looked just like a burst plum . . . and as for Thrago before him—well, men said it wasn't for nothing that he was known as the Horse Lord.

Vaylo's smile faded as the corridor widened ahead of him and he entered the coldness of the vault. The same blue light that spotted the corridor lay soft upon the standing tombs of Dhoone. They lined the great circle of the vault wall, stone coffins the size of men, with the likenesses of kings carved deep upon them, each one raised upright, as if they bore living, standing flesh, not dust. It made Vaylo's hair rise to see them. The clanholds had been settled for three thousand years and the Dhoone Kings had reigned for a third of that. One thousand years of kings, sealed within the silence of stone.

Now, at last, he realized the weight of Ayan Blackhail's sin. To bring an end to this with a Hailish arrow, carelessly loosed to the throat.

The Dog Lord shook his grizzled head, feeling the weight of his braids at his back. He wasn't one for wonder, and could recall having felt it only twice in his life. The first time was at Cedarlode, when the mist parted before him to reveal the mounted might of the Sull.

The second was here, in this tomb.

The air was dry and it moved strangely in the lungs. Vaylo could taste the age of it. It made him feel young and unimportant, a fish inside a whale. There before him, dominating the center of the space, stood the stone table that Jamie Roy had brought across the mountains during the Great Settlement. It had taken an army of men to move it, had occupied ancient roundhouses that no longer stood, had spent a hundred years rotting at the bottom of the Flow, and now it lived here, with the bones of the Dhoone Kings. Vaylo had no desire to touch it, yet his hand moved toward it all the same.

"I wouldn't do that if I were you, Dog Lord. Last I heard that table was cursed."

Vaylo stayed his hand and turned to face the man who had entered the vault.

Angus Lok shrugged. "Of course, if you have a fancy for your hair falling out and your manhood falling off, go ahead and stroke it. Just be sure to step into the shadows if you do, as I imagine it's not a pretty sight."

Vaylo huffed . . . yet he did not touch the stone.

The ranger ignored him and began looking around the vault. "So these are the famous standing tombs of Dhoone? I see a few of them have gone to their knees." It was true enough. Some of the older coffins had crumbled and fallen open, revealing nothing but blackness inside.

Vaylo said, "Only your first time here, ranger? I'd have thought you'd have skulked your way in before now."

"Skulk?" Angus Lok showed his teeth. "That's a fancy word, Dog Lord. How long have you been saving it for?"

Vaylo showed teeth of his own. "Since I caught you and the clansman at Ganmiddich."

If Angus Lok was stirred by Vaylo's anger he did not show it. He merely moved across the vault to inspect one of the more hideously carved tombs. The eight weeks of his confinement had gone easy upon him, and he looked little changed from the day Vaylo had seen him sealed in the pit cell beneath the chief's chamber at Ganmiddich. His kind always prospered. He had the gift of turning enemies into friends, could coax extra rations from the most heartless of jailers, draw information from the most tight-lipped of guards. Even when Ganmiddich had been beset by Blackhail and retaken, the ranger had managed to talk Hammie Faa, his jailer, into letting him take up a sword. Angus had given his word that he would make no attempt to escape, merely defend himself against attack. He had kept it too, Vaylo had to give him that. And Hammie swore that the ranger had kept open the retreat at the Crab Gate, whilst the old Bludd retainers rode through. Vaylo himself had seen none of it, though he never doubted a Faa man's word.

Now Angus was here, at the Dhoonehouse, held in one of the strange and echoing moleholes under Dhoone. The Dog Lord had considered calling for him many times, yet had only today decided firm.

Slapping his side in search of the small leather pouch that held his chewing curd, he said, "Since we're talking of words, Angus Lok, mayhap you can help me with the meaning of one of them."

"If I can."

The Dog Lord softened a cube of black curd in his fist. "You can tell me what exactly it is that a ranger does."

Angus was inspecting the stone likeness of some ancient and unknowable king, and did not turn as he said, "A ranger *ranges*, Dog Lord. Surely you know that." Admiring the curve of the king's intricately carved greatshield, he crouched and ran a finger across the boss. "We ride wide and far, bearing messages and small goods where we can, spinning tales for our supper and trading news for our keep. We take day labor where we find it, trap game if we're so inclined. I even knew one man who made his living teaching clanwives how to dance like city bawds." Angus straightened his spine. "As for myself, well I'm no dancer, and the last thing I trapped with a wire was my own left foot, so I mostly rely on trade."

An easy smile warmed the ranger's handsome face. "Why, you wouldn't happen to have a proposition for me, Dog Lord?"

Indeed Vaylo did, but he'd be damned if he'd let this clever-spoken dog trick him into speaking before he was ready. Crossing the vault, he made his way toward the effigy of the Dark King, Burnie Dhoone.

The man who had destroyed Clan Morrow had been carved without eyes. The stonework on his greathelm was so fine that Vaylo could see the join where the nosepiece had been welded to the crown, yet, on either side of the smoothly planed stone, the carving gave way to sockets of jagged rock.

Vaylo touched the powdered guidestone at his waist. *Who had ordered him carved so, and why?*

"The Thistle Blood ran thick within him," murmured Angus, coming to stand at the Dog Lord's back. "It's said that he got it from both sides."

Vaylo had never heard such a thing before. "How so?"

"His mother was raped by her father, the king."

"*Stone Gods.*" Vaylo suddenly wished for the company of his dogs, yet he and Angus were close to the heart of the matter now: how a ranger came to know more about the clanholds than a clan chief himself. So he said, "I remember the summer I turned seventeen. It was hot enough to bake mud, and the sky had that haze to it that only comes with long days of sun. I couldna keep myself in the roundhouse, so hot and restless was I, so I'd ride out every day at dawn to cool myself in the forests south of Bludd. There's old trees in that forest, and man-cut stones and ruins amongst them. When it got too hot to hunt I'd take my stick and fish for trout. I was not a patient fisherman, and doubtless scared more fishes than I caught, yet I liked it well enough. There was green water, and it was cool, and some ancient bit of archway shaded me, and one day when I came to my secret place I met a ranger there."

Angus Lok didn't stir, though Vaylo knew he had the man's attention in full. So he took his time with the telling; let no one say the Dog Lord couldn't spin a tale when he chose to.

"He called himself Hew Mallin, though I learned later he was known by many names. Sitting right on my spot, he was. Bold as brass, with a line in the water. Greeted me by my name, and told me that I'd best pick another hole next time as I'd never pull anything bigger than sticklebacks from this. *Why do you fish here then?* I challenged him. And he looked me right in the eye, cool as milk, and said, *Because I'm here to hook men, not fish.*

"Well, I was young and suspicious and hard to impress, yet I felt a thrill all the same. He knew about me, this man. Knew what kind of bastard I was, and what kind of father had begot me. *There's no love for you in that roundhouse*, he said. *Come south with me and I'll show a place where your strengths won't go unrewarded. There are fights to be fought and a world that needs watching, for even as we speak the enemy masses at the gate.*"

Vaylo turned to face the ranger full on. "Aye, Angus Lok. Your fine, secret brotherhood thought to have me in their fold."

A moment passed, and then Angus said quietly, "I can see why."

It was not the response Vaylo had expected. He had been prepared for derision or disbelief—but not grace. It lightened something within him to receive it.

Angus watched him closely. "How did you answer them?"

Vaylo waved his fist. "I told Hew that I might be a bastard but I was a Bluddsman to the core, and that I'd shrivel and dry to nothing the moment I stepped on land that wasn't clan. Oh, don't think I wasn't tempted—bastards dream of little except grabbing glory far from home—but the desire was already in me to make myself Lord of the Clans." He shrugged. "Besides, I had a small idea to steal the Dhoonestone from Dhoone."

Angus nodded. "Fishing will do that to a man—give him ideas."

"Aye, I've learned so."

Silence grew then, as the ranger waited for the clan chief to name the terms of his deal. Vaylo did not fool himself about who was the cleverer man here: Angus Lok had had him pegged from the start. Vaylo could see it in the blandness of the ranger's face. Old Ockish Bull had looked as bland as that, and no one had ever risen early enough or stayed out late enough to put anything over on him.

Outside it was growing dark, and the filtered light dimmed to the deepest blue. *Sull blue*, Vaylo thought. Gone was the light, grayish thistle-blue of Dhoone. The Dhoone Kings were probably spinning in their graves.

But if they were you couldn't hear them.

Vaylo spoke into the silence they created. "You know Spynie Orrl was killed after visiting me, here, in the Dhoonehouse." A nod from Angus; no surprises there. "And did you know what he came to tell me? This old man who was no one's fool, and knew exactly what he risked to come here."

Angus did not nod this time, but Vaylo saw awareness in his copper-green eyes.

"He came to warn me. The Sull are preparing for war."

The words did not rest easy in the Tomb of the Dhoone Princes; cold currents caught them and blew them against the walls, creating sharp little echoes that hissed, *Sull. Sull. Sull.*

Vaylo sucked on his black and aching teeth. He could not rid himself of Spynie Orrl. The old goat haunted him, he was sure of it, whispering words in the black of night as if Spynie hardly knew he was dead. *There are outside forces at work here, Bludd chief. I know it. You know it. And the question that now remains is, are you content to let it be?*

Suddenly tired with games, Vaylo cried, "What is going on here, ranger? There's secrets beneath secrets, plots inside plots. I'm not a scholar or a seer. I look at the sky and see only sky. How am I to protect my clan against dangers I cannot see?"

"You already know the answer to that, Dog Lord," Angus said, his voice soft and dark as the shadows that gathered about him. "Return to Bludd and marshal your forces and wait for the Long Night to come. Forget about Dhoone and this round-house, and your fancy of naming yourself Lord of the Clans. Days darker than night lie ahead, and no amount of land or titles will stop the shadows when they come. Chiefs may die as easily as pig herders, yet they're nowhere near as blameless. Men look to you to lead them. So *lead*. Leave this place, set aside your battles." Angus's gaze flicked to the seventy stone coffins lining the walls. "It's all small purchase in the end."

Vaylo had his hand on the wire grip of his sword. Anger was hot within him, and he thought of many things to say to this man, but in the end there was only one. "I will not relinquish Dhoone."

The ranger nodded. "Aye, I had an inkling you'd say that."

The anger puffed out of Vaylo, leaving him feeling weary and very old. By rights he should call Hammie Faa or Drybone and have them take the ranger away—and not gently at that. Yet he feared Angus Lok, feared the knowledge he held and the counsels he kept. Feared them, and wanted them for himself.

Resting his weight against the tomb wall, Vaylo said, "You know the Surlord offered a sow's weight in gold for your head?"

"What, only *one* sow?" Angus scratched the stubble on his jaw. "I'd have thought this chin alone was worth more than two."

Vaylo did not take the bait. "And the Lord Rising of Morning Star sent one of his White Helms to bid for you. I daresay I could make a pretty profit if I chose to, auctioning you off for the high-est price."

"Yet you *choose* to do something else." The humor left Angus now, quick as if it had never been there at all. Vaylo reminded himself that this man was one of the best longswordsmen in the North, marksman and assassin, expert horseman and field surgeon. Friend of the Sull.

Vaylo thought carefully before speaking his next words. Pride was at stake here, both the ranger's and his own. "I choose to offer you a deal. The Mountain Lords are no friends of mine, and if I thought so once then I was a fool. I'm old enough now to admit my mistakes, but not so old that they cannot shame me. The clanholds are at war, and I will not deny my part in that, nor will I surrender my gains, but I canna say that I sleep well at night. I have lived too long on the edge of things not to recognize when those edges change. Bludd is a border clan and I am a border chief. You know our boast. *We are Clan Bludd, chosen by the Stone Gods to guard their borders. Death is our companion. A hard life long lived is our reward.*"

Vaylo looked carefully at Angus Lok. The moon was rising now, silvering the standing tombs so they looked like men of ice. The ranger's face was deeply shadowed, and looked leaner and hungrier for it. *He wants this*, Vaylo thought, and so he spoke his deal.

"Help me guard my borders. I don't need might or swords or warriors—Bludd has them in numbers—I need knowledge from a man I can trust. I know you will not name the brotherhood that claims you, and can guess well enough what breed of oath they made you speak. Yet there is middle ground here, between a chief's oath and a ranger's oath, and though our wars may be different our enemies may one day prove the same."

Angus stood silent and unmoving, his weight balanced evenly between his feet. Time passed, and then he said, "And in return?"

"I'll see you released."

The two watched each other, each mindful of what was at stake. Angus Lok might be a clever and amiable prisoner, well able to coax information and favors from any man who guarded him, yet he had to know that no Bluddsman would ever set him free. Sixty days of captivity had taught him that.

"I know you travel these lands," Vaylo said, "speaking with clansmen and city men alike. What I ask is that you share your knowledge of the clanholds with me."

The ranger's eyes glittered cold. Any other man and the deal would be done by now, for talk was cheap and confidences easily betrayed. Yet Angus Lok was not any man . . . and he had lived twenty years with the Phage. He said, "I am no petty traitor, Dog Lord, and I go running to no man with news given to me in confidence. Nor would I speak a word that endangered friends or kin." A pause, while the ranger allowed Vaylo time to remember that the man standing before him was kin to Raif Sevrance, murderer of Vaylo's own grandchildren. "Yet there are matters where our interests meet—" a dangerous smile "—not least of which is setting me free."

Vaylo inclined his head. The deal was done. Neither man would insult the other by haggling over terms.

"So," Angus continued briskly. "You would have information from me. Well, much though I hate to come courting with swords, I should warn you to watch your back."

"Blackhail?"

"No. Dhoone."

The word seemed to warm the vault, Vaylo swore it. All around stonework creaked and settled, sending spores of blue sandstone to seed the air. "How so?"

Angus shrugged. "The battle for the chiefship is coming to a head. On one side you have Skinner Dhoone, brother to the slain chief Maggis. He names himself chief-in-exile and gathers men about him at the Old Round outside of Gnash."

"Aye." The Dog Lord nodded. He had Skinner's measure. The Dhoone chief-in-exile put no fear into Vaylo Bludd. Skinner had a high temper and he blew hard and long, but he had lived too many years in the shadow of his brother and no longer had his jaw. Any other man would have tried to retake

Dhoone by now. A month ago Skinner might have seized it if he'd had the balls, for Vaylo and Drybone were housed at Ganmiddich, and the Dhoonehouse was held by Pengo Bludd. Vaylo snorted air. He had nothing but contempt for a man who had a chance but failed to seize it.

"And on the other side you have Robbie Dhoone," Angus continued. "The golden boy of the Dhoone warriors, who claims chiefship through some questionable second-cousining and the Thistle Blood through his dam."

Vaylo pushed himself off from the wall with force. "A young pretender, nothing more."

"Not from what I've heard, Dog Lord." Angus's voice was strangely light. "Then again, perhaps you have better intelligence than I. After all, there are limits to what a man can hear in a cell."

Put in his place, there was nothing for Vaylo to say other than, "Go on." They both knew who was master of secrets here.

"Robbie Dhoone has the golden hair and fair eyes of the Dhoone Kings, and he knows how to cut a figure with them. They say he's born to the sword, but the weapon he draws in battle is the great ax, much loved of the old kings. By all accounts the Thistle Blood runs true within him, and he can trace his line back to Weeping Moira. And I've heard it said by more than one man that he signs his name Dun Dhoone."

Dun. "Thistle" in the Old Tongue, the name the Dhoone Kings took as their own.

Unease must have shown itself on Vaylo's face, for Angus said, "Aye, Dog Lord. You see the way the lake drains now. He's young and ambitious and well loved in Castlemilk, and he's puffing himself up to be a king."

"He quarters in Castlemilk?"

Angus nodded. "He raises an army there."

Vaylo turned his back on the ranger to give himself time to

think. The likenesses of the Dhoone Kings watched him, stone eyes alive with moonlight. *The pretender will try to retake this place*, he thought. *That is the warning Angus Lok would have me heed. All talk of kingship is hollow unless a king holds the land he claims.*

Behind him, Vaylo heard the sound of Angus crossing to the far side of the vault. Shadows lay deep there, amongst the oldest of the standing tombs. All edges had been worn to curves by nothing more than air. "And there's more, Dog Lord," Angus said softly, causing Vaylo to turn. "The border clans best ready themselves against raids from the Mountain Lords."

Vaylo grunted. There was always more. "The Surlord and the King on the Lake have long had an eye for the green hills and black mines of Bannen and Croser. Spring raids are nothing new. Heron Cutler led a sortie five years back, and took a blade in the kidneys for his trouble."

Angus squatted to inspect the capstones surrounding the effigy of an ancient and faceless king. As he spoke he ran a finger along the mortar lines, testing. "If I were you, Dog Lord, I'd watch the clans nearer home. The Lord Rising of Morning Star stands close enough to HalfBludd to smell the staleness there."

This was news. "Cawdor Burns plans to strike against the Bluddsworn clans?"

The ranger did not look up from inspecting the wall as he said, "Who can say? The Lord Rising is no man's fool. He'll sit and watch the clanholds crumble from the safe haven of his Burned Fortress, and as soon as he spies a weakness he'll move. HalfBludd is past her glory. She's been in decline since Thrago HalfBludd deserted his birthclan to name himself chief of Bludd."

Vaylo found himself nodding. It was so. Thrago HalfBludd was his grandfather, the Horse Lord who brought back glory to

the Bluddhouse after the defeat at Crumbling Wall. Yet whilst
Thrago was in the field winning victories for Bludd, his birthclan suffered for want of a strong chief, and Bludd's gain was
HalfBludd's loss. "I'll send word to Quarro at the Bluddhouse,
get him to send a crew of hammermen to HalfBludd's southern reach."

"Do that. But be sure to keep your watch."

Vaylo bristled. He did not care for advice from any man, let
alone from some cocksure, trusty runner for the Phage. He was
the Dog Lord, and he had lorded his clan for thirty-five years,
and a chief did not hold his place that long by being anybody's
fool. "Get up, man," he commanded. "Go and present yourself to Drybone and tell him the nature of the deal we have
struck. He'll return your arms and provision your drypack and
see you on your way."

Still Angus did not rise. "And my horse?"

The magnificent bay gelding. As soon as Vaylo had set eyes
upon it he had known it for a Sull horse. "It will be returned."

"I thank you for that, Dog Lord." The ranger stood and faced
him. His fingertips were white with mortar dust, and Angus saw
Vaylo's gaze upon them. "'Tis nothing," he said, with a small
shrug. "I heard once that a tunnel led from this tomb all the
way north to the Copper Hills. It's said that it was dug so long
ago that not even the Dhoonesmen can remember it."

"Yet you and your brotherhood do."

The ranger brushed the dust from his fingers. "We remember the old words and the old rhymes, nothing more. *In the
Tomb of the Dhoone Princes there be/A bolthole for those who
canna look nor see.*" He grimaced. "Poetry was never a Dhoonish
art."

"Nor patience a Bluddish one."

Angus accepted the reprimand with a bow. "Well, I'd best
be on my way. Let no one say Angus Lok outstayed his welcome

in the Dhoonehouse." He offered the Dog Lord his arm, and after a moment Vaylo stepped forward to clasp it. "I shall call back when I have more news. Expect me when the wind blows cold and from the North."

"That's near every day in the clanholds."

Angus grinned. "Then I'll be sure to pick an especially stormy one."

Vaylo released his arm. "Aye, I'm sure you will." He made himself wait until the ranger was long gone before following him out of the tomb.

FOUR

The Beast Beneath the Ice

Raif pushed the sealskins from him and swung his feet onto the floor. The band of ice sealing the door glowed blue and milky in the growing light. The little soapstone lamp was dead, the whale oil in its chamber long congealed to a wedge of fat. A fur of hoarfrost had grown on the ceiling above where he had slept, each rising breath adding crystals to the mass. It was bitterly cold. And he was alone.

Ash was gone.

Raif waited, but the panic didn't come. He would go after her, that was all. Wherever she was, wherever they had taken her, he would find her and bring her back.

His head hurt when he moved his eyes, and the skin on his face was tight and numb. Something dry and scaly coated his tongue, and he remembered the *oolak* the Listener had bade him drink. *Strong brew, and like a fool I drank myself into oblivion. I should have known what Ark Veinsplitter wanted. The truth was in his eyes.*

Raif pressed his fingers into his face, trying to banish the numbness. They'd had it all planned, the two Far Riders and the Ice Trapper. Make him drink until he'd passed out and then steal away with Ash. From the look of the hoarfrost over the bench, he'd slept longer than one night . . . and that meant that Ash could be leagues away by now. No one could travel further in white weather than the Sull.

But a clansman could always try.

Standing, Raif tested his body for aches. There seemed too many to count so he ignored them and concentrated on his thirst instead. A small copper pot stood beside the lamp, its rim caked with caribou hairs and frozen soot. Snapping surface ice with his knuckles, he discovered liquid water beneath. The water was so cold it smoked from his mouth as he drank, and he could feel it sliding down to his gut. The horn bowls and the stone warming basin that had contained the *oolak* were gone. The only evidence that Ash had been here were the footsteps stamped in rime on the floor.

How could I have let them take her?

A soft chuffing sound broke his thoughts. The raven. The Listener's great black bird stood to attention on its bone perch, its wings tucked and folded, its sharp-eyed gaze upon Raif. Raif thought he would like to swipe it with his fist, but seriously doubted that he was faster than the bird, and didn't think it would be dignified to miss. So he turned his back instead. He was sick of ravens and their omens. And he didn't want to think about his lore. Ash had it, that was enough. The last time he'd seen the hard piece of bird ivory, it had been suspended from twine at her throat.

Suddenly eager to be gone, Raif kicked the driftwood door. The ice seal cracked, and the thick sea-salt-cured planking swung back to reveal a twilight landscape of day-burning stars and ice. The sun was somewhere north of the horizon, unseen, but sending out rays of red light that stretched across the floes toward the sea. The air smelled of a coldness beyond frost.

When Raif exhaled his breath whitened so violently it seemed to ignite.

"*Sila. Utak.*" The small hunched figure of the Listener was heading toward him, leaning heavily on a staff of twisted horn as he made his way across the cleared space at the center of the stone mounds. His words sent a young girl racing off to do his bidding, and made two older hunters who were hacking frozen meat by a cache hole stand alert.

Raif stepped forward to meet him. The man's finery and tokens of power were gone, replaced by grubby sealskin and stiff furs, yet he appeared no smaller for it . . . and he did not look repentant.

Anger sparked within Raif. "Where have they taken Ash?"

Close now, the Listener shook off Raif's question as if it were nothing more than snow on his back. Coming to a halt, he repeated the words he had spoken to Raif when first he saw him: "*Mor Drakka.*"

Raif felt the same strange thrill, almost as if he were hearing a god speak his name, yet he would not let himself be distracted. "The girl. Where is she?"

The Listener crooked his mitted fist and turned. Slowly, he walked away, heading for the hills and frost boils that rose sharply to the north of the village. A low wind buffeted the snow and set the sea ice creaking. Raif did not want to follow. He'd been trapped once in this place. How difficult could a second entrapment be? He was a stranger here. An outsider, and without warmth and food and knowledge of the land, he'd be a dead man within a day.

Reluctantly, he grabbed his Orrlsman's cloak from the ground and followed the Listener north. There were no choices at the edge of the world, and a clansman could do well to remember that. The Stone Gods' power was stretched thin here; the earth and rock they lived in was buried deep beneath the ice.

The Listener led him north across treacherous ground. Ice fog had frozen the top snow to glass, and it shattered with tiny explosions underfoot. The cold made Raif weary, and the bleak whiteness of the landscape drained the willpower from him. It was hard to imagine journeying alone in this place.

Frost boils broke through the ground like shrunken volcanoes, their stone rims too sharp and narrow to bear snow. The Listener stepped around them with ease, prodding at drifts and suspect ice with his staff. When the land began to rise he slowed his pace, yet Raif still found it difficult to keep up. He could barely hide his relief when the old man came to a halt by the leeward edge of a frost boil. Raif clambered up the slope to reach him.

"Turn around, Clansman. Tell me what you see."

It took Raif a moment to realize that the Listener had spoken in Common Tongue. How could this be? What had happened to the old man who had not understood a word he'd said the other night, and had needed Ark Veinsplitter as a translator?

Seeing Raif's surprise, the Listener's eyes glinted with satisfaction. "Never assume you know your enemy until he is dead."

Feeling heat come to his face, Raif said, "You can't learn anything from a corpse."

"You can learn that only a dead man cannot surprise you."

Something hard and ancient shifted behind the Listener's eyes, and Raif knew he had been told a truth worth remembering. Yet it didn't mean he had to like the old man for it. Turning to face the way they had come, Raif looked out across the Ice Trappers' territory and the frozen sea. His gaze traveled to the stone grounds of the village, then toward the shore, where a second village, built of wood and whalebone and mounded earth, stood abandoned close to the ice.

"Our summer life," said the Listener, following his gaze. "Soon it will be eaten by the ice. A storm will move the sea, and the shore ice will break its mooring and come crashing onto the beach. Much will be destroyed. So we gathered our lamps and harnessed our dogs and took refuge in the old places." His eyes flicked to Raif. "It's a foolish man who thinks he can stand in the way of fate or moving ice."

"How can you know this?"

"I listen while others sleep." The Listener poked a mitted finger at the remains of his left ear. "Gods and things older than gods whisper in the darkness, telling the tale of what has been and what is to come. If you are lucky you cannot hear them. You grow, you hunt, you enter a woman, and the world you live in is a knowable place where a man can make his own way and find his own death.

"If you are unlucky you learn more. Oh, men will honor you for it, send the women with the best cuts of meat and their daughters with animal skins beaten till they run through your fingers like grains of sand. And all the while they fear you. And though they need the knowledge you bring them, they do not love you for it. For you have heard whispers from the beginning of the world, and no man can listen to those echoes and remain unchanged."

The Listener rested his weight on the yellow and twisted horn of his staff. His face was dark and knowing, lit by the farthest edge of the sun. When he spoke again there was anger in his voice, and his breath crackled in air that was suddenly still. "Days darker than night lie ahead; that is the truth here. That is the answer to your question. The girl has gone and you cannot follow her. How can you track someone in utter darkness? What good would it do to find her, when you can no longer see her face?"

"Where have they taken her?" Raif heard the stubbornness in his voice. He could not let this man's words distract him. It was a trap, like the *oolak*. Fine drink. Fine words. He just wished they sounded less like the truth.

"Better ask *why*, not where, Clansman. Follow me." The Listener raised his staff to the hummock wall and began the final ascent to the rim. He moved like a spider, light and skittering, stepping sideways more often than forward. Raif envied his technique. The little tribesman was full of surprises.

The frost boil was a crater of raised rock, forced upward by earth that had expanded as it froze. Raif had seen their like in the badlands. They were good places to set camp by, and Tem said that clansmen used to fight duels in their hollows as they were reckoned a worthy place to die. When Raif gained the rim he saw the crater's basin was filled with snow-crusted ice. Hard black basalt ringed the core.

The Listener wagged his head toward the ice. "Drop down and scrape off the snow."

Raif had half a mind to tell the Listener to go to one of the nine spiraling hells. He was getting tired of games. And he feared another trap.

"I am an old man," snapped the Listener, "and the women tell me I must save my strength for winter's end. So if I had a mind to kill you I'd have done so closer to home." He bared tiny brown teeth. "Save myself the trouble of hauling back your body for the dogs."

Raif let out a breath. Why was it that all holymen thought they had a right to taunt him? Inigar Stoop had been no different—but at least he was clan. Laying a mitted hand on the crater's rim, he vaulted onto the ice. He landed hard, ten paces below the Listener, on a basin of ancient water that was frozen to its core.

"Here. Use this." The Listener dropped a flat-bladed knife onto the ice. "*Ulu*. Woman's knife. Should serve a clansman well."

Raif stabbed at the snow. The top layer was hard and brittle, but softer grains lay beneath. The little knife, with its center tang, had been designed for scraping skins, and it made good progress toward the underlying ice. Raif decided it wasn't worth thinking about why he was being made to do this. The Listener reminded him of one of those spiteful little imps who always guarded bridges in crib tales: they'd never let you cross until they'd humbled you first.

Fumes rose from the ice as he worked. When he reached the final layer of snow, a chill went through him. Something was casting a shadow on the ice. Turning, he looked up at the Listener and the twilight sky beyond. Neither the sun nor the moon had risen high enough to cast shadows. Yet it was there, a darkness upon the ice.

"Finish what you started, Clansman." The Listener's voice was thin and hostile. "You wanted answers; dig for them."

It occurred to Raif that he could kill the man standing above him. Raif was armed now, and though the Listener possessed a wily sort of strength, he would be no match for a fitter, younger man. A blow to the heart would finish him. Not sure if he was comforted or unnerved by the thought, Raif turned back to his task and resumed scraping. The final layer of snow was hard and frozen, stuck fast to the ice by frequent thaws. The knife blade bent as he worked, and he could feel the sweat trickling between his shoulder blades as he put the force of his body behind each blow. The area he was clearing was roughly circular, the size of a man's chest. When he'd chipped away enough of the surface crust he set down the blade and brushed off the loosened snow.

Something deep inside his spine, the nerve that Tem said was the first thing of a man's to grow within the womb, sent Raif a warning of pure fear.

The darkness was not upon the ice, it was *within* it.

Instinctively, his hand rose to his waist. Only the tine containing his measure of powdered guidestone wasn't there. He experienced a moment of panic as he slapped his hip, searching for the hardness of elk horn, before remembering he had used his last portion on Ash. It had summoned the Sull for her.

Oh gods.

Raif bit off his mitts and spat them away. Holding his hands to his face, he blew warm air upon them. He was aware of the Listener standing above him, perfectly still now, his breaths coming slow and silent. Raif put his hands upon the ice. He felt the coldness leap toward his fingers, questing for fluids to freeze. Quick frost fastened to his skin, but he pushed against it, dragging his palms across the small area he'd cleared, turning opaque ice transparent.

He saw the teeth first. A dark mouth gaped wide beneath the surface, lips pulled back to reveal a jaw of broken teeth. Raif recoiled. Something lay dead and frozen beneath him, something that could not be called a man.

Slowly, he returned his hands to the ice. He was shaking now, and there was little heat in him, yet he had no choice but to carry on. He would not let the Listener see his fear.

An eye socket was revealed next, the skin black and mummified, the eyeball long exploded with the pressure of the ice. Evil was frozen in the densely layered muscles of the face. The shadowy mass of the creature's body was buried deep beneath the surface, its shoulders and chest receding into grotesquely twisted shapes. Raif told himself the distortions were due to ripples in the ice; he almost believed it until the Listener spoke.

"*Thaal Sithuk,*" the Listener said, his voice soft with hunter's awe. "From the War of Shadows. Xaluku of the Nine Fingers killed it with a spear thrust to the heart."

Raif struggled to find his voice. Beneath his fingers, the last portion of darkness waited to be revealed beneath a crust of white snow. "How long has it been here?"

"Five thousand years."

Raif closed his eyes. The time seemed too vast to comprehend.

The Listener waited until Raif's gaze returned to him before saying, "There are many things more terrible hidden beneath the ice."

I don't want to know, Raif thought. *I just want to find Ash.*

"Men and kings, and weapons they forged and cities they built and beasts they slew in the darkness. Ages have passed and most think only the legends remain . . . yet most never look beyond the surface of the ice. All things that die fall upon the earth. The musk ox is eaten by the wolf, the shored whale is plucked apart by gulls, the warrior is found and burned or thrust deep within a tomb. Yet sometimes the ice finds them before scavengers or the hands of men do. Sometimes the ice claims them and bears their bodies away."

Raif pushed his hands across the snow, clearing the last of the crust. He didn't want to hear this. His fingers ached, and patches of skin around his knuckles had started to yellow with frostbite. He wanted his clan, and Drey and Effie . . . and Ash. Yet even as he wanted them, he polished the ice under him so he could see what lay beneath.

A hand, with thick black talons that ended in razor points, reached out toward the light, its fist packed with ice. It was so close to the surface Raif could see the fine dark hairs that ran along the skin. Suddenly cold, he said, "Why are you showing me this?"

The Listener jabbed the point of his staff into the snow. "Because telling the truth is seldom enough. A man must see it with his own eyes. The shadows are rising, and beasts and taken men will walk this earth once more. Now is no time to be chasing after things you cannot have. The girl has gone. The Sull have taken her, and what the Sull take they never give back. She's theirs now. Let her be. Save your strength for the battles you can win. The Long Night has come, and those who thrive in darkness must step forward to fight."

Raif felt his face stiffen at the Listener's words. He wanted to deny them, but the little tribesman thrust out a hand to stay his reply.

"Yes, Clansman. I know who you are. I have seen the raven riding on your back. I have heard the sound of footsteps at your heels. Death follows you. She named you. Watcher of the Dead. Yes, you are cursed. But you are young and whole, and I am old and have no ears and can find little sympathy for you. We cannot choose our skills. A boy with a gift for nets and lines must fish. A man with a hunter's eye must hunt. If you're born to the darkness, claim it. Find yourself a weapon and fight."

Raif pushed himself upright. He was stirred, but didn't want to be. This was not his world, this place of shadows and darkness and beasts held in ice. He had no weapon, no training. How could you banish shadows except with light? Kicking the mound of snow at his feet, he scattered dry crystals across the clear and gleaming ice. *Ash, think of Ash.* Where was she now? Had they harmed her? Was she waiting for him to come?

He said simply, "Where are they taking her?"

The Listener watched him closely before answering. "They will carry her east to the Heart of the Sull."

"Then I'll go east."

"Men have died searching for the Heart of the Sull. The ways are long and twisting, and there are forests where every tree looks the same. Some say time itself is woven into the paths, but the Ice Trappers know little of that. We know the legends, some of them. And I can tell you that although Bluddsmen have been known to cross the borders of the Sull Racklands no clansman has ever entered the Heart."

"Then I'll be the first."

The Listener almost seemed to smile. "You are young, and

your arrogance becomes you so I won't tell you all the reasons why you are wrong. Know this. I have walked this land for a hundred years, from Wrecking Sea to Endsea, from the Ice Horn to the Lake of Lost Men, and not once in that time have I found the Sull ways. They ride for the mountains—I know because I have watched them, even followed them in my youth—but as soon as they pass into the foothills they cease to be. Now your eyes may be good, but mine were better, and I never discovered where they went."

Raif bowed his head. He couldn't argue with the Listener's words; he knew all about Sull ways. He wouldn't be here if the two Far Riders hadn't deigned to leave a trail. Still. He could make his own way east. Softly, almost to himself, he said, "I *will* find her."

"What makes you think she *wants* to be found?"

Raif glanced up at the hard ice-tanned face of the Listener. What he saw made him wary. "She was taken against her will. Drugged, snatched away in the night, forced to ride east to gods know where. Of course she wants to be found."

The Listener tapped snow from the tip of his staff. "*Oolak* is bitter and stringy, and stinks like dead fish. Only men are fool enough to drink it."

Again, Raif felt a stab of wariness. "Why are you telling me this?"

"Your friend was not drugged. She only took one sip of the *oolak*. She went of her own free will."

"No."

"They did not force her. She is the One With Reaching Arms. She knew she had to go."

Raif shook his head savagely. She wouldn't leave him without saying a word, not after all they'd been through. Not after the Cavern of Black Ice. He said coldly, "You lie, old man."

The Listener nodded. "Often, about many things. The kind

of truths I know destroy men. Mothers do not want to know that the child they carry will be born dead, or that their sons will die before they do, and that their husbands will be maimed during the hunt. You cannot be a Listener without knowing how to lie." As he spoke, the old man reached into the soft inner furs that lay beneath his sealskins and pulled something out. "But to you I speak the truth."

Opening his fist, the Listener let something small and dark fall upon the ice. "She asked me to return this."

Raif stared at the object by his feet. Black and hooked, as long as a child's finger, with a hole bored through the bridge for threading string. Raven lore. *Here it is, Raif Sevrance. One day you may be glad of it.* No matter how hard he tried to lose it, it always came back.

It changed everything, and both he and the Listener knew it. Calmly, because there was nothing else to do, Raif bent and picked up his lore. It felt thin and brittle, like something he could crush in his fist. Instead he pulled a short thong from the Orrl cloak and fastened the lore around his throat. It was his and he would wear it . . . and he would not think of what Ash had done.

"She made her choice," the Listener said. "Now it's time you made yours."

Raif found himself looking at the ice, at the dark and monstrous shape rippling beneath him. *Guard yourself,* she had said, her last words. How could he do that when the things that cut the deepest couldn't be fought? After a moment he crossed to the crater wall and began to pull himself up. His choice was made.

FIVE

Into the Fire

Effie Sevrance crouched behind the great copper distilling vat and watched as Gat Murdock sampled the low wines. The low wines were the halfway point in the distillation, Longhead said: too weak to be named a full malt, but strong enough to send a man to his knees if he sampled too often and too long. Effie wished Gat Murdock would drop to his knees . . . *soon*. It was hot and dark in the distilling well, and vapors bubbling from the cauldron made everything clammy and damp. Effie could feel the heavy wool of her dress sticking to her back like wet oats. *Stupid thing*. Why hadn't she thought to wear her linen shift instead?

Gat Murdock closed the spill hole on the bell-shaped vat and held his final sample up to the lamp. The sea-glass cup glowed green, revealing liquid still cloudy with dregs. Effie willed him to swallow and be done. She was on a mission for Bullhammer and Grim Shank, and she didn't want to disappoint them. They'd chosen *her* to brew the iron juice. There were a score of boys in the roundhouse, all doing nothing more than waiting around the Great Hearth each day in the hope of sanding the rust from a hammerman's chains or mending the shearling that couched the hammer itself. Yet when it came to the matter of the stain for the hammermen's teeth, Bullhammer had decided that Effie Sevrance would do a better, quieter job than any one of them.

"Effie's your girl," Bitty Shank had said to his older brother Grim last night, as they stood in the dry and dusty shadows of the stable block. "She's clever with her hands, knows how to keep a secret, and she's sister to a hammerman herself." Bullhammer and Grim had nodded gravely, the dim glow from the safe lamp sparking strangely off their tarnished plate. A hammerman's sister was good enough for them.

Iron juice, Bullhammer had explained, was as black as the Stone Gods' tears and only a little less likely to kill you. It had to be strong enough to stain a hammerman's teeth, and keep them good and black for a season. "It's no good using lamp-black or ashes—the stain barely takes for a week. And as soon as a man sets to frothing at the mouth his spittle's likely to run black." Effie had nodded in understanding. If you were going to stain your teeth so you looked fierce in battle then it would be better if the stain didn't wash off halfway through. Else you might end up looking foolish instead.

The problem was that Blackhail hammermen hadn't stained their teeth since Mad Gregor had led three hundred men to their death in the fast-rising waters of the Flow. All but a dozen of their number had been hammermen. Their bodies had been dragged downstream by the spring rush, across the rocky shallows known as Dead Man's Ribs and over the towering, misty drop of Moon Falls. Effie had heard it said that the river rock had peeled the flesh from their bones, and the only things left for the widows to wrap were white skulls with grinning black teeth.

Effie frowned. It seemed to her that there were far too many clan stories involving skulls and violent deaths. Still, it *was* interesting how afterward no Blackhail hammerman would stain his teeth for fear of riling the gods, and the recipe for iron juice had been lost.

"Sour as piss," Gat Murdock pronounced to the now-empty sampling cup. "Good enough for a tied clansman—or his wife." Satisfied, he upended the cup onto a basswood rack and spat to clean his mouth. Like many older clansmen he was missing fingers, yet he moved no slower for it, and sealed the taps and dimmed the lamp as quick as if he had ten fingers, not eight. Effie watched as he moved to leave then stopped himself before reaching the stair. Turning to face the very corner that concealed her, he sent his gaze darting this way and that, checking if he was being watched. Effie held her breath, imagining herself still as the very stone the well was built from.

Long seconds passed before the clansman's pale-eyed stare passed her by. Satisfied that no one was looking, Gat Murdock reached for the high shelf where Anwyn Bird kept her twenty-year malt and slipped one of the precious wax-sealed flasks under his coat. Effie forgot she was being still as a stone and let her mouth fall open in amazement. Anwyn's twenty-year malt! Wasn't there a curse upon it? Anwyn swore that any clansman who drank her malt without her blessing would find himself short of his man parts within a week. Effie closed her mouth. She had learned all about man parts from Letty Shank. Any man who lost them was bound to be sorely displeased.

Uttering a small grunt of satisfaction, Gat Murdock put his foot to the stair and began the short climb from the well. Effie forced herself to listen for the sound of his feet treading the floor above before emerging from her place behind the vat.

Her arm was stiff and she rubbed it softly as she squeezed past copper pipes. Other parts hurt too; places where Cutty Moss's knife had sunk deep, opening ragged hard-to-heal wounds that still wept water at night. She wouldn't think about those now, though. She was a clanswoman of nearly nine winters, and men returning from the Clanwars had worse hurts to bear.

She just wished Cutty's knife had spared her face.

Effie stopped her treacherous hand from rising to touch her cheek. *Wouldn't have been a beauty even without the scars, Mace Blackhail said so.*

Quickly, she turned her thoughts to iron juice. She needed good strong liquor to proof the potion. Anwyn's twenty-year malt was too mellow—and too cursed. She needed something that could burn a man's gums, and possibly his tooth enamel as well. Thoughtful, she scanned the flasks on the highest shelf. Will Hawk's Dhooneshine in its odd sparkly flask stood beside Dagro Blackhail's Chief's Malt, and Shor Gormalin's Gutbreaker with its crossed swords burned into the wood. So many dead men's brews. Then she saw it, in the darkest corner, its leather flask hairy with cobwebs, its wood stopper near forced-out with age: Tem Sevrance's Special Brew. Da must have distilled it himself.

It was late: the roundhouse had grown quiet and Effie knew she'd better hurry, yet she couldn't seem to stop herself from reaching for Da's flask. It smelled like him: leathery and horsy. And when she pulled the stopper out she nearly laughed. *This* would do the job. It surely couldn't kill anyone, not after this long, and Da had been a hammerman himself. He'd help her with blackening his companions' teeth.

Something behind Effie's eyes began to hurt, and she recorked the flask with a hard thump and began the short climb from the well.

It was an odd night in the roundhouse, dark and still with only half the torches lit in preparation for the Feast of Breaking. It had seemed like a good idea to gather the ingredients for the iron juice tonight, for few liked to travel the halls on the night the Stone Gods walked the earth. Now, though, as she wound her way through the roundhouse's crumbling lower reaches, she began to feel little prickles of unease. Her lore felt cool against her skin.

The small granite stone was suspended around her neck once more, heavy as a new-laid egg. Inigar Stoop had found it, clutched in a severed hand. It had been the clan guide's job to gather the remains of Cutty and Nelly Moss. Back bent double against the wind, wicker basket in hand, he had pried their frozen flesh from the snow. Effie had heard it whispered that nothing whole remained, that the dogs had eaten Nelly's eyes and tongue and torn out Cutty's spleen. She supposed she was lucky no dog had swallowed her lore. Inigar would not let her wear it at first. Instead he had taken the lore to the guidehouse where he'd spoken words of power over it, and then laid it atop the guidestone where it could draw strength and be renewed.

It felt different now. Older. Harder. Inigar said lores changed and grew with their wearers; so did that mean she was older and harder too?

Nearing the oil-blackened stair that spiraled up to the clan forge, Effie slowed her pace. Normally she liked this part of the roundhouse, with its low ceilings and narrow ways. It was darker than normal, but she didn't mind that. No Sevrance had ever been afraid of the dark. Still. There was something else . . . something watchful and waiting. And her lore didn't move, didn't push, but something inside it shifted as if a drop of liquid mercury had flash-hardened in its core. She stopped. Listened. Almost she heard something, but it was probably just a fancy. You couldn't *hear* the sound of a man holding his breath.

Go back, Effie, said a little voice inside her. *Run to your room and lock the door.*

No. She was on a mission for Bullhammer and Grim Shank. And she wouldn't bolt like a rabbit every time she was afraid. Besides, things were different now she was armed. Bitty Shank had given her a knife. A maiden's helper, he called it. "As nice a piece of flint as you'll find strapped to a goodwife's thigh." He taught her how to use it, too. It wasn't like stabbing someone with a sword. A flint knife's strength was in its blade, not its tip, and unless you fancied the tip breaking off as soon as you hit bone it was wiser to slash than stab. Effie had practiced slashing moldy and worm-holed sheepskins in the tannery, reducing the thick, useless rams' hides to strips. The knife's edge had been knapped to a sharpness beyond steel, so thin in parts that light shone through the stone. It was spoils, Bitty said, seized from a group of Ille Glaive trappers caught setting wires on Ganmiddich soil.

Effie touched her waist, feeling for the smooth horn sheath that held her knife. She loved Bitty Shank. He and his brothers would hear no talk of her being a witch.

Careful to let her thoughts go no farther, Effie started up the stair. All was quiet except for the groaning of ancient timbers and stone. Normally the clan forge was kept busy through the night, and although Brog Widdie, master smith and exiled Dhoonesman, would allow no man without an oath to work with hot iron, unsworn smiths and wireworkers would be busy socketing arrowheads and riveting coats of mail.

Tonight was different, though. The Eve of Breaking. All clansmen, sworn and unsworn, were gathered close around the Great Hearth, chanting the old songs. The Breaking was sacred to the Stone Gods. If they were not given their due this night they might send a frost so hard and so long that ice would grow in the heart of all guidestones, and the clanholds would shatter to dust. Castlemilk's guidestone had taken the frost nearly two thousand years earlier, and that ancient and venerable clan—who had once been great enough to challenge Dhoone for the kingship—had been in decline ever since. Many tales of the clanholds had been lost, even to Withy and Wellhouse who kept the histories, but the story of the Milkstone shattering, of how the Milkwives gathered the broken shards in their skirts and carried them to a place their menfolk would never know, sent chills down every clansman's spine. All knew that if the women hadn't hidden the fragments the men would have used them to cut out their own hearts.

Effie touched her little pouch of powdered guidestone, giving the Stone Gods their due.

Beneath her feet the stone steps were slippery, greased by graphite and calf's-brain oil from the smith's feet. The air grew warm and dry, thick with the stench of sweat and sulfur and smelted ore. Ahead, the great lead-plated doors were drawn closed. Water casks stowed to either side of the threshold told of the clan's great fear of fire. The forge bulged out from the north face of the roundhouse, shielded from the core stonework by a dark, airless tunnel called the Dry Run. The main entrance to the forge was cut from the exterior north wall, a towering arch as tall as two men, guarded by doors force-hardened with salt water and studded with steel heads to deflect blades. A clan's forge was its wealth and its strength. Raw metals were stored here, swords and arrowheads were forged here, and war spoils awaiting refiring and refitting were piled in great stacks along the walls.

Effie walked the length of the Dry Run, then put her hand to the lead door. It was neither locked nor bolted—she hadn't expected it to be—and half a ton of wood swung easily on hinges that Brog Widdie had tooled himself. The orange glow of the furnace lit the cavernous space of the forge. A circle of anvils dominated the room; horned and blocked and mouse-holed, they sent strange shadows to flicker at Effie's feet. Tempering baths filled with brine and refined tallow stood warming close to the furnace. Beyond them lay the worktables and work-blocks piled with striking hammers and bow tongs and other vicious-looking tools. Beyond those lay the stores: tubs of oil and slack and pig's blood, sacks of charcoal, sand

and raw ore. Iron rods were stacked as carefully as if they were gold, and cords of quartered lumber were piled like a bonfire to the rafters.

Effie took a step forward, hesitated, then called softly, "Message for Brog Widdie." No one answered. Something in the far corner, next to the redsmith bench where Mungo Kale worked copper and bronze, rustled and then was still. *Rat after tallow*, she thought, feeling braver by the minute. Letty Shank and Florrie Horn might scream at the very thought of rodents, but Effie could find nothing within her that was afraid of things so small. Quietly, she crossed the circle of anvils and headed toward the stores. One of the tallow baths had claimed a rat. As the temperature from the furnace dropped and the tallow congealed, the rodent had been set in fat. Tomorrow morning one of the Scarpemen would likely scoop it up, roast it in the furnace, and eat it. Everyone knew Scarpes feasted on rats.

As she passed one of the nail-punching benches, she paused to empty a supply of nails from a brass bowl. As the little iron spikes tumbled onto the wood she thought she heard something creak in the Dry Run behind her, but when she turned to look all was still. Probably just a beam settling—yet she moved a little quicker because of it.

The sacks of charcoal were easy to identify, as the pallet they were set upon was furry with soot. The charcoal-burner's mark was a tree above a flame; Effie noticed it as she unsheathed her knife and set flint to the hemp. The sack split easily and a thick stream of charcoal spilled to the floor. She moved quickly to catch the fine powder in the bowl, marveling at the richness of the charcoal . . . surely the darkest, blackest thing that ever was. If this didn't stain the hammermen's teeth then she might as well try to bottle the night sky, for nothing else was darker.

When the bowl was half full she drew it back and let the sack spill until it found its level. Her lore shifted uneasily against her skin, but she was too excited to pay heed. What if she tested a potion now? Did iron juice need iron? Or was it just a name? Yes, she probably needed acid to etch the charcoal into the hammermen's teeth, but it wouldn't hurt to try without it first . . . and it might save somebody's gums. *And*, she thought, becoming even more excited, *I'll test it on one of the shankshounds tonight. Old Scratch won't mind. His teeth are so yellow and chipped that it really might be an improvement.*

Grinning at the thought of a dog with black-stained teeth, Effie set down her knife. She pulled out Da's flask, uncorked it, and then poured half its measure into the bowl. Crouching by the charcoal sacks, she stirred the mixture with a chip of wood she found on the floor. Da's special brew darkened in an instant, and a fine black dust rose from the bowl like the opposite of steam. As she stirred she had visions of rank upon rank of Blackhail hammermen, armed and mounted, their hammer chains rattling in a quickening wind, their lips pulled back to reveal night-black teeth. Drey would be one of them, too. And perhaps if she made the iron juice dark enough and he looked fierce enough he wouldn't have to fight. Perhaps the Bluddsmen would turn and flee rather than raise their axes against him.

The men seemed to come from nowhere. A harsh cry raised Effie's head, a lead door was sent cracking against a wall, and then clansmen burst into the forge. Breathing hard, glittering with drawn steel, they moved to circle the room. Effie had once witnessed a group of hunters surrounding a wounded boar before a kill, and she recognized the same nervous excitement; the sucked-in cheeks and wet lips. The fear of drawing too close to their prey.

"Stay your ground, witch."

Effie recognized the speaker as Stanner Hawk, brother to Will and uncle to Bron who had both been slain in the snow outside of Duffs. Tall and pale like his brother, Stanner bore no love for anyone bearing the Sevrance name. Something hardened within Effie as he looked upon her. Raif had fought to save the lives of Will and Bron, yet that one fact had been twisted and ground down, and now all that could be remembered about the night outside of Duffs was that Raif Sevrance had spoken out against his clan.

Effie raised her chin. This was a coward before her. They all were. Two dozen men to capture an unblooded girl. They didn't even have the jaw to do it in full daylight on open ground; instead they had watched and sneaked and waited. Like weasels after eggs.

There was not a hammerman amongst them. No man who bore a hammer would raise a hand to harm his own. Instead there were Mace Blackhail's cronies; old and hard Turby Flapp bearing a sword so badly weighted he couldn't keep the point off the floor, lean and dark Craw Bannering clad in the cured hides and swan feathers of Clan Harkness, known as the Half Clan, his long tattooed fingers resting easily on a blade. The longswordsmen Arlan Perch and Ichor Roe moved with practiced stealth to take positions behind Effie's back. Many of the men were older Hailsmen, too long cooped up in a roundhouse at war and eager for any kind of blood.

And then there were the Scarpemen. Uriah Scarpe and Wracker Fox and others she did not know. Lean men, dressed in the black leatherwork and weasel pelts of Scarpe, watching her as if they had something to fear. *They really believe I'm a witch.* The thought came quickly and with it another: *This trap was carefully set.* No Shanks or hammermen had been told, no one who was friend to Drey.

"Stand up, witch." Stanner Hawk's voice was cold, and for the first time Effie wondered if he had something more than capture on his mind. With his sword fist he made a gesture to Craw Bannering. The dark bowman moved toward the woodstack and selected a cord of wood.

"I *said* stand up, witch." Stanner Hawk lashed out with his foot, sending a tub of brine crashing to the floor. Salt water splashed Effie's face.

Effie felt the calm leaving her. Her lore began to twitch against her skin, and she noticed sharp-eyed Uriah Scarpe glancing at the wool around her throat. Looking away, her gaze came to rest on her flint knife, there on the stone floor beside the pallet, only three paces from her foot. Uriah Scarpe was still watching her so she quickly turned her gaze. Slowly she began to rise, setting the bowl of iron juice on the floor.

Craw Bannering had drawn on the thick cowhide gloves of a hot-metal worker. The cord of wood now lay unbound beside the furnace, and the yearman was using both hands to pull back the cast-iron door that guarded the charging hole. Heat from the furnace leapt into the room as air was sucked into the hole. Craw fed the fire below it, choosing only the driest, densest wood.

Old men shifted their weights, whether with unease or excitement Effie didn't know. One of the Scarpemen said, "Pump the bellows, Crawman."

Stanner Hawk's eyes glinted orange in the growing blaze. "You are charged with being a witch, Effie Sevrance. Confess now and receive the swift judgment of my blade."

Someone at her back whispered, "It'll be a mercy for you, lass, in the end."

Twenty-four pairs of eyes watched her. Turby Flapp took a hand from his poorly made sword to wipe the saliva off his lips. Effie looked at every one of them; Hailsmen and Scarpemen and strangers alike. She was shaking, and she couldn't seem to speak, so all she could do to show her innocence was look them in their faces and meet their stares. One or two had the decency to look away. Arlan Perch found something to study on the knuckleguard of his sword.

"Speak, witch." Stanner Hawk was playing to the room now, his back turned toward her as he walked the circle of anvils. "I'll hear something from you before I put your feet to the fire."

Effie heard the belch of popping mud-bubbles as the mud trough surrounding the furnace began to boil. Ridiculously, she thought of the shankshounds. They made sounds like that whenever they were given greens instead of meat. Thoughts of shankshounds helped, and she suddenly found her voice. "Stanner Hawk, my Da said you once cheated him out of a kill, swapping his spear for yours so you could claim the she-bear as your own. My Da never lied, and nor will I. I am not a witch. The shankshounds saved me out of love and loyalty, not sorcery. They'd do the same for their master Orwin Shank, just as Mace Blackhail's hellhounds would save him."

Several grunts of agreement echoed around the forge. Many men here kept hounds, and all took pride in their dogs' fierceness and loyalty.

Stanner Hawk's face had lost what little color it had been blessed with. Two points of anger burned in his eyes, and Effie knew she had made a mistake attacking his honor. He would see her burned for it.

In three quick strides he was in front of her, the point of his sword pressing against the plump flesh of her lower lip. "Open your mouth, witch. Let me see the tongue that lies so easily. I'd heard witches could charm the sword from a man's hand, but I never thought to see such a thing myself." His last words were directed at the gathered clansmen, and to a man they straightened and raised their swords. No clever-speaking witch was going to fool *them*.

"Your father was a good man, Effie Sevrance," cried hard-eyed Turby Flapp. "You do him a disservice by defending yourself at his expense. What man here hasn't clashed with another over kills? It's not something you bring home to the women.

Let them tend to their traps, not the hunt."

Cries of *"Aye!"* circled the room. Turby Flapp was old and shaking, yet Effie could still see the triumph in his eyes. He'd insulted her and her father, and fired the men with righteous rage.

Mace Blackhail had chosen well.

Oh, she knew why he wasn't here, in this room. His hands must be seen to be clean. When Drey came to him, as Drey certainly would, Mace could say, *Drey, if I'd been there I would have stopped it. I was holding vigil around the Great Hearth. I had no idea what these men would do.*

Effie felt the bite of Stanner's sword as it split her lip, sending a line of blood trickling down her chin. Immediately a shift took place in the room. Breaths came hard and fast as sweating palms made it necessary to alter grips. Blood had been spilled. All hope of mercy was lost.

Stanner Hawk's mouth tightened in satisfaction, and with a kingly gesture he withdrew his sword. "Wracker," he said to one of the Scarpe swordsmen. "Feed the hound through the hole."

Wracker Fox was powerful in the way Shor Gormalin had been powerful: small and lean and so swift to movement that it was like watching a hare bolt from a set. In an instant he was gone from the forge. What seemed like seconds later he was back, something wrapped in a blanket held fast against his chest.

Effie thought her heart would stop when she heard the first frightened whimper. They had caught and bound one of the shankshounds.

Wracker Fox dropped the dog onto the floor to free it from the blanket. The dog's legs had been hobbled and its snout tightly muzzled with tarred rope, and the creature landed badly on its side. Effie flinched. It was Old Scratch, the gentle, dignified elder of the pack. Wounds around his eyes and jaw told he hadn't been taken without a fight.

Stanner Hawk said, "Put him in feet first, like we will the girl."

A sound left Effie's throat, a sound so soft and powerless that no man in the room paid it heed . . . but it was enough for Old Scratch to hear her and know that she was there. Slowly and at great cost, he turned his large amber gaze upon her.

Never, ever, not even if she lived for a thousand years would Effie Sevrance forget that look. Terror, faith and love touched her with such force it was as if she were inside the dog's head. Suddenly it was hard to breathe. The shankshounds had saved her life.

"Stop," she murmured to Stanner Hawk. "Set the dog free and I'll give you what you want."

Stanner ran a pale hand over his dark beard, and then exchanged a brief satisfied glance with Turby Flapp. Turning his back on her once more he said, "So you admit you are a witch as charged. And that you aided Clan Bludd in the attack upon Dagro Blackhail in the badlands, and the assassination of Shor Gormalin in the Wedge. You admit also that you helped your brother Raif Sevrance desert this clan, and heard him confess that cowardice drove him from the ambush on the Bluddroad. Lastly you confess that you bewitched Orwin Shanks's hounds and forced them to attack an innocent man and woman for no other reason than you feared they knew you for a witch." Stanner Hawk was suddenly there, back in front of her face, his smile so cold it chilled her. "Do you admit these sins, Effie Sevrance, before the faces of nine gods?"

Da, I didn't do them. Effie looked at Old Scratch, then quickly looked away. She found she couldn't face the dog and lie. Stanner Hawk was something different. She tilted her chin, raised her gaze and looked him full in the eye. "I admit I am a witch before the faces of nine gods."

Breath was sucked in around the room. Some of the older

clansmen touched their tines. One man, ancient and stoop-backed Ezander Straw, began to name the nine gods: *Ganolith, Hammada, Ione, Loss, Uthred, Oban, Larannyde, Malweg, Behathmus.*

Flames from the furnace leapt high, sending waves of heat switching wildly around the room. The mud in the trough boiled madly, slapping and sucking as the water within it turned to steam. Stanner Hawk's pale lips twitched. His knuckles were white where they curled around his sword. Still holding Effie's gaze he said, "Craw, send the dog to the fire."

"No," she breathed. Then, louder, "NO!"

"Yes," he hissed. "I make no covenants with a witch."

"But . . . you said . . . The dog—"

Turby Flapp stepped forward and slapped her face. "Hush, girl. 'Chant us no more with your lies."

Frantic with terror and helplessness, Effie didn't feel the pain of the blow. She couldn't find the words to save Old Scratch. *They said . . . they said . . . Old Scratch isn't used to the heat. He's afraid of lit candles . . . I'm sorry, I'm sorry, Da. Didn't have the words.*

Craw Bannering hefted the dog against his chest. Air venting from the charging hole shimmered with heat. The fire crackled and roared, releasing showers of white-hot sparks. Twenty-four men fell silent. No one except the bowman moved. The smith's gloves reached as high as Craw's upper arms, protecting him from the flames as he fed the dog to the furnace.

The heat was so great in the smelting chamber that fire ignited from dry air. Old Scratch screamed, thrashing and jerking, his eyes wide with terror as he fought to buck himself free. When the first flames found his flesh he let out a terrible moan. Effie watched, waited, knowing the dog's gaze would come to her, determined in every part of her that she would not look away.

Old Scratch's eyes were dimming when he found her, yet the same thing she had seen in them before was there. Faith. He thought she could save him. Even now.

Effie felt tears run down her face as the last of the dog went to the fire. Something hard and terrible was growing within her, and she felt the first stirrings of rage. Eyes darting, she studied the men who formed a circle around her. Their attention was given fully to the thrashing thing alive with flames. Slowly, slowly, she moved two paces to the side, put her foot on Bitty's flint knife, and sent a hand down her leg to scratch her knee. In an instant the knife was hers. Straightening, she checked the two Hailsmen behind her; their gazes hadn't shifted from the smelting chamber.

As the smell of singed fur and roasting meat filled the room, Effie found her grip on the blade. Men were shifting now, rubbing their eyes as if they had woken from a dream. When Stanner Hawk turned to face her she was ready.

"Witch. May the fire go no gentler on you." He motioned to the two Scarpemen, Uriah Scarpe and Wracker Fox. "Seize and bind her. Let her go awake and repentant to the flames."

As the two Scarpemen moved to flank her, Effie showed her knife. Sweeping the blade in a circle in front of her, she spoke in a shaky voice. "Stay back. You'll not find me as defenseless as a dog."

Someone close to the door snorted. Uriah Scarpe stretched thin weasel lips to a smirk. Wracker Fox danced back in mock fright. "Well, well, my little Blackhail hellcat. I see you've a fancy for a fight."

Stanner Hawk wasn't amused. "Burn her and be done."

"Aye," added Turby Flapp. "Allow her no chance to do more witchery this night."

Effie felt her face burn. *Stupid, stupid.* How could she have thought they'd be afraid of a girl with a stone knife? That was

when she saw Uriah Scarpe's gaze return to her lore. The granite stone was twitching with force, moving the wool fabric of
her dress. She watched fear enlarge the Scarpeman's pupils . . .
and then she knew what she must do.

Remember, they think I'm a witch.

Still holding the knife firm, she swept down and grabbed
the bowl of iron juice from the floor. Before any clansman had
a chance to react she dipped the blade of her knife into the
swirling fluid. A thousand pores in the flint soaked up the
black. The blade emerged glistening and smoking, like a piece
of frozen night. Almost when she saw it she felt afraid herself,
for the look of it stirred memories within her that she did not
know she had. But then Da's smell was upon it; the smell of
barley too old and honey nearly off and peat that had been
burned, not smoked. It gave her strength and heart, and when
she spoke all fear was gone.

"This," she said, holding up the coated blade for all to see,
"is dark magic I distilled myself. One drop upon your skin and
your soul is mine. Your teeth will rot and your sword hands will
wither, and your man seed will come out black." She paused,
sending a silent prayer of thanks to Letty Shank for inspiring
that particular horror, and then carried on, imagining Anwyn
Bird in a rage over something to help her voice come out right.
"If you value your lives you'd best let me walk free from this
place, or I swear I'll cast this bowl down and splash every one
of you, and take your souls with me to hell."

Silence. Someone coughed. Turby Flapp started to speak,
then was still. Some of the younger men began to edge back.
Uriah Scarpe brought his sword hand down to protect his man
parts. Effie waited, knife in hand, bowl tucked into the crook
of her arm . . . and stared every one of them down.

Stanner Hawk's face was a tight mask. Of the twenty-four
men in the room he was the only one who knew she was no

witch. She saw him weigh all possible outcomes. Call her a trickster and everything that had taken place here was voided. She was either witch or trickster; she could not be both. To speak up would be to contradict himself. And then there was the distinct possibility that they'd pay him no heed. Real fear lived in this room; if Effie could see that so could he.

In the end his decision was taken for him. Wracker Fox stepped away from her, saying to Stanner, "*You* take care of the Hailish bitch. I'm not going to touch her." As soon as he spoke, murmurs of agreement passed through the room, and the four men securing the doorway moved aside. Other clansmen stirred and within moments a path toward the door had cleared.

Something terrible must have been showing on her face when she walked between the ranks of clansmen for not one of them would meet her eye. Turby Flapp let his poorly weighted sword clatter to the floor and grabbed the tine containing his measure of powdered guidestone with both hands. The Scarpemen made gestures she did not recognize, strange wardings in the shape of poison pines. As she passed Stanner Hawk he whispered, "Never sleep in this roundhouse again, Effie Sevrance, else my knife will find you the moment you shut your eyes."

She said nothing in reply. She did not trust herself to speak. Everything in her was intent on making it toward the door. Thoughts of Old Scratch kept her hands steady and made her eyes blaze with their own kind of fire.

Later she could remember nothing of the journey along the Dry Run and out of the roundhouse. Only two thoughts held her: Old Scratch's faith that she could save him, and the dull and terrible certainty that the Stone Gods would send ice into the heart of the Hailstone for the wrongs done by clansmen this night.

SIX

Becoming Sull

They entered the mountain on the fourth day and, although it was virtually impossible to tell in which direction they were moving, Ash had a feeling they were no longer traveling east.

"We head east to the Racklands, then south to the Heart," was all Ark Veinsplitter had said about the journey. Ash had not questioned him. It had been the morning of their departure, when the sun barely showed itself on the eastern horizon and starlight lit the ice and turned it blue. There had been no sleep for her the night before in the Listener's ground, just terrible hours of wakefulness, knowing that she would soon leave Raif, and knowing also that she could not explain why. Speak to him of it and she would have been undone. He would have argued, persuaded, changed her mind. And he would have done it because he loved her. And it would have been a mistake.

She was Sull now; their battles were hers. Her flesh was *rakhar dan*, reachflesh. And it owed a debt for what it had done.

She could not bring Raif with her on this journey. The Sull Far Riders would not have it; they had no love for the man they called the Clansman. Yet their reasons were not *her* reasons. She would not have Raif because he had already done enough, risked enough, and she was traveling into darkness . . . and she would travel that road alone. She would not endanger him. It was as simple and as complicated as that.

She knew he could not follow her. Ark Veinsplitter had only contempt for clannish tracking. "Clansmen see only what is there. They do not see what has been. Like children they look only at their feet. Does an eagle leave footprints as it flies, or a squirrel as it leaps from tree to tree? No. They leave trails that must be smelled and tasted and heard. Clansmen track with one sense, the Sull use five."

Ash slowed for a moment, weariness suddenly weighing her down. *He cannot track me.* The thought almost broke her heart. He'd protected her for so long, carried her in his arms when she could no longer walk. Yet all his strength and determination meant nothing in the face of the Sull. They'd fooled him as easily as if he'd been a green boy . . . and they'd make sure he could never find her again.

Ash breathed deeply, controlling the hurt. She just wished she could stop herself looking for him whenever she first awoke.

Noticing that she had slowed her pace, Ark Veinsplitter slowed his own to match. Nothing went unobserved by the Far Rider; she had to remember that and guard herself closely. "How much farther before we make camp?"

Although they had been inside the mountain for a full day, Ark Veinsplitter was still wearing pale, milky scale armor beneath his wolverine cloak. The armor gave off light, shimmering in the darkness of the mountain as if it stored radiance from the moon. Ash had seen the armor up close when the Veinsplitter cleansed himself with stone-heated water; it was warm to the touch, and strange—rings of fire flickered within each scale. It was bone, that much she guessed, sliced in cross sections so thin they should have been easy to break. But when Ash had held one piece between her fingers she felt steel-hardness there.

Ark Veinsplitter turned to look at her, his scale armor rippling like silk. His ice-tanned face picked up little light from the torch Mal Naysayer bore several paces ahead, yet his eyes were plain to see. Something was hidden there. "We journey late this night."

What time was it? Ash couldn't be sure. Her only guide was the sense of hours passed walking beneath rock. The mountain muffled time and light. Narrow tunnels twisted through the rock, winding down through granite and glistening ores, past pools of standing water and caverns where small bulb-eyed creatures scattered from the light. They moved down, always down. Sometimes the ways were so low they had to double back to find a path for the horses. Other times the Naysayer had to guide the mounts over stone bridges and crooked stairs. Echoes followed them like shadows. No sound ever left the mountain; instead it circled round, bouncing from wall to wall, growing lower and deeper and splitting into fragments of itself. Once Ash stopped and listened. She heard her own voice, eerily distorted, saying quite clearly, "I'll take a piece of the waybread." Words she had said half a day earlier, when they had stopped for their mid-morning meal.

Suddenly chill, Ash drew her coat about her. Ahead, Mal Naysayer led the horses through a natural archway stippled with quartz. The giant Sull warrior hadn't spoken in hours. It fell to him to find whatever path Ark Veinsplitter sought, and to bear the torch that lit the way. His broad back was spanned by the diagonal slash of his longsword, holstered across his shoulders due to its extraordinary length. He was cloaked in differently pieced furs to those of his *hass*, but the armor beneath them was the same shimmering scale. On his left hand he bore a great leather mitt, like a falconer's glove, that shielded his fingers and wrist from the spitting tar of the torch. As if aware Ash's gaze was upon him, the Naysayer turned. Always his ice-blue eyes were a shock. They pierced you.

Knowledge—and knowing—burned within them, and Ash wondered what tragedies had happened in his past.

"Is the path open?" Ark asked, moving forward to where the Naysayer stood in the archway.

The great Sull warrior shook his head. "Nay. The rock ceiling lowers, and there is uncertain ground ahead."

Ark nodded, but not lightly. He regarded his *hass* with eyes that were almost black. Ash could see him thinking. Five days ago they had left Ice Trapper territory, traveling through ice storms and whiteouts, across black hackled ice and snowbound foothills, and in all that time she had seen nothing but certainty on his face. Now there was something else.

"Settle the horses. We go on alone."

As the Naysayer pulled rope from one of the packs, Ash forced her way through the arch and regarded the territory ahead. Shadows were deep, and concealed much. A stair had been cut into the rock, but she could not see where it led, only that it spiraled down into the mountain's depths. A breeze lifted the hair from her face, and she caught the unnerving scent of copper ore. *Like blood.* Suddenly uneasy, she returned to Ark Veinsplitter's side.

The Far Rider was studying markings tattooed into the archway's vault. Ash recognized Sull signs; full moons and half-moons and diagrams of night skies. *Everywhere that is deep and lightless they have claimed.* Ash shivered. She knew so little about the Sull. How could she ever hope to become one?

Ark must have seen some of the uncertainty on her face, for he drew close enough for her to see the letting scars on his cheekbones, ears and jaw, and said, "The night's journey will soon be done."

"We're not going to camp, are we?"

"No."

Something warned her not to ask the next question. She

studied the Far Rider closely. He had the ability to be perfectly still, to stand unmoving and unblinking, biding his time between breaths. Since they had left the Ice Trappers' territory little had been said between them. Talk had been of food and weather and other small matters between travelers. Nothing had been mentioned about the reason for the journey. As with each carefully measured breath, Ark Veinsplitter was biding his time.

She surprised herself by saying, "The skin on your neck, below your jaw, why are there no letting scars there?"

Muscles in Ark's face shifted, and when his voice came it was so low she had to strain to hear it. "*Dras Morthu.* The Last Cut." He touched the unblemished flesh. "When it is time for me to depart for the Far Shore I will cut the last great vein."

"And if your life is taken by another?"

"Then my *hass* will not rest until he has found me and made the Last Cut himself."

Ash looked down. Something too private was showing in the Far Rider's eyes.

"The horses have been fed and watered. Let us go." Mal Naysayer pulled the torch from its mooring between two rocks. The Sull stallions and the packhorse stood their ground. Tall and proud, they needed no hobbles to prevent them from fleeing. Ash knew without question they would wait for their riders' return. As she passed through the archway she scratched the gray's nose. "Good boy," she whispered. "One day I'm going to find out your name."

The going was slow and treacherous, the steps wildly uneven and slick with graphite. Ash slipped many times, and many times the Naysayer put out a hand to steady her. The great Sull giant saw things that she could not: fissures and slicks of oil and crumbling rock. She wondered if he needed the torch. The rock was dark and grotesquely folded, and at every opportunity it ate the light. Shadows flickered and lengthened, and soon

Ash could see no farther than a few paces ahead. Yet the Naysayer never slowed.

The two men were bearing light packs. A few days' food, blankets and medicine, she guessed. Why had they brought her here? At first she'd thought they meant to pass through the mountain, a short cut that would protect them from the ice. Now she knew they had a specific location in mind, a place nestled beneath a mountain of rock. *Raif, I wish you were with me.*

At first she could not quite believe it was getting warmer. Time passed as they made their descent, and Ash became aware of a prickly film of sweat above her lip. She brushed it away, and it came back. Soon she had to remove her cloak and haul it over her back. And it wasn't just growing warmer, she realized, glancing at a rock beaded with moisture; it was getting damper, too. The two Sull warriors appeared impervious to the changes, yet they had to see the tendrils of mist creeping up the stairway to meet them. And they had to hear the sound of dripping water.

Down they went, their footsteps muffled now, their echoes nearly silent. The mist stayed low, washing around their ankles like foam. Every so often Ash would see signs etched in the rock. Once she thought she saw a raven, and didn't know whether to be comforted or afraid. Exhaustion made her stumble, and the Naysayer offered his arm for support. Leaning on him she reached the bottom of the stairs and entered the mountain chamber.

The chamber was dark and alive with shadows and it stretched farther than she could see. A pool of green water lay in its center, the source of the smell and the mist. Great piers of glistening rock rose around its banks, their bases barnacled with deposits of copper ore.

"*Hass*, light more torches." Ark Veinsplitter did not sound like a man happy to reach his destination. For some reason Ash thought that he might open a vein and pay a toll, but he did not. Instead he walked heavily toward the pool. The Naysayer made sure Ash was steady on her feet and then went about the task of lighting sticks. Ash had little choice but to follow Ark to the water.

By the time she reached the pool's bank, the Far Rider had already laid down a blanket for her. "Sit," he said. "Rest."

Ash did just that. This close to the pool the mist was stifling, and she realized for the first time that she was sitting by a natural hot spring. Suddenly she was taken with the desire to wade, fully clothed, into the water and let its warm waters soothe her aches. *They haven't brought me here for a bath*, she reminded herself, snuffing the small spark of joy.

"Ash March, Foundling. Drink this." Ark Veinsplitter was holding out a ram's horn filled with clear liquid. When she didn't immediately reach out to take it, he said, "It will not make you sleep."

They were both thinking of the night in the Listener's ground, of the *oolak* that had rendered Raif senseless. She said, "Will it harm me?"

"No. It will lend you strength."

She took it but did not drink. The Naysayer was moving in a circle around the pool, planting torches between rocks. This simple act woke fear in Ash: why did they need so much light? Because she was afraid she spoke. "Will we have a fire? I could roast the last of the goat."

Ark shook his head slowly, and for a moment she saw sadness in his eyes. "We do not eat this night, Ash March. Tonight you become Sull."

The words echoed once around the chamber, and then stopped. Ash felt as if they had entered her, like a knife. She found she was trembling. Liquid from the horn splashed her leg, and she forced herself to be steady.

Ark Veinsplitter continued in his softly powerful voice. "We cannot bring you to the Heart unless you are Sull. You are *rakhar dan* and you are needed for the long night to come. We are the only ones left who fight the darkness. Whilst clansmen and city men feud amongst themselves over land once claimed by the Sull, we will ride out and battle with the Endlords and their taken. Make no mistake, Ash March, I offer you little in return for your soul. *Maer Horo* lies ahead—the Age of Darkness. It is not a good day to become Sull. If we are lucky we shall fight until we die; if we are not we shall be taken and our souls will walk lost into the grayness.

"Much I cannot say to you now. Such things that I know cannot be spoken to an outlander and a stranger to our ways. Our secrets come at too great a cost, like our blood, and whenever we speak them out loud we risk much.

"Know this, though. If you become Sull we will protect you and honor you, and give our lives to spare you from harm. You are as precious to us as a newborn, and like a newborn you bring us new hope."

Ash let the Far Rider's words work upon her. Seven torches now flickered around the pool, turning the water orange and green like the Gods Lights in the northern sky. She could hear the torch resin crackling . . . and the measured breaths of the two men. Stirred, but unwilling to reveal it, she said, "So you offer me a choice?"

If the Sull warrior noticed the shakiness in her voice he did not show it, merely nodded.

"And if I refuse?"

"We shall escort you from this chamber."

"And then?"

She'd asked the question the Far Rider had hoped not to answer; she saw it written clearly on his face. He and his *hass* exchanged a glance. The Naysayer moved from his place on the far side of the pool. The grace and size of him struck her anew, and as she looked into his ice-blue eyes she knew without a doubt that she was looking into the face of the man who would kill her.

He said softly, "I will take you without hurt."

Ash believed him. It struck her that there were worse ways to die than at the hand of a master swordsman; a man whose blade was so sharp that not even a human hair could fall upon it without being cut. Strangely she found she was calm. "I am a danger if I live."

Ark Veinsplitter nodded, though she had asked him no question. For the first time she saw the age of him, and realized that he was older than she had ever thought. "If the Naysayer did not take you now, and we walked away from this place and left you to find your way back to the Ice Trappers, others would come after. We are the first to find you but we shall not be the last. If you are not with us you are against us, and as such no living, breathing Sull will let you live."

Ash let the chamber fall to silence rather than speak. If the Far Rider spoke the truth, then these two men before her were offering a mercy that future Sull would not. Something in the dark lines of Ark's face and the way his fingers curled around the chain that connected his letting knife to his belt told her what his words would not: The Sull who came after him would tear her limb from limb.

Seconds passed and the mist rose, and then she said, "What is it to be Sull?"

"Sull is home," said Mal Naysayer.

"Sull is heart and life and soul," continued Ark. "The Heart Fires burn for us and all the ancestors who have gone before. We have traveled far across oceans and continents and places where time itself stretches thin. We are beyond family and country, life and death—as you know it—and all our histories and battles are carried within our blood. Our children are born with memories of the Far Shore, and it is our one desire to return there. We are more ancient than mankind, and have borne witness to the creation of mountains and the fall of empires and the extinction of many living things. Our ancestors knew the Old Ones who once walked this earth, and we can remember our own creation at the hands of the First Gods."

The Far Rider watched Ash, his great dark gaze pulling something from her. Time passed, and then finally he added, "We are your brothers, Ash March, and we would have you for our sister. Join us and become a daughter to the Sull."

Pain flared in the space behind Ash's eyes. *Am I that transparent, that he can see the desire within me?* She said in a small voice, "You would have my soul?"

"You cannot become Sull through flesh alone."

"And my life will not go unused?"

"*Maer Horo* lies ahead. Your life will be fulfilled."

Ash nodded, understanding the grim promise of those words. She was a Reach and she had forced a rift in the Blindwall; become Sull and her life would be dedicated to battling whatever came forth. *I do not go into this blindly. I just wish Raif were here.*

The two Sull warriors waited. The Naysayer stood tall and unmoving, without so much as a hand upon a stone column to steady his great weight. A torch flared to his side, but even its warmth and golden light couldn't reach the ice in his eyes. Ark Veinsplitter sat on a carpet of night-blue silk, his wolverine cloak draped over a rock, his sword and dagger and eating knife fanned out behind him like a steel tail. Strange that both men's reflections glowed silver in the green pool.

Ash gathered the breath within her. *I am Ash March, Foundling, left outside Vaingate to die.* As always the words, *her* words, filled her with a stubborn kind of strength. She was unwanted and had no family, and so had exactly nothing to lose. Yet the two Sull warriors would change that. *Sister*, they called her. And not *almost-daughter*, but simply *daughter*.

She belonged with them. She had known it from the moment Mal Naysayer had prostrated himself in the snow in front of her, and spoke words for her ears alone. *Welcome, sister, I have never seen a moon so bright as the one that brought you to us.* Ash held herself still as she remembered his blessing. She was proud, like these men, and she would not cry. It was easy to stand then, easy to meet their eyes and say, "Make me Sull." In many ways that counted she was already one of them.

The night changed then, grew smaller and darker as shadows surrounding the pool merged to form a wall. Suddenly there was nothing but seven torches and two men. Mist rose and fell, rose and fell, as she put the horn to her lips and drank. The liquid was cool and sharp, and there was a sweet aftertaste to it that reminded her of cloves. Her vision blurred for an instant and then restored itself, and then Mal Naysayer was beside her, reaching out a hand to take the horn. Ash stood and let the sharpness of the liquid move through her. Already things were falling away. Fear seemed some impossibly faraway object that she could see but was unable to grasp. Time seemed even farther beyond reach and Ark Veinsplitter and the Naysayer appeared to move great distances in the time it took to complete a blink.

Slowly, deliberately, Ash began to pull off her clothes; they were so much unwanted weight on her back. Naked she faced them, her chin high, her hair unpinned and brushing against her breasts. Mist coated her skin and collected in the dimples at her throat and lower back. The two Far Riders had stripped to their waists, revealing hard-used muscle and networks of scars. With an even, much-practiced motion the Naysayer was drawing his white-metal letting knife through his fist. At first Ash thought he was polishing it, and then she saw he held a slice of whetstone between finger and thumb. Honing the blade.

I'll take you without hurt.

Ark Veinsplitter was speaking, but Ash's mind had to labor to make sense of the words. "Nothing of worth can be won without peril. To be born Sull you must first know death."

"I will guard you, Ash March," murmured the Naysayer. "You will not walk alone to the world's edge."

The protectiveness in his voice reached her before his words, and she heard herself say, "What do I risk here?"

"Your blood is not Sull blood. It must be drained so new blood can be made."

Ash nodded, comprehending at last what they meant to do. *And I thought I'd taken the easier choice.*

Pulling her hair back behind her neck, she turned and began to wade into the pool. The water was hot and she saw her feet and then her legs turn pink. Copper vapors sheathed her, spreading warmth and drowsiness as they curled around her arms and throat. When the water reached her waist she opened her arms wide and laid her hands on the green, still surface. Behind her she heard the Far Riders entering the water, swift movements that roused the mist. She saw the glint of silver sparking off the rocks, and felt a stab of fear. Knives were drawn. Then hands were on her arms, forcing them behind her, twisting her wrists toward the light of the torches. Fingers encircled scalded flesh, probing for veins.

When the cuts came they made her gasp. She was glad she couldn't see the men who had made them, gladder still that she could not see the wounds. Watching the torches and the shadows beyond, she listened for the sound of the men withdrawing. Water moved, rising as high as her breasts, then all grew quiet. Dimming. Lifting her feet from the pool bottom and tilting her spine, she allowed her body to float to the surface. Dark blood bloomed in the water, forming plumes like rare flowers. She smelled their sugary odor.

Dimming. The rock ceiling sparkling with hidden ores . . . red spreading to the edges of the pool, sliding across the bones of her hips and into the hollow of her navel, where it lapped in and out, in and out. So tired . . . so tired. *The Naysayer was right. No hurt.*

Darkness. Floating. Peace and warmth embraced her. *This. This is what I want.* No weight or worries, just peace.

Let me go.

The darkness shifted, thickened into shapes. Things moved within it, ghost-children bending to feed upon her soul. Someone laughed, a woman. A voice soft and tinkling said, *Welcome, my daughter, I wondered how long it would take you to come.* Ash felt a touch so cold it burned. Pain sharpened her awareness, and she knew with perfect clarity that she was not ready for this place. Not yet. Turning, she fled. Tinkling laughter followed her.

The landscape was gray now, but ahead lay the first glimmering of white. The Far Shore. And as soon as Ash said those words to herself, she felt the first pang of longing. *It is our one desire to return there.* She saw a sea so blue it was like a wholly new creation, breaking softly on a curving shore. Tall trees grew beside moss-covered rocks and glimmering pools, and beyond them a golden forest stretched to a horizon where something secret and everlasting shimmered just beyond her ken. Ash laughed with the sheer joy of seeing, watched as a yellow butterfly fed from a flower dripping with dew. *This is why they fight the darkness,* she thought, *because one day they will return here and know perfect joy.*

With that she turned again. She felt herself growing, filling up with a new kind of strength. Memories sparked, and the first seeds of knowledge were born within her. Overcome with a breathtaking sense of belonging, she cried out.

Becoming Sull.

SEVEN

An Arrow With a Name

The girl laid a hunk of bear meat in front of him. "Eat." She giggled nervously, covering her teeth with both hands, and then tried another combination of the words he had taught her. "Good. Eat."

Raif found himself smiling despite his mood. He was going to have to teach her more words; either that or she'd drive him half mad pointing to blankets, pots, lamps and strips of cured hide, saying either, "Good", "Bad" or "Eat". The blanket he was sitting on was "bad". Something to do with flying birds and many feet; at least, that was the best he could tell from her sign language. Suddenly inspired, he tugged at the corner of the blanket and pulled it high against his face. "Warm." Rubbing the blanket against his cheek, he repeated himself. "Warm."

The girl darted forward, touched the blanket lightly, then darted back. "Warm." He could see her thinking. A moment later she pulled a dark glossy fur from a storage chest and ran a hand down its silky nap. "Warm."

Raif nodded. To please her he took a knife to the meat. It was purple and part-frozen, having been heated in a skin above the lamp for a time so short it barely counted as cooking at all.

He chewed the fibrous morsel, attempted to swallow, then chewed again.

"Good," the girl encouraged.

But not "warm", he added gently to himself.

They were sitting in the Listener's ground, the whale lamp between them casting the softest kind of light. As far as Raif could tell it was early evening. The Listener had been gone for two days, for the hunters were out upon the ice and they had spotted no seals in half a moon. Sadaluk had been needed to listen for them. The old man had seemed pleased at the opportunity to leave Raif alone, and had extracted a solemn promise that Raif would not leave until he returned. Raif hadn't understood the sly twinkle in the Listener's eye, but looking at the girl dressed in soft sealskins before him he thought he might now. Her name was Sila, and she was plump and beautiful with waist-long hair and black eyes.

Only a dead man cannot surprise you. Raif made a sound in his throat. It seemed the Listener made a habit of such surprises.

The girl had brought him food for the past two nights, and had visited many times to tend the lamp. The long wick needed to be carefully managed so it didn't die out or smoke, and Raif noticed there were many opportunities for Sila to show off her plumpness, bending and crouching as she fed the little wick-seeds to the oil. She was as unlike Ash as it was possible to be: warm-skinned and warm-eyed, and ready with shy laughter. *Ash is gone. Gone.* So why couldn't he smile at this girl and enjoy her simple attentions without feeling as if every act of companionship were a betrayal?

Sila took the tray of meat from him, observant of the fact that he had little appetite for it. "Bad?" she asked, making a question of her newly learned word. Dimples appeared like small blessings in her cheeks.

Raif tried to resent her, but could not. What was the Listener thinking, to send her to him? Did the old man seek to make amends over his part in stealing Ash? Or did he think that one girl could make Raif forget another?

Still waiting for an answer, Sila plucked at the golden fur around her collar, all the while frowning doubtfully at the meat. This small sign of her nervousness affected Raif and suddenly he wanted to be kind. Patting his stomach, he said, "Full."

The girl was quick to mimic him, rubbing the swell of her belly with one hand whilst covering her teeth with the other. "Full," she said proudly. "Full."

They sat and looked at each other, shyly at first and then more boldly. Sila was dressed in a close-fitting coat decorated with fish-bone stitching and musk-ox fur, its neck-opening tied back to reveal a necklace of tattooed skin. Raif saw her gaze alight on his frost-scarred hands, and then rise to the lore at his throat. She surprised him by reaching out to touch it.

"Warm."

He smelled her, and he could not speak. She smelled of seal oil and sea salt and sweet heather, and it made the blood rise in him. Suddenly it was hard to think. She leaned closer to inspect the lore, her breath condensing on the down-facing planes of his face. He could see the back of her neck, where soft baby-hairs had worked free from her braids. And then she was kissing him, gently, tentatively, her lips moist with seal oil. Raif thought he would lose himself. He wanted to crush her to him, to feel her forehead grind against his. Something desperate came alive within him, and with it the real fear that he would hurt her. Not gently, he pushed her away.

She was breathing hard, and there was hurt in her eyes. She touched her lips. "Good."

Shame and need sent hot blood to Raif's face. Seconds passed where he fought to regain self-control. He didn't know what he was doing anymore. *Ash, why did you have to leave me?*

Sila waited, watching him. When he made no move to pull her back she unfastened the ties of her coat. Her gaze met his as she bared small brown breasts and laid her hand upon her heart. "Full."

Ridiculously, Raif felt himself close to tears. He had struggled for so long for so little that he had forgotten what it was to receive a gift. He did not deserve her . . . but that knowledge did not stop him from wanting her. With swift movements he pulled off his own borrowed coat, rough bearded-seal hide that shed many hairs. Pushing the thing away he let her look at him; at the great white scars the Bludd swordsmen had raised outside Duff's, and the weals and marks of torture he had received at the Dog Lord's hand. Time and healing had done little to prettify his flesh. Angus Lok's thick black stitches, that had been made with boiled horse-mane, had long since gone— winkled out by Angus's diabolically sharp knife—yet their uneven tracks remained puckered in his flesh.

Sila studied him. If he had thought to repulse her he was mistaken, for she looked with curiosity and some knowledge of scarred flesh. When she reached out to touch him he moved back.

"Bad," he said, laying her hand on the center of his chest. *Watcher of the Dead.* Close to losing himself, he stood. His head was light with confusion and he knew he couldn't stay here any longer and not seize her. Stumbling, he snatched his coat off the floor and made his way into the night.

The blinding cold could not cool him. He was too deeply roused and shamed. Unable to bear his thoughts, he headed out toward the sea ice, drawn by the terrible noise of it and the great glowing blueness of its mass. Starlight lit a path. Mountains lay quiet to the north, marking territory where no clansman had ever been. The Lake of Lost Men was out there, and beyond that the Breaking Grounds and the pale endless ice of Endsea. Raif thought of Tem. He had taught his sons and his daughter about the land, making maps in the dirt and the snow. His broad fingers would draw lines marking coasts and forests, and sometimes to please Effie he would raise little dirt mounds to represent mountains. Always he spoke of clan. *This is the Milk River that runs into the Flow; when clansmen first arrived on its banks its waters ran milky with stone dust from the White Mines of the Sull . . . Here lie the Floating Isles; when Arlech Dregg, the Restless Chief, first laid eyes upon them he set his men to making boats so he could see the isles first-hand. Yet Dreggsmen are no watermen and the boats they built were green and flawed, and halfway across the channel they foundered and killed all hands . . . Beyond these hills lies the part of the badlands known as the Rift Valley; the Maimed Men make their home there, and send their dead, eyeless, into the Rift.*

Raif stepped onto the hard plate of shore ice that rose like a stone pier from the beach. The great body of ice created its own weather, and currents spiraled around him, channeling up his legs with each step. For the first time since leaving the Listener's ground he felt the cold. Shocked by its depth and fierceness, he hastily tied the fastenings on his coat. Part of the ice had been hacked here, smashed and then picked out for use in the village. All salt had long since drained from the topmost layers, leaving pure freshwater ice. Raif supposed the sea beneath to be saltier for it, its waters concentrating through the long winter to a stock of strongest brine.

It was time to leave this place. The worst of the white weather had passed, and the unclouded sky promised stillness for the first time in many days. Ash had a good head start on him; their paths were unlikely to cross. He needed supplies, warm clothing. A weapon. Guidance to set him on the right track. Too much to ask from strangers, yet he had no other choice. He could not stay here. He had seen the way the Ice Trapper hunters looked at him; he needed to find a place where men would not fear or distrust him.

He needed to be amongst clan.

"The Gods Lights burn this night."

Raif turned at the sound of the voice and saw the Listener, well wrapped in several shaggy furs, standing behind him on the ice.

"You look the wrong way, Clansman. The Gods Lights always show in the north."

Raif could find no answer to that, other than to turn his face north. He didn't see the Lights at first, so slowly did they move, rising behind the mountains like green smoke. Then the horizon itself began to glow. It was easy to believe that a forest fire in some distant and unreachable valley had to be raging to give off such light. Even in the clanholds, where the lights were rarely seen, it was known that strange unclannish gods sent them at times of change. Raif didn't want to think of it. He said, "When did you return, Listener?"

"Last night."

Raif should have been surprised, but wasn't. The little old man was full of tricks. "Did you listen for the seals?"

"Yes."

"And?"

"They did not come." The Listener moved forward so he stood alongside Raif. His hard, wrinkled face glowed green as the Gods Lights brightened. "They swim west, away from the land, and the fish and krill go with them."

Sensing an accusation there, Raif said, "I leave tomorrow."

"Good."

"I'll need to be shown the path east."

"You cannot follow her."

"I know . . . but I can't return to my clan."

"So you head to the badlands?"

Raif nodded. "I go in search of the Maimed Men."

The sea ice groaned and lifted, as the sea beneath swelled. Somewhere far in the distance two plates ground together, making a sound like the sawing of wood. It did not occur to Raif that the Listener had not heard of the Maimed Men; the set of the old man's jaw spoke for itself. The Maimed Men were clansmen, most of them. Tem said they had first come into being the year Burnie Dhoone destroyed Clan Morrow out of jealousy for his wife, Fair Maida. Hundreds of unhoused clansmen had nowhere to go, and no clan would take them in for fear of the Dark King's anger. They headed north, legend said, to the vast bleak spaces of the badlands where time and hardness changed them. No man amongst them was whole; the terrible dry cold and fierce badlands predators saw to that. Every clansman knew they had no honor, for they raided villages, outlying farms, guard posts and hunt parties, and they had no guidestone to offer shelter to the gods. The living was hard, and little was known of them, and Raif thought they would suit him well enough. Traitors and outcasts had few choices.

Raif thought the Listener would say something, some caution, but after many minutes of silence Sadaluk turned for home. "Come," he said. "The lights burn red and it disturbs an old man to stand beneath them."

Raif hesitated.

"The girl has gone. I sent her home with the last of the meat."

Oh gods. Remembering made Raif want her as strongly as before. His face heated as he wondered how much the Listener knew.

The old man could read thoughts, Raif swore it, for the Listener frowned deeply and shook his head. Unspeaking, they returned to the warmth and the heat of the Listener's ground.

The first thing Raif noticed was that the mute raven had

been returned to its whalebone perch. The big black bird made a retching sound at Raif's entrance, throwing its head back and forth as if it were a jester playing sick. Raif took it for an insult and scowled. *Insolent bird.* The soapstone lamp Sila had diligently tended for two days was now smoking from lack of care. Raif thought he would try and adjust it, but the Listener brushed him away. "Sit," he said, pointing to the bench against the wall. "Perhaps the next gifts I offer will not be so willfully refused."

The old man crouched in the center of the chamber and began pulling away the blankets and grass mats that covered the floor. Clawlike hands pried up four stones that concealed a cache hole. Out of a sense of honor Raif did not watch as the Listener pulled out a long chest and struggled with its metal latches. After a minute of watching shadows, the Listener complained to him, "Can you not see when an old man needs your help?" Chastised, Raif moved quickly to aid him.

The chest was not Ice Trapper-made. Fine wood had been carved and steamed into curves, and filigreed ironwork protected the corners and was mounted as latches on the lid. The latches were badly corroded, and Raif had to take a knife to them to pry them open. At once the smell of dust and age hit him; old parchment, old metal and mold. The Listener drove his hands deep into the opened chest, scattering clumps of parched brown moss that had been used for packing and for keeping the contents dry. "Two things, Clansman. Tell me which is the greater, the arrow or the sword?"

Raif replied without thinking. "The arrow. You can kill at distance without endangering yourself or your companions."

"So you do not want to look into the eyes of the man you kill?"

Feeling tricked, Raif said, "I would prefer not to kill at all."

"A wistful sentiment from a man named Watcher of the Dead." The Listener raised his gaze to meet Raif's. "Do not look at me that way, Clansman. I'm old enough to have earned the right to speak my mind. You, on the other hand, are at an age when it would serve you well to listen and speak not at all. Now, what if I were to tell you I have an arrow that would be wasted if you used it to kill a man?" The Listener did not wait for an answer. "You would ask what is it for. And I would give the only answer I have: Not many arrows have names, no blacksmith toils months over their making, no jeweler mounts stones upon their hilts, and no fine clansman lovingly oils them each night. Swords have names—Daybreaker, Fear Me, Taker of Lives, Ghostfriend, other such foolishness as that—arrows do not. Well, very few. I possess one of them."

The Listener's hand closed around an object in the chest, drew it up through the layers of moss. "Here she is: Divining Rod."

Bright metal caught the light. *Silver*, Raif thought. *No steel, or white gold force-hardened with arsenic and nickel like the arrows loosed by the Dhoone Kings.* Then he looked more closely, and saw he was wrong. It was the hard, white-blue metal of the Sull. Clans did not know its name or where to mine it. Some whispered that it fell from the stars in great rocks that had to be cracked open like eggs. The arrowhead was three-bladed, slender as if for hitting targets, not game, and held to the shaft not by thread or metal wire like clannish arrows, but socketed by a banded ferrule so expertly tooled that it made Raif's breath catch to see it. A skeleton ferrule: he'd heard tell of them from Ballic the Red, but never until now had he seen one. Such a socket added stability and accuracy to the arrow, holding shaft and point more surely than a bobbin's worth of twine. He couldn't help himself—he had to reach out to touch it.

"Ha!" gloated the Listener, offering it up. "I see you are capable of wanting something without guilt."

Raif accepted the reprimand; he deserved it. He had acted like a fool and treated Sila badly, and he wouldn't blame her if she hated him. Yet he hoped she didn't. For a reason he couldn't understand her good opinion was important to him.

The Listener pressed the arrow into Raif's palm. "Take it."

The instincts of a bowman overcame Raif, and he weighed the arrow in his hand, reading it for draw and height. It was surprisingly light; a windcatcher, Ballic would say, needing little height to aim it. The shaft was strangely made—bone, it looked like, with the kind of inlay work Raif was accustomed to seeing on bows, not arrows. Such tooling, if wrongly done, could greatly affect the arrow's flight, for any flaw in the shaft would create drag. Yet when Raif ran his fingers over the bone he felt only perfect smoothness. It had once been stained red, for traces of color hid within minute striations in the bone. The arrow's flights spiraled along the bottommost third of the shaft, and as Raif traced their course he felt his excitement growing. A *spinner*. This arrow would rotate in flight, spinning the moment it left the plate, protecting itself against the random buffeting of air and the gradual curving trajectory of all thrown missiles by its own spiraling motion. He wanted to loose it now, set its point against the riser and release the string. No arrow he'd ever held had been so exquisite.

"I see you've marked the spiral course of the flights," the Listener said in an unusually quiet voice. "Yet have you also marked their substance?"

Raif had not. Turning the arrow, he studied the pale, translucent hairs that had been set into the bone and trimmed to an inch in length. "Ice-wolf hair," he guessed. Then, seeing the Listener still waiting, "Lynx . . . snow tiger." Still the old man waited and as he did the answer came. "Human hair."

"Not quite human, no, but close." The old man studied Raif in the silence that followed, seeming to judge his readiness . . .

for what? With a small shrug, he finally spoke. "Have you heard tell of the Old Ones who once walked this land before Men? Some say they were like us, in that they had eyes and mouths and stood on two feet, and were as beautiful in their way as the Sull. This land wasn't always hard froze, you must remember that. In ages past the Great Want was green with trees, and blue water flowed there along riverbeds so broad and deep that entire villages could be tossed into their centers and sink without a trace. The riverbeds are still there, if you know where to look for them, and many other things lie abandoned too. There are halls in the heart of the Want, raised from ancient timbers that take an Age to rot. The Old Ones built them, and some say their skills grew at great cost to their defenses, and they built a beautiful but flawed fortress where the Last Battle was fought and lost. *Ben Horo*, the Sull call it. The Time Before. The Sull think they are the only ones who honor and remember the Old Ones, but they can be blind in their arrogance and they forget that old men such as me can hear many things that they cannot."

Pride shone briefly in the Listener's eyes and then was gone. Raif turned the named arrow in his hand as Sadaluk continued speaking, and it seemed as though the night turned too, spinning like the arrow in flight toward a point the old man had long since set in his sights.

"*Mor Drakka*, Watcher of the Dead, I name you. I saw you long before you knew yourself and took your first life. The Sull see you as a threat and a curse, for it is written that one day *Mor Drakka* will bring their doom. They are a proud and ancient race and their numbers have been declining for ten thousand years, and they fear you are the one who will watch their end. You live only because they need as well as fear you. And because when you loose an arrow it finds a heart.

"No, do not gainsay me, Clansman. You forget who I am." Again, the pride was there, flashing bright like lightning before dimming to nothing at all. "Take this arrow named Divining Rod that has been fletched with the Old Ones' hair, take it and use it to find what you must. It seeks—what, I cannot tell you for the echoes from things so old are weak. I have guarded it for sixty years and Lootavek for a hundred before me, and before him Kullahuk, and before him the great Tungis himself. Many hands have touched it. None have set it to a plate and drawn power behind it. *Wait*, they said. *One day someone will come and we will know from his hands and his spirit that he will use the arrow well.*"

The Listener returned his attention to the chest, pushing his hands once again through the moss. "I cannot say I was glad to see you come here, and I fear that even when you leave the seal will not return. Yet how can I change such things? What choices do we have, you and I?"

Raif held the old man's gaze. He felt sad and weary, and suddenly the arrow seemed less like a treasure than a debt. Quietly, he slipped it into one of the many game pouches sewn within the seal coat.

"Grow wide shoulders, Clansman—you'll need them for all your burdens." The Listener pulled something out of the chest, something heavy and long and wrapped in old skins. The old man looked up, and there was a twinkle of mischief newly come to his eyes. "You might think I'd give you a bow to match that fine arrow of yours. You might think it, but you'd be wrong. I'm old and contrary and have a fancy to give you a sword. And, as there's no one but gods here to stop me, I will." He handed it to Raif. "Unwrap it. It's time you learned how to kill someone and look them in the eye."

Raif winced at the insult. He had drawn a sword against men before today. Three had died by his hand outside Duff's . . . and yet he had no memory of that night; all his knowledge came secondhand from Angus Lok. Perhaps the Listener was right: he had taken refuge behind the bow, distancing himself from his heart-kills, and denying his enemies the simple grace of being able to look into the eyes of the man who killed them. Ayan Blackhail had learned that lesson at the loss of both hands. *An arrow is no way to kill a king. You should have used your sword or naught at all.*

Raif unwrapped the sword. Could he heart-kill a man with this? And if he did, would the death be more honorable for it?

The old man watched in silence as Raif inspected the sword. It was foreign-made of fine blued steel, neither clannish nor Sull-like in design. A span short of a true longsword, double-edged with a hand-and-a-half grip, it was forged for close combat on foot. Raif held the weapon up to the lamp, watched as the patterning of the blade scattered the light. Taking the unpadded wire grip in his hand he tested for the sword's balance, then touched the wooden chest with its point to proof its temper. The blade was well fitted and sound, though its edges needed grinding. The sword's hilt formed a plain cross, and its pommel was surmounted by a faceted chunk of rock crystal as big as a child's eye. Holding it, Raif thought of Tem, of Tem's humble halfsword that Drey had given him after Da's death, and that had been taken by Cluff Drybannock on the slopes of the Bitter Hills. *Da would have loved this.*

"You'll have to make yourself a scabbard for it, find a skin to wrap around the grip. It should serve you well enough until you find a better one."

Raif looked up.

"What, Clansman? Did you really think this will be the sword that makes you?"

"No. I . . . I don't know . . ." Raif heard himself stumbling. "Thank you. It is a fine sword."

"It should be. I took it from a knight's corpse. Don't worry, I didn't kill him. Poor soul was on a pilgrimage to the Lake of

Lost Men, got lost himself and died." The old man sealed the chest and then stood. "Quite useful, really, the Forsworn. At least one of them gets lost here each season. We Ice Trappers depend upon it." Pushing the chest back into the cache hole, he said, "I'll see you receive clothes and provisions in the morning. Tonight, I promised a certain widow I would visit her for the benefit of our mutual health. Sleep well and remember what I said: learn to use your gift through the sword. It will be better for you in the end." With that Sadaluk sealed the cache and made his way toward the door. "I do not envy you, Clansman, though I find myself wishing I could join you on your journey. I could eat many suppers on the tales you will spin."

Raif bowed his head, unable to find words to reply.

The Listener took his leave, and Raif closed the door behind him. He found himself hesitating to seal the cracks around the doorframe, though he did not want to admit why. The sword lay on the stone bench; he picked it up and began to polish it with a scrap of skin. The raven watched him, wings tucked behind its back, mimicking the motion of a skater in time to Raif's strokes. Raif balled the skin in his fist and threw it at the bird. He was beginning to hate the thing.

A sword, he learned, was poor company at night. He polished and waited, yet Sila did not return. He told himself it was for the best, but his body was restless with need and longing and dawn could not come too soon.

When morning finally came, he rose early and set off east in search of the Maimed Men.

EIGHT

The Thorn King

The forest south of Bludd was dark and ancient, with oaks slithery with moss and basswoods roped with ivy, and great white willows grown weak from the effort of surviving in stagnant water, eaten alive by spongy growths and rotting slowly from the roots up. Ruins stood here; a pale footstone half sunk into the loam, a section of standing wall protecting nothing but trees, a crumbling arch grown over with rapevines, a stretch of man-laid road running parallel to the path.

Bram noticed these things while most in the raid party did not. Or perhaps they saw but looked away; if a man had war and fighting on his mind it was better not to think too closely about those who had died before. Bram could not help himself, though. His brother said he had been born in the wrong place, and instead of being birthed amongst the thistle fields of Dhoone he should have been brought into the world in the Far South where a man could grow to be a warrior monk or a soldier scribe. Robbie Dhoone liked to tell men what they should be and where they should have been born, and although Bram was reluctant to admit it his brother was often right. Take their great-uncle, Skinner Dhoone. Robbie said the man should have been born on Topaz Island in the Warm Sea, where men owned slaves and kept concubines, for all Skinner was good for was controlling loose women and men in chains. Skinner had been furious when the insult had been relayed back to him, supposedly shaking so hard veins broke open in his face. In response he had named Robbie the Thorn King, claiming anyone who offered him loyalty would be torn to bloody shreds. Unfortunately for Skinner, Robbie had taken a liking to the name and had since claimed it for his own. And it hadn't taken long for Skinner to realize the full breadth of his mistake: he'd been the first man alive to name Robbie Dun Dhoone a king.

Robbie, riding at the head of the line on his fine honey stallion, raised a fist and called a halt. Bram was torn between relief that he could rest at last and misquiet over making camp, however briefly, amid these quiet, twilit trees.

It was late in the day, and a red sun was sinking fast in the west. The sky was clear and it was bearably cold, without a wisp of wind to stir the thistles braided into the Dhoonesmen's hair. A perfect night for a raid. *I shouldn't be surprised*, Bram thought. *Even nature herself can't help but be charmed by Robbie Dhoone.*

Twelve days ago they had left Castlemilk and headed east toward Bludd. Sixty warriors and two women, war-dressed and battle-mounted (except for the elder woman whom everyone knew as Old Mother, and who stoutly refused to wear anything thicker than boiled wool, or ride anything taller than her white mule), they had skirted the pathways and forest lines of Haddo, Frees and Bludd. On the fifth day they had forded the Flow on horseback, not trusting any of the river crossings manned by Bludd-sworn clans. It had been an exercise that none except the warhounds enjoyed, for armor and weapons and heavy leathers had to be removed and floated across on makeshift rafts to prevent canker. Bram shivered to think of the coldness of the water rising against his thighs. This far east the Flow was a league wide, disturbed by strong underpulls and sucking pools, quite unlike the narrow stately river that flowed south of Dhoone.

"Bram! Robbie says you're to attend him—and quickly." The voice belonged to Guy Morloch, a Castlemilk swordsman lately come to Robbie's cause. Like most of Robbie's inner circle, he was handsomely mounted on a high-bred stallion and dressed in the finest cloths. Bram noticed that his cloak of heavy, felted wool had been newly fitted with thistle clasps. Turning his mount smartly, Guy headed back through the dry camp.

Bram hated to leave his horse without grooming, but he knew that Robbie wouldn't suffer waiting gladly, so he tethered the sweet-natured gelding to a gorse brush and set off on foot for his brother's tent.

All around, Dhoonesmen were preparing to sit out part of the night. No fires were to be lit, not this close to the Bluddhouse, and men had to content themselves with drawing their cloaks close and eating cold fare. The big ugly axman Duglas Oger had made himself comfortable on a fallen log and was inspecting the head of his ax. Other men were wetting their swords with tung oil, and reflections from the pure Dhoonish steel flickered coldly through the trees. Water steel, it was called, due to the shimmering waves of iron and blistered steel that ran beneath the metal's surface like lake water.

Bram had once hoped to own such a blade himself, for his father had been the swordsman Mabb Cormac, and he had left two such swords for his sons upon his death. Robbie had been sixteen at the time, ten years older than Bram, and Bram thought that when his brother claimed both swords the night of Da's deathwatch, he did so with the intention of giving one to Bram when he reached an age to use it. Bram was fifteen now . . . and still there was no sword.

"Damn you, Old Mother, go gentle with me! I swear you treat me worse than your mule!" Robbie Dhoone sat on a wooden camp stool outside the only tent in the camp, his legs stretched out in front of him, his booted feet resting upon an ale cask, offering up his face to an old woman brandishing a needle as thick as a nail.

As Bram looked on, the woman dredged the needle through the contents of her hip flask, causing a coat of bluish powder to cling to needle and thread. Unsmiling, she brought the needle close to Robbie's eye and pierced the skin between his eyelid and brow. Blood welled. Robbie, knowing the attention of several of his companions was upon him, winked as if it hurt him not at all. Old Mother plunged the needle deep, depositing powder beneath his skin, making a mark that would last as long as Robbie Dhoone's life.

The blue tattoos: no Dhoonesman could call himself a warrior without them. They took years, sometimes decades to finish, for no man could stand the pain longer than two or three strokes. Yet here was his brother, choosing to add to his warrior's face in the middle of an armed camp, as calm as if he were being shaved, not stitched. Bram shuddered. He had received his first warrior's mark at midwinter; the pain had kept him awake half a night.

"Bram." Robbie finally noticed him. "Take a look at Oath's hoof irons for me. I think he picked up a stone. You know he won't give his hocks to anyone but you and Flock."

Bram kept his face still. *Show no disappointment; Robbie has burdens enough.* Nodding, he turned to leave.

"Oh, and Bram." Robbie drew him back, turning his brilliant blue-gray gaze upon him. "Muffle your gelding's bridle. You ride with me tonight."

As Bram turned out a stone lodged in Oath's hoof horn, he tried to control his excitement. It was dark now, and half a moon had risen above the trees. All about him Dhoonesmen were strapping on plate and adjusting ax harnesses: making grim preparation for war. They looked fierce, his fellow clansmen, big men with pale faces and yellow braids. Bram only had to look at his hands to know he wasn't one of them. Dark and small, like the rest of him, his hands hadn't been made for wielding an ax. Still, he was good with horses and other living things, and people had told him he could ride well enough.

And he was known to have good eyes.

Even now in the half-light, he could see what others could not. Old Mother had walked from the camp for privacy's sake and was relieving herself behind a bush. Bram saw her eye-whites glinting. He saw also that the clearing Robbie had chosen for a campsite had been used countless times before, and had once even been built on. Despite the snow cover, his eyes detected a ridge of earth that ran too straight and narrow to be natural: the foundation for something lay beneath. And then there were the trees themselves: limbs hacked off at man height for firewood, a hoof print stamped low on a white oak, a series of marks splitting the papery bark of a gray birch, indicating where some would-be archer had once practiced shots.

Sometimes Bram wished he could see less. To see was to think. He couldn't look at something without asking questions about it. Right now his brother was sitting in the darkness of his tent, thinking the shadows concealed him as effectively as any tent flap. They didn't, at least not from Bram's eyes. Robbie was speaking with the woman warrior Thora Lamb, laughing softly, judging from the tilt of his head, and resting his hand upon her thigh. Quickly, Bram looked away.

Moments later Robbie emerged from the tent, and began to walk a circuit of the camp. Men waited for him. Bram watched them form small groups, their eyes following Robbie as they weighed their weapons in their grips. Robbie spoke with every man, naming them, clasping fists, listening to advice from the battle-seasoned warriors, and offering words of comfort to the green untested boys. The mood in the camp changed as Robbie walked amongst them, became charged and vital and grave. Bram could see it on the faces of the men.

Robbie Dhoone gave them a cause.

"So, Bram," Robbie said when he reached him. "Are you ready for your first raid?"

Bram nodded. How could he expect Robbie to remember that this wasn't his first raid, that he'd ridden on one two months back, when Duglas Oger struck a caravan of Ille Glaive merchants on the Lake Road, winning the very horse that Guy Morloch sat this night? Bram's hand rose to his face. He'd earned his first warrior's mark that night, though in truth he had done little except untether the horses and scare a little girl who'd taken refuge in one of the trunks.

Eager to thank his brother for including him in the raid party, Bram cleared his throat to speak.

Robbie Dhoone had already moved on.

Bram stood and waited a little while, then went to tend his horse.

As he fastened strips of felt to his gelding's bit, he watched as Robbie and his close companions held a war parley outside the tent. Bram didn't know what action his brother planned to take this night. He thought at first it would be a simple raid; striking farms for livestock or travelers for goods. But there was too much risk here for that. They were in the heart of the Bluddhold—dangerous territory that no Dhoonesman could claim to know. It seemed madness to draw so close to the enemy, yet no one had openly questioned Robbie's judgment, and the morning they'd ridden forth from the Milkhouse there had been a hundred more willing to come. Visibly moved, Robbie had shaken his head at them. "It's a small thing I ride to do and I must risk the fewest possible men."

Bram wondered about those words now. It was surely no

coincidence that a week earlier Skinner Dhoone had forced the clan guide to declare Robbie and his companions traitors to the clan. Everyone in Castlemilk had been expecting Robbie to make a countermove, perhaps raid the Old Round outside of Gnash where Skinner and his followers were quartered. Yet Robbie had been strangely restrained on the subject, saying only, "First I must win back Dhoone's heart."

"Here, boy. Dull your face." Old Mother's rough voice cut into Bram's thoughts. The stout, big-breasted matron stood in front of him, thrusting a pouch of lampblack into his hand. "Be sure to work some into the draft horses' whites."

Bram did as he was bidden, smudging the dark powder along the white noses and skirts of the four workhorses. Old Mother watched for a moment, satisfying herself that boy and horses were now invisible by moonlight, then moved to the next man. She had a curious hold over the Dhoone warriors, Bram noticed. She never strategized or offered opinions on battle— though she had ridden on more campaigns than most Dhoonesmen—but she was a powerful mascot to all. She had been the first of the clan elders to declare herself for Robbie and his cause. Bram thought she smelled strange, but he kept that opinion to himself.

"Bram!"

Spinning round, Bram saw Jess Blain heading toward him. Jess was Bram's age, though he was taller and stronger and fairer, and the considerable number of battles in which he'd fought showed themselves on the long tattoo spiraling across his left cheek.

"There's to be a split. I'm heading east with Iago Sake." Jess drew his sword and made imaginary strikes through the air. "We're setting light to the sacred wood where Thrago HalfBludd and all those other barbarian chiefs are earthed. Robbie reckons they guard it day and night. Imagine that! It's hardly a proper tomb or anything, just a load of old trees."

Bram thought Jess made too light of the sacred wood. Any ground where chiefs were laid was hallowed. You could hardly blame a clan for having nothing to match the splendor of the Tomb of the Dhoone Princes. Few did. Still, Bram's mind was already working on something else. "How far from the wood does the Bluddhouse lie?"

Jess shrugged. "A league or so."

So they'll see the flames. Robbie means them to see the flames. "How many in your party?"

"A full score and more. We're to be quick about it. The Nail says we ride in, kill the guards, douse the trees with naphtha, torch them, then ride out."

That explained the many barrels of fuel oil they'd brought. Bram was quiet for a moment, thinking. "Who rides with you?"

Jess named the sworn warriors in a nonchalant voice, pretending to be more interested in practicing his downstroke. "The Nail, of course. Ranald Vey, Diddie Daw, Mangus Eel, Guy Morloch . . ."

Bram listened as Jess listed the twenty-four best horsemen in the raid party. When Jess had finished he asked casually, "Which way will you make your retreat?"

Jess waved his sword to the east. "We're to head east and north until we come to the Hell's Road, and then turn west for Milk."

It's a distraction, Bram thought with certainty. *Robbie doesn't care about the sacred wood. The Nail's party is meant to draw attention away from . . . what? Surely not the Bluddhouse? No.* They didn't have the manpower to take it. Even with the Dog Lord housed at Dhoone, the Bludd Gate was well defended. Quarro Bludd, Vaylo's eldest son, was said to be a hard and terrible warrior who meant to keep the Bluddhouse for his own.

"Jess, what's Robbie's party to do?"

The golden-haired boy looked at Bram with barely concealed superiority. With an elegant gesture borrowed from Robbie Dhoone, he recouched his watered steel. "Oh, Robbie's only told his trusted companions what he plans to do. And *we're* all sworn to secrecy." With that, Jess Blain swung his yellow braids behind him and headed off to find his horse.

Bram watched him go. *Robbie chose me to be in his party*, he told himself. *Me, not Jess*.

Around him the camp was being dismantled in preparation for the raid. Robbie's tent had been leveled and stowed, feed-bags removed from the horses, and all the remaining supplies gathered in a pile to be bound once more upon the draft mares' backs. Bram thought he'd better start work on it. Moalish Flock, the horsemaster, was already looking for him. Taking the first of the four draft mares by the reins, Bram walked into the center of the camp and began loading.

The horsemaster approached him and spat. "Nay. Don't go loading any of those drafts up, Robbie's orders. What's left here has to fit on the pack mule."

Bram glanced at the two mules standing by the makeshift horse post; the fat white one was Old Mother's mount, the little angry one had been brought here tethered to the horsemaster's reins. With four big workhorses in the party, Bram had assumed it was merely a spare. Puzzled, he packed the animal with as many of the supplies as the creature could possibly bear. When the mule could take no more—letting its displeasure be known by braying and throwing kicks—Bram decided to slip away and prepare himself for the raid.

He owned no ax, nor had he been trained to wield one, so his only weapons were the sword Robbie had called his own before their father's death, and the alien-looking twin-bladed katar he had earned for his part in the Ille Glaive raid. The sword had been oiled and honed countless times during the journey, yet Bram couldn't help but inspect the blade one last time. His stomach churned as he tested the edge. Robbie was right in a way; this *was* his first proper raid. At Ille Glaive he had just been carried along by the other clansmen, drawing his weapon yet not using it. Tonight would be different, tonight he would act like a man.

Excited, and determined to ignore the twisting in his gut, Bram went to take his place in Robbie's crew.

Robbie was already mounted and giving orders. "Flock, take Old Mother and the pack mule and lead them west. Find that old paved path we crossed at noon and wait there. I'll send Bram for you when we're done." Moalish Flock, who seldom had a good word to say to anyone and was known for finding fault with the most flawless plans, nodded obediently and went on his way. Robbie had that effect on men. He made you want to do your best.

He should be chief, Bram thought with pride.

"Duglas, you're with me. I want that wickedly sharp ax of yours as close to my neck as humanly comfortable, though I'd take it for a blessing if you managed to stay downwind. That raw onion you had for breakfast is just as deadly as any blade."

Everyone laughed. Duglas Oger grinned, showing large broken teeth and gums as pink as a baby's. "Anything you say, Rab."

Robbie bowed his head toward the big axman before sending his gaze over the entire raid party. "Men. Dhoonesmen, Castlemen, Wellmen, brothers to me this night. We ride not for blood or killing, but for simple justice. The Dhoonehouse is ours, and tonight we begin winning it back."

"*Aye!*" breathed the party, stirred by Robbie's words yet aware of the need to stay quiet this close to the Bluddhouse.

When the men had quieted to his liking, Robbie nodded and went on. "We're small in number yet, and we'll need more men and more sway before we're ready to claim Dhoone. But make no mistake, we *will* take it. We, the companions. Not Skinner and his band of old men. Never forget that we've got what Skinner hasn't—"

"Blood of the Dhoone Kings!" cried the fierce little swordsman Diddie Daw. "That Skinner's only got chief's blood pumping through him—and that runs thin as piss. Our Robbie's got kings in his veins!"

"Aye," cried another. "Blood of kings!"

Robbie let the men go on, his eyes hard and glittering, his hand resting princelike upon the hilt of his sword. After a time he said, "Enough. We must first win a war before we speak of kings."

Bram sighed with relief. He didn't like talk of kings.

"Tonight we *begin* the war. Here. Now. On Bludd-cursed soil we make our first strike." Robbie's hand rose from his sword to his neck, where his measure of powdered guidestone lay suspended in a copper horn on a copper chain. Eyes closed, chest rising and falling, he brought the horn to his lips and kissed it. "Stone Gods be with us!"

"Gods be with us!" came the reply from sixty men.

With that the raid party split into two groups, drawing up their horses into ranks, fitting their great helms and their hourglass gauntlets, closing their visors and spreading their capes. Bram had only a pot helm and boiled-leather gloves, but he hardly cared. *Tonight we begin the war*, Robbie had said. Excitement and fear burned in him like a fever, and when Robbie drew his weapon, so did he.

With shining eyes he watched Iago Sake's party ride east. Robbie spoke solemn words of farewell to the deathly pale axman known as the Nail. He called Iago his "brother in all things save blood", and Bram thought he saw the sparkle of tears in the Nail's hard, colorless eyes as he rode forth.

Quiet descended on the forty remaining men. Minutes passed as they waited, giving Iago Sake the lead he needed. All eyes were upon Robbie. The would-be chief sat high on his thistle-barded stallion, his blue wool cloak trimmed with fisher fur spreading gently in the barest breeze. Bram couldn't help himself, and he worked his way up through the line to be next to his brother.

Robbie spotted him as he reached Oath's withers. Bram saw his brother's forearm rise in welcome, watched as the gaze of those famed Dhoone-blue eyes took him in. And then Robbie hissed, "Sheathe that sword, you fool. You're not here to fight. Get down the line and handle the drafts."

Bram had no memory of riding back down the line. It seemed as if he was suddenly there, by the horsepost, receiving the driving reins for the four fully harnessed draft mares from Moalish Flock. "Let them run ahead o' your gelding, and keep 'em on a close rein. Ropes are on Milly's back when you need 'em."

Bram could barely make sense of the words. He felt as if he'd been stabbed.

Silently, he dismounted and formed the four mares into a team, checking their traces and collars. They were good horses, gentle and eager to snuffle Bram's coat for treats. Bram spoke soft words to them, telling them that no, he had no treats but he'd find apples for them later if he could. It was a difficult task, positioning the four drafts ahead of the gelding. The drafts were massive creatures with deep chests and powerful shoulders, bred for pulling carts. Bram feared they'd pull him clean from the gelding's saddle if he gave them an inch too much head. The gelding was wary of their closeness, twitching its tail and showing teeth.

And then suddenly they were under way. Robbie's cry came low and clear—"*North to Bludd!*"—and forty men and forty-four horses rode out from the clearing toward the Bluddhouse.

Tack jingled, hooves thudded, and axes wielded in anticipation made *snick*ing sounds as they cut air. Bram brought up the rear. The path was narrow, and he immediately regretted forming the drafts into double, rather than single file. Still, they were moving well enough, and there was little tension in the reins. He just wished he wasn't falling behind so quickly. The main body of the party had already raced a quarter-league ahead.

The forest was dark, fragrant with the odors of old trees. The loam beneath the horses' hooves was rich and black beneath the top layer of snow. Bram felt sweat trickle along his neck. Holding the team made his shoulders ache, and he kept searching the darkness ahead for lights, hoping to spy the Bluddhouse.

He saw the fire first, the barest glow above the trees, hardly brighter than starlight. Minutes passed, and then the cry came from ahead: "The Nail's fired the wood!" Dhoonesmen cheered. Digging steel into horseflesh, the raid party quickened their pace.

Other noises soon broke through the darkness: a horn blast, low and chilling, coming from due north. Gears whirred. Something monstrously heavy shook the earth as it moved, and then came the unmistakable rumble of many horsemen riding forth . . . *to the east. Bluddsmen. Robbie's luring them away.*

Bram felt for his earlier fear but found it gone. Robbie had killed it.

Bram could smell the fire now, see the orange flames dancing high above the canopy. Armed men were on the move, calling instructions to each other in their thick Bluddish tongue. Bram could hear but not see them. The forest was thinning now, ancient sentinels giving way to man-planted maples, red pines, smoke trees and scarlet oaks — trees chosen for the blood-red foliage. Suddenly the path broadened and turned. And there, before him, rose the hideous bulk of the Bluddhouse.

It was a massive, flaking cyst on the earth. A scab of stone, the brown-red color of dried blood, rising four storeys high and spreading immeasurably wide. Seeing it, seeing its total lack of symmetry and grace, its carbuncled outbuildings and blistered stonework, its strangely smoking gate towers and misshapen archers' roosts protruding from its roundwall like sores, Bram knew why the Dog Lord wanted Dhoone. This place was not fit for a king.

Mounted Bluddsmen in their dull plate, rough leathers and sable cloaks were racing across the roundhouse's forecourt, heading east toward the fire raging in the sacred wood. Chaos reigned. Bram's sharp eyes saw it all. Stablemen trotting out mounts tangled with armsmen bearing torches and youths bearing steel to the sworn men. Women were screaming, and a line of children and maids were running east with buckets and other vessels meant for filling with water and dousing flames. Someone, possibly the clan guide, was naming the Stone Gods in a high, wavering voice.

Robbie's done a good job surprising them, Bram thought, feeling an unfamiliar bitterness rising in his throat. *It's as if we'd torched the heart of their clan.*

Ahead, Robbie and his companions rode low in their saddles, water-steel and ax-iron drawn and moving. The woman warrior Thora Lamb hefted the hollow-tipped throwing spear she was known for, her cool gaze ranging ahead in search of game. Quietly, the war chant began, a drumbeat with two notes. *Dun Dhoone! Dun Dhoone! DUN DHOONE!*

Realization of the trap rippled through the Bluddsmen like a cold wind. There was a moment when everything was still, when buckets hung suspended in mid-swing and smoke ceased to rise from the torches. And then the cry went up.

"Close the gate!"

Into the scrambling chaos of women, warriors, children and youths rode Robbie Dhoone and his forty men. Oath had pulled thirty paces ahead of the other horses and Robbie's ax drew first blood. A yearman, poorly mounted on a sunk-backed pony, had one of his hands hacked off. Encouraged by the sight of spurting blood, the Dhoonesmen grew wild with fury, killing and slashing and riding men down. Douglas Oger rode through the lines of retreating Bluddsmen like a fallen god, savage and stinking, dealing death with his three-foot ax. Beside him rode Robbie Dun Dhoone, the Thorn King, fair as Duglas was dark, graceful as his companion was barbaric, his plate armor and great helm black and dripping, his braids whipping around him like golden chains. Together the two men drove the remaining Bluddsmen back as others in the party scattered women and children, axes and swords moving in and out of Bluddflesh to the rhythm of the Dhoonish chant. *Dun Dhoone! Dun Dhoone! DUN DHOONE!*

Bram watched as a horse slid in a pool of gore, crushing its rider and breaking its own back. He felt a fine mist of blood spray across his face as Duglas took a man's head, smelled human shit and urine and horse stale as men and beasts lost themselves to fear. Something close to relief overcame him when the Bludd Gate finally closed, its black iron hinges and pulleys straining as they swung two tons of iron-studded bloodwood back into its frame. Women and children and old men ran but did not make it, and as bars were shot home with the force of crossbolts firing, they threw themselves against the wood, scratching and pleading, tearing their nails.

Duglas Oger slowed his ax swing and looked to his leader. Robbie pulled off his great helm to reveal a face red with exertion and stained bloody around the eyes. His braids were dark now, drenched with sweat. He seemed to wait until everyone, even the panicking Bluddsfolk, stilled, and then said in a clear voice, "No. Let no one say Robbie Dhoone kills innocent women and children like the Hail Wolf. Let them run free to the woods."

Duglas Oger nodded, grabbing a fistful of mane from his horse's neck and using it to clean his ax. All around Dhoonesmen lowered their weapons and removed their helms, panting for breath.

Wary relief spread through the crowd gathering at the Bludd Gate. One toothless old hag bobbed a curtsy to Robbie, calling him a clansman good and true. Impatient, Robbie waved her away. Slowly, the Bluddsfolk stepped clear of the gate, eyes down, arms around the shoulders of small children, buckets still in their hands.

"No," Robbie said suddenly, pointing to a red-haired boy of perhaps twelve. "He carries a sword—so is a man."

Duglas dealt the boy a clean blow with his newly shined ax, cleaving the youngster's chest from shoulder blade to heart, crushing a dozen bones. A woman fainted. Children began to whimper. A group of maids broke free from the gate and ran screaming through the Dhoone ranks. Thora Lamb amused herself by cracking their knees with her spear. By the time the gateway was clear, five other corpses lay on the ground. Three more youths and two old men.

An archer high up in one of the roosts began taking shots, and an arrow glanced off Robbie's plate. "Come, men," he said abruptly, turning his horse. "Let's finish what we came here for. Bram! Bring the horses."

Bram obeyed the order, struggling to set all five horses into motion at once. The party moved west of the Bluddhouse, toward a series of outbuildings that lay clustered on the banks of a small stream. Robbie rode ahead of the group, searching. All the buildings looked the same to Bram—squat, red-stoned, hastily built with neither mortar nor chinking—yet Robbie came to a halt before one.

The moon broke through the clouds as Robbie waited for his companions to draw abreast, and Bram saw that he had been wrong: not all the shanties were red-hued. This one was pale, built from blue-gray stone.

And then Bram knew what his brother meant to do.

"Bram," Robbie murmured, his voice dark with feeling. "Put the ropes on the horses and tear this thing down."

The Dhoone ranks parted to let Bram and the drafts through. Bram's hands shook as he fastened the wrist-thick ropes to the mares' harnesses, surprised by the strength of his emotion. All around, men had dismounted and were murmuring the names of the nine gods. Duglas Oger had tears in his dark eyes, and a fellow axman moved to lay a reassuring hand on the big man's shoulders. Watching them, Bram was overcome with an aching love for his clan. *How can Robbie not be chief after this?* The sadness came slowly, as he walked around the little stone shanty, pulling rope through his fist. *I no longer love him as I did.*

With his heart aching softly, Bram cracked the whip and set the four massive draft horses in motion, bringing down the building that the Dog Lord had raised thirty-five years ago from the rubble of the lost Dhoonestone.

NINE

A Broken Stone

Raina Blackhail sat on the edge of the stone bed and bound her honey-brown hair. The tresses were soft and heavy, and the familiar movements of weaving the long braid calmed her. Dagro had always loved her hair. *Unbind it for me*, he had whispered, that first night in the barley field when they had come together as man and woman whilst his first wife lay dying in this very chamber. Norala had wished it, knowing her husband needed the comfort of a woman and wanting him to pick one worthy of being his new wife. Still, Norala had died a week later, earlier than expected and in terrible pain, and Raina knew it was the knowledge of their union that had killed her. Picking a new wife for your husband was one thing; living with the knowledge that the new pair were in love and well matched was another, and the anguish had been too much to bear.

Sighing, Raina stood. It all seemed like a hundred years ago now, and she had been such a child. How could she ever have believed that the world was good, and that everyone within it wished her well?

Thrusting sharp silver combs into her hair, she coiled her braid around her scalp. It wouldn't do for her to be seen with it unbound or even hanging down her back in a single plait. She was chief's wife, and there were many around her who were eager to find fault. Already the whispers had begun. *Mace no longer sleeps in her chamber. Ayla Perch says she drove him out. Who can blame a man for looking elsewhere for favors his wife won't grant?*

A hard little smile that Raina did not like on herself was showing when she looked in the glass. *Always he twists and maneuvers, killing the truth.* It was he who had walked out on their marriage bed. Mace, not her. Gods knew she had not loved it, but she had found her capacity for endurance was like a great hollow space inside herself, always able to swallow a little more. Now Mace had let it be known that she had turned cold and frigid, and had shut her door against him. Lies, all lies, but they sounded so much like the truth.

And they weakened her position in the clan. The clanswomen were her backbone and support; she birthed their sons, taught their daughters how to be women, offered counsel when their marriages grew strained and mourning in times of grief. Always it was said of her that she was a good woman and a loyal wife. And now Mace Blackhail was taking that last thing from her.

If you refused to share your bed with your husband, it meant you were no longer a loyal wife.

She was too proud to deny it, for she would not speak aloud what others delighted to whisper, nor was she sure that such a denial would be believed. She had always been cool to Mace, and the women had doubtless observed this, as women always did, and the rumors would be easier to believe. *After all*, they would say, *she's never shown much love for him in the past. It was only a matter of time before she drew away.*

Frustrated, Raina tugged at the straw-filled mattress on the bed and began shaking some air into it. She really should make a new one, for this one had grown limp, and doubtless many small creatures had made their home within it, and it no longer cushioned her spine against the hardness of the stone bed.

Stone, stone, stone. She was sick of Blackhail and its hardness; its dark oppressive roundhouse, and its corpses left to rot on open ground. Look at this chamber: stone bed, undressed-stone walls, stone flags worn thin where two thousand years of chiefs had stepped upon them. Where was the lightness and the music? Growing up in Dregg there had been dancing and mummery, the great hall gay with candlelight, the men with their kilts a-skirling, the women with sprigs of rosemary in their hair. Just to look at the walls made you glad; plastered smooth and painted umber, and swaddled in homespun fabrics they hardly looked like stone at all. Blackhail had ten times the wealth of Dregg, so why did it have none of its joy?

Raina let the straw mattress drop to the bed. *I am young yet, only thirty-three winters passed, yet why does this roundhouse make me old?*

It was a question she had no time for. Inigar Stoop had called her to the guidehouse, and she did not want to go yet knew she must. Already she had kept him waiting.

Her chamber was located high on the western wall of the roundhouse, as far as it was possible to be from the guidestone and the guidehouse, and it seemed today that the walk was especially long and tiring. Some of the Scarpe women had set up a cook chamber in the old granary, where the damp had risen too sharply to continue storing grain. Raina smelled the sharp, unfamiliar scents of another clan's cookery, and it made the gall rise in her. *How do we stand it, this slow invasion by Scarpe?* At that moment, she spied Anwyn Bird crossing the entrance hall on her way to the kitchen. She thought of stopping the older woman to ask her, but she noticed an unfamiliar stoop in the clan matron's shoulders and too many loose hairs pulled free from her bun. *She suffers too*, Raina thought, and wondered what it must be like for Anwyn to have her clean, well-ordered domain taken over by strangers. You could fight and fight, but little was won in the end. Mace Blackhail would have his way.

As she approached the narrow tunnel that led out to the guide-house, Raina smoothed her dress and checked her boots for mud. Foolishness, but she could not help herself. There would be a battle here—she sensed it—and she had long learned to fight with whatever weapons she had at hand. Inigar would see her as chief's wife, not some scared little maid he could bully and cajole.

Pulling composure about her like a mask, she entered the Blackhail guidehouse.

The cold struck her first, the sheer depth and deadness of it. How long ago had the freeze set in? Ten days? Surely now it was passed. Just yesterday she had watered Mercy at the Leak, and she was sure she had felt the first whiff of spring. Yet here, in the guidehouse, time seemed to have stopped at midwinter. Chilled, she rubbed her arms, wishing she had thought to bring a shawl.

As her eyes grew accustomed to the dimness, the massive bulk of the Hailstone emerged from the shadows like some-thing conjured up from another world. Its bulk and power humbled her, and despite her best attempts to discipline her feelings she felt the old stirrings of awe.

Then she saw the stone was steaming.

Fear, instant and so concentrated she could taste the salt in it, leapt from her throat to her mouth. The Hailstone was steam-ing like a side of frozen meat.

"Yes, Raina Blackhail. Eagle lores always know when to fear."

Startled by the clan guide's voice, yet determined not to show it, Raina straightened the curve of her back and said, "How long has it been like this?"

Inigar Stoop stepped free from the shadows and smoke. *He*

has aged, she thought as the two regarded each other. The clan guide's eyes were as black and hard as ever, but his body seemed shrunken and dry, sucked clean of blood. She tried not to show her shock, but Inigar Stoop was not an easy man to fool.

"You find me changed, Raina?" he said, his voice as sharp as ever. "Then perhaps you should have come here before now."

She made no reply. *I am chief's wife and will offer no excuses to this man.*

He knew what she thinking, she was sure of it, and for a moment the two faced each other as adversaries: chief's wife and clan guide, gazes locked and bristling. Then, abruptly, Inigar shrugged. Strangely, he pulled off the pigskin gloves he had been wearing and held them out toward her. "Take them. Touch the stone."

Annoyed that she had lost control of the situation, but also affected by the grimness in Inigar's voice, she hesitated.

He offered the gloves once more. "You cannot touch the stone without them. It would skin you."

How can it be? she wanted to ask. But she feared that question more than touching the stone, so she took the gloves from him and drew close to the guidestone's eastern face. Cold breath rose from the monolith, making her teeth chatter like a little girl's. This close she could see the living surface of the stone, the valleys and fissures and weeping holes. Normally it was damp and oozing, but now a frost covered it like scale. Wary, she reached out and laid gloved fingers upon it.

Oh gods. It was like touching a dying man. Always when she had touched it before—at the end of her girlhood, after both her weddings, and Dagro's death—its power had leapt toward her fingers like heat. Now it was cold and all power had withdrawn from the surface. She sensed it buried deep. As she took her hand away she felt a faint stirring, as if something reached toward her . . . but failed.

The loss numbed her.

Inigar Stoop stood silent, watching. After a time he said, "The gods send ice into the heart of the stone. It will shatter before the year's out."

Raina touched her measure of guidestone, held in an embroidered pouch at her waist. She had heard the tales of guidestones cracking, but they had always seemed more like legends than truth. Quietly, she said, "The Eve of Breaking?"

Inigar nodded. "The night Stanner Hawk sent a hound to the fire."

She bowed her head. It was too much to see the weight of knowledge on his face.

Slowly, she backed away, feeling for a wall to support her. The guidehouse was in disarray, the smoke fire almost burned out, grit and ashes littering the floor, chisels scattered like sticks. Even the clan guide's clothes had been neglected, and his once fine pigskins were stained and torn. Suddenly she felt pity for him, but knew better than to show it. "Have you told Mace?"

"You know I have not. What good would it do to strike fear amongst the clan?"

"Yet you show no such scruples to me?"

"You are a woman and do not fight."

She wanted to strike him for his arrogance. How dare he! She fought. Gods knew how she fought for this clan. Shaking, she said, "I wonder why you brought me here since you think so little of me." With that she turned to leave.

"Stay," he commanded, his voice calm with practiced authority. "I said only that you do not fight, not that you hold no power."

Tired of games, she threw the pigskin gloves onto the floor. "What would you have of me? The stone is broken and I cannot fix it. I'd have to be a god for that."

Still he did not rise to her anger. Moving to pick up the

gloves he said, "Do you know all stones have lives? Ask any farmer. Stones can appear in their fields overnight, cast up by the restless earth. Mountains calf and move them, rivers and glaciers carry them, and heat and ice destroy them when all else is done. Whenever a guidestone dies a new one must be found to take its place."

Inigar Stoop grew silent, and Raina found herself wondering when he had ceased talking of stones and begun talking about himself.

"I want Effie Sevrance, Raina. Tell me where she is."

So this was what he wanted. Effie. She should have guessed it. "You cannot protect her, Inigar."

"I am clan guide. I watch over this clan, and will watch over her."

Yet you did not watch over her the night Stanner Hawk tried to burn her in the forge. And then the damning thought, *None of us did.* Anger at her own failing made her sharp. "You are only one man, Inigar Stoop, one amongst thousands. Effie is no longer safe in this clan."

Inigar's hawk nose whitened across the bridge. "She is needed. I choose her to be the next guide."

Raina stopped herself from replying sharply. Looking at the guidehouse, at the smoke-blackened walls, stone troughs and stark benches, she knew Inigar did not see this place as she did. Again the pity came. *He is sick and will one day die, and there is no one to take his place.* She said gently, "You must choose another, Inigar. Effie will soon be gone from here; I'm sending her south to my sister at Dregg."

Cold anger burned in the guide's eyes. "So the girl is more important to you than clan?"

It was not a fair question, and she could not answer it. All she knew was that when Bitty Shank came running to find her on the Eve of Breaking, telling of how he'd found Effie outside in the dog cotes, shaking with cold and fright, she had thought her heart might break. No child had lost as much as Effie Sevrance; Raina was determined she would lose no more.

Inigar spoke over her thoughts. "I have searched for five years for someone to train as my replacement. Every time a boy was born I hoped. Whenever a child took a special interest in the guidehouse I watched and waited and dreamt . . . but no new guide ever came. And then Effie began to come here and sit beneath that bench. No child has ever disturbed my dreams like she has. There's power in her, Raina. Power this clan can use. She is young yet, but she will grow and learn more. I will teach her myself.

"I know you see only the bleakness of this guidehouse. Don't deny it. It's plainly written on your face. What you don't see is the life behind it. When I stand here and take a chisel to the guidestone I deal in men's souls. Every man and woman in this clan holds steel fired by Brog Widdie and powdered guidestone ground by me. Which is the most powerful, Raina? Tell me. That which kills or grants grace?"

He paused, not for her to answer, but to allow her time to think. The Hailstone smoked behind him, a giant slowly dying as it froze.

"It would not be a bad life for her. Sparse and solitary, yes, but ordered and meaningful too. I think if you were honest you would say it would suit her. She came here often enough of her own free will. You know she is happiest in closed, dark spaces. Let me take her and teach her. She can sleep on one of the benches, and take her meals with me."

Almost he persuaded her, for there was much truth and sense in his words. Effie feared open spaces—Gods knew how they would get her to Dregg. But get her there they would. What Inigar offered was a kind of half-life, led amidst darkness and quiet and smoke. Raina would not have it for her. She had raised Effie as her own child, taught her how to speak and hold her spoon, and she wanted simple happiness for her. She wanted her to dance at Dregg.

Inigar read it all on her face, and she was prepared for his anger, but in the end there was only resignation. "Take her, then," he said. "No matter if she ends up in Dregg or the farthest badlands, you cannot change her fate. She was born to the stone, Raina Blackhail, she wears it around her neck. You're an eagle and can see clearly and know I speak the truth."

Raina nodded, and there was nothing else to say, so she left Inigar there in the darkness, a broken man with a broken stone.

She couldn't get out of the roundhouse quick enough. Running, she made her way along the tunnel and out through the entrance hall. People saw and tried to hail her, but she paid them no heed. She needed light and wind and freshness, and she raced to the stables to saddle Mercy.

Sweet-faced Jebb Onnacre trotted out her mare. "I thought you might be taking a run," he said. "Be careful around Cold Lake, the ice is rotting there." As she took the reins from him their gazes met. "I'll be telling anyone who asks that you headed south to the Wedge."

She thanked him, glad in her heart for the small kindness. Jebb was a Shank by marriage, and the Shanks' loyalty to Effie remained unchanged. Orwin Shank knew where the girl was hidden, and Jebb had doubtless guessed that Raina was on her way there. Well, she was, but she'd lay a little ghost trail first. Mace had her watched and she had to be careful.

Little mice with weasels' tails.

Shaking off her unease, Raina gave Mercy her head.

Oh, it was glorious to ride! To feel the mare's muscles beneath her, and the wind buffeting her chest. She grinned with the joy of it, sending Mercy galloping over a series of hedgerows for no good reason at all.

South first, must be careful, she counseled herself, somehow afraid that her joy might make her careless. *Turn west only when you reach the trees.*

They had tried to find Effie, of course. Mace and Stanner Hawk and Turby Flapp. They suspected Raina and the Shanks had concealed her, but the Shanks and the Blackhail hammermen had closed ranks: Effie was one of their own, and no one was going to find her, so help them Gods. Mace had questioned Raina about it, casually asking why she'd rode out so often these past ten days, especially given the freeze. He knew she was lying, but could not press her. After all, his interest in Effie had to be seen to be purely honorable, a chief concerned for a little girl. He did not fool Raina. She knew whose hand lay behind the burning of the hound. She had heard the threat herself.

Slowing her pace to a canter, Raina turned for Cold Lake. All about her stone pines and black birch showed signs of the sudden freeze. Ten days back the temperature had dropped so low so quickly that you could hear the trees exploding. A thaw had begun a week earlier and the winter-starved trees had begun drawing water. Longhead said that the freeze couldn't have come at a worse time, for the water in the pines turned to ice and split the trunks clean open. Over five hundred mature trees had been lost in the Wedge alone, the worst anyone could remember in a single season.

More bad omens, thought Raina grimly as she turned onto a little-used dogtrot to the lake. Two hours passed as Mercy worked her way through a mire of half-frozen bulrushes and mud. Raina found herself thinking longingly of the fine trail that led directly from the roundhouse to the lakeshore and could be traveled in less than an hour. *Damn rushes!* They tore her ankles to shreds, and Gods only knew whether firm ground or water lay beneath them. When she finally spied the ugly little crannog extending out across the lake, she let out a great sigh of relief.

Mad Binny was out upon the pier, waiting for her, cool as if she'd known all along Raina would come. The old clan spinster was dressed in black, and she held a wooden mallet in her hands. "For the fishes," she said in greeting, seeing Raina's gaze upon it. "They come up to the surface by the poles, and they're slow at this time of year."

Raina could think of nothing to say to that, though she did notice that several fair-sized bull trout lay skipping at the spinster's feet. Dismounting, she looked over the queer little crannog Mad Binny had claimed as her own.

Raised on stilts above the water, it commanded the southernmost shore of the lake. It had been built by Ewan Blackhail in the time of the River Wars, when every clan chief worth his guidestone had been obsessed with running water and the need to defend it. Looking around, Raina could not understand the crannog's position, for none of the streams that fed the lake looked wide enough to hold a boat. Still, men would be men, and if other clans were building defensive crannogs then so, by Gods, would Blackhail.

Trouble was, this one hadn't been built well at all—Hailsmen not being rivermen and so unfamiliar with the challenges of building over water—and forty years later it had fallen to ruin. The roof sagged, and had been mended here and there with bulrushes and animal hides, the window frames were rotten and broken, and an entire wall of outbuildings had half sunk into the lake. Gods knew what lay beneath the water. It was a wonder the thing still stood.

"You'll be wanting to see the bairn, then?" Mad Binny squatted and hit one of the skipping trout with the mallet. "She's inside, learning how to make a broth to boil a fish."

Raina was growing accustomed to being speechless in this woman's presence. It was hard to believe that this strange, big-boned woman had once been a great beauty, betrothed to Orwin

Shank. Birna Lorn, her name was, and some old men in the roundhouse could still recall the day when Orwin and Will Hawk had fought for her hand in the graze. Not much later she had been named as a witch, for she had correctly predicted that Norala's unborn child would be born dead. *If I ever turn into a prophet*, Raina thought dryly, *I'll keep all the bad news to myself.*

"You should learn how to kill a fish, Raina Blackhail," Mad Binny said, clubbing another trout. "It's good practice for killing men." Brilliant green eyes caught the light, and Raina couldn't decide if she saw madness or cleverness in them.

"Take me to Effie."

"Take yourself. Door's right there, what's left of it. I'll be in when I've headed the trout."

Knowing that was one thing she definitely did not want to see, Raina climbed the rickety ladder and made her way inside the crannog. The room she entered was dim and warm, scented with the mulish odor of wet rot and lit by a tiny iron stove. Effie stood by the stove with her back toward Raina, stirring a little pot. She was singing as she did so, some song about the shankshounds and how they had once saved a baby from the snow. Standing at the doorway, watching her, it occurred to Raina that she had never before heard Effie Sevrance sing. When a board beneath Raina's foot creaked, Effie started, spilling the broth.

Fear changed to recognition in an instant, and Effie ran to Raina with arms outstretched. "Raina! I've been making broth! Did you know you put carrots and onions in it, and then boil them till they nearly disappear?"

Raina nodded. She was still seeing Effie's start of fear in her mind and her chest was too tight to speak.

"Binny says it won't be done until she brings the trout and I boil their heads in it. Is Drey back yet?"

Raina had visited Effie three times in nine days, and each time she did so she was greeted with the same question: Where was Drey? Disentangling herself from the girl's embrace, she thought what she should say. *It suits Mace to have Drey away at the moment while he decides how best to deal with you. So he keeps coming up with things your brother can do that will keep him far from home.* No, that wouldn't do. Aloud she said, "I heard word from Paille Trotter's son. He saw Drey ten days back at Ganmiddich, and thinks Drey will head home soon."

Effie was not fooled by Raina's forced optimism, and she returned dispirited to her broth.

Raina wanted nothing more than to comfort her, but she knew better than to speak lies to a child. "So, what has Mad Binny been teaching you?"

"Lots of things. Cooking. Herbs. Do you know that maggots can eat the pus from a wound and make it heal faster? And that piles shrink when you put vinegar on them?"

Raina laughed. In many ways the clan guide had been right: Effie needed to learn. Suddenly tired, Raina sat on an old chicken crate, content simply to watch Effie chop onions and stir broth. She had to believe she'd done the right thing. The guidehouse was no place for this bright and lovely girl.

In this light you could hardly see the scars. Effie's long lustrous hair covered most of them, and the one on her cheek had been so expertly stitched by Láida Moon that it looked as if a fine feather rested there. Some would think it beautiful. Raina did.

"Here we are. Trout. Effie, put those heads in the pot. Yes, they have eyes. Too bad they didn't use them." Mad Binny took command of the room, detailing how the broth should be made and the fish cooked, directing Raina to the woodpile for firewood, and Effie to the storage chest for hard liquor. It was a relief to let someone else take charge for a change—even if she were a madwoman—and Raina found herself surprisingly happy to be told what to do.

When they had eaten a good plain meal of trout in its own broth and black rye bread smothered in honey, Mad Binny told Effie to go outside and try her hand at stunning passing fish with the mallet. "But it's nearly dark," Effie observed.

"Even better then. They'll be half asleep already."

Effie had no argument for that, and she picked up the mallet and let herself out. Raina had her money on the fish.

"So," said Mad Binny, pouring a double measure of malt into Raina's cup. "Has that old sourpuss Inigar Stoop made a play for the girl yet?"

Raina couldn't stop her eyes from widening.

"You needn't look so pelt-shorn, Raina Blackhail. Why d'you think they drove me to this mud bucket in the first place?"

"I . . . well . . ."

"Aye. I'm either a madman or a witch. Possibly both." Mad Binny slammed the malt flask onto the table, flattening a fly. "I'll tell you this, Raina, that girl can't stay in Blackhail. And if you don't know that you're a fool."

Raina nodded, still reeling from the turn of the conversation. "I'm planning to move her to Dregg."

"When?"

"When her brother returns. She won't leave without seeing him."

Mad Binny raised the malt flask and studied the squashed fly. "Well, she'll be leaving soon, then, since Drey Sevrance is on his way here this night."

Raina felt a rush of pleasure and relief, then told herself she was a fool. "You're making it up."

"Am I, now? Well, we'll see about that. In the meantime I'm going to tell you what you should do with that child, and you're going to sit there and listen." Mad Binny spoke with the calmness of one who had seldom been contradicted. Raina supposed it was a benefit of living by oneself.

"Effie Sevrance should be delivered to the cloister at Owl's Reach. It's in the mountains, east of Hound's Mire—the locals can tell you where. They teach the old lores: herb and animal, far seeing and far speech, summonings and compulsions and other ancient magics. She has the quickness for it, and I need not tell you she has the power. The sisters there will value her, and she'll grow to become one of them, accepted for what she is."

Raina stood. She was sick of people telling her what to do about Effie. This was a child they spoke of, not some dangerous animal that must be either trained or caged. "I'm not sending Effie to a place full of strangers who are not clan. Who will love her? Not some cold-eyed sorceress who seeks to control her. No. Dregg will be good for her. I was only a year older than she is now when I was fostered from my birth clan; it will be no different for her. She'll make friends, and all this sorcery nonsense will be forgotten." In her agitation, Raina knocked over her cup.

Mad Binny caught it before it rolled to the floor. "It's a pity to see a woman as clever as you fool herself. Look at me. Thirty years alone here. Would you want the same for the child?"

No, Raina would not. The two women looked at each other, the older one calm, the younger one shaking. Raina almost knew what Mad Binny would say next, and she did not want to hear it.

"Dregg is a young clan," Mad Binny said quietly. "Its warriors are fierce and they wield the heavy swords with the broad blades. Its women are held to be passing fair, and dress in bright cloths they weave with their own hands. It's said their chief is a good man, and their roundhouse is well set and well built. All this is known, yet clan is still clan. Tell me, when was the last time you were there, Raina? Ten years ago? Twenty?" The spinster's green eyes were knowing and there might have been pity in them. "Do you really think they will treat Effie any differently than Blackhail once they know the power of her lore?"

Raina made a small gesture with her hand, pushing the words away. *It will be better for her at Dregg*, she told herself. *There's no Mace Blackhail there.* Yet the thought gave her little comfort, and she found her mind returning to the morning after Effie had fled. In her haste to escape the roundhouse, the girl had dropped the bowl of liquid she had used to threaten the men. It had landed on the great court, just outside the clan door. Effie had since told Raina that the black liquid was nothing more than charcoal mixed with malt liquor, and Raina believed her . . . yet it had burned the stone clean through.

Raina shivered. She was afraid, and she had run out of words to argue with this woman. When Effie's voice came from outside she was relieved.

"Drey! Raina, it's Drey!"

Mad Binny had the decency to look only slightly triumphant. Raina Blackhail left her and went outside to greet Drey.

TEN

Condemned Men

Penthero Iss stood on a stone platform cushioned with silk and horse hides, waiting to sentence a grangelord to death. The man was charged with high treason, and so rightly the trial and the execution should have been held within Mask Fortress, and the man's head laid upon the obsidian block known as Traitor's Doom. But Iss, Surlord of Spire Vanis, Lord Commander of the Rive Watch, Keeper of Mask Fortress and Master of the Four Gates, had thought to assemble a larger crowd. You could only fit so many bystanders into the quad. Whereas the Quarter Square spread out before Iss, with its circle of gibbets know as the Dreading Ring, its baiting pits, statue garden, market stalls, cattle folds, gaming courts and slave blocks, could accommodate half a city.

And today it nearly did. Even though the sky was steel gray and a high wind was blowing off Mount Slain, the city had come out in force. Thousands of merchants, apprentices, laborers, prostitutes, priests, pot boys, mercenaries and lords milled around in the great expanse of the square, growing restless. They had eaten from the cook stalls, gamed at dice and sticks, drunk beer and strong white liquor, inspected the corpses strung high on the gibbets, watched the spectacle of a hundred grangelords assembling on the steps of the Quarter Court, and now they were ready for blood.

Iss sympathized with them. John Rullion, the High Examiner, was reading a list of the charges, and the man's dour and powerful voice rose high above the noise of the wind. "Maskill Boice, Lord of the Hunted Granges, and Master of the River Crossing at Stye, you are here today charged with high treason against the lord of this city and its people. Knowingly you met with others at the Dog's Head in Almstown, and knowingly you plotted to assassinate the surlord on the last day of Mourns as he made his progress through the city, bequeathing alms. Seventeen days later you made contract with Black Dan, master bowman of Ille Glaive, and paid him ten gold rods for his service. Furthermore, on the same day you reached agreement with the coarsehouse bawd Hester Fay, otherwise known as Big Hetty, thereby allowing Black Dan use of her three-storeyed house on the Spireway, which overlooks the surlord's progress, in return for a payment of six silver spoons. How say you?"

The crowd stilled, restless and ready for anger. Corpses on the gibbets swung wildly in the rising wind as the throng waited to hear what the accused man would say.

Maskill Boice stood at the foot of the Quarter Court, an iron collar around his neck that ran chains down to his wrists and ankles and forced him to keep his head up. Boice was a big man turned fleshy, with the high color of one who drank too much and the contemptuous sneer of a grangelord. He had been held in custody for the customary twelve days, and Iss had made sure the man was well treated, even going so far as to have Caydis Zerbina deliver cooked pheasants, fortified wines and hothouse plums to his cell. Caydis had also seen to his attire, ensuring that of all the grangelord's considerable wardrobe, it was the richest, finest cloths he wore today. Rubies glittered on the grangelord's doublet, and the unmistakable opulence of ocelot could be seen lining his cloak.

It was an interesting picture he made, standing there below his fellow grangelords. There could be no denying Maskill Boice was one of them, with his riches and arrogance displayed for all to see. Indeed, if it weren't for the matter of his chains he might simply have mounted the steps and taken his place amongst them. And Penthero Iss sincerely doubted that this irony went unnoticed by the crowd. They knew a rich lordling when they saw one.

By contrast, Iss was dressed moderately, his robe of swansdown a stark gray trimmed with executioner's black. At his back Marafice Eye was cloaked in maroon leathers that had seen battle and hard travel in their day.

The Commander General of the Rive Watch had brought his men out in force for the trial, and the deep red of their forge cloaks could be seen in numbers, patrolling the crowd. Iss was gratified by their presence. The population of the city had swelled these past months, taking in mercenary companies, men-at-arms, knights, footmen, sappers, engineers, armorers, and every farmer's son within five hundred leagues who thought to make his fortune seizing battle trove rather than sowing grain.

Marafice Eye was doing as he had promised at midwinter: raising an army to invade the clanholds in late spring.

Iss was well pleased with what his Knife had accomplished so far. Camps had been established to the north of the city: makeshift towns where men lived under canvas and spoiled the neighboring fields. Training was under way, with large groups of men-at-arms being drilled in how to fight in formation with shields and spears, and raids for provisions and arms had been mounted as far east as the Hound's Wall. Still, there was danger in having so many free lances in the city. Danger also in those hundred grangelords assembled in costly splendor upon the

Quarter Court's limestone steps. And a wise man could see further danger in Marafice Eye and his red cloaks.

All in all, Spire Vanis was a hazardous place to be in.

And for no one was that more true than for Maskill Boice.

The accused man looked defiant, rattling his chains as he declared himself innocent of the charges. Iss felt Boice's gaze come to rest upon him, challenging him to meet his eye, but Iss was not about to engage in such theatrics. It was time to move the proceedings along. He nodded once to John Rullion.

"Bring forth the witnesses," ordered the High Examiner in response. Rullion was a hard man, not gently born, and he bore no love for the grangelords. His arrogance came from his belief in the One God, and although he had been High Examiner since the time of Borhis Horgo and had amassed vast wealth over the past thirty years, he still dressed like a priest.

Two brothers-in-the-watch brought forth the whore, handling her with some care as they knew her to be a favorite with the crowd.

Hester Fay winked at Marafice Eye as she passed him, drawing a great guffaw from the front ranks. She was a large woman, dark and bejeweled like a gypsy, with hoops in her ears and a bodice perilously laced. She had the audacity to call the High Examiner by his first name and ask him how his gout was faring, as she'd heard he'd had an attack at midwinter.

The High Examiner kept his dignity by ignoring her remarks and clearing his throat. The crowd quieted in anticipation: a priest examining a whore. This should be high sport.

"Hester Fay. Do you recognize this man before you?"

"I do." A small adjustment to her bodice accompanied the words, bringing forth cheers of appreciation. "Used to come into my establishment every week, he did. Liked 'em young. Willing to pay for 'em, too. And let me tell you, those kind don't come cheap."

"*What about you, Hetty?*" cried someone from the crowd.

Big Hetty thrust out her hips. "Darlin', you can have *me* for two silver spoons!"

The crowd roared with laughter, pushing and jostling for positions closer to the steps. Iss suppressed a smile. This was going very well. Who could have guessed the whore would be so amusing?

"Quiet!" commanded the High Examiner. His authority was such that he was immediately obeyed, and his voice soared into the growing silence. "Is it true, Hester Fay, that Maskill Boice caused you to come to the Dog's Head seventeen days back, and there requested that you rent one of your upper rooms to the bowman, Black Dan?"

The whore nodded. "That he did. Though I can't say as I knew Black Dan for a bowman at the time. Master Boice said he was a carpenter, lately come from the Glaive, who had need of a small room."

"And was Maskill Boice particular in his request for a room?"

"That he was. Wanted Kitty's room, right at the top o' the house, with the overlook to the Spireway."

The crowd drew breath. All knew the surlord was due to ride the length of the Spireway the next morning.

The High Examiner, sensing triumph, moved quickly to finish Boice off. "And when did you learn that Black Dan was indeed a bowman, not a carpenter as reported?"

Big Hetty looked contrite. She appealed to the crowd. "Well, you know how it is when a stranger moves in. You don't know him, you're worried about your girls. Has he got the means to pay? It's only natural you'd want to inquire into his finances. All I did was slip into his room when he was out taking his supper—just a quick look through his effects."

"And you found the crossbow?"

"Aye. A real big 'un. All fancy, with a hand crank and

trigger. And ten good quarrels with barbed heads."

The crowd erupted into a frenzy, drawing weapons and stamping their feet. Marafice Eye made a spreading gesture with his gloved hand, signaling a thousand red cloaks to close ranks around the square. Right on cue the chant began and was quickly picked up by the masses, becoming a thunderous roar for justice. *Kill Boice! Kill Boice!*

Iss kept himself still. It was a nice touch, those ten barbed quarrels. The whore had earned her money well.

On the steps of the Quarter Court the grangelords grew pale with fury. They were powerful in their granges—those vast ranging estates they held outside the city—but when faced with an angry mob they were vulnerable. The people loved them not, and from time to time it served a surlord well to remind them of that fact.

Iss looked over their ranks. All the great houses were there: Crieff, Stornoway, Mar, Gryphon, Pengaron. And Hews. There he was, that young princeling Garric Hews, with the badges of his granges surmounted on his shoulder-guards, and the sword named for his great-grandfather strapped to his muscled thigh. The Whitehog. He was the only one of the hundred who had had the forethought to wear armor this day.

Iss felt the familiar burn of resentment as he looked over at the Lord of the Eastern Granges, a mere boy of eighteen, untested in battle and statecraft, yet so certain of his own worth. House Hews was ancient, stretching back to the time of the Quarterlords, when Harlech Hews bore the standard for the Bastard Lord Torny Fyfe. Harlech had been granted lands along the Sheerway following the Founding Wars, and his ancestors had been adding to their holdings every since. Rannock, Owaine, Halder, Connor, Harlech the Second, Third, Fourth, Fifth and Sixth: all had amassed wealth and titles for the house. And all had been Surlord before Iss. Now this arrogant son-of-the-Hewses thought it was his birthright to take Iss's place.

Raising his hand high, Iss brought the attention of half a city upon himself. *Watch very carefully, Garric Hews. Maskill Boice's fate might be yours one day.*

"Grangelords!" Iss commanded the hundred men on the steps. "What is your decision: freedom or sword?"

The grangelords stared at Iss with fury. They were trapped, and they knew it. Only grangelords could stand in judgment of high treason, and here they were forced to judge one of their own. They did not like it. Most surlords would have taken justice into their own hands and had their attempted assassin summarily executed. But not Iss. He would make a show out of this. The whole of Spire Vanis would learn just what they risked if they lifted a finger against him.

Ballon Troak, Lord of Almsgate, stepped forward from the grangelords' ranks. Troak was grossly fat and dressed in sparkling green samite. He held one of the oldest granges within the city and was not so easily intimidated by angry mobs. "Surlord," he said in his high, nasal voice. "Surely you know we need more evidence before we condemn a man to the sword. Where is this bowman, Black Dan? Bring him forth. Let him be examined before the city."

Iss let his face show no emotion. The crowd had grown settled again, and the chant of *Kill Boice!* was nearly lost to the wind. Pointedly, Iss let his gaze rise to the nearest of the six gibbets where the headless remains of a man were strung. "There's your bowman, Lord of Almsgate. Perhaps you should ask him how he lost his head."

Uneasy laughter rippled through the crowd. Blood rushed to Ballon Troak's cheeks. "You dare to take—"

"I dare much," Iss hissed, directing his voice solely to the grangelords. "Be grateful I don't dare more." Then, to one of the pages, "Bring the bowman's weapon. Hold it up for all to see."

The weapon, a fine crossbow made from costly limewood varnished to a high sheen, drew murmurs of appreciation from the crowd. When a second page raised the arrows, they went wild. Ten deadly points, barbed and of Glavish design, just as the whore had said. Stronger than ever, the chant was renewed. *Kill Boice! Kill Boice!*

He's mine now. Satisfied but unsmiling, Iss returned his attention to the grangelords. "I ask again. How find you? Freedom or sword?"

Sword! Sword! Sword! screamed the crowd.

The grangelords moved to form a rough circle on the steps. Fergus Hurd, Lord of the Fire-River Granges, and appointed Speaker, went from man to man, collecting pieces of killhound bone from each. White for freedom. Red for the sword. Iss could hear them rattle in the Speaker's silk pouch, watched as the Whitehog unclenched his fist and added his bird bone to the tally. When the hundred lords had cast their ballots, the Speaker descended the steps and came to stand before the accused.

Maskill Boice's head was high, but there was fear in his pale blue eyes. The rubies set into his doublet glittered in time to the pumping of his heart. Fergus Hurd was old and white-haired, yet he still had power in him . . . and he would not look Maskill Boice in the eye.

As the Speaker shook the silk pouch the city stilled. The mob ceased chanting and the dogs stopped barking. Even the wind died down. Fergus Hurd spoke into the silence, his voice sharp and bitter as he repeated the old words. "The grangelords are servants of the surlord, and the surlord is servant of the city. We speak in the voice of our forebears and we mete justice on behalf of Spire-Vanis." With that he pulled the pouch open and cast its contents at the prisoner's feet. Bones rattled and jumped. The crowd pushed forward to *see*. "Look you, Maskill Boice," directed the Speaker. "Count the bones that speak your fate."

Red, all red. Iss let out a heavy sigh of relief. *Strange*, he had not realized he had been holding his breath. He had known all along the grangelords would not dare defy him before an angry and indignant mob. But still. You could not be Surlord in Spire Vanis without knowing uncertainty. It was a quicksilver city, and its loyalties ran with the wind.

Sword! Sword Sword! shrieked the crowd.

Iss shivered. The triumph had gone out of him, and all that was left was the need to see this thing through. "Examiner!" he commanded. "Bring forth the mask."

Hearing the command, Maskill Boice began to scream. Awkwardly, with movements hampered by his leg-irons, he kicked at the bones at his feet. "Cowards!" he screamed at the grangelords. "Spineless fools! You'll be next!"

Iss barely heard him. His gaze had been caught by one of the bones that Maskill had sent flying toward the surlord's platform. White, not red; it must have been buried beneath the rest. Immediately, Iss looked up—to see Garric Hews watching him. The man who had named himself the Whitehog was dark and compact, with hair cropped to a soldier's shortness, and the unjeweled fingers of a man who expected to use his sword at short notice. Almost the name did not fit him . . . until you saw the craving in his small black eyes. With an elegant gesture, he bowed low to the surlord, acknowledging the white bone to be his.

So he has declared himself against me. Iss returned the man's gaze coolly, not bothering to return the bow. Danger upon danger. First Marafice Eye, now the young princeling: both thought they could take his place. Was this how it had been for Borhis Horgo, that year before he was slain on the icy steps of the Horn? Enemies closing ranks around him. The thought chilled Iss. Fourteen years ago he had stood on those same steps, and had looked at the aging surlord with the same keen ambition. Anything was possible in this city of spires and Bastard Lords, and a surlord had to remember that and give his rivals reason to fear.

John Rullion approached the platform, bearing the hideously carved Killhound Mask beneath a sheet of plain white linen. The High Examiner retained all the instincts of a priest and he knew how to awe a crowd. He held the mask high, letting all see it, before pulling back the cloth. A collective breath was drawn as the mask's blackened metals caught the light. It was the likeness of no living bird, warped and fanged and scaled like a dragon: the Killhound of Spire Vanis.

It weighed as much as a child. Even though Iss had handled the mask many times before, he was shocked anew by its heft and coldness. The last killhound had fled Spire Vanis fifty years ago, and no one but madmen had seen one since. The great predators' likenesses were carved on gate arches and corbels around the city, and the surlord's seal was a killhound rampant. It was said the great bird of prey could kill an elk with its foot-long claws and bear it aloft to its mountain aerie. Iss thought of the creature's power as he fitted the mask over his face and felt the cold-forged iron encase his cheeks. Wearing it, Iss knew what it would be like to be sealed inside a tomb.

It filled him with the desire to live. Raising his masked face to the crowd, Iss pronounced sentence on the condemned man. "Maskill Boice, Lord of the Hunted Granges and Master of the River Crossing at Stye, you have been found guilty of high treason, and I hereby sentence you to death by the sword. May the One True God forgive you."

The crowd cheered. Priests in the viewers' gallery made the sign of redemption. A woman watching from one of the Quarter Court's many balconies fainted; by her dress and appearance, Iss guessed her to be Boice's wife. Boice himself stood silent and unmoving, finding his dignity at last. Quite unexpectedly, Iss remembered that the man had two young sons. Too bad their father had a liking for loose talk.

Boice had talked for years of assassinating the surlord, always when drunk and in his cups. It had been easy to conspire against him, to create an offense from his drunken boasting. Caydis Zerbina had seen to the details. Black Dan, the Ille Glaive crossbow, the meeting at the Dog's Head: all fiction. God only knew whose corpse swung from the gibbet. The only thing real had been the whore. And Caydis would slip poison into her milk ale tonight. A pity, really, as she had put on such an excellent show.

Iss gave the matter no more thought. The executioner—brought overland from Hanatta in the Far South at great cost—was taking his place by the block. The man's skin was dark as night and his bared arms were thicker than most men's thighs. Still, it wasn't his strength that made him famous; it was the fact that he had no eyes. Barbossa Assati needed no executioner's hood to shield him from the sight of death. The exotic gods of the Far South had done that for him, bringing him into the world with two empty sockets where most men had eyes. Watching him, Iss wondered what Marafice Eye must be thinking. The Knife had lost an eye himself, and surely, upon seeing the hollow orbits dominating Barbossa Assati's striking face, he must value his remaining one eye all the more.

Marafice Eye showed nothing but hard efficiency as he commanded his guards to take charge of the prisoner and escort him to the block. Six red cloaks flanked Maskill Boice, never once laying a hand upon him. Condemned flesh was cursed—everyone in the city knew that.

The block was hewn from a hundred-year oak, rectangular in shape and cut with a curved depression for the laying of a head. As Iss looked on, some aging grange widow brought forth a cloth-of-gold and draped it over the wood. When the prisoner drew close she held out a hand and named him: "Son."

The crowd was so quiet now, Iss could hear the breath wheeze in their throats. Barbossa Assati had drawn his sword from its felt-lined scabbard, and the sight of the heavy fern-curved blade sent a ripple of excitement through all present.

Maskill Boice would not look at it, though he did press something—a gold coin or a jewel—into the executioner's hands. "Take me in one stroke," he murmured.

Barbossa Assati spoke one word in his beautiful, strangely accented voice. Iss thought it sounded like "Always."

And then Boice knelt on the black-stained cobbles of the Quarter Square, and laid his head upon the block. As his hands reached out to steady himself against the cloth-draped wood, his throat moved in prayer. Grange ladies, viewing from the safe distance of the Quarter Court's balconies, sighed with the tragedy of it all.

Barbossa Assati found his place and settled his weight evenly between his straddled legs. One powerful black hand came down briefly to bare Maskill Boice's neck. Then the executioner raised the sword with two hands, and let it fall. Steel *chunk*ed into wood. Blood fountained. The head rolled, for no one had thought to place a basket to catch it. The crowed *Aah*ed. Maskill Boice's torso jerked once, then slumped at the executioner's feet. The great dark blindman spoke words over it before hefting his sword free of the block.

Within his mask of black iron, Iss felt curiously removed from the scene. He saw the looks of horror in the grangelords' faces, watched as the little beetle-like gallows-master retrieved Boice's head and dipped the stump into a pan of salt before impaling it upon a pole. All around, women were wailing and wringing their hands, yet the men in the crowd seemed strangely restless, exchanging glances and short comments as if they had expected more.

Very well. I shall give you one last thing.

Iss turned to face Marafice Eye and commanded, "Bring out the traitor's gravegoods and distribute them amongst the people."

A huge cheer shook the crowd. They had not expected to share in the grangelord's wealth and this was unheard-of bounty. Jostling for positions close to the front, they shouted Iss's name in praise.

At the Knife's word, four pages struggled down the steps of the Quarter Court, bearing a heavy litter suspended between two poles. Armor and jewels and fine silks were heaped upon it, glittering gold and crimson in the failing afternoon light. Cries of outrage united the grangelords: How dare Iss send a nobleman's wealth to the crowd! It was unthinkable. Yet one look at the front ranks of the mob, their faces dark with greed, hands twitching in readiness to seize bounty, was enough to know that it could not be stopped. Even before the four pages had set down the litter, the crowd surged forward.

What happened next was ugly and bloody, as grown men fought tooth and nail over scraps. People slid in Maskill Boice's blood, kicking and screaming, beating each other in their frenzy to grab gilt cups and bolts of cloth. One man seized a sword and ran into the crowd, running a small child through in his haste to get away. Iss stood above it all in the Killhound Mask, holding everyone—Marafice Eye and his red cloaks, John Rullion, the priests in the viewers' gallery, the women on the balconies, and the Whitehog on the Quarter Court's steps—in their places. None could leave until he dismissed them, and it suited him to have them watch.

He held power in this city, and as the weeks wore on and he lost influence in other spheres, it was important to demonstrate that power for all to see. Asarhia had gone, fleeing to the north and taking her Reach strength with her. The Nameless One was growing weak and had withdrawn to the dark spaces inside himself where beatings and isolation could not reach him. More and more it was growing harder to use him, and Iss knew that the day was fast approaching when he would smother the Nameless One with a soft cushion and take the life from him. A bound sorcerer was only useful as long as he had strength to steal. And this one, in his weakness and madness, was keeping every last drop for himself. It had been many weeks since Iss had visited the twilight world of the Gray Marches, and he no longer had sway over what happened there. Influence had been lost. Knowledge had been denied him. He knew the Blindwall had been breached, but after that nothing.

The future was uncertain once more, and the only advantages he had were earthly ones. Today had been a demonstration of those powers, and a warning to his enemies. Dark times were coming: land would be lost and claimed, and great lords and clan chiefs would fall and be made. Marafice Eye thought to make himself Surlord by winning success in the clanwars; Garric Hews thought to do the same by treachery. Well, let them both look upon this ravenous mob . . . and know who knew it best.

Stepping down from the platform, Iss walked into the heart of the looting. Men ceased fighting as he passed, jeweled buckles and silver boxes in hand. One old man bowed, and then another, and then the entire crowd fell to their knees. Iss moved through them, feeling no fear. He was wearing the Killhound of Spire Vanis and he was filled with the great bird's power.

The mob closed around him as he made his return to Mask Fortress, letting no one else through.

Deep down beneath a mountain, in a space carved and blasted two thousand years before, a man awakes. This far below the surface, the cold of the firmament gives way to the warmth of the earth's core. It is humid, and although the sky is sealed off five thousand feet above, the man can remember times when accumulated moisture has dropped like rain on his back. The memory brings delight and pain, as all his memories do. It is a slow, painful process, this reclaiming of his life.

Shifting in his iron pit, he seeks comfort that custom has long taught him he will never find. Not here. He smells his own shit. The chains that shackle him chafe his raw flesh, drawing lines of watery blood. He is less well tended now, and has not been fed in several days. It has been even longer since a hand tended his sores and cleaned his skin.

Sometimes he despairs, since it seems he has traded memory for life. What good is owning a name when you are slowly starved?

Baralis, he mouths, using the word as a charm to drive away the monsters in his thoughts. *Once a continent turned upon my deeds. Or did I dream it?* Uncertainty plagues him. It is difficult to tell where dreams end and truth begins. Almost he has forgotten how to think. Eighteen years bound and broken. *How can I be sure I am sane?* Surprisingly the thought makes him smile. He remembers someone once telling him that any man capable of asking himself that question is already saner than most.

The man's smile fades, and the loneliness returns with such force it is like a dagger in his heart. Hours stretch ahead in the unchanging darkness. Days pass and he does not know it. When will the Light Bearer come and bring him food and touch and light? He sleeps and wakes, then sleeps again. Sometimes caul flies eat their way through his skin, and crawl over his face in search of light. They will not fly in the dark, he has noticed, and soon tire and die. Sometimes he saves his strength by not moving, gathering power to him bit by bit, like beads upon a thread. When he has enough he looses himself, letting his mind rise to a place where his body cannot follow.

Once it had been still in those gray places, like mist hanging above a lake. But now dread creatures walk there, stirring the calm. When you are dying it is difficult to be afraid of anything except death, yet still the man feels fear. Those monstrous shadows know his name. *Baralis*, they call. *Heart of Darkness. You are ours and we want you. Wait for our touch.*

The man shivers. He had done many terrible things in his life, but cannot decide if that makes him evil. His past hardly seems to belong to him anymore; can he still be judged by it? He recalls a sprawling castle peopled by kings and queens. The touch of a child's thigh. Poison slipped into red wine. And fire, always fire, catching on the corner of his robe and igniting in front of his face.

Still shivering, the man rests his head against cold iron. How long before the creatures who own the voices come? What will he become if he allows one to touch him? Already they lure him with promises of revenge. *Your enemies are our enemies. Burn their hateful flesh.* Such words are tempting to a helpless man, and he does not know how long he can resist them. If it hadn't been for one certainty he might already have given in.

Someone, somewhere is searching for him.

How he knows this he cannot say. Where the knowledge comes from is something he will never learn. He just knows that he is loved and searched for, and it gives him the will to carry on. Slowly his eyes close and sleep takes him, and he dreams he sends a message to the one who loves him. *I am here. Come to me.* And the one who loves him hears and comes.

ELEVEN

The Forsworn

Raif looked down through the blasted remains of a dying forest, down to a lake where lines of charcoal had been laid upon the ice, and he knew that he had entered the territory of living men. He had seen lines like that before. Once, during the Long Freeze ten years back, when all running water in the clanholds had frozen, clansmen had laid lines of soot upon the ice. The darkness of the soot absorbed the heat of the sun's meager rays and the ice beneath the black lines had melted over several days, opening precious leads. Raif had not expected to see such a thing here, only five days east of the mountains, and he felt the first stirrings of fear.

No one was supposed to live in these pale twisted forests that bordered the Western Want. Clansmen called them the White Wastes, and said that only elk and caribou dared pass through on their way to the purple heather fields of Dhoone.

Raif shouldered his pack, shifting the weight so it was borne evenly on his back. It had taken him many days to cross the mountains—even with the help of Sadaluk who had directed him toward a pass. He counted himself lucky that the weather had held, and that the only storm he'd been forced to sit out was one that had hit at altitude just east of Trapper's Pass. The wind had been his greatest problem, for it blew continuously, stripping him of warmth and strength. It blew now, rolling the edges of his Orrl cloak and raising the hair from his scalp. The Listener had given him many precious gifts of dressed skins, and three layers of seal hides protected his chest from the cold, yet the biting deadness of the Want still got through.

It lay out there, to the north, stretching farther than any clansman had ever seen, stretching as far as time itself, unknowable, uncrossable: the Great Want. Raif shivered. Of all the maps Tem had ever drawn for his children, not one had contained any details about the Want. It was a place of ghosts, clan said, dead and freezing and dry as a desert, and not even the Gods knew what walked there.

From his position above the lake, Raif turned his gaze north. Since he had left the mountains he had noticed the peculiar clarity of the landscape. There was no dust or warmth to warp the air. Faraway trees and rocks looked close enough to reach in half a day. But they weren't. Distance was distorted here, and Raif was beginning to realize that landmarks on the horizon might take weeks, even months, to reach. When he'd first spotted the lake from a position high in the pass, he'd thought he'd gain the shore by sunset. It had taken nine days: six to clear the mountain's skirts and a further three to cross the tree line.

Now he was here he felt no satisfaction of a goal reached. The Great Want disturbed him. It was too close, and too vast. League upon league of nothingness, broken only by tortured rock formations, glacier tracks and calderas.

And now there was evidence of strangers, lately here, settled enough to spread charcoal on lake ice for access to fresh water. Raif studied the lake, scanning the shore and surrounding woods for further signs of life. No smoke rose from among the trees. No piers or boats were frozen into the ice. He was too far away to spot footprints. Should he descend the slope and search for them? Or should he turn south and move on?

Uncertainty made him hesitate. He was beyond his bounds now—he knew it plainly by the look of the trees. Nothing so dry and twisted could live in the clanholds. One spark and they'd go up in flames. So who *was* down there? Not Maimed Men; they lived closer to the clanholds, in the badlands northeast of Dhoone. Raif peered into the tree cover, deciding. It was growing late and he could feel the willpower draining from his limbs. He had not rested since mid-morning, and his knee joints ached with the constant strain of descent. Drey had once told him that descending hills was more tiring than climbing them, and he hadn't believed it until now. *Drey* . . .

Abruptly, Raif started down the slope.

He told himself there was a good chance that whoever was down there had already spotted him—a lone traveler on the rise above the lake—and he drew his mitted hand inside his cloak, feeling for the makeshift sealskin scabbard that held his sword. He'd scraped the rust from it as best he could, using the dull gray emery stone that could be found freely in the high mountains. Without a millstone he could do no better. And he found a grim kind of pleasure in imagining that whilst the blade might enter a man well enough, it wouldn't so easily come out.

Resting his hand upon the sword's grip, he wound his way down through the trees. Pine needles and ice crystals crackled underfoot, and somewhere to the south an owl called out at the approaching night. Darkness rose as slowly as mist, hovering close to the ground while the sky still glowed red with the fading sun. Stars winked into existence. First a few dozen, then *thousands* . . . more than Raif had ever seen in his life. The wind dropped, and then suddenly it was quiet enough to hear the lake ice groaning. Raif grew cautious, deciding against walking the open land at the lake's shore.

Silent now, he skirted the lake, keeping to the cover of the trees. Dimly he was aware of his hunger, sucking his insides tight. The air was perfectly still. No tree limb moved. When he stepped on something warm he nearly cried out. *Fox*, he told himself, rolling the carcass over with his foot. *Dead less than a day.* Wetting dry lips, he walked on. When he reached the foot of an ancient dragon pine, he spied two dead crows lying in the debris beneath its twisted lower limbs. And then he saw the footprints. Many pairs, some fresh from the look of them, stamping a trail that led to and from the lake.

Raif was not aware of drawing his sword. It was just there, in his fist, its blade running silver in the starlight. Ahead, the trail widened into a makeshift path, and there were signs of men and horses upon it: a thrown hoof-iron, a mound of frozen dung, a piece of trail meat crooked like a finger. Raif suddenly wished he wasn't so tired. Weeks of hard travel had taken their toll, and it seemed as if his thoughts and his reflexes were moving a beat too slow. He thought he smelled something, a coldness filled with potential, like air charging before a storm.

The edge of a building loomed ahead. As he drew closer, Raif made out the eerily pale form of a palisade raised from timber and then sprayed with water to form a protective wall of ice. He'd seen such winter-built strongwalls in the city holds, and admired their simplicity—the ice repelled fire and rendered the wall almost unscalable—yet he had never known clan to build one.

Abruptly, the path rose, and he saw what lay beyond the palisade. A rock-and-timber redoubt, square-shaped with a roof of hammered logs and the rough beginnings of a battlement ringing its northern wall. No light showed through the narrow, defensive windows. A lone shutter had come loose from its mooring, and it creaked back and forth on rusted hinges. Raif smelled old fires and cook oil. And then he saw the first body, lying facedown in a trench where there was a gap in the palisade to make space for a gate.

Fear dried Raif's mouth. Cautiously he approached the body. Already he could see the man was well-armored, in a backplate of painted steel. Some design had been beautifully worked in purple and gold. An eye. And then suddenly Raif realized what he was looking at: a Forsworn knight, with the Eye of God upon him.

The man had been slain in a single thrust, run through with such force and such an edge that both breastplate and backplate had cracked open. Turning the body over Raif saw where the jagged edges of the punctured breastplate had been driven deep into the meat of the knight's heart. He had never seen such an entry wound before, not even that day . . . that day in the badlands with Tem. The flesh was black and seared, as if it had been cooked, and something dark oozed from the wounds.

Raif turned away. He thought he might be sick. The purge fluid stank of the same alien odor he'd smelled earlier. The knight had been lying facedown, and yet fluid had not drained off. It hung in his mouth like smoke. Instinctively, Raif reached to touch the tine at his waist . . . and felt emptiness instead. He would give his sword to have it now, the comfort of gods and clan.

Traitors aren't allowed to bear the stone. Bitterness welled up in him, and he was glad because it shrank his fear.

Even without a measure of powdered guidestone, Raif knew he could not leave the dead man before him unblessed. The corpse belonged to a Forsworn knight, and so was an enemy to clan and clannish gods, but he had died alone and untended. Like Tem. Closing his eyes and touching both lids, Raif murmured, "May your god take your soul and keep it near him always."

It was all he could do. Bending low, he tugged at the knight's purple cloak, freeing it from beneath the man's shoulders and covering the face. The knight's eyes were open and the irises had rolled back in his head, showing nothing but white. It was a relief not to look at them any longer.

Straightening, Raif inspected the gate. Unstripped logs, tarred and bound, mounted on an X-shaped frame. The outpost had not been established long. Everything about it had the look of something hastily erected. No clansman would raise a defensive structure with raw timber. So why had these knights?

Raif considered what he knew about the Forsworn. They were wealthy, it was said, with temples known as Shrineholds scattered throughout the North. They called themselves the Eye of God and made war against heretics in his name. The Listener said they made pilgrimage to the Lake of Lost Men, but Raif did not know why. He didn't know much, he realized. Clan had few dealings with outsiders, and Blackhail had even fewer than most. Growing up clan meant learning little of other men.

Raif dropped his pack and walked through the gate into the narrow, packed-earth bailey beyond. His breath was doing strange things in his windpipe, hurting his back as he breathed. He felt like a child carrying a grown-up sword, and found he could not remember a single form Shor Gormalin had taught him. *The Listener was right; I need to learn how to use this. But not tonight. Gods, not tonight.*

He almost passed the second body, so deep were the shadows that surrounded it. The redoubt had been built on a ground-sill of rubble and timber to keep it raised above the frozen tundra and protected from sinkage during spring thaw. The first floor of the structure overhung the foundation pile, creating a trap for shadows and moss. This body lay in two pieces beneath the overhang, sheared through the gut so that only strings of sinew and intestines joined the two halves. Raif retched. *Be thankful for the shadows*, he told himself, spitting to clean his mouth. *Without them I'd see worse.*

There was nothing to do but speak the same blessing over the dead knight and cover his face.

Slowly, Raif mounted the quartered-log stairs leading to the redoubt's main door. Time and effort had been spent on the door: the timbers were dressed and sealed, the joints shod in lead. The Eye of God had been painted above the arch, and someone had even brought gold leaf to burnish the pupil so it looked as if God were gazing upon a golden field. Raif felt the Eye upon him as he put a hand to the door and pushed.

Darkness and stillness waited on the other side. The stench of accelerated rot and strangely charged air made him doubt that anyone within had been left alive. Seconds passed as he stood on the threshold, letting his eyes grow accustomed to the blackness. He appeared to be in a small defensive ward, fashioned with louvered floorwork to slow an enemy's charge. One wrong step and a man's foot would slip through the boards to the groundsill below, halting and trapping him, and possibly breaking his leg. *Who did they fear?*

The Eye was here too, painted huge upon the walls. Only now it was not something watchful and benevolent, it was an angry eye, fearsome, shot with red veins. Raif found himself discomforted beneath it, and felt a pang of guilt at being so easily awed by a foreign god.

Carefully, mindful of his steps, he crossed the ward and entered the main chamber of the fort. The inner door had been torn from its hinges and two dead knights lay to either side of it, swords drawn and visors down: they'd had more warning than those outside. But it had not saved them. Beautifully worked scale armor made one man's corpse glitter like a faceted jewel. He bore the spiked collar of a penitent, and all his metalwork had been greased with reddish-brown bone oil. The weapon that had killed him had struck so deeply that Raif could see the floorboards beneath his chest; they had been ripped up and splintered as the weapon was pulled free. Raif shuddered. What creature could break down a strongdoor and do this to a man? Bullhammer, the most powerful man Raif had ever known, had never torn the middle from an enemy in a single strike.

Raif spoke blessings to both men and moved on. The main hall of the redoubt made him sad, for he recognized the pain these knights had taken to honor their One God. The only local resources were timber and rock, and they had used both to raise a massive altar block that had been draped with cloth of purple. Here the Eye was not a crude wall-painting but a crystal set into an almond-shaped mounting of pure gold. Seeing it, Raif felt the sword move in his hand. *Of course, a knight's blade.* The rock crystal surmounted on the pommel seemed to pulse in time with the Eye.

Light poured in from a window high in the hammer-vaulted roof as the moon rose overhead. Raif saw crudely carved chairs and box pallets, prayer mats woven from coltgrass, oak coffers lining the far wall, a rope ladder leading to the external battlements, and an ancient book laid open on a dragon-pine stand. They had not been here long, these men, and he could not understand what had brought them to this place.

More knights had fallen in the farthest reach of the hall, defending, it seemed to Raif, the small Eye-carved portal beyond. Seven men dead. Seven blessings given. All of the knights' eyes were open and rolled back, and all had the same black fluids oozing from their skull cavities and wounds.

Breathing thinly, Raif made his way through the Eye portal and into the small chamber beyond. In the same way that the Hailstone was heart of clan, this chamber was the heart of the fort. Raif felt its power. The timber walls had been stained white, and in the center a font hewn from speckled granite held a pool of water in an eye-shaped bowl. Instinctively, Raif kept his gaze from alighting too long upon the water. Something told him he didn't want to see his own face reflected there.

A soft noise made him start. Spinning, he raised his sword.

"Morgo?" came a weak murmur. "Is that you?"

Raif peered into the shadows in the corner behind the portal. Someone, a knight, lay fallen in a pool of blood. He saw immediately that the man was not dressed like the other knights, in fine armor and cloth of purple, but was unarmored and mantled in a cloak of skin. Dimly, Raif remembered that as the Forsworn rose through the ranks they cast more and more of their worldly possessions aside, until they were left with nothing more than their swords and what clothes they could stitch with their own hands. That meant this man lying before him was of a high order, possibly even the commander of the fort.

Raif dropped to his knees beside the knight. The man's wounds were terrible to see. His left hand was gone and his left thigh had been laid open by a series of chopping blows. His skull had taken a slicing cut, and part of his right ear hung from a flap of skin. The same purge fluids that leaked from the other knights' wounds leaked from his, mingling darkly with his blood. On his right side lay a sword not unlike Raif's but of finer make, with a bluish crystal surmounted on the pommel. The sword's edge was warped and blackened, as if it had been held to a flame and burned.

The knight's face was gray. His lips were parched, and bits of skin flaked from them as he spoke. "Morgo?"

"Hush," Raif said, not gently, stripping off his inner coat of seal fur and bundling it to form a pillow for the knight's head. "I'll bring water."

"No," murmured the knight, suddenly agitated. "Don't leave me."

He had once been powerful, Raif saw, with the lean muscle

of one who fights rather than trains. He was not young, for there was much gray in his close-cropped hair, but his strength of will persisted. Gods alone knew how he still lived. Raif tore a strip from the soft rabbit fleece he wore next to his throat. Almost he did not know where to begin to tend this man, but he knew that he could not leave him like this.

The knight, seeing what Raif meant to do, waved him away. "No." He paused for breath. "You cannot save me, not this way."

Gray eyes dull with pain met Raif's, and Raif found he could speak no lie. Silently, he let the rabbit strip fall to the floor. "What happened here?"

"Evil walked amongst us . . . broke down our door."

"How many attacked?"

The knight's eyes clouded. His fist clenched and unclenched. After a time he repeated, "Morgo?"

Raif folded his own fist around the knight's, forcing his flesh to be still. Helplessness roughened his voice. He was clan, and every clansman knew what was owed to a fatally wounded man. "No. Not Morgo. A friend."

"Then why do you have Morgo's sword?"

Raif felt the world switch beneath him. He glanced at the sword Sadaluk had given him, resting now on the plank floor, well clear of the knight's blood.

The knight's gaze sharpened. "Tell me you did not kill him."

"I did not." Raif thought quickly. "Morgo lost his way on his journey to the Lake of Lost Men. The Ice Trappers found his body, and gave me his sword." He had no idea how long the Listener had held the sword, but he'd imagined it lying in that foreign-made chest for decades. He asked, because he could not help himself, "Who is Morgo?"

The knight's throat began working but words took long to come. ". . . took the Lost Trail. A boy . . . only fifteen. I told him to wait. *Wait.*"

Something in the knight's voice made Raif say, "He was your brother."

"Dead now, long dead."

Forty years dead, Raif guessed, feeling weary and suddenly old. "Rest now," he murmured. "I'll watch you."

Time passed as the knight slept. Raif crouched by his body, thirsty and hungry but unwilling to move away. The font in the center of the room cast a shadow that circled the chamber as the night passed. Sometimes the water rippled and *plink*ed, though Raif could detect no breeze. The knight rested fitfully, jerking and shivering, each breath gurgling wetly in his throat. He awakened before dawn, and Raif could see the livid fever lines spreading up his neck.

"Only one," the knight rasped. "A shadow that was not a shadow, bearing a sword as black as night."

Raif felt his gooseflesh rise. The knight was answering his question from earlier, and the words of Heritas Cant sounded in his head. *They ride the earth every thousand years to claim more men for their armies. When a man or woman is touched by them they become Unmade. Not dead, never dead, but something different, cold and craving. The shadows enter them, snuffing the light from their eyes and the warmth from their hearts . . . Blood and skin and bone is lost, changed into something the Sull call* maer dan: *shadowflesh.*

Slowly Raif's hand rose to his lore. When he looked up he saw the knight watching him.

"Take me," he said. "Before the shadows can."

Raif breathed and did not speak. Although he had not wanted to see it he knew that the purge fluids had collected in the knight's wounds, sending tendrils of darkness smoking across his skin. *Oh gods. The other knights are lost.*

But not this one, not yet. Raif found his strength and his voice. "Tell me one thing. Why did you build this place?"

The knight raised his clenched fist. "We search."

"For what?"

"The city of the Old Ones. The Fortress of Grey Ice."

Raif felt himself begin to shake, not strongly but intensely, as if something within him were vibrating. As he looked on a wisp of shadowy fluid rolled over the knight's eye, and he knew it was time to reach for his sword.

The knight knew it too, and drew himself up a fraction against Raif's coat. Raif hefted the sword, testing its weight. Drying blood sucked at the soles of his boots as he took his position above the knight. He was still shaking, but he didn't think it was from weakness or fright. Gravely, he raised the point of his sword to the knight's chest. The knight's eyes were open, and they were clear and shining, and Raif found a measure of understanding there.

Kill an army for me, Raif Sevrance.

Putting the weight of his body behind the blow, Raif thrust his sword through the heart.

He must have lost time after that, for he could not remember freeing the sword from the knight's flesh, or closing the man's eyes, or entering the main hall and taking the purple cloth from the altar and laying it over the knight's corpse. He remembered only a feeling of terrible weariness and, as he stumbled over a pallet in the main hall, deciding then and there he needed rest. He remembered the luxury of curling up in wool blankets, and then nothing but the deadness of sleep.

When he woke many hours later, sunlight was streaming down on his face. For a long moment he did not open his eyes, merely lay still and enjoyed the play of light and warmth on his eyelids. How had he not noticed such a beautiful thing before? Hunger and the need to relieve himself eventually roused him, and he swung his feet onto the floor and looked out across the hall.

All that remained of the bodies were skeletons and gristle. Longbones were darkly stained, and the tendons still attached at their heads curled strangely in the freezing air. Wisps of smoke rose from the ribcages like fumes. Seeing them, Raif thought he must be the greatest fool in the North. How could he have fallen asleep here? It was madness. And for some reason he found himself thinking of Angus. His uncle had once told him that the best way to stay alive in a hostile city was to walk through its busiest streets jerking your arms and muttering wildly to yourself. No one would interfere with a madman. Perhaps not even fate.

Feeling strangely light-headed, Raif skirted the knights' remains and made his way outside.

Retrieving his pack near the gate, he decided to walk the short distance to the trees. The sun was low and weak, but it felt good on his back. It felt good also to drink the meaty-tasting water from his seal bladder, and to feast on the Ice Trappers' peculiar idea of travel food. There were cakes of caribou marrow streaked red with berries, rolled strips of seal tongue, and the last of the boiled auk. Raif sat down amidst the pale gray needles of the dragon pines and ate and rested and did not think. Overhead the sky was the rich blue of twilight, though it was barely midday. An osprey was rising on thermals channeled by the lake, and the warning cries of small birds pierced the calm.

Raif packed and stowed his provisions. He was feeling the lack of his inner coat now, and the bitter cold sank against his chest. He didn't want to return to the redoubt and had no intention of retrieving his seal coat from its position beneath the dead knight's head, but he had to know if the knight had been spared the fate of his companions. And he had to bear witness for them all.

In the low light that passed for day the redoubt looked little more than a fortified cabin. Eight men had crossed hundreds of leagues to build here and now they lay dead. What had the knight said last night? *We search.* Raif felt the sadness of those words. And the hope. Grimly, he crossed the defensive ward and reentered the main hall.

The cold, otherworldly odor to which his slumbering body had grown accustomed rose to meet him anew. It was subtly changed now—staler and less concentrated, like smoke dissipating after a fire. The knights' remains had stained the timber flooring in dark, man-shaped patches. Raif thought he would like to torch this place, but the knights were not clan and he did not know if such an act would honor or further defile them. The marrow had been sucked from their bones, and their skulls were hollow except for the black liquid trickling from their teeth and eye sockets. It was hard to believe these men had been dead less than a day. Raif thought about the blessings he'd spoken over them, and then quickly turned away. *I arrived too late.*

The knights' souls were already gone. Taken.

Crossing to the stone and timber altar, he raised a hand to touch the Eye of God. Its price was unimaginable, so heavy and pure was the gold that surrounded it, yet it seemed to Raif that it would be safe here. It would cost a man much to walk through this hall and steal it in sight of the dead. The crystal in the Eye's center sparkled so brilliantly Raif wondered if it might be a diamond. But he had little knowledge of gems and doubted if something the size of a sparrow's egg could be anything other than rock crystal. Hesitating at the last instant to touch it, Raif stepped back. He already knew what it would feel like: ice.

His gaze found the carved wood of the dragon-pine stand, and the book laid open upon it. The book was very old, bound in animal hide that had been inexpertly tanned so that a nap of fine hair remained. The pages were yellow and warped, and their edges had been darkened by countless generations of fingerprints. The book was opened to a charcoal drawing of an icebound mountain and a passage of ornately rendered script. Meg Sevrance had taught both her sons to read, but Raif still had difficulty deciphering the words. They were set down in High Hand, an archaic written form of Common, and they bore little resemblance to anything he'd learned at his mother's knee. *Mountain* he thought he recognized, and the phrase *North of the Rift*, but the script was too stylized for him to be able to read much more. Frowning, he turned his attention to the drawing. It was of no peak he had ever seen, craggy and spiraling, with nothing green or living upon it.

He thought about turning the pages and seeing what else the book held, then decided against it. It seemed to him that while he stood here, first at the altar, now at the lectern, the hall was changing around him, settling into the silent deadness of a tomb. *This place should be sealed.*

Suddenly eager to be gone, he went to fulfill his final obligation.

The small chamber the head knight had fallen in was so cold Raif's breath whitened as he entered. The water in the font should have been frozen, but it wasn't. Raif worked to keep his gaze from settling upon the gently rippling liquid. He still did not want to see what it showed.

The knight lay where Raif had left him, his body wholly covered by the altar cloth. Taking the corner of the cloth in his fist, Raif began naming the Stone Gods. *Ganolith, Hammada, Ione, Loss, Uthred, Oban, Larannyde, Malweg, Behathmus. Please may this man be whole.*

A sharp tug on the cloth was all it took to reveal the knight. The livid pink flesh of a frozen corpse met his gaze. Plump flesh, whole and at rest.

Raif closed his eyes. He could find no words to give thanks, and as he let the cloth float to the ground, something wound tight inside his chest relaxed.

I have done no harm here.

It was a comfort he took with him as he passed through the redoubt and continued his journey east.

TWELVE

Fair Trade

"Y ou'd better move faster next time, you big ox, or I'll take the legs right off you."

Crope cowered by the roadside, waiting for the wagon train to pass. The head drayman had a whip, and Crope's gaze stayed upon the six-foot curl of leather until it was nothing more than a line in the distance, and the mud flung up by the wagons' wheels had settled once more upon the road. He did not like whips, or the men who wielded them, and the dread beat hard in his chest.

It was morning and it was icy cold, and he had thought to enter the next town and trade his goods for warm soup and crusty bread, but the drayman and his wagon train were headed in the same direction, and Crope feared to have that whip raised against him. *Stupid, thick-headed fool. I always said you had no guts.* The bad voice made him climb from the ditch and brush the mud and twigs from his coat. A waystone marked a fork in the road ahead and since he could think of nothing better to do he headed toward it.

His feet hurt, for although diamond-miners' boots were made sturdy and tipped with bronze to deflect glancing blows with an ax, they were not meant to be walked in. Yet he had walked in them now for many days—exactly how many he could not say, for the numbers kept getting muddled in his head. Very long, it seemed. Past frozen lakes boiling with mist and queer little villages where men armed with pitchforks and cudgels had lined up along the roadside until he'd passed. Always the mountains followed him, a world of peaks rising sharply to the south. It was cold in the shadow of their snowy slopes, and the wind blowing off them shrieked like pack wolves at night. He did not like to sleep anymore. He took shelter in ditches and abandoned farm buildings and once in the rubble-filled shaft of a dry well, but he could never get warm or feel safe. The bad voice always told him he'd picked a poor place to rest and as soon as he closed his eyes the slavers would come and chain him.

Crope shivered. He missed being in the pipe. Men knew him there, and no one looked at him with mean eyes and shouted bad things. He was giant man, and when a hard wall needed breaking everyone knew to call upon him. Now there were no walls to break, and after seventeen years of wielding an ax—first in search of tin, then diamonds—he did not know what he was good for anymore.

Arriving at the waystone, he knelt on the roadside and brushed the snow from the worn, thumb-shaped marker. He could not read the words scored into the stone's surface, but he recognized the arrows and signs. One arrow pointed due north, and there was a number with several slashes marking a great many leagues by it, and a seven-pointed star atop that. *Morning Star*, Crope thought, a small flush of satisfaction rising up his neck. Bitterbean said that Morning Star was two weeks west of the pipe. Now he was north of it . . . which meant he'd traveled quite a way. The second arrow pointed southwest, and the number alongside it was even longer than the first. A dog's head surmounted the point, and Crope tested the image against his knowledge of the land. *Dog . . . Dog Lord*

. . . *Clan Bludd.* No, all clans lived to the north, everyone knew that. *Wolf* . . . *Wolf River.* No, Bitterbean said that was north, too.

Suet for brains. Wouldn't remember your own name if it didn't rhyme with rope. Crope's shoulders sank. The bad voice always knew what he was thinking. It made him feel small, but it also made him try harder, and he frowned and concentrated as fiercely as he could. *Dog . . . pup . . . hound. Hound's Mire!* That was it. Hound's Mire.

Slapping a hand upon the waystone, Crope raised his great weight from the road. His back ached in the deep soft places where his ribs met his spine. Diamond back, Bitterbean called it. Said that once a man had dug for the white stones his bones knew it for life.

Turning slowly, he surveyed the surrounding land. Ploughed fields lay to the north, their furrows tilled for onion and turnip planting come spring. A small flock of black-face sheep was nosing through the snow close to the road. The town lay to the west, its buildings raised from timbers and undressed stone. Most of the houses had thatched roofs, but one or two were tiled with slate or costly lead. Crope had traveled enough with his lord to know that money lay beneath such roofs, money and comfort and hot food. His stomach rumbled. The last thing he had eaten had been a meal of six stolen eggs. He felt bad about that—though the farmer he had taken them from hadn't known enough about hens to cut off their wattles and combs in such a climate. Some of the hens had gotten frostbite, for they were tender in those unfeathered fleshy parts, and Crope feared the black rot might set in. He would have liked to stay and tend them, but he could not ignore the call of his lord.

Come to me, he commanded, his once beautiful voice cracked and raw. He was trapped in a dark place, broken and hurting, and he needed his sworn man to save him. How Crope knew this he could not say. He had dreamed during the night spent in the dry well, a strong and terrible dream where flies broke free from his living flesh and shackles circled his wrists. Suddenly there was iron, not stone, beneath him and the darkness was so deep and black it felt like cold water upon his skin. He woke up shivering, and as he blinked and worked to still his racing heart his lord's voice sounded along the nerve that joined his ears to his throat. *Come to me*, it said. And Crope knew he must.

Eighteen years had passed since the day in the mountains when his lord's burned body was taken from him by men wielding red blades. *Unhand him*, a cold voice had commanded. *If you fight you'll die.* Crope remembered the man's pale eyes and the hairless shine of his skin. Baralis's body was bound to the mule, his bandages wet and stinking. The fever was upon him and he had not spoken in three days. The left side of his face was burned and his hair and eyebrows were gone. Crope feared for his lord's life, and doubted his ability to save him. It was one thing to heal creatures. Another to heal a man. The rider with pale eyes commanded his red blades to circle the mule, and then spoke again to Crope. *Your lord's so close to death I can smell it. Fight and the struggle will kill him—don't make the mistake of guarding a corpse.*

But Crope had fought anyway, for he could not abandon his lord. He remembered the pain of many cuts, the laughter of the red blades, and the taste of blood in his mouth. Still he fought, and he hurt many men, dashing their bodies onto the rocks and ripping their arms from their sockets. He could see the fear grow in them. They had thought him simple, but they did not know that a simple man with one thought in his head and one loyalty in his heart could be transformed into a force of nature. Crope felt his own strength burn like a white light within him, and when a mounted red blade charged him, he stood his ground, waited until horse breath puffed against his eyes, fixed his hands upon the stallion's neck and wrestled the creature to the earth.

All fell silent after that. The red blades fell back. The man with pale eyes reined in his mount, his face thoughtful, a gloved hand stroking his chin.

Crope dropped to his knees by the downed stallion. Its rider was pinned beneath the beast, his scalp torn open and showing bone. The man was struggling for breath, and a froth of bile and blood was bubbling from his mouth. Crope only had eyes for the horse. The creature was jerking horribly, its hoofs clattering against the rocks, its eyes rolled back in its head. Crope felt shame pierce him. *Fool! Look what you have done! Told you to look, not touch.* Shoulders sinking along with his rage, Crope reached over to where the red blade's sword had fallen upon the ground. He did not like swords, and never used them, but he knew what to do to kill a horse. Gently, he comforted the creature, whispering soft words that only animals could understand. *Sorry, sorry, sorry,* he murmured as he opened the stallion's throat.

The first arrow pierced him high in the shoulder, and the pain and surprise of it winded him. He fell forward into the horse's blood. More arrows hit. One entered the meat of his upper arm, another grazed the tendons of his neck, and a third pierced the flank of muscle beneath his ribs, puncturing his kidney with its tip: All shot from behind, at the order of the pale-eyed man.

A day later when Crope awoke to find himself in a gully halfway down the mountain, the red blades long gone along with the mule bearing his lord, he realized it was the stallion's blood that had saved him. He was drenched in it from head to foot, and it did not take a clever man to see that the red blades had mistaken it for his own. They thought they had mortally wounded him, and had simply rolled his body down the mountain to be rid of it. They did not know that Crope had the ancient blood of giants in his veins, and it would take more than four arrows to kill him.

Abruptly, Crope started down the road to the town. He would not think of what came later—not here, out in the open, with the selfsame mountains so close. All that mattered for now was following those mountains west, to the slopes where his lord had been taken and the place where the red blades lived.

The road was well traveled by carts and cattle, and a season's worth of cart oil and dung had been trampled into the snow. The sheep grazing by the wayside scattered as Crope approached, and he saw that many were ready to lamb. This small sign of approaching springtime warmed him, and he picked up his pace and began to sing one of the old mining songs:

"O Digger John was a bad seed and he carried a big bad ax,
O Digger John was a bad seed and he kept all his grudge
in sacks,
One day he came upon a seam, made his eyes gleam
And he hit it with a whack. Yes, he hit it with a whack."

By the time Crope got to the third verse where he couldn't remember all the words, just the bit about Digger John's toe falling off, he'd arrived at the town's outer wall. Many of the towns and larger villages that he'd passed along the way had sections of earthwork and masonry defending them. This wall was mostly mounded dirt, with a trench behind it filled with dirty water that had hardened to brown ice. Crope was relieved to see there was no gate, for he had a fear of gatekeepers and their suspicions and clever words. As he stood inspecting the earthwork, an old man wheeling a handcart passed him by. Crope immediately looked away, for he knew how easy it was for lone men to fear him, and he had no wish to cause a stir.

The old man was dressed in the bright clothes of a tinker, with a red woolen coat held together by a great deal of showy lacing, and patched green-and-yellow hose. Crope was surprised when the man didn't alter his course as he approached. More surprised when the man addressed him.

"You. Yes, you busy pretending not to see me." The tinker waited until Crope met his gaze, and then motioned to the town with a finger gloved in sparrow skin with the feathers still attached. "I wouldn't go there if I were you. Sweet Mother, I would not! They're an ill bunch, these goatherds, and they don't take kindly to outsiders. Think they'd welcome a bit of trade, stuck out here in the hinterlands with only goats and ground-chuck for company. The women are still dressing in stiff corsets, for heaven's sake! But would they look at my nice lace collars— all the rage in the Vor? No, they would not, thank you very much. 'Fraid of looking like whores, they said. Whores, I ask you—with *this* stitching?" The old man pulled something white and frilly from beneath the tarp on his cart and thrust it toward Crope's face. "See the openwork. Finest to be had in the North."

Crope politely inspected the lace thing. It seemed a bit flimsy, but he didn't say so since he wasn't quite sure what it was for.

The old man took Crope's silence for agreement. "You're a man with an eye, I see. Wouldn't care for a pair yourself? Gift for your lady mother and your . . . er . . . lady."

Crope shook his head.

"A fellow trader, I perceive. How about the pair for the price of one?"

Feeling a little overwhelmed, Crope continued to shake his head.

"A more wily negotiator I have never met! Very well, out of respect for your obvious discernment I'll give three for the price of one. Just five silver pieces. There! The deal's done." The little man held out his open palm, twitching his fingers for payment.

Crope began to feel the first stirrings of panic. Somehow it seemed as if he'd agreed to this without speaking a word. He felt hot blood rush to his neck, and he swung his head back and forth, looking for escape.

The old man's eyes narrowed. "Don't you be looking to run out on a lawful agreement. You owe me five silver pieces, and I'll take you to a magistrate if you don't pay up this instant."

The word *magistrate* struck more fear into Crope than the sight of a dozen drawn blades. Magistrates meant jail and chains, and cells with iron doors. It meant being locked up and never let out. In full panic now, he put his hands upon the tinker's handcart and turned it over. Ribbons and lace goods and all manner of twinkly things went tumbling into the snow. The wheel axle snapped and a wheel went bouncing down the slope toward the ditch. Crope felt his chest squeeze tight. *Look what you've done! Told you not to touch.* The old man was gabbling on, pointing at the cart and hopping up and down in rage. Crope looked around wildly. He had to get away, but he didn't know what he feared more: an open road where bad men could ride him down and hurt him, or a town full of strangers who could 'prison him.

His mind was made up for him when a pig farmer and his boy appeared on the road driving six winter-thinned sows before them. The way back was blocked. The tinker would call to the pig farmer for help, and the pig farmer would be glad to, and a cry would go up and more men would come and circle him and beat him with sticks. Crope knew how these things went. Seventeen years in the mines wasn't long enough to forget.

Crushing wood beads and painted brass trinkets beneath his feet, he fled toward the town. Behind him he heard the tinker shout, "Stop! Come back here!" But Crope didn't stop—he ran with his head low and his shoulders hunched forward as if he were about to break down a door.

People stared at him as he entered the shadows of the streets. A goodwife dragged her two children into the nearest doorway to avoid his path. A handsome youth in a pointed hat shouted out to no one in particular, "I'll be damned! Is it man or bear or both?" A scrawny white dog with a black mark over his eye came racing from a dunghill, yipping and wagging its tail like a mad thing as it chased after Crope's heels. Crope felt his face redden with shame and exertion. Everyone was looking and laughing. He had to get off the main thoroughfare and find somewhere dark where he could catch his breath and think.

Turning corners at random, kicking up clods of muddy snow and skidding on patches of ice, he wove his way in toward the oldest part of town. The buildings here were low and in ill repair, their cross-timbers greasy with rot, the iron ore in their stonework bleeding rust. An old woman on a street corner was boiling horse hooves in a pot. The caustic stench brought tears to Crope's eyes, and its after-whiff of meatiness made him feel both hungry and queasy at once.

Panting, he slowed his pace to a walk and spat out a wad of streaky black phlegm. Digger juice. Bitterbean said it was the mine's way of striking back: you entered the mine, the mine entered you. Realizing that the scrawny dog was still following him, Crope turned and told it to shoo. The dog sat expectantly, thumping its tail against the cobbles and cocking its pointy ears.

"I said *go*." Crope raced at the dog, raising his hands and stamping his feet.

The dog skipped back, yipped in excitement, then launched an attack on Crope's diamond boots. Crope pushed the creature away, but just as quickly it came back, dancing and pouncing, delighted with this new game. Crope frowned. His back and neck were sticky with sweat, and he suddenly wished for the comfort of a closed room and a hot bath. Deep down in the underlevel of the tin mines, below the shaft the tin men called Devil's Throat, there were caverns filled with steaming hot water. Once you got used to the bad-egg smell, you could soak in the pools until your fingertips wrinkled and your back muscles relaxed like jelly. Crope knew better than to wish himself there—life in the tin mines was dark and crippling and the life of a digger was worth less than an ax—but there had been good things along with the bad. Food. Songs. Fellowship. Now there was nothing—just running and hiding and fear.

Spying a tar-stained door with the sign of the rooster hung above it, Crope turned his back on the dog and made his way across the road. The rooster door was set in a squat structure that bore the marks of recent fire upon it. The stonework was blistered with soot, and great cracks in its mortar had opened up where the heat of flames had touched upon it. Timbers framing the door were charred and crumbling, and a stang of green wood had been hammered into place to prevent collapse. As he approached, Crope felt the old wariness grow within him. The sign of the rooster marked an alehouse where men came to trade. He needed to trade. Badly. He had no food or coinage, and a chicken tarp instead of a cloak. Yet trading meant dealing with men, and Crope could recall few times in his life when men had treated him kindly. They either feared or despised him. Often both.

Letting out a slow breath, he shrank himself, curving his back and slumping his shoulders and bending his legs at the knee. He lost perhaps half a foot that way, but it was enough to give him courage to push open the door.

The alehouse was a one-room tavern reeking of goat tallow. Gobs of fat in the lanterns hissed and sputtered, giving off musty green smoke. Tables and stools hewn from unmilled timber were crowded around a copper cook stove. Old men in goat fleeces and pieced skins turned to look at Crope as he made his way toward the front. A big man in a leather apron shouted, "No dogs!" and it took Crope a moment to realize that the white dog had followed him indoors. Crope didn't have the courage to explain that the dog wasn't his, so he simply turned around, picked up the dog and deposited the creature outside. By the time he shut the door everyone's attention was upon him, and it took all his willpower not to turn and run. One of the old goatmen made a warding sign as he passed, and the man with the leather apron folded his great meaty arms and spread his weight evenly between his legs as if bracing himself for a fight. Eye signals passed between him and a young bravo standing at the ale counter.

"What's your business, stranger?" The man in the leather apron, the tavern-keep, looked Crope up and down, his gaze lingering on the bird lime that spotted Crope's cloak, and the raised white scars on his neck. "If it's trouble you're after I'll see you get it, and if it's ale and warmth I'll weigh your money first."

Crope felt the blood rise in his face. He didn't like being the object of so much attention, and he had a fear of speaking in case he tied himself up in knots. As he thought what to do, he noticed the bravo at the counter casually reaching for his knife.

"Trade," Crope said softly. "Come to trade."

Again, glances passed between the tavern-keep and the bravo. "Come back here, then," said the older man. "Let's see what you've got."

Crope was glad to get away from the goatmen and the heat of the stove. He was sweating and the ceiling was so low he had to bend his knees further to pass under it. The young bravo moved alongside him as he approached the counter, pulling too close for comfort. Crope edged away, only to find the man with the leather apron on the other side of him.

"Right," said the tavern-keep. "Show us your goods."

Crope touched the hem of his tunic, checking for the one thing he had to trade. The smell of meat and gravy simmering on the stove filled his mouth with saliva, and he swallowed several times. The bravo saw this and followed Crope's gaze to the black pot on the stove.

"Reckon he's hungry, Sham. Reckon he's willing to trade for a bowl of meat and a hunk of bread."

The one named Sham refolded his arms with vigor. "He's getting nothing from my stove until I see the measure of his goods."

The bravo began picking dirt from his nails with the tip of his fancy quillioned knife. Dressed in felted wool and finely napped suede, he shrugged without making a sound. "I don't know about that, Sham. I'd bring him a bowl. A man's better able to bargain on a full stomach."

The two men stared at each other for a moment, and then Sham gave way and went to fill a bowl with stew. The bravo watched Crope watching the food. "Come a long way, have you?"

Crope shook his head. He knew enough not to give this man any information about himself.

"Seems you've taken a good few whippings in your time." The bravo's eyes were knowing. Abruptly, he sheathed the knife. "I don't think this would be much use against a fellow like you. Reckon you can take care of yourself."

Crope was relieved of the need to reply by the tavern-keep returning with the stew. It was rich with blood and fat, and smelled strongly of goat. He felt the eyes of both men upon him as he drank from the bowl. The stew was finished too soon, and seemed to leave him more hungry than before. His eyes strayed back to the pot, and the bravo, seeing this, smiled knowingly at the tavern-keep.

"So," said the bravo, leaning forward. "I'm sure you'll agree we've shown goodwill by feeding you. And I daresay Sham would be happy to fetch you a second bowl when our business is done. What say you, Sham?"

Sham eyed Crope with displeasure. "If the trade warrants it."

Crope's stomach rumbled. He was trapped between hunger and obligation, and he couldn't think what else to do other than show the men his trade. With a slow and ponderous movement he plucked the item from his coat hem, tearing half a seam away in the process. Raising his closed fist to the counter, he was aware of both Sham and the bravo leaning forward in expectation. Crope thought his fist looked huge, big as an aurochs's skull, and he was anxious to remove it from sight. Quickly, he opened his hand.

The diamond seemed to capture every beam of light in the alehouse, sucking it in like a pump and using it to burn as cold and blue as the stars. Sham's leather apron creaked as his chest expanded to draw breath. The bravo was silent and unmoving, yet his eyes glittered with the reflected brilliance of the stone.

Hadda's diamond. The Crone Stone, Bitterbean called it, chipped from Hadda's front tooth as the life and warmth drained from her body where it lay at the top of the pipe. The gem was the size of a baby's fingernail, table-cut and clear as water; a fitting reward for the woman who had found the biggest diamond ever to be mined west of Drowned Lake. Crope had not wanted to take it, yet Hadda had grasped his buckskin pants as he set her down on the wet, muddy ground above the pipe. "Take the stone from me, giant man," she murmured, gasping for breath. "If you don't *they* will. And I won't have the first Bull Hand who finds me break my face in his haste to get it."

Crope had shook his head. He didn't want a dying gift from Hadda the Crone. Hadda sang strange songs . . . and had summoned the darkness into the pipe. Any gift she gave would be cursed.

The crone had become agitated then, her hands clenching and unclenching as she fought the death closing upon her. "Take it. You earned it . . . you bore me from the pipe."

So Crope had taken it, using the blunt edge of his ax to knock out the tooth and winkling the stone free from its enamel mounting. The Bull Hands had loosed the hounds by then, and Crope could hear the fearful sound of their howling. Pushing the diamond into his mouth for safekeeping, he ran for the refuge of the trees. The last sound he heard before entering the dark and tangled silence of Minewood was the ripping and sucking of hounds upon prey.

Now the stone lay twinkling in the palm of his hand, and two men stood over it, silent and unmoving as if the diamond had cast a spell upon them. Crope had a sudden wish to close his hand and flee, but Sham reached out and plucked the stone from his grasp.

"How do we know it's real?" said the tavern-keep, squeezing the diamond between finger and thumb as if he meant to crush it. "Could be rock crystal or glass."

Crope shook his head vigorously. No one was going to tell him the stone wasn't real. He'd mined diamonds for eight years; he knew gems from glass. As he gathered breath for a heated denial, the bravo put a hand on his arm.

"Why don't you bite it, Sham?" he urged. "If it breaks a tooth it's real."

The tavern-keep looked suspiciously from the bravo to Crope. After a moment, he raised the diamond to his lips, opened his jaw to bite down, and then thought better of it. Offering the stone to the bravo, he said, "Seems you're so knowledgeable, Kenner, why don't *you* test it?"

The bravo nudged the older man's hand away. "Because I'm

not a damn fool, and know genuine goods when I see them. Why don't you set that stone down, and fetch me and my friend here a drink."

Sham's cheeks reddened in indignation, but Kenner ignored him and began speaking to Crope, leaving the tavern-keep little choice but to do as the bravo said. Sham did not go quietly, slamming the flat of his hand on the counter as he deposited the stone and muttering peeved curses. Minutes later a tired-looking alewife dressed in a man's tunic belted with a length of rope brought a jug of ale and two wood cups. She would not look at Crope, and addressed her words to Kenner. "Sham says the ale's to come out o' your share."

Kenner nodded, dismissing her. Pouring two cups of ale, he continued speaking to Crope. "I hear the snow at Drowned Lake's been passing light this year. Too cold for it, they say. Have to keep setting fires on the ice to keep the lake from freezing solid."

Crope nodded. He was beginning to relax now that he was alone with Kenner, and it didn't occur to him to wonder how the bravo had managed to pinpoint his place of origin. The ale was delicious, warm and nutty, with swirly bits of egg yolk, and he could feel it loosening his tongue. "We had bother drawing the water 'cos of the frost. Had to bring me up to man the pumps." Pride made his ears glow pink. "Said no one could get them moving, only me."

Kenner poured Crope a second cup of ale. "I can see that, big strong man like you. Free miner, are you?"

Crope shook his head without thinking. "Miners don't pump water. That's diggers' work." As soon as he spoke, he knew he had said too much. Bitterbean had warned him to tell no one who he was and what he did. *Slave hunters will come and get you, giant man. Chain you, and haul you back for the bounty. And the Pipe Lord'll be so pleased to see you he'll give you an iron kiss that rips out your tongue, and caress you real nice with his branding* iron. *Oh, make no mistake you'll still be able to dig when he's done, but you'll never break rock without pain again. And the terrors'll wake you every night.*

Quickly, Crope glanced at Kenner. The bravo was skimming froth from his ale, and his expression was relaxed and pleasant. Not the face of a man who would deal with slavers. Even so, Crope couldn't quite stop the fear from rising. *Fool,* chided the bad voice. *Told you to keep your great mouth shut* Nervously, he glanced at the door, checking to see that no one had moved to block his escape. Slavers and slave hunters were everywhere, with their whips and chains and purses full of coin. They could hunt you down in a town full of taverns, circle and whip you, and then chain you to the axles of their wagons . . . and drag you along behind them if you didn't keep up.

"Whoa, big man. Settle down." The bravo's voice seemed to come from a very great distance. Only when his hand touched Crope's arm, gently restraining him, did Crope realize he had stepped toward the door. "What's your hurry, big man? We haven't finished our business here yet." The bravo's voice sharpened. "And lest you forget, you owe a debt of ale and vittles to this tavern."

Crope let himself be drawn back to the counter. His heart was pumping wildly, and it was suddenly hard to think. Kenner said he was in debt. *Debt.* Debt meant magistrates and jail. Locked up and never let out. The overwhelming urge to flee came upon him. But everyone was looking at him, and all the goatmen had mean eyes and leather stock-whips. *Great stupid chicken-head, gone and got yourself trapped.* He was gulping so much air, he could barely make sense of what the bravo was saying.

"Now I see the problem, big man. What you've got there is contraband. Mighty troublesome stuff is contraband. Sooner gotten rid of the better."

Crope didn't know what contraband was, but he seized upon the last thing the bravo had said—*Sooner gotten rid of the better*—and nodded fiercely in agreement.

Kenner's gray eyes gleamed with satisfaction for an instant, but just as quickly his expression changed to one of serious thought. Leaning forward, he lowered his voice to a whisper. "This stone is trouble. Trouble for you. Trouble for me. I take it off your hands and suddenly the very same people who are looking for you start looking for me. I know, I know, we won't name them here and now. Best thing we can do is get this trade over and done with quickly, and go our separate ways. Now, I'm willing to keep quiet about where you've been and what you've done, but that silence is a risk. It'll cost me dear, and that cost must be factored into the trade."

Crope was trying hard to understand what Kenner said, but there were big words here, and it was easier to focus upon the smaller ones he knew. *Risk. Silence. Trouble.* Hadda's diamond twinkled on the counter, attracting a lone moth who mistook it for a light. Looking at it, Crope was overcome with a powerful urge to be free of the thing, and he put his thumb upon the stone and pushed it toward the bravo. Kenner became very still. His gaze met Crope's and his eyebrows lifted in question. *Are you sure?* Even before Crope finished nodding the diamond was gone, pocketed away in a compartment concealed beneath the bravo's gear belt. Crope felt as if a great weight had been lifted from his shoulders. For a moment he forgot to stoop, and his head bumped against the rafters. He grinned at his own foolishness, and Kenner grinned too, and suddenly it was easy to speak.

"Trade?" Crope prompted, nodding toward the bravo's gear belt. Seeing the blank look on Kenner's face, he elaborated, "Trade, like you said . . . for the stone."

Kenner made a minute gesture to the tavern-keep who stood

watching by the stove. A rustle of movement disturbed the room. Goatmen shifted forward in their seats. Someone let the tail of a whip drop against the floor. The bravo pushed himself away from the counter. "Look, stranger. We don't want no trouble here. The door's there. Use it."

Crope was confused. Kenner's voice had changed, and he was acting as if they weren't friends. "Trade," he repeated uncertainly. "For the stone."

"Get out!" shouted the tavern-keep, sliding an iron poker from the stove. "Won't have no dirty freaks in my alehouse."

Crope looked to Kenner, but the bravo had already moved away. The tavern-keep took advantage of his momentary distraction and lunged forward with the poker, stabbing Crope's shoulder with the smoldering point. Crope yelped in pain. Wheeling around, he lashed out at the thing that had hurt him. He caught only the tip of the poker, but his weight and momentum were enough to send it flying from the tavern-keep's hand and clattering into the huddle of goatmen sitting about the stove. The tavern-keep cried out in fury, nursing his twisted wrist. One of the goatmen, a scrawny herder in a fleece hat, rose from his seat, the tail of his stock-whip bunched in his fist. Others followed his lead, edging forward, careful not to step within the turning circle of Crope's massive seven-foot arm-span. The bravo watched from a safe position behind the counter, his fancy quillioned knife nowhere to be seen. Crope stared and stared, but Kenner wouldn't meet his eye.

Crack. A whip struck down at Crope's feet, its leather tail slithering on the floorboards before its handler snapped it back. Suddenly Crope was back at the pipe, and the Bull Hands were closing in around him. Fear came so quickly he could taste it. It tasted of leather and salt. Through a haze of rising panic he spied the tavern door. The oblong of light seeping in around its frame looked like the sky overhead in the pipe. It meant escape. A second whip lashed his foot, and another licked the hamstring at the back of his calf. Raising his hands to protect his face, Crope barreled toward the door. If the goatmen had been carrying man-whips instead of the shorter, finer stock-whips they could have stopped him. For the man-whips were twelve-footers, their leather cured to the hardness of steel ribbons, and when they curled twice around a man's leg their handlers could bring that man to the ground. But the stock-whips didn't have the length for it, and they snaked Crope's ankles but didn't catch.

Crope fixed his sights on the door. When a goatman failed to move out of his way quickly enough, Crope blasted into him, flooring the man instantly. Ribs in the goatman's chest snapped with wet, explosive cracks as Crope tramped over his torso to reach the light. The delicate slot-and-groove mechanism of the doorlatch proved too much for Crope's big, shaking hands and he smashed that too in his haste to be gone.

Finally the door swung open. Cool mountain air touched Crope's cheeks. Sunlight dazzled him and he blinked many times, his miner's eyes weak when struck by the sudden light. It seemed impossible that it should only be midday after so much had happened in the tavern. A pain in his chest in the place where his breaths came from made him press a hand against his ribcage. He would have liked to sit down right there, upon the tavern's stoop, and rest until he caught his breath and all the trouble had passed. But the goatmen in their greasy skins and fleeces were driving him on with the crack of their whips.

"Get off with you, you filthy monster."

"Go back to your hell-cave where you belong."

Crope put his hands over his ears to shut out the noise. Hadda's diamond gone. *Fool*, taunted the bad voice. *Suet for brains. One day someone will talk you into walking off a cliff.* Angry at himself, he lashed out at the air. *Stupid, stupid, stupid.*

As he wheeled around he saw the goatmen watching him from inside the tavern. Something about the way they had gathered in a half-circle to watch him, their lips splitting in ugly leers, their fingers stroking the tails of their whips, shifted the anger in him. They weren't slavers or Bull Hands. They were men who herded goats.

The first stirrings of white rage moved within him, and he felt the skin across his back tighten and the blood pump into his eyes. The white rage was bad, he knew that, but it was hard to remember why when the pressure pushed all thoughts from your head. He had to act. Nasty men had stolen Hadda's diamond. Nasty, laughing men.

As he sprang toward the tavern door, the leers on the goat-men's faces faltered. The herder in the fleece hat stepped back. Crope recognized the man's fear, but took no satisfaction from it. People had been afraid of him all his life.

The desire was in him to run the goatmen back into the tavern and rip the whip-arms from them, but an old warning pierced the haze of his rage. *Use it. Don't let it use you.* It was his lord's voice, rich and beautiful, as calming as water dripping into a deep pool. His lord was the wisest of men. He got angry too, but he rarely let that anger rule him. He would never storm a tavern when outnumbered many to one. No. His lord would bide his time, watching and waiting, only striking out when his enemies least expected it and could be taken unawares.

Thinking of his lord cleared a space in Crope's mind. The white rage still burned, contracting his muscles and making him fever-hot, but now there was a pocket of air. Abruptly, his gaze alighted on the stang of green wood that was bracing the charred and rotten timbers above the door. The stang was taller than he, a fifteen-year growth of black spruce, three feet round and oozing pitch, and looking at it Crope knew what he must do. Wrapping his arms around the gray and papery bark, he hugged the stang fast against his chest. The men inside the tavern, realizing what he meant to do, began shouting and cracking their whips. Crope barely felt the leather lick his skin. It was like the day when he'd brought down the horse: once the white rage was upon him he could not be stopped.

Deep down he reached, beyond the caverns of his five-chambered heart, deep into the blood that looked as red as any man's but would burn like fuel when set alight, down into the muscle-meat where the memories of his giant ancestors waited to be sparked. A tremor of power charged the great saddles of muscle in his shoulder and lower back. His lungs pulled in enough air for six men. Tendons whitened. A dozen tiny capillaries forked like lightning in his eyes. He heaved the stang to him, hearing the creak of unstable timber as half a ton of wood moved like an oiled crankshaft in his hands. Men were quiet now, backing off into the dim smoky recesses of the tavern, their whips flaccid by their sides. Flakes of charred matter fell on Crope's head as he yanked the stang free of the doorframe.

The stang dropped to the ground with a mighty *crack*. The entire building shivered. Timbers framing the door, badly weakened by fire and then rotted by water, groaned under the strain of masonry above. A strange *whirr*ing noise, like the sound of an arrow in flight, rose higher and higher, until something deep within the masonry snapped. And then the entire front wall of the tavern began to collapse.

Crope did not stay to watch the destruction. Turning on his heels, he retraced his steps out of town. The scrawny dog with the black eye caught up with him along the way, and after Crope tried many times to shoo it away, he gave up and named it Town Dog, and together they made their way east toward the shelter of the mountains and the trees.

THIRTEEN

Blue Dhoone Lake

Blue Dhoone Lake lay a quarter-league due south of the Dhoonehold, within sight of the chief's chamber and the two gate towers known as the Horns. It was a large and glassy body of water; some said it had been artificially dug and filled by order of the first Dhoone King. Others said huge chunks of lodestone, rich with copper ore, had been dragged south from the Copper Hills and sunk into the lake's depths so that the minerals bleeding from them would turn the lake water a vivid, unearthly blue. The Dog Lord didn't know about that, though he had to admit the waters of Blue Dhoone Lake were passing queer. They never froze, glowed a strange and milky hue when the moonlight caught them just right, and nothing but albino eels and the prey they hunted swam there.

Disgusting things, those eels. Scunner Bone had netted one last month, before the deep frost. Pale as wax it was, and a full five foot in length. Old Scunner had thought to honor his chief by offering him the head. Vaylo could still see the monstrosity now; the pink eye, the half-circle of teeth, the wolfish band of muscle around the throat. Vaylo chuckled, remembering the look on his grandchildren's faces as they inspected this oddity. "You're not going to *eat* that, are you, granda?" his grandson had exclaimed. "Of course he is, stupid," his granddaughter had contradicted with all the authority of someone eight years old speaking to someone just four. "It's the food of the Dhoone Kings. And if it's good enough for them it's good enough for our granda."

Vaylo found he could not shrink in the face of such fierce pride, and he had eaten the eel, teeth and all.

He was sure it was still inside him, thirty days later, its teeth fastened to his gut wall like a leech on skin, as he rode a circuit of Blue Dhoone Lake at sunset with the wolf dog trotting at his heels.

The sun was red and engorged, its edges wavering in response to some faraway dust; a Blood Sun, Ockish Bull used to call it. Said it meant that change was coming, and swiftly at that. Watching it sink below the heathered slopes and thistle fields of eastern Dhoone, firing the lake surface in its descent, Vaylo reined in his mount. Would this land ever be home to him? Would the brittle satisfaction of acquisition ever give way to something deeper?

The Dog Lord sighed deeply, his breath whitening in the cracking air. He did not love this land, with its neatly tilled oatfields and walled-in grazes and tracts of cleared brush. Just yesterday he'd ridden out to the sloping plains north of the Flow. What had once been an old-growth forest, with ancient oaks, horse chestnuts and elms, was now a field of stumps, the timber felled for either fuel or defense. It looked like a grave-yard, and it made Vaylo hunger for Bludd. No forests in the clanholds could match Bludd's. A man could ride north or south for a week and still find no end of them. And there was no telling what he might glimpse in the quiet glades: lynxes, ice wolves, ancient woodsmen long forsaken by their clans, deep fishing holes, Sull arrows still vibrating in tree trunks, spotted mushrooms as big as hammerheads and just as deadly, ancient ruins smothered by vines, and dim caves alive with bats, eyeless crickets, and ghosts. Bludd was a border clan. It shared edges with the Sull. Fear came with that, Vaylo could not deny it, but alongside fear lay wonder and excitement. No man could ride in the forests east of Bludd and not feel the thrill of being alive in such a place. Looking out across the vast expanse of the Dhoonehold, with its man-planted thorn beds and ploughed fields, Vaylo doubted he would ever feel such a thrill riding here.

Suddenly impatient with himself, he tossed his steel-gray braids behind him and dug his heels into horsemeat. Too much thinking would turn him soft. He had possession of Dhoone, that was enough. Childhood fantasies about ancient forests and mysterious glades had no business in the mind of a man who had lived out five decades and more.

As he turned the dog horse for home, he spied Cluff Drybannock on his big charcoal stallion, riding out from the Dhoonehouse to meet him. From this distance it was impossible to make out the expression on Drybone's face, but Vaylo felt a stab of misgiving all the same. Unlike the seven sons of Vaylo's blood, Cluff Drybannock was not a man to seek out his chief for idle gossip or self-advancement.

Speaking a word of command, Vaylo brought the wolf dog to heel and rode clear from the slushy banks of the lake. "Dry," he called, his voice hoarse from the cold and lack of use. "What brings you?"

Ever since he had taken the Ganmiddich roundhouse with a troop of only two hundred swordsmen, Cluff Drybannock had taken to braiding his waist-length hair with rings of opal. It was a small thing, one of those countless little rituals that warriors used to mark their progress, yet it had not gone unnoticed. Some in the roundhouse whispered that he was showing his true nature at last, and that pride and ambition could be read in the hollow, pearly rings. Vaylo didn't believe it for an instant. Yet seeing Dry now, watching as his blue-black braids lifted in the rising wind and the pieces of opal woven amongst them glimmered like slices of moon, he wondered if there wasn't some truth to the whispers after all. Not the part about pride and ambition—Vaylo knew he had Dry's loyalty for life—but rather the part about his true nature. *Moon and night sky.* Discreetly, perhaps unconsciously, Cluff Drybannock was taking on the colors of the Sull.

"Word's arrived from the Bluddhouse." Drybone reined his mount, and the two horses halted head-to-head, nostrils steaming. "Quarro sent Cuss Maddan. Dhoone raiders attacked the Bluddhouse fourteen days back. Torched the Chief's Grove, and slew twenty men. They struck at night with no warning, and retreated as quickly as they came. Quarro mounted a pursuit, but the mist rose and they slipped away."

"Stone Gods." Vaylo touched the oxblood leather pouch containing his measure of powdered guidestone. His father's bones lay in that grove, sealed in a skin of lead that had been poured like molten wax onto his still-warm corpse. It was the way all Bludd chiefs met their gods. One day Vaylo knew his own flesh would be cremated by the searing metal and then set to cool beneath the black and loamy earth. He shivered. "Who took loss?"

Drybone named the men. Some were old retainers, well past the age of bearing arms. One was a boy of eleven.

The Dog Lord dismounted. He could not hear such news and remain seated. "Did we take any of their number?"

Drybone swung down from his own mount. "Two men were unhorsed in the Chief's Grove. Quarro spiked them both."

It sounded right. Quarro was his eldest son, the fiercest swordsman of the seven, and the one Vaylo judged most likely to claim the chiefship when he was gone. Vaylo had ceded him command of the Bluddhold in his absence, and Quarro had doubtless acquired a liking for playing chief during the seven months his father had been at Dhoone. He'd had it easy until now. Vaylo reached for the cloth bag that held his chewing curd as he looked out upon the darkening glass of the lake. Behind him, he heard Dry squat to rub the wolf dog's neck.

"Your sons ride forth to meet you," Dry said, and Vaylo looked up to see three horsemen closing distance from the Horns.

Pengo Bludd, hammerman, bearer of the shrike lore, and second amongst Vaylo's sons, was the first to reach his father. Unlike Drybone, he did not dismount when faced with his standing chief. Instead he pulled the bit deep into his stallion's mouth and forced the great warhorse to stillness. The dog horse, who had been quietly nosing through thistle grass at the end of its tether, took offense at the stallion's closeness, and spun to bite the creature's neck. Pengo was flung back in his saddle as he battled his rearing mount.

"For gods' sakes," he cried to Vaylo. "Can't you control that beast?"

Vaylo looked coolly at his son. Pengo was past thirty years of age, big and powerful, with the flushed skin of an ale drinker and his mother's striking eyes. As usual he had taken little care with his appearance, and his braids were plastered with horse-hair and congealed grease. He was not dressed for war, though his spiked and lead-weighted hammer was cradled and chained at his back. Forced to retreat to a safe distance from Vaylo's horse, he scowled at his father. "I suppose *he*—" a dismissive snap of his head indicated Cluff Drybannock "—has told you the news from Bludd."

"Some of it." Vaylo pushed a cube of black curd between his lips. He did not love his sons, and wondered what kind of father that made him. Other men, he knew, looked at their sons with pride and affection. Vaylo looked, but saw nothing other than seven men who had taken from him all his life. And still wanted more. He waited until Gangaric and Thrago rode abreast of their elder brother before adding, "Dry has told me enough to ice my blood. Is Cuss sure the raiders were Dhoone?"

Gangaric, Vaylo's third son and the sole axman of the seven, brought his gelding to a banking halt, sending clumps of soft mud flying through the air. "They were Dhoone for a certainty. Faces inked like savages and the blue steel upon them."

Pengo, already growing restless, waved a gloved fist toward the Dhoonehouse. "It's retaliation for this. If Skinner Dhoone thinks—"

"It wasn't Skinner," Drybone said quietly. "It was his nephew Robbie Dhoone."

Pengo glared at Drybone, furious at being contradicted. He looked to his two brothers to gainsay Cluff Drybannock, but both men held their tongues. Drybone watched Pengo dispassionately, infuriating him more. Finally, Pengo exploded, "Go back to the roundhouse, bastard. This is Bludd business, not yours."

"Son," Vaylo said, deceptively calm. "If it's bastards we're sending back to the roundhouse then mayhap I should ride right along with Dry and leave you and your brothers to fight amongst yourselves."

Pengo's face reddened. Not with shame, Vaylo knew, but with anger he didn't dare let out. Gangaric, who had styled himself a HalfBludd in memory of his great-grandfather and had taken to wearing a collar of woodrat skins in the manner of HalfBludd axmen, regarded his father with open dislike. Only Thrago, Vaylo's fifth son, the one who was the mirror image of Gullit Bludd, had the decency to look ashamed. *Yes, Thrago. Your father is a bastard. So what does that make you?*

Vaylo spat out the wad of chewing curd, its bitter burned-cheese taste suddenly sickening in his mouth. Usually he knew better than to dwell upon the failings of his sons—it gained him nothing but a stabbing tightness in his chest—but tonight his feelings were harder to set aside. He turned his back on the company while he mastered his thoughts. Someone was lighting torches inside the Dhoonehouse, and windows set deep into the sandstone began to glow with orange light. The sun had gone, and a full moon was pulling at the waters of the lake, raising ripples that traveled west. Vaylo let the moon breeze cool his skin, and after a time he said, "Is there anything else I need to know about this raid?"

Leather creaked behind his back as his sons shifted in their saddles. Cluff Drybannock moved alongside him and murmured, "They brought draft horses to tear down the blue shanty."

Vaylo closed his eyes. So this was it. This raid hadn't been some daring spur-of-the-moment strike. Robbie Dhoone had ridden to Bludd with one purpose: to destroy the building erected from the remains of the stolen Dhoonestone. No matter that what he pulled down was nothing more than quarry-bought rubble, and that the real Dhoonestone lay at the bottom of this very lake. No one knew that except the fifty Bludd warriors who had stolen it—and half of them were dead. No. Robbie Dun Dhoone had struck a blow for Dhoonish pride. He didn't have the manpower yet for all-out battle, but that would change soon enough. Skinner would lose ground when word of Robbie's feat got out. Few clansmen could resist the lure of such reckless and prideful bravado. Vaylo knew that. It was the reason he'd stolen the cursed Dhoonestone in the first place. Clansmen loved jaw. Robbie Dhoone had it, and Skinner Dhoone did not.

It was just as Angus Lok had said. The golden boy was puffing himself up to be a king. *He warned me about Robbie Dhoone, and I did not heed him.* Vaylo was suddenly overcome with a deep possessiveness for the very land he had earlier dismissed. He might not love Dhoone, but he would not relinquish it. He was the Dog Lord, and once he had fastened his jaws upon an object he'd never let it go. They'd have to kill him first.

Turning to face his sons, he said, "We must not be caught unawares again."

Gangaric nodded his large and part-shaved head. He was all axman now, sure and powerful in his heavy crimson cloak, the weight of his broadax straining the leather harness at his breast. Thrago, named for his great-grandfather yet the least self-willed of the three, followed Gangaric's lead and sat ready on his mount. Pengo met Vaylo's gaze, his ungloved hand smoothing his horse's mane. "So, Father. What would you have us do?"

Vaylo chose to ignore the arrogance in his second son's voice. He shifted his position slightly to include Cluff Drybannock in the circle. "We must increase our watch. Success at the Bluddhouse will leave Dhoone thirsting for more. They'll strike again. And soon. Robbie Dhoone's eager to make a name for himself. He's after his uncle's sworn men."

"The Bluddhouse, more like," contested Pengo. "We've claimed his clanhold, now he's after claiming ours."

Vaylo shook his head, growing impatient. "Robbie Dhoone had no intention of taking the Bluddhouse. He didn't have the men for it. Aye, it was doubtless pleasing to see the Sacred Grove go up in flames, but this raid was more about Dhoone than Bludd. The young pretender's sending a message to the Dhoone warriors at Gnash. *Come, join me. Leave Skinner. He's an old man with an old man's ways, and he doesn't have the jaw to retake Dhoone.*"

Pengo's face twisted. The scar on his cheek, caused when he'd fallen through a trapdoor at Withy, stretched to an ugly white line. "If you're such an expert on what the Dhoonesman thinks, how come you didn't think to guard our roundhouse against him?"

The wolf dog, perceiving an insult to his master, began to growl very softly from behind a screen of withered bulrushes. Vaylo, seeing something familiar and disturbing in the hard lines of his son's face, lashed out. "Get off your horse. I am your chief. Don't you dare speak down to me from the high comfort of your saddle like some grand city lord. I've led this clan for thirty-five years—and I can't remember one of them when you've performed any service to earn your keep."

Pengo's nostrils flared. His eyes burned with a force that made him shake. Vaylo saw him look to his brothers for support, but both Thrago and Gangaric managed to stay occupied with stilling their jittery mounts. Pengo snatched up his reins and pulled back his horse's head.

"Ride away now," Vaylo warned, "and you forfeit your say in this clan." As he spoke he knew it was a mistake—give a man no way to back down and you either lose or humiliate him— but the unsettling vision of seeing his dead wife's features living beneath Pengo's own made him angry, not wise.

Pengo turned the great gray warhorse, forcing a path between his brothers. As he put spurs to his mount, his gaze alighted on Cluff Drybannock, who stood tall and unmoving by the water's edge. With a sudden heft of his weight, Pengo swung his horse to charge him. The two men, one mounted and one afoot, stared at each other for the scant seconds it took the horse to cross the distance between them. The Dog Lord held his breath. There was a moment, when something ancient and fearless sparked in Drybone's eyes, when Vaylo realized how little he knew of his fostered son. Cluff Drybannock was not his real name. He had been called it by Molo Bean, who had laughed as the young and starving orphan had stuffed himself with dry bread at Molo's table. Who Dry was, what he'd seen and done before coming to Clan Bludd, was unknown. The one and only time he'd spoken of his father was that first day, when he claimed the man was a Bluddsman so Bludd must take him in. His mother was a Trenchlander . . . and Trenchlanders were Sull. Vaylo saw that Sull in him now, and was overcome with the sudden certainty that if Dry chose to, he had ways within his power to halt the horse.

Yet he did not. At the final instant, Cluff Drybannock moved aside. Lake water seeped around his boots as he stepped onto a floating bed of mallow grass at the lake's edge. Pengo's horse entered the water with a great splash, quickly rearing back at the shock of its coldness. Pengo easily gained control of the beast and turned it back onto the shore.

"Aye," he said to Drybone. "It'd suit you well enough if I rode away." Abruptly, he dismounted. "But I don't think I'll give you the satisfaction of taking my place just yet."

Drybone did not speak. After a moment he turned his back on Pengo and bent to collect water from the lake. Vaylo watched as Dry released cupped hands above his forehead and let the dark, oily water run down his scalp. *He stopped Pengo from losing face, yet he needn't have. Why?* When the answer came it made Vaylo feel old. *For me, just for me.*

Pengo raised his voice to his brothers. "Gangaric. Thrago. You lazy sons-of-bitches. Get down from your saddles. I'll be damned if I'll stand here alone."

Vaylo looked on with distaste as his two younger sons did Pengo's bidding. Sometimes he wondered if he hadn't brought the curse of his sons upon himself. *I married my half-sister. No man can come that close to trespass and remain unpunished.* Stone Gods! But Angarad was fair then! The color of her skin, the way her eyes crinkled when she laughed. Old Gullit Bludd had adored her. He'd grunt at his sons, ignore his bastard, and shower his daughter with gifts. The only time Vaylo could recall seeing his father pay coin for anything was when a Far South trader had shown him a sea pearl as black as night. Angarad was thirteen then, more lovely than a thousand pearls, and when she'd held the jewel to her hair it disappeared, so closely were the two matched in sheen and hue. Gullit had bought the jewel on the spot, and named it for her. Angarad had worn it till her death. Vaylo had it now, yet he'd never once looked upon it in the nine years she'd been gone. Strange how he had once thought it beautiful. Now he knew it for the dark omen it was: no girl of thirteen should be given a black jewel.

She had not wanted him. How could she? She was fifteen, in the fullness of her beauty, and the man who claimed her had slain the father she loved. Worse than that somehow was Vaylo's bastardy. Angarad was her father's daughter: she had grown up believing in his word. She had seen firsthand how Vaylo was treated, and that seeing had darkened her feelings for the rest of her life.

The Dog Lord sighed deeply. He could not blame her. She was proud, as a Bluddswoman should be, and she had borne him seven healthy sons. Toward the end, during the last few months of her life, when she insisted on being carried out to the Bluddcourt each morning in her wicker chair, there had been a softening. All she had to do was show him one small sign of affection to steal the heart from his chest. He had wanted to love her all along.

It was an effort to drag his mind from the past.

To Thrago he said, "Take a crew of thirty south to Withy. Warn Hanro of what passed at the Bluddhouse. Tell him to double watches on all borders—especially in the east where the Withy hunt-runs cross into the Ruinwoods. You'll stay with Hanro until I call you back. And before you say it I'll hear no argument about which of you is to take command of the Withyhouse. Hanro has it. He's been there for ninety days, and he should know how best to defend it by now." Vaylo couldn't resist a jibe at his second son. "And be sure to watch your step, else you'll fall through a trapdoor and end up with a hole through your head."

Pengo scowled.

Thrago nodded. "I'll leave on the morrow."

"Good." Vaylo turned to Gangaric. His mind was fully engaged now. Angus Lok had warned him that Robbie Dhoone was cunning and hungry. Vaylo had been cunning and hungry himself once; it shouldn't be difficult to put himself in the Dhoonesman's place. "Gangaric. I want you back at the Bluddhouse. Take a small crew with you. No more than two dozen spearmen and bowmen. You'll be working with Quarro to secure the Bluddhold. I want three hundred yards of timber cleared around the roundhouse. And take Scunner Bone with you. He's old, but he's devious, and he knows how to lay horse traps and strangle lines." *And it'll stop him from catching any more damned eels for me to eat.* "Send him to Withy when he's done."

Gangaric was not so pleased with his assignment. He had styled himself a HalfBludd axman, and had plans to travel south to the Halfhouse and take up arms there. Now his father was commanding him east, and at the head of a crew of archers and spearmen, no less. Every axman Vaylo had ever met had nothing but contempt for weapons that relied on piercing, not chopping, blades. Gangaric fought his dissatisfaction. Deeply scarred and blistered hands flung back his braids. "Aye. I'll go east. Though I'll be taking a half-score of axmen as escort."

Vaylo forced himself not to object. Six axmen were neither here nor there. If it pleased his third son's vanity to have them, then it came at a small price. "Well enough. I'd have you leave at dawn. All in the Bluddhouse must know our hearts are with them."

Gangaric bowed his head, a strangely courtly gesture that lay at odds with his manner and dress. *He's learning grace from the HalfBludds*, Vaylo thought, pleased despite himself. HalfBludd axmen were renowned for two things: their reckless joy on the battlefield, and their gallantry with clan maids off it. It certainly wouldn't hurt Gangaric to pick up a few manners whilst learning how best to chop off a man's head.

Vaulting into his saddle, Gangaric said, "I'd best get back. There's much to settle if I'm to be gone by first light."

Thrago followed after him, and the two of them rode at gallop to the Dhoonehouse. The moon was high now, silvering the thistle fields and moving deep within the lake. The wind carried the scent of resin from the western pines, a smell that reminded the Dog Lord of surgeons' tents and wound dressings. Underfoot the first dew of nightfall was crisping to ice.

Vaylo was aware of the silence that grew between the three remaining men. Cluff Drybannock and Pengo Bludd seldom had much to say to each other, but tonight the hostility running between them crackled in the air.

"Pengo," Vaylo said eventually. "I want you to take a company of a hundred men north. Ride overnight to the Dhoonewall and secure—"

"No," Pengo hissed. "I'm not leaving this roundhouse while *he's* still in it." He snapped his wrist in Drybone's direction. "Send *him* to those blasted rocks—he's not one of us. He won't be missed."

"*Silence!*" Vaylo roared, taking a step toward his son. Fifty-three years old Vaylo was, yet Pengo still flinched before him. "Cluff Drybannock is your brother by fosterage and a warrior of this clan. You will show him due respect, or as the gods are my witness I'll beat you where you stand."

Pengo took a step back, his face flushing with blood. "That bastard thinks he's as good as a chief since he took Ganmiddich.

But what good did it do us? He held it for less than a month."

Cluff Drybannock regarded Pengo with such a depth of coldness it made hairs rise on Vaylo's neck. It was not Dry's fault Ganmiddich had been lost—Vaylo knew that blame lay with himself for sending Dry north to Dhoone when they were already undermanned—yet Dry did not speak up in his own defense. His pride allowed for no excuses.

Addressing himself to Vaylo, Dry said, "I will take command of the Dhoonewall."

"No, you will not!" Vaylo replied hotly. "That charge falls to my second son."

"Let him take it, Father," urged Pengo, sensing an advantage. "He's unwed. He has no wife to drag north for his comfort."

Vaylo halted for a moment as he made sense of what his son said. Pengo couldn't be thinking of taking his new wife to the Dhoonewall. The Dhoonewall was a defensive rampart spanning two major passes in the Copper Hills. It had lain unused since the time of the River Wars—and then manned only briefly. Built by Hawker Dhoone, it had once been a source of Dhoonish pride; a means of protecting the Dhoonehold and Dhoone's precious copper mines from Maimed Men raiders, and preventing hostile clans from mounting northern attacks. Now the copper mines were mostly sealed. Iron had long since taken over as the metal of choice for forging weapons, and the number of Maimed Men had been declining for decades. As far as Vaylo knew, only one of the original hill forts was livable and that was a broken-down tower of crumbling mortar and mossy stones. No woman could be taken there. Especially one as heavy with child as Pengo's wife.

Vaylo heard his voice fall dangerously low as he said, "You *will* man the Dhoonewall and you will *not* take your wife."

"I don't think so, Father. You may command the Dhoonehold, but *I* command my wife." Pengo flicked a piece of straw from one of his braids. "And while I think on it, I'll have her bring the bairns along as well. They've been so long in your care they think they've an old man for a father."

Vaylo wanted to strike him. Pengo's two children were his sole remaining grandchildren. To even speak of putting them in danger was unthinkable. It made Vaylo see spots of red rage before his eyes. "Your wife stays here. She's with child. You can't drag her and the bairns to some broken piece of rock-wall. I forbid it."

"She. *She*. You don't even know her name, do you? All Shanna is to you is a means of restocking your grandchildren. A brood mare. Well start looking for someone else to do your rutting, Dog Lord, for if you send me north to the Dhoonewall you'll never see Shanna or the bairns again."

Gods help me not to kill him. Vaylo grabbed his braids in his fist and tried not to grind his teeth. There was truth in what his son said, he could not deny it. He couldn't remember the name of Pengo's new wife, though she had been a daughter of the clan for twenty years. Oh, he knew her well enough by sight—a striking girl with the dark skin and black eyes of her sister, Pengo's first wife—yet the only time he'd spoken to her was when she became visibly heavy with child. It had been the same with all his sons' wives: he valued them, but only as mothers of his grandchildren. Now Pengo's wife was six months pregnant, soon to bring forth the clan's first newborn since the massacre on the Bluddroad. Every effort must be made to keep her safe. Vaylo wanted that child.

"So, Father. What's it to be? Do you send a wifeless bastard from the roundhouse, or me?"

Vaylo looked to Cluff Drybannock. Since he'd taken his final oath six years back Dry had gathered a troop of loyal swordsmen about him. His skill with the longsword was unmatched in the clanholds, and no swordsman could watch him in battle and remain unmoved. He was Vaylo's right hand, silent and uncomplaining, and he would fight to the death to protect his chief. *Yet I have given him so little; a sword, a bed, brotherhood in a hostile clan. I should have taken him as my son formally, spilt my blood over his. Yet he never asked for it, and I always thought there'd be time enough for such sentimental fussing when all wars and conflicts were done.*

The Dog Lord's hand closed around his measure of guidestone, weighing the gray powder in his fist. He wanted Dry here, with him. When an attack came, and he knew one would, he would fight easier knowing Dry was at his back. Pengo was a fierce warrior and he rode with a fierce crew, but he lacked loyalty and obedience . . . and something else that Vaylo couldn't name. Perhaps the cold and deadly grace of the Sull.

Drybone's gaze rose to meet his chief's. Moonlight sheened his hair and ran along the sharply defined bones of his face. He was wearing a cloak of auburn wool, its hem weighted with bronze chains so it would not move with the wind; a gift from Ockish Bull upon his deathbed.

Dry, I love you like a son.

But I love my grandchildren more.

The Dog Lord turned to his son. "You will stay here at the roundhouse with your crew. You'll take charge of securing the perimeter. I want a station on the Flow to the south, and one on Lost Clan Field to the east. Plan for ranging parties to ride as far west as the Muzzle, and make sure every scout's equipped with fire arrows and horns."

Pengo stood straighter. "Aye."

Vaylo was glad he said no more. Glad that his second son chose not to gloat, for he didn't think he could have borne it. Weariness stole over him, and suddenly he wanted very much to be with Nan. Glancing over at where Drybone stood facing the lake, his beautiful long fingers resting gently upon the wolf dog's neck, he knew he wasn't done.

"Pengo. Go now."

He meant to say more, to warn Pengo of the importance of his task, and advise him to learn the lie of the land—for Robbie Dhoone knew it only too well. Also he knew he should force a reconciliation between Pengo and Dry, make them clasp hands and speak hollow words so at least a semblance of unity could be maintained. But he didn't have the strength for it.

Pengo waited, and when no further words were forthcoming he grunted in dissatisfaction and led his horse from the lake.

He wanted to stay, Vaylo knew. Listen to what he and Dry said to each other, like a jealous husband eavesdropping on his wife. Vaylo waited until horse and rider reached the torchlight and cobbled stone of the Dhoone greatcourt before turning to face Cluff Drybannock.

"Dry. I'm—"

"Don't say it." Dry's voice was quiet, but there was no comfort in it. "I'll take a hundred north. We'll leave at dusk tomorrow."

"Take the full two hundred—at least until you make the hill fort livable."

"No. I would leave half at your command."

So much to say to each other, yet we can only speak the language of fighting men. "If you must leave some, leave only twenty. If you judge the post a folly send word and I'll call you back."

Drybone nodded, once. "Chief," he said, and Vaylo recognized the finality in it. The word was both an acknowledgment and a farewell. Dry clicked his tongue to beckon his horse and before Vaylo knew it he was on his way.

Vaylo watched him leave. The wolf dog, torn between staying with its master and trotting alongside Drybone, raced back and forth in the growing distance between them. Time passed, and eventually the great orange-and-black hound came to heel. As Vaylo scratched and pinched its ears, he saw the lake was glowing. It reminded him of the chorus to an old clannish lament.

Give me a maid at full moon, and on the banks of the Blue Dhoone we'll dally as if it were day.

With a heavy heart the Dog Lord turned for home.

FOURTEEN

Awakening

L
ight pulsed against her eyelids, a breeze rippled across her face. Somewhere far in the distance a bird chirred, and then someone said, "She's coming awake." *Am I?* she thought lazily. *I really don't think I want to. It's so much easier to sleep.* The voice wouldn't let her go, though. It called her name, and there was a force behind that one word that seemed to propel her straight from her dreams.

"Ash."

She opened her eyes. Weak dawn light shrank her irises, and spots of light floated across her field of vision like bubbles in water. A face loomed over her. Dark eyes inspected her, and warm rough hands probed the pulse points in her neck. "Welcome home, daughter. I thank the gods for sending you back."

They were the most beautiful words Ash March had ever heard. She tried to reply, but her head felt woolly and her throat was so dry it hurt.

"*Hass*, bring water."

Water was brought, and a thin stream of it trickled into her mouth. She swallowed. Hands slid under her, raising her head and slipping something soft under her back. She saw two faces now, both stark and subtly alien, the plates of bone beneath their cheeks somehow different from her own. Ark Veinsplitter and Mal Naysayer. She was pleased when the names came to her. It meant she wasn't mad.

She found her voice, and grimaced when it cracked and squeaked like a boy's did when he came into manhood. "How long have I been asleep?"

The two Sull warriors exchanged a glance. "Many days," said Ark Veinsplitter.

Oh. Ash couldn't think why she wasn't more surprised. She glanced around. A crown of peaks surrounded her, purple and blue, jagged as split bone and heavily freighted with ice. She felt as if she were floating amongst them like a cloud. A fuzzy, aching cloud. Directly ahead lay the trappings of a well-laid camp: a tent stretched on poles, a horse corral, a firepit, even a line suspended over the flames for thawing game and drying clothes. *It should be cold*, she thought abruptly. *This high in the mountains, at dawn.* Yet she did not feel cold, she felt numbed and protected. Only the gentlest breezes got through.

"There was a cave," she said as she took in the saddle of rock they were camped upon; the tufts of yellow goatgrass growing from chinks in the boulders, the rippling course of a dry streambed, the ledge that sheared away into thin air. "You took me there, into the mountain . . . I . . ."

"We bled you."

With those three words she remembered everything. The pool. The razor on her wrist. Blood dyeing the water red. She shivered. Her arms lay beneath heavy white fox pelts and she labored to free them. They were thinner now, the veins showing like gray wire beneath her skin. Slowly she turned her palms to the sky. *Oh god. The scars.* Bands of livid pink scar tissue crossed her wrists.

"*Hass*, breathe the blue."

Mal Naysayer rose and walked toward the horse corral. Ash saw the bright glint of metal as he drew his letting knife. She did not want to see as he knelt before the breathtaking blue stallion and sliced open the skin above its coffin bone, but she found she couldn't look away. Horse blood bubbled from the gash, and the Sull warrior moved swiftly to catch it in a copper bowl. Mal's hands were gentle upon the horse's calf as he massaged the vein to keep it open. Ash couldn't believe how still and calm the horse was; its great sculpted head held as steady as if it were being shoed. The bowl filled quickly, and Mal set it down whilst he stanched and then greased the wound. Before retrieving the bowl, his lips moved as he spoke words of thanks or blessing.

Ash wasn't surprised when he brought her the bowl. "Drink," he said, in his low-timbred voice. "Grow your blood."

Ash took the steaming bowl in both hands, smelling the sugary, grassy odor of horse. She did not want to drink it, and had a brief desire to tell Mal that she hadn't agreed to have her lifeblood drained for it to be replaced with horse blood. Yet when she brought the warm liquid to her lips a terrible craving overcame her, and she drank greedily, letting riverlets of blood spill down her chin in her haste. Only when she'd drained the bowl did her normal senses return. Sheepishly, she offered the empty vessel to the Naysayer.

"It is the iron," he explained. "Your body thirsts for it."

"You must sleep now," Ark said, standing. "We will speak when you are rested."

But I don't want to rest, Ash protested. But just as quickly she felt a wave of lethargy pass over her, weighing her eyelids and making her exhale. The horse blood was a delicious heaviness in her stomach, the fox pelts as soft as breath against her skin. She slept.

When she woke the sun was gone. The glow from the fire

created a cave of light around the camp. Mal Naysayer was butchering a carcass, a huge bird-shaped thing, skinned and slick with blood. He used a broad cleaver to smash open the skull and hack off the feet. Ark Veinsplitter was a short distance from the camp, sitting upon the ledge that jutted out into the dark mountain night, a woven rug pulled like a cloak around his shoulders, his gaze directed northward to the great white star.

Ash rose cautiously, testing her legs before allowing them to bear her weight. She felt she had sponge for muscle, and it was really just as well she was light as a feather, since a feather seemed to be the limit of what they could lift. Mal Naysayer paused in his butchering to indicate a rocky depression screened by oilbushes to the rear of the camp. The jacks. Ash found she had no embarrassment within her, and calmly found a place to urinate. She wore no smallclothes, just a shift of coarse wool and the fox pelts, and it was easy to pull up her skirts and pee. When she was done she returned to Mal Naysayer, and received a beaker of water and a flatcake crusted with seeds. She ate in silence, watching Mal smash individual bird vertebrae to get at the pink marrow.

"Walk now," he said, after a time. "Work your legs before we eat."

She knew a dismissal when she heard one, and stood and looked around. There didn't appear to be anywhere particular to walk to, since the camp was sited hard against the mountain face, and boulders and dark crevasses formed natural boundaries, limiting the number of paths a girl could take. Overhead, clouds sailed silently between the stars. The moon was somewhere, cloaked from view though close to full, judging by the diffused and silvery light that backlit the sky. Ash began walking a circuit of the camp, heading first for the corral to greet the horses. It occurred to her that she could now feel the cold when earlier she could not. *Sull sorcery?* she wondered, remembering how once she had seen Sarga Veys push back the mist on the Black Spill. Had Ark or the Naysayer pushed back the cold to keep her warm?

She decided she didn't want to know, and let her mind fill instead with the warmth and companionship of the three Sull horses. They had woken from sleep to greet her, and now pushed their warm dark noses forward for her to touch. It was good to stand there, by the canvas-hung posts, and speak nonsense horsy stuff to three enormous beasts. It healed a little of the strangeness that had become her life.

When she was ready she made her way to Ark Veinsplitter. The ledge was a pointed spar of granite jutting out from the mountain, and when Ash stepped upon it she could see nothing else before her, only sky. A dizzying sense of displacement made her lean toward the edge.

"Sit," warned Ark Veinsplitter, without looking around. "I do not think you are ready to lean into the wind just yet."

Ash sat, a safe distance from the edge, her heart beating strongly. "What do you mean?"

"There are some I have known who consider it a rite of manhood to stand upon a ledge such as this and wait until the updrafts rise. When they feel the warm air upon their cheeks they lean into it, and let the wind push them back to standing."

"That doesn't sound like such a good idea."

"We have lost some that way," Ark conceded.

"So it's a test of being Sull?"

Ark shook his head. "No. Of being alive." She noticed for the first time there was gray in his sable hair. "The moon burns full this night. Soon it will show itself and we shall begin."

A speck of fear moved in Ash's chest. She wanted no more cutting.

The Far Rider must have sensed her fear for he said, "Tonight you begin learning the ways of the Sull." For the first time he looked at her, his dark eyes appraising. "What? Did you think the dreams they sent you were all there is?"

How did he know about the dreams when she barely remembered them herself? The images were fleeting, blurred. A silver shore. A land lit by moonlight. Flashes of battles so strange and horrific they could not belong in this world. Chilled, Ash gathered the fox pelts close. The stars suddenly seemed cold and bright.

The two sat in silence, watching them, and after a time the scent of roasting game bird drifted across on threads of smoke. Ash swallowed. She had a sense that she was moving through the sky, that the clouds were static and she was passing beneath them. Dimly she became aware that the moon was revealing itself, its rays sliding like fingers across her face.

"Light the flame."

Ash was drawn back by Ark's words. It took her a moment to understand that he was speaking to Mal Naysayer, not to her, and that the Naysayer had joined them on the ledge and was crouching a short distance behind them. Ash felt a small thrill of unease. She had not heard him come.

Mal turned the key on a strangely shaped pewter lantern, releasing a hiss of what sounded like gas. He held an ember from the firepit above the lamp's chimney, and a strong yellow flame burst into life. As she watched, Mal adjusted the valve at the chimney's base and the nature of the flame changed. It blued, growing smaller and fiercer, sissing softly like the wind. Ash could see halos of color within it; pale lilacs and vivid blues. Only the outer corona was yellow now.

"Sull is the heart of the flame," Ark Veinsplitter said softly. "The cold blue center that gives rise to light and heat." As Ark spoke, the Naysayer settled the lamp upon the stone ledge and pushed up the sleeve of his silvery hornmail and the padded silk tunic beneath. "Fear is the enemy that will destroy us. It lessens and distracts us, clouding our judgment and losing our battles before the first blow is struck. To fight we must cleanse ourselves of fear, find the stillness that lives within us. The search for this stillness is called *Saer Rahl*, the Way of the Flame. Just as the flame blows hot and uncertain so do we. Yet every flame ever struck has blue in its heart, and it is this we strive to reach.

"*Mas Rhal*. The perfect state of fearlessness. The flame at the center of all things."

As Ark said "*Mas Rhal*" Mal Naysayer raised his left hand to the flame. Slowly, steadily, he slid his living flesh into the pale blue radiance. Ash forced herself to watch as he held it there, unmoving, unblinking, the flame shimmering around his fingers for long seconds after Ark fell silent.

In his own time he took his hand away. Ash looked into his dark, ice-tanned face searching for signs of pain. He surprised her by offering his hand for her inspection. Ash almost feared to touch it, yet when she did the skin was cool and unmarked, the muscles and veins hard. Gingerly, she raised her own hand toward the flame, but even the air surrounding the lamp was searing and she quickly snatched it back.

The two Sull warriors watched her impassively. Ark said, "The air is hot, but the core of the flame will not burn you. Losing fear takes many things. Trust is one of them."

"So am I to trust you? Thrust my hand through the hot air in the hope you're right?"

"Not this day."

Mal killed the flame.

Perversely, Ash felt disappointed. She knew herself well enough to realize how hungry she was to be included. *Daughter*, they had called her. She wanted to hear that word more.

Mal Naysayer was the one who read the disappointment on her face. "Nay, Ash March, we are not finished with you yet. Come. Stand."

Ash did as she was bade, and the two Far Riders stood also, Mal collecting the lamp and stepping clear of the ledge and onto the safe ground of the camp, and Ark taking the few steps necessary to put himself at the very tip of the ledge. Ash joined Mal, eager to put a safe distance between herself and the sheer drop. The Naysayer handed her a strip of silk, three feet long and a hand-length wide. "Tie it over your eyes."

Her hands shook as she laid the smooth black silk over her eyelids and secured it with a knot behind her head. She felt Mal's hands come down upon her shoulders, turning and positioning her. Facing her out toward the ledge. A bubble of panic worked its way toward her heart. *No. It can't be . . .*

"Walk toward Ark. He will guide you."

Ash shook her head. "I can't."

"Ash March, I have journeyed with you twice. I know what you can do."

A gust of cool air brushed against her face. She could see nothing but blackness, utterly flat and without depth.

"Seek the flame. Trust yourself and trust Ark. He will not let you fall." With that, Mal Naysayer stepped away from Ash, stripping her of her bearings. She listened, but was unable to tell the direction in which he left. An instant later she realized she had moved her head to track him, and now she was no longer sure if she had moved her body as well. Which way was she facing? She made what she thought was the correct adjustment, but her foot settled upon a raised lip of granite. *That wasn't there before, was it? Where's Ark? Why doesn't he say something?* Again, she listened, but not even the wind was moving now. Without realizing it, her body had begun to sway, and it was only when the blackness before her eyes began to spin that she spread her arms wide to steady herself. Fright had made her rigid.

Calm. I need to be calm. She had to be facing in the general direction of the ledge—she hadn't moved that much. If only the wind would come again. That way she would know for certain. *Seek the flame*, Mal had said. But it was too new a concept and she didn't know where to look.

Taking a shallow breath, Ash stepped forward. Nothing bad happened—no roots tripped her, no previously unseen crevasse swallowed her up. Emboldened by this small success she took another step and then another. During the third step, she noticed the granite smoothing out beneath her. Did this mean she'd reached the ledge? What if she were off track by even a few feet? She was suddenly overcome with the fear that she'd veered dangerously far from her path, and was now headed for the shallowest part of the overhang, not the promontory where Ark now stood. One step and she could be over the edge.

Afraid to move, she tried to calm herself. The Naysayer had told her Ark would not let her fall. She had to believe that. He had called her daughter: what kind of father would risk his child?

One named Penthero Iss. Ash hardened herself against thoughts of her foster-father. He had not loved her. Oh, he'd said it and she'd believed it. But that made him a liar and her a fool. She had been nothing to him but a means to more power.

Anger and hurt made her take unplanned steps. And then she felt it: the updraft rising along her body, billowing her skirt and lifting her hair. *I'm on the edge.* Her heart froze. Muscles inside her body slackened, and she was suddenly glad she had emptied her bladder earlier. Where was Ark? Why didn't he speak?

She couldn't move. Her mind showed her the long drop

down the mountain, the jagged edges of rock that would skin her legs as she fell, and the dark and quiet place where she would land. No man or Sull would ever find her. She shivered violently. *I should have touched the flame. It would have been easier. You'd have thought I would have learned by now that when the Sull give you a second choice it's always worse than the first.*

Strangely, madly, she found herself smiling. She was Sull herself now; her own blood drained to nothing to make way for theirs.

Seek the flame.

How? They had not told her where to find it. The updraft swelled against her chest, rocking her back. The stars were out there, burning beyond the ledge, and she was taken with the idea she could feel them. They danced like blue raindrops upon her skin. She could imagine that blueness now, not on the silk pressed against her eyes, but deep within her, in the caverns where her Sull blood now pumped. It was a tiny flickering, a beacon lit to guide the way. Slowly, gradually, her heart relaxed, finding a rhythm close to sleep.

I have nothing to fear. Ark will save me if I fall.

And with that she took a step. For one brief instant the world fell away beneath her and she knew how it would be when she met her death—and then Ark's strong hands were upon her, his arms fastening around her waist, catching her and pulling her back. She hugged him fiercely, joy and exhilaration coursing through her blood. He smelled good, like horses and wood smoke, and that faint alien pungency that meant Sull.

"Daughter," he said. "I have never met a Sull warrior with a worse sense of direction than you."

She laughed giddily, pulling the silk from her eyes to discover how true his words were. She had missed the ledge's spur completely, and had come to stand upon the shallowest lip, as she'd feared. The speed with which Ark must have moved from his position to intercept her defied thought.

He smiled grimly as he carried her to the safety of the camp. "*Hass*," he called to the Naysayer. "We must begin teaching this warrior the path lores, for I fear we'll lose her if we do not."

He settled Ash down upon a soft blue rug before the firepit, and Mal Naysayer, the great ice-eyed warrior with the face of stone, winked at her and said, "Nay. Ash March knew where she stepped. She had a mind to test the reflexes of an old man like you."

Ark Veinsplitter chuckled softly. "You conspire against me, Naysayer. I'll not forget it next time I draw steel in your defense."

"Then I'll be sure to fight with two blades. One for my enemy and one for you."

The words had the cadence of old and much-repeated banter, and the two Far Riders contemplated each other with lively sternness. "So," Ark said, conceding victory to Mal for outstaring him, "Do you propose to feed us some of that mountain duck you brought down? Or just torment us with the smell?"

"Golden eagle," corrected the Naysayer with dignity. "This Sull has not heard of such a thing as mountain duck."

Ash had to push her lips together to stop herself from grinning. She was shaking with relief. The death her mind had shown her was so real she wondered if the world hadn't split in two, and one Ash had died while the other had lived. The Naysayer handed her a bowl of broth and bird meat, a mildly affronted look on his face. The broth was delicious, strong and dark and flavored with cardamom and seedpods. The leg meat was lean and gamy, with a sharpness that reminded Ash of wild boar. She ate all of it, and held her bowl out for more. As she ate her second helping, Ark spoke.

"Do you know why we made you do it?" Ash shook her head.

"Walking blindfold on the edge is how the Sull make war. We battle in darkness, with the abyss beneath us, and every step we take is uncertain. War against the Endlords is a dance with doom. Battle men, and we risk our lives. Battle the Endlords, and we risk our souls."

"And race," added the Naysayer quietly.

"It is so." Strong emotion weighed Ark's face. He shifted his position near the firepit, rising to sit upright so that firelight and shadows flickered across his face. "Ash March, you are Sull now. Rules of men no longer apply. You must learn a new way of being: how to walk the farthest edge and not falter, and live within your *Rhal*. Forces are awakening within you, and it is our job as *Mayji* to guide and teach you."

Ash traced a finger around the rim of the bowl. It was a thing of beauty, glaze layered over glaze until the color had such a depth and translucence to it that it was like looking at the night sky. "*Mayji*?" she asked, preferring to deal with this small detail rather than the greater truths he had told her.

"Men have no word for it. You may think of it as master or elder."

"Why didn't you help me on the ledge? The Naysayer said you would guide me."

"Perhaps I did, and you did not hear."

Ash closed her mouth, silenced. All her earlier triumph at stepping from the ledge and being caught drained from her, and she now feared that she had been reckless, not brave.

Ark Veinsplitter saw all in her face and spoke no words to deny it. He began placing logs in the firepit, banking the fire for the long winter night. "There is much to learn and little time. Tomorrow we resume our journey east. The wind is rising in the Want, and these lands are no longer safe. Sleep and gather your strength. We wake before dawn."

Ash felt dismissed. She rolled one of the fox pelts into a

pillow, and settled down to sleep. Through half-closed eyes she watched the two Far Riders rise and walk a short distance from the camp. They spoke briefly, their voices low. Once, Ark turned to look at her, and she knew they spoke of her. After a time, the Naysayer returned to the firepit, settled himself into a crouching position facing out from the fire, and unsheathed his sword.

The blade shone with the purest light. Meteor steel, she recalled it was named, as the iron and trace metals it was forged from came from rocks that fell from the stars. When Mal noticed her sleepy gaze upon it, he brought out a squirrel skin and a pot of tung oil and began greasing the edge. Ash saw it for the deception it was. He guarded against an enemy so swift and invisible that he feared to lose even a moment to unsheathing his sword. He stood ready to fight, yet went through the motions of tending his blade.

Ash turned to see what had become of Ark Veinsplitter. It took a moment for her eyes to grow accustomed to the darkness beyond the firepit, and even longer to make out the figure of the Sull warrior, moving silently around the camp. He held something weighty in a cloth pouch, and every few seconds he halted his circuit, drew something small and pale from the bag and laid it on the ground. As he worked, Ash was struck with the sense that it was growing warmer and calmer in the camp, as when she'd first awakened that morning. *Wards*. Unease pricked the base of her spine. Two men, neither sleeping, both taking action to secure the camp.

Against what? Ash knew she could not think about it and sleep. Slowly, she let her mind drift. She wondered where Raif was that night. Was he on his way home to the clanholds? Did he hate her for what she had done? She tossed and turned in the fox pelts, sweating. When her dreams came they were murky and fleeting, and offered no peace.

Ark Veinsplitter woke her in the layered darkness of pre-dawn. Already, the camp had been dismantled and the spare horse loaded with supplies. It was bitterly cold once more, and tendrils of mist slid across the rocks. Mal Naysayer was nowhere to be seen. "He scouts ahead," Ark said, handing her a bowl of steaming broth. "We'll follow his trail and meet him at noon. He can move more swiftly in the mountains afoot."

Ash accepted this, unsure of what it meant. She thought Ark looked ill-rested, and said, "Those things you laid on the ground last night, what are they?"

The look he gave her was not friendly. He stood. "Your travel clothes are warming by the fire. Be ready by the time I've fed the horses."

Ash felt his brusqueness as a slight. It hurt her to realize there were some secrets the Sull warrior wasn't ready to tell. Raising the bowl, she let the steam rise across her face. Somewhere on the slopes below a snowcock was whistling in the dawn. The wind was restless, and rising, and there was a wetness to it that promised sleet.

Standing, she worked the stiffness from her muscles and tried to decide if she felt stronger than the day before. A bit, perhaps. Her gaze traveled to the pile of furs and clothing warming beside the remains of the kicked-in fire.

Something bright and silvery flashed atop her woolen dress. A hair ring. Ash moved quickly to retrieve it. The metal was white and gleaming, smooth as a wedding band and cool as ice. She had seen the same kind of rings in the Far Riders' hair, and marked how they flashed more brightly in moonlight than sunlight. Now one had been given to her. She searched her belongings for a comb, eager to dress her hair. As she threaded the thumb-sized ring through her pale locks, Ark approached, leading the horses.

He was dressed in full armor beneath a wolverine cloak, his

weapons arrayed ready for drawing in a many-chaneled harness upon his back. Ash counted two swords, a recurve longbow, a dagger and a hatchet. A six-foot spear was mounted on the blue's saddle strap, its butt secured in a shoe of yellow horn. Motioning toward the hair ring, he said, "The Naysayer thought to make you a gift. He wanted you to know that after the First Gods created the moon they made this metal to catch its light."

Moved, Ash fitted the soft ring around her ponytail.

"It disappears in your hair." Ark's voice was low. Abruptly, he mounted the blue. "I'll await you at the streambed."

Ash dressed quickly, and packed the Naysayer's exquisite gray stallion with her blankets and meager supplies. Buckles on the gray's bardings shone bright as mirrors, and Ash caught a glimpse of herself in one of them. She started. Why had no one mentioned her eyes were now blue?

Dawn light was showing on the horizon as she and Ark broke camp. The path led them east and then south down the mountain, past frozen gullies, matted ground-willow and meadows of ice-killed grass. To Ash's eyes the trail was all but invisible, yet Ark told her the Naysayer had freshened it, and directed her to look for his sign in the hoarfrost. Ash looked at the underbellies of granite boulders and the boles of dead trees, but saw nothing. Just when she was growing impatient with the game, she spied something—a pale thumbprint, barely perceptible and easily mistaken for a natural variation in the frost—pressed into the north-pointing branch of a prostrate pine. Ark nodded, pleased. "He tells us there is running water to the north if we choose to break the trail."

Ash was intent on guiding the gray down a difficult rock stair, yet she still managed to throw Ark a disbelieving look.

The Far Rider saw it and grew cold. "The path lores make us vulnerable. If an enemy learned to read them he could track us. Ways known only to us would be revealed to him; sacred sites and waystones, paths laid down by the first *Mayji* and the Old Ones in the Time Before. When I show you the most basic workings of the lore it may seem a small thing, but small things can grow quickly and become much. Once I teach you the inner workings of the path lores I arm you with a weapon to destroy us."

Ash bowed her head, chastened. Ark rode on ahead of her, his spine stiff with Sull pride. She knew better than to draw abreast with him, and instead settled into place at the rear. She felt she was no closer to knowing these people than she had been when she first encountered them . . . but she would learn and grow wiser. And become one of them.

The morning passed slowly, as mist gave way to sleet, and gray stormlight darkened the snow. Ash only realized it was midday when Ark called a halt. They were riding through a narrow valley that sheltered the first upright trees they'd seen all day, and Ark rested the horses while he waited for the Naysayer to join them. They lit no fire and cut no meat, and Ash was forced to search her pack for waybread. She was hungry and tired, and her thighs ached from sitting astride the gray. The Far Rider barely noticed her. He walked the length of the valley, his gaze traveling along the tree line, his cloak of gray wolverine shedding sleet.

Time passed, and still there was no sign of the Naysayer. Ash felt rather than saw Ark Veinsplitter's growing apprehension. The Far Rider stood still now, a booted foot resting on a spur of basalt, his hands clasped around the six-foot spear he used as a staff. When a dark shape broke through the tree line, Ark hefted the spear from the snow. There was a moment when Ash thought he would loose it, but he recognized his *hass* and let the butt drop to the ground.

The Naysayer moved swiftly through the swirling sleet. Ash saw he'd drawn the longsword with its raven-head pommel, and she knew something was wrong. When Ark stepped forward to meet him so did she. The Naysayer's ice-cold eyes looked only at his *hass*. "We must take another path east. A *maeraith* guarded the entrance to the Rift Road."

Ash glanced at his sword, and saw something black as night trickle down the edge and drop like acid into the snow.

FIFTEEN

Stillborn

R aif crouched behind the ridgewall and picked out his prey. It was mid-morning, dry and bitterly cold, with a wind blowing that sucked all the moisture from the snow and sent it sweeping across the tundra as dry as salt. He was lucky to encounter a herd here this late in the season. Luckier still that he had spent the night three days back whittling a spear. The spear was a six-footer, cut from white holly he'd found growing in the shelter of a dry canyon, its point hardened by fire. Clansmen called such spears "whore sticks" as they were only good for one shot and if you missed you'd go to bed starved. Raif wasn't starved yet, but he was weary of dried seal tongue and rendered lard. He was hungry for fresh meat.

And even hungrier for the hunt. He'd traveled too long without a kill.

East, always east, along the hard, rocky margin that lay between the badlands and the Want. This was canyon country, east of Blackhail and north of the Copper Hills: the land hideously buckled by some ancient calamity, raised into rocky bluffs and windswept ridges, and sunk deep into dry riverbeds, canyons and things deeper than canyons. All sharp and desolate and shimmering with a layer of hoarfrost that collected on everything like limescale. Raif had no firsthand knowledge of this land, and little but sparse rumor to go on. Dhoonesmen mounted longhunts here in autumn to claim their portion of the vast herds of elk and moose that moved south with winter. From where he crouched on the ridge, Raif could see the Copper Hills rise to the south, their bald peaks hazy with distance and purple with heather, their slopes scored with dark lines that might mark game tracks or the ancient masonry of the Dhoonewall.

Raif had lost count of the days he had traveled. He did not like to think about what had happened at the Forsworn redoubt, and his memories of the days after were not good ones. Passing through the Blackhail badlands was not something he ever wished to do again. He had tried to avoid the campsite, had walked leagues out of his way, swerving northward into the great ice desert of the Want, yet he had still known when he passed it. The place his father died.

He seldom slept well now, and woke from dreams unsettled and ill-rested. His pace had slowed, and he knew he was riding the ragged edge of energy—swinging between moments of extreme alertness and complete lapses of thought—that came with lack of sleep.

He was alert now, focused upon the herd as it snuffled for pine bark and willow in the gorge below. Elk, sixty head of them, led by an ancient and scarred bull with a rack of antlers as wide and darkly stained as a hangman's gibbet. They were moving north, and some of the cows were heavy with calf. Others were old and ribby, their cheeks hollow and their coats fouled by running wounds. Raif picked a young dun cow, barely out of her calf-spots, who had found a fallen trunk to strip bare and lingered behind the herd. The wind was with him, driving his man scent east. The cow was almost directly below the ridge, lipping bark from the log.

Raif eased his pack to the ground, freeing his hands to loft the spear. The dead man's cloak lay flat across his back like a layer of virgin snow. Orrlsmen were white-winter hunters without peer, and their cloaks were things of wonder in the clanholds. Some said they were cut from the tanned hides of rare white aurochs, their leather lacquered with a secret glaze that shifted color with the wind. Strange that he'd possessed one for so long and yet never hunted beneath it until now.

The head bull lowed as he began the climb out of the gorge, warning stragglers to pick up their pace. The little dun cow hesitated. Raif began his move forward, gliding over the ridge top, mimicking the movement of sliding snow. The dun's head came up, alerted by the sound of a single tumbling piece of scree. Raif stilled. He felt a breeze pass over his Orrl cloak, watched as the dun's gaze passed over it too, her dark eye focusing instead upon the stone he'd dislodged in his descent. Seconds passed. The dun finished chewing the strip of bark she'd pulled from the log. Raif waited. Wary now, the dun didn't return to the log and turned instead to the north to check the progress of the herd. Raif moved as she turned, rippling down the ridge face like the wind. Almost without thought, his eyes focused on the dun's breast, searching out the pale underfur that concealed the ribs.

As the dun's ears twitched in response to some subhuman sound, Raif locked on to her heart. Bigger than a man's and beating more quickly, the dun's heart filled his sights like a torch held to his face. Elk heat enveloped him, and knowledge of her fear took his breath.

The dun bolted. Raif sprang. The downslope sped his acceleration, and for a brief moment he found himself moving faster than the deer. He hefted the spear, leapt. Air passed beneath him as he closed the distance between man and beast. The spear tip found the space between the third and fourth rib, and with eyes focused on a point beyond seeing, he drove the spear home. To the heart.

The elk dropped, and he tumbled forward with her, the spear cracking in two as his weight came down upon it. Blood fountained over his face. The herd panicked, tramping up the north face of the gorge, ripping out bushes and tumbling rocks as they stampeded. A cloud of snow and dust rose around their hooves. Raif slumped over the dun, exhaustion hitting him hard. For several minutes all he could do was breathe. There was a tang of metal in his mouth, but he didn't have the strength to spit.

Eventually his breathing calmed, and he lifted himself up from the dun. His furs and cloak were soaked in blood that was rapidly cooling. He felt light-headed and not at all ready to butcher a three-hundred-pound carcass, but he heard his father's voice utter an old warning—*If you kill it and don't eat it, then it's a shameful waste of life*—and his hunter's instincts took over.

In no mood to preserve the hide, Raif made a cut from throat to groin to spill the guts. The heart slid out atop the lungs, a hunk of muscle with his spear tip still attached. Raif tried not to look at it as he freed the liver and dragged the carcass away from the offal.

Glancing up at the gorge wall, he knew he didn't have the energy to carry the elk to the ridge, so he decided to follow the dry riverbed south until he found a protected area to camp. He ate the liver as he worked, unable to find the usual hunter's joy in savoring the bloody and highly flavored flesh. When he came upon a crop of rocks choking what had once been a tributary of the dead river, he halted. This would do.

It was noon, and the sun was low and very small, almost white in a bone-pale sky. Raif collected firewood with haste, not bothering to search out finer-burning deadwood when greenwood was closer to hand. He knew he shouldn't be making camp so early, but he told himself it made sense. There was a carcass to quarter and meat to cook and cure; slowing himself down for half a day would make little difference.

His knight's sword made short work of the butchering, though it lacked the finesse to winkle meat from between ribs and was as good as useless for skinning. Once he'd built a makeshift firepit of mounded stones, he placed a leg on the fire to roast, and hung strips of meat on willow poles downwind to catch the smoke. That done, he found he had a mind to drink something other than plain water, and filled his only pot with scraps of birch bark, dried berries and springwater and set it upon a warming stone to steep.

Next he set to cleaning his sword. The rituals of hunting were familiar and oddly comforting. Kill. Butcher. Clean. He had carried them out so often he could do them without thought, and that suited him. Or at least he thought it did, until his mind began wandering back to other hunts. He remembered the summer when Dagro Blackhail and his ten best men had ridden south on the rumor of a thirty-stone sow and her sixteen piglets. It was a giant among boars, they said, marked black and silver like the Hailstone itself. Raif grinned at the memory of himself and Drey riding concealed in the hunt party's wake, determined not to miss out on the excitement of bringing down such a beast, and thinking themselves undetectable. By the Stones! They caused mayhem when the sow was finally flushed. Dagro himself drove the beast . . . straight toward the very spot where Raif and Drey were hiding in the wood. Raif learned more curse words that day than in an entire year at his father's hearth. Both their horses bolted, but Drey, all of twelve and still awaiting his man growth, had the presence of mind to fling his spear.

That spear saved their hides. For a mercy it found the sow's throat, and the pain of impact and the shock of bolting horses drove the creature back the way she'd come.

Later, when the kill was made and the great quantity of hog's blood turned the forest loam into mud, Drey and Raif were called into the chief's presence. Raif could still remember Dagro Blackhail's fearsome face, the way the skin on his nose was bubbled with sun blisters and sweat. "Which of you threw this spear?" he demanded, putting his foot to the sow's neck and yanking the Sevrance-marked shaft from sow flesh. "Speak," he roared, when no answer was forthcoming. "If the truth's not given freely I'll whip it from you." Raif clearly recalled Drey touching him then, a brush of fingers against his hip, a warning to stay silent come what may. Then Drey stepped forward.

"Lord Chief," he said, his thin boyish voice making the words sound oddly formal, "the spear was thrown by two hands. My brother's and mine."

Dagro's eyes had narrowed. A full minute passed, and then he grunted. "Aye. 'Tis well said, lad. Here. Take my knife. Cut you and your brother the hunter's portion."

Raif realized many things as he watched Dagro Blackhail watch Drey open the carcass. Dagro *knew* Drey had thrown the spear, and he also knew that Drey had shared the credit to prevent any punishment falling on his younger brother. Drey had won himself immunity from the terrible act of interfering with the chief's hunt. But Raif had not. The full force of Dagro's wrath would have fallen upon him if Drey had not protected him. And Dagro saw that act of protection and was moved by it.

The sow's liver was the sweetest thing Raif had ever eaten. He could still taste it now; the taste of sugar and acorns and love.

Raif felt a prick of pain in the exact center of his spine. Hairs on his scalp rose as a voice said, "Hmm. Legmeat. I think I'll have me some of that. Cut me a portion, boy, and cut it slow as your mam squatting for a leak."

The voice was rough and soft, and it came with a breath foul with salt meat. The sun was in Raif's face, and the man stood behind him so Raif didn't have the benefit of a shadow to gauge his size. He had approached from behind, doubtless drawn by the smoke and scent of fresh meat roasting on the fire. Raif cursed himself for a fool. He'd been so caught up in thinking about Drey he'd lost himself in the past and forgotten that he was camping alone in a place on the farthest edge of clan. Even so, he had ears. And any man who could move along a dry gorge bed and draw a weapon without sound was dangerous.

Still looking dead ahead, Raif said, "Stranger, why don't you put your weapon down and join me? I'd be glad to share my food."

He felt the point of a sword touch his backbone a second time. "So the wee clansman would be glad to share, would he? After he's taken down one of me own elk and scared the rest so witless that they won't come back in a month. Well, excuse me while I piss myself with gratitude. Now cut, boy, before I get tired of holding my sword just so and decide to run you through instead."

Raif leant forward slowly, his mind racing. The stranger had been watching him take down the elk. He sounded like a clansman. Almost. But no sane clansman would lay claim to a herd of elk; they ranged too widely and traveled too swiftly for anyone to own them.

At least he was alone. *I can't let him master me.*

"Not the sword, Clansman. Use your knife."

Raif's hand hovered above the rock-crystal pommel of his sword. "I don't own a knife."

"Well, that's a pretty state of affairs. A fine cloak, a fine sword, and no knife. Why's that, I wonder? Haven't had a chance to steal one yet?"

"No. I lost it in a man's throat." With that Raif grabbed the sword and spun to standing. He found himself facing the ugliest man he had ever seen. Middle height, but grossly broad, with thick shoulders and a fat neck. His upper arms were so wide they stood out from his body like sacks of grain. He was dressed in armor cobbled together from metal pieces and once-living things. Turtle and oyster shells were mounted alongside steel discs and copper rings on a coat of boiled hide. His lower arms were squeezed like sausages into spiraling bullhorns, and his legs were clad in fleece pants beneath a fleece kilt.

But it was his face that made him who he was. He had very black hair, and it was shocking to see it growing in a line down the middle of his face. The tissue of his forehead, nose and left cheek was deeply folded, and scalp hair and lumps of flesh grew from the face-length cleft.

"What's the matter, pretty boy? Never seen a Maimed Man before?" The man touched blades with him; a lightning-fast ring of steel that for some reason made him grin. "Oh. Oh. Oh," he cried, stepping back. "You did steal that sword, I knew it! Damn! I should have put coin on it." He parried forward effortlessly, matching Raif cut for cut.

Raif realized he'd made a mistake. The sword wasn't his weapon of choice, and whilst Drey and his fellow yearman had spent hours every day on the practice court drilling with master-swordsman Shor Gormalin, Raif had only practiced for the bare minimum. Shor Gormalin had warned Raif that once he'd taken his yearman's oath, he'd expect Raif to report to the drillcourt every morning at dawn. But Shor Gormalin was dead. And Raif Sevrance was a traitor to his oath.

The stranger mounted a series of rolling attacks, moving his blade in ever-decreasing circles around Raif's sword. When Raif stepped back, dropping his sword against his body in readiness for a vertical cut, the stranger performed a dancelike move and was suddenly at Raif's blade-side, slashing Raif's knuckles and stealing the momentum from his attack. Angry, Raif struck wide. The stranger danced easily away, only to return with breath-taking quickness and apply his point to Raif's chest.

Blooded twice. What am I doing? Raif turned a jolting attack, both blades touching at their sweet points to produce a strange moaning sound and a handful of sparks.

"Nice blade," commented the stranger, showing no sign of strain. "I think I'll take it in payment for the elk." Exploding into motion, he executed a double turn that drove him side-ways and backward into Raif's unprotected left side, striking Raif with enough force to take the wind from his lungs and drop him to one knee. As Raif rolled back for a counterattack, the stranger drove forward with his sword, opening a hairline cut in Raif's arm and smashing his sword's basket guard into Raif's elegant and unprotected crosshilt. The momentum of the strike sent Raif's blade flying from his grip.

Shor would kill me for losing my weapon.

Before Raif could make a grab for the blade, the stranger hooked the tip with his sword edge and sent it skittering over the rocks. Raif looked wildly around in the free second this gave him. A chunk of unburned log protruded from the firepit. One leap and his hand was upon it. The wood was hot enough to make him wince, and it ignited pain in the old frostbite scars on his palm. The far end of the log was red and smoking, and the stranger looked less happy to see it than if it had been just another blade.

The two circled each other. Raif felt light-headed from lack of sleep, and he could smell the elk blood on him, making him stink like something already dead. When the stranger struck, Raif was ready, barreling forward with no finesse whatsoever, trusting that the man's fear of fire and scorching would force him into stepping back. He was right. Sort of. The stranger did step away . . . but sideways, managing to score a glancing touch on Raif's shoulder as he danced past the smoldering log. Stung with pain and frustration, Raif resisted the urge to lash out. *Think of the elk.*

His gaze met and held the stranger's. The man's eyes were hazel, fine and clear as two drops of rain; it was unnerving to see them in such a face. Deliberately, Raif dropped his gaze, skimming past the strange growths on the man's forehead and cheek, down along his throat . . . to the heart.

The strength of the man's life-force was staggering. Raif felt it hit him like a blow to the gut, forcing him to fling out an arm to steady himself.

He'd forgotten what it was to heart-kill a man.

Metallic saliva squirted across his tongue. Things became known to him, strange things that he could barely understand. The scar on the stranger's face was just the start. Organs and blood vessels were warped and displaced, the lungs mismatched and the spleen elongated like a fish. The heart was large and beating strongly, but it was scarred above the valve, as if an old wound had healed over. And it bulged gently to one side.

Raif calmed himself. However misshapen, the heart was his. Settling the smoldering log in a two-handed grip, he charged. He saw the stranger's eyes widen, saw him raise his basket-hilt sword in defense. An instant passed when Raif smelled scorching leather and he knew he had him, but bright pain exploded in his head, and then he knew nothing but diminishing circles of light as he fell.

Raif awoke retching, and turned his head to vomit. The sight of regurgitated pieces of liver made him vomit again. His head throbbed, and his eyesight was strangely slow to react; he could feel muscles in his irises working to focus his gaze. It was sunset, and the cook fire he'd built earlier was still burning, but now there was nothing but a gnawed bone upon it.

"Don't make me feel bad now," came the voice of the stranger. "You're hardly in a fit state to eat."

Raif blinked. He couldn't understand why one of them wasn't dead.

"I did save a splash of the berry tea. Even took it upon myself to improve it with a bit of hard liquor." The stranger moved into Raif's line of sight. He was holding Raif's sword up to the firelight, inspecting the edge for dents. "It's over there if you want it. 'Course, it's a coin toss whether you should drink it or rub it on that lump. I'd sod it if I were you. Drink the whole damn lot and find myself a hat." He looked thoughtful for a moment. "One of those furry ones made from beaver, with the tail still attached."

Raif felt too queasy to speak. The stranger's face looked hideous in the firelight, the deep cleft swallowing shadows and bristling with coarse black hairs. Raif looked away. He put all his strength into levering himself into a sitting position. Muscles that had lain upon cold stone for several hours were stiff and unresponsive, and his left calf threw a violent cramp.

The stranger did not seem displeased by Raif's pain. Nor did he offer to help. The pot containing the tea was well within his reach, yet he made no effort to pass it. "Nasty things, blows to the head. I've seen men walk about as frisky as spring lambs right after them, only to keel over and die the next day."

Raif could think of nothing to say to that. He looked around. His pack had been rifled through and the contents scattered. The Listener's arrow had been unpacked, handled, judged unworthy, and thrown on the lumber pile ready to be burned. Raif's seal-skin blanket was currently unrolled by the fire, and it had the rumpled look of recent use. The stranger's own pack stood close to the fire, and a weapon stand containing a bewildering array of cloth-bound shapes stood beyond it. A stout hill pony was pin-hobbled to a cleft in a boulder, and was contentedly browsing on mash. Overhead, the sky was rapidly darkening and the first stars were coming to life. The wind was restless with coming night, channeling along the gorge in sudden bursts only to die as quickly as it came. The gorge itself glowed red, revealing layers of ocher and blood marble deposited within its walls.

Raif said suddenly, "What did you do to me?"

The stranger grinned, showing surprisingly even teeth. "That's for me to know and you to bribe from me. Though as I already own your most valuable possession I don't think you've got much to work with. 'Course, I could take that fancy cloak. But I'll have to insist on you washing it first. A great dirty blood-stain tends to spoil the look." He continued to study Raif's sword. "I'll have to say, though, you're pretty fierce with a burning log. God-awful with a sword, but a real demon with raw timber. What are you? The last living member of some clannish woods-men's cult? As you're no knight, that's for sure."

"How come you're so sure I'm clan?"

"Can smell it on you, boy. Clan turned sour. Stinks like all the hells I went through as a bairn."

"So you're clan, too?"

The stranger raised an eyebrow, and for just one moment Raif found himself forgetting about the scars. "There you go again. Asking when you should be bribing." Abruptly, he turned the sword point down and thrust its tip into his pack. "Does it have a name?"

"The sword? No."

"Good. That means I can give it one." His eyes narrowed as he ran his fingers across the hilt, looking for inspiration. After a moment he glanced thoughtfully at Raif. "I think I'll call it Finger."

Raif found his temper coming back as his queasiness subsided. "What makes you so certain you can keep it?"

"I'm not," said the stranger softly. "I saw what you did to that cow. A man capable of such a thing can certainly manage to win back a sword when he has a mind to. The game is seeing when and how."

The stranger sat, the cobbled armor of plate and turtle shells chinking softly as he bent at the waist. He retrieved the little iron pot containing the fortified tea, and drank deeply. He did not pass it to Raif when he was done. "So," he said, wiping his mouth. "Let's see if I can guess your story. Orrlsman, by the look of that cloak—though I wouldn't put it past you to have killed and robbed one. As we've seen today you're no swordsman, and you ain't got the arms of a hatchetman, so I'd say by the look of those callused fingers you're a bowman good and true."

The stranger looked to Raif for confirmation, but didn't seem in the least put out when all Raif did was frown. "So, bowman. Now, you'll excuse me for saying so but you look soddin' rough. Oh, you're pretty enough under that beard and muck, but you ain't had the attentions of a good clanwife in quite a while, I can tell."

"You don't look too good yourself."

The stranger put a palm to his chest. "Me? Not look good? So I take it the love charm hasn't worked. Sod it! That witch swore I'd attract half the young maids in the clanholds. Or was it half the men? I forget."

"I hope for both our sakes it's the maids."

The stranger laughed, throwing back his head in delight. Raif saw evidence of a second band of misshapen flesh, curling down his neck and disappearing beneath his collar. Something white and pearly like a tooth grew just below his ear. Raif shivered. The stranger saw this and his smile ended.

"Oh, you're clan all right. Never seen nothing that wasn't perfect before, eh? Everyone pretty as girls and whole. Gods forbid that a bairn like me could be born amongst you. Little evil troll must have fucked my mother, for no fine clansmen could have fathered me."

Raif dropped his head. Nothing was happening how it should. This man before him should be dead, not shaming him. "I'm sorry."

"Don't be. The world's a hard place, and not once in my life have I known it to be fair. Only thing that's even between men is death; we all get our share of that in the end. Me, I'm lucky to be alive, lucky that this god-ugly face inspired guilt as well as revulsion in me mam. Guilt saved me when me father would not. He was all for setting me on a rock and letting the vultures peck me, yet me mam wouldn't let him. Oh, she wanted to, make no mistake about that. She wanted her teats to dry up quick so she could make another bairn and forget the first one ever existed. But she was gutless when it came to it. Didn't want the stain on her conscience. She would have been glad if me father had stolen me from my crib in the dead of night and murdered me, but he chose to make her party to the deal. And that she couldn't have. Sent me out to the woods to be fostered. Right from one hell into another."

Full night had risen while the stranger spoke, and only the dimming fire provided light. Grains of salt from the earlier cookery ignited every so often, turning the flames green.

"What clan are you from?" Raif asked.

The stranger shook his head. "Ah. Ah. Ah. No questions, remember."

"Fair enough. So how about a trade? Your name for mine?"

The stranger considered this. He wasn't as old as Raif first thought, and there was something vaguely familiar in the set of his jaw. Just as quickly as Raif was seized with the idea, it fled, and he saw nothing but a stranger before him.

"You go first," replied the stranger. "First name only. And if I like the sound of it I'll trade mine."

"Raif."

The stranger opened and closed his mouth, almost as if he had bitten the name from the air and was tasting it. "Raif. Rhymes with safe, and it's good and short and not a bit fancy. I'll take it."

Strangely, Raif felt pleased by this odd pronouncement. No one had ever said anything—good or bad—about his name before.

"Goods for goods, then. I'm Stillborn." The stranger stilled, awaiting a reaction. Raif thought the name suited him, and said so. Stillborn suddenly looked dangerous. "A monstrous name for a monstrous man?"

"No. A strong name. Not easy to forget."

Stillborn thought on Raif's words a long time, and then nodded. "It'll do."

Raif held out his arm and Stillborn leaned over to clasp it.

"So," Stillborn said, straightening up. "You'll be wanting the last of the tea?" Raif nodded. The bull-horns clasped around Stillborn's forearms gleamed wickedly as he deposited the pot by Raif's feet. "Drink deep. Remember what I said about head blows; tomorrow you might be dead."

Raif drank. The liquor was very strong and bore little resemblance to any kind of tea. It stripped the lining from his throat on its way down.

Stillborn watched approvingly, and then reached out toward the timber pile to load more logs on the flames. When Raif saw his hand close around the arrow named Divining Rod he put down the pot. "Don't burn that. It's very old. It was a gift from . . . from a friend."

"A gift, eh?" Stillborn inspected the arrow, running a finger along the flights. "I'll keep it, then." He shoved it in his pack, and resumed loading logs on the fire. "I suppose you're out here looking for Maimed Men?"

Raif didn't answer straight away. The liquor had passed swiftly into his blood, and he reminded himself to be cautious. Tentatively, he felt for the source of pain on the side of his head. A lump, hard and exquisitely tender, made him suck in his breath. "And if I were?"

"Well, you'd need to know a few things first."

"Such as?"

"Maimed Men is what clansmen call us. And if we heard those words on your lips we'd likely kill you for it. We name ourselves Rift Brothers, and you'd be a fool to think we're just another clan."

"I didn't."

"Good." Stillborn pried Raif's sword from his pack and began to oil it with a bit of rag. "The Rift's no pretty clanhold with fine oatfields and clipped grazes. And men harder than clan chiefs rule there. We get the throwaways and the bastards and the oathbreakers—and not just from the clans. We get them all: foreigners, city men, pot boys, whores. They all come north in the end. It's a desperate man who'll travel to the far ends of the earth in search of shelter, and desperate men don't make good friends."

Raif met Stillborn's gaze levelly. The warning had been given . . . and received. The fire was crackling fiercely now, as a new green branch went to the flames. The wind had calmed with the onset of night, and now it blew the smoke through the space between the two men.

"I wouldn't expect much of a welcome if I were you. No one's gonna light a fire for one more clansman. They'll want to know what you can bring them, and as I've already taken your one decent possession you're going to have to think fast about your answer. Oh, and another thing. You're too whole."

There was a light in Stillborn's eyes that made Raif wary. "What do you mean?"

"You know what I mean. Pretty boy like you. All your fingers and toes, and that fine whole nose. The first thing the brothers will do is hold you down and maim you."

"No one's ever called me pretty before. I've taken my share of scars."

"Maybe so. But they won't see that. They'll just see a whole clansman. Nothing missing, nothing bent out of place, and they'll hate you for it. They'll have you pinned and under a knife before you can say *God help me*. And that's one place you definitely don't want to be. I've seen them take an arm off a man in their frenzy. Hands. Earlobes. Eyes. Depends whether the raiding's been good. Good season, plenty of spoils, everyone happy and drinking themselves soft, and they might let you off with a toe. Poor season and they'll take a hand. And I'm sorry to tell you this, Raif, but winter's been a long, dry season."

Raif watched Stillborn's eyes as he spoke, searching for signs of deception. The Maimed Man's face was hard, but there was nothing hidden within it.

"You have to decide how much it's worth, becoming one of us. Can you go back? Accept penalty for whatever trespass brought you here, and live a different kind of life? Because if you can, *do*. There's nothing noble or heroic about being a Maimed Man. The only reason to be here is because you've got no options left."

Raif almost smiled. Bitterly. He wanted to ask Stillborn what brought and kept *him* here, but he was learning the ways of the Maimed Men already: no questions about a man's past. He said, "If I returned to my clan they would kill me. I have nowhere to go and no one to turn to. I'd say I have no options left."

Stillborn nodded slowly, weighing the resolution in Raif's

eyes. Abruptly he seemed to come to some decision and stood. "Drink the rest of the brew. It'll go easier on you that way."

Raif read the intent in Stillborn's eyes, and it almost made him bolt. *I made my choice when Ash left me. If this is the price, then so be it.* He cupped the pot in his hands, but in the end decided not to drink. Stillborn was drawing close with the sword, and Raif wanted to savor the blood throbbing through him. He wanted to remember for always what it felt like to be whole.

SIXTEEN

Leaving Blackhail

Efie spotted a fly buzzing in the rafters and set her gaze upon it. Mad Binny was naked and she didn't know where else to look. Of course, that treacherous fly would go and start flitting past Binny's head . . . and oh dear *no* . . . it landed on Binny's shoulder. And that meant she had to look at those breasts. Effie tried to keep her face from reacting, but it wasn't easy and she felt distinctly wooden as she listened to Mad Binny speak. All she could think of was: *I hope I don't grow any of those.*

Mad Binny was sitting in a copper bath with only the shallowest depth of water to cover her, cleaning herself with soapweed and a cloth. She'd filled the bath for Effie, but Effie had refused to use it—she wasn't about to be naked while Mad Binny stood over her and watched—so Mad Binny had called her a fool and took to the water herself. Now she was working up a lather on her neck, talking all the while about various herbs and potions that could be added to a person's bathwater to make them sleepy or refreshed.

"Then there's the curatives," advised Mad Binny. "Some of the finest skin cures are best taken in the bath. Let me see now . . ." Mad Binny soaped a deep and extremely hairy armpit while she thought. Effie felt an uncomfortable mix of repulsion and fascination. Once she'd started looking she couldn't seem to stop. In theory she knew about all the changes a girl went through to become a woman; Letty Shank and Florrie Horn had drawn pictures in the dirt, placing little burrs of thistle where the hair was supposed to grow. But the reality was so much more unsettling. Mad Binny was a large woman and line drawings didn't do justice to all the squelchy flesh and bristly hair. Effie frowned. She was quite sure Raina wouldn't look like that. Raina would be beautiful, and quite bald except for her head.

". . . And then there's pokeroot. Toss a few hands of the rootflesh in a tub, let it steep a while, and you'll have a bath for curing scabies. Now this—" Mad Binny leant over the side of the bath and snatched up a handful of fragrant dried flowers "—is for nothing other than making a woman feel like a girl. Sweet lavender. Raises the spirits and makes you unaccountably attractive to men." Crushing the dried stalks in her fist, she scattered them into the bathwater, releasing a light and pointy scent. "I may steal Drey away from you yet."

Effie was immediately attentive. "Drey's coming?"

"Oh, yes. Didn't I say? That's what the bath was for. Today's the day you leave for Dregg."

No, she had *not* said, and she knew very well she hadn't. Mad Binny was like that: sly and contrary. She liked to keep her visitors in a perpetual state of confusion. Effie knew better than to let her irritation show: she *would* have taken a bath if only Mad Binny had told her the truth. She'd only seen Drey once since he'd returned to the roundhouse, and that was only for a few minutes since he feared to stay too long and run the risk of discovery by Mace Blackhail.

"Hand me the drying cloth, Effie. And you needn't look so crab-appled. Not my fault you weren't listening when I explained about today."

Effie handed Mad Binny the cloth. She was beginning to realize there were advantages to being considered mad. No one could take you to task. You could say whatever you liked, tell lies till your face turned blue, and everyone would dismiss it with an "Aah well, Mad Binny *is* mad." Effie didn't think Mad Binny was mad at all. Effie thought Mad Binny was one of the cleverest people she had ever met. She lived exactly how she wanted to, got clansfolk to traipse leagues through the snow to bring her fresh meat and supplies in return for one of her cures, and she had no responsibilities whatsoever and no one but herself to care for. Effie glanced around the crannog's main hall, looking admiringly at the low ceilings, the blackened beams and damp-warped walls. *And* Mad Binny got somewhere wonderfully cavelike to live in.

"I haven't made you a pack for the journey," Mad Binny warned, thankfully pulling on a dress. "I'm not your mother, you know. If Raina doesn't bring anything then you're on your own. No one's paid me for your keep, and I can't recall as anyone's thanked me either."

"Thank you, Binny," Effie said innocently.

"Oh, you're a devilish minx, that's for sure. Run outside and watch for Drey—and stun me some pike while you're at it."

Effie was glad to do as she was told. Outside, on the little rotting pier that stretched over Cold Lake, you could see for leagues in all directions. It was mid-morning, and a light wind blew off the lake, thinning the last of the mist. The lake's surface was a battleground of wet and breaking ice, with hackled plates riding atop each other and free ice floating against the wind in stretches of open water. Effie liked the sounds the ice made as it disintegrated: the snapping of plates and the fizzing of bubbles as air escaped to the surface. Almost it wasn't bad to be outside. She was aware of her heart beating a fraction more strongly than usual, but that was all. She was close to the crannog and to safety, could run back any time she chose—and, more importantly, Drey was on his way.

She missed her brothers fiercely. Nothing had been the same since Da had been killed in the badlands. They had been four then; her, Da, Drey and Raif. Now they were down to two.

Soon to be one, said a little voice inside her. *After today you're on your own.*

Effie picked up the mallet and wished for fish. It would have been good to hit something just then. Now she didn't know whether to look forward to Drey's arrival or not. She was going to Dregg. *Dregg*. A stranger's clan, leagues to the south, with a roundhouse built from birdseye limestone, and the words *We fight as easily as we dance* as their boast. Oh, Raina said it was a fine place and Xander Dregg a fair chief, but it wasn't home, and the shankshounds weren't there, and there'd be no Drey to look out for her. Effie ran thin fingers over the mallet head. What was it Raif used to say about Drey? He always waited, that was it. Now there'd be no one for him to wait for anymore.

Feeling something stinging behind her eyes, Effie smashed at the lake water with the mallet—just in case there were fish below the surface.

As she rubbed droplets of icy water from her sleeve, she spied a mounted man approaching from the southeast. Crouching very still, she waited until she could be sure it was Drey.

"Effie," he called, when she stood up. "I swear you've grown as tall as this horse."

He reined in his mount and dismounted, and Effie dashed down the pier to hug him. He smelled of neat's-foot oil and tanned leather, and he remembered she didn't like to be kissed and hugged her double hard instead. When he pulled back and held her at arm's length to study her, she studied *him* as well. He looked older now, more like Da. His chestnut hair was braided into a warrior's queue, and it was woven with silver wire. His plate armor was old but well made, its glancing surfaces free of embellishment, its rolled edges lightly silvered to ward off canker. Da's elkskin greatcoat lay well on his shoulders, the large felted collar brushed and gleaming. Seeing Drey like this, war-dressed and fully armed, it struck her for the first time that her eldest brother was a grown man, not unpleasing to look at, and sure to attract attention from clan maids. An unworthy stab of possessiveness made her want to drive the imaginary girls away. Drey was hers, not the property of some silly and fluttering maid.

He took her hand, and she felt the calluses and scars there. He glanced at the sun still rising in the east and then at the door of the crannog. Effie could see a decision being made on his face. "Little one," he said finally, sitting down on one of the pier posts so he could be at eye level with her, "you don't have to go to Dregg, not if you don't want to. Tell me now, and I'll put you on Fox's back and we'll ride straight home. No one will hurt you, I swear it, even if I have to camp outside your chamber every night."

That was a lot of words for Drey, and he didn't speak them easily. The sons of Tem Sevrance had never been good with words. Even so, Effie knew what it cost him to speak them. He was a Blackhail hammerman, a sworn warrior of eight seasons, celebrated for saving Arlec Byce on Bannen field and holding the Ganmiddich roundhouse with a force of just eleven. Now he sat before her, proposing to tie himself to the roundhouse like an old man—for they both knew that he could not be absent for as much as one night and hope to keep her safe. Mace Blackhail would not allow it.

Drey reached for her hair, curling one of the auburn strands around his finger. "You and me, little one. Just you and me."

Effie looked down at her feet. She couldn't look at him or speak. He felt it too: the loss of Raif and Da. They were the only two left, and she'd been a selfish ninny to think that their parting would affect only her. A sudden memory filled her: the sight of Drey striding through the greatdoor on his return from Bannen. Men surrounded him, pulling him this way and that, wanting his opinion on wounded men and damaged blades, yet he had stopped in the midst of it all, his gaze sweeping across the entrance hall . . . in search of her.

Effie breathed deeply. She knew with unshakable certainty that she must be strong. She could not allow him to halve his life because of her. "I'm looking forward to going to Dregg," she said, aware that the words were coming out a little too fast but unable to stop them. "Raina's told me all about the dancing and . . . and the bones. And she said that after a few months all the fuss would die down, and then you can come and bring me home, and everyone would have forgotten what happened to Cutty and Nelly Moss, and everything will be all right."

Drey's steady gaze almost undid her. He looked as if he knew just how little it would take to make her cry. "I was ten when our mother died," he said quietly. "It happened suddenly. No one was expecting it. She carried you well and high, and everyone guessed you'd be a girl, and when she went into labor we didn't know to be afraid. Then what should have taken hours turned into half a day, and Anwyn came out to speak to Da. That's when I snuck in to see her. She was so pale, Effie, and scared. There was no blood, not then, but she knew she was failing. She smiled when she saw me, and you know what she said?"

Effie shook her head.

"She said, *Drey, you're the eldest and that means you've had the most love. This little one I'm carrying will have the least. Make up for it. Love her for me when I'm gone.*" Drey was very still for a moment—the only thing moving was a muscle deep within his neck. "The loving is the easy thing, Effie. It's knowing how best to look after those you love that's hard." He looked at her knowingly. "Now I realize I'm your slightly slow-witted elder brother, and you've probably fooled me many times. But not in this. Bones? You're excited about going to Dregg because of bones?"

Effie smiled; it was a bit shaky but still counted. "*Fossils*, Drey. They have this pit outside the Dregghouse that started out as a defensive trench, but they kept finding old bones and treasures in it, and now it's as deep as a mine."

"Mm."

Drey didn't say anything else, and his silence made her speak the truth. "I don't mind going to Dregg, not really. I'll be frightened a bit at first, but Raina said her sister and the chief's wife will look after me, and I won't have to worry about anyone hurting me."

Drey nodded slowly. All the while they'd been speaking he had been curling a strand of her hair around his finger, and now he let it go. "I know you'll be safer there, little one. That's why I agreed to let Raina arrange it. It doesn't mean I have to like it, though. And it doesn't mean that I can't ride to Dregg any day I choose and bring you back." He stood. "Come on. Let's say your farewells to Mad Binny."

Effie followed him down the pier. She'd won, but it didn't feel like much of a victory.

The interior of the crannog smelled like flowers. Mad Binny was cooking up a love potion, either that or a batch of pollen butter. Effie hoped it was the butter. She didn't believe the love potions worked, of course, but that didn't mean she wanted Mad Binny using one on Drey. Thankfully, Drey seemed unaffected. He bowed his head respectfully to Mad Binny, and thanked her for taking care of his sister. *His* thanks were accepted a lot more graciously than hers, Effie noticed. Mad Binny was a different person when there was a man about, and even went so far as to serve Drey a cup of best malt with her own two hands. She surprised Effie even further by handing her a full measure of the honey-colored liquid. "Down it in one, girl. For the journey."

Effie knew a command when she heard one, and threw the liquid into the back of her mouth. It smoked on her windpipe, its vapors rising straight to her head and releasing a tension that she hardly knew was there. As she went to fetch her cloak and meager bundle, Drey and Mad Binny exchanged a knowing glance.

"What's couch grass good for?" Mad Binny asked as Effie came to stand by the door.

"For the kidneys and anything to do with making water. You boil the root to make a tincture."

Mad Binny folded her arms across her chest. "Good enough." Despite the gruffness of her voice she seemed pleased. "You've a memory like a Withyman, Effie Sevrance, I'll give you that. Now. See that cloth bag on the peg. That's yours to take. No food, mind. Just a few herbs and simples for doctoring. I've heard you can't gather much except dandelions around Dregg." She sniffed her disapproval. "Well, best be gone now. I won't wish you a good journey, as we both know you're not likely to have one." With that, Mad Binny ushered Effie and Drey out the door.

By the time Effie had thought of a reply the door was closed behind her. Drey held her hand. "Best pull up your hood. There's clouds moving south from the Want." Effie stuffed the little cloth bag containing the herbs into her pack and let Drey lead her to his horse.

The malt liquor had been a clever trick, she thought as she clung to Drey's waist whilst he galloped Orwin Shank's fine black stallion south across the Wedge. She was outside with the open spaces of the clanhold spread for leagues around her, and she knew she should be feeling the first stirring of panic—the nearest building was now an hour's ride to the north, and that meant terrible things could happen and she wouldn't be able to run for shelter—but all she could feel was a sort of sleepy sense of concern. She hiccuped. Outside wasn't really so bad, not when you were on a horse and your brother's head was blocking the forward view. Couldn't really see much from the sides, either, with your hood up.

When she heard Drey say, "Slide down, little one. We're here," she could hardly believe they'd arrived at the farthest edge of the Oldwood. Drey grinned and told her she'd been asleep, but she didn't believe that for one second. Effie Sevrance *never* slept outside.

Still, she yawned unaccountably when Raina came forward to help her from the horse. "Your cheeks are flushed," she said. "And you smell of hard liquor. What's that madwoman been doing to you?"

Effie shrugged. She wasn't sure she liked Mad Binny, but she wasn't about to rat on her either.

Raina's gray eyes looked especially dark and flinty, and Effie suddenly realized she had spoken sharply because she was worried. Looking around the timbered bank, Effie saw two men standing by a covered wagon hitched to a pair of matched ponies. The smaller of the two men she recognized as Druss Ganlow, Merritt Ganlow's son, and the second had the look of an Orrlsman, if his pale cloak and antler bow were anything to go by. Druss saw Effie watching him and raised a hand in greeting. He was a stoutly built man with the beginnings of a belly, and a baby fluff of fine red hair. Effie did not think he'd given his oath to the clan, nor was he likely to. Druss Ganlow was known as a trader. When Drey walked over to meet him, Druss clasped his arm and the two men fell into easy conversation. *Of course, Drey was at the badlands when Druss's father died.*

Sometimes it was easy to forget the deep and silent connections that bound Blackhail as a clan.

"There's food and blankets and spare clothes in the wagon," Raina said to Effie. "I thought the journey would go easier on you if you had a roof overhead. Of course, you don't have to stay in the wagon if you don't want to. You can always ride up front with Druss and Clewis Reed. The journey will be pretty slow by pony cart. Druss reckons that with good weather he'll have you there in under a week. He's a good man, Effie, and he needn't have done this for us. He's got a nice little run heading west to Orrl for fresh meat, and the last thing he needs is a dogleg to Dregg this time of year. Be nice to him. And pray the weather holds."

Effie nodded. She was beginning to feel a bit sick.

Raina saw this and smiled—her first since Effie had arrived. "Oh dear," she said, brushing hair from Effie's face. "Whatever you do, *don't* throw up in the back of the wagon. We don't want to try Druss's goodness *that* far."

They both laughed, and all three men turned to look at them. Raina put an arm around Effie and guided her toward them. "Come on. I don't believe you've met Clewis yet."

Drey watched Raina approach, and there was something in his look that gave Effie a small thrill of realization. He'd dressed in his finest clothes for Raina Blackhail.

"Have you told Drey about the Maimed Man at Black Hole?" Raina asked Druss as she came to a halt by the wagon. If she had noticed Drey's attention, she did not show it, merely put her foot upon the mounting step and gave her attention to Druss Ganlow.

Druss shrugged. "Nothing to tell, except I heard that one of the miners spied a lone horseman on the ridge east of the pit. Said he was riding one of those shaggy little ponies the Maimed Men are known for."

Drey immediately became serious. Black Hole was the last open silver mine in the clanholds. Blackhail had mined silver in the balds for two thousand years, and the clan's wealth had once been dependent upon it. Mordrag Blackhail, the Mole Chief, had dug the first foot of earth from Black Hole with his own two hands and had used the first nugget of silver mined to forge a bracelet for his child bride. The trouble with the silver mines was their location: in the balds far north of Blackhail. They were four days' hard ride from home. Effie didn't know much about Black Hole for the men who lived there kept themselves separate from the rest of the clan. They lived in queer little shanties with sparkly lodestone walls and only a few of them had oaths. The miners came to the roundhouse twice a year, trading cartloads of raw ore for supplies.

"Did the miners give chase?" Drey asked.

Again Druss shrugged. He was dressed strangely for a Hailsman, with no colors or badges to show his clan, just a short cloak of brown greasewool and a set of bleached leathers beneath. "Can't say. I only heard the story briefly." His green eyes, so like his mother's, twinkled brightly, and for a moment Effie was reminded of her uncle, Angus Lok. "Probably nothing to worry about. No one's going to make raid on Black Hole. Only thing they'd come away with is a wagonload of raw ore. No smelting gets done up there."

Effie watched Drey nod in agreement, and wondered why he couldn't see what was obvious to her: Druss Ganlow wasn't speaking the truth.

"Still," Drey said. "I'll speak to Mace about it. Get him to run a patrol from the northern borderhold. Check on the miners every few days."

Druss nodded. "That's as well." He rubbed his nose with the back of his hand. "I think we'd best be off. Clewis doesn't like the look of those clouds. What d'you call 'em, Clew? Dark horses. Says there's no way of telling what they'll bring and when they'll bring it." Scratching the stubble on his chin, Druss looked to the Orrlsman for confirmation.

Clewis Reed had positioned himself to the rear of the wagon, and from the way he stood and the manner in which he held his horn bow, Effie guessed he was standing guard. His Orrl cloak was pale as mist, softly shadowed with the color of storm clouds and old snow. Clewis himself was tall and gaunt, and he carried the longest bow Effie had ever seen. It was a good foot taller than he was, backed with clarified calf's hide that let the greenish tint of the horn show through. He nodded mournfully toward the sky. "Day's half done. Be lucky if we can put two leagues of road behind us afore dark."

Druss smiled easily at Drey as he swung himself up onto the driver's seat. "An Orrlsman has spoken, and you learn quickly to ignore them at your peril. Effie, be a good lass and squeeze yourself in the back. I knocked together a little pallet for you to sit on. Should be good and snug as long as you watch for nails."

Effie looked to Raina and then Drey. It was happening too quickly. There had to be something more before she left.

Raina guided her toward the back of the wagon, finding little excuses to touch her hair, her arm, her cheek. "I'll come and visit when all the fuss dies down. I'll be there by spring thaw, just you wait and see."

Raina wasn't speaking the truth either, just saying wishes out loud. Effie looked down at her feet. The wagon's wheels had gouged tracks in the soft mud bank, and some enterprising blackbird was scouting the ruts for worms. Strange how she didn't feel sick anymore, just sort of heavy and achy in the head. *Wintergreen leaves boiled in water would cure that*, she thought inanely.

"Take care. And give my love to my sister."

Effie nodded. She didn't look up. After a long moment Raina squeezed her shoulder and walked away.

"So, little one," came Drey's voice. "Are you going to promise you won't forget me?"

More nodding. The blackbird was pulling a worm from the mud.

"You know, I don't think I've ever told you how much you look like our mother."

That made her look up.

Drey smiled, but it was a serious thing, quickly done. "What I remember most is her hair. The exact same color as yours."

He looked at her and waited.

He was good at waiting and this time he won, for she couldn't bear the quiet and the stillness and broke it by rushing forward to hug him.

"Just you and me," he murmured before he pulled away.

And then Clewis Reed's hands were upon her waist, hefting her into the back of the wagon, and pulling the oiled canvas closed behind her. In the sudden darkness she could see nothing and smell much. Men had pissed here once, and the air was scratchy with hay spores and sawdust. She smelled the food Raina had packed for her before her eyes could make out the shape of the pack. Honey cakes, roast goose and fresh bread. A supper fit for a chief, not a child.

It was a shock when Druss cracked the whip and the wagon lurched into motion. Everything except her and her packs had been tied down, and Effie scrambled for something secure to hold on to. She could feel the wagon turning, hear Druss's voice as he coaxed a better pace from the ponies. Wheel axles squealed underfoot, and everywhere wood creaked and shuddered as the wagon rolled down the bank.

As her eyes grew accustomed to the dimness, Effie leaned forward to push back the canvas flap. Then something stopped her. She knew what she'd see if she looked out and knew how it would make her feel. Better to go like this. Knowing Drey was standing at the top of the bank, waiting until the wagon passed beyond sight was one thing. Seeing it was something else.

Settling herself on the pallet Druss had constructed, Effie gave herself time to grow accustomed to the motion of the wagon. Looking down the length of the wagon bed, she saw she wasn't the only cargo Druss was hauling south. Sealed crates and lidded wicker baskets were stowed to the ribbing. Idly, she tried to open one of the baskets but found it bound with knotted rope. She sniffed it. No smell. Lacking anything better to do she untied the cloth bag Mad Binny had given her. Inside she found comfrey, woundheal, lily of the valley, cowslip, barberry, witch hazel and willow: all tied neatly into little sprigs. Effie smiled. Mad Binny had given her the basics of a healer's chest.

The day wore on, and the wagon turned onto a flat trail and the ride eased enough for Effie to feel hungry. She ate three honey cakes and one goose wing—in that order. Afterwards she felt thirsty but she couldn't find any water, and felt shy about calling out to Druss or Clewis Reed. Pulling Raina's blankets about her, she settled down to sleep.

It was growing dark, and the gentle rolling of the wagon made her drowsy. Effie thought about what Drey had said as she drifted into sleep. If she looked like Mam and Drey looked like Da . . . then who did Raif look like?

Her dreams had no answers, and when she woke later to the sudden stilling of the wagon, she'd forgotten even asking the question.

SEVENTEEN

Maimed Men

"How about a trade?" Raif said to Stillborn as they walked the little black pony down a steep gorge. "You tell me something I want to know and I'll tell you something in return."

Stillborn thought carefully on this. It was something Raif had come to appreciate about the Maimed Man during the three days they'd been traveling together: Stillborn was one of the few men he'd ever met who actually *thought* about what you said and then thought some more about his answer. After a time, Stillborn nodded. "I get to ask first. And I don't guarantee an answer if I don't like the sound of your question."

Raif nodded gravely as if he'd considered the counteroffer carefully. They both knew he had no bargaining power here, but there were rules of form to be maintained. "Go ahead."

Stillborn was quiet for some time as he led the pony down a slope of crumbling shale. It was mid-morning, or close to it, and a tide of dark clouds hid the sun. Sharp little winds gusted along the gorge wall, rolling scree and uprooting weeds. They were close to the bottom of the gorge, and there was little to see except cliffs of rock rising in warped lines above them. There had been water here once, Raif guessed, for the lower rocks were smooth and the scree at the bottom had been rounded into pebbles. Overhead, the cliffs were rougher and the making of the world was exposed. Tiers of stone, minerals, sand, fossils and ancient lava flows could be read like history within the rock.

When they reached a level platform just above the detritus-filled trough at the bottom of the gorge, Stillborn turned to eye Raif. As always, there was the shock of seeing the man's face, the flesh stretched and seamed as if someone had cut a strip out of his face and sewn together the remains. Stillborn saw Raif's reaction, and a hard sort of weariness showed briefly in his eyes.

He surprised Raif by asking, "Do you have brothers?"

Raif nodded. "One."

"And do you love him?" Something else was now lighting Stillborn's eyes, but Raif couldn't tell what. Hunger, perhaps. But that made no sense.

Raif thought of Drey. He said quietly, "Yes."

"And have you ever hurt him, this brother who you love?"

Here was the question Raif was trading for; he could see it in the way Stillborn put his hand on the pony. There was too much tension in the fingers for a man just patting a horse. But what to say about Drey? What brothers didn't hurt each other growing up? Fights and irritation were the other side of love. Still, Raif knew what Stillborn meant by the question: He didn't want to hear if Raif had bruised Drey's shins or called him names in anger. No. It was the larger thing Stillborn was concerned with: Have you betrayed his love and trust? Raif recalled Drey that day on the greatcourt, stepping forward to second his brother's oath. The old pain moved like a sword tip in his chest. "I've hurt him. Yes."

Stillborn nodded very slowly, as if Raif had given him an answer to a problem he had considered for years. "Yes, that's how it is," was all he said. Reaching inside one of the pony's saddlebags, he took out the last of the roasted elk. The tenderloin was lean and bloody, and Stillborn bit into it like a sausage. "Well," he said through red teeth. "Claim your debt."

Raif considered his question. Strange how he no longer thought he'd got a bargain. "How did you stop me," he said, "when I went for your . . . chest . . . with the log? Your sword was too far back, and I was moving too fast."

The Maimed Man grinned. "Hold this," he said, thrusting the tenderloin into Raif's right hand. With a lightning-fast movement he pulled a small round-faced hammer from his belt. "This beauty did the damage." Stillborn nodded toward Raif's head. "Can draw her faster than a Sull draws his sword—and with me left hand, no less. Soon as you reached for the log, I smelled trouble. You had that mad look in your eye, you know, the one that says *You're mine, bastard*. So I drew the old bonecracker and had it moving by the time you charged. Your fault you looked only to the sword. 'Course, it's only to be expected. Clansmen never imagine a man will fight two-handed. Now the Sull are another thing. Sword and longknife, that's how they fight in a bind. Beautiful it is to look at. Blade and shield. The tricky part is knowing which weapon is playing the part of the blade and which is the shield. And when you've got that figured they go and switch it on you—right in the middle of a fight. Right unsporting it is."

Raif looked at the hammer. It looked like something Longhead would use to knock in nails.

"You're right. It's no pretty longknife, that's for sure. But I find nothing works better when it comes to breaking a man's head." Stillborn's gaze was almost loving as he returned the hammer to his belt. "I'm renaming it in your honor, by the way. I think I'll call it Skull."

Raif couldn't quite manage to look honored. For the first

time since they'd started down the gorge wall the pain of his missing finger threatened to unman him. It flared white-hot where Stillborn had cut with the Forsworn sword. Raif sucked in breath. *Don't look*, he warned himself. *Nothing to see but bandages and fresh air*. But still he looked, down at his left hand, where the smallest of his fingers had been halved. It had stopped bleeding some time during the second night, but fluid still wept from the stitches and the bandages were damp. Stillborn had been careful with the skin, making his first incision just below the nail and then rolling back the skin to the middle knuckle so there was enough to cover the bone stump. Raif had not been conscious during the stitching. Blinding pain had robbed him of his wits. He awoke later in the night from a nightmare where his hand was being eaten by the monster the Listener had shown him beneath the ice.

Reality was worse. That first night the knuckle swelled to the size of a kidney, so full of blood the skin seemed almost black. Now the skin *was* black, necrotizing around the edges of the cut. Raif hadn't slept through the night in three days. And he did not expect to sleep through this one when it came.

Stillborn saw the whiteness of his face. "Had to do it, Raif. Either that or let them take you for an arm."

With an effort of will Raif mastered the pain. "I see *you're* whole."

"Me? I'm fuck-ugly. That counts as a missing leg."

There was nothing Raif could say to that, and he handed the tenderloin back to Stillborn to free up his hand for the waterskin. Raif drank while the Maimed Man ate. They'd filled the waterskins at a small rill they'd found emptying into the gorge. The water was salty and left him just as thirsty as before. "When do we get to the Rift?"

Stillborn wagged his head at the cliff wall. "This *is* the Rift. Beginnings of it, anyway. Land splits in two. This trench keeps getting deeper and deeper until there's no end to it. Goes right down to hell, they say, and the abyss that lies beneath."

Raif glanced down at the gorge floor with its house-deep litter of scree, petrified trees, elk antlers, bones and rocks. "Shouldn't we be heading up, then?"

"No. We're on the right path. Be there before dark." Stillborn smacked the pony's rump. "Come on, girl. You know the way from here."

The little party moved forward, and Raif realized that they were indeed on some sort of path. At first he thought it was just a natural staggering of the cliff, but when they rounded a projection and he saw the path curving eastward for leagues, keeping its level while the gorge dropped away beneath, he began to wonder. Could this have been cut by man? For some reason he thought of the Listener, and the people he had spoken of. The Old Ones.

The path was narrow, but it didn't seem important until the drop grew deep enough to kill anyone falling into it. Raif felt the updrafts rising, drying his face and setting his damaged hand on fire. He was walking behind Stillborn and the pony, and he found himself hugging the cliff. After an hour's trekking the drop became so deep and sheer that Raif could no longer see where it ended. Shadows had taken the place of the gorge floor. *A man wouldn't just be killed if he fell now*, he thought. *He'd be lost.*

Stillborn and the pony seemed unaffected by the danger. The Maimed Man had stripped off his makeshift armor and now walked in felted tunic and kilt. The Forsworn sword hung at his waist, the chunk of rock crystal mounted on its pommel gleaming darkly in the gray light. He was eating again, this time some of the crackling he'd built a special hot fire to fry last night. The matched bullhorns encircling his forearms had been oiled with the leftover grease, and the black horn looked rich and newly taken. Raif watched him. He knew Stillborn was a strong man, and quick, but he still wasn't sure how the Maimed Man had managed to best him. Never before had Raif had a heart-kill thwarted. He'd thought, foolishly perhaps, that once he had a man's heart in his sights that was it. Now he knew different. He wasn't as invincible as he'd thought.

Unsure how that made him feel, Raif trekked the next few hours in silence, his head low, his thoughts circling around his past.

Afternoon darkened into dusk, and what little moisture the air held began condensing on lone weeds that grew from cracks in the path. Scents deepened with the coming of night, and Raif could smell metal ores bleeding salts into the rock. When the wind changed he detected pitch smoke. The scent deepened as the path rose and swung out to accommodate a great bulge in the Rift Wall. Raif felt vulnerable in the darkness, too exposed to the Eye of God in this place where the continent split. Even Stillborn seemed to feel something, for his steps were less hearty and his hand went often to the pony for comfort.

The sky was alive with stars, thousands upon thousands, teeming like ants across the night. Raif watched them, noticing what he had never seen before; not all of them shone blue-white. Some were red as blood.

When the small party rounded the curve in the Rift Wall, Raif was not prepared for what he saw. Hundreds of torches burned in a city honeycombed into the cliff. Immediately Raif thought of the time he'd broken into a termite mound with Bitty Shank, recalling how the dust had risen like smoke as swarms of white insects poured from the break. He remembered the cross section he'd broken into with the pine log; the warren of passageways and cells that had riddled the mound like mine shafts. That's what the city looked like: the inside of that mound.

The Rift Wall was tiered into vast ledges hewn from live rock. Scores of caverns pocked the cliff wall, their interiors dark as pits, their outer rims cratered and flaking. The ledges and caverns were accessed by a shambling web of stone steps, cane ladders, rope bridges and hoists. Great portions of the city had caved in to rubble, and further to the east an entire tier had collapsed, creating boulders the size of barns. Cracks ran and forked through the remaining structures like fault lines, black as the Rift itself.

Raif's gaze traveled across deep-set halls and stone arcades. Nothing he had ever seen, not even the city of Spire Vanis, was less like clan than this place.

"Aye. It's pretty in the torchlight," Stillborn said, continuing forward.

Raif had little choice but to follow him. As they drew nearer he saw Stillborn was heading toward a cleared space in the middle terrace where a massive bonfire burned, and men flickered in and out of darkness as they moved around the flames.

Suddenly a sharp retort sounded on the path ahead, a crack like shattering glass. Fire flared into existence twenty paces ahead of the pony. Stillborn shouted something at the top of his voice as he worked furiously to calm the little horse. Raif stood his ground. He guessed that whatever substance had been dropped or fired had been done so expertly, to both warn and illuminate the intruders. During the brief seconds when heat and light touched his face he knew he was being watched.

The fire quickly died, and the pony danced warily over the smoking rock. Stillborn was not happy. The scar on his face pulsed ominously. "It's that fat bastard Yustaffa. Knows it's me. Yet sends his cronies to scare the life out of the pony."

"Where did the shot come from?"

Stillborn waved an impatient hand. "Above. Above. There's lookouts on the cliff." Angry as he was, he spoke soft words to the pony, ushering the little creature forward at a careful pace. "I warned you, Clansman," he said, turning on Raif quite suddenly. "Whatever comes of this don't say you weren't warned."

Raif tucked his head low. There was nothing to do but carry on.

A meet party gathered around the bonfire as they approached. Live steel glowed orange, and hammers and weapons stranger than hammers cast eerie shadows across the rock floor. All present were silent, waiting. A few were armored, but most were cloaked and wrapped in skins against the coldness of the night. You couldn't see that none of them were whole, for the flickering light cut pieces from them all. Raif found his attention drawn to one man, a small wiry figure who stood away from the main body of men yet still managed to be its center.

"Stillborn!" came a high male voice. "I heard your pony got a firing. Too bad you didn't make yourself known sooner." A fat man dressed in beaver fur stepped forward. "Could have saved a little hoof."

Someone snorted. A few near the back laughed. The slight figure in the shadows did not move.

Stillborn stared at the fat man, and in his own good time looked away. "Unload the meat," he said to Raif.

Raif was glad of something to do. The attention of the Maimed Men was making him sweat. Now he was close enough to them to see their imperfections: a missing hand, a clubbed foot, a broken and badly reset jaw, cheek flesh eaten away by the bite, a humped and twisted back. The pain in Raif's missing finger flared hotly as he unpacked the sides of frozen elk he and Stillborn had cached from his kill. There was a lot of meat, even considering he and the Maimed Man had roasted whatever they fancied and been none too careful with what was left. The pony was glad to be relieved of her load, and began bucking and shaking her head. She'd need to be scrubbed to get rid of the smell.

Stillborn stood silent whilst the elk was unloaded at his feet. His face was hard and his gaze never left one man: the figure waiting in the shadows. When all the pieces of iced-over carcass had been arrayed, he dropped his fist toward them. "I bring meat, new-killed. Enough for sixty men. What have you brought since I've been gone, Traggis Mole?"

The Maimed Men around the fire grew very still. The fat man in beaver fur opened his mouth to speak, then thought better of it. All eyes turned to the figure in the shadows. Uncloaked and seen in silhouette, Traggis Mole seemed whole. Light from the flames did not touch him as he said, "I don't make account of myself to any man, Stillborn. And if you ask that question again I'll see you dead for it."

Tension lit the crowd. Men shifted weight between their feet, sword hands twitching and tongues flicking out to wet dry lips. The fat man drew a sword breaker—a foot and a half of spike-toothed steel forged to trap and break a longsword—and suddenly he didn't look fat any more. "Will you take the floor with me, Stillborn?" he asked in his high, musical voice. "I see you found a new sword for me to kill."

Stillborn's gaze flickered from the fat man's face to his weapon. Raif had only seen one other sword breaker in his life; the treasure of the Gnash chief, Nairry Gnash. Clan did not possess the knowledge to make them. They were said to be forged only in the city of Hanatta in the Far South, by a guild of smiths who guarded the secret of their unbreakable teeth as if they were hoarding gold. Stillborn's face was controlled, but the weapon made him wary, Raif could tell.

"Put it away, Yustaffa," he said. "You step too quickly into this fight. Anyone would think the Robber Chief couldn't speak for himself."

The fat man smiled as if Stillborn had said something amusing. He did a little dance, surprising Raif with his speed and grace, and in the space of an eyeblink the sword breaker was gone. "It'll be a sad day when you go to the Rift, Stillborn. Who will make me laugh when you're gone?"

Stillborn made no response, save to let his gaze return to the Robber Chief, Traggis Mole.

The man in the shadows bided his time. He had the ability to be very still, Raif noticed, like a hunter coaxing game to draw nearer so he could get a better shot. He waited until a pile of logs in the fire-stack collapsed, creating a wall of heat and sparks, before he spoke. "Stillborn," he warned in a hard, rough voice. "Your tongue's this close to being added to that meat."

Suddenly there was a blur of motion. Raif tried to follow it, but waves of heat from the fire blurred the air . . . and Traggis Mole moved inhumanly fast. When Raif's vision cleared, he saw two things: Traggis Mole had a knife at Stillborn's throat.

And the Robber Chief was not whole.

Brown leather straps formed a "v" across his forehead and slashed diagonally across both cheeks . . . holding a wooden nose in place. Traggis Mole breathed, letting the knife rise with his chest until it pressed against the apple of Stillborn's throat. The Robber Chief's face had once been handsome, with a finely shaped brow and cheekbones, and absolutely black eyes. He was small in the way cragsmen were small; hard and flinty as the crags they walked, with nothing spare to slow them. His eyes flicked once to Raif, saw all, then looked away.

"Do you yield this meat to me, Stillborn?" he said, his gaze dropping to the cache of frozen elk.

Stillborn's hand was on the wooden handle of the hammer hooked to his belt. Muscles in his arms were so tense that flesh bulged between the bullhorns. He breathed lightly, for to do anything else would be to push his own throat against the knife. Raif glanced around. More Maimed Men had come to the fire, and a group of women had gathered near the rear. Their faces were hungry and pitiless, and Raif wondered what they wanted most: meat or blood. He cursed his own lack of a weapon. No one here would step forward to defend Stillborn. You could see it in their eyes.

Just as Traggis Mole began pulling the knife blade across Stillborn's skin, Stillborn spoke. "I yield the meat," he said quietly.

Traggis Mole bared his teeth, and for a moment Raif thought he would make Stillborn repeat his words—louder this time, so all gathered could hear. Yet the Robber Chief took his pound of flesh another way, opening Stillborn's throat with an expert hand. Blood quickly filmed the length of the foot-long hunting knife, and Traggis wiped it clean on Stillborn's shoulder.

"Rift Brothers!" he cried, turning to his men. "I bring meat. Let the women come forward and put it on the fire."

A cheer went up. The fat man started a chant, and others quickly joined him. "*Mole! Mole! Mole!*" Someone hammered a wedge into a barrel, and ale began to flow. Within seconds the atmosphere around the blazing fire changed as women scrambled forward to hack at meat, torches were dipped and lighted, and a little clubfooted child began plucking a tune from a stringboard.

Stillborn did not move. The blood from the hairline slit on his throat was already drying, so shallow was the cut Traggis Mole had made. His scars were twitching with the effort it took to master himself, and Raif could clearly see the tooth-like thing growing from the side of his neck moving in some hideous imitation of a bite. When he noticed Raif watching him, Stillborn tilted his head back fractionally, warning Raif to keep his place in the background.

But Traggis Mole was watching, and even though his nose was wooden it twitched as if he'd sniffed something out. Wholly black eyes came to rest upon Raif.

"I'm taking him as my hunt partner," Stillborn said casually. "Orrlsman. Found him in Grass Gorge, heading this way. He's a fair hunter. He'll earn his keep."

"Will he, now?" Traggis Mole looked Raif up and down. "I see you took half a finger from him, Stillborn. Thought to rob me of the pleasure of taking a full hand?"

"I thought to leave a man with what he needs to hunt." Stillborn's voice was dangerous now, all attempts at sounding casual gone. "Or are you so afraid of anyone with four limbs that you'd see a man made useless rather than risk raising a rival to your chiefship?"

Traggis Mole laughed; a hard, short crow that had nothing to do with joy. "A rival? To this maggots' nest on the edge of nowhere? If someone wanted it enough to put a point through my brain don't think I wouldn't welcome it. We're all damned here. The frosts eat us alive and the shadows are rising. Show me a man with balls enough to take me and I'll go willingly into the Rift."

As he spoke, the wind began to rise along the cliff wall, whipping at the hems of men's cloaks and beating a fierce heat from the fire. Raif looked out toward the edge and saw little but blackness. The land fell away to nothing, and the distance between the north wall of the Rift and the south one seemed as cold and empty as the space between stars.

"I know you hate me, Stillborn," came the Robber Chief's voice, cutting through the wind. "But you don't quite hate me enough. How long have you been here? Fifteen years? Yet you still haven't learned how to stab a man in the back. Look at Yustaffa. Calls me his liege lord and makes my fights his, yet I wouldn't trust him near me with a knife. All the men here tonight, every last broken one of them, dreams of slitting my throat while I lie abed with my whore atop me. Fear stops them . . . but that's not what stops you, is it?" The Robber Chief looked shrewdly at Stillborn, the shadow of his wooden nose lying black against his cheek. "That last dram of clannish honor is always the hardest to lose."

Stillborn shook his head slowly and heavily, yet he spoke no words to deny it. Instead, he let his gaze travel to the base of the bonfire, where men were reaching in with bare hands to grab at the half-cooked meat. "The Rift Brothers are hungry, Traggis. If I were you I'd set my mind on that. Send men out to hunt, not raid. A coffer full of gold is worth nothing to a starving man. There's elk three days west of here, and if you were any kind of chief you'd mount a hunt party and bring down as many as you could. And if you were any judge of men you'd bring this lad along with you, for no other reason than I say so."

Others in the crowd heard what Stillborn said and stopped to listen. Some drew nearer. One man with frost-rotted cheeks was quick to nod at the mention of elk. Traggis's black eyes saw all.

"If you had any love for your life, Stillborn, you'd keep your notions to yourself. I'm lord of this hole in the earth. Not some bullhorned gargoyle who was born dead and should have stayed that way." Quick as a flash, Traggis Mole's finger and thumb were on Stillborn's chin, squeezing the flesh till it whitened. "And I tell you something else, my scarred friend. That Orrlsman's mine until he's proven himself. He's brought no weapons, no goods. Whatever he eats and sups he robs from the mouth of a Rift Brother. And I'll take my own eyes if you can find one man here tonight who'll welcome him for it."

No one spoke. All the Maimed Men were listening now, hands and mouths greasy with elk juice, the firelight making masks of their faces. Raif felt their hostility like a drying wind against his skin. Traggis Mole had easily directed all their hunger and frustration onto him, an outsider, and Raif knew he'd been trapped by a master.

Traggis Mole broke his hold on Stillborn, but continued to maintain eye contact for long seconds afterwards. When he was satisfied that whatever silent warning he'd issued had been received, he turned his attention to Raif. "Orrlsman. What skills do you claim?"

Raif was careful not to make the mistake of looking to Stillborn before answering. "I'm a white-winter warrior. Bowman. Longbow and shortbow. I once brought down a dozen kills in one night."

A ripple of interest passed through the crowd, but the Robber Chief was unmoved. "You're young for a white-winter warrior. Last I heard, it takes ten years to make one."

Something in Raif rose to the challenge of those hard black eyes. "Then you heard wrong."

Interest moved briefly across Traggis Mole's face. "Yet you have no bow, and from the looks of it Stillborn didn't relieve you of one."

"He broke it in two in his rush to get my sword."

A titter of amusement rippled through the crowd, and Raif knew he had read Stillborn true. The great bullhorned Maimed Man was no bowman; his arms were built for wielding steel, not firing wood. And if the large number of weapons in his weapon stand was anything to go by, he was a collector of steel, too. The Forsworn sword, even sheathed as it was with only its cross-hilt and pommel showing, was clearly a treasure to be hoarded.

Raif felt relief, yet did not show it. Looking into Traggis Mole's small and fatally flawed face, he got the distinct impression that he had fooled everyone in the crowd except him.

Yet for reasons of his own Traggis Mole kept the truth to himself. He said only, "Well, Orrlsman. How shall we test your claims?"

Raif held the man's gaze and said nothing. He knew the second trap was about to be sprung.

"I've an idea," offered the fat man, pausing in the business of sucking marrow from a chunk of thigh bone.

"Speak it."

Yustaffa waived airily with the bone. He had the copper skin and almond eye-whites of a Far Southerner, and although his beaver furs were finely dressed and gleaming he did not sit well in them. He looked like a man dressing up as a bear. "Let him shoot against Tanjo Ten Arrow or whatever he's calling himself these days. Archer against archer. Bow against bow. Could be quite amusing. Certainly better than watching this rabble throw another dead man to the Rift. I said only this morning—"

"Enough," warned Traggis. "Find Tanjo and arrange the match for first light. And you," he said, addressing a frost-eaten swordsman dressed in the rod-and-slat armor of a seafarer. "Take this Orrlsman to the caves, and hold him overnight. Feed him naught but dirt and water, and make sure *he*—" a quick glance to Stillborn "—doesn't get by you. Bring the Orrlsman to the High Mantle at dawn."

The swordsman nodded brusquely, and Raif felt an ungentle hand upon his arm. He was not given the chance to speak a word to Stillborn before he was led away.

EIGHTEEN

The Tower on the Milk

The five Dhoone warriors entered the old riverhouse under heavy guard. Iago Sake's face was white in the starlight, his dread half-moon ax drawn and ready. He and Diddie Munn escorted the five warriors through the strange roofless arcade that formed the entrance to the broken tower at Castlemilk.

Bram was surprised to see the five men still armed, and wondered why his brother Robbie had not given the order for their weapons to be ransomed. Water steel flashed at their backs and thighs, making river-like ripples upon the blued surfaces of their breast and back plates. The tattoos on their faces showed them to be veterans of many campaigns. One of their number, whom Bram recognized as the master axman Mauger Loy, had whorls of ink so densely sewn across his cheeks that you could not see the true color of his skin. Even his eyelids were blue. All five had the fair hair of the Dhoones, and Bram realized that he was one of only a handful in the room with dark eyes and dark hair.

"Couch your ax, Iago," came Robbie Dhoone's voice from the tower's vast circular chamber. "These men are our brothers. They'll offer no fight."

Iago Sake, the deathly pale axman known as the Nail, nodded but did not speak. He and Mauger had been companions of the ax before the slaying of the old Dhoone chief, yet all the years spent training and campaigning meant nothing to Iago when compared to his loyalty to Robbie Dhoone. Iago thrust the three-foot ax under his gear belt rather than couch it against his back as ordered. Bram knew other men might mistake Iago's lack of obedience as defiance, but Bram knew it was done out of love and protectiveness for Robbie. If weapons were drawn, Iago Sake would get to his first.

The five Skinner Dhoone-sworn warriors could not hide their interest as they stepped into the principal chamber of the broken tower. It had once risen thirty storeys above the Milk, legend said, higher even than the tower on the Ganmiddich Inch. But the living was harder here in the northern clanholds—storms could rage for weeks and frosts had been known to last for half a year—and the tower had long since fallen. All that was left were a few lower storeys, and all but the ground one were broken. Even that let in moonlight and rain, and if Bram looked up he could see great cracks and absences of stone. If he looked down he could see a pool of water as large as a fish pond that had formed in a pocket of sunken flooring. The water had been frozen when they'd first occupied the tower ten days back, but it was thawing now under the sufferance of torchlight and man heat. Once or twice Bram had seen things flitting beneath the glaze of ice, and had wondered briefly how fish had made their way in here.

Few had answers to questions concerning the tower, not even the Castlemen who had lived with its closeness all their lives. The Milkhouse was barely a league to the west, its rounded walls and domed roof constructed for the most part from stone quarried from the tower. When the first clan settlers had come upon the ruins north of the river, they had named the pale, pearlescent blocks they were built from milkstone. Centuries later, when the first roundhouse was raised in the shadow of the tower, the clan chief had forsaken his old name and called himself Castlemilk instead.

The Milk River still ran white each spring, when rushing water and thawing ice ate away at the remaining deposits of milkstone that lay in a series of open quarries upstream. Bram had once heard said that the quarries were now overrun by forest and pokebrush and near impossible for anyone but crags- men to find.

Even now, after months of living in Castlemilk where milk- stone was plentiful and many structures were built from it, Bram still found the pale rock beautiful. It glowed like teeth in firelight.

The five warriors crossed the round chamber to where Robbie was sitting at the head of a camp table. Robbie was uncloaked and unarmored, dressed in a fine wool shirt and linen vest, his moleskin pants tucked into high leather boots, and a heavy belt of beaten copper plates circling his waist. His hair had been recently washed and braided, and wet strands still clung to his neck. Another man might look disarrayed in such a state, but Robbie Dun Dhoone looked like a king.

He watched the five men gravely, his hands resting on the leather-bound armrests of his chair. "Mauger. Berold. Harris. Jordie. Roy," he named and greeted them, clearly surprising them by this feat of memory. "Come. Sit. It's a hard ride from Gnash, and the river banks are thick with mud. Have your horses been fed and watered?"

Mauger and his companions exchanged glances. They were not men easy with such courtesy. "Aye," Mauger said gruffly after a moment. "'Tis well done. A stableman took our mounts."

Robbie made a small gesture with his hand. "Good. Now

warm yourselves by the brazier. Bram, bring bread and ale. And be sure to tell Old Mother who has come. She would not thank us if these men came and left and she'd missed the chance to greet them."

"Old Mother is here?" Mauger asked, turning his head to look for her.

"Yes. Out by the river. She gave us her blessing three months back when she came to join our cause."

"We thought her dead." Mauger was clearly perplexed. "She went missing with that sorry mule of hers, and Skinner said she'd rode out to the ruinwoods to die."

Robbie raised an eyebrow, but said nothing, leaving the five warriors to name Skinner Dhoone a liar for themselves. Bram loaded nutbread and a flagon of black ale onto a wood platter, and carried it to the camp table. A cloth map of the clanholds was spread across the length of the table, and Robbie nodded impatiently when Bram hesitated to set a tray upon it. As Bram poured ale into drinking horns, the five warriors sat reluctantly.

"So you are no longer quartered at the Milkhouse," Mauger said to Robbie, glancing around the tower chamber. "A pity, as it's a fine fortress."

"We grew too big for it." Robbie took the first horn of ale for himself. "Wrayan asked me to stay, but a man would be a fool to overburden his host."

Mauger grunted his agreement. He was a big man, with all his strength in his shoulders, and a stubble of white-blond hair poking through the blue skin on his neck. Bram saw him take note of the men gathered around the cook fires sanding their armor, fixing pieces of tack, or turning out damp clothing to dry. More men squatted by the doorless entryway, playing knuckle-bones and taking bets, and still others formed small groups around the chamber, speaking softly amongst themselves. Bram took pride in their numbers. Not a day had gone by since the raid on Bludd when a man or small company hadn't presented themselves to Robbie for service. His fame was growing, and the name Skinner Dhoone had coined for him was known throughout the clans. The Thorn King.

"Count if your master bids it, Mauger," Robbie said lightly, stretching his legs. "But don't expect an accurate tally, as you're seeing less than half of us here tonight."

It was a lie, but it was well done. Bram marveled at the calmness of his brother's face. *Strange that I never realized before how good Robbie is at deceit.*

Mauger colored hotly.

The man named Berold spoke to cover his companion's discomfort. "We bear messages from Skinner. Would you hear us now, or would you prefer to parley in private?"

It was a challenge and Robbie rose to it. "I hide nothing from my companions. Speak up, man, so others can hear."

Berold glanced at Mauger. "It was agreed my brother would speak for all."

Bram looked anew at Mauger and Berold, and saw what he had failed to earlier: the same features occupied both faces. *My brother*, Berold had said. The words pricked something in Bram, but he did not know what or why.

Mauger held his horn out to be refilled before speaking. "First. Skinner demands that you no longer name him uncle. He has looked into your bloodline and found you to be no cousin to a chief. You are nephew to him by neither blood nor marriage, and any claims you stake are false."

Whilst Mauger was speaking, men around the chamber turned to listen. Many bristled at this insult to their chief. The big axman Duglas Oger bared a mouthful of broken teeth, and came to stand at Robbie's back. Even in the company of other axmen, Duglas had no rivals for strength or bulk, and his presence at the camp table caused the five visitors to exchange wary glances. Duglas Oger saw this and casually reached behind his back for his ax.

Robbie gentled him with a hand to his arm as he addressed himself to Mauger. "I take no umbrage. I know the words you speak are not your own. I can't say I'm surprised by Skinner. It pleased him to call me nephew when it suited him, now it pleases him not to. A nice trick. A pity he's never tried it on his wife."

Laughter rippled around the chamber. Duglas Oger chortled; it sounded as if someone were trying to strangle him. The visitors were less easy with this jest at their chief's expense, and all but one of them kept their faces guarded. Young, white-eyebrowed Jordie Sarson couldn't quite manage to keep the grin from his lips.

Robbie's won him, Bram knew with certainty. So far his brother had done everything right: disarming the visitors with courtesy, impressing them with his cool-headedness, and now refusing to take insult where it was most definitely intended. Bram felt a wave of pride rising, and with it the familiar sinking sensation in his chest. *How can I feel so proud of him, and yet not want him to succeed?* It was disloyalty of the worst kind, and Bram knew it shamed him. With an effort of will he set his mind away from it and concentrated instead upon the simple task of keeping the visitors' horns topped with ale.

"Is there more?" Robbie asked.

Mauger shifted uneasily. "Aye. Concerning the kingship." He downed more ale to give himself courage. "Skinner says your dam was a whore, and if every man who's seen the inside of her cunt claimed kingship from it then a good half of the clanholds should be crowned."

Robbie's blue-gray eyes turned cold. "No," he said quietly to Duglas Oger who was in the process of raising his ax. Across the room Iago Sake stalked the visitors, his deathly pale skin and winter furs rendering him almost invisible against the milk-stone walls. Robbie stood. "No," he repeated again, this time to all the men in chamber. "Don't send our brothers back to Gnash thinking we don't know a lie when we hear one. All here knew and honored my mother Margret. Everything fair and golden lay within her, and she went to her death with the grace of the Dhoone Queens. The words of a scared man cannot change that. Skinner Dhoone is growing desperate, and he sinks to new depths. Does he think me a dog to fight at his command? Insult my lady mother and I'll froth at the muzzle and strike out without a plan?" Robbie shook his head. "Don't mistake me, Dhoonesmen. I won't forget this insult, but I won't drag one extra sword into this fight. This is between me and Skinner, and it'll be settled between two men, no more."

Many in the crowd nodded. Iago Sake rested his ax. Robbie was right. Only a son could defend his mother's honor, no matter how keenly that son's companions felt the insult. Bram found he could look no one in the eye. None had looked at him since the visitors had entered, and he did not want to invite their scrutiny now.

Margret Cormac nee Dhoone was not his mother. The golden hair and blue eyes she possessed went solely to her first and only son, along with a well-documented claim to the Thistle Blood. Even before the old Dhoone chief was slain by Bluddsmen, Robbie had forsaken his father's name and started calling himself Dhoone instead. Bram could still remember hearing the name Robbie Dhoone for the first time, and think-ing how much grander it sounded than Rab Cormac. He had been six. *"Can I call myself Dhoone, too, Rab?"* he had asked on the weapons court as Robbie cleaned pig blood from his sword with a fist of hay. *"No, Bram,"* Robbie had said, squinting down the length of his swordblade to check for trueness. *"We share the same father, but not the same dam. My mother was a great lady with ancestors stretching back to Weeping Moira. Your mother's just a rabbit trapper from Gnash."*

Bram rested his hand on the camp table for a moment. He told himself Robbie had meant no insult, that his words were just the thoughtlessness of a sixteen-year-old boy. Yet Bram was fifteen himself now, and he knew he wouldn't have spoken the same words in Robbie's place.

Mauger was speaking, but it took a moment for Bram to understand him. "Skinner's tired of the wait," said the seasoned warrior. "He calls for a meeting with swords, to settle the matter of the chiefship once and for all."

The call to swords stirred the men. They had taken part in little but raids since the attack on Bludd, and they were hungry for battle. It mattered little that Skinner Dhoone's forces outnumbered them, for success at Bludd had made them bold, and their faith in Robbie's leadership was unshakable. Bram saw and understood all—and he also saw the glint of calculation that passed across his brother's face.

Still standing, Robbie made a gesture to quiet the men. "Brothers. Companions," he said quietly. "I'll not meet Skinner Dhoone on a field of his choosing. He may be willing to set Dhoonesmen against Dhoonesmen, but I am not. Who here tonight can cast eyes upon our visitors and not know them for our clansmen? Kill them and we kill ourselves. Every Dhoonesman dead is one less man to fight against Bludd. Tell me, whose blood is better served on our blades? Dhoone's or Bludd's?"

Silence settled on the tower chamber like a spell. Light from the torches hissed and dimmed as the first mists of evening stole through cracks in the tower. The Milk lay less than thirty feet to the south, and river ice could be heard fracturing as air cooled above the surface. Inside the chamber all Dhoonesmen had grown grave. Duglas Oger raised the copper horn containing his measure of powdered guidestone to his lips. Others followed. Iago Sake bowed his head, and began speaking the names of the Stone Gods. Robbie joined him, and by the time the third god was named the entire room was chanting them in prayer.

. . . *Ione, Loss, Uthred, Oban, Larannyde, Malweg, Behathmus.*

The words brought tears to men's eyes, for Robbie had somehow reminded them that Dhoone was the beloved second son of the gods.

The visiting clansmen chanted along with Robbie's men, and Bram wondered how many would return to Skinner at Gnash. Jordie Sarson would not, for his gaze seldom left Robbie and there was a light of devotion within it. The bald and big-knuckled spearman Roy Cox, known as Spineback, also looked as if he might succumb to mutiny, for there was a troubled look on his thin, bony face and his gaze traveled around the tower chamber as if assessing it as a potential home.

Mauger and Berold also looked troubled, but Bram did not think they would entertain the thought of switching sides. Loyalty and honor ran too deep within them, and just as they were cautious of Robbie's courtesy, they were cautious of his well-spoken words as well.

Mauger broke the silence by asking, "Have you any message to send to my chief?"

Robbie reached behind his neck to handle his braids. Bram doubted he was unaware of the figure he cut, the length of muscle in his arm and shoulders, the fine long fingers, unbitten by any ax. "I have no message for Skinner. Any man who would set clansman against clansman is not worthy of my respect. I would speak only to those who follow him. And I would tell them this: All are welcome here as brothers. What has been done and said in the past is forgotten. Join me, and we'll return in force to our clanhold and reclaim Dhoone."

Mauger nodded brusquely and quickly, as if wary of the effect of Robbie's words on his four companions. "A fine speech, but I'll not do your campaigning for you, Rab Cormac. If you have no message for our chief, then you have none for us." He turned to his companions. "Come, men. We need to cross the Milk afore moonset." Mauger bowed his head in farewell to Robbie and Duglas Oger, and then crossed the chamber. Berold and the three others followed him, but not before Robbie had made eye contact with Jordie Sarson and Roy Cox.

Only when those two men had turned away from him did Robbie allow the anger to show on his face. He had ill-liked being called Rab Cormac. Bram had once witnessed him beating Jesiah Shamble bloody when the simple-minded luntman had forgotten Robbie's new name and called him by the old one instead. No one had dared name Robbie a Cormac since, and no one but Duglas Oger ever called him Rab. Yet it was clear from Mauger's remark that they were calling him both at Gnash.

Bram Cormac slipped out of the tower unnoticed. He had no wish to witness his brother's anger over the name their father had given them.

The mist had risen to man-height on the riverbank, and there was a deep chill to it that penetrated every layer of Bram's clothing and then lay wetly against his skin. Hunching his shoulders, he made his way toward the mossy bank where Old Mother kept a tent and fire. She would not sleep or take meals in the broken tower, and would only enter it at Robbie's command.

The smell of woodsmoke guided him through the mist. The land east of the Milkhouse was wild and heavily forested, and Guy Morloch said that if a man built a hunt lodge among the trees and left it unattended for a year he'd never be able to find it again. The forest would destroy it. Castlemilk's farmland and grazes were to the north and west, leaving the land that bordered Bludd-sworn Frees free to create a thick and impenetrable barrier to keep enemies at bay. Even here, only a league west of the Milkhouse, the forest claimed every space it could, and willows and bog oak sent bare limbs out across the river as if they could claim the very water itself.

Old Mother was sitting on a tree stump by a green-log fire, warming sotted oats in an iron pot helm and chewing on a stalk of rue. Her only greeting was, "Does Robbie call me?"

Bram wondered if she knew his name. Her teeth were yellow from the rue, and she smelled unpleasant, like river water trapped too long in a hole. "Robbie said to let you know that Mauger and others from Gnash are here. He thought you might want to greet them before they leave. They're out by the horse tent. I'll take you to them if you want." Bram didn't truly believe the offer, made in courtesy, still held, but Robbie had not gainsaid it so he decided it was worth the risk.

"Mauger was a colicky baby," Old Mother said, rising stiffly. "Bald as a vulture that first year and screaming up a storm every night."

Bram couldn't think of anything to say to that so he nodded. Old Mother was strange, but he had come to understand that she knew things that others did not. Mostly it was tales about how grown clansmen were when they'd been babes and the scrapes they'd got into as boys, but sometimes she said things that made you think. The day that Robbie had proposed moving from the Milkhouse to the broken tower, she'd been dead set against it, and had flatly refused to sleep there. "Sull stones, Sull bones," she had murmured, shaking her large, fleshy head. "The smell of it will draw them like flies."

Bram found he didn't like to think about who *they* were, but there was something in the words that excited him. Every clansman knew that the land between the Bitter Hills and the Copper Hills had once belonged to the Sull, but no one spoke of it. It was a mystery. If the Sull were the fierce and death-stalking warriors everyone held them to be, then how had the settling clansmen managed to best them? Bram frowned. Withy and Wellhouse kept the histories: one day he'd travel to both roundhouses and discover the answer for himself.

Holding his arm out for Old Mother to take he guided her back along the bank. For no discernible reason the mist had begun to fail, and Bram found he could see through the retreating wisps. Ahead, the Sull tower sat strange and unlovely upon the riverbank like a broken tooth. At its highest point only four storeys remained, at its lowest less than one.

Out of the corner of his eye Bram spotted the five visiting Dhoonesmen grouped in a circle around their horses, engaged in last-minute preparations for the ford across the river. The horses were irritable, and would not stand easy while their riders greased their flanks against the cold water. The warriors should have stayed overnight and rested them, but Bram knew Mauger was eager to get away. He had seen and heard for himself how seductive Robbie Dhoone could be, and he feared to test the loyalty of his men.

Mauger was tightening his mount's girth when he saw Bram and Old Mother approach. His smile was genuine upon recognizing the old woman, but there were signs of weariness around his eyes. "So it's true, Old Mother. You have left us . . . and now we must fight alone." He bent to lay a kiss on her forehead, and then seemed to force himself to speak lightly. "In truth, I'm glad that you and that ugly mule of yours are still alive."

Old Mother accepted the kiss as her due, with her arms folded over the great barrel that was her chest and her mouth pressed into a line. She showed so little emotion that Bram wondered why she had come. Then she said, "He'll use Skinner. He canna help it, it's just the way he is."

Mauger's gaze flicked to his companions, checking that he and Old Mother could not be overheard. "How will he use him?"

It was telling that no one mentioned Robbie by name.

Old Mother wagged her head. "Ride on his back, that's how. Have Skinner for a workhorse, and himself for its master. He always was a canny child, quick to get others to do his bidding. Year of the long drought he had Duglas and his crew dam the Fly. Stayed away all day practicing with his ax, then came and took the credit when it was done."

Mauger frowned. He did not look comfortable with Old Mother's ramblings. "If you cannot say anything clearer, Old Mother, then best speak naught at all." He thrust a foot into a stirrup and hefted his bulk over his stallion's back. His companions did likewise, and began trotting close to hear what Old Mother had to say.

"Be careful you and Skinner don't fight his fights for him, Mauger Loy. Else I'll be laying heather on your cairn afore we're done."

Bram bowed his head. He wished he had not brought her, for she had picked the worst possible moment to lay a doom upon Mauger—when his brother and three companions could hear.

Mauger breathed hard, his bronzed and ax-dented breastplate rising along with his chest. With a short rein he turned his horse. "Brother. Men. West to Gnash!" Kicking spurs into horsemeat, he forced a starting gallop from his stallion and led his party west along the Milk.

Bram watched him disappear into the swirling, unsettled mist. *Brother*, he had said again, and for the second time that evening Bram felt something inside him freeze at the word.

Brother. And then, quite suddenly, he understood. It had been over a year since Robbie had said that word to him.

Bram blinked. At his side he was aware of Old Mother watching him, her arms still folded across her chest. An anger that surprised him made him say, "You didn't have to do that to Mauger. He's a good man."

"So you'd have him go unwarned?" asked Old Mother placidly, not rising to his anger.

She had answered him with his own argument, but Bram was unwilling to let go of his anger. He didn't want to think why. "Why did you have to come to us? Why not stay with Skinner at Gnash?"

"You know the answer to that, lad," she replied, unperturbed. Something in her voice made Bram turn to look at her. Her face was bland and old-womanly, but her eyes were the purest Dhoone blue he had ever seen, with the violet ring around the irises that revealed a high concentration of Thistle Blood. Only direct descendants of kings had those eyes.

"I've never known Robbie not to win," she said.

NINETEEN

City on the Edge of an Abyss

Raif awoke to the sensation of cold water dripping upon his face. He opened his eyes, and it took a moment for him to understand that a man was standing above him, slowly wringing drops of water from a damp and twisted rag. The man smiled pleasantly, displaying little demon teeth in a brown and fleshy face. Yustaffa.

"Morning, Archer Boy," he said gaily, wringing more drops from the rag. "You failed the test, you know. If you were a prince good and true you'd wake after the first drop." With an elaborate sigh, he twisted the rag with all his might, sending a torrent of freezing water over Raif's face. "Let's hope you do better with the second test of the day."

Raif sat up, furiously shaking his head. The cliff cave was dark and freezing, and the portion that opened to the sky showed a world still black as night. "It's not dawn yet. Go away."

Yustaffa shuddered theatrically. "Orders! And from a master archer, no less. I quake in fear, I really do."

"I'm a bowman, not an archer." Raif didn't know why he said this, but the fat man was beginning to annoy him. Raif's shirt was soaking, and he was cold and tired, and his bandaged finger was throbbing. The missing tip and knuckle still felt as if they were there, and the sight of the digit's shortness, the vacant air where flesh and bone should be, made him feel like he might be sick. With an effort he forced his mind elsewhere. Stretching his legs, he began working the stiffness from his limbs.

"Well, *bowman*," Yustaffa said pointedly, looking for somewhere to sit. "Perhaps you'd like to tell me something about yourself, since we find ourselves with a few minutes alone." Unable to find anywhere that was not naked rock, the fat man settled on shrugging off his beaver-fur collar, rolling it into a ball and sitting cross-legged upon it. A tiny sniff of discomfort let Raif know what he thought of his surroundings.

Raif wondered why he had come. Recalling his exchanges with Stillborn, he said, "I'll trade you for information."

Yustaffa raised an eyebrow. "My, you learn fast, for a clansman. And here was I thinking you'd be willing to trade for food." The fat man pulled a soft package from his black beaver coat and laid it on the floor by his feet. With exaggerated delicacy he unfolded it with his fingertips, revealing squares of fresh-baked bannock, oatcakes wrapped in bacon, a wedge of crumbly white cheese, three heads of butter-braised leeks, and a tiny stoppered pot known in the clanholds as a tonicker because it held just enough malt to revive a man's spirits without rendering him drunk.

"Clan food. Coarse, but strangely appealing." Yustaffa bit the head off a leek. "Now, where were we? Yes, information. How about we start with your name and clan?"

Raif tried not to look at the food. He wouldn't allow Yustaffa the satisfaction of knowing how much he wanted it. "You know my clan. And my name's no secret—it's Raif."

Yustaffa nodded as he poured a measure of malt into the

hollow stopper. "Orrlsman, yes. Yet you haven't that look about you." He downed the malt and then looked Raif directly in the eye. "As long as you shoot like one I suppose it doesn't really matter either way."

Raif forced himself to return the fat man's gaze steadily. "I do."

Yustaffa bowed his head in acknowledgment of Raif's confidence. He seemed pleased, and raised the remaining dram of malt in toast. "To Raif. May I share in the excitement of your life, but never the danger." Again, the fat man did his trick of throwing the malt down his throat and then snapping his gaze back to Raif. "You know in my country the word *raif* means stranger?"

A drop of cold water slid down Raif's spine. He willed himself not to react, but Yustaffa was quick and saw something in Raif's face that made him smile.

Cheek fat pushed against Yustaffa's eyes. "I see you haven't heard of the legend of *Azziah riin Raif*, the Stranger from the South who spent his life searching for heaven only to find the Gates to Hell instead? A sad tale with a sad end, but then most tales from my country are like that. We're a strange race, we Mangali—we'd rather weep than laugh."

Raif dropped his gaze to the food; he found he could look at it now without desire. For seventeen years he had owned his name, and somewhere in the back of his mind he had always known it wasn't clan: no one but himself was called it. Still . . . *Stranger from the South.* It made no sense, and Raif cautioned himself to be wary of what the fat man said. Maimed Men did not make good friends.

Abruptly, he said, "How about repaying the debt, Yustaffa? A question for a question."

The glint in Yustaffa's eyes was knowing. "In my country it is considered the height of good manners to shift the topic of conversation from oneself to one's guest." He waved a fleshy arm with surprising grace. "So, please. Go ahead."

"Why come all the way from the Far South to join the Maimed Men when you are whole?"

Yustaffa's laughter was high and tinkling. "Me? Whole? Dear boy, you flatter me." With a quick little hop the fat man was on his feet, bunching the hem of his beaver coat and tunic in his fists. Unceremoniously, he raised both garments to the waist and bared his loins. His cock was intact, but there was a thick white scar where his scrotum had once been.

Raif tried not to shudder as he looked away.

Letting the coat and silk tunic drop, Yustaffa said, "My Song Master cut me when I was a boy. It was my very bad luck to have a voice like a nightingale's, and my unforgivable weakness to be proud of it. I'd still be whole today if only I'd learned enough modesty to step back and lower my voice. Fool that I was, I thought only of the praise and rewards . . . nothing of the price. Oh, they drugged me, of course, and I woke four days later with a splitting headache in my groin, and an unbearable lightness where my balls had once been." Something cold and angry flash-hardened muscles in Yustaffa's face, but just as quickly it was gone. "I never sang again. As far as revenge goes it was a petty one, but it was all I could think of at the time— I *was* only eleven, after all. Later I thought of more."

Raif followed Yustaffa's gaze down to his gear belt where the sword breaker and a curved scimitar were sheathed and hung.

"They called me the Dancer later. Do you know why?" Raif shook his head. "Because when they found the bodies of the Song Master and his surgeon a man's footsteps were stamped in the surrounding gore. To all who saw the footsteps it looked as if the killer had danced in their blood. He had. And I did. And my only regret is that I didn't dance longer and kill more."

It was a warning, then, this tale Yustaffa told. Raif felt better for knowing the reason behind it: one man warning another that he was not to be fooled with was something he understood.

"All of us here are missing something," Yustaffa said, squatting to collect the leftover food in the cloth. "We may not look it but we are. Traggis Mole had his nose ripped from him by a Vorlander armed with a plate-piercing spike, but that's not what makes him a Maimed Man. His scars run deeper than that. You'd do well to remember that, *Azziah riin Raif*. And perhaps next time when a man owes you a debt you won't waste it on foolish questions."

Raif nodded, accepting the reprimand. In truth, he didn't consider his question wasted, but he wasn't about to argue. Yustaffa was too clever for that.

Outside, the patch of sky above the cliff cave was lightening from black to charcoal and the stars were fading from it. The air in the cave was switching and unsettled, and Raif detected the subtle freshness of dawn. Restless, he stood and walked to the cave entrance. The same frost-eaten swordsman who had brought him here last night stood at the head of the tunnel, barring the way out. When he saw Raif he motioned toward the sky, "Best get ready. Traggis'll be expecting you good and soon."

Raif almost smiled. *Ready?* He had no weapon or armor to prepare. All he had to do was put on his cloak and piss.

"I'll be wishing you well, then," Yustaffa said, straightening up. "I enjoyed our little talk so much I think I'll give you some free advice. Tanjo Ten Arrow loves a bet. Wager for something you want and if the gods are willing you'll get it."

"And if they're not?"

Yustaffa tutted as he walked through the tunnel and away from Raif. "And here I was hoping to leave on a high note. Dear boy, if you lose the contest you die. You don't really think Traggis would allow an outsider to lie to him in public and live? Traggis Mole is as good as a king in the Rift, and a king's pride is a terrible thing. You've told him you're a white-winter hunter—so hunt. I'll be watching from the toeline, and I'm sure it'll ease your mind to know I'm rooting for you." Yustaffa turned at the cave entrance and bowed low to Raif. "Until later."

Raif made no reply except to run a hand across his face. *Oh gods.* What had possessed him to tell Traggis Mole all those lies? Last night it had seemed a simple choice: appear strong or die. Now he knew better. The Robber Chief had been leading him all the way. Traggis would gain much by today's spectacle. He'd unite the Maimed Men in hatred of an outsider, and prove to Stillborn once and for all who was chief.

Resting his weight against the cave wall, Raif exhaled deeply. It was difficult to fight off the idea that coming here had been a mistake.

Ash. Why did you have to leave me?

When the swordsman with the frost-eaten nose and cheeks came for him a few minutes later he was ready. His Orrlsman's cloak was fastened at his throat and his hair had been freshly smoothed and braided. Water had been left for him in a cattle trough, and he'd used it to drink his fill and wet his face. Birds were calling now, crowing and chittering at the increase in light. The sky was the color of deep water, and rays from the rising sun picked out ice crystals suspended in the air and made them sparkle like tiny fish.

As soon as Raif straightened his spine after leaving the tunnel, he read the wind. The head wind blew south, steady and persistent, at a speed to raise the braid off his back. Nothing unusual there. It was updrafts rising from the Rift that worried him. They'd give an arrow lift, but he lacked the experience to judge them. He could feel them now, pushing at the hem of his cloak as the swordsman led him across a barren, rocky ledge. Spreading the fingers on his undamaged right hand, he let the air pass through them. The updrafts were a few degrees warmer than the surrounding air, and they buffeted wildly, blowing and then dropping to nothing in the blink of an eye. As he watched, a kittiwake rose on them, only to flap its wings furiously to maintain height when the thermal fell away.

Raif grimaced. Ballic the Red had names for winds like that and all of them were curses. Land where warm air and cold air met was no place for a bowman to shoot from.

"Up here," came the gruff voice of the frost-eaten swordsman, indicating a rope-and-cane ladder that dropped from the ledge above. The man thought himself nobody's fool, and waited for Raif to start the climb before putting foot to the ladder himself. Raif dimly recalled making the descent last night on his way to the cliff cave, but it had been pitch black and calm, and he hadn't realized quite how close he'd been to the Rift.

The great black chasm in the earth lay below him as he climbed, and though he did not look at it his mind kept playing tricks on his eyes. He could *see* the sheer face of it, the way it ran deep and shadowed to a place where living earth ended and molten core began. Pockets of mist hung like vertical pools in the pitted clefts of its faces. Somewhere deep and profoundly quiet, in the oldest and most inaccessible cracks, steam was venting. The sulfur-and-ash smell of it rose to Raif's nose, where it pushed through blood and membranes to enter his brain. Raif's grip loosened on the cane rung. *Azziah riin Raif . . . spent his life searching for heaven only to find the Gates to Hell instead.*

Blinking as if he'd woken from a dream, Raif forced his clenched hand to hold steady on the rung. Two-thirds of the climb was done, but he found he had no memory of the ascent. A stitch on his halved finger had split and clear fluid leaked through the yellow bandage down to the web of skin that joined his fingers. He ignored the pain of it as he finished the climb.

As he levered himself up onto the ledge, he saw the smoking remains of last night's bonfire ahead of him. The circle of ground surrounding the burn was black with tar, and small children darted in and out of the still-hot timbers, playing a game of dare. One child, a brown-eyed girl with a halo of wiry hair, found a charred joint of meat amongst the embers, and with the kind of furtive side glances that were a child's idea of stealth, she slipped it beneath her tunic and ran away.

Raif glanced around the honeycombed city as he waited for his handler to top the ledge. *Effie would have loved this.* The entire cliff face was mined with caves. Some of the chambers were closed off by stretched oilskins or cane screens, but most were left open to the wind. The lower dwellings looked hard used, their ledges piled with refuse and stained black by countless fires. Many of the higher caves were sealed off by giant boulders, and many more still had collapsed. Raif wondered how long it had taken to create such a place. It must have required some kind of inspired madness to build a city on the edge of an abyss.

The frost-eaten swordsman followed Raif's gaze. "No one lives up high since the east face collapsed," he said, nodding toward the buckled and contorted terraces in the far east of the city. "We lost two hundred that day."

Raif nodded slowly. He would have liked to ask about their numbers now, for it was impossible to gauge how many Maimed Men lived here, but he judged his chances of getting an answer as low. Stillborn had warned him you never got anything from a Maimed Man unless you gave him something first.

In silence they crossed the main terrace of the city, heading for a stone stair that led to the level above. Raif was aware of many gazes upon him as he walked. Old men watched him from the shade. Hardened warriors stepped out of their caves to stare him down, and groups of tired-looking women paused by their cook fires as he passed. By the time he'd reached the stair he'd gathered quite a following. Children mostly, a band of sullen-faced youths who bounced stones in their fists, and a handful of young girls who thought it amusing to dart forward and poke him and then run away.

With a sizable crew at his back, the swordsman judged it safe to take the lead up the winding steps. Raif followed him. As the stair spiraled through the cliff face he got a spectacular view across the Rift. Birds swooped in flight two hundred feet below him. The purple mounds of the Copper Hills shimmered on the horizon against a sky blushed pink with dawn. The clanholds. Strange that he could be so close to them yet feel farther away than he had in the land of the Ice Trappers. The Rift was probably seven hundred paces across at its widest point, yet it might as well have been a thousand leagues, so absolutely did the crack in the continent separate the clanholds from the badlands in this place.

The Lost Clan lay directly to the south, what was left of it. The clanhold itself had been claimed by Dhoone, then contested by Bludd and Wellhouse in the War of the Three Clans. Raif wasn't sure how the borders sat now, but Tem had once told him that no clan who claimed the territory of extinct Clan Morrow got any joy from it. The lands and forests surrounding the razed roundhouse would yield neither crops nor game.

Raif raised his hand to his throat and touched his lore. No clansman could name Clan Morrow—even in his thoughts—without showing due respect.

"Take your hand from your lore."

Raif looked up at the sound of the voice to see Stillborn awaiting him at the top of the stair. The Maimed Man looked well rested, and had changed from his travel clothes into dressed

skins edged with rat fur and a rat-and-coon-fur kilt. The
Forsworn sword hung from his waist, and if the gleam of its
cross-hilt was anything to be judged by the weapon had been
expertly ground and polished. Even the grip had been
remounted, and the piece of rough sealskin Raif had wrapped
around the hilt had been replaced by oiled and crosshatched
leather. Seeing the hiltwork so splendidly finished, Raif thought
he'd like to have the sword back. Right about now *any* weapon
would have been a relief.

Maimed Men had gathered in numbers to watch the contest.
The High Mantle was a massive ledge of pale green rimrock,
stretching from the west of the city to the caved-in terraces in
the east, and extending thirty feet out over the cliff face. The
crowd was double what it had been last night, and still growing, as men lowered themselves on ropes and hoists and crossed
swaying bridges to join it. The central lane of the ledge was
clear of people, and a series of man-high wooden beehives had
been placed along the lane at various lengths. Targets. Raif
forced his gaze to move away from them without showing any
reaction. A little beyond the targets and closer to the cliff face,
a second, smaller group of people had gathered around a stacked
cook fire. A whole hog—snout, trotters and all—was spitted
above the flames.

It was to be a festival, then. With him as the mummers'
show.

"I *said* take your hand off your lore. They won't love you
for reminding them that you're clan and they're not."

Raif obeyed Stillborn's hissed order, but not before a few
sharp eyes in the crowd had seen the blackened piece of bird
ivory that was his raven lore.

The frost-eaten swordsman began leading Raif forward, but
Stillborn put out a muscled forearm to halt him. "I'll take it
from here, Wex." Without waiting for the man to agree, Stillborn

guided Raif away from the stair and led him toward the cleared lane where a small body of men waited.

"Right," Stillborn said as soon as he and Raif were out of earshot. "This ain't gonna be pretty. Tanjo's the best archer amongst us, but he's arrogant and liable to underjudge an opponent. Play possum if you can, make him think he doesn't have to try too hard to beat you." Stillborn gave Raif a quick appraisal. "It's probably your best chance."

Raif could find little to be heartened by in this statement, but Stillborn was looking at him expectantly so he nodded.

"And another thing." Stillborn lowered his voice as they approached the meet party. "You'll be offered a choice of bows. Pick careful now, as that fat bastard Yustaffa laid them out. And the only thing you need to know about him is that he'd stick out a foot to trip his own mother if he thought he'd get away with it." The Maimed Man began moving away from him. "Shoot true. And mayhap the touch of the Stone Gods'll reach out across the Rift."

Raif shivered. He did not welcome the touch of any god.

"Aah. Here he is, Raif Twelve Kill. Is he a white-winter warrior as he claims, or just an impostor with a quick tongue and no bow?" Yustaffa, newly resplendent in a tunic of bronzed leather inset with panels of saffron-dyed fleece, heralded Raif's arrival to the crowd. "Only the test of arrows will tell. An arrow cannot lie. A bow will break if it's bent too fast. If our visitor speaks true then the proof will be found in the distance between his arrows and the bull. If he speaks false may he go to the Rift."

The crowd murmured restlessly as Raif walked through them. They were dressed in a strange motley of dressed skins, foreign-made armaments and city finery. The men wore mismatched pieces of armor: wooden knuckle-mitts, articulated steel greaves, hornmail, ringmail, pot-helms, spike-helms, metal plate, boiled leather, coats of shell and bone. One man wore a fantastic spiked and hooded greatcloak that clicked as it rose in the breeze. Some of the women were armored too, but most wore furs or skins over shabby woolen skirts. Trade in women's dresses must be slow.

A low-breasted hag near the front hissed at him. Raif ignored her, but found his attention drawn to the young woman she was standing next to. The girl was heavily pregnant. A slab of slate had been strapped high on her belly, pressing upon the bulge that was her unborn child. *Latening*. Raif shivered. He'd heard of the practice of slowing an unborn child's development by bringing weight to bear upon the fetus, but he'd never thought to see it until now. Clan had done it at one time, it was said, during the Great Settlement when no mother wanted to bring a child into the world whilst the Wars of Apportionment were being fought.

The woman cursed him as he passed. Raif accepted her words without reacting: he didn't know what else to do.

Yustaffa smiled gaily as Raif approached the clearing. "Hope you like the name," he confided. "I thought of it myself. More numbers than Tanjo—it's sure to get him riled."

Raif let Yustaffa's words slide over him. Already something was changing within him, responding to the hostility of the crowd and the challenge that was to come. He would not let these people affect him.

Standing some way back, close to the crowd yet set apart, stood the small dark figure of Traggis Mole. In the light of day Raif could see the drill holes in his wooden nose. The Robber Chief watched the proceedings in silence, holding himself uncannily still, only moving what it took to breathe and see. All felt his presence, Raif was sure of it, for the Maimed Men seemed to turn around him like a wheel around its axis. Traggis was aware of Raif's attention from the moment Raif's gaze swung toward him, and his own gaze snapped back with such force that Raif almost flinched. For a moment he knew what it would be like to have Traggis Mole attack him, saw blood spraying from his nose and eyes at the blinding speed of the Robber Chief's first strike.

Suddenly the crowd began to cheer, and the image fled. Raif hoped never to see it again.

"Here he comes!" Yustaffa proclaimed in a voice pitched to soar above the noise of the crowd. "The finest archer ever to loose an arrow in the Rift. Once shield to the Emperor of Sankang across the Unholy Sea, youngest man ever to send an arrow through the Eye of Mount Somi, slayer of two hundred on Blue Yak Field, archer-assassin of Isalora Mokko, the Glittering Whore, and taker of first blood from the Great Gray Wolf of the Rift: Tanjo Ten Arrow!"

Maimed Men roared. The crowd drew apart to let the archer pass, and Tanjo Ten Arrow walked into the clearing.

TWENTY

A Test of Arrows

*B*urned, was Raif's first thought. Tanjo Ten Arrow's face
was mottled pink and tan, inhumanly smooth in parts
and hideously seamed in others. The whole left side
of his brow was stretched and shiny, the scalp oddly puckered
and out of alignment. Patches of missing hair revealed ring scars
where blood blisters had once formed.

Raif recalled the old Hailsman, Audie Stroon. Drunk one
night in the greathearth and bickering with his wife, Audie had
reached for a jug of ale on the mantle but had seized upon a
pitcher of lamp oil instead. As he raised the pitcher to his mouth,
a spark from the fire caught him and lamp oil ignited in his
face. Clansmen had rushed to smother him with bear hides,
and the flames were snuffed within seconds. But later, when
time came to pull the hides away, Audie's skin peeled right off
with them. Heat had fused it to the hides. Audie lived for a
year, but by all accounts it wasn't a happy one, for when he
wasn't in pain from the burns, he was suffering the revulsion
of the clan.

Revulsion. That had to be part of Tanjo Ten Arrow's story,
but not all of it. A master archer did not end up in a place like
this unless he'd run out of choices.

Raif glanced quickly at Yustaffa, who was presenting Tanjo Ten Arrow to the crowd with the oily glee of a pimp displaying his whore. How much of what he said could be trusted? Raif had never heard of Sankang or Mount Somi. Clan had no knowledge of what lay beyond the Unholy Sea, and what little Raif knew had come from Angus Lok.

Tanjo Ten Arrow himself was slender and finely boned, with the spare muscle of a man who knew shooting sticks was as much about concentration as strength. The unburned portions of his skin were a color somewhere between copper and olive, and they gleamed from a combination of hairlessness and rubbed oil. His scalp hair was black and straight, and his eyes were the color of dark plums. They were striking, his eyes, elegant and elongated, with the cool and focused gaze of a bird of prey.

Coming to stand in the clearing he bowed low from the waist, never once taking his eyes off Raif. Ten arrows were inserted into the stiff silk sash that was bound high around his chest and ribcage, making it seem as if he had been shot in the back many times. Snow-goose feathers fletched all ten arrows, and the shafts had been expertly tapered toward the nock and then lacquered to a brilliant red. Grass cords dyed the same color bound Tanjo's topknot into fat beads of hair. No effort had been taken to disguise the burned portions of his scalp, and strands of black hair lay taut over scalded flesh.

Raif bowed to him. For a moment they were alone: an island of unmoving calm in the noisy and restless sea of the crowd. Seconds earlier, Raif had doubted the claims Yustaffa had made on Tanjo Ten Arrow's behalf, but now he wasn't so sure. This man in front of him stood with the poise and self-assurance of someone who had achieved great things.

"Archers," Yustaffa said, bowing his head first to Tanjo and then to Raif. "To your bows, and let the contest begin."

Raif was the first to break eye contact. Tanjo Ten Arrow's gaze was steady and piercing, and Raif recognized the man's will to win even in the matter of outstaring his opponent. It should have been a small thing to concede, but it felt like more. *First round to Tanjo Ten Arrow.*

Yustaffa beckoned imperiously, signaling a young boy wheeling a cloth-covered cart to come forward. The crowd quieted in anticipation as Yustaffa's chubby fingers descended upon the stained yellow oilcloth. "Raif Twelve Kill comes to us with neither bow nor the means to beget one. Therefore, *I* have agreed to supply him with a choice of three." There was a pause while Yustaffa accepted the gratitude of the crowd. Then, "Choose well, Orrlsman, for while a good bow cannot make an archer, a bad bow can destroy one."

With great flourish, Yustaffa pulled back the cloth.

Three bows, already strung, lay side by side on oaken boards. A Far South recurve. A clan yew-wood. An elm flatbow. One built, and two self. The recurve was built, made of horn and sinew glued onto a wood frame. The other two were self bows, cut from single staves. The clan yew drew Raif's gaze first. Drey had one similar; kiln-dried and hand-tillered, cut whip-thin to bend like a whalebone in the hand. The last time Raif could recall seeing it had been on the day Tem died. Abruptly, he switched his gaze to the elm flatbow. The elm was thick and sturdy, board-cut, and a few hands short of a true longbow. It was the weapon of cragsmen and herdsmen; reliable and unlikely to break, capable of firing an arrow with enough heft to stop a rushing wolf in its tracks. But it was not a bow made for distance. The Far South recurve *was*. Light and wickedly curved, its ox-horn belly was dimpled in the center to form the shape known as "two hills". Raif recalled Ballic the Red once saying that such bows were used by the warrior hordes who'd invaded the vast grasslands of the Far South. Ballic had never been one for lauding foreigners, but he had respect for the men who drew two-hill recurves. "They know how to make an arrow fly," he'd said once, grudgingly. For him it was high praise.

Which to choose? Flatbow, longbow, or recurve?

Raif glanced quickly at Yustaffa. The fat man was ready for him, his palms raised skyward in a showy pantomime of *I can't possibly give anything away*.

A second glance at Tanjo Ten Arrow showed the burned man accepting charge of his own weapon from a small child who looked like his son. The boy bowed formally as he offered the six-foot longbow to his father on a cushion of tasseled and embroidered silk. He was beautiful, the child, smooth-skinned and somber-faced, with the large watchful eyes of someone eager to learn. His right earlobe had been expertly excised, leaving a half-moon scar in the place where jaw met skull. Raif recognized the scar for what it was: a mercy cut. If a father didn't take a pound of flesh from his son, someone else might take more later. You couldn't trust a Maimed Man around a whole child.

All thoughts fled Raif's mind as he set eyes upon Tanjo Ten Arrow's bow. The weapon was built, made of wafer-thin layers of wood and horn laid down in alternating strips. Thin as a reed and barely recurved, it had the slightest suggestion of ears where the tips flared outward to accept the string. Its belly was stained deep blue, and designs in a milky shade of silver had been stamped below the riser.

A Sull bow.

Raif felt an odd fluttering in his stomach. He wanted that bow. It was finer and more beautifully worked than the one Angus Lok had given him—the one he'd lost on the southern slopes of the Bitter Hills. Almost he knew how it would feel to draw it: the extreme tension in the string, the tick of wood and horn as the belly flexed within his grip. For a brief moment he imagined setting the arrow Divining Rod against its plate and releasing the string . . .

A dizzying sense of displacement made him stagger forward, and he had to thrust a hand against the cart yoke to stop himself from falling. Pain from his halved finger cut through his thoughts. Something, a sense of knowledge almost gained or a future almost glimpsed, fled from him like a small animal at night.

Behind him, Maimed Men were drawing breaths and murmuring softly. All had seen him falter, and Raif could not tell if this pleased or disgusted them, just that it excited them in the way that the first drop of blood excited a hunter.

The Orrlsman was on the run.

Ignoring them, he focused his attention on the three bows. Flatbow. Longbow. Recurve. The yew longbow was the obvious choice; Yustaffa had to know that as a clansman it would be the one Raif would be drawn to first. The recurve was the most valuable and showy, and would probably be the favorite of the crowd, but Raif didn't like the look of the memory marks on the wood backing. Some looked deep enough to split. That left the elm flatbow. A workhorse, but nothing to excite a distance shooter. Reluctantly, Raif moved his hand toward it.

As he did so, he became aware of Yustaffa *stilling* at his side. The fat man's dark eyes glittered as his breath hung, unexhaled, in his mouth.

He wants me to pick it, Raif knew with sudden certainty. *He guessed how my mind would work, and bet that I'd reject the two superior bows.*

Raif let his hand hover above the flatbow as he studied the wood. Smooth, well-oiled elm met his gaze. But there. A sunken knot on the back of the bow, partially concealed by the skin-wrapped grip. Ballic the Red called such knots doom holes and said any bow made with such flawed wood would break sooner or later. Looking at it, Raif thought he detected a series of tiny indents around the edge of the knot. Yustaffa had been busy with a needle.

Smoothly, Raif pushed his hand from the flatbow and let it fall upon the yew longbow instead. The slight shrinking of the fat man's lips told Raif all he needed to know. *Beat you, Yustaffa.*

Now all he had to do was beat Tanjo Ten Arrow.

"The choice is made!" Yustaffa proclaimed, easily regaining his good humor as he motioned for the cart to be wheeled away. "Archers. Prepare to take practice shots."

Tanjo Ten Arrow's son moved behind his father, drawing back Tanjo's short archer's cape and fastening it so that it lay flat against his back like a beetle's wings. Tanjo ran two fingers down the Sull bowstring, warming the twine and checking its tension. Two rabbits' tails had been fastened to the twine to suppress recoil.

Raif unhooked his own cloak, noticing as he did so the brief flash of interest in Tanjo Ten Arrow's cool, alien eyes. Always the Orrlsman's cloak made men look. Thoughtful, Raif tested the bend of the yew longbow. He was relieved when a bow case containing five dozen arrows was placed at his feet by a tiny, ancient bowman who caused Yustaffa to frown. Good. That meant the fat man had not been given a chance to interfere with the arrows.

While Raif was making last-minute preparations, the meet party edged back, giving both contestants room to draw. Yustaffa was last to go, directing a young boy to snap the chalk line that would form the starting mark.

All was quiet except for the wind. Raif and Tanjo Ten Arrow stood eight feet apart, bow cases at their feet, bows rising like ship's masts at their sides. The rising sun sent shadows slanting westward over the Rift. Light shone on the wooden beehives, illuminating the red bull's-eyes painted at the height of human hearts. Yustaffa was addressing the crowd, explaining how the contest would proceed, but Raif had little patience for his words. Fear and anticipation mingled in his blood, making him quiver with nervous force. His stomach sucked against his spine as he filled his lungs with air. *How am I going to do this?*

"Archers. Take your practice shots."

Even before Raif slid his first arrow from the case, Tanjo Ten Arrow was already firing. The burned man was a blur of movement, pulling the decorated arrows from his sash one by one and firing them high into the air. As Raif nocked his first arrow the count began:

"One!" chanted the crowd.

"Two!"

"Three!"

By the time the crowd called "Four!" Raif knew how Tanjo Ten Arrow had won his name. He meant to send all ten arrows into the air before the first one landed. And he was going to do it, too. Raif had never seen anyone shoot so fast. Tanjo's arms dropped and pulled, dropped and pulled, with the speed and efficiency of a war engine. The arrows cut air, whistling softly as they shot toward the target. Tanjo had taken the head-wind into account, and angled his arrows slightly northwest of the first beehive, letting the strong southern current correct their flights. The updraft from the Rift aided him, for he had chosen a moment when the thermals were rising and they buoyed each arrow, keeping it in the air for precious seconds longer.

"Eight!"

"Nine!"

"Ten!"

Thunk. The first arrow hit the beehive as the tenth cleared the riser. The crowd erupted into a frenzy of cheering and stamping their feet. *Thunk, thunk, thunk . . .* it went on as each of the remaining arrows pierced wood.

Tanjo Ten Arrow stood very still, his bow edge resting against the rimrock, his burned head held high and his gaze upon the target. He heard the appreciation of the crowd but in no way responded to it. The only sign that he had pushed his body hard was the fierce flaring of his nostrils as he expelled air.

Raif watched as the last of the arrows struck the wooden beehive. None of them had hit the bull's-eye or even the inner circle, but that wasn't really the point. Undermining your opponent's confidence was. No bowman could watch such a display of shooting and remain unaffected. There was true skill here. Tanjo Ten Arrow had been touched by a god.

Perhaps that was why he'd been burned.

As the crowd quieted and Yustaffa heaped ever more fantastic praises upon Tanjo Ten Arrow's head, Raif drew the yew longbow. Pain in his little finger stabbed sharply as he braced the bow with his damaged left hand and pulled the string to his cheek with his right. It didn't matter. It was as if he had never stopped firing arrows at all, so quickly did the discipline of eye and hand return to him. How long had it been? Half a winter ago? Yet it felt like no time at all. The muscles in his shoulders felt stiff, but it was a good stiffness, a reminder that they were the source of the bow's power and though they hadn't been used in many months they hadn't forgotten their role.

Then everything fell away. Raif's eye fixed on the target, the red bull's-eye as big as an apple a hundred paces to the west. It was the heart. All archery targets were the heart. They might be circles or crosses or even cabbages lined up on a fence: to a bowman they were always the heart.

Raif did not attempt to *call* the target to him. It was dead wood and there was nothing but fresh air and then a second target a hundred paces behind it; there was no life or heart to respond to his call. Instead he forced his mind to focus on the target, sending an invisible thread from the hole in his eye to dead center of the bull. A fisherman casting a line. The circle came into sharp relief, and when the redness filled his vision he released the string.

The soft *thwang* of the recoil was all he heard for a moment. Unlike Tanjo Ten Arrow, he hadn't made a large adjustment for the wind. His arrow traveled close to the ground where the worst of the headwind couldn't catch it. The thermals were another matter, and lacking the ability to judge them he had simply waited until there was a break in the updraft.

Besides, he told himself stubbornly, this was just a practice shot: it didn't really matter either way.

Thunk. The arrow hit. Speckled hawk-feathers blew wildly as the arrow-shaft vibrated. The iron head had sunk deep into the pitch-soaked pine of the beehive . . . incredibly, miraculously, grazing the edge of the bull.

Maimed Men jeered. Yustaffa started up again, fluting praises to the lone Orrlsman, Raif Twelve Kill. Raif would have liked to punch him. Far beyond the target lane, two women began to turn the iron spit that suspended the whole hog above the cook fire. Raif smelled the fatty, meaty aroma of roasting pork as he accepted the hostility of the crowd. Like Tanjo Ten Arrow before him, he willed himself not to react. He didn't want to betray his own amazement at his practice shot. Let them think he placed arrows like that every day.

Two men on the fringes of the crowd were watching him intently. Raif turned his head slightly and exchanged gazes with Stillborn. The great, thick-necked Maimed Man nodded enthusiastically, his eyebrows up and working. Briefly, Raif wondered what had possessed Stillborn to befriend him. True, he had stolen Raif's kill, his sword and his named arrow, yet Raif still thought of him as a friend. He was the only man here who wanted to see him win.

Traggis Mole did not.

The Robber Chief was the second man watching Raif intently. He hadn't seemed to move all the time Raif had stood on the rimrock, yet something behind his eyes had changed. He had not liked Raif's shot, but there was more. Out of a crowd of perhaps eight hundred, he was the only one who saw it for what it was. A lucky hit. *Do it again, Orrlsman*, his eyes seemed to say. *I dare you.*

Raif swallowed, then looked away. The crowd had grown quiet again as Tanjo Ten Arrow prepared for his first official shot. The same boy who'd wheeled the handcart was kneeling in front of the beehive, tugging the practice arrows from the face of the target. Pitch oozed from the holes.

"You have killed wolf."

Raif's head turned at the sound of Tanjo Ten Arrow's voice. The burned man spoke in low tones, fired as expertly as his arrows. The words were for Raif's ears alone. And they were not a question.

Fixing his gaze on the targets once more, Raif asked, "What makes you say such a thing?"

Tanjo slid an arrow from his bowcase and nocked it. "Your eyes. The wolf is in them."

Raif thought of the great ice wolf, Pack Leader, spitted on a willow staff that had sundered its heart. He closed his eyes for a moment, reliving that final, desperate blow. Ash's life had depended upon it.

"Kill a wolf, and the gods look up." Tanjo Ten Arrow released the string, sending a lacquered arrow high into the air. Snow-goose feathers caught glacial winds blowing south from the Want, and used them to bend the flight of the arrow as surely as if they were still attached to the bird. *Thunk.* The arrow landed in the bull, a fraction short of dead center. "Kill a wolf with a blow to the heart, and the gods make play with your fate."

Raif kept his face still. *Words, just words.* The burned man was trying to throw his concentration. He took several deep breaths, then slid his own arrow from its case. As he fitted the string into the arrow's nock, he remembered something Yustaffa had said. Not dropping his gaze from the bull, he murmured, "How about a wager, Tanjo? Just you and me?"

Tanjo Ten Arrow was silent. Raif could not see him, but he felt the burned man's interest. After a moment, Tanjo said, "Name what you would have."

"Your bow."

Two words, and Raif knew he had spoken them too quickly and given away exactly how deeply he desired the Sull bow. At his side, Tanjo Ten Arrow was very still. Seconds passed. Raif gripped both arrow and string and pulled the yew longbow to full draw. Only when he reached full tension did Tanjo speak. Raif was prepared for it and held his draw. Let the burned man try to distract him. Let him try.

"What do you offer in return?" Tanjo Ten Arrow spoke Common with the solemn precision of someone who had learned it as a second tongue, and it was hard for Raif to gauge the level of his interest.

Dancing ice. That was what Angus had called it when his horse had carried Ash to safety over the frozen waters of the Black Spill. Raif felt he was doing the same here, negotiating with Tanjo Ten Arrow. It was a dance, and timing was everything. The negotiation must be completed before he released his first shot, while Tanjo's arrow was the only one in the bull. The burned man would not risk wagering his bow if he thought there was a chance he could lose it.

"The Orrl cloak." Raif made a brief motion with his head, indicating the cleared area behind him where the iridescent blue-white cloak lay fanned out upon the rimrock. It was a worthy prize, a treasure for any man who hunted in snow and ice. But for a bowman, nothing was more precious than his bow.

It was hard to hold the draw while he waited to hear Tanjo's response. Raif's shoulder muscles began to quiver and his thumb and bowfinger whitened as the pressure drove blood out. Tanjo saw this, and Raif swore the burned man counted to a hundred before declaring, "Done."

Raif released the string.

The arrow shot from the plate, delivering a recoil that sent the bow snapping against his bandaged finger. Wincing, he did not see where his arrow landed. The pain was so fierce he hardly cared.

The crowd told him what his eyes did not. The women hissed, and the men muttered in dissatisfaction. Yustaffa issued a throaty sigh, enjoying himself immensely. Raif's arrow was in the bull. *This* was starting to get interesting.

As the cart boy ran forward to measure and retrieve the arrows, Raif glanced at Tanjo Ten Arrow. The man showed only his profile to Raif, his gaze cast far in the distance. Burned skin twitched once, then was still.

When the cart boy was finished with the measuring stick he signaled to Yustaffa.

"Raif Twelve Kill has it!" pronounced the fat man, his face reddening with excitement. "He wins first shot by a margin of— what, boy?"

The boy held the measuring stick above his head. Made of a hollow reed and seared with marks at short intervals, the stick resembled a flute. Grubby fingers marked the spot. "Two notches."

Raif did not expect what happened next. Tanjo Ten Arrow turned to him and bowed so low that the tail of his topknot touched rimrock. When he straightened his spine Raif saw he was smiling. Like a shark. "And now we will see who the true master is."

Raif could prevent his muscles from reacting, but he had no power over the blood leaving his face. He'd been so pleased at foiling Yustaffa's attempt to trick him that he'd not realized he was being tricked by someone else. Tanjo Ten Arrow's first shot had been a fake.

Tanjo seemed well satisfied. In a single, elegant sweep he slid an arrow from his bow case and fitted it to his bow. Barely waiting for the cart boy to clear the target, Tanjo let his arrow fly. *Thunk.* Dead center of the bull.

Oh gods. Raif barely registered the cheering of the crowd. At the far edge of his vision he saw Traggis Mole move. A small motion, executed with enough speed to defy the eye, delivered his right hand to the hilt of his knife. *I won't see the blow that kills me.*

Raif nocked his second arrow. He felt his concentration alight like a fly upon the bow. The slightest thing would send it elsewhere. Best be done with the shot quickly, while the bull was in his sights and before his arms began to shake.

The moment his fingers released the string he knew he'd made a mistake. The bow recoiled dully, the twine flapping loosely against the riser. A puff of wind on the underside of his chin told him the updrafts were rising, and his arrow was lofted into the path of the southern headwinds. Raif dropped his gaze. Turbulence was making the arrow-shaft wobble, and he didn't need to see it complete its flight to know it was going wide.

Thunk. Cheering erupted for Tanjo Ten Arrow.

Raif stared at the rimrock beneath his feet, waiting to hear the sound of the cart boy pulling arrows from the beehive. The next shot would be the final one at this target. Winning the first round was not vital in winning the contest, but Raif had watched enough archery contests to know that once you started losing it was hard to stop. He breathed hard, trying to settle his thoughts. At his side he was aware of Tanjo Ten Arrow scratching an imagined defect from his bow with fingernails as long as waxed beans.

The third arrow Tanjo fired entered the hole made by his second. Pitch sprayed into the air, spattering rimrock and trickling down the target like cold syrup. Raif set his sights on the white snow-goose feathers protruding from the center of the bull. The updrafts rose and dropped, and then Raif released the string.

The shot was good, and the arrow landed within the bull, but it was wide of dead center where Tanjo's arrow stood upright like a needle on a sundial. Maimed Men cheered as Yustaffa pronounced the burned man the winner of the first round. A handful of small children rushed into the archery lane to help wheel off the first beehive, clearing the way to the second target. The second beehive was set at a distance of two hundred paces, the bull nothing more than a dot in Raif's sights.

Clay pots of beer and trays piled high with greasy oatcakes and whole roast onions were distributed amongst the crowd during the lull. Women around the hog fire rolled up their sleeves and loosened the strings on their bodices as the heat from the flames made them sweat. The hog was black now, its outer skin cracked and flaking. When one of the women pierced its belly with a pitchfork a fountain of juices spurted forth. Raif looked away. The festivities left him cold. He was anxious to begin the second round, and every extra minute he had to wait was torture. Nervously, he ran a hand down the yew longbow. At a hundred paces an archer could shoot straight. At two hundred paces he needed height. There'd be no avoiding the headwind this time.

"Archers. Take your practice shots."

Raif was ready with his arrow, and he didn't wait to see if Tanjo was about to launch another ten-shot spectacle. Quickly, he fired an exploratory arrow high into the air. The wind caught it and gently curved its flight southward, sending the head into the far edge of the beehive, a good two hands wide of the bull. Raif exhaled in relief. *At least I didn't miss.*

Tanjo Ten Arrow chose to launch only one practice arrow, expertly pitched to exploit the wind. Even from two hundred paces Raif heard the satisfying *thunk* of an arrow piercing the hollow center of the bull.

"I think I will enjoy wearing your cloak, Clansman," Tanjo said as he relaxed his grip on the Sull bow. "It should bring me much luck in the hunt."

Raif had no reply for him. He was running out of shots and time. He knew he was a good bowman, but it would take a master archer like Ballic the Red to match arrows with the burned man. He'd thought the extra hundred paces might even things out between them, but Tanjo's last shot had proved him wrong. His only hope now was blind luck.

Tanjo made his next shot easily, placing his arrow a fraction high of dead center. Raif almost matched him, and hawk feathers and snow-goose feathers scissored together the arrows landed so close. Yustaffa did a little dance of glee as he waited for the cart boy to make the call. Raif wondered how much the fat man had wagered on Tanjo's head.

The next two shots went quickly. Both Raif's arrows placed well—one firmly in the bull and the other grazing its rim—but Tanjo's arrows were better.

By now the crowd was going wild. "*Tan-Jo!*" they shrieked. "*Tan-Jo! Tan-Jo!*" Much ale had been drunk, and Maimed Men were pressing close on all sides. Raif could smell them and see their weapons. The pregnant woman with the slate bound to her chest looked at him and sneered. "Be a long, cold night in the Rift."

The Gates to Hell. Raif shuddered as Yustaffa's words came back to him. From where he stood, twenty paces from the edge of the rimrock, he couldn't see the vast gap in the earth. The sky above was a clear and perfect blue, and the only sign that the world wasn't right here was the sun. It shone too pale and small, and all its warmth and half its light were swallowed by the Rift. Why send men over the edge? Dead or alive, what good did it do?

Raif barely heard the sound of the second beehive being wheeled away.

The third and final beehive was the largest of the three. Built from pine boards, it was drum-shaped and tall as a horse. It had to be. At three hundred paces few archers sought to hit a man. Most would be happy to clip a rider's mount. Still, the bull's-eye was there, a red circle at the height of a stallion's heart.

Beyond the target, the hog fire roared as pork fat fueled the flames. Raif found it hard to center himself on the bull. Archery contests were all about the final round. Win here, and he could force a draw with Tanjo. It wasn't going to be easy, though. The headwind was gusting now, and more difficult to gauge for it. The distance between archer and target was so great that the bull was the merest fleck of red in the distance. Raif glanced at Tanjo. The burned man was keenly focused on the target, the damaged skin around his eyes pulling taut as he squinted.

Practice shots were taken, and for the first time Raif got the sense that Tanjo's arrow was exploring, rather than homing. The burned man fired his arrow a few degrees short of vertical, and the headwinds fought its arc and robbed power from it. The arrow landed on the face of the target, a good three feet below the bull. The crowd murmured their surprise. Tanjo's shot had fallen short. Raif was quick to correct Tanjo's error, and angled his bow lower and drew more power behind it, straining the twine until it hummed. His arrow landed high, making a solid *thunk* as it struck the beehive, demonstrating it still had power to spare. Someone in the crowd cheered. Probably Stillborn.

Raif almost grinned. It took jaw to cheer a hated man.

The next shot went better for Tanjo, but in his eagerness to counter his opponent's show of strength, he overpowered his arrow, blasting it from the plate. Like Raif's arrow seconds earlier, Tanjo's landed high, missing the bull by a handspan. For a shot taken at three hundred paces it was remarkable, but Tanjo Ten Arrow took no joy from it. The burned man clenched his fist and sent a look of cold hatred to Raif.

Raif thought he was probably going mad, for that look filled him with hope. With an easy hand he drew his bow, squinting to set the faraway target in his sights. Lightly, he released the string, and watched as his arrow battled headwinds and updrafts to land on the rim of the bull.

Malign energy rippled through the Maimed Men like a storm cloud passing overhead. Raif felt their dark looks and hostile mutterings like mosquitoes landing to feed. They would have harmed him then and there if it hadn't been for the unmoving presence of Traggis Mole. The Robber Chief seemed to control the crowd by the act of stillness. No one wanted to be the first to make him move.

"First shot to Raif Twelve Kill!" cried Yustaffa, breaking the tension by fanning a chubby hand beneath his chin as if the air had suddenly become very hot. "Two more shots left. May the gods help me survive them."

Tanjo Ten Arrow ignored the fat man's theatrics, and slowly pulled back his bowstring. He'd won the first two rounds, but the third counted for more. If Raif were to win here there'd be a tie, and a fourth target would be set. Waiting for a break in the wind, Tanjo held the Sull recurve at full draw as easily as if it were a child's first bow. The jade bowring he used to protect his long fingernails glinted in the rising sun. When the release came it was so quiet on the rimrock you could hear the arrow fly. Raif knew straightaway the shot was good, but he didn't realize *how* good until his eyes far-focused on the target . . . and saw the arrow enter the red territory of the bull. It wasn't dead center, but it was close enough to send gasps of amazement through the crowd.

Raif forced a calmness he did not feel onto his face. Any man who could make a shot like that was worthy of respect, but he knew he couldn't afford to admire Tanjo Ten Arrow. You had to hate a man who had the power to deprive you of life. Raif plucked an arrow from his bow case. A pulse had started throbbing in his neck, and it seemed to him that there were too many calls upon his thoughts. As he sighted his arrow he waited for the calm to come. Strangely, all winds had dropped and for the first time since he had awakened he heard the sound of the city itself. It groaned. Deep within its hand-hewn caverns bedrock was moving. Low wails and barely audible creaks rose from the hollow orbits of its many caves, making a sound like something tearing open.

A memory came to Raif unbidden: the gas geysers exploding as he and Ash approached Ice Trapper territory. The earth he walked on wasn't stable any more.

With the briefest kiss, he released the string. As he braced against the recoil he realized he had held his draw too long and relaxed the tension unwittingly, and the arrow sped forth underpowered. Angry at himself, he watched as the arrow flew too low and reached its zenith too soon. Lazily, it dropped to the foot of the target, barely carrying enough speed to pierce wood.

"Second shot to Tanjo Ten Arrow!"

A small satisfied smile briefly stretched the pink and tan skin of Tanjo's face. He did not look at Yustaffa or the cheering crowd, only Raif. "Did you think I would let you win this, Clansman?" He lifted the Sull bow so that it caught the light, causing the dyed horn to ripple like molten glass. Silvery markings which had shown earlier as faint lines suddenly leapt into sharp relief: moon and stars. And a raven. A raven screaming at the night. "I would die first."

With that Tanjo Ten Arrow took his final shot. The arrow moved in the exact same arc as his last one, almost as if it were following a trail. The only difference was a fraction of extra pull to the right that guided the iron head even closer to the center of the bull.

Raif flinched as the arrow hit. Maimed Men began pounding rock with the butts of their weapons and booted feet, chanting a word that it took him a moment to understand. For an instant he thought they were calling his name and he wondered what had happened to change their allegiance—but then he realized they were speaking his death sentence instead.

"Rift! Rift! Rift!"

Grimly, Raif nocked his arrow. A sort of dark calm was descending upon him, and the pulse in his neck began beating with the quiet force of a second heart. He knew Death. He'd met her. Did they think they could scare him by threatening to send him back?

The arrow flew hard from the plate. Whatever force had possessed Raif's body had transferred to the bow, and the recoil lashed against his hand. The pain barely registered. He'd sent his arrow too high, and all its power was being wasted as it climbed almost vertically toward the sky. Raif cursed himself. It was all over. Arrows like that peaked and then fell. They were good for taking an enemy's eye out on the field, but not for hitting targets. Already the Maimed Men were closing on him, their chant rising as the arrow dropped.

"Rift! Rift! Rift!"

And then the updrafts rose. Suddenly the air moved, lifting cloak hems and scalp hair and filling the women's skirts until they puffed like bells. Raif felt a drying warmth upon his eyeballs, and then his warrior's queue lifted from his shoulders like a pennant.

Invisible columns of force rose from the hole in the earth, making the air ripple as if it were melting, and catching in the flight feathers of Raif's arrow. It happened in less than an instant, but to Raif it seemed as if he watched the path of his arrow change over minutes. Air buoyed the shaft and nudged the point upward, shifting the flight from a sheer drop to an arcing fall. All was quiet for a moment as the arrow traveled westward on the thermals. Eight hundred faces turned skyward. Breath was held. The updrafts blew steadily for perhaps another second, and then died.

The arrow dropped with the wind.

Thunk. Dead center of the bull.

Silence. A stillness possessed the Maimed Men. It was as if no one wanted to be the first to move or speak into the void created by the receding wind.

Defiantly, Raif rested his bow, causing the wood to tap against the rock. He couldn't understand what had just happened, but he sensed danger, and he knew he would be a fool to show these men his fear. Steadying himself, he turned to Yustaffa. "Announce the victor."

All animation had drained from Yustaffa, leaving him looking fat and charmless. His tunic strained at the seams, and grease in his over-coiffed hair had attracted stray filaments from the arrows' flight feathers. He cleared his throat, and Raif did not miss the glance he sent to Traggis Mole before daring to open his mouth. "Third and final round goes to Raif Twelve Kill."

The crowd surged forward, mouths shrinking, fingers closing around air. Someone threw a stone.

Yustaffa raised his palms skyward and rushed on, his voice

almost squeaking. "Now, Rift Brothers, we mustn't be hasty. The contest isn't done yet. In the event of a tie we fall back on that most glorious and perilous tradition: sudden death. Yes, my friends. Sudden death. One target, one shot per man. Best shot wins." Yustaffa swung his head back and forth, looking for an appropriate target. Clearly, none had been arranged. No one had thought the outsider could win.

Raif looked away. For some reason he found himself thinking of Ash. Where was she this moment? Did she ever wonder if leaving him had been a mistake?

"Let them shoot the hog."

The sharp, rough-edged voice of Traggis Mole brought him back. Raif looked up to see the Robber Chief's black gaze upon him, and he was almost glad of it. Glad because it took his mind away from Ash.

Charged silence followed Traggis Mole's words. Maimed Men eased back, but did not appear eased. Their chief's voice stirred them, and Raif could see the need for violence in their eyes. *They're not clan.* He'd been told it by Tem and Angus and a dozen other people he knew. Three nights ago Stillborn had told him the same. Yet he'd listened without truly hearing them. Now he knew they were right. The Maimed Men looked and sounded like clan, most of them, but there were no gods living in this stone city and nothing but shared desperation to bind it.

"I yield first shot to the clansman." Tanjo Ten Arrow bowed to Raif as he spoke, his face a mask of politeness as his shoulder blades sliced air.

Raif did not return the courtesy. It was a sham. The hog was perhaps three hundred and fifty paces away, far wide of the central lane, suspended above a snakepit of flames. Heat distorted the air, and smoke clouded it. Tanjo had not relinquished first shot out of kindness. No practice shots were allowed in sudden death. The man who loosed his arrow first would be shooting blind. How much pull and height would be needed? Was the heat of the fire great enough to affect the arrow's flight? Any experienced bowman was capable of making such judgments, but the decisions were that much easier when you could learn by someone else's mistakes. Tanjo had decided to stand back and let Raif make some.

There was nothing to be done but shoot. Raif flexed the longbow and waited for the women to clear the cook fire. The hog had been turned to present its flank to the archers, and although the animal was large it was winter-starved and bony. Raif wondered where it had come from, for Stillborn had said the Maimed Men were short of meat. Did raid parties ride south and seize livestock from tied clansmen? How did they cross the Rift?

He fitted an arrow to the longbow. The carcass was hideous. Heat had shrunk the tendons, and all four limbs were raised and contracted. The tail looked stiff enough for a child to swing on. The snout had split and split again, and glimpses of steamed pink flesh could be seen beneath the char. Raif tried not to shudder as he focused his gaze upon the flank.

Dead. Something deep inside him, in the place where his brain fused with his spine, sparked darkly like a single beam of moonlight moving across black water. Saliva wetted Raif's mouth. The cooked gray chambers of the hog's heart sucked him in. Suddenly he couldn't breathe. He was surrounded by reeking flesh. Nothing of life remained here, just a spongy mass of exploded cells, and arteries choked with boiled blood. *Dead.* And even though it was hot inside the chamber, an immense and merciless coldness lay beneath. Waiting.

Fear squeezed Raif's stomach. He had to get out of here. Now. Death was moving closer, its tendrils uncurling like drifts of smoke as it reached out to touch his mind. *The Gates to Hell.* He could feel them pulling him in: the sucking blackness of swamp water, the fumes and taint of death. There was no bottom to the swamp, just a lifeless, eternal void. Once he went under he'd never stop falling.

It wouldn't let go. The hog's heart was a sprung trap. He should never have entered. A pumping heart was a force of nature. A still one was a portal to death. And it pulled, it *pulled* him. Roaring filled his ears, and his thoughts began to twist around themselves as the tow grew stronger. The smell of cooked flesh faded, replaced by the sparkling blue odor of ice. Shadows moved at the periphery of his vision. Something sighed. The weight of corrupted flesh, soft and liquid with rot, bore him down.

Yet his mouth still watered, and deep within his brain stem something quickened. He could feel his retinas dilating. This territory was known to him. Coming here was like coming home.

Afterwards he could not remember releasing the string. He recalled only the shock of emerging from the darkness and the dizzying confusion of feeling sunlight on his face. His breaths were coming hard and fast, and he felt the iciness of the wind as keenly as if he were naked. He blinked like a man shaken suddenly awake, and his eyes showed him a sight it took his mind several moments to understand.

A crowd of people, so still and silent they might have been clothed statues, were staring beyond him to the spitted carcass. An arrow—*his* arrow—had plunged deep into the creature's heart. The force of impact had split the crisped hide in a star-burst pattern, and flaps of blackened flesh blew in the breeze, curling back to reveal the fatty hoops of the ribcage and a fist of shattered bone. It looked as if someone had taken a hammer to the ribs that lay directly above the heart and smashed them like pieces of pottery. The steaming gray mound of the hog's heart could be glimpsed beneath the shards. It had been split clean in two.

Raif swallowed. A sour taste was in his mouth. The yew longbow stood upright in his grip like a staff, yet he had no memory of resting it. He thought he should perhaps act; force Yustaffa to pronounce the shot good, acknowledge the fearful quiet of the crowd with an easy wave of his hand, bow smartly to Tanjo Ten Arrow and say, *your shot, I believe.* Yet he couldn't move.

Strangely, he recalled a tale Angus had once told him, of how the people who wandered the hard, red desert of the Far South named their sons. The father would choose a name but tell no one, not even his wife, of his decision and the child would grow to manhood never knowing what his father had named him. The son's mother and siblings would call him by pet names until he became a man, strong enough and brave enough to challenge his father to a fight. The fights were bloody, Angus said, for the pride of the desert men was a terrible thing, and no father wanted to lose a fight to his son. To win, the son must be merciless and beat his father to the ground. Standing over his father, he must say, *I claim my name. Give me what is mine.* And the name is spoken, and the son walks away, leaving his father on the desert floor for the women to tend to, and departs the camp to hunt. There is magic that first night, Angus said, and animals will throw themselves onto the son's spear and the gods send visions to guide him.

Raif did not expect visions or animals lining up for the honor of being killed by him. But still.

I claim my name.

Looking at the carcass, at the arrow splitting the cooked heart, Raif knew that somehow he had claimed his name. *Mor Drakka.* Watcher of the Dead. How many arrows had he sent into beating hearts? He didn't know. But this . . . this was the first arrow he'd sent into a dead one.

He looked away, gazing down at the rimrock without seeing it. From what seemed like a very great distance, he heard Yustaffa speak. "Well. A shot, a shot, certainly a shot. Leaves a few less bones for Old Bessie to carve." He made an odd hiccuping sound. "Well. I suppose we'd better write an end to this. Tanjo. When you're ready."

The crowd began stirring as Tanjo prepared to take his shot. Maimed Men murmured, their leathers and metalwork creaking as they stretched numbed limbs and worked cricks from their necks. Raif heard an arrow being fitted against the plate, and looked up in time to see Tanjo draw his bow. Tanjo Ten Arrow's burned face was made golden by the morning light. The Sull bow shimmered with power as it curved in his hands. Tanjo breathed once against the string and then lifted the jade bowring clear of the bow.

The shot was beautiful, Raif would remember that for always: Tanjo's release, his perfect stance, the particular sound—the trill of the discharged arrow—that said the shot was flawless. It flew high and then dropped like a hawk onto the carcass. Almost it matched Raif's arrow. Three hundred and fifty paces through smoke and warped air, and it landed in the bulb-shaped aorta that exited the hog's heart.

Even before the Maimed Men had a chance to react, Tanjo Ten Arrow turned to Raif and bowed. Pride kept his face muscles taut as he straightened his spine and held out the Sull bow. Out of the corner of his vision, Raif saw Tanjo's son weaving through the front row of the crowd, moving urgently toward his father. Someone, a big fair-haired hunchback, put out a hand to halt him. The boy kicked and fought, but the hunchback held him firm. An old hag near the front handed the hunchback her wool cloak and bade him cover the child's face.

Raif knew Tanjo Ten Arrow had to be aware of what was happening to his son, but the burned man did not react in any way. His gaze held steady on Raif. "Take the bow. It has served me well."

Yustaffa had begun speaking, his voice rising in high drama, but Raif did not hear the words. The Sull bow was no longer something he wanted, yet he moved his hand toward it all the same. *I claim my name.* And now it seemed to him that he understood why the sons of the desert men walked away and left their beaten fathers on the ground. Shame burned both men, yet neither could let it show. Raif met Tanjo's pride with pride of his own, and their hands touched briefly on the belly of the bow.

I owe you respect, Raif wanted to say. *You are the greater bowman.* Yet the words would never be said. Instead, Raif bowed low as he took possession of the bow, and pretended not to see the darkly moving shadow of Traggis Mole sliding toward them, and the brief flicker of fear in Tanjo Ten Arrow's eyes.

"*Rift! Rift! Rift!*" the chant began as Traggis Mole pulled his knife from its sheath of fossilized wood. Tanjo straightened his spine and turned to face him. The fear was gone now, and the pride that remained made the women weep.

"Unhood my son."

As Raif heard those words he felt a hand touch his shoulder. "Come on, lad. Step away. Best give them chance to forget you." Stillborn gripped Raif's arm and tugged him back. Raif thought for a moment he would fight him, but Tanjo's son now stood quiet and free from restraint, his face uncovered, his small body quaking with the effort of matching his father's pride. The child was younger than Effie, and Raif let Stillborn draw him back.

"*Rift! Rift! Rift!*"

The cry of the crowd rose to a frenzy as Traggis Mole descended upon Tanjo Ten Arrow. There was a movement too quick to follow with the eye, and then the Robber Chief yanked

Tanjo to his chest. A violent wrench broke bones in Tanjo's neck and spine, and then two streams of blood jetted across the rimrock as Traggis Mole's knife took the lids from Tanjo's eyes. The burned man's body slackened and twitched in Traggis's grip. The white globes of his eyeballs rolled forward, the corneas sheeting with blood. Raif's hand dropped to his waist, searching for a measure of powdered guidestone that wasn't there. *Please, gods, take him now*. But the Robber Chief had broken only the bones needed to paralyze, not kill, and when the crowd surged forward to take possession of the body, Raif clearly saw Tanjo's gaze focusing upon his son.

The Maimed Men fell upon him. Raif had once seen a man torn apart by a pair of horses at Gnash, and the same forces that worked to rip limbs from sockets and the pelvis from the spine came to bear on the burned man's body. The mob pulled him apart. They dragged him to the edge of the rimrock, heaved him high on to many shoulders and then threw him violently over the brink.

Tanjo Ten Arrow's eyes were open and no sound ever came from his fall.

Raif shivered and walked away.

TWENTY-ONE

The Nine Safe Steps

"Alongsword is no weapon for a girl. You could train for a year and still not grow the muscle to use it." Ark Veinsplitter held out his hand. He wanted his longsword back. Ash had slid it from his weapons holster while he'd been busy covering the fire. The fire had burned through the night, and like most fires started by the Far Riders it had barely smoked, and had produced scarcely enough soot to stain the snow. Now that Ark was done with it Ash couldn't detect the exact patch of ground where it had been. For some reason this annoyed her, and she decided she wasn't about to give up the sword.

Ark was right: it *was* too heavy for her—and long, too. About two feet too long. And the weight of it seemed to shift from tip to pommel as she tilted it this way and that, as if it had something liquid in its core. It was so very beautiful, though, shining as brilliantly as a mirror so that sometimes you couldn't see it, just the things it reflected like mountains and sky. Ash's arms began to wobble with the weight of it, so she rested the tip in the snow. "Mal said he would begin teaching me how to defend myself today."

She expected Ark to be irritated by her refusal to give up

the sword, but instead he nodded gravely. "The Naysayer is right. Sometimes I forget you were not always Sull."

She nodded quickly, not wanting him to know how much she valued his words. *Tell me how much you love me, Asarhia.* The old request came to her unbidden, spoken as always in her foster-father's voice. It was a warning, that request, for when you let someone know how much you loved and wanted to belong to them, they could hurt you and shut you out. Casually, she tugged the Sull blade from the snow and handed it, grip first, to Ark Veinsplitter.

He watched her for a moment, and then recouched his steel.

Dawn light slid across the ice fields, revealing melt holes and pockets of gravel frozen just below the surface. Overhead the sky was deep blue, streaked with high clouds that were heading out. Ash shivered as a low wind set her lynx fur rippling like a field of grass. She did not know where she was. To the west lay the shimmering phantoms of the Coastal Ranges, white peaks that floated weightlessly above the horizon as if they were no longer anchored to the earth. In every other direction there was nothing she knew or recognized. The land was flat, almost featureless except for the steaming beds of ice that surrounded her. Sometimes she thought she saw shapes—ridges and rock forms in the distance—but if they existed they lay at the far edge of her perception and she could not trust her eyes to show the truth.

Mal Naysayer had left the camp sometime in the long night. The Far Rider was often away. Ash imagined him scouting for landmarks and drinkable water, standing on raised ground and peering into the territory ahead. She did not want to think about the black substance on his sword that day in the high valley, the way the liquid smoked as it melted snow. No. Better to imagine Mal surveying, rather than protecting. Safe, not in harm's way.

"Ash March. I would take on the promise my *hass* made you."

Ash looked over to see Ark Veinsplitter coming toward her. He had left his packs by the horses and shrugged off his heavy furs, and was bearing a small arms case covered with blue silk. Ash realized he was making a formal gift of the case and its contents when he placed the case on the ice at her feet rather than directly into her hand. It was the Sull way. They were sensitive about gifts, she'd noticed, adhering to rules she didn't quite understand.

"Take them out," Ark said. "Tell me how they feel in your hand."

Ash knelt on the ice. The case was the length of her forearm, made of cured hide judging by its stiffness, softened by an outer shell of padded silk. Someone with a fine hand had woven tiny silver threads around the clasp. Inside, resting on a pillow of down, was a slim dagger the length of the case, and a small, sickle-shaped weapon with a nine-foot chain attached. The chain was the thickness of her middle finger, forged from smoke-gray steel so finely worked that she could not see the joins between the links. It looked as if it should be heavy, but when she took it in her hand she was surprised by its fluid lightness. A glittering weight shaped like a giant teardrop was attached to the farthermost link, giving the chain heft. Ash ran fingers over the weight, wondering at its substance. Metals had been violently fused in its making, leaving some parts smooth and others cankered, and the entire surface rainbowed with smelt lines. Strangely faceted peridots studded its outer face, glowing weirdly like cat's eyes. To Ash's fingertips they felt as hard and sharp as diamonds, and she found herself imagining what they could do to a man's face.

"Take the sickle in your left hand and whirl the chain with your right."

The grip of the sickle fitted her palm perfectly and for the first time she realized this was not a weapon forged for a man. Letting out three feet of chain she began whirling the weight overhead. The metal *whump*ed as it gathered speed, its appearance changing from a solid object into a blur. The metal teardrop spun so swiftly that the peridots drew a ring of green fire in the air.

"Good. Now let it slow. Hold your arm straight. Move only the wrist."

Ash did as she was told, watching as the chain slackened and dropped. The weight descended rapidly, and she cried out in surprise as it hit the soft underflesh of her upper arm and the chain coiled around her forearm like a snake. Her eyes watered with the sting of impact, and when Ark stepped toward her she moved back in fright. He was too quick for her, and in an instant he had disarmed her and taken the sickle into his own hand. A quick tug on the chain and he floored her, wrenching her trapped arm down toward the earth. Even before she had time to register surprise he was upon her, applying the sickle blade to the roof of her jaw. Blood was drawn, squirting like hot urine against her skin.

The Sull Far Rider dropped the sickle and the chain's slack upon the ice. "Rise," he commanded.

Ash sat up but did not stand. She was shaking, and she felt betrayed. Raising her hand to her jaw she went to stanch the flow of blood.

"No," he warned her. "Let it run. It is *Dras Xaxu*. The First Cut."

She touched her jaw and brought bloody fingers to the light. "I've been bled before."

"Not with Sull blood."

He offered his hand, and after she'd made him wait a moment she took it and let him pull her upright. Ice crystals shed from her furs floated between them like dust. "Why did you do that?" she demanded.

"We are Sull, and we stand ready to fight. Before a child comes to manhood or womanhood blood must be drawn in friendly combat. We wound ourselves so that we might deprive our enemies of the satisfaction of delivering the First Cut."

Ash frowned at the Far Rider. She wanted to know why he'd chosen now to cut her. Who did he fear might cut her first? But his face was hard and his eyes issued a warning from their deep wells of bone. *Do not ask me more.*

Reluctantly, she picked up the sickle and chain. Her arm was sore and blood was trickling down her throat, and she thought for a moment she might like to scream at him. *Why do you hold so much back? You made me Sull—trust me.*

As she whirled the chain overhead Ark Veinsplitter moved to where the horses were feeding on oiled millet and pulled one of the birchwood corral posts from the ice. Planting the post closer to Ash, he bade her strike it with the chain. Tendons in Ash's wrist strained like guide ropes as she fought the torque. She cast the chain a beat too late, and the metal teardrop skimmed wide of the post and swung violently back toward her. The weight struck her spine, punching air from her lungs and gouging out a wedge of lynx fur.

Ark Veinsplitter watched coolly as she struggled to catch her breath. "Cast the chain properly and you can trap an enemy's arm, his weapon, his horse's leg. The weight can kill a man if it strikes with enough force in the temple or throat. And when the chain itself is held taut between two hands it becomes a shield, able to deflect an oncoming blade."

The Far Rider approached Ash and took the weight from her. Stepping backward, he reeled out the length of the chain until it was fully extended between them, and then dropped the weight onto the ice. "Watch," he directed, drawing his sword.

Close to six feet of Sull steel struck like lightning in front of her face as he wielded the blade from the distance created by the chain. Strike followed strike so swiftly that the space crackled with discharging energy, and the gashes carved out by the blade left afterimages hanging in the air. Yet the edge did not touch her.

"It is *Naza Thani*. The Nine Safe Steps. Keep the length of the chain between you and your enemy and their swords cannot reach you."

Ash nodded stiffly, unable to take her gaze from Ark's sword. The point of the blade moved so close to her eye she could see the crystalized "x" where the edges met. The Far Rider wanted her afraid. It was a test, and she feared failure more than getting hurt. She was Ash March, Foundling. She'd been abandoned once. She wouldn't give this man before her reason to walk away. Tilting her chin upward she stood unmoving and unblinking under Ark Veinsplitter's onslaught.

Ark's eyes narrowed, and he executed a series of forward thrusts, shearing off stray hairs that had risen around her face. Abruptly he halted, and recouched his sword. He was breathing hard, and when his voice came it was not gentle. "You should have stepped back. When I thrust forward I took a step toward you. *Naza Thani* was breached. My sword could have taken your head."

Ash felt her cheeks burn. She'd mistaken the nature of the test. And failed.

The expression on the Far Rider's ice-tanned face remained cold as he turned toward the corral. "Practice striking the post while I break camp."

She watched him saddle the gray and tighten its cinches. The wind skirled around the stallion's forelegs, raising whirlwinds of ice that would have chilled another horse to the bone. Not the gray, though. It was protected by deep feathering that fanned out from its knees in long, silky skirts. Ash pulled her arms around her chest, suddenly cold. She didn't want to pick up the sickle and chain and start again. She wanted to run to the gray and nuzzle him and slip bare hands beneath his mane to feel the warmth hidden there.

By the time the Far Rider had stowed the corral and equipped and watered both horses Ash had mastered striking the post. It was easy, really, as long as you didn't loose the chain too late. Once the chain was spinning rapidly it coiled around anything thrown in its path. The noise the links made as they wrapped around the birchwood post made hairs rise on Ash's neck. It was the sound of a snake rustling through grass. And then the weight fell with the soft *thunk* of a sprung trap, locking the chain into place. Aware that Ark's gaze was now upon her, Ash grabbed the chain in both hands and ripped the trapped post from the ice.

The Far Rider nodded, once. "Clean the chain and sheathe it. We need to be gone from this place."

Telling herself she didn't really expect praise, Ash did his bidding. The sun was rising swiftly now, bouncing rainbows of light off the ice. The frozen surface beneath her feet cracked and popped like firewood just set alight. Last night Ark had explained that the rock underlying the ice field was black chert, the same stone they knapped flints from, and its hard glassy core provided poor drainage for standing water. Pockets of ice melted during the day and refroze at night, as the entire valley held water like a bowl. It wasn't drinkable, for the water was old and gray, and poisons leached up from the rock. Looking down at the ice, at the withered things suspended just below the surface—the ancient pine needles where trees no longer stood, the claw of a predator, yellow and segmented like a maggot, the slivers of flint scattered like fish scales on a beach—Ash suddenly knew where she was.

The Great Want.

She thought she might shiver, but the bones inside her spine locked into place. The Great Want. The vast nothingness that lay at the top of all maps of the Northern Territories. No one knew how far it stretched, only that no man who had gone in search of its end had ever returned. Audlin Crieff, twenty-third surlord of Spire Vanis and Forsworn knight, had been lost here. He'd been taken by madness while on pilgrimage to the Lake of Lost Men, and had simply left his tent one morning and walked east. They had searched for him for ten days and ten nights but his body was never found.

Ash sat the Sull horse that was her mount when the Naysayer was away on the blue, and turned her thoughts elsewhere. The white gelding was a few hands shorter than Ark's gray, with a deep girth and muscular legs. Panniers mounted on its rump and shoulders held tent felts, ropes and poles, and the many other items required for raising camp. It was a heavy load, and Ash worried about being an added burden to the gentle beast. "Sorry, boy," she murmured, rubbing its nose.

"He was bred to bear aurochs home from the hunt," Ark said, surprising her by swinging the gray alongside the white. "Your weight will not trouble him."

Ash nodded uneasily. The Far Rider was always watching her.

"Reach down under his stifle."

Puzzled, she obeyed, running her hand along the horse's belly until it met the muscled ramp of its thigh. A leather trace ran the length of its torso, a harness of some kind, and she wondered at its purpose.

"Do you feel the buckle?"

She found it, yet it felt wrong to her fingers, lumpy and unguarded, and there was an extra piece of leather sticking out.

"If we are pursued pull the strap." The Far Rider looked ahead as he spoke, as if what he said wasn't as important as the task of crossing the ice. Ash wasn't fooled. She could hear the intensity in his voice. "If the Naysayer or I are engaged in combat pull the strap. It will release the horse's burdens and allow you to flee at speed. He has been *maygi*-spoke. He will carry you to safety and only return on my say."

"And what if you can no longer 'say'?" The words were out before Ash could stop them, and her first instinct was to soften them with an apology or more words. Yet she thought of her foster-father and didn't.

Time passed and then the Far Rider said, "Then you must continue east and find the Heart Fires for yourself." He held his head high and with great dignity, and watching him she learned something new: she had the ability to wound him.

Sobered, she asked, "What is a *maeraith*?"

"A beast of shadow." High clouds passed over the sun. The Far Rider's wolverine-fur-wrapped fingers did not tighten on the reins, yet some measure of tension must have passed from rider to mount, since the great Sull horse lowered its ears and twitched its tail.

Ash felt her own mount lose its rhythm. "And that was what Mal killed that day in the mountains?"

Ark nodded. "The Naysayer believes it was a sentinel, set to watch the Rift Road. It has started. Where there is one there will be others. We must be careful."

It has started. She felt a soft stab of pain beneath her jaw, in the place where Ark had drawn blood. "Is that why we're traveling through the Want?"

He turned to look at her. "What do you know of the Great Want, Ash March?"

"I know we're within it—and heading deeper."

"Look behind. Tell me what you see."

Ash twisted in the saddle. She saw mountains and ice and sky, and said so.

"So you see the Coastal Ranges?" She nodded, and he continued, his voice strangely controlled. "And you think it possible to stand within the Want and look out upon a landmark you know? You think it possible to say to yourself *I am in the Want and if I turn west toward those mountains I can head out whenever I choose*?" He paused, waiting for an answer.

She had none for him.

The Far Rider stretched the silence until she questioned her assumptions on many things. Satisfied by the uncertainty he had created, he resumed more gently. "We head along the edges of the Want, the margins where the land is solid and unchanging, and the stars may be trusted at night. Make no mistake, Ash March: ride north for half a day and you would be lost. Any mountains you saw then could not be trusted. Ride toward them and they could lead you in circles until your palms crack open from dryness and your horse falls lame beneath you. You do not travel through the Want, you are set adrift. We call it *Glor Skallis*. Land of Fallen Sky. Landmarks that seem solid drift like clouds. A moon appears and sheds light, and then a second looms on the horizon and you cannot know which is real and which is false. Light bends. It scatters and creates, and even the Sull cannot tell a light-made landscape from a god-made one until we touch it with our hands and say, *Here is air* or *Here is soil*."

Ark's words were hypnotic, spoken to the rhythmic bunching of the muscles in his horse's shoulders, and Ash knew she was hearing things that no clansman or city man had ever heard.

"We follow the path laid out by the Naysayer. He rides ahead and around us, searching for way markers and holding us upon the edge. It is not a simple task, this holding, for the edges of *Glor Skallis* are fluid in places and a tracker must be vigilant or risk becoming lost."

The Far Rider spoke a word to his horse, increasing its speed to a trot. Ash saw some tension in his face, and realized his thoughts were with his *hass*. She said, "He's not just tracking, though, is he? He's watching for them."

Lines around Ark's mouth tightened and he kicked the gray into a canter. Watching the space open up between them Ash suddenly feared she'd be left behind and scrambled to catch up. She'd pushed him too far. The Sull never spoke their fears out loud.

Morning passed quickly into midday. Freezing winds numbed Ash's ears and sucked the moisture from her lips, leaving ridges that felt like scars. The sky grayed and after a time so did the ice. Boulders and the crumbled remains of petrified trees littered the path. The high clouds fled west, and a cold haze set in like the thinnest of fogs. They rode in single file, with the Far Rider taking the lead, and although Ash couldn't see his face she sensed his constant vigilance from the stiffness of his back.

It has started.

She closed her eyes for a moment and breathed in the dark. The gift of weapons, the drawing of first blood . . . even the instruction on how to release the gelding's panniers: they were all measures taken for her protection. The Far Riders expected something to come after them, and had planned for her survival if they died.

I can't think of it. Opening her eyes she let the harsh light pierce her. She hated this place. The Naysayer had chosen it as an alternate route to the Rift Road, but any fool could see it wasn't safe. They'd be better traveling through warring clan-holds than this desert of mist and ice. Anger warmed her, and took away some of the fear, but it took too much energy to sustain and she felt her shoulders slump and her spine bend as day moved toward night. Inside her mitts, her fingers had stiffened into hooks, and she knew she needed to work them to prevent the sickening numbness of frostbite.

Reaching down into her lynx fur, she searched out the hide pouch that contained her waybread. She wasn't hungry, but it gave her hands something to do.

When she looked up she saw a mounted figure on the path ahead. She stiffened, and then recognized the shape of Mal Naysayer. It was twilight and not yet full dark, and Ash couldn't understand where he'd come from. The way ahead had been clear moments earlier.

The Naysayer trotted the blue forward, and then fell in step with his *hass*. Ash heard the two Far Riders exchange words, and then the Naysayer swung the blue north, indicating a change in their path. Ash followed. She wondered why they were heading deeper into the Want, but didn't think she'd get an answer if she asked. The Naysayer was a hard man to read, but she thought she detected some urgency in the way he handled his horse.

They rode at a canter into the darkness. There was an instant when Ash thought she heard something, a low howl that seemed to carry through the ice, but the combined noise of twelve hooves drumming against frozen earth soon drowned it out.

Night came swiftly, bringing a depth of darkness so great Ash could no longer see the head of her horse. It was strange, riding in the gloom, and she found it difficult to relinquish control to the gelding. Underfoot, the ground became rougher as ice gave way to permafrost. It had been cold before, but it had been a passive coldness, the kind that layers of clothing and willpower could fight. Now it went beyond that. It hurt to breathe, and when the air was inside your lungs you could feel it moving toward your heart.

Ash would never know how much time passed before the Naysayer finally signaled a halt. At some point she had fallen into a trancelike state, driven into herself by the cold and the darkness like an animal sleeping out the winter. The gelding halted of its own accord, and Ash felt strong arms lift her from the saddle. She looked up to see Mal Naysayer's hard and beautiful face close to her own. His scale armor was shimmering softly, casting an eerie light under his jaw.

As he set her down, her legs buckled, and he signaled his *hass* to bring a blanket. "Drink this," he said, after she'd been wrapped in soft rugs and laid on the ground.

Ash took the small silver flask from him, and then didn't have the strength to pull the cork. Her muscles were tight and close to cramping, and her mind floated lazily from thought to thought. The next thing she knew, the Naysayer was kneeling before her, forcing the neck of the flask between her teeth. Liquid as warm as her own body filled her mouth. It tasted sweet and metallic, like honey ground with metal filings, and it immediately cleared her head.

"*Manshae*," the Naysayer explained. "You would call it ghost-meal. It will help replenish your strength." With that, he recorked the flask and left her to see to the camp.

Ash wiped a hand across her mouth; the ghostmeal had a bitter aftertaste. She looked around, and it took her a moment to realize that although it was still dark she could now see. They were in a shallow depression surrounded by low-lying rock walls and dragon pines. Living trees in the Want? She dropped a hand to the ground to touch the dry, scaly grass that lay beneath her. She couldn't quite believe it was there.

"It is an ice oasis."

Ark Veinsplitter laid a rug next to her and sat. "There are many such places in the Want if you know where to look for them, places where the frost and darkness are held back."

By what? she wanted to ask but didn't. She realized it was warmer here, as well as lighter, and she stretched her legs out in front of her and took a deep gulp of air. "Will we be able to get back?"

He nodded. "The Naysayer marked the path."

She watched Mal brushing down her horse on the far side of the hollow. "There'll be no fire tonight."

"No."

"They've found us, haven't they?"

Ark looked at her for a long time without speaking. Finally he asked, "What did you see?"

Four words and Ash felt her understanding of the world change. Here it was, the reason these men had made her Sull. *What did you see?* How could she have been so stupid not to realize why they wanted her? They hadn't hid it. They had told her she was needed and must fight. She just hadn't understood what her role would be. She still didn't . . . but she was learning.

What did you see?

Ark Veinsplitter was very still as he waited for her reply. His hands were bare, and she could see the tracework of letting scars around his fingernails.

"I didn't *see* anything," she said. "I *heard* something—a howl. It never came again." She watched him relax visibly, and wondered if he knew he'd given himself away.

Perhaps he did, for he rose abruptly and told her to get some sleep—there were only a few hours left before dawn.

Ash smoothed one of the rugs into a sleeping mat and rolled a fox pelt into a pillow to support her head. She felt strange— weary, but abnormally alert. Her mind was racing with what she'd learned. *They believe I can sense them, the shadow beasts, see them before they do. Is that what a Reach is, a finder of shadows?* The thought unsettled her, and she tossed and turned, looking for answers that didn't come. Time passed, and she drifted into an uneasy sleep.

Animal calls disturbed her dreams. Something howled to the south, and after the beat of a few seconds something else answered. Ash opened her eyes. Her skin was cold and tingling, and she could still hear the last traces of the answering howl ringing in her ears. Turning her head, she searched for the figure of Ark Veinsplitter. He was there, as always, crouching at the edge of the camp, facing out. His sword was sheathed. He was standing guard, but not on alert. If the calls had been real he had not heard them.

Telling herself it was just a dream, that they were safe here in the Want, Ash settled back in her blankets and tried to force herself to sleep. It didn't work. Her heart was racing and the slightest noise unsettled her. When one of the horses whiffled she stiffened. Snorting softly at her own fright, she told herself she was a fool . . . but still she couldn't sleep.

Through the dark night she lay awake, listening for *maeraiths*.

The hunt was on.

TWENTY-TWO

Treason

Raina held out the chunk of rock salt for the cow to lick on. The creature lipped at her palm in its eagerness, tickling her and slobbering her fingers with saliva. After checking to make sure that only she and Anwyn Bird were in the cattle shed she laughed out loud. Cows had no manners.

"Don't you go upsetting my beauties, Raina Blackhail," Anwyn warned. "There's little enough butter in their milk as it is."

Raina quieted herself and regarded Anwyn. The clan matron was looking old. The thick rope of hair pinned in a circle around her scalp was completely gray. When had the gold gone out of it? Raina could still remember her first sight of Anwyn Bird, that summer when she'd arrived at the Hailhouse from Dregg.

All the clanwives had come out onto the greatcourt to inspect her. Raina's uncle had arranged the fosterage, her second in under three years, and although he was a genial and well-meaning man he had a weakness for red malt. And when he was drunk he was prone to boast. He must have gotten drunk the day he visited Blackhail to purchase her fosterage, for later that evening he'd told a chamber full of clansmen that his niece

356 † J. V. JONES

was not only beautiful, but more graceful than Weeping Moira herself and as smart as Hoggie Dhoone. Raina still flushed at the thought of it. Naturally, when she'd arrived the clanwives were inclined to dislike her. Thirteen, she was, and already in possession of her full height and a woman's fullness. The fact that she *wasn't* as graceful as Weeping Moira became quickly apparent when she dismounted her little gray pony and slipped in the mud. But still. Her uncle's words had done their damage and Lally Horn, the woman who'd accepted a milk cow and its calf in payment for Raina's keep, turned around and refused to take her. The Dregg girl was a temptress, she said, who'd woo suitors away from her daughters. Lally Horn had been deceived! And though she might very well return the cow, she'd keep the calf for her trouble.

That was when Anwyn had stepped in.

Only Raina hadn't known her name then. She saw a stout-built woman with aggressively plain features and a curtain of golden hair falling thick and heavy past her waist. Anwyn had been about to braid it when she'd heard the commotion on the court. The clan matron had quickly taken charge of the situation, telling Raina she could stay in the kitchen with her, and informing Lally Horn that she was off to feed the wee visitor, and when she returned she'd expect to see a cow *and* a calf on the greatcourt, or so help her gods she'd break Lally's nose and lock Laida Moon in a wet cell so the healer couldn't set it for a week.

The strategy worked. Lally was known to be proud of her short, perfect nose, and Anwyn Bird was a genius with threats.

Raina dropped the rock salt into a pouch in her apron. "Remember Lally Horn?" she said to Anwyn, suddenly needing to talk about the past.

Anwyn was in the process of greasing a sick cow's shrunken teats, yet something in Raina's voice caused her to halt her doctoring and look up. She studied Raina's face for a moment. "Aye. It's a shame. No one in the clan could set soap quite like her. Used to grind strawberry blossoms in that little pestle of hers and add the oils to the ashes. All the maids would beg for a wedge whenever they went courting. Made them smell like summer fruit."

Raina nodded, feeling small and mean. Trust Anwyn to remember the good over the bad. Lally had been dead these nine years, taken in childbirth at an age when most women had long withdrawn from their husband's beds. Yet her husband had wanted a son, and Lally had been so desperate to give him one she'd risked her life . . . and given him another daughter instead.

So many deaths. When will it end? Crossing over to Anwyn's milk stool, Raina laid a kiss on the clan matron's head, right in the middle of the gray.

"While you're handing out kisses, Raina Blackhail, how about saving one for me?"

Raina looked up to see Angus Lok standing in the entrance to the tunnelway, the deep black passage that ran from the cattle sheds down to the fold. She had not heard him come. The ranger was dressed in layered buckskins the color of wheat. Water stains ringed the hem and cuffs of his coat, and his soft riding boots were spattered with mud. Sliding back his otter-fur-trimmed hood, he bowed to her as if she were a great city lady, and then bowed again to Anwyn.

"Mistress Bird. I see you're expecting me. Got your hands all nice and greasy to salve my chin." The ranger ran a hand along his jaw. "Well, get moving, woman. Wind's near chapped it to the bone."

Anwyn frowned with force. "The only thing about you that needs curing, Angus Lok, is your tongue. Anything that stricken needs pulling out."

Angus laughed heartily, surprising Anwyn by leaping over to her and catching her up in a huge bear hug. The clan matron protested, throwing her hands wide to avoid smearing the ranger with grease, all the while shuffling backward with her feet.

Angus winked at the sick cow before releasing Anwyn. "Sorry, Daisy. I tried, but I couldna keep her off you a minute longer."

"Her name's not Daisy," Anwyn said, awkwardly brushing hair from her face with her forearm. "It's Birchwood. And I'll thank you to leave us both in peace."

Angus stepped back in mock obedience, but not before slipping a small, slim package beneath Anwyn's belt. Anwyn ignored it and settled herself down on the stool to finish her doctoring.

The ranger turned to Raina. "Will you walk with me a while?" he asked.

Raina lifted her eyebrows in mild surprise, but nodded her agreement. As she stepped toward the shed's double doors, he spoke to halt her. "It's a mite cold on the greatcourt for a thin-blood like me. What say we take the low road instead?"

It was midday and unseasonably mild out, but she didn't contradict him, and let herself be led across the cattle shed to the tunnelway. The cows bellowed as she passed them, sensing the retreat of the salt. The giant stone trough that ran the length of all seven cattle sheds and tapped into the Leak south of the roundhouse was brimming with icy water. Raina spied the speckly froth of frogspawn floating upon it, and thought, *I must tell Effie; we're rearing frogs in the cattle shed!* And then remembered Effie was no longer here.

The tunnelway was dark and unpleasant-smelling. It had been dug to evacuate livestock from the vulnerable timber-roofed outbuildings to the safety of the underground fold in the event of sudden attack. Some ancient clan chief or other had commissioned it. Obviously a man who cared more about cows than the people who tended them, Raina thought hotly, for the incline was sharp and she stumbled several times. Angus offered her his arm, but she refused it. She couldn't afford to be seen holding a man who wasn't her husband. *Little mice with weasels' tails.*

Shivering, she put a hand on the wall to steady herself. When had she begun to let Mace Blackhail rule her life?

The air soured as they descended. Thawing mud oozed through cracks in the masonry, and entire sections of tunnel wall had buckled inward from the pressure of moving earth. Black-shelled beetles battled in the rubble, their mandibles clicking as they fought over the putrefied remains of a drowned mouse. Raina increased her pace. She hated the dark, rotting underspaces of the roundhouse. They had stood empty and unrepaired for decades, waiting for war.

The Blackhail fold was the largest standing hall in the clan-holds, capable of holding five thousand head of livestock in times of siege. Giant bloodwood stangs with girths so wide it would take three men to circle them rose from floor to ceiling like a forest of charred trees. The ceiling was deeply groined and barrel vaulted, cantilevered in part by the foundation wall that braced the perimeter, and by a huge central stone shaft. The entire weight of the roundhouse rested upon the walls and stangs of the fold, and every craftsman who had ever hammered a nail in the clanholds held nothing but awe for the men who had raised it.

It had been several weeks since Raina had last been down here, and she was shocked to see that it had become a camp-ground for tied clansmen and their meager stocks. Makeshift tents were pitched against the stangs, and rickety cattle corrals of wicker and woven bark held lone calves and ribby sows. Dung fires smoked heavily, giving off the sickly-sweet odor of partially digested grass. The air was so thick with soot it made Raina's throat itch to breathe it, and her first instinct was to rush to the nearest shutters and throw them open. But there were no windows this far belowground, and little ventilation to be had. What were these people doing here? Surely there was space enough above?

"Not a Scarpe amongst them."

Raina turned her head sharply as Angus spoke. She had almost forgotten he was beside her. Why had he come? Tem was dead, Raif and Effie were gone, and Drey had been sent south to Ganmiddich. The ranger had no kin left here. So why make Blackhail business his own?

"What's it to you who's down here, Angus Lok?" she challenged him. "Last I heard, you live in a city, not a clan."

The ranger stopped to look at her. His face was deeply tanned and lined, and the blood vessels in his eyes were feathered with fatigue. He was a fine-looking man, she had always thought so, but she did not envy his wife. Angus Lok reminded her of a treader fly, one of those spindly brown insects that settled on the surface of the stew ponds around Dregg. You wondered how they could stand on water, until you looked very closely and saw their legs: ten times as long as their bodies, thinner than threads of silk, probing wide in all directions, their tiny hairs bristling in response to the slightest change in current.

What change in current had brought him here? Raina wondered. *I must be cautious*, she counseled herself, *speak little and listen much.*

Angus watched her a moment longer—his copper eyes taking in such depth of detail that she had to suppress the urge to smooth back her hair and straighten her dress—before turning his attention to the campground.

"What's it to me if tied Hailsmen raise their tents belowground, whilst sworn Scarpemen sit in the comfort of stone chambers above? You know what it is, Raina Blackhail. It's imbalance. Even a Hailsman without oath should be given precedence over an outsider in his home clan."

She could not disagree with him. She thought the same thing every day, when she came across Scarpe women using the dyeing vats to blacken their husbands' fronts, Scarpe children sneaking into the cold stores to raid the apple barrels, and Scarpe men eyeing her with insolence whenever she entered the Great Hearth. She said, "And is that why you're here, Angus, to address that imbalance?"

He smiled at her then, a genuine showing of warmth mellowed by weariness. "Come now, Raina. When a man asks you to dance do you stride into the middle of the floor and place his hands upon you? Or do you at least allow him the pleasure of leading you forward? We're sensitive fellows, we men, and though we know very well we're not in charge of much we like it when you pretend that we are."

Raina had to smile. He'd pinned her precisely. She was mistaking defensiveness for caution. Spreading her arm before her, she invited him to walk a circuit of the fold. Angus Lok was a man who liked to be courted, and at one time long she had been good at courting. Dagro used to tease her about it, but Dagro was gone now. And she could barely remember the woman she used to be. With an effort, she put her smile into her voice and inquired about his wife.

"Darra." Need darkened his eyes for an instant and then he blinked and it was gone. "She's well, I hope. I haven't been home since midwinter. I've been, as they say, unavoidably detained. The Dog Lord took a fancy to me and decided to keep me in his cellars along with his favorite malt and cheese. I wouldna have minded normally, but the cheese tasted like foot fungus and the malt ran out after a week."

So the rumors were true: the Bludd chief had held the ranger prisoner. "Longhead says the weather will break any day now. You should head home while you can."

Angus shook his head. "Not to be. I've fallen a wee bit behind in my affairs."

Raina knew better than to ask what those affairs were. Angus Lok would doubtless give a charming answer that hid more than it revealed. *Play his game*, she reminded herself. *We're two old friends chewing the cud.* "How did you find the clanholds on your journey west?"

"Troubled. Gnash is slaughtering its breeding stock, and the black rot has spoiled the grain stores at Dregg."

"You've been at Dregg?"

"Ten days back. They were burning the meal on the court; great hills of it, giving off the blackest smoke. Xander had to mount a guard to stop the tied clansmen from rioting."

Raina kept her face impassive; she was getting good at that, she'd noticed. "Does Xander expect more trouble?"

"Don't all the chiefs?"

Hope was like breath, she thought: when it left your body it made you slump. Dregg was her birth clan; its future was part of her own. When her work and duties at Blackhail were done, when she was an old widow with wispy hair and no teeth, she'd pay one of the tied clansmen to take her to the Dregghold in a cart. She'd be an elder at Dregg, cousin to the chief, and the clan maids would rush to bring her hot apple possets and the inner loins of meat. Someone would offer a shawl for her shoulders, spun with as much air as wool. And she'd sit in the finest painted hall in the clanholds and watch the young ones dance.

"Here, chief's wife. Wet your lips with this."

Raina turned her head to see a tiny, hard-faced clanwife holding out a horn of ale. The woman had the look of the wild clan from Blackhail's far west, and Raina did not know her by sight or name. Still, she took the cup and drank. A chief's wife learned early never to refuse humble courtesies—you could never be sure when an insult might be taken. The ale was mead thinned with pond water and tasted brackish and flat, but she finished it down to the skim. The clanwife watched her swallow, and when Raina offered back the cup she shook her head.

"Nay. Keep it, chief's wife. Give it to your husband—save him seizing it for hisself."

The thin voice carried far across the stone vault, and dozens of heads turned toward it. The woman straightened her spine, waiting until silence had passed from man to man, then spat at Raina's feet. With a hard, satisfied nod of her jaw, she turned to make her way back to her camp. Small dark-skinned men, her sons by the look of them, made space for her around the fire.

Raina felt the blood rise to her face. Spittle trickled from her skirt hem to her boot, and she scraped it away awkwardly against the floor.

"Here," Angus said quietly, holding his hand toward the cup. "Let me take that from you."

Raina shook her head with a snap. "Nay, Angus Lok. It is my clan and my cup, and I'll keep it as she said." Her fingers trembled as she threaded a silver hook through the horn cup's rimhole and hooked it onto her belt. When the task was done she took a deep breath and raised her head. Every tied clansman in the fold was watching her, and her instinct was to hunker down and flee. There were currents here she didn't fully understand. But she was wife to two chiefs, first woman in the clan, and she could live with much worse than hostile stares.

"Angus," she said a little too loudly. "Let me show you the north wall. The builders of the fold set a block of moonstone into the masonry and carved their kin marks upon it. The sandstone blocks are strong, but their faces quickly wear, and the builders wanted to be sure to name themselves for posterity."

Angus was all attention. "Indeed," he said, as if he'd just

learned the most interesting fact in all the clanholds. "Lead on."

She heard him fall into place behind her, and thanked him silently for his understanding. Holding her shoulders square and looking directly ahead, she crossed the length of the fold, defying the tied clansmen to find fault.

The moonstone glowed in the darkness like a ghost trapped in the wall. Raina reached out to touch it, aware that the noise level was slowly returning to normal. She and Angus were alone here, separated from the open space of the great hall by a blood-wood stang as wide as a smoke tower. Angus made a show of squinting to interpret the kin marks carved deep into the stone. Someone had once rubbed silver leaf into the carvings, and odd lines and curves reflected light. The ranger halted when his gaze fell upon the mark of the armed bear.

"Sevrance," he said quietly. "Tem's ancestors helped build this?"

Raina nodded. "The Sevrances are one of the oldest families in the clanholds. Ned Sevrance was a table bearer for Jamie Roy."

Angus nodded with interest, though Raina would have bet coin on him having known that fact before. Making a tiny gesture to the fold behind her she said, "Do you know what all that was about?"

He continued studying the kin marks, keeping his face toward the wall. "I'm sure you heard that Mace sent outriders to the western farms a few months back, urging all tied clansmen to take shelter in the Hailhold. Well, it seems a few of the outriders were a wee bit overenthusiastic about their task. Let's call them Scarpes. Not only did these 'Scarpes' claim Mace had ordered a full-scale evacuation to the hold, but they—how should I put it?—*aided* in the evacuation process. Took horses, livestock, belt buckles, sacks of grain—anything they could rope or heft. Told the poor farmers all goods would be returned to them at the Hailhold. Only nothing but carcasses and empty sacks were returned. Now there's a rumor going around that the farms themselves are being overrun, and that Scarpes are moving into the empty crofts and settling down for spring."

"Does Mace know about this?"

Angus turned to look at her. "What do you think?"

"He wouldn't dare sanction it."

"Aye. But knowing about something and choosing to look the other way is much the same in the end."

Catching a spark of green in Angus's coppery eyes, Raina wondered if this was the reason he'd brought her here.

He executed a kind of half bow in acknowledgment of the understanding dawning on her face. "Small things like dispossessed crofters have a nasty habit of bringing clans to their knees."

He was right. Tied clansmen—farmers, woodsmen, traders, miners—might not swear to die for their clans, but they brought goods to the table in return for the defense of themselves and their families. It was a fact no warrior cared to admit, but a clan could survive longer without swords than scythes. Even so. It occurred to Raina that she shouldn't have to listen to such wisdom from an outsider.

Pulling away from the wall she said, "Well, I'd best be off now. I'll be sure to speak to my husband when you're gone."

Angus's fingers snapped around her wrist. And she did not think, did not stop to wonder why the entire surface of her skin erupted into violently cold gooseflesh. She simply reacted. Twisting her arm against his grip, she pulled down with enough force to send the ranger stumbling forward. As her trapped hand broke free, the other came up to strike him. Angus righted himself in an instant, but he was not quick enough to stop her open hand from striking his face. The impact made a dry crack, stinging Raina's palm and raising an immediate welt on Angus's jaw. His gaze jumped to her face, and he did not retaliate, did not move at all.

Raina let her hand fall awkwardly to her waist. Her heart was racing, and the gooseflesh on her arms and chest was so extreme that the entire surface of her skin felt tight. An image came to her of a woman lying amid the sword ferns and blue gorse of the Oldwood. Raina could feel the snow melting beneath the woman's buttocks, hear the ragged gasps of breath as the man above her held down her wrists and thrust her legs apart with his knee . . .

"Raina. Raina?"

Angus's voice was gently questioning. She knew she should respond to it, *wanted* to respond, but there was the woman in the Oldwood. Hurting. Alone.

After a time she heard her voice say, "Angus. Forgive me. I don't know what came over me."

The ranger tapped his jaw lightly. "What, this? Was nothing. My own wife warned me about my tongue. Angus, she said, when you attack a woman's good name always be sure to duck."

Raina nodded stiffly. She was aware that Angus was speaking loudly for a reason, and that many ears were listening to what he said, but she couldn't find the strength to play his game.

She wanted to run away.

"Here." A rabbit-fur-covered flask was pressed into her hand. "Drink deep."

She did as she was told, filling her mouth with sweet scalding alcohol so pure it barely registered as fluid at all. When the liquor hit her brain it made the woman in the Oldwood recede into the distance, and she was finally free to think. Sweat drenched her back and buttocks, cold as melted snow.

"Let's go," Raina murmured, making for the stairs. She'd thought the past was behind her—had *forced* it behind her—so why had it all come flooding back? A strange, high sound left her lips as she ran from the fold. *Gods, don't let it ruin me now.*

She found herself in the great stone dome of the entrance hall, possessing no memory of climbing the many ramps and stairs that rose toward ground level. Angus was close behind, flanking her. Biddie Byce rushed by, a basket of winter-grown carrots pressed against her chest. A group of new-sworn year-men, Perches and Murdocks and Lyes, were sitting against the stair wall, disassembling their gear belts and scabbards for cleaning. When they spotted their chief's wife they slowed their labors to watch her. Raina ignored them. Her gaze fell on the iron-banded clan door, and she had to fight the urge to run outside. She wanted desperately to be alone.

"Angus Lok."

Mace. She didn't need to turn toward the stair that led down to the chief's chamber to know who stood upon it.

"Wife."

He made her turn anyway, for he would not be ignored in front of clan. Mace Blackhail was dressed in an elk-suede tunic dyed black, collared with a heavy mantle of ice-wolf fur that still had the tail and leg sheaths attached. His beard and moustache had been newly trimmed, shaved narrow to match the long planes of his face. Climbing the last remaining steps to the entrance hall, he addressed himself to the ranger. "My scouts informed me you entered the Hailhold two nights back—yet you did not see fit to present yourself at my hearth?"

Angus stood his ground behind Raina, his face bland. "Aye, well, Hail Lord, if I'd have known you had a hankering to see me wild pigs couldna have kept me away."

Mace's mouth tightened. He suspected he was being made

light of, and Raina knew he could not allow that in such a public place as the entrance hall. "Ranger. Enter my clanhold one more time without my knowledge and be forewarned to watch your back. Blackhail is at war, and any intruder on my soil must be judged enemy rather than friend."

The yearmen by the stair wall stopped all pretense of cleaning. They were chief's men, all of them. Red-necked Elcho Murdock had just been betrothed to some hollow-cheeked niece of Yelma Scarpe.

Angus nodded, the blandness in his face holding firm. "I'll be sure to remember that, Hail Lord. Watch my back. A pity no one offered such a warning to Shor Gormalin. Now that I recall, didn't he take two quarrels in the back of his head?"

Raina heard one of the yearmen gasp. Foolish child. Had no one taught him to school his reactions?

Mace ignored the outburst, his attention solely upon Angus Lok. Both men were matched in height and build, though Angus carried a bit more fat. They were both swordsmen, too. And as that thought occurred to her she realized both men's sword hands were resting on the hilts of their sheathed blades. Silently, she cursed Angus. What madness had possessed him to mention Shor Gormalin's name?

A second or two, no longer, was all it took for Mace Blackhail to weigh all possible outcomes. He was a clever swordsman, but he had to know that Angus Lok might better him—wasn't he rumored to have spent two years with the Sull? And besides, what would a duel win Mace? It would only add credibility to the ranger's outrageous claim. Shor Gormalin had been killed by a Bludd-sworn cowlman. Everyone in the clan knew it.

Holding his gaze upon Angus Lok, Mace Blackhail commanded his yearmen. "John. Elcho. Stiggie. Graig. Escort this city man from the Hailhold and deposit him on the border. His welcome here just ran out."

The four yearmen scrambled to strap on their gear belts and weapon cradles. Young Graig Lye, cousin to Bludd-slain Banron, buckled his sword harness so ferociously he struck sparks. Others had entered the hall whilst the two men were speaking—a gaggle of clan maids wheeling a laundry barrow and two ancient oasters from the brewhouse who stank of yeast—and all eased back against the walls, sensing the tension in the entryway like livestock sensed a storm. At her side, Raina was aware of Angus breathing evenly, even as he shifted his weight forward onto the balls of his feet.

Please do not fight, she willed him. *You may win one-on-one, but after that you'll die—and I don't think I can take any more blows today.*

Perhaps Angus Lok could read minds, for slowly he eased his weight back down upon his heels. He bowed his head once toward Mace, and then to the four yearmen. "Gentlemen," he said. "Lead on."

Raina's ribcage slumped forward with relief, feeling at the same time a terrible kind of disappointment. She had wished Angus not to fight, but now that he had backed down and she saw how her husband's lips came together in a cold, triumphant smile, she could only think, *Is there no one in the clanholds who can stop him?*

She had no time for answers, for Angus was addressing her as "Lady" and bidding her a nonchalant farewell. Wordlessly, she bowed her head toward him and watched as the four yearmen moved to flank him as he made his exit. Once the clan door closed behind him, a brisk draft circled the entryway and died.

No one moved. One of the clan maids who'd been dragging the laundry barrow hiccuped nervously. Mace's black-and-yellow-eyed gaze found his wife. "Raina," he said, his voice strangely gentle. "I'm sorry you had to witness that. I know he's kin to the Sevrances, but it was necessary to remove him from the clan."

Raina couldn't understand Mace's gentleness. Was it an act of husbandly solicitude for the benefit of onlookers? Or was there something showing on her face that genuinely worried him? *You were a partner to Dagro. Be one to me.* The memory of his words in the chief's chamber made her shudder, and for a moment she thought she saw that same desire writ plainly on his face. Suddenly it was all too much for her, and she made a break for the door.

Mace's demeanor abruptly changed, and he put out a hand to stop her.

Don't touch me. Don't you dare touch me. She swerved to avoid him and, perhaps aware that he'd look foolish trying to grapple with his wife, he let her pass. That tiny victory gave her courage, and she found words springing to her mouth that she had not planned.

"I'm going to see Angus off. His wife embroidered a tunic especially for Drey, and I'm not letting him come all this way and not deliver it." She hardly knew where the lies came from, but as soon as she spoke them she felt their rightness. Let him try to challenge her over them. Let him try.

Mace watched her carefully for a moment, aware that he too was being watched. "There's no need for you to go to the stables. One of the girls can retrieve it."

But Raina was ready for him. "I don't think so, husband," she said briskly, her hands already pushing the quarter-ton clan door into motion. "Darra Lok's embroidery is known throughout the north, and I'm not going to have it passed from hand to hand without giving proper thanks."

The clan maids, bless them, nodded in agreement and understanding. There wasn't a woman in the clanholds who didn't value beautiful needlework. Mace saw this and must have realized he was in danger of looking foolish. A clan chief never concerned himself with women's affairs.

He waved a hand toward the door. "Go, then."

She finished pulling the oak door in its oiled track, all the time knowing what he would say next and waiting to hear it.

"But, wife," he warned when the door's motion was complete. "Such a piece of work as this tunic . . . I'd like to see it for myself. Bring it to me when you're done."

Raina stepped outside. "I'll be happy to—tomorrow, when it's been properly pressed and aired." *And once I've raced upstairs to the widows' hearth and begged Merritt Ganlow and her widow-wives to stay up all night embroidering something for me.* Thank the gods Mace was a typical clansman and wouldn't be able to tell clan-sewn pieces from city ones.

Almost dizzy with satisfaction, Raina hurried to the stables. She had to caution herself not to skip like a girl.

By the time the short walk was complete, her euphoria had drained away, leaving her feeling vulnerable and shaky. The early sunshine had gone, closed off by swift-moving clouds, and the air was misty with rotting ice. Spikes of new greenery— snowdrops, by the look of them—had pushed through the slush piled to either side of the stable's double doors. Raina supposed that meant spring was here, and could find nothing in her that was glad.

Inside the stable all was dim and warm, the air kept well above freezing by Jebb Onnacre's carefully tended safe-lamps. It was easy to tell which box held Angus Lok's mount, for six men were gathered around the half-gate, admiring the beast within. Four of them were the yearmen sent to escort the ranger off Blackhail territory, and the others were Angus himself and Orwin Shank.

The wealthy clan overlord was speaking, a red and ax-bitten hand resting on the horse's neck. "Aye, it's a pity he's gelded. Could have charged the gods' own eyeballs for stud."

"I heard the Sull cut any horse that leaves their heart fires," sniped Elcho Murdock. "Won't have outsiders breeding down their stock."

"Is that so?" Angus said mildly. "An expert in our midst and I didn't know it."

Elcho, who was small-eyed and bulb-nosed like his grandfather, suspected an insult but couldn't prove it, and scowled childishly. Young Graig Lye, who was brighter by far but no more self-restrained, sniggered at him under his breath.

"Gentlemen," Angus said, ignoring the obvious signs of their youth. "I wonder if you'd do me the honor of waiting for me outside whilst I talk to your chief's fair wife?"

Until he spoke, Raina had thought her entrance had passed unmarked. She should have known better. It was the treader fly again, sensing the slightest ripple on the water.

Elcho puffed out a disbelieving breath. "I don't think so, ranger. What if you mount your horse and escape us?"

"Then I'd be off your hands and away from your clanhold just as your chief commanded."

Raina had to smile at the befuddled looks on the yearmen's faces. Angus was tying them up in knots. Luckily, Orwin Shank stepped in before the poor lads could be sold a dead horse. "You boys run along outside. I'll stand second to the ranger's word."

Orwin Shank was father to four living sons and one daughter. He was the greatest landholder in the clan and keeper of the most gold. He kept a stable of thirty horses and more sheep than there were days in winter. He'd fought at the Griefbringer's back at Middlegorge and lost two grown sons to Bludd: no man in the clan was worthy of more respect. Even young, untested yearmen knew better than to doubt him.

Raina smiled her thanks at the aging axman as the four yearmen filed out through the stable door.

"'Twas nothing, Raina," he replied brusquely. "If two people can't speak in private without watchers then what sort of clan are we making?" His hazel-eyed stare seemed to challenge her. "I'll be waiting over there by the pump. Speak quiet now, for there's no such thing as trying not to overhear."

She watched him cross to the far side of the stable wall and begin drawing water to wet his face from the crank-pump. Behind her, she was aware of Angus breathing lightly, waiting for her to speak. Now that she was here and had her way, she was no longer sure of her motives.

First things first. "Angus," she said, turning to him. "You must give me a package, one large enough to hold a man's tunic."

He did not ask for an explanation, merely leaned forward to search his leather saddlebags that had been hooked over the stall door. The beautiful Sull horse, his coat as dark and glossy as tree syrup, popped his head over the half-gate to watch. Raina scratched him gently on the nose as Angus laid a smooth, linen-wrapped package at her feet.

She did not thank him. Quite suddenly she knew they were about to speak treason of the chief. She took a breath. "Why did you infer Mace had something to do with Shor Gormalin's death? Everyone knows he was killed by a Bludd cowlman."

It still hurt to mention Shor's name. *"Wed me, Raina,"* he had said, the night before she rode west with Effie to the Oldwood. *"I know it's too soon after Dagro's death, but I would not see you unprotected. I . . . I would not expect to share your bed, but in time I hope you'll come to love me as I love you."*

And she had not answered him. Fool that she was, she'd made him wait, though in her heart she'd already said yes. And by the next day it was too late . . . and Shor had ridden to his death thinking Raina had rejected him for Mace.

Angus cleared his throat. "Raina, what if I were to tell you that Bludd has not raised one cowlman these past thirty-five years? That the Dog Lord has little patience for the sort of wars where trained assassins bivouacked in the snow can terrorize an entire clan? I know him, and he's not that sort of man."

Hay crunched beneath Raina's feet as she shifted her weight. "What of a cowlman gone wild? They live in the field for years, often with little or no contact with their chiefs. Isolation drives men insane."

The ranger nodded. "You speak the truth, but the only living cowlman in Bludd is over sixty. His name is Scunner Bone and he's afflicted with an arthritic right hand, and he fishes and raises chickens for his keep."

The truth of Shor's death was there to see in the ranger's steady gaze, but she couldn't face it just yet. "And what of another clan? Dhoone? HalfBludd? Gnash?"

"Gnash has cowlmen, that's for sure, some of the best in the North. HalfBludd . . . well, if you're undersized in HalfBludd and can't raise one of their giant war-axes shame might well turn you to stealth. As for Dhoone . . . well, I'm sure once young Robbie takes over they'll have them by the cartload. He's the kind who'll need assassins."

Gods, what doesn't he know about the clanholds? Suddenly Raina wanted very much for this to be over. "Have you any proof Mace was involved in Shor's death?"

"I've handled the two quarrels he was shot with. Beneath the new red paint I saw the work of Anwyn Bird."

Many things went through her mind at once. Who had shown him the arrows? Why had they even been kept?

Angus was looking at her closely. "Anwyn's workshop was ransacked a week before the shooting. Several items were stolen, including a set of a dozen quarrels she'd made especially for the Lowdraw."

Raina put a hand against the half-gate to steady herself, and as she did so she began to realize how deep Angus' connections ran in this clan. Others had aided him in this. She was aware of her body cooling, despite the warmth of the mica-covered safe-lamps.

Shor had been killed by his own clansmen.

Oh, Mace's hand would never have loosed the arrow. He was too clever for that. Always he used others for his dirty work; meetings by the dog cotes and stoke holes, words whispered in a willing ear, denials ready on his lips. Shor had been a threat to him, both for the chiefship and Raina's hand. So Mace had spoken soft words and loosed an assassin, and killed Shor before he could claim either.

Dagro, help me. Raina raised her gaze to meet Angus's. In Dregg she had been taught that hell was a place without stone or earth to stand on, that souls sent there drifted for eternity, in search of a place to rest their feet. Until this moment it had always seemed a pleasant concept, that floating. Now she knew that to float was to be powerless. A man or woman could do nothing without their feet upon the ground. There was a choice here: float with the rest of the clan, following the current created by Mace Blackhail. Or plant two feet on the earth and take a stand.

Angus read the decision on her face almost the moment she made it. His nod was barely perceptible . . . and it made her shiver with fear.

She knew he would leave her to speak first. Although he had led her this far, with this one goal in mind, the treason must be hers.

Letting her thoughts come to rest upon the woman in the Oldwood, Raina found the words to say:

"My husband must be removed. It's time Blackhail had a new chief."

TWENTY-THREE

Hauling Stones

Effie had a feeling Druss wasn't taking her to Dregg. Back at Blackhail he'd promised Raina and Drey he'd have her in the clanhold within a week. Well, seventeen days had gone by since then, and Effie was pretty sure that if Druss Ganlow wanted to reach Dregg he should have turned east by now.

Rising upright, she hooked a hand through one of the bale rings to steady herself against the wagon's motion, and peeked out through the canvas flap at the farthest southern reaches of the clanholds.

It was all very confusing.

Rain was falling in slushy spits, and the wet-dog odor of snowmelt rose from the earth like steam. The land rose all around in forested ridges. Ancient stands of hemlock and stone pines grew tall and lush on the southern exposures, and there— far behind them now—rose the strange purplish canopies of Scarpe's poison pines. Somewhere far ahead, water was rushing and crashing through rocks. The Wolf River, Effie guessed, newly swollen with the first of the spring thaw.

She sealed the flap and sat down on an empty chicken crate. So. They were south of Scarpe and just north of the Wolf.

Certainly nowhere near Dregg. Frowning, Effie Sevrance settled down to think.

The journey hadn't been nearly as bad as she'd expected. It was the covered wagon, of course. It was dark and cozy, and whoever had oiled the canvas last for weatherproofing had used beeswax instead of elk lard and it made the interior of the wagon smell like Longhead's carpentry workshop. And *that* made it smell like the roundhouse. Sometimes when Effie woke she'd forget where she was, and she'd think to herself, *I'll beg some bone ends from Anwyn and head over to the dog cotes.* Then her eyes would open and she'd find herself looking up at the wooden ribs of the wagon. Remembering was the worst. Even if she were back at the roundhouse and Anwyn were to give her bone ends, Old Scratch couldn't eat them. A burned and dead dog *was* bone ends.

A queer, unhappy laugh jerked her shoulders. *Enough*, she told herself sternly. *Time to eat.*

Food had been good and plentiful since leaving home. Druss Ganlow was fond of saying he couldn't cook a sausage on a stick, but the Orrl marksman Clewis Reed was wondrous good with herbs and spices, rubbing the plucked skin of pheasants with yellow mustard and cracked peppercorns, and stuffing the neck cavity with leeks. Clewis Reed was nearly as good as Raif with his bow so there was always fresh rabbit and fowl. Reaching down to the wagon floor, Effie sorted through her cloth bag. Finding a cold pheasant wing from last night's supper and the last of the honeyed hazelnuts, she settled down for her morning meal.

Druss and Clewis had eaten already. Men did that, she concluded, ate as soon as their eyes were open. They needed their strength to shave.

If she pushed the empty chicken crate to the front wall of the wagon and stood on it, she could peek over the break in the canvas and see Druss and Clewis on the driver's seat. Sometimes Druss was peering back. Effie wondered about that, the watching. She didn't think Druss was interested in her at all. Sometimes he forgot her name and called her Eadie, and once he'd clean forgotten she was there at all and had begun eating her share of meat and oats, and Clewis had to elbow his ribs to make him stop. No. Druss Ganlow was concerned solely with his load.

He often came back to check on it, tightening ropes and cinches that hadn't slackened a bit since he'd last looked. Once, he ordered Effie from the wagon whilst he restowed the entire load. Effie had stayed close to the wagon, trying not to look much further than her feet. When Druss was done and she was allowed to return she saw that the lidded baskets had been moved to the back and the chicken crates stacked all around them. Druss had sweated for hours afterward, and later that day when they'd stopped to camp he'd complained about his back.

Suddenly, the wagon lurched woozily as the ground beneath the wheels changed from hard dirt to a swampy mire of mud and melting snow. Hazelnuts bounced from Effie's hand, pinging like hailstones as they scattered across the floor. Quickly, she wrapped the wing bone in a cloth and fell to her knees to retrieve them. Druss wouldn't like nuts loose in the wagon bed; he'd yelled at her once for spilling ale.

Late-morning light filtered through the front canvas flap, too weak to be any help at all. Down on the floor the shadows were deep, and Effie had to squint to see the nuts. When she found the first one she brushed it against her sleeve and ate it. The next got crushed beneath her boots and she didn't fancy eating that at all. Others had fallen between the crates and she had to wait for the motion of the wagon to roll them out. One particularly pesky nut had lodged itself between the crates and the lidded baskets at the back. She tried pushing the front crate to the side to reach it, but the cargo was too heavy to budge.

Must be hauling stones. Effie decided she'd leave the hazelnut where it was. If Druss were to turn around in the driver's seat and see her unsettling his cargo he'd be mad. Besides, perhaps a mouse might eat it. Da had once told her vermin could live anywhere—even boats.

Thinking of a mouse on a boat made her smile, and she hardly noticed the wagon was slowing. It was funny, though, the way your body could do things without asking your mind, for by the time the wheels had creaked to a halt, her hand was on her lore. Checking. It wasn't usual to stop before midday.

The small, ear-shaped chunk of granite was still except for a faint . . . aliveness. There was no other word that would do. It was like finding eggs in the chicken yard; you could tell straightaway which one held chicks and which were just yolks and white. The ones with the chicks had a special heaviness, a way of lying in your hand, perfectly still, yet not passive. Her lore was like that now. Alive. Aware.

In the quiet that followed the halt she heard Druss curse to all the gods. "Damn river. Moving faster than a spooked herd. Only thing crossing that today is birds."

Clewis Reed's deep, mournful voice was slow to respond. "Then we'll have to set camp and wait."

"Wait? *Wait?* With a cargo in the back and that girl ten days late to Dregg? I say we head upriver to the Bridge of Boats. See if they've crossed there."

Effie sensed a slow shaking of the Orrl marksman's head. "Bannen will have beached its rafts. Anything left to ride water will have broken its mooring and be halfway to the Wrecking Sea by now."

Druss let out a frustrated growl. "I told you that girl would slow us."

Stung by Druss's unfairness, Effie leant forward to hear

Clewis Reed defend her. But the Orrl marksman merely pointed out that the river had been running high and fast for several days and that any delay would not have mattered.

"Hell and high water," Druss proclaimed loudly, losing his anger. "Stone Gods save me from both."

Effie heard the thud of his feet hitting ground as he vaulted from the driver's seat. When he had walked a fair distance from the wagon, Clewis Reed added softly to himself, "Gods save me from hell alone. A man can drown but once in high water."

Effie let her lore drop against her chest. It was growing cold.

The wagon shuddered as the Orrlsman alighted, and Effie stepped to the back of the wagon to peer out. She couldn't see the Wolf from where she stood, but she could feel its icy spray, and smell the strange, aged-meat odor of its water. The two men were talking, but their voices didn't carry above the rush. Druss had halted the wagon on a muddy bank high above the water, and the first wild oats of spring were sprouting in the snowmelt. Trap-rock boulders tumbled down toward the Wolf in a natural stair, and a daring pair of harlequin ducks were heading for a swim.

Wanting very much to see the ducks enter the water, Effie took a deep breath and pushed herself through the canvas slit. As always when she ventured outside somewhere unknown there was that dizzying sense of falling. The ground was solid, she *knew* it was solid—once, as a toddler, she'd made Drey fetch a spade and dig it to a depth of four feet so she could be sure—but somehow it never felt quite substantial enough to hold her. It was as if there were pockets of air—traps—lurking just below the surface. Oh, she knew she was a pelt-shorn fool, told herself that all the time, yet it seemed to Effie there was always a battle going on between things you knew and things you imagined. And things you imagined were stronger.

She was careful where she put her feet as she rounded the

side of the wagon. When she was sure she was facing the river full on, she slid her gaze from her toes to the water twenty paces below.

The Wolf was churning and roiling, its waters so dirty with mud that not even the crests frothed white. Branches and chunks of ice tossed wildly on the surface, and below, in the gravy-colored murk, the bloated green mass of a stag carcass floated eerily on the undertows. Far upstream, in the bottomlands east of Croser, forty thousand elk were said to cross the Wolf each spring, heading due north to the Summer Steppes and the vast unending forest of the Boreal Sway. Effie remembered Da telling her that Jamie Roy himself had named the Wolf. He'd camped for a whole season on its northern bank, and in that time he'd counted more than a hundred carcasses passing downstream. Others in the party had wanted to name the river the Greenwater in memory of the old homeland, but Jamie had shaken his head and said, *No. We must name this river for itself, not in memory of a place that no longer exists. I name it the Lone Wolf, for it claims more prey than any man and heads west when all other rivers flow east.*"

Effie shivered. The gusts rising from the water were sharp and drenching, and she felt her hair and cloak quickly soak through. Below her, the pair of mated ducks were gauging the current from a slimy ledge overhanging the water. When a fast-moving swell crashed against the ledge, it buoyed the plain brown hen and she let it carry her into the current. Her showy blue-and-green mate honked in excitement and then dove in straight after her. Effie leant forward, trying to track them, but the water's surface was a mountain range of foam and the pair were soon lost from sight.

"They'll live," Clewis Reed said, surprising Effie with his nearness. "Queer birds, harlequins. If they were men they'd be berserkers."

Effie turned to face him. The Orrlsman's face was pale and gaunt, and about as long as a person's face could possibly be. His hair and beard were silver and wavy, both worn loose in the old-fashioned style of the Western Clan Lords. His Orrl cloak was old-fashioned too, cut long to brush grass as he walked and pieced so narrowly it dropped straight from his shoulders without flaring. The whole thing served to emphasize his height, and Effie felt like a mushroom beside him.

She couldn't think of anything to say. Awareness of being outside, far from any stone shelter or familiar landmark, was slowly taking command of her thoughts. It was like the water soaking through her cloak, making her feel goosepimply and unprotected. When something touched her shoulder she jumped.

"Steady, lass," Clewis said, tightening his fingers about her collarbone and guiding her firmly away from the bank. "You wouldn't want to be following those ducks downstream."

No she would not. How had she got so close to the edge? Had she taken a step and not known it? To cover her agitation, she asked, "What are berserkers?"

Clewis Reed studied her for a moment. "Head back to the wagon, lass. Heat yourself some ale. I imagine we'll be here quite a time, and if I'm setting to tell a tale I'd rather my listeners be warm and dry."

She searched for humor in his face, but saw only graveness. Suddenly she missed Drey and Raif so much it made her stomach hurt.

"Get along, lass. I'll be in to shake my cloak soon enough."

Effie did as she was told. It was hard not to break into a run. Her hands shook as she unhooked the little safe-lamp from its bale hook and lit the wick with a flint and striker. The interior of the wagon had grown damp whilst she'd been outside and the flame fizzed and shrank. Druss feared fire in the wagon above all things, and had insisted that Effie place the lamp on a slate tile and keep the flame covered at all times. She wasn't allowed to light it for warmth or illumination, only to heat ale and broth; and never when the wagon was in motion. As she sifted oats into the smoky brown ale to thicken it, she thought about the wagon. It was well made, compared to other wagons she'd seen. The curved lasts that formed the ribbing for the canvas were as smooth as table legs, and so expertly steamed that you might have thought the trees had grown that way. And then there was the canvas itself; woven as close as a chief's own field tent, and proofed against the finest rain with beeswax. Such things came at a price, Effie knew, and she wondered how Druss and Clewis Reed could afford them.

Just as the ale began to shimmer with heat, Clewis's large gloved hands parted the canvas. Stepping into the wagon he brought the rain with him, for the coating of his Orrl cloak shed water as quickly as the smoothest glass. Nodding toward the copper pan above the heat, he indicated he was ready to take a cup of ale. Effie poured a large measure into a turned wooden cup, hoping he wouldn't see how nervous she'd suddenly become. This was the first time she'd been alone with him in the wagon. Normally he and Druss slept outside, under cover of a small tent rigged to the side of the wagon. They took their meals outside, too—around a stone-ringed cook fire, like elk hunters.

The Orrlsman sat on the empty chicken crate, his spine straight and his free hand spread wide upon his knee, and drank deeply. The apple in his throat moved once, like a pump, as he swallowed. "It's well made," he said when he was done.

Effie felt her cheeks flush. "It's the toasted oats and the nutmeg, and the . . ." She hesitated, wondering if she should mention the dram of Mad Binny's rubbing alcohol she'd dumped into the pot on impulse. "The heat," she finished lamely.

Clewis looked at her as if he saw all she had not said. "So you're Sevrance-born, daughter to Tem and granddaughter to Shann and great-granddaughter to Moag the Hammer?" He paused, waiting for her to nod, and then continued in his deep, methodical voice. "It's a strong line. A warrior's line. I fought at Shann's side during the River Wars, at the Battle of Shaking Bridge."

Effie could only blink at him. She had never known her grandfather and knew next to nothing about him. The River Wars were nearly fifty years in the past; most of the men who'd fought in them were dead.

"Shann was lamed as he held the center. A Dhoone lance unhorsed him, and his foot became caught in his mount's trappings as he fell. The beast panicked and trampled his free leg. I don't believe Shann felt the ankle break, though we all heard the cracking of the bone. The battle frenzy was upon him, and he fought his way back onto the stallion and held that line until sundown. It took three of us to pull him from his horse. His foot and ankle were swollen like water bladders, and we had to saw off his boot. His toes were as black as plums, and the bone had shattered into so many pieces that the surgeon had to keep the wound poulticed for nine days. Every night Corrie Moon would remove the poultice, and there, embedded in the moss, would be a dozen tiny slivers of bone."

Effie hardly dared to move, less she distract the Orrlsman from his tale. She had never heard tell of her grandfather being a hero—Da never bragged about his kin. Da hardly talked at all. And then there were the interesting details of the wound. She wondered what Laida Moon's father had spread on the moss to draw out the bone fragments. Mad Binny said honey would draw out splinters, and purified meat jelly seasoned heavily with salt. If Effie closed her eyes she could almost see the splinters oozing out.

"Well, pour me some more ale, lass. In Orrl, we knew to keep our bards' throats oiled."

Shamed by her lack of manners, Effie hastened to do his bidding.

Clewis Reed drank deep a second time, yet the strong brew did not relax him, and his back remained stiff as he spoke. "Shann was carried home after nine days, and though I never saw him again I heard tell of him from time to time. He learned to walk with a stick, and by all accounts could ride well enough to be useful in the training of hammermen. He took up wood-working, fathered a son, and died a few years later in his sleep. Not a bad life. He never took to the field again, yet that hardly mattered after Shaking Bridge.

"Blackhail and Orrl won victory over Dhoone that day, and you'll not find a man in the clanholds who won't give Shann Sevrance his due. Without him Dhoone would have routed us. They were so close to the bridge they could see the splinters on the rail. Yet Shann fought them like a man possessed, I know because I watched him with my own two eyes. It was cold that day, yet the air around him rippled. It was like watching a man underwater. The distortion, as if you were seeing everything he did a moment after he did it."

The Orrlsman halted in his telling to look at Effie full on. His eyes had the washed-out color of a man in his sixties, yet his gaze had a force that pinned you. A marksman's gaze. "Your grandfather turned berserker that day at Shaking Bridge. He fought like a Stone God, unseating Dhoonesmen, smashing the weapons from their hands. All you had to do to make a kill was fight in his wake, for the men he matched hammers with were left dazed and bleeding. I was fourteen, a self-anointed swords-man for the day. I'd seen so little of battle until then that I thought that what Shann did . . . what he *became* was normal. Time has taught me otherwise."

Effie had to look away. For no good reason she felt guilty, as if Clewis Reed had caught her in a deception. To distract herself she studied his hands. Thick bowman's calluses had misshapen all the fingers of his drawing hand, and his knuckles were blotched with liver spots.

"Shann's sister was with him, that morning in the tent. Breeda, a plain lass, but devoted to her brother. We were waiting outside for him. We were a small company, all Orrlsmen— none of us had made white-winter warrior yet and we were divvied up at the Hail Lord's pleasure. When Shann and Breeda came out, Breeda kissed him full on the lips and wished him well. I've remembered that kiss for over forty years, yet to this day I hardly know why."

Effie shifted uncomfortably. Outside, the rain had turned heavy, and it drummed against the canvas roof. The tent flap hadn't been secured, and the curled edges of the canvas began to funnel water into the bed of the wagon. Effie turned up the wick on the safe-lamp—Druss wouldn't be pleased about that at all—and heard herself ask, "What was Breeda's lore?"

Clewis leant forward to adjust the tent flap, so he wasn't looking at her as he said, "I can't say as I remember. As far as I know, all you Sevrances are bears."

How do grown-ups do it? she wondered. *Lie so badly and get away with it?* He had led her this far, hinting at things she could hardly imagine, and now he was leaving her stranded. Well, she wouldn't let him. Grabbing hold of her lore, she held it out toward him. "Did she wear a stone like this?"

The Orrlsman breathed deeply, and after a time nodded. "Aye, she may have done."

Effie let the stone drop against her breastbone. She had won an admission from him, but she regretted her tactics. She could see from the faint drawing-in of his long dignified face that she had overstepped herself. Here was a subject to be fished for not hunted. He stood.

"I'll be off to check on the ponies."

She dropped her head in something like a nod, and then listened as he left. Confused guilt made her quick to snuff the lamp.

"Effie Sevrance."

She looked up, and there was Clewis Reed again at the tent flap, peering in, returned after less than a minute. His expression was somber and resigned.

"There's one last thing you should know about your grandfather. Shann took to the field that day a young man, his warrior's oath new-spoken, his shoulders so thick with muscle that his plate had to be held on with horse straps. By first light next morning he was someone else. His muscles were gone. Burned up. His skin rested loose on his face and neck, and his fingers were curled like an old man's. He'd aged twenty years. I've never seen the like before. It was as if the battle at Shaking Bridge had consumed him."

Sorcery. There it was, the unspoken word between them. Effie understood his reticence now. Clansmen could not—would not—talk of such things out loud. Clewis was telling her in his roundabout way that Shann Sevrance had traded his youth for skill in battle. Only *telling* wasn't the right word for it. *Warning* was a better one. Questions jumped into her throat, but she closed her lips to stop them coming out. Clewis Reed would not be hunted. Instead, she busied herself with the lamp, scraping hot soot from the vents with her thumbnail, and waited.

She felt the Orrlsman hesitate, heard him clear his throat. "The old stories, they need passing on. Time may come when we need them, and how will we survive if we've forgotten how to fight?"

He left her then, carefully sealing the tent flap behind him, shutting out the rain and the light.

Effie pushed the lamp away, and set her bottom on the warm spot it had created. Her thumbnail was black and gummy, and for a brief moment she wished she was back at the roundhouse so she could go running to Letty Shank and Florrie Horn and tell them her thumb was gangrenous and would soon be falling off. The thought of their screams made her smile for a bit, but it wasn't enough to make her forget about Clewis Reed.

Why tell me? That was the question she wanted to ask him.

Her hand found her lore and weighed it. Hauling stones, that's what it felt like to wear it. Both she and Breeda Sevrance had hauled stones. It should have made her feel better to learn she wasn't the only one to bear the stone lore, but it didn't. Breeda had been strange—that was something else Clewis Reed had managed to convey without actually coming out and saying it—and that meant she, Effie Sevrance, was strange as well. She didn't want to be strange. She wanted to be like Letty Shank and Florrie Horn, pretty and careless and afraid of normal things like mice and gangrenous fingers.

That made her snort and come to her senses. She didn't really want to be afraid of gangrenous fingers. It was just . . . the weight of everything, that was all. Longhead once said that the trouble with carrying stones was they never got any lighter, just heavier and heavier the longer you carried one. He should know—he'd spent forty years hauling stones around the roundhouse for repairs. Today Effie knew what he meant. Her lore had just got heavier. Somehow the weight of Clewis Reed's story was now resting upon it.

Well, she wasn't going to think about it. Standing, she began to tidy the bed of the wagon. Her chicken crate and sleeping pallet were shoved noisily to the side, and the lamp was set to cool on its bale hook. She slid the slate into place between the lidded baskets, and then began sopping up the puddle of rainwater that had collected below the tent flap. As she leant out of the wagon to wring the rag, Druss Ganlow called to her.

"Girl. You best not have spilled more ale."

He was standing by the back wheel, kicking a brake block into place. Rain had plastered his hair to his scalp, collapsing his normal baby fluff and revealing all the bald bits in between. His ale belly shuddered as he drove the cedar wedge into the mud. "I'll tell you now, if you've wet one of those baskets I'll see you tanned for it."

"It's nothing. Just a few drops of rainwater, that's all."

Druss huffed at her. "You best get your arse down here. We're setting to stay the night and I need to check the lode."

Effie grabbed her cloak. She'd come to realize that Druss Ganlow was one of those men who looked soft on the outside but was all hard stuff within. And he lied. He'd lied to Raina about the trip to Dregg, and to Drey about Black Hole. As she passed him on the wagon step some contrary bit of wickedness made her ask, "Did Raina pay you to take me to Dregg?"

He drew back his hand to show he was ready to smack her. "Let's get this straight, girl. I took no coin for you. It was a widow's favor, set between my ma and Raina. You should be grateful you got out of that roundhouse alive, not stirring up the piss in the pot. And I'll tell you another thing. Once we get to Dregg: First word of this dogleg leaks to Raina, and I'll haul you back to the Hailhold so fast Stanner Hawk won't have time to fire the forge."

Effie frowned as Druss pushed past her to enter the wagon. "So we *are* going to get there, then?"

She heard him growl as she ran away. Fear was a strange thing, she'd noticed. Your head could only hold so much of it at once, and there just wasn't enough room left to be afraid of Druss's threats.

The rain had begun to ease, but she still had to pull up her hood to keep from getting soaked. Clewis Reed was nowhere to be seen, so Effie checked the driver's seat to see if he'd taken his bow. The long, waxed-leather bow-sleeve lay as limp as a shed snakeskin on the boards. So he'd gone hunting, then. In the rain. Which was a bit strange, really, as everyone knew you couldn't bag any game in a downpour. Still. *I suppose he could shoot the ducks.* Somehow she didn't think he would, though. Harlequins were berserkers, he'd said so. They'd only carry on swimming if they were shot.

Not wanting to move far from the wagon, Effie went to see the ponies. The hitch was still in place, though the traces had been loosened to allow the pair to feed, and both animals were busy cropping the new green oats. They lifted their heads in interest when she approached, and let her scratch behind their ears and try to guess their names. Bacon and Eggs. Hammer and Nail.

Just as she decided upon Killer and Outlaw, Clewis Reed came running from the trees. The tall Orrlsman was holding his six-foot longbow aloft like a spear, and moving without a sound. He spotted Effie straightaway, and put a hand to his lips to silence her.

"Tighten the traces," he ordered, as he neared the wagon. He was breathing hard, and his hand went briefly to his heart. Sliding an arrow from his bow case he turned to face the trees. "Where's Druss?"

"Inside the wagon," Effie whispered, stretching over Killer's haunch to tighten his waist cinch. Clewis Reed had to be an old man—he'd fought in the River Wars—yet he didn't move like one. And he didn't panic, either. Not taking his gaze from the trees, the Orrlsman issued a high-pitched whistle, managing to sound just like a grouse marking its territory. Druss emerged from the wagon immediately. His face was red with exertion, but his eyes were sharp with comprehension, and he'd drawn his city-made longknife. His gaze followed Clewis's to the trees, but there was nothing to be seen except rain-weighted boughs of hemlock, too heavy to move in the wind.

When he turned back to the wagon and saw Effie, his expression hardened. "You. Inside," he hissed, kicking the brake block clear of the wheel.

Feeling the final buckle snap into place beneath her fingers, Effie moved clear of the ponies. Druss was already mounting the driver's seat, the reins pulled taut in his fist. "What did you see?" he asked Clewis.

The Orrlsman held his position at the rear of the wagon, his green-antler bow part-drawn, an iron-headed arrow trained upon the trees. "City men. Trappers like as not, caught in the clanholds by the thaw. Had some fine horses, though, for skin men. Swords, too."

Druss clicked the ponies to alertness and began guiding them through the delicate half-turn needed to steer clear of the river-bank. Effie got the feeling that both men had gone through this before. There was urgency without alarm; a mutual under-standing that one man's job was to move the wagon—the other's to protect it.

As she raced to catch up with the back of the wagon, she heard Druss ask, "How many?"

"Five. Quarter-league downstream."

"Have they spotted us?"

"Only the gods know that."

Effie leapt onto the step just as the wagon turned along the path. Clewis was sidestepping with his bow, losing distance to the wagon as he covered its retreat. Wagging his head at Effie, he encouraged her to move inside the canvas, leaving the step clear for him. She would have liked to stay put, but knew better than to ignore a clansman, and pushed forward into the dim interior. The wagon was picking up speed, and the load creaked and shifted, but Effie was more interested in watching Clewis

Reed mount the step. He had to run to match the wagon's pace, but even then he didn't relax his part-draw until the moment before he jumped. Swiftly, with his back turned to Effie, he fastened a guide rope around his waist, anchoring his torso to the wagon. Within seconds he had his bow back at part-draw, and his gaze trained once more on the receding tree line.

Effie observed him through the canvas flap. His fine silvery hair was floating on the breeze, revealing the flesh at the back of his neck. Engorged veins had turned the skin gray. He must have sensed her attention for he turned toward her briefly and said, "Sit down, girl. Nothing to see but an old man with a bent stick."

Reluctantly she moved back. The wagon was traveling over a rocky path, and the wooden ribs began to sway wildly from side to side. The lamp clattered noisily against the bale hook, and the chicken crate she normally sat on kept sliding backward and forward like something not battened down on a boat. It made her feel a bit sick. Crouching in the corner, she tried to settle the rolling in her belly.

Minutes passed and there was still no sign of pursuit. Effie thought it strange that clansmen in their own territory had reason to fear city men, but then she knew little about the border clans. Perhaps Bannen was more dangerous than Blackhail.

Suddenly, she heard Druss *Whoa!* the ponies, and the entire wagon lurched massively to the left. Effie was thrown forward as the ponies pulled to a halt. Leather whined, then snapped. One of the lidded baskets broke free from its mooring and fell with a heavy thud by Effie's head.

"Are you in one piece back there?" came Clewis Reed's voice through the canvas.

Effie groaned an affirmation. She was lying face down on the bed of the wagon and her left ear was on fire.

"Standing water on the road," he said. "Nothing more. We'll be taking a turn for the trees now anyway. I'd say we've seen the last of the trappers." He shouted ahead to Druss, and the wagon jerked into motion once more.

Effie raised a hand to her ear and winced. The basket had clipped her as it fell, and her earlobe felt strange and swollen. As she lifted her head from the floor she noticed a flickering yellow light on the canvas. Blinking slowly, she tried to work out its source. It was beautiful, warm as sunshine. Magical in its brilliance. Perhaps she'd been knocked out and this was a dream. Only ears didn't throb in dreams, she was pretty sure of that. Turning her head slowly she checked to see if the canvas flap was gaping, letting in light.

That was when she saw it. The lidded basket had burst open, and five rods of metal had slid out.

Gold.

TWENTY-FOUR

A Surlord's Progress

"We can reach the clanholds in twenty-four days, weather permitting. A good scout can halve that."

"Not at this time of year, with the floods." Penthero Iss halted in his progress of Spire Vanis's northern wall to look Marafice Eye in the face. The Protector General of Spire Vanis was clothed in the red leather cloak of his office, with the great lead killhound broach at his throat, and his black iron birdhelm crooked in his left arm. His one small eye was squinting against the whiteness of the morning mist and the strange disembodied rays of sunlight that shot through it like enemy fire. Marafice Eye ill liked being contradicted, but they were alone here, upon the limestone, and the Knife was learning to school his responses. Any man who sought to be Surlord had to choose his battles carefully.

Iss watched him drop his shoulders with an effort. "The dark-cloaks I sent out at Atonement should be back any day now. I'll have better intelligence then."

The word "I" sounded a warning to Iss. It was a tug on the reins of power. Marafice Eye was demonstrating the range of his influence, now grown diverse enough to command companies of notoriously volatile darkcloaks and gather intelligence from sources far beyond the city. But not far enough. With the minutest stretching of his lips, Iss turned smartly on his heels and continued his progress, leaving the Knife no choice but to follow him. *Later he will see just how much farther a surlord must reach.*

The Almsgate progress had begun before dawn. From high atop the northern wall it was possible to look out upon the vast tent city erected to accommodate Spire Vanis's ever-growing army. A ragged patchwork of hide and canvas tents spread wide and unlovely across the Vale of Spires below, turning furrowed fields to lakes of mud and crushing the first new grasses of spring. The stench of horse manure, unwashed bodies and woodsmoke rose like marsh gas from the encampment, and there was at least one grangelord in the progress who held a scented pomander to his nose to void the stink. The progress had been requested by Marafice Eye so he might show his surlord the full breadth of the army he was massing. It had been intended as a small affair—ranking generals, masters-of-arms, and a select few grangelords who were not wholly unsympathetic to the Knife—but word had spread, as word was wont to do, and half the grangelords in the city had turned up.

Marafice Eye was furious. And he'd made the mistake of showing it. Iss was an old hand at these things; knew all about the delicate egos that vied for influence in the city, and knew to expect greater numbers. Any attempt to exclude powerful grangelords from a public procession was doomed from the start to fail. The Knife would have been better served inviting them all along from the beginning—the progress would never have taken on its air of secrecy and exclusivity and hardly anyone would have bothered to turn up—but then, the Knife had much to learn.

Iss was conscious of a falling in his spirits as he headed

toward the great iron edifice of Almsgate. The wall was fifteen feet deep here, swelling to accommodate the gate towers. Lead-capped merlons and roofed archers' roosts protected the walk-way, yet Iss himself did not feel fully protected. At his back, at a carefully gauged distance of three feet, walked the Knife, and behind him, out of earshot as custom demanded, walked the eighty or so grangelords and generals who formed the remain-der of the progress. Lisereth Hews was in attendance, mother to the Whitehog and the only woman in the party. Iss had spied her earlier, dressed in the white and silver of House Hews, her ermine cloak paler than the limestone she walked on, her ungloved fingers glittering with a dozen surlords' rings. She had been daughter to the surlord Rannock Hews and now fancied being mother to one too. Many counted her a beauty, with her pale green eyes and unlined skin. Iss counted her dangerous. Her father had been slain before her eyes in Hound's Mire. She knew what it took to make a surlord.

It was only a matter of time before she sent her assassins out.

Briefly, Iss turned his head and acknowledged her with a small bow. She returned the gesture in kind, her own bow displaying the proper degree of genuflection even though her gaze never dropped once from his. House Hews was ever subtle in its defiance.

"Lady of the Eastern Ranges," he addressed her on a whim. "Walk with us." Turning his back, he did not wait to hear her acknowledgment. The brisk swishing of her silks and furs told him how eager she was to be included in the surlord's party.

Marafice Eye was not gentle around women, and he made no courtly show of welcome, nor did he give up his place for her, forcing the lady to walk around him to draw abreast of the surlord. She was a little breathless when she reached him. The morning light shone directly on her face, showing Iss that while her many admirers were wrong about her unlined complexion, they were right about her eyes. They were green like a cat's.

"I trust Garric is well?" he said. "I notice he's not among us this morning."

Lisereth Hews made a small gesture toward the encampment. "My son has duties with his hideclads. He leads the cavalry drills at dawn."

Her pride was unmistakable. Iss chose to inflame it. "I've heard he's begun styling himself the Whitehog, after his great-grandfather. It's gratifying to see a young man honor his ancestors. Let us hope *their* fates do not befall *him*."

Lisereth Hews stiffened. Diamonds woven into her hair-veil threw sparks. "My ancestors' fates have never been less than glorious. House Hews has given rise to forty-seven surlords. And you are mistaken, Surlord, if you imagine I would discourage my son from following them."

Iss raised an eyebrow. Lisereth Hews was a clever woman, but she had the unhappy habit of turning shrill when defending her son, and it was remarkably easy to goad her. "My dear lady. I make no mistakes regarding your ambitions, you can depend upon it." With a flick of his wrist he dismissed her, walking briskly forward with the Knife so that she stood alone on the limestone until the larger company met her.

Almost it was a relief to have her intentions out in the open.

Ahead lay the first of the northern gate towers, drum-shaped donjons built to house a hundred men. The wall was five storeys high here, but the towers were higher by another three storeys, and they dwarfed the gate they warded. Almsgate was cast from pure clannish iron, and no device had ever been built that could raise it. Manpower was needed. Two hundred brothers-in-the-watch raised it every morning on ropes as thick as a child's thigh. When it was dropped at night the sound of iron hitting iron could be heard as far away as the Quartercourts. Whores timed their shifts to it, and young men tested their manhood beneath it, standing in the gate trough until the very moment the warden called the drop. A gold coin left in the trough as the gate fell would be flattened to the thinness of parchment and stamped with the impressions of gate bolts. It was legal tender, and highly regarded, and many contracts within the city stipulated payment by Almsgold.

Iss thought the gate ugly and barbaric, ill fitted to the creamy limestone walls it was set within. Still, he had to admit its efficacy. Not once in the thousand years since its forging had an invading army breached it.

Pausing by the entrance to the western donjon, Iss made a show of asking his Knife questions regarding the army arrayed below, allowing Marafice Eye the chance to point and gesture and demonstrate his command. It was part of their deal. *Lead an army for me,* Iss had said at midwinter in the Blackvault. *And in return I'll name you as my successor.* It was far too early for such a reckless declaration—even Marafice Eye would admit that—yet small things such as this parley led toward it. Eighty of the most powerful men in the city stood watch as the surlord paid deference to his Knife.

Marafice Eye was aware of it, but his mind was a soldier's mind, and he was soon engrossed in the details of wagon trains and supplies. "We'll need provisions along the way," he said, his huge dog hands pushing northward. "The northern granges are wary of our passage. I've had Ballon Troak and Mallister Gryphon raising hell over it, threatening to withdraw their hideclads if we pass through either of their granges. Mother of bitches. They fight me at every turn."

They're playing a game with you, Iss thought to say but didn't. *This is about compensation, nothing more. Gold would solve it; that or the promise of first spoils on some lesser roundhouse like Harkness.* It was an unusual thing, this raising of a surlord, and Iss was unsure how to accomplish it. There were benefits—he could not deny it. Marafice Eye was the most feared man in Spire Vanis, his name spoken with awe on the streets and with outrage in the granges. If a man counted on being Surlord for life he needed such a second at his back. But there were dangers, too. How long would Marafice Eye be content to wait for his prize? Butcher-bred in Hoargate, he had the kind of hard, practical ambition that seldom overlooked chances. He'd move at the first smell of blood. They all would. Lisereth Hews and her son the Whitehog, the Forsworn who'd been expelled from the city since Borhis Horgo's death, John Rullion and his hardliners, and the ancient houses of Crieff, Gryphon, Stornoway, Pengaron and Mar.

Iss shuddered, though cloaked in velvet-lined vair the winds from the mountain barely touched him. It moved a man strangely to contemplate his own death. The absurdity of favoring one candidate for murder over another did not diminish the fear.

Nodding to the gate warden, Iss indicated his intent to enter the donjon. From his years of service in the Rive Watch he knew the city's gate towers well. They were damp and cold, the stairs and ways built narrow to exclude the passage of more than one man. The grangelords would have to pick up their heavy cloaks and travel in single file. Let them wonder as they rounded dark corners if an assassin was waiting in the shadows on the other side. That would be the closest most would get to becoming Surlord, that knowing of a surlord's fear.

Marafice Eye commanded the gate towers and knew all about their dangers. Without waiting for his surlord's permission, he stepped to the head of the party, his sword hand descending to the hilt of his red blade, his voice barking a command to the warden. The warden took possession of the Knife's blackened birdhelm, then ran ahead to arrange the firing of torches.

Shouted calls to order accompanied the surlord's entrance. Inside the donjon the temperature and light level dropped. The smell of old rankness, of fluids spilled by torture and cog grease long soured, sweated from the stones like groundwater. Iss descended swiftly, the anxious murmurs of grangelords falling soft upon his ears.

When Iss reached ground level Marafice Eye stood waiting by the donjon's sole entrance, a doorway so narrow that a large man like the Knife had to face side on to enter. A sept of sworn brothers flanked him.

"Surlord," he said formally, his gaze flicking over Iss's shoulder to check that they were alone and that the rest of the party still straggled far behind. "I present your personal guard. Good men, picked by my own hand. Sworn to protect you in my absence."

A personal guard? What mischief is this? Iss knew better than to show surprise. Coolly, he inspected the sept, taking his time to note their weapons and their faces. They were big men, cloaked in black rather than their dress reds, their killhound brooches set with ruby eyes denoting ten-year service. Iss recognized two of them. Axal Foss was known as the Knighthunter, for the great number of Forsworn he'd slaughtered during— and after—the Expulsions. He was a veteran of twenty years, and had risen to the rank of Captain Protector. The other man was Styven Dalway, blond and handsome and much admired by grange-bred ladies. Iss had recruited him in Almstown sixteen years earlier after seeing him fight singlehanded against the King of Pimps and two of his cronies. Apparently, Dalway's sister was a seasoned whore who'd failed to pay her cut to Edo Shrike, the self-styled King of Pimps, and the King of Pimps had seen her flogged for it. Dalway had killed him on the Street of the Five Traitors with half of Almstown watching.

Hearing the footfalls of the remainder of the progress

approaching, Iss ordered the sworn brothers at ease. "Knife," he commanded, slipping through the portal and into the gate court beyond. "Attend me."

Almstown was famous for its markets, and the open area south of the gate was bustling with activity as merchants set down tables and rolled out canvas for the day's business. Brazier men were lighting their grills, setting sausages and knuckles of pork to char in their own fat. A steady stream of mule-drawn carts was passing beneath the gate, bearing staples of grain and winter roots from the northern granges, while dark-skinned acolytes of the Bone Temple hefted baskets of forced plums and honey melons from the temple's heated garden. All slowed their labors to watch the surlord and the Knife.

"So you'd see me thrice-guarded whilst you attend the clans?" Iss turned on Marafice Eye, caring little if his voice rose. "I already possess an honor guard of sworn brothers and a company of darkcloaks. Tell me, would you set guards to watch my guards?"

The Knife shrugged his massive shoulders. "I would see you alive on my return, Surlord. No more."

Iss breathed deeply. The Knife spoke hard and true. The worst that could happen for Marafice Eye would be an assassination in his absence. Spire Vanis would not wait on his return. By the time word reached him in the clanholds a new surlord would be made. What then for the Knife? New surlords were full of fear; they had to move to smash their rivals. The Knife would find himself shut out of the city. Or worse. He might never make it back to Spire Vanis alive.

Iss stepped farther into the market square, making space for the crush of grangelords and brothers-in-the-watch that was rapidly assembling behind him. On his movement the sept of sworn brothers rushed forward into the crowd, clearing a space of fifty feet around their charge. Iss almost smiled. So the Knife would keep his surlord alive until *he* was ready to kill him. Absurdity heaped on absurdity. But then, what would one expect from a city founded by bastard lords?

"The sons of many granges ride north with you," Iss said as the Knife drew level with him. "It is a good thing to take one's rivals to war."

Marafice Eye grunted. "Good for both of us, Surlord."

Iss could not deny it. Looking south across the city toward the boiling mists of Mount Slain, he said, "Keep the Whitehog close on the journey."

"I plan to." Marafice Eye ran a hand across the hollow socket that was his left eye. It pained him some, Iss had heard, yet he refused to take anything for it. "I'd sooner watch the son than the dam."

Then you are a fool, Iss thought with some satisfaction. Marafice Eye was a butcher's son, bred in the stinking shanties of Hoargate. His taste in women ran low. He was comfortable amongst maids, whores and alewives. He didn't know how to act around grange-bred beauties. And he didn't know how to gauge them. Iss knew the son to be more dangerous than the mother: Lisereth Hews ran hot and cold and seldom hid her emotions; Garric Hews ran only cold. Yet the Knife could not see that. He saw Lisereth Hews's arrogance and finery and knife-edged tongue. He saw and felt threatened by them.

"Knife," Iss commanded, feeling at last a lightening of his spirits. "Send for the horses. This progress has ended."

While he waited for the horses to be led into the gate court, Iss called for his Master of Purse. Behind him he was aware of the grangelords growing agitated and impatient. They couldn't send for their own mounts until their surlord was under way and they felt their lack of dignity keenly. Mallister Gryphon, Lord of the Spire Granges, was fuming. He'd tried to move forward out of the crush, only to have Axal Foss restrain him with an unweaponed hand. Lisereth Hews had managed to spirit five of her personal hideclads into the fray, and though she wasn't unwise enough to have them escort her from the gate, she used them to clear the area immediately before her, so that she stood arrayed in all her House Hews finery for every merchant in Almsgate to behold.

Iss admired her nerve. Taking a bag of mixed coin from his Master of Purse, he stole the merchants' attention from her.

"Gentlemen traders," he addressed them, using the skills of voice he'd honed under Borhis Horgo. "I've heard tell the goods sold in Almsgate Market are the best to be had in the city. I would sample such excellence myself. Ready a basket of your finest wares, and my Master of Purse will purchase them in my name and bear them south to the fortress."

An excited murmur rippled through the marketplace as merchants and traders reckoned the profit from this unexpected boon. Iss loosed the purse's drawstring, allowing the gold and silver coin to catch the light.

"And you'll pay us fair value?" shouted a suspicious vintner near the front.

"A silver over," Iss replied, throwing the purse back to its master.

It was delicious to ride through Almsgate to the accompaniment of so much cheering. At his side, mounted on his massive black destrier trapped with Rive Watch red, Marafice Eye watched and learned. As they turned their horses onto the wide expanse of the Spireway, he said, "That was nicely done, Surlord. They'll love you better for buying their wares than they would if you'd given them charity."

Iss nodded. Sometimes he didn't know if he was teaching the Knife or warning him.

The Spireway was the widest thoroughfare in the city, running north to south, from Almsgate to the Quartercourts. In the time of the Bastard Lords it had been known as the Street of Spikes, for traitors and petty thieves alike had been impaled on iron shafts along its three-league length. Later surlords had enlarged and improved it, commissioning decorative arches and stone statues and private limestone palaces to house their whores, their bastards, their gold. Theric Hews had excavated the great stone warrior's pit that lay at the halfway mark, and Halder the Provider had built a folly of mock canals and sunken gardens that froze to an icesheet every year until spring. Still. Not even *he* had dared remove the spikes. The Impaled Beasts were the war badge of Spire Vanis. This city had been built on stakes and spikes and poles.

Iss absently counted the iron shafts as he rode. Black and ugly, they were, some broken by frost and rust, others tied with the red ribbons of marriage banns, announcing to anyone who cared to look that a marriage between two parties was taking place, and any objections or prior claims should be lodged with the officiating priest. It was a popular outing on holy days to travel from spike to spike, reading the ribbons. Every betrothed couple in the city had to publish banns, and it was counted a fine game to judge highborn marriages from lowborn solely from the quality of ribbon used.

Shifting in his saddle so he could look at Marafice Eye, Iss said, "It's time you were wed, Knife. The man who would be Surlord needs a grange."

Marafice Eye made a noise. Iss took it as a sign that he would listen.

"You cannot hope to rule this city without the grangelords. Yes, you could take the power, but could you *keep* it? The grangelords control the trade routes. They grow the grain and raise the livestock. You could fling open the gates but nothing would come in. The city would starve. Then where would your brothers-in-the-watch be? You could send them out against the granges, but they'd be fighting hideclads on their home ground. And whilst you're waiting to hear news of battles and sieges, Almstown and Hoargate would riot. And would they riot against the grangelords? No. Because the grangelords would be holed up in their granges, well out of the city."

Reaching the end of the Spireway, Iss guided his gelding east along the muddy course of wells and mineral springs that bubbled up from Mount Slain and was known as Water Street. An uneasy mix of bathhouses, tanneries and slaughterhouses made use of the natural springs, and the sept of sworn brothers swept wide as Iss and Knife rode through. The rising sun was just passing behind Mount Slain as it did every morning in winter, providing a false dusk for the short time it took to clear the peak. Iss tugged soft deerskin gloves from his belt and slid them on.

"You need to control a grange, Knife. And the only way to do so is to marry into one. Wed a grangelord's daughter and you become one of them. Fight them from the inside. That way they'll respect as well as fear you."

The Knife's nostrils flared as he breathed and thought. "So it's about respect, is it, Surlord?"

"You know it is."

"Then *you* must know that marrying a grangelord's daughter will not make me a grangelord. Those bastards have their estates and titles bound up tighter than a bathhouse whipping boy. It would take an Act of Ascendancy to allow me to inherit the title of grangelord on my father-in-law's death."

"Then you shall have one."

Marafice Eye turned to look at him at last. The hollow eye socket was full of shadow, a hole with nothing coming out. "I have your word on it?"

Iss nodded.

"Speak it."

"You have my word on it." Iss felt his anger rising, but tamped it. He wasn't done here yet. Increasing his gelding's pace to a trot, he said, "I've been giving mind to whom you might wed. Suitable candidates are few and far between, but I believe I've found one willing to have you. Katrina Mallion of the Needlewood Granges is in need of a husband. She's an only child, heir to her father's estates, and her first husband died without issue."

Iss waited for the Knife's response. Seconds passed. A flock of snow geese passed overhead. Marafice Eye made a gesture to Styven Dalway, ordering the sworn brother to flank the surlord as they entered the bustling expanse of Pengaron Square.

Just as Iss was ready to explode, Marafice Eye put a hand to his chin and said, "Needlewoods. Aren't those the trees that grow in swamps?"

Iss was having trouble containing his anger. "They may be. I hardly see that it matters. The Needlewood Granges lie at the western foot of the mountain, near Loon Lake. A portion of the holding may lie in marshland. What of it? Katrina Mallion is young, noble, and willing. And her father has need of hard cash."

"So you've approached him?"

"Tentatively. Yes." It was more than that, but Iss knew better than to admit it. He'd been working for over a month toward this match. Edward Mallion was a drinker and gambler, a wastrel who'd run his inheritance into the ground. The Needlewood Granges produced reeds, fowl and turf. Only production had been dropping these past ten years and now the granges barely paid for themselves. Mallion had already accepted a hundred count of Almsgold from the surlord's coffers. In return, he'd given his word that he'd seek no further suitors for his daughter. Iss judged the match a good one. The Needlewood Granges were a minor holding in decline: they would suit his purposes well.

Iss said, "Katrina Mallion attended the Winter Feast at the fortress. Even dressed in the black of mourning she turned many heads."

Marafice Eye grunted. "You have given no promises?"

"No," Iss lied.

"Good," the Knife said, digging steel spurs into horsemeat. "As I've given my word elsewhere."

Iss felt the world turn out of focus. The jewelers, silversmiths, redsmiths, blacksmiths, armorers and wiremakers whose market stalls filled Pengaron Square became a blur of light and movement. Iss could almost feel the knives at his back. *This is what I will know at the moment of my death; this revelation of betrayal.*

With an effort of will he forced his mind from that dark place. The sun had emerged from behind Mount Slain and was sliding its rays across the square. A table piled with pewter bowls and cook pots flashed like treasure as the sunlight touched it. Ahead, Iss saw the Knife in conversation with Axal Foss. The other six men in the sept had drawn close around their surlord, reacting to the slowing of his mount and the slight stiffening of his face.

Iss was aware of his heart as a living, moving weight in his chest. *I have been duped.* Tilting his chin upward he sent a sworn brother to purchase a jeweled cup from the nearest stall. He did not want it, would never even handle it, but he would not let the Knife know what his words had done. Let him think his surlord slowed to inspect silverware, nothing more.

He'd move at the first smell of blood.

Trotting his mount forward, Iss joined the Knife and they turned onto the great white-paved promenade that led south to Mask Fortress.

"So," Iss said after a time. "Who is the lucky maid?"

"Liona Stornoway."

Stornoway. *Stornoway.* One of the five Great Houses of Spire

Vanis. Roland Stornoway could trace his ancestors back to the Bastard Lords. His family had birthed a dozen surlords and countless Masters of Purse, Chief Examiners, Protector Generals and warlords. The Stornoway holdings were vast. They owned lands so far east they bordered on Hound's Mire, and their coffers were rumored to be brimming with Sull gold.

Iss kept a tight reign on his features. "A good match."

Marafice Eye lifted the massive bulk of his shoulders in his version of a shrug. "I think so. The bitch is well seasoned and not quite right in the head, but I daresay she'll suit me well enough. I'll keep away from her and she'll keep away from me, and once we've fucked to seal the match we'll be done."

"Such romance."

Marafice Eye barked a laugh.

Iss wondered how he had done it. True, Stornoway and Hews were longtime rivals, and the Knife might have gained much by promising that Garric Hews would never make Surlord. But still. Stornoway was a proud house. How had they agreed to marry one of their own to a son of Hoargate? Then he remembered. "Liona, you say?"

"Aye. And if you're thinking is she the one who got caught straddling the bookbinder's son, then you'd be right."

"Quite a scandal, as I recall."

Marafice Eye executed another one of his shrugs. "Her scandal is my gain. Roland Stornoway has been wanting to be rid of her for months. No decent man would have her." Stretching his lips into a savage smile, he added, "That's where I come in."

He was clever in low ways, the Knife; you could never forget that. This was a clever trick he'd pulled off, taking on the unwanted slattern of one of the city's finest houses. Roland Stornoway must be pissing himself laughing. But then Roland Stornoway was a shortsighted fool. His death warrant had just been signed.

"Refresh my memory," Iss said, his voice casual. "Liona is one of three daughters?"

"The eldest. And there's a son. Also named Roland."

"Sickly?"

"He will be."

Iss nodded. So many fools here, and he himself was one of them. Not an hour earlier he'd given his word to pass an Act of Ascendancy, allowing the Knife to inherit his wife's titles and holdings. Once father and son were out of the way the Knife would find himself Lord of the High Granges, Lord of the Highland Passes, and Lord of the Rape Seed Granges. Not a bad tally for a butcher's son. Not bad at all, considering the current Surlord of Spire Vanis was heir solely to the Sundered Granges.

Something sour began to burn in Iss's stomach. He said, "And when shall I expect the happy event?"

"Soon. Afore I ride north. John Rullion's agreed to wed us. Said we can exchange bread and vows at the Shrine of the Sister 'neath the Quartercourts."

The High Examiner knows of this? And has agreed to wed them? Iss could barely keep the surprise from his face. John Rullion was in alliance with the Knife? No. Surely not. More likely the great dour man of God was playing all sides. Hadn't he burned the amber for Garric Hews's Affirmation? And didn't he teach Mallister Gryphon's two young sons their Pieties? As a man of Holy Orders, John Rullion could never be Surlord, but that did not stop him from wielding power. His first priority was keeping the Forsworn out of the city: he would tolerate no rival for men's souls.

Such thoughts calmed Iss. The Knife hadn't been especially singled out by John Rullion. No. That wasn't the issue here. The issue was that the Knife had suddenly grown crafty and devious enough to pose a real threat to his surlord's power.

Iss shot Marafice Eye a sideways glance. The Protector General of Spire Vanis was picking a deer tick from his stallion's neck. His thumbnail was the size of an arrowhead, and he used it to lance the tick like a boil.

"I'll have to think of a suitable gift."

The Knife wiped his fingers on his sheepskin numnah. "There's one you can give."

"And that would be?"

"I would have you host the wedding feast at the fortress."

So all the grangelords and men of influence in the city would be bound to attend. It was one thing to refuse an invitation from the Protector General, another thing entirely to refuse one from the Lord Commander of Spire Vanis. "It shall be done."

"I thank you for it."

For the first time Iss heard a hint of relief in the Knife's voice. *He hadn't been so sure of me after all.*

Horns sounded, first one and then a chorus, as sentries positioned high on the Mask Wall spied their surlord approaching. The northern edifice of Mask Fortress lay directly ahead; a walled city within a walled city, its four ill-matched towers spiking the sky. The winds from Mount Slain hadn't started up yet, and the Killhound banners flying from the ramparts sagged listlessly against their poles.

As Iss neared the stable gate a company of sworn brothers rode out to escort him into the fortress. Marafice Eye fell in step with one of them, falling back from his position now that the surlord was safely delivered.

"Knife," Iss commanded as he passed beneath the mud-coated iron teeth of the portcullis. "Attend me in the Horn."

Not waiting on the Protector General's response, he headed to the stables to dismount.

It was cold in the fortress, and mist still swirled in the quad. Great cracks in the paving stones had opened during the thaw and the odor of mountains escaped from them. Iss was approached by several supplicants as he headed toward the Horn. Every tenday the fortress was thrown open to those seeking boons or justice from the surlord, and dozens of tradesmen and lesser folk had been kept waiting in the quad while the surlord completed his progress. Iss waved them away. Later he would see that the jeweled cup he'd purchased in Pengaron Square went to one of the paupers who'd waited patiently in place whilst he passed. The rest would get naught.

The Horn, at two hundred feet, was the second-tallest of the four towers in the fortress. It was a strange construction, flat-sided where the other three towers were rounded, its stonework clad in an intricate grille of metalwork and sheeted lead. It had been built after the Cask but before the Bight, and it suited no purpose well. Theron Hews had intended the Horn to combine both defendability *and* beauty, but had sadly fallen short of both. Iss leased the lower storeys to ranking grangelords, for it was ever fashionable to claim apartments in the fortress, and the income helped cover repairs.

The upper two chambers and the walled roof enclosure he kept for himself. Climbing the worn, shallow stairs he headed for the roof. By the time he'd reached the halfway mark he could hear the *kaaw*ing of the rooks.

Passing through the hatchery and the game room, Iss emerged onto the stone landing of the roof. An area the size of a dance circle was carefully furnished with settling posts, wicker cages and walls of wooden cubbies. Everywhere along the ramparts the big crows known as rooks danced in mock battles and shows of bravado, bobbing their heads aggressively and spreading their dirty-black wings. The noise was deafening. The Master of the Rookery had just brought out a bucket of maggots, farmed from a decomposing deer corpse kept in the game room, and the rooks were starting to flock. A few rogue birds took to the air, and began swooping perilously close to the Master's head. None swooped at Iss. They could smell the faint tinge of sorcery upon him—even now, after he'd not drawn power in many days.

Corwick Mools, Master of the Rookery, dug his hand deep into the bucket and brought out a fistful of squirming maggots. Flinging his arm out, he scattered the fat white larvae wide, and the rooks fell upon them like locusts on a cornfield. Contests were fought. Eyes were pecked out, and feet were bloodied as questing beaks speared maggots from between clawed toes.

Into this feeding frenzy walked the Knife.

Iss knew straightaway that Marafice Eye was nervous, for he hung back close to the door and would not join his surlord in the center of the circle. Iss let him stew. For sport, Corwick Mools threw a handful of maggots high into the air and the swiftest rooks caught them on the wing. The Knife ducked his head unhappily, cursing under his breath. When he could take it no longer he said, "You wanted me, Surlord?"

"You know the keeping of birds is sacred in Spire Vanis," Iss said conversationally, ignoring the question. "Three of the four towers house hatcheries. I keep my hawks in the mews atop the Bight, and the Splinter was once home to a family of killhounds. They perched on the spire and laid their eggs in the roof vault. It must have been quite a sight to see them, gliding above the fortress. Their wingspans were as wide as thirty paces, did you know?"

Marafice Eye took a swipe at a crow that got too close. "I did not."

Iss nodded. "Only surlords were allowed to eat their eggs."

"Say what you would have of me, Surlord," roared the Knife, goaded at last to anger and growing increasingly nervous of the crows' razor beaks near his one remaining eye.

Iss exchanged a knowing glance with Corwick Mools. It was remarkable how easily birds could unman one. "It's not what I'd have of you, Knife. Rather what you need from me."

"And that would be?"

Iss signaled to Corwick Mools to bring the bird that had homed this morning from the clanholds. "Intelligence."

Corwick Mools cut the bundle from the bird's leg in full view of his surlord. The message had been rolled in a lamb's bladder to protect it against water and sealed with a pinprick of red wax. Iss's hands were well practiced in the handling of such things and were quick to unravel the thin strip of pigskin that bore the message. He read it, nodded once, then fed it to a big male crow.

Banishing Corwick Mools with the words "Leave us," he turned to face the Knife.

Now you will see just how far a true surlord must reach.

"You must ready the army to leave within the tenday. The Wolf is cresting early this year. By the time you reach it the flooding will have passed and you'll be guaranteed easy crossing into the clanholds. A flat barge awaits to give you crossing at Mare's Rock."

All the Knife could do was nod.

TWENTY-FIVE

Spilling Sand

"No. No. No. No. Don't bother with all that pretty stuff. Hack the wee lassie to pieces."

Raif wiped the sweat from his forehead with the back of his sword hand and bent his legs at the knee, waiting to see which way Stillborn would swing the quintain. Even though he was prepared for it, the dummy came hurtling toward him with force. It was an odd construction, torso-shaped and filled with wet sand, armored in consecutive layers of felted wool, boiled leather and ring mail, and armed with spikes like a porcupine. Heavy as hell, it hung from a thick chain anchored to the rock ceiling. Stillborn controlled its movement from a ledge just above Raif's head. The Maimed Man could send it in lazy circles around Raif or he could shove it toward him with enough force to knock him off his feet.

Raif rolled to the side to avoid being smashed, but as he spun back to strike he felt the tell-tale sting of the quintain's body-spikes rake his arm.

"You're dead, archer boy." Stillborn smiled with satisfaction as he reeled in the guide rope, causing the quintain to rise toward him. "It's a sad state of affairs when a dummy—and a female one at that—can beat the crap out a living, breathing man."

Raif thought of many things to say, but his arm was stinging and he was out of breath. Briefly he wondered what manner of irritant had been applied to the spikes. Salt, lye, ground glass— something to bring tears to his eyes. Resting the flat of his borrowed sword against his thigh, he nodded toward the quin-tain. "That's female?"

Stillborn chuckled. He was dressed in his rat-and-coon-fur kilt, rawbuck pants and a tunic made from two whole sheep-skins. A leather belt with a square-shaped pewter buckle was the only thing upon him that didn't look as if it had been dragged straight off a carcass. "Can you not see her dugs? Stuffed them myself, I did." Wrapping his thick fingers around the quin-tain's waist, he kissed the stump where its neck ended. "She's a feisty lass. I think I'll call her Yelma."

"After anyone you know?"

Stillborn raised an eyebrow. "Maybe."

"The Scarpe chief is named Yelma."

"Is she now?" Stillborn's clear hazel eyes glittered in the darkness of the cave. With a lightning-quick movement he thrust the quintain at Raif.

Raif was ready for it this time, and slashed the torso with a sideways cut as he cleared its path. The sword contact slowed the quintain's backswing, and Raif risked diving forward to thrust at its belly on the return. He knew it was a mistake the moment he struck. The quintain was moving in the same direction as his sword, robbing momentum from the blow, and his sword tip entered with an awkward jab, catching in the dummy's ring mail. It took a twisting wrench to free it, and Raif didn't even need to look at the blade to know how badly he'd damaged it. Shor Gormalin would have skinned his knuckles for less.

"It'll have to go to Bledso for a firing," Stillborn said amica-bly, nodding toward the sword. "No harm done. It was a piece of whore's steel to begin with." He stilled the quintain with the guide rope and vaulted down from the ledge. Drawing the Forsworn sword, he waved Raif out of the fight circle.

"You have to learn to spill the sand, boy. Go for the guts. You're so busy weaving and ducking and remembering whatever pretty steps your sword master taught you that you forget the whole point of the game. Kill ugly and kill fast."

Suddenly Stillborn exploded into motion, kicking the quintain from him with all his might. The suspension chain creaked as the armored dummy swung away, halted for the briefest instant, and then came barreling back. Instead of sidestepping the dummy's swing, Stillborn spread his weight and stepped forward to meet it. Wrapping the haft of the sword in an overlapping two-handed grip, he raised its point to the dummy's gut and ran the quintain through. The dummy's forward momentum brought it right up the sword's blade to the crosshilt, and its spikes squealed against the tempered steel as it came to a grinding halt. Stillborn didn't blink. In one easy movement he slid the blade free, barely causing the quintain to stir. Globs of dark, wet sand oozed from entrance and exit holes.

Turning to Raif, Stillborn executed a self-satisfied bow. "Ugly and fast. Introducing a man's intestines to his spine is the best way invented to win a fight."

Raif ran his thumb over the chewed-up tip of his borrowed sword. "Not the heart?"

Stillborn gave him a quick look. "No. Path to the heart's guarded by the ribs and the heaviest armor. The belly's vulnerable. There's skin—" he punched his gut, making it ripple "—and fat and precious little else. Few men have the money or patience for full plate. Most would rather bend at the waist. Oh, they cover their bellies with hard leather and ring mail and enough hinged pieces to tile a roof. But that's nothing to a longsword. One good thrust below the ribs and you're done."

Stillborn smiled lovingly at the Forsworn sword and then sheathed it.

Shadows were deepening in the cliff cave with the approach of night. The sunset had turned bloody and the granite walls sparkled with flecks of red garnet. The chamber was long and low, its ceiling mined to a height uncomfortably low to most men. Only the fight circle and the cave's entrance were vaulted. Outside, in the vast space where the continent split, the wind piped and wailed. Stillborn called it Rift Music, and had lit a fire against it, like a woodsman warding against wolves. He tended the fire now, feeding goat chips and closed fir cones to the flames. The fuel hissed and cracked, competing with the wind.

Stillborn settled down against the cave wall, took a piece of brown bun from his pack and began eating it. In between crushing nuts with his teeth, he said, "It's time we took you raiding. Traggis has his nose set on you. Watches you like a flea in his curlies, and unless you're doing something useful he'll set you a bastard's task instead. You're new here, and so far you've done naught but split a hog's heart in two—and cause a brother's death. Some are saying you're bad luck. And bad luck best go to the Rift."

Raif ran a hand through his hair. He had no argument to counter Stillborn's words, so instead he said, "Take me raiding, then."

Stillborn nodded as if Raif had spoken wisely. Pushing the last of the brown bun in his mouth, he asked, "Have you a head for heights?"

Raif thought about crossing the Ranges, about the heart-stopping altitude of Trappers' Pass. "I manage," he said.

"Good." Stillborn stood. The seam of flesh that ran down the center of his face was black with shadows and grizzled hair. "I'll see you at dawn on the Rim. Best if you stay here tonight.

There's not much fuel for the fire—so burn sparingly. And if it's food you're wanting you'll have to fend for yourself. Just be sure to keep your distance from the Mole."

Raif watched him collect his pack and climb the rough-hewn steps to the cave entrance. Just before he disappeared from sight, he waved a hand toward the quintain. "And a few extra rounds with Yelma wouldn't hurt."

Raif raised his damaged sword in salute. He had been with the Maimed Men for nine days now, yet he wasn't any closer to understanding them. Mostly Stillborn kept him in the background, making him sleep in the lower tiers of the city and spend his days in the caved-in eastern quarter, out of sight and out of mind of Traggis Mole. So far Stillborn had kept him busy caring for his equipment: sanding armor, oiling steel, repairing tack. Sometimes he shared his food. Sometimes not. Always they would spend the sunset hours training. Raif's deficiencies with a sword made Stillborn nervous.

Idly, Raif crossed over to the quintain and set it swinging. The missing portion of his finger was aching tonight, and he grimaced as his hands closed around the haft of the sword. If he tired himself out perhaps he would sleep.

The cave darkened as he fought the quintain. Strike followed strike, and after a time he found his rhythm and it became easy to thrust his sword between the spikes. There was a numbness to the combat he welcomed. The quintain had no heart. It made things simple. Purer. *This is how other men fight.* Encouraged, Raif began a new barrage of sword thrusts, tracking the quintain as it swung around the fight circle. He discovered that Stillborn was right. There was a lot to be said for stepping *into* your opponent's strike. It turned fear into action, met aggression with aggression. It was not what Shor Gormalin had taught . . . but then, Shor Gormalin had never been a Maimed Man.

Time passed and the Rift Music rose from the divide. Cold winds skirled around the cave but Raif barely felt them. Within her triple coat of armor, Yelma sagged. She was losing sand from a dozen holes and her ring mail looked as if it had been chewed by dogs. Raif abandoned her tattered belly, and began work on her throat. Tomorrow he would have to stitch and restuff her, but for now it felt good to imagine the spot where the great red arteries rose toward her brain. Imagine and destroy them.

Just as he was finishing her off, a high-pitched cough echoed from the cave entrance. Raif slackened his pace, sticking out his sword to slow Yelma.

"Don't stop on my account, Twelve Kill," came Yustaffa's piping voice. "I can't speak for anyone else, but personally I never pass up the chance to watch a man beat a bag of sand."

Raif halted, and stilled Yelma. His breaths were coming hard. Sweat plinked from the tip of his nose.

"What? No welcome. And here I came all this way to invite you to a little supper. I've quails' eggs, you know. But I see you have no appetite for them. Well, never let it be said that Yustaffa the Dancer stays where he's not wanted. Two's company and all that. You and the dummy make a lovely couple, by the way."

Raif heard silk rustle and the pad of soft-shoed feet. He took a breath. "Wait." The feet ceased padding. "I'll come with you."

Yustaffa resumed climbing the stair. "Well, hurry up, then. I'm passing fond of quails' eggs and I can't guarantee there'll be any left unless you're there when I divvy them up."

Raif grabbed his Orrl cloak from the ledge and followed Yustaffa from the cave.

The night air stung his skin. It was black in the Rift after sundown, the stars shedding the barest memory of light. Smoke drifted in gray patches, forming shadow terraces that lay above the real ones like ghosts. The Rift was quiet now, the wind strangely becalmed, the stench of underworld metals rising in its place.

Yustaffa held a mica lamp on a stick for illumination and moved swiftly through the city, climbing stairs with ease and hoisting his considerable weight one-handed up rope ladders. Raif struggled to keep up.

Maimed Men were gathering in small groups, cooking and drinking around bonfires, fortifying themselves for the night's business. Many fell silent and stared as he passed, and he could feel the accusations in their eyes. He wanted to shout at them *I did not kill Tanjo Ten Arrow*, but somehow it didn't feel like the truth. Less than ten days in a foreign city and already they knew what he was.

When they reached the western edge of the highest terrace, Yustaffa slipped into a gap in the rock wall. The stench of sulfur assaulted Raif's senses as he followed the fat man through. Steam curled forward to meet him, and it took some time to adjust to the dimness and the haze. A stone grotto cratered with hot springs and lit by green-burning lanterns lay before him. The rock floor was wildly uneven, creating ridges and crevices and stone chimneys that rose like ancient, deformed oaks to the roof. Men and women languished naked in small pools, their deformities and missing limbs cloaked by the water and the steam. No one spoke. Water gurgled and sloshed. After the cold dryness of the Rift, Raif found it difficult to breathe.

"This way." Yustaffa beckoned him to a plank gangway that led over the rock floor and between the pools.

As they moved deeper into the cavern, the pools became fewer and more secluded as the rock floor warped to create half-walls and hollows and closed-off rooms. Yustaffa left the gangway and ducked beneath a low arch. "Here we are. My own private little steam bath. Strip off and take a dip. You've been hanging around with Stillborn far too long—picking up his habits and his fleas."

Raif glanced around the small chamber. A narrow ledge circling the pool was the only place to stand. Steam rising from the water made him drowsy, and for a brief instant he was reminded of the Listener's ground, of the *oolak* he'd drunk there.

Yustaffa shed his furs and silks and slipped naked into the bubbling water. Raif followed him, throwing his clothes against the wall, and sucking in his breath as the scalding liquid enveloped him. Almost immediately, all the aches and stings of sword fighting floated away. He found a ledge beneath the water and sat on it, tilting back his head against the rock.

"Good, eh?" prompted Yustaffa, seeming pleased.

Raif nodded. "Good."

Yustaffa reached out a fat, scalded arm and slid a package from his furs. "The quails' eggs. I think we'll have them cooked." One by one he lowered the small, speckled eggs into the water, resting them deep below the surface.

Raif plunged his head underwater, emerged, and then slicked back his wet hair. He couldn't remember the last time he'd felt so good. *Now*, he could sleep. Right here, buoyed by the water. Sleep and not dream of Tanjo Ten Arrow . . . or the bodies of the Forsworn. Stretching out his arms, he closed his eyes and let the hot water ease him.

He must have drifted off for a moment, for when he opened his eyes again he saw Yustaffa was watching him. Steam had sprung the Maimed Man's hair into tight curls.

Yustaffa stirred the water. "I never finished telling you about *Azziah riin Raif*, the Stranger from the South, did I?" He looked at Raif for a moment, not waiting for a reply or expecting one, and then continued, turning the quails' eggs as he spoke.

"*Azziah riin Raif* came to the Mangali in the year of the

Burning Tree. The gods had not sent rain for many seasons, and the frogs had dug themselves into the mud at the bottom of the dry lake. Scorpions tormented us, for they alone can live on dust. We were hungry when he came, yet the women took him in, for he was fair to them, tall and pale, with god-touched eyes. His feet were blistered and his back bore the mark of the whip. We told him he was a fool to come here for there was nothing but death and scorpions waiting in the sand. And he said, *The scorpion's kiss cannot kill me for my soul is already dead.*

"We Mangali know of such things, and the women wept for his soul. *I search*, he said. And we knew he searched for heaven and the loved ones he'd lost in a faraway war.

"We gave him our best guide. Mehembo, He With Little Teeth. Mehembo was wise and knew all the best places where heaven might be. He took the stranger into the baking heat of the Glass Desert, into the darkness of the Cave of Bats, and up the sheer face of Goat Mountain. Years passed and Mehembo died of heat sickness, and still heaven wasn't found.

"That was when the stranger began to turn. He demanded another guide from us, a girl, Illalo. She of the Fair Voice. And when she failed to find heaven after one year, he wrapped his fingers around her neck and cried, *Lead me there, Illalo, for I send you on your way.* Illalo died by his hand and found heaven, but he could no longer follow where she led.

"He left us after that. Years passed and in time his story returned to us. He'd headed north, across the Soft Lands and the mountains, farther than any man had ever trod. A siren called to him, they said, promising him the afterlife he'd earned. Eventually he came to a land that was as empty as the sky. Great gaps had opened up in the earth, and he knew he was close to the world's end. The day finally came when he spied a lone mountain in the waste, and although he was weary beyond knowing he climbed it. Above him he saw a shining gate. All day he climbed toward it, his heart breaking with joy. He reached the gate at sunset, and he could hardly bear to look upon it, so golden it was in the failing light.

"He put his hand upon the gate as the sun sank beneath the earth. *I die and am glad*, he said, as the gate began to swing. And in that moment the last rays of sunlight died and the gate grew blacker than the blackest night. He screamed but it was too late, and the Gates of Hell opened and sucked him in."

Raif shivered, rippling the water.

Yustaffa smiled, showing little demon teeth. "As I said, a sad tale. They say it marked the beginning of the War of Blood and Shadows, but we Mangali don't know about that. Quails' eggs?"

Raif woke before dawn, his hair stiff with mineral salts, his mouth gluey with the taste of eggs. The hot water from the springs had loosened the bandage he kept around his halved finger and he was forced to look at the livid stump as he rewound the cloth. After he and Yustaffa had eaten last night, Yustaffa had lent him the lamp to find his way back through the city. He had been so exhausted he'd fallen asleep in the fight circle, with Yelma floating above him like a bubble. The quintain creaked on her chain, moving with the wind, as he sat upright.

He had not dreamed; that seemed like something to be thankful for. He stood and went in search of his pack.

Tanjo Ten Arrow's bow was wrapped in cloth beside Raif's belongings. Stillborn had lent him a knife and a sword, but somehow they weren't enough. They left him vulnerable. He needed the certainty of a bow.

Raif splashed his face with water, scrubbed his teeth with sand, and braced the Sull recurve. The old man who had brought him arrows for the contest had let him keep them, and Raif rigged a makeshift bow case and quiver for his back. By the time he was done, the weak light of dawn filled the cave. A low mist washed over the rock floor, and he stirred it as he left.

Outside all was quiet. A young boy with a stump where his left hand should have been was quietly moving from cave mouth to cave mouth, raiding the burnt-out fires for usable fuel. When he spied Raif he flattened his body against the Rift Wall and made the sign of the evil eye. Frowning, Raif continued the climb toward the Rim.

The raid party was already assembling on the easternmost ledge of the city when he topped the stair. A ragged band of men, unmounted and in motley armor, stood stamping their feet against the cold. Raif recognized few of them. The rangy spearman in Glaive plate was one of Yustaffa's cronies, and the little cragsman in the horsehair-crested helm got drunk with Stillborn every night. Neither man acknowledged him as he approached.

"Raif. Over here, boy." Stillborn stepped away from a huddle of men to beckon him over. "I brought you a sword to replace the one you damaged. Nice and quick, she is. Took the spleen from a Hailsman once."

Raif felt blood drain from his face. How could he have lived here ten days and avoided the fact these men killed clan? A moment must have passed while he controlled himself, for when his vision cleared he saw that all in the raid party were watching him. He stepped forward and took the sword from Stillborn's hand. It was a single-edged footsword, hollow-bladed and light. Stillborn's hazel eyes tracked him as he made the expected practice blows, cutting air to test the blade. Only when Raif had praised its quickness did the hazel eyes turn elsewhere.

"Here. Swallow this."

Raif spun around to see the little cragsman holding out a leather flask. He took a mouthful and tasted the sweet black treacle of Rift-brewed mead. As he wiped his mouth clean, Stillborn gave the call to march out.

The Rim ended abruptly in a tumble of collapsed rock, and Raif didn't spot the path threading east through the rubble until the first man in the party stepped upon it. The way was treacherous, littered with slabs that rocked underfoot and mounds of loosely piled stone. A broken arch led to a ramp and soon they were climbing to the very edge of the abyss. Fragrant smoke drifted from the way ahead, and as the path turned sharply an old hag squatting by a fire came into view. Stillborn tossed her a carved trinket as he passed, and bade her pray for them. The hag cackled, revealing a mouth with no tongue, and threw the trinket on the fire.

Raif tucked his head low and kept to the rear. Thick clouds blanketed the sky, and Raif could feel the air pressing down on him. South across the Rift the clanholds floated in a sea of blue mist.

The leather flask was passed from hand to hand as they followed the path along the edge. The Maimed Men had lost all fear of the drop, and took pride in walking along the brink. One man, a big southerner with a bald head, struck up a dirge for them to march by. Raif couldn't catch the sense of it, but at the end of every chorus the entire raid party echoed the words, *Gods take my eyes before I go to the Rift.*

As the song continued Raif became aware of something, a quiet pulsing in his temples like the beginning of a headache. Ahead a lean-to had been rigged to a rocky outcropping and Raif saw a man leading out ponies: hill garons, with stout legs and short tails.

"There's no picking ponies for the new man," Stillborn said, falling in with Raif as they approached the lean-to. "You'll get what the others don't want."

Raif counted the men in the raid party. Fifteen, including

himself. He said, "Why stable the mounts here?"

Stillborn tapped his nose knowingly. "Because this is where we cross the Rift."

A quarter-hour of activity followed as men chose mounts and hefted saddles from the lean-to. The stableman had a clubfoot and was slow about his business. He gave Raif an agitated mare with a scarred flank, and a saddle that was too small. As Raif buckled the pony's belly strap, he saw an olive-skinned outlander detach himself from the raid party and approach the edge. Wind lifted the man's black hair and billowed his wool cloak. He was lean and long-limbed and appeared whole. Others noticed the outlander's movements and fell silent. One man touched the space below his hip where his portion of powdered guidestone had once hung. Clan.

The pulse in Raif's temples deepened. The earth fell away at the outlander's feet, leaving nothing but gray sky. Six hundred paces in the distance the southern face of the Rift towered like the wall of a giant fortress. Steel flashed as the outlander drew his knife. His lips were moving, chanting, but the words belonged to no tongue Raif had ever heard. Something creaked. The air at the outlander's feet rippled. All the Maimed Men were quiet now, still as stones.

The outlander raised the knifepoint to his eye. His voice rose as he spoke a command, and the smell of blood metals, of iron and copper and sodium, puffed from his mouth like smoke. The updrafts died. Time hung. Something vented deep within the Rift, like the sighing of a child. And then, with the tip of the knife touching the center of his eye, the outlander stepped into the Rift.

And did not fall.

Air thickened at his feet, spooling out in a line across the Rift, and then a substance that was not air or mist or daylight parted, and a bridge came into view.

Raif blinked. How could he have not seen it before? The bridge was a rickety construction of tarred rope and wooden lats, suspended from iron posts sunk deep into the cliff wall. It creaked in the breeze. The outlander turned to face the raid party, and Raif realized that his pupil was so enlarged you could see what lay behind it. The man swayed. Stillborn moved swiftly onto the bridge to steady him. "Make way, lads," he said as he guided the outlander back. "Our brother needs rest."

The outlander raised his gaze to Raif as he passed him. Blood slid across the white of his eye.

"He will not come with us?" Raif asked the cragsman, as Stillborn led the outlander into the lean-to.

The cragsman shook his head. "He'd be naught but a burden. He'll wait, though, if he knows what's good for him. Uncover the bridge when we return."

Raif heard the distaste in the cragsman's voice. Another clansman. He said, "How long has this bridge been here?"

The cragsman spat. His saliva was streaky with mead. "We don't keep no fancy histories in the Rift."

Stillborn called the men into file. As they were forming up, he thrust a length of brown wool into Raif's hand. "For the pony," he said, responding to Raif's puzzlement. "No horse will take the bridge unless it's blinkered."

Raif watched the other Maimed Men fashioning makeshift blinkers from pieces of leather and felt. Following their lead, he bunched and tucked the length of wool around the mare's cheek straps until she was allowed only a limited field of view. The mare fought him as he led her forward, her stout little legs locking at the knees, and he had to slap her hard on the rump to get her going.

In single file, the Maimed Men led their ponies across the Rift. Later that night, Raif would think of the dizzying height, the black drop beneath him, and the awful swaying of the bridge—he would think of it and his heart would knock in his chest. For now he managed to stay calm, as much for the pony's sake as his own, and put one foot in front of the other until he was done. His legs shook as he stepped onto the hard rock of the clanholds.

Stillborn grinned at him and punched him cheerfully in the back. "I'll win coin on you tonight. Addie had you down as a jumper."

Addie was the name of the cragsman, Raif recalled. "Men jump from there?"

Stillborn nodded merrily. Now that they had completed the crossing, the Maimed Men were pleased with themselves and showing it. One man took out his cock and pissed into the Rift. "Aye. Mostly green boys like you. Takes them in the middle. They start looking down, and the next thing you know they're hearing the Rift Music . . . and it's all downhill after that. And never was there a more considerable way downhill than jumping into the Rift."

The Maimed Men laughed as they mounted their ponies. Raif made himself as comfortable as it was possible to be on a saddle that was too small, and looked around. The badlands were narrow here, the flat plains warping gently into the Copper Hills. Heather clung to the rocks, and whitebark pines growing low to the earth provided nurseries for ironweed and mistletoe. Glint lakes and muskegs shone silver in the morning light, telling of a recent thaw. It was a different world than on the north side. Alive. Changing. Raif felt as if he'd emerged from a tomb.

As they rode south for the hills, Stillborn explained that they were heading to a village of free clansmen, lately settled in the woods northeast of the Lost Clan. By rights it was Dhoone territory, but Dhoone was no longer around to defend her turf. Settlements of free clansmen often sprang up in times of war. A settlement could grow quickly into a village, attract more people, and in time might declare itself a clan. Clan Harkness had begun that way, and Otler, and the tiny Dhoone-sworn Clan Croog. Raif remembered Tem telling him that it was a natural cycle of the clanholds. *"Clans rise and fall. Some fail, some are lost and some are cursed. New ones must be born to take their place."* Clan Innis had failed, and Morrow had been lost, and everyone knew Gray was cursed. Perhaps one day this settlement would grow to take Morrow's place.

But today I go to rob it. Raif pushed the thought down. Inigar Stoop had cut his heart from the Hailstone: Raif Sevrance was no longer clan.

They rode east of the Dhoone hills, entering instead the highlands of Morrow. Smoke had been spotted coming from the old fort that defended the Dhoonewall, and pitched battles with armed clansmen were not the Maimed Men's way. At midday they stopped in the hills to rest and water the horses. Stillborn joined Raif by the tiny stream that cascaded down from the hilltop.

"Gods! This water is cold," he declared, scooping up two handfuls and splashing it over his face. "Tastes good, though. Clean, like nothing in the Rift." He glanced around, checking that they were out of earshot of other men, and said, "Stay close to me when we hit the village. First time out's always hard— especially for a clansman. Just don't do anything stupid, and don't run scared. See the blackbeard over there, the one with the pretty cloak?"

Raif nodded. He'd noticed the man earlier.

"He's Linden Moodie, Traggis's spy. You can't so much as take a leak without him knowing. Now, as far as raids go this'll be a dull one. I'm running the show, so there'll be no unusual punishment, if you get my drift. We go in. Seize the grain stores and livestock. And ride out. Everyone here's ridden with me before. They know I won't waste time breaking into strong-chests and chasing down women in fields. It's food we need, not trouble. And I aim to get the first and avoid the other. Is that clear?"

Raif nodded again. He could feel the quails' eggs resisting digestion in his stomach. Searching for a safe place to send his thoughts, he asked, "Don't your arms get cold, wearing nothing but the bullhorns?"

Stillborn raised a hairy forearm to the sky, letting light gleam along the wickedly curved horn, and laughed. "Nay, lad. If your mam's intent on setting you on a rock in the dead of winter, you learn early on how to make your own heat." The Maimed Man stood. "Now, let's get moving and head east."

The Copper Hills were losing their snow. The ground was softening, and in the deepest valleys, below translucent crusts of ice, bogs were forming. Uprooted saplings and newly churned-up rocks littered the slopes. The hill ponies made short work of the terrain, and the cragsman Addie Gunn knew the ways. Within half a day they were on the southern slopes, descending into the farthest reaches of the Lost Clan. The tree cover deepened as they passed into the foothills, and day gave way to night.

Raif's breath whitened in plumes. Addie Gunn slowed the party as they approached another of the little streams that veined the hills. "We follow this south," he whispered to Stillborn. "Let the noise of the water mask our progress."

Without a single command spoken the Maimed Men drew their weapons. Raif slid from his mount, and led the pony forward. As he yanked his new sword from its sheath he was aware of someone watching him. Linden Moodie's gaze was like a finger on his spine. Traggis Mole's spy had a full black beard that almost hid the garrote scar that circled his throat. His rich, plum-colored cloak swished against his body armor as he drew his broadblade.

Somewhere close by a lamb bleated. Stillborn extended his arm, slowing the raid party, and looked to Addie Gunn.

A cragsman's business was sheep. "There'll be a dog," Addie warned.

Stillborn nodded. He turned to Raif. "Go with Addie and shoot it. Leave your pony here."

Raif felt Linden Moodie's gaze upon him as he slid the Sull bow free of the pony's saddle strap. Addie Gunn grabbed his arm, guiding him away from the raid party. "You do naught but silence the dog. I'll take care of the sheep."

Raif pulled an arrow from his makeshift quiver. It was dark amidst the pines, the rising moon barely silvering their trunks. Addie moved swiftly along a path only he could see. Dry needles that crunched beneath Raif's feet barely whispered beneath the cragsman's. When a second lamb cry sounded, Addie signaled a slowdown. Directly ahead the established pines gave way to scruffy brush of black-rotted saplings and berry canes. Something in the shadows moved. Raif halted and drew his bow.

"Ewe," Addie hissed. "Cover me while I hog-tie her."

Raif held his draw.

Addie navigated through the brush, a little man in a big crested helm. He must have spoke some sort of sheep talk, for the ewe did not shy from him as he approached. She was heavy with lamb and burdened with a shaggy winter coat. Addie cooed, and then in a flash he was upon her, felling her with a body blow and pinning her to the ground as he wound rope around her legs. And then two things happened at once.

A dog streaked from the brush toward Addie, its hackles raised in spikes and its lips pulled back to its gums. Yet even as Raif tracked it, a twig snapped to his left and a man called, "Drop the bow."

Raif froze. The dog reached Addie and sank its teeth into

his leg. The ewe bucked furiously, squealing in panic. Addie released his hold on her, letting the rope spool through his fist. He snatched off his crested helm and slammed it into the dog. The dog yelped and sprang back, and then immediately pounced forward for more. The ewe was free of Addie now, but its back legs were hobbled and it thrashed through the berry canes in panic.

Raif saw this and felt nothing. He couldn't see the stranger in the shadows, hadn't even turned his head toward him, but already he'd marked the man's heart. Fear jolted Raif's chest . . . but he didn't think it was his own. *Herdsmen carry bows. They need them to shoot wolves.* Chances were the stranger had an arrowhead trained upon Raif. Chances were that arrow would be loosed the instant Raif made a move. Raif knew he'd be lucky to get in a single shot.

Man or dog?

"Drop the bow!"

Raif dropped along with his bow, rolling onto his side so that the bow fell parallel to his body and the ground. His weight came down on his bracing hand, and he struggled to hold the entire length of the six-foot bow free of the earth. He managed an awkward twisting half-draw. And chose his heart.

The arrow loosed with a noisy twang, crossing paths with the arrow released by the herdsman. The herdsman's arrow whistled over Raif's head and stabbed the earth behind him.

Raif's arrow shot through the brush . . . and entered the sheep's heart.

The ewe stiffened for an instant, blood jetting from the entry wound between its ribs, and then collapsed into the canes. The dog hesitated for that same instant, giving Addie long enough to drive his crested helm deep into its snout. The herdsman let out a terrible cry and rushed toward the ewe.

Raif dug his heel into the ground and spun his body around

to face him. He could barely manage a half-draw this time because his trapped arm was shaking so badly. Yet, even so, the man's heart was his. Raif felt its galloping beat, felt it catch in terror as the herdsman realized his mistake. Even as the man halted and drew his bow, Raif let his arrow fly.

It was a poor shot, but it still floored its target, passing through the upper inch of the herdsman's shoulder, gouging out a flap of muscle as it continued its flight to a point far beyond the clearing. Grunting, the herdsman fell.

Raif let the bow drop from his grip and rested his head against the earth. All of him was shaking now. His body felt fevered, cold with sweat. He spat the taste of metal from his mouth and then braced himself to stand.

Addie was already on his feet, his left leg bloody at the shin, his doeskin pants torn through. The dog was on its belly, whimpering as it crawled toward its master. Part of its nostril slid from Addie's helm. Addie's chest was rising and falling rapidly. The look he gave Raif was full of rage, but when he spoke his voice was quiet. "She was wi' lamb."

Raif nodded. A lactating ewe and her lamb would be worth much in the Rift. Now she'd have to be butchered and hauled back as meat.

In the distance another sheep bleated.

Addie hesitated, his gaze hard on Raif. He looked weary. Blood seeping from the dog bites on his leg was collecting in his boot. Reluctantly, he reached a decision. "Take care of the herdsman and the dog. I have to find the other sheep."

"Should I butcher the ewe?"

"No. That's my job." Addie Gunn turned in the direction from where the lamb's cry had sounded. "I'll be back later to open her up."

Raif dragged a hand across his face. He left the Sull bow on the ground and drew his sword.

The herdsman had fallen on a pine sapling, bending the immature tree in two. The dog had reached its master and was sniffing at the arrow wound. As Raif approached, the dog shrank back onto its haunches, saliva leaking in strings from its ruined jaw. The herdsman's eyes were open, blue as Dhoone and focused on Raif's sword.

Raif killed the dog with a single strike through the larynx. Spilling sand. He turned to the herdsman. "Get up."

The man didn't move.

Raif kicked his leg. "I said *get up!*"

As the herdsman struggled to his feet, Raif pulled a shammy from his waist pack. He waited until the herdsman had dragged himself to his knees, and then shoved the shammy in the man's mouth and gagged him. Needing something to tie the man's wrists, he slid the blunt edge of the sword against the herdsman's belly and cut his belt. The belt fell away from the man's gut, sending his horn of powdered guidestone thudding to the earth. The horn was yellow and chipped. Its neck was sealed with a silver cap.

The remains of the quails' eggs curdled in Raif's gut. "Where did you get this?"

The man shook his head, unable to answer the question with a gag in his mouth

"Is it Hailstone?"

The herdsman widened his eyes, confused.

Raif grabbed him by the arms and shook him. He couldn't understand where his anger came from, but he couldn't stop it either. "Does the horn contain powdered Hailstone?"

Understanding dawned on the herdsman's face. He gargled a denial through the gag, and then attempted a word that sounded like "ith".

"Withy?"

The man nodded furiously. Raif let him go, and he slumped

back to the ground with a groan of pain.

Not a Hailsman then. Thank gods, not a Hailsman.

Raif closed his eyes for a moment. When he opened them again he secured the man's wrists and helped him to his feet. "Go," he said. The man was wounded, gagged and tied: He could issue no warning or pose any threat. Addie had ordered Raif to take care of him, and Raif told himself it was done. He watched for a while as the herdsman lumbered south through the brush. Then Raif turned to join the raid party.

A cloaked figure was heading away through the trees.

Raif plucked the Sull bow from the loam. How long had Linden Moodie been watching? Had he seen Raif angle his bow *away* from the herdsman's heart? Had he seen him let the man go? A tremor of fear altered rhythms in Raif's chest. Had he heard the word *Blackhail* spoken?

Thoughts dark with foreboding, Raif went to join the raid.

TWENTY-SIX

Spire Vanis

Town Dog was digging for field mice. Crope would have liked to carry on walking until midday, but a mouse was a mouse, and he wasn't in any position to turn down food. The little dog dug furiously, kicking up dirt. Crope could tell when she found the first mouse, for Town Dog had a special noise that she made, like the squeaking of a bat. It wasn't a very doggy noise—but then, Town Dog wasn't a very doggy dog.

Crope sat on a fallen spruce log and waited for Town Dog to bring him the mouse. It was sunny in the foothills, the sky as clear as a diamond, and you could almost believe it was warm. There was a bit of shade under the great firs, and the *kuk-kuk-kuk* of a hairy woodpecker sounded over the rise. Ahead lay the shimmering phantom of a city, all pale walls and high spires, like cities in legends. It was *his* city. The bad place. The site where his lord was being held.

Dutifully, Crope took the mouse from Town Dog's jaw, and shook it clean of dirt. The little dog looked expectantly at her master, her tail thumping the mat of spruce needles that carpeted the slope. Crope looked at the dog and the dog looked back. With an elaborate sigh, Crope threw the dazed mouse into the trees, sending Town Dog tearing after it with tail-wagging joy. It was easier stealing eggs, he reckoned. By the time Town Dog was through with the mouse there'd be little but the head left. And mouse brains were passing small.

Still, he couldn't help grinning as he watched the little dog dive into a bush. It was good to have a companion, and mostly it felt better being hungry than alone.

Crope stretched out his legs and groaned. His feet were hurting, and he was tempted to pull off his boots and thrust his toes into the cool loam of fir needles and melted snow. He'd never get his boots back on again, though—experience had taught him that—and he had to get to the city by sundown. He could not fail his lord.

Come to me. The words echoed in Crope's dreams, softer now, losing their strength a little each day. His lord's voice was more beautiful than he remembered: softer, more complex. There had always been wisdom and command within it, but now you could hear other things as well. Crope knew he wasn't good at words, but the one he kept returning to was *loss*.

Abruptly, Crope stood. Some things he could not bear thinking about. Like when the slavers had cornered him on a slope like this one, how they had driven him hard against the rocks and cast a rope net over him, and how his feet had tangled in the lines and the slavers had laughed as he stumbled and fell. His ankles still bore the marks of their ropes. They had driven him east in their wagon train, getting drunk on pure grain alcohol and congratulating themselves over their catch. *He's as big as three men*, they had said of him. *He'll fetch a fine price in the mines.*

Crope's chest began to heave. *You entered the mine, the mine entered you.* He spat out the black phlegm, and felt better after a while.

Town Dog had returned with the mouse and now sat patiently

at Crope's feet. Crope bent slowly at the waist and pocketed the limp brown rodent. Town Dog nosed his hand, and Crope scratched her ears and tussled with her until he was ready to carry on.

After the incident at the alehouse, Crope had kept far away from settled land. When he spied a village he walked leagues out of his path to avoid it, and when he smelled the woodsmoke of mountain men he quietly altered his course. The journey went easier, having Town Dog. Longer, but easier. Worrying about Town Dog stopped him worrying about himself. Town Dog wasn't a very accomplished hunter. The one time she'd flushed something worthwhile from the brush, she'd been so startled that she'd let the raccoon hotfoot up a tree and get away. Crope tried to be fair about it—it *was* an unusually big coon—but visions of sweet roasted meat made him eye Town Dog accusingly for several days.

The storms were the worst. The mountains bred them, whipping up winds and clouds, sending sleet driving into Crope's face and blinding him with swirling snow. He'd lost some days to fever, holed up in a depression banked with snow south of Hound's Mire. The only way he knew later that time had passed was by the number and assortment of small rodents that Town Dog had brought to him while he slept.

Things were bad for a while after that. His chest was weak— Bitterbean said that diggers had lungs like sea sponges soaked in tar—and the going was slow for many days. He and Town Dog had descended from the mountains into the foothills. It was riskier here—bad men and slavers might find you—but at least it was easier to breathe. One morning he'd walked past a birch sapling as straight as a spear and cut himself a staff. It was good having something to lean on, and even when he regained his health and strength he decided not to lay it aside. Travelers in illustrated books carried staffs. He knew this because his lord had once possessed many tomes. A staff gave a man something to do, Crope discovered; good for prodding snow to test its depth and ice to test its fastness. And he had never learned to love blades. It was comforting to have a weapon on hand that relied on strength instead of edge.

Crope felt his heartbeat quicken as he and Town Dog wound down the slope. Part of him wished that he and his dog could just carry on walking, watching the season warm into spring and listening to the mayflies buzz around his face. Back in the diamond pipe, he'd dreamed of owning the perfect length of land. Just enough for a man to cross on foot in the hours between sunrise and sunset on a summer day. He'd grow wheat and radishes, and seed a meadow for sheep, and perhaps later lay a hard standing for milch cows. Sometimes the details changed . . . but the length of land never did. Long enough for a man to walk in a day.

But that was a dream for another life. In this one he belonged to his lord.

Crope could no longer count how many years he'd known Baralis, but he'd never forgotten that first meeting, a continent away in the Far South. It was burned in his memory the way his slave brand was burned into his flesh.

Baralis had spied him on Green Spinster Street in Silbur, being stick-whipped by a gang of youths. A stallholder had accused him of stealing a bolt of wool, and had raised a hue and cry. A mob formed quickly, as mobs did when he was about, and he was chased through the market and into the street. He was hurting badly when Baralis approached, his nose broken and bleeding and his right eye swollen shut. Jail was a certainty, for he could never find the words to defend himself. Baralis was walking along the street, dressed in scholar's black, a tall young man with an arrogant face. Crope called out to him, though he could not say why, and instead of passing by Baralis stopped.

And that was when the miracle happened. Somehow the man who would become Crope's lord brought an end to the beating—with nothing more than words. He never raised his voice, never drew a weapon, yet he turned Crope's attackers cold.

All his life, until that very point, Crope had never known anyone to defend him. He'd been attacked and jailed, hunted down and tormented, made scapegoat for a dozen different crimes. He'd been thrown into the baiting pits of Lynch Town and made to fight bears. He'd been used as a pack animal to carry baskets of damp salt from the Dead Shores. He'd dug graves, logged forests, performed as a curiosity with a troop of black-skinned mummers, and laid down on surgeons' mats whilst physicians tapped his blood. He'd slept in holes, caves and locked cells, lived on rats and chicken bones and the ticks off his own skin.

When Baralis turned to him on Green Spinster Street and murmured, *Come, follow me home*, the black-clad young man became Crope's savior, his protector—his lord.

Baralis was owed Crope's soul.

Crope dug his staff into the earth and rested his weight a moment. Town Dog was ranging far ahead, and her skinny tail was the only part of her visible above the scrub.

The city was mere leagues away now. Crope could see the gray haze of smoke and mist it created, and the way it sprang from the base of the mountain like a newborn peak. To the north lay rolling grassy plains, dotted with villages and crossed with roads. Close to the city's north wall he could just make out the flapping brown edges of a camp town. Here in the east, entire hillsides had been clearcut for timber. Somewhere not far below him, Crope could hear the *whir* of pit saws, and he remembered how it was to be the man standing below in the pit, how the sawdust rained on your face and shoulders every time you pulled down the saw.

Bitterbean said a man's past was like a ghost, and it would haunt you if you let it. Crope had thought about that a lot on his journey, and sometimes he thought Bitterbean was right, yet mostly he hoped he was wrong. Once, one summer when the pumps had failed, Crope had been hauled up from the pipe to unclog them. As he disassembled the crank on the lakeshore, a bass fisherman nearby launched his boat. Crope remembered glancing at the boat as he went about his work, watching as it slowly pulled away. *That* was what he hoped the past was like . . . a boat sailing away as you stood upon the shore.

Suddenly anxious to be moving, Crope called Town Dog to him, and together they headed down toward the land of men.

They passed the logging camp at midday, and by late afternoon they had joined the road leading west to the city's walls. Farmers, drovers and wagon trains jostled for space on the road. Occasionally, horns would ring out and everyone would clear the center while troops of men-at-arms rode through. Crope fell in behind a high-sided wagon ricked with hay, content to let the height and breadth of the load conceal him. Bits of straw and hayseeds floating down from the bales made him sneeze from time to time, but he didn't really mind it. Town Dog grew tired as they neared the gate, so he picked her up and tucked her under his cloak.

The gate seemed a very fine thing to Crope, tall enough for five men standing on each others' shoulders to pass through. It was carved from giant blocks of granite, the kind that Scurvy Pine said he'd quarried before they set him to tin.

There was a great stirring in the city, Crope learned, as he waited in the crush of people petitioning for entry. Someone high and mighty had been wed that very day, and now there was to be a feast and dancing in some important fortress. The driver of the hay wagon was made much of, for his load was due to be delivered to the stables of that very place. Crope listened for a while, but he couldn't keep up with all the unfamiliar accents and long names.

So far no one had challenged him or even stared too hard, but that didn't stop him from feeling anxious. In his mind he rehearsed what he would say to the gatekeep. It was only a few words, but he worried he'd get in a muddle and they'd come out wrong. As the line shortened he experimented with his staff, trying for a pose that seemed unthreatening. Tucked under his belt or slung on his back it seemed too much like a weapon ready to be drawn, and in the end he settled on holding it in his hand as if it were a flagpole.

Just as he was about to reconsider the flagpole hold, the hay wagon trundled under the gate, and a voice called out, "Next."

Crope moved forward into the shadow of the gate tower, glad of Town Dog's warmth near his heart. A man-at-arms cloaked in red leather with a bird broach at his throat presented his spear.

"Name?"

"Crope of Drowned Lake."

The man had to tilt his head to look at Crope's face. The guard's gray eyes glanced over the ragged beard that had grown on Crope's face since he'd left the pipe, and the thick scars on his ears and neck. He said tersely, "Trade?"

Crope could no longer stand the scrutiny. "Free miner," he replied, looking down.

"You're too late for sapping. Army's moving out within the week."

Crope didn't understand what he meant. Slowly the panic began to rise.

The guard was losing patience. He lowered his spear. "On your way, big man. The Spire's been closed to freebooters and mercenaries since yesterday at noon, under order from the surlord himself."

Knew you had suet for brains. Crope struggled to make sense of the guard's words, but it was difficult with the bad voice speaking in his head.

Someone in the queue behind him shouted, "Stop holding up the line."

The guard turned toward the sentry post to summon more men. As he took a breath to make the call, Crope mumbled, "Not mercenary. Not here to fight."

The guard hesitated. "What you here for, then?"

This was the question Crope had practiced for. Although he didn't much want to, he raised his head. "Here to visit with the priests in the Bone Temple."

Something behind the guard's gray eyes changed. He raised the spear. "Best get going, then," he said quietly, stepping aside.

Relief made Crope's ears glow with heat. Half a century later and the words taught to him by the black-skinned mummers of the Ivory Plains still worked like magic. *Learn them,* long-limbed Swalhabi had commanded. *There is not a city in the Known World that does not possess a Bone Temple. And when we travel north to new places and pale men bar our way, we speak these words and watch the pale men step aside. Bone Temples house powerful magic, and no man, pale or dark, will risk that magic being turned against him.*

Every night for thirty days Swalhabi had made Crope repeat the words until they soaked into the fabric of his brain. Swalhabi had sold him half a year later to the salt mines, but Crope had never blamed him for it. Once the giant-slaying masque had grown old there were no more parts for him to play.

Mumbling his thanks to Swalhabi and the other mummers, Crope entered the city of Spire Vanis.

It vibrated with the presence of his lord. Hundreds of miles west, over mountains, frozen lakes and tilled fields, and somehow the journey had overshadowed what he sought. He hadn't meant to let it, but the world above the diamond pipe was unknown to him, terrible and fraught with danger, and during his travels he'd drop to the ground exhausted at night and spare barely a thought for his lord. Tears of shame filled Crope's eyes.

Come to me, his lord had commanded. And now, at last, he had.

An early dusk was setting in behind the walls. Candles were being lit within buildings, filling the blank squares of windows with golden light. Ahead, the driver of the hay wagon had stopped to light his driver's lamp. Crope watched the careful precautions the man took before striking his flint, using his body to shield the load from stray sparks. By the time the job was done and the horn guard was secured over the flame, Crope had caught up with the rear of the wagon, deciding to follow in its wake for a while.

The city was very large and grand. It seemed more orderly than most he'd known, and the ways traveled by the hay wagon were wide and open. Mounds of slush were melting along the roadsides, sending little streams of water spiraling down drains. The air was still between the high buildings, and mist was beginning to form.

Town Dog grew restless and wriggled against Crope's chest until he set her down. As they followed the wagon west and then south, he was overcome with the conviction that he was drawing closer to his lord. It had been the same with Mannie Dun, who always knew the best place to dig for diamonds. Crope had asked him once how he did it, and Mannie had tapped the bridge of his nose and said he felt them in his bones. That was how it was for Crope: Baralis was in his bones.

The wagon seemed to be heading toward the massive, high-walled structure that dominated the south of the city. The fortress. Torches burned from the ramparts and the wailing of horns blasted from the walls. The streets grew busier, and it seemed to Crope that everyone was moving in the same direction as the wagon. The bad voice began to whisper to him, telling him that he'd better be careful or he'd make some thick-headed mistake and fail. Crope curved his neck and shrank his shoulders, praying for something he'd never known in his life: obscurity in a crowd.

He was so close to his lord now—he could shut his eyes and *see* him. His lord was in the dark place . . . and he hurt. Crope could not bear to think about how he hurt.

"Make way! Delivery for the stable!" The driver of the hay wagon stood on the running board and cracked his whip. He'd arrived at a gate in the fortress wall, but couldn't approach it due to the press of revelers who were standing in front of the lowered portcullis.

One of the men-at-arms manning the wall shouted a reply. Six heavily armed red cloaks emerged from the gate station and began moving back the crowd.

Come to me.

Crope suddenly knew he had to be inside the fortress. While everyone else was moving back, he moved forward. Grabbing hold of the wagon's ring hook, he hoisted himself onto the tail-gate that ran along the rear.

The wagon lurched forward, traveled a few paces, and then halted. Booted footsteps sounded. Someone called, "Check the hay," and a series of sharp crunching noises followed as one of the red cloaks stabbed the bales. Crope kept very still, but he knew it was only seconds before he was spotted.

A spear blade passed close to his knee. Town Dog growled. A man's voice called, "Driver! Is this your man?"

Crope heard the rider shout, "Ain't no one pitching hay but me"—and then a spear tip jabbed the back of Crope's neck.

"You'd best step down, hay man. And while you're at it you can tell me what business you intended in the fortress."

Knew you wouldn't get it right. Crope raised his arms and turned slowly to face the red cloak. His ears were hot, and he couldn't think of any words.

Two other red cloaks joined the one with the spear, and all three men kept their weapons raised as Crope jumped from the step. The revelers were quiet now, sensing entertainment. The driver of the wagon peered around the back wheel to get a look.

The red cloak with the spear said, "Do you want to spend the night in jail?"

Crope shook his head.

Someone in the crowd piped up, "He came to try his chances with the bride!"

Laughter spread in an ugly wave. A woman shouted, "He's almost as handsome as the Knife."

Crope felt the color rise up his neck.

"Enough!" shouted one of red cloaks. And then, to Crope, "Speak up for yourself, man."

"Wedding. Come to see the wedding."

The red cloak rolled his eyes. "You're too late for that. Wedding took place this morning. It's the feasting tonight."

As the red cloak finished speaking, horns blared within the fortress, sounding a call to attention. Crope looked up along with everyone else, and saw the heralds in all their finery atop the wall. Torches blazed around the flat-sided tower closest to the gate, throwing light and shadows across the stonework. At the halfway point of the tower an embrasured balcony had been draped with a silk cloth that showed a fearsome red bird on a silver ground. As Crope watched, two heralds stepped onto the balcony and sounded a fanfare before stepping aside. A moment passed and then a man and a woman came into view, and the crowd began cheering and stamping their feet.

The woman was dressed in stiff red silk that glittered with diamonds—even from a distance Crope knew them for real.

She was black-haired and pale, and she did not smile. The man standing at her side was large and broad, and when he took her hand in his it was like watching a wolf eat a chick. One of his eyes was gone, and he wore no device to conceal it.

The pair stood uncomfortably, and suffered the attention of the crowd. After perhaps a minute had passed, another man stepped into the light . . . and robbed the very breath from Crope's throat.

It was the pale-eyed man, the one who had taken his lord. Eighteen years later and Crope knew him as surely as if he'd looked into the man's face every night. His lord's captor. His enemy. The man who had left him to die.

The pale-eyed man drew renewed cheers from the crowd. He was dressed in quiet finery of subtle hues; butter-soft suedes in gray and maroon, all edged with bands of gold. He was carrying something heavy in a small cloth-of-gold sack, and when he shifted it to ease the weight the crowd cheered. The pale-eyed man smiled but did not show his teeth. His gaze swept down to the gate, taking in the great crush of revelers. Instinctively, Crope stepped into the shadow of the wagon. He saw the pale-eyed man's gaze track the movement, saw him peer into the shadow, and then look away.

The pale-eyed man appeared to lose a beat of concentration before leaning forward to lay a kiss on the bride's lips. The cloth-of-gold sack had passed into the bride's keeping, and she seemed to gain some color now that her hand was no longer in her husband's grip. As she untied the sack's drawstring and reached inside, the crowd began a singsong chant.

"Fair bride, share your bounty. Cast the grain."

The bride took a handful of something gold out of the sack, and showered it on the crowd. Crope felt little pellets, like hailstones, *ping* off his shoulders and bounce to the ground. He caught a glimpse of one as it fell at his feet: a tiny nugget of gold cast in the shape of a wheat germ. The crowd surged forward, a cry went up from the red cloaks, and Crope found himself in the middle of a feeding frenzy.

When he looked up next the pale-eyed man had gone. The bride cast one more handful of golden grain and then withdrew into the tower with her husband.

Crope stood for a moment, watching the space the pale-eyed man had vacated, and then turned away. The red cloak who had challenged him waved him along with his spear. In the madness of the grab for gold he had more important matters on his mind. Crope whistled for Town Dog, and worried like a mother until the little dog appeared. Taking no chances, he scooped her up and tucked her under his cloak. Ducking his head low, he pushed gently through the crowd.

Come to me, his lord had commanded. Now Crope had arrived he had to figure out how.

TWENTY-SEVEN

The Rift

T he infant's body was laid on a board, and the Maimed Women crouched beside it and washed it with spirits. The mother stood apart, her belly distended, her bodice stained dark with seeping milk. A Maimed Man was oiling the crude winch fixed to the edge of the rimrock, hunching his shoulders against the swirling snow.

Raif stood beside the cragsman Addie Gunn and watched as Traggis Mole approached the newborn's corpse. The infant's eyes had already been removed, and the eyelids sewn shut with black thread. Traggis Mole scattered the women with the briefest movement of his wrist, and knelt alone beside the board. Gently, and with great care, the Robber Chief lifted the newborn's head. The baby's scalp was covered with a fine down of auburn hair, and Traggis Mole ran his fingers through it before reaching for the hood. The Robber Chief's face was dark. At the left side of his temple Raif could see the pressure line where the straps that held his wooden nose in place had dug into his skin.

Charms had been sewn into the little woolen hood: glass beads and drilled coins and sprigs of dried touch-me-nots. As Traggis Mole pulled the hood over the infant's face, all who had gathered became quiet. The Robber Chief nodded to the man with the winch, signaling for him to come forward and take possession of the board. As the winchman secured the board to the cable rope, the Maimed Women began to keen. Raif felt hairs rise on the back of his neck. He had never heard such a sound made by humans; a deep and joyless howling, as if the wind itself blew through them.

When Traggis Mole gave the word, the winchman began turning the crank, and the board holding the stillborn infant was lowered into the Rift.

The mother did not move as the barrel turned. She was no longer young, and Addie Gunn whispered that this bairn would likely be her last. A boy stepped forward and handed Traggis Mole a burning torch, and the Robber Chief moved to the edge of the rimrock. It was late morning, and a cold snap had brought the high white clouds bearing snow. Snowflakes danced on the Rift's updrafts, swooping and soaring; hissing into nothingness if they strayed too close to the Robber Chief's flame.

"Poor thing," Addie Gunn said quietly, dropping his head in respect. "Wasn't whole enough to live."

As the winchman cranked the barrel, Traggis Mole touched the cable rope with the torch. The rope's tightly bound fibers crackled and charred, and then hot yellow flames caught light. The winchman continued cranking, and the burning section of rope dropped from sight as the infant was lowered deeper into the abyss. The Maimed Women bellowed, their song growing stranger and more terrible until the moment the tension left the rope.

The mother jerked forward as the rope sprang back. Traggis Mole called out in a harsh voice and the Maimed Women rushed forward to steady her. As the Robber Chief turned away, his gaze met Raif's. Traggis Mole's eyes were black and haunted, and there was such a force behind them Raif fought the desire to step back. *Harm us and die*, the Robber Chief warned him, and then swept his gaze away.

Raif breathed softly and held himself still. The crowd was beginning to break up. The winchman wound back the rope to the burned stump and cut off the blackened portion with a knife. An old woman the size of a child led the mother away. Someone on the upper terrace began roasting lamb, and the bloody aroma of meat juices drifted down.

"One of ours," Addie said, with a look that might have been pride.

Raif made himself nod. The raid had been a success: three ewes, two with lamb, a newborn, an old pollard good for mutton, plus grain and rendered elk fat, salt, horsemeat, cheese, two dozen bantams, and a keg of young malt.

Stillborn had commanded the raid with an iron hand, driving the villagers into the sheep pen whilst the looting was under way. Some villagers had taken wounds. One of them was dead. Raif had watched as Linden Moodie rode him down; a big aging Dhoonesman trained to the ax. The Dhoonesman had made the mistake of organizing a defense, perhaps imagining that Maimed Men on hill ponies were no match for fully-mounted clansmen. He had not counted on the Maimed Men's complete disdain for horses. Horses had no currency in the Rift. They could not be made to cross the swing bridge, would not take to the heights, sudden drops and rocky stairs of the cliff city, and needed absurd amounts of feed to sustain them. A hill pony lived on what he could tug from the cliffs and scrounge from the grain stores, and they suited the Maimed Men well enough.

Raif and a second archer, a city man with spider-veined hands, had been commanded to target the horses. They shot the clansmen's mounts from beneath them, and then Linden Moodie and his crew rode the clansmen to ground. Moodie's crew possessed self-control enough to stay their hands when the Dhoonesman and his companions surrendered, but Linden Moodie himself had passed beyond reason to rage.

"Thought you could best us, eh?" he screamed, closing in on the Dhoonesman with his broadblade. "We're not clan like you. Not perfect. Not whole. Well, let's see how *you* fare when I cut something from you. See if you can put up a fight."

Linden Moodie had hacked off the man's arm at the shoulder before Stillborn and the other Maimed Men could restrain him. Stillborn gripped Moodie in a mighty bear hug, squeezing the breath and anger from him. As he gradually eased his hold, Stillborn commanded Raif to escort the remaining villagers to the sheep pen. When Raif hesitated, his gaze flicking to the wounded Dhoonesman, Stillborn snapped in a harsh voice, "Him. He's already dead."

It was true, Raif knew it—the Dhoonesman was losing too much blood—but there was something else here. Stillborn never rebuked Linden Moodie for his violence, and as Raif led the clansmen to the pen, he heard Stillborn call for the liquor flask, shouting that a Rift Brother had need.

The rest of the night had passed swiftly. The clansmen's stone cottages were looted, the grain cellars pried open, the coops emptied. The horses were slaughtered for meat. Raif butchered a gelding and caged the bantams. By the time dawn came he was shaking with exhaustion. The penned clansfolk were quiet, some sleeping. There were not many, really, perhaps six families in all. Raif had taken his turn guarding them, along with every other man in the raid party. He walked circuits of the stone-walled enclosure, his borrowed sword ill-balanced in his hand, a band of muscle in his chest strangely tight.

Stupidly, he had thought the villagers would know him for clan. Yet when he looked into their eyes he saw fear and contempt.

He was just another Maimed Man.

It was daylight when his watch ended and the raid party broke camp and headed for the hills. The return journey took two days, the ponies were so heavily laden. Linden Moodie and his crew got drunk on young malt the last night. They'd made camp amidst the bald hummocks and sedge barrens that formed the northernmost swell of the Copper Hills. The first wave of black flies had hatched from the snowmelt and the ponies were under assault. The Maimed Men huddled around the longfire for protection, passing the sheep's bladder from hand to hand. Linden Moodie drank deep and often. The thick black beard that covered his lower face was a trap for flakes of food and ash, and he raked his knuckles through it as his gaze fell on Raif.

"To clan," he said, raising the flaccid sheep's bladder above the fire. "Gods damn the lot of them."

Releasing his grip, he let the sheep's bladder fall to the fire. The small quantity of alcohol remaining ignited instantly, *whump*ing as it shot up a ball of violet flame. Addie Gunn, Stillborn, and the rest of the Maimed Men nodded tersely, their faces lit grotesquely by the pure-burning alcohol. Stillborn murmured, "Gods damn them all," and after a moment others echoed him.

Raif felt the blood come to his face. He wanted suddenly to run, to escape these men who were not whole in ways he was just beginning to understand. But he didn't. He sat and stared into the fire, and knew with cold certainly that if any man tried to push him just then he'd go straight for their heart.

Perhaps Stillborn saw the intent in Raif's eyes, for he drew attention to himself by plucking a blood sausage from the heart of the fire and dancing the scorching offal between his fingers like a hotcake. Soon the Maimed Men were laughing and making jest, and the subject of clans was dropped or forgotten. Only Linden Moodie remembered. He sat and watched Raif from the far side of the fire, his fingers rubbing the garrote scar that circled his throat.

Raif pulled his Orrl cloak close as he walked the length of the rimrock with Addie Gunn. They'd made it across the Rift by sundown the following day, and a feast had been planned for tonight to spread the bounty. Stillborn would be celebrated. He informed Raif the salt would be divvied up—a thimbleful for each man, woman and child—and the horsemeat would be smoked and portioned. Raif, as a member of the raid party, was entitled to extra, but he knew better than to accept it. An outsider shouldn't take more than his share.

"I set a piece of that ewe to roast this morning," Addie said to him. "There's enough for two."

Raif started to shake his head, but stopped himself. Addie Gunn had once been clan. "That sounds good."

He let the small, dark cragsman lead the way to his fire. Addie slept close to the collapsed east wall, high on the cliff where eagles made their aeries and winds from the Want smoothed the edge of the rimrock into glassy waves. By the time they'd completed the ascent the snow had stopped falling, and Raif's heart was pumping hard.

"Aye," the cragsman said, noticing Raif's shortness of breath with satisfaction. "It takes newcomers that way."

Addie kicked a handful of loose stones out of his path as he headed for the fire that burned low at the entrance to his stone cell. They were close to the edge here, and Raif could see white cranes in flight below him, turning great circles in the Rift as they paused on their journey north. Addie squatted by the fire and started turning over the embers with a moose bone. A shoulder of mutton, covered in a creamy skein of fat, sat upon a little iron trivet above the flames. Addie took a handful of dried leaves in his fist and crumbled them over the meat. Almost immediately the sharp fragrance of mint rose with the smoke. Addie looked expectantly at Raif, and Raif showed his appreciation with a solemn nod. He was beginning to understand that many things were rare in the Rift, and when a man crumbled herbs into a dish you would share that man did you honor.

Taking a chance, Raif leant against the cliff and asked, "Were you from Wellhouse?"

Addie said nothing, merely prodded the meat joint with his moose bone, testing to see if it was done. Pink juices hissed into the flames. Just as Raif thought he'd made a mistake — asking a Maimed Man about his past — the cragsman said, "Is it the ears that gave me away?"

"They *are* big," Raif conceded, grinning. "And the eyes, too," he added hastily, not wanting to insult Addie further. "Like Dhoone's, only grayer."

Addie nodded. Wellhouse had been sworn to Dhoone for fifteen hundred years, and intermarriage had bred similarities between them. Wellhouse called itself Dhoone's Hand, and its boast was *Our past bears witness to our glory. The future is ours to write.* They kept the histories of the Great Settlement and the age before it, when clans lived in the Soft Lands to the south. Rumors told of a great, lead-lined strong room sunk so deep into the bedrock below the Wellhold that groundwater now surrounded it, sealing it shut for the past hundred years. The Wellhold had been built around an ancient stone well known as the Kings' Fount, for every Dhoone king had been laved in its water before being crowned. The Kings' Fount was said to hold the purest water in the clanholds, and in the dark times following the Wars of Apportionment, when clan upon clan fell victim to river fever, only Wellhouse pulled through without loss. Tem always said that Wellmen brewed the best malt in the clanholds because of that water.

"It was a long time ago," Addie said, spearing the meat joint with his hand-knife and lifting it from the fire. "And I never took the oath."

Raif recognized the pride in the cragsman's words. *I might have deserted my clan*, he said, *but I broke no oath*. Even a Maimed Man had his self-respect. Raif exhaled softly. He knew what that made him.

"I was never one for clans and clannish business," Addie continued. "Rooms with closed doors were too much like prisons to me. Was always drawn to the heights, to the uplands and the bluffs. Would rather spend the night camped on a rock, with nothing but a green-burning fire to protect me, than sleep within four walls. Everyone said I was moon-touched, and my Da tried to beat it from me. He was a fountsman, one of the ten best warriors in the clan, and gods help him if his middle son was going to turn into a herder of sheep. He got his way, o' course—my Da always did—and I was trained to the ax." Addie snorted. "A short-arsed fool like me! 'Course, when it came time to take the oath my mind was set. Ran away the night before my swearing. Ran for the hills and never looked back."

As he was speaking Addie had been shaving the fat off the joint, revealing the tender gray-pink mutton beneath. He sliced deeply against the bone, freeing a wedge of meat. "Here," he said, offering it to Raif with his knife. "Best eating to be had in the Rift."

Raif came forward to take it. Kneeling by the fire, he tore a piece from the mutton and pushed it in his mouth. The meat melted on his tongue, shedding the strong pungency of mint and sheep. "It's good."

Addie nodded, unsmiling but pleased.

"Did you stay in the clanhold," Raif asked, "after you ran away?"

"Mostly. Cragsmen live by the oldest laws in the clanholds,

the Sheep Laws. We move through the territory of every clan, following our flocks. If our flocks graze in a foreign clan for over nine days then we owe that clan a sheep—that's why we're always on the move. 'Course, if you're herding the bighorns, like I did, you favor the high country. And in the high country there's few to tell whose toes you're treading on and whose heather your sheep are grazing. There's freedom, or something like it. You're close enough to know you're clan, yet not so close as to be ruled by it."

"Then why did you leave?"

Addie set down the joint. His fingers were coated in grease and he wiped them against his tunic as he spoke. "Leave? *Leave?* No one leaves the clanholds. You're either driven out or shunned. Look at Stillborn. Finest swordsman in his clan—but did they love him for it? No. They saw a monster, not a man. Me, I caught the bone fever the winter the Flow froze over. A pair of Blackhail cragsmen stole my sheep while I was passed out in the snow. When you get the bone fever real bad it takes years to rebuild your strength. You shake. There's days when your vision shrinks to dots. And your legs, your damn legs, are like twigs soaked in water beneath you. And every time you take a step you fall, and every time you think to yourself *I'm going to get the bastards who stole my sheep* you make it as far as the first hill and your vision turns dark and your legs set to wobbling, and you might as well be dead."

Addie stopped and took a breath. When he spoke again his voice was softer, almost puzzled. "I wasn't driven out so much as . . . disregarded. A cragsman who loses his hill legs is about as much use a pitchfork with no tines—at least, that's what you're told. I drifted around for a few years; spring lambing at Wellhouse, husbanding at the Dhoone Fair. But there'd be lapses, and my legs would go, and it wasn't long afore no one would hire me for day-work.

"That was the autumn I had my worst lapse. Walking east of Wellhouse, in the home of the Lost Clan. A fair name, I suppose, since I was lost myself. Woke up to find I'd been carted north to the Rift and left for dead. They call it a Cragsman's Farewell. If you're old, sick, or injured they cart you there and leave you. They give you a day's food, and a choice. Either throw yourself in the Rift or cross it, become a Maimed Man."

Addie stood and faced the Rift. The white cranes were forming up for the flight north, and their mournful whoops filled the air. The cragsman didn't seem to hear them. His attention was set upon the gray mists and stony peaks of the clanholds. He was quiet for a long time, and Raif waited, knowing he wasn't done.

"And you know what was the worst thing?" Addie said when he was ready. "The worst thing was that I actually believed I should jump. I cracked open my horn of guidestone and walked to the edge. Drew the circle, named the gods, and . . ." He snorted softly. "I couldn't do it. Thought myself a coward at the time, but not anymore. I survived. And it seems to me that when you judge a man's worth his ability to survive should be no small part of it."

Addie turned to face Raif. The cragsman looked worn and strangely vulnerable, but the pride was back in his eyes. "In the clanholds Stillborn was a monster and I was a fever-addled weakling. But look at us, look at every man, woman, and child in the Rift: we not only endure, we *thrive*."

Raif felt the cragsman's words stir him, but he didn't want them to. *I am clan*, he wanted to cry. For the first time since Tanjo Ten Arrow's death he touched his lore. The raven ivory was smooth and warm, lighter than he remembered. The lightness frightened him. What had been lost?

Addie saw what Raif held in his fist. He said, "Clan is just one way of being. They have their warriors and guidestones—

all manner of fine things—and if you grow up one of them it's hard to believe that anything else can compare to it. But ask yourself this: Is clan better or worse for Stillborn's loss . . . my loss . . . yours?"

Raif tried to shrug but found he couldn't. Addie's sharp gray gaze wouldn't let him. Raif squeezed his lore, and then let it drop against the hollow of his throat. "You and Stillborn would be an asset to any clan," he said, knowing it for the truth.

"And you?"

"You don't know me."

"I know you outshot Tanjo Ten Arrow when your life depended on it. I watched with my own eyes as you made a choice between three targets, and though you killed a fine ewe we're both here to tell of it. I'd say that makes you a survivor."

Did it? Raif thought of Duff's stovehouse. Six men dead . . . but not him. And the badlands. Tem dead, a chief dead, thirteen others dead. Yet he and Drey had survived. Raif stood. Cold drafts from the Rift had stiffened his joints and he had to put a hand on the cliff wall to steady himself. Air beat against his eardrums as pressure built for another snowfall.

"You mourn your clan, I can see that," Addie said. "But does your clan mourn you?"

Raif searched desperately for a reason not to shake his head. *Drey. Only Drey.*

"Set it aside. Take what you've learned and move forward. A clansman can never be anything other than clan. We can be more."

How could that be possible on the edge of the world, with no kin, no guidestone, no gods? Men came here because they'd run out of choices, not because they sought something more. Addie's words were self-deception. Yet why didn't they sound like it? And why, after Stillborn had warned him that Maimed

Men didn't make good friends, had Stillborn acted as a friend to Linden Moodie?

Raif took a breath to calm himself. He needed answers.

"Why was the newborn lowered into the Rift?"

"It's our way."

"And Tanjo Ten Arrow?"

"That is also our way."

Raif recognized the stubbornness in Addie's voice, and was glad of it. It gave him something to fight. "Why were his eyelids taken from him?"

"So that he would see his own end."

"And the newborn? Her eyelids were sewn shut."

"She was innocent. She shouldn't have to—" Addie stopped himself.

"Shouldn't have to what?" Raif pressed. "*See?* What's down there, Addie? What are the Rift Brothers afraid of?"

The cragsman looked Raif straight in the eye. "You don't want to know."

"Don't I?" Raif heard the coldness enter his voice. He plucked his lore from his throat and held it out for the cragsman to see. "My clan named me Watcher of the Dead. My father and chief were slain in the badlands. I broke an oath to my brother, and abandoned my sister. And you'd be a fool to think I have anything left to lose."

Addie stepped back a fraction. The large chunk of cartilage that formed the apple of his throat quivered as he studied Raif carefully. After a few moments he seemed to come to some decision.

"You know Wellhouse keeps the histories?"

Raif nodded.

"In the Wellhold you grow up hearing the old songs, the ones everyone else has forgotten. If your father's a fountsman then you have access to the Kenning Hall where many old scrolls and documents are kept. It gets inside you, knowledge. Even if you've a brain as holey as an old fleece some portion of it sticks. You canna help it. You learn things despite yourself. Our old clan guide was Rury Wellhouse, uncle to the chief, and the most learned man in the clanholds. Rury was a canny man. He knew how to wake a boy's mind. He'd tell us stories of the great chiefs, of battles and treaties, and fierce duels where neither opponent was left standing. He slipped the histories into our heads and we never even knew it. At night, after the hunt, he'd lead the singing. Such a fair voice, he had, mellow and filled with knowing."

Addie halted, remembering. Snow had begun to fall whilst he spoke; big white flakes that seesawed down like feathers. Raif wondered what had become of the cranes.

"It's funny how songs stay in your head," Addie said. "You can forget the name of your first herd dog, and the color of your mother's eyes, but some piece of nonsense from forty years ago stays with you like it's been scribed into your skin."

Raif heard himself ask, "What have you remembered?"

Addie hesitated. He was standing close to the fire, and the rising heat formed a shield around him, warding off snow. "Something. A fragment of an old song."

"About me?"

"Perhaps." Addie shrugged, discomforted. "It was what you said, put me in mind of it."

"Tell me."

"I'm not much of a singer. I—"

"Say the words."

"Aye." The cragsman pushed at the air testily. "I see you'll not rest till you've had your fill." Letting out a breath he calmed himself, and then began to speak in his rough, smoky voice.

"Though walls may crumble and earth may break
He will forsake

Though night may fall and shadows rise
He will be wise
Though seals may shatter and evil grow
He will draw his bow
Though a fortress may fall and darkness ride through the gate
He will lie in wait
And when the Demon emerges and all hopes depart
He must take its heart."

The snowfall thickened in the silence following the cragsman's verse. Raif was aware of icy flakes catching in his hair and in the collar of his Orrl cloak, but he was numb to their coldness. He felt made of stone. *They're just words*, he told himself, but he knew it wasn't the truth, and the echo came back to him. *My words.*

He understood what they meant. Almost. They lay on the edge of his perception, like a high-pitched birdcall that began within normal range, then passed beyond hearing. And they sent charges along his nerves, firing off scraps of memory and making images flicker behind his eyes: Drey pressing the swearstone into his fist; Sadaluk holding out an arrow; the Forsworn knight murmuring, *We search.*

Raif blinked and the images fled. He was aware of the cragsman, watching him and waiting, an expression that was half fear and half resignation lying heavy on his face.

Abruptly Raif moved, shrugging off snow. "Tell me about the Rift, Addie."

The cragsman nodded, acknowledging the inevitability of the question. Glancing around, he assured himself that they wouldn't be overheard before speaking. "The earth's thin here. The Want, the badlands, the Rift: they lie on rotting crust. There's canyons, frost boils, gas geysers, hot springs. All flaws. And the Rift is the greatest flaw of them all. It's deep, *deep*, and there are those who say it's too deep, that it bores down to the place where worlds meet. The gray place, where life and death are separated by a lamb's breath. Wellhouse knows some of it, but most of the old knowledge has been forgotten or sealed away. And it's the same with the Rift Brothers: they know just enough to be afraid."

Addie paused, his worn hands reaching out to steady himself against the cliff face. "We don't speak of it. We're like clan that way, always burying the old troubles deep. I'm hardly the man to ask. I herded sheep for my living, now I thieve them. What do I know of the dark days ahead?"

He looked at Raif, and Raif met his gaze without flinching.

Addie blew air from his mouth, beaten. "You asked why the brothers send their dead to the Rift. That I can tell you. They're trying to seal it. They believe that if they throw enough bodies down there, and enough blood is shed, they can stop the Rift from tearing open. What's down there I canna say. Innocents like the newborn are allowed the privilege of never finding out. Their eyes are taken so they never have to see what awaits them. Now Tanjo, he dishonored Traggis Mole. He was supposed to win the duel of arrows and make a liar of you. 'Course, it didn't play out that way, and the crowd was all riled up for a killing. Traggis had no choice but to send him to the Rift. It's a hard land we live in and the Maimed Men respect a hard man. Traggis dealt Tanjo Ten Arrow the worst death in the Rift. Sent him down there alive, without eyelids to shut out the horrors that bide there." Addie's hand went to his waist, questing for a portion of powdered guidestone that was no longer there.

Raif pretended not to notice. Some things were between a man and his gods.

He asked, "What do the brothers believe will come through the rent if the Rift tears?"

Addie snorted softly. "Imagine your worst nightmare, then reckon it tenfold. That'd be a start."

Raif nodded. The cragsman was speaking a language he understood. "The Rift isn't a fortress, though," he said.

"Aye," Addie replied, knowing immediately what Raif meant. "The song was most particular about that."

"You said there are other flaws?"

"The Want is riddled with them. Just because the Rift's greatest doesn't mean it will be the first to give."

"Just the worst."

Addie chuckled grimly, not disagreeing.

Ash. It all began with Ash. Raif tilted his head back and let the snow fall on his face. They had failed, both of them, and now the darkness was forcing its way out. Addie's verse hinted that it could be slowed or delayed, but that would mean finding the fault most likely to give. *We search*, the Forsworn knight had said. Could it be for the same thing?

Raising his hand, Raif scrubbed his face clean of snow. The skin around his eyes was beginning to numb. He was *clan*. He didn't have the book-learning of the knights or the tracking skills of the Sull. What made Addie think he was the one do it?

We can be more. Raif shook the cragsman's words away from him. He didn't want them to be true.

Hearing footfalls on the steps below, Raif calmed himself. Later. He would think about it later, after dark.

Addie moved back to the fire, and began fussing with his joint of meat. Motioning for Raif to join him, he spoke in a voice meant to be overheard. "Will you be taking a little tea before you go?"

As Raif shook his head, a call came up from below.

"Addie! Is Twelve Kill up there with you?" Stillborn.

"Aye," Addie cried back, relaxing imperceptibly. "Come and join us. We're sharing a spot of supper."

Stillborn's big, ruined face came into view at the far end of the ledge. He was sweating and out of breath. "Haven't got time, Addie. The Robber Chief's got me running errands like a girl." He turned to Raif. "I don't know what you've done this time, lad, but I'm betting it's nothing good. You're to come to the Chief's Cave at midnight. Traggis Mole wants to see you alone."

TWENTY-EIGHT

Dealing in the Milkhouse

The Milkhouse was a strange place, Bram concluded as he walked through its lower corridors bearing a heavy, covered platter. Parts of the building were hardly like a roundhouse at all. Where most other roundhouses had large vaulted halls, accessed by wide walkways and stairs, the Milkhouse was built like a maze. Leagues of white-walled corridors spooled off in countless directions, each one looking the same as the last. You had to look carefully to figure it out.

Milkstone was impervious to mold, soot, damp or decay, so although parts of the Milkhouse had been standing for three thousand years, it had an ageless look about it. No rooms or vaults existed belowground. Bram had wondered about that until Guy Morloch had explained Castlemilk's strategy for defense. The Milkhouse lay in a shallow depression, two hundred yards north of the river. A system of ancient pumps and cisterns, built by the great Milk chief Huxlo Castlemilk, allowed the ground floor of the roundhouse to be flooded in times of war. The milkstone held water, Guy confided, and all of the principal rooms of the roundhouse were located in the upper two storeys. The clan would move upwards for safety, an invading force would be thwarted, and the water pumped out when the threat had passed.

Bram thought it was a clever idea, but he wondered about Guy Morloch's willingness to tell it. Guy was a Castlemilk swordsman, newly come to Robbie's cause. How had Robbie managed to command his loyalty so completely?

It was a question Bram wasn't sure he wanted answered. Besides, there wasn't time for it now. He'd already fallen behind the others, and he didn't want to risk losing sight of them. Robbie was on edge at the prospect of this meeting, and his temper would likely flare if everything didn't go to plan.

Only a handful of men had been chosen to accompany Robbie Dun Dhoone on his visit to the Milk chief: Iago Sake, Duglas Oger, Guy Morloch, and the swordsman newly deserted from Skinner Dhoone's camp, Jordie Sarson. Bram and Jess Blain brought up the rear as pages.

It was sunset and the failing light somehow found its way into the roundhouse, casting long, complicated shadows, and rippling like fluid within the milkstone. Guy Morloch led the way. He and Robbie were the only ones not bearing goods. Bram didn't know what lay within the various sacks and baskets the others carried, but he could guess their purpose. Bribery. Robbie Dhoone wanted something from the Milk chief.

As they wound their way higher through the roundhouse, Bram noticed that the milkstone began to be supplemented with sandstone. The two didn't lie easily together, and pale, uniform walls gave way to a checkered mismatch of light and dark stone. Bronze torches had been hammered into the softer sandstone, and a Castlemilk luntman was busy filling their fuel reservoirs with pure-burning rape oil.

At this time of day clansmen were at their hearths, supping ale and taking their supper, and Robbie's group passed few people on their way to the Brume Hall. Guy Morloch set a brisk pace. Like all of Robbie's chosen companions he wore a a floor-length cloak of heavy Dhoone-blue wool fitted with thistle clasps. Robbie wore one too, only his cloak was edged in gold-and-black fisher fur, like the mantles of the Dhoone Kings.

After climbing a steep cantilevered flight of steps they arrived at a pair of doors guarded by two Castlemilk spearmen. The spearmen crossed their weapons barring the way. "Who comes here, and on what business?" demanded the elder of the two.

Guy Morloch stepped forward to speak, but Robbie put a hand on his shoulder, halting him. "Robbie Dun Dhoone comes here," Robbie said. "On the business of kings and chiefs."

The exchange was a formality—the meeting had already been set between Robbie and the Milk chief, and the Castlemilk guards had to know that—but Robbie's words made it more. Only eight weeks earlier he had camped on the ground floor of this very roundhouse, a guest and supplicant of the Milk chief. Now he stood by the great Oyster Doors to the Brume Hall, demanding to see the chief on an equal footing.

Bram watched as the two guards drew to attention, unconsciously responding to the authority in Robbie's voice. The elder spearman rapped against the door with the butt of his spear. "Open up! Robbie Dun Dhoone to see the chief." The double doors swung back on his command and the party moved forward into the Brume Hall.

Like the Tomb of the Dhoone Princes, the Brume Hall at Castlemilk was held to be one of the wonders of the clanholds. Situated at the very top of the roundhouse, it occupied the dome at the apex. The chamber was built entirely from the finest grade of milkstone, known as "brume". Brume, Bram recalled being told, was the old clan word for "mist". And that was what it looked like to him as he entered behind Jess Blain: as if he were walking into a chamber walled and roofed with mist. Almost you could see outside, observe the darkening sky and pale globe of the rising moon. As he looked up, he saw a shadow pass over the roof. A night hawk, flying south to its hunting grounds along the Milk. Bram was filled awe. The stone blocks forming the great dome of the roof had to be at least three feet thick, yet it was like looking through a sheet of cloudy glass.

"The Builder Chief, Hanratty Castlemilk, spent a lifetime fitting the dome. It took him ten years alone to develop the mortar."

Wrayan Castlemilk, the Milk chief, raised herself from the Oyster Chair and moved forward to greet her guests. A rank of swordsmen flanked her. She was dressed plainly but finely in a robe of pale blue wool, letting the silver-and-russet braid she was known for fall straight down the front like a chain. Now that Spynie Orrl was dead, she was the second-longest-reigning chief in the clanholds. Only the Dog Lord himself had held his chiefdom longer.

"Robbie," she said, inclining her head. "Welcome. I see you've brought Guy back to see me."

Robbie grinned almost sheepishly. "He was homesick."

Wrayan Castlemilk threw back her head and laughed. It was a good sound, vigorous and throaty, and it broke the tension in the Brume Hall. "Duglas. Iago. Bram."

Bram wondered how she knew his name. He bowed formally at the neck, as his father had taught him, and for some reason this pleased her and lengthened the duration of her smile.

"I saw you admiring the dome," she said to him. "Hanratty may have fitted it, but truth be told it wasn't really his own work."

"The Sull?"

She nodded. "You've a smart brother here, Robbie. I see why you keep him close."

Bram felt hot blood flush his face. Quickly he glanced at his brother, and saw that Robbie was unsure how to react. By the time he'd settled on a bland smile, Wrayan Castlemilk had already registered his discomfort and moved on.

"The dome was found in pieces in the heart of the Ruinwoods," she said to Bram. "It had fallen from a structure we think may have been a temple. Of course, there's nothing left of it now. The forest's broken it down and swallowed it up." For a moment Wrayan Castlemilk's deep brown-eyed gaze held Bram's, appraising him, before turning her attention to other things.

With a few brief commands, she relieved the party of their burdens, arranged for sufficient chairs to be assembled around the chamber's central firepit, ordered the fetching of ale and milk, and the tamping of the fire, so that they could parley more easily across the firewell. Such arrangements could have been made earlier, Bram realized, but then Wrayan Castlemilk would not have had the advantage of command.

When all was settled fifteen chairs circled the firewell, the camps almost evenly divided. Yet again Wrayan Castlemilk had surprised Bram by providing chairs for him and Jess Blain. As a clanwife passed from man to man, pouring the traditional dram of milk into their ale horns, Wrayan leaned back in her chair and addressed Robbie.

"So, Robbie Dhoone. What would you have of me?"

Robbie was ready for this. Placing his hands on his knees, he breathed deeply and easily. "I need to retake Dhoone."

Wrayan Castlemilk did not react. She had been a clan chief for nearly thirty years, and Bram reckoned she must have reached the point where little surprised her.

"It's time Bludd was driven out," Robbie continued. "They hold too much power, and the clanholds are collapsing around them. Without Dhoone there is no center. No heart. The clanholds are vulnerable, and none more so than the middle clans.

Wellhouse, Withy, Gnash, Croser—" He halted to look the Milk chief in the eye. "Castlemilk."

Wrayan pressed her lips together in a gesture that might or might not have been agreement. "Go on."

Robbie leaned forward in his chair. "Power must be returned to the Dhooneseat, you know that, Wrayan. When was the last time you slept through the night, knowing that Bludd sat at your door?"

The Milk chief's smile was surprising gentle. "You're young, Robbie, else you'd know that a clan chief rarely sleeps through the night. As for Bludd sitting at my door, you forget that Castlemilk is well guarded to the north. We have the Flow and the gorges to protect us. And—" a quick, knowing glance at Guy Morloch "—as I'm sure you've heard, the Milkhouse itself has never been taken."

Guy Morloch colored hotly. Robbie, on the other hand, remained calm, amused even. He shrugged winningly. "It's my duty to gather intelligence where I can."

"And it's my duty to protect my clan."

It was a warning, Bram realized, and Robbie was wise enough to accept it. He took a moment and used it to calm himself, his blue-tattooed face settling in grave lines. When he spoke his voice was urgent. "I need your help, Wrayan. You were a friend to me when I broke relations with Skinner and needed a base to rally support. You lent your house, your protection, your blessing . . . and you must know I have wondered why."

The hall was very quiet. Heat rising from the tamped embers warped the air between Robbie and the chief. The men in Wrayan's party were hard-bitten warriors, powerful and graying, in the late years of their prime. Bram saw that one of them had a glass vial hanging from his sword belt. Gray liquid moved gently within the vial as the man breathed. So it was true, then. The head warrior of Castlemilk carried his measure of powdered guidestone suspended in water, so he might drink it before he rode to war or died.

Wrayan Castlemilk looked to the head warrior, and the two exchanged a brief, telling glance. Squaring her shoulders, Wrayan said, "Robbie, this clan has helped you because we believe Dhoone must have a strong leader if she is to win back her house. Skinner is not that man. I myself provided intelligence to him when the Bludd chief and his forces moved south to occupy Ganmiddich. The Dhoonehouse was left vulnerable for fifteen days, yet Skinner chose not to act. I will never forgive him for that. I have led this clan for twenty-eight years, and time has taught me many hard things. And none harder than this: A chief who hesitates kills his clan."

Of course, Bram thought. *She's speaking of Middlegorge.* Blackhail slew five hundred Castlemilk warriors that day. And all because the old chief—Alban Castlemilk, Wrayan's brother—delayed choosing his ground.

Bram saw that Wrayan was watching him, registering the understanding on his face. He looked away quickly. For some reason he didn't want Robbie to notice her interest.

Robbie raised a hand to his throat and unhooked the thistle clasps, letting his cloak drop to the back of his chair. He said, "When the time comes you need not worry that I will hesitate, lady. I am young, yes, and some might say untested. But know this. I *will* retake Dhoone. The Dhooneseat is mine, and I would sit her sooner with your help. Yet if you refuse, know you only slow, not stop me."

As Robbie spoke a subtle change took place in the Brume Hall. Iago Sake and the rest of Robbie's party sat straighter, stiffening their spines and raising their jaws. The giant axman Duglas Oger actually nodded when Robbie had finished and murmured roughly, "Aye."

Wrayan Castlemilk betrayed no sign of having heard him.

Her warriors shifted uncomfortably in their seats, and for the first time Bram realized why she had allowed no younger men to attend this meeting. It was hard for a fighting man to resist Robbie's confidence. Every word he spoke promised glory.

Robbie eased himself back in his chair, taking time to arrange the cuffs of his shirt. As a self-named chief, he was the only one of the Dhoone party who had been allowed the privilege of bearing arms in the Brume Hall, and his hand came to rest on the cross-hilt of his sword as he waited for the Milk chief to speak. Watching his brother, Bram suddenly understood that Wrayan Castlemilk had little choice here. Guy Morloch and a score of other Castlemen had already deserted their clan for Robbie's cause, and it wouldn't take much to lure away more.

Wrayan Castlemilk must have understood it too, for there was an edge to her voice when she said, "So. What would you have of me?"

"I need two hundred hatchetmen—either hammer or ax— and double that number of swords."

Wrayan's warriors stirred uneasily. Six hundred men. It was unheard of. Even Robbie's chosen companions were surprised. Duglas Oger's mouth fell open, and Guy Morloch looked positively stunned. Only Wrayan Castlemilk and Robbie Dun Dhoone remained calm, appraising each other across the fire like rival swordsmen.

The Milk chief shook her head. "Can't be done, Robbie. Ask again."

"I think it can, and I think you'd be wise to grant it."

"How so?"

Robbie leaned forward in his seat. "You grant me the men I need, here, now, and I'll accept them under the Liege Laws. Under these laws, as you know, the men will be mine to command only for a limited time, their oaths to Castlemilk will remain intact, and they'll return to your house when the campaign has ended." A draft circling the room stirred the embers into flames, and suddenly Bram could see the coldness in Robbie's Dhoone-blue eyes. "Refuse, and you leave me no choice but to take men as they come, bind them to me with oaths and make Dhoonesmen from them. They'll never see Castlemilk again."

Wrayan Castlemilk stood, sending her chair scraping against the stone floor. "You play with fire, Robbie Dhoone."

"I must, to win back my house."

She nodded slowly, acknowledging the truth of his words. "I take it you have already spoken to some of my men?"

Robbie's smile charmed but did not warm. "You know me well, lady. I admit I've taken promises from perhaps a hundred. But don't damn them for it. They're young. They want to fight."

Wrayan's hand found the tail of her braid. There, wound tightly to the leather fastening, hung the broken tip of an antler. Elk lore. She weighed it as she thought. Bram wondered how much of what Robbie said was true. Could it be possible that a hundred Castlemen were willing to forsake their oaths to join him?

With a heavy sigh, Wrayan dropped her lore. "What do you offer in return?"

Robbie stood. "Jess. Bram. Bring forth the gifts. We must show this chief how highly we value her."

Bram felt Wrayan's gaze upon his back as crossed to the wall where the packages had been stowed. Robbie and Iago Sake had packed the sacks and baskets in secret, selecting items from the great war chests that had been removed from the Dhoonehouse the night of the Bludd strike. They were heavy, Bram knew that much, and he prayed to the Stone Gods that he wouldn't make a fool of himself by dropping them. Jess Blain seemed to have a sixth sense concerning weight, for he managed to choose the packages that could be lifted with ease, leaving Bram with the ones that felt like rocks.

When all had been brought forward into the firewell, Robbie dismissed Bram and Jess with a nod. And then he drew his sword. In an instant the Castlemen stood and drew their weapons, but Robbie was already raising his arms in a gesture of no-contest.

"For the packages," he said. "The ties must be cut."

The Castlemen returned to their seats, their faces dark and disgruntled. Robbie had made them look foolish—his first mistake, Bram realized—and now he moved quickly to put it behind him. With a single movement he sliced the length of the first sack, letting bolts of cloth-of-gold, crimson damask, silver tissue and amber samite spill out. The clanwife who had served them their ale and milk and now stood in waiting close to the door gasped. Robbie turned to her and smiled. "For the ladies of the clan."

Bram recognized some of the cloth from the raid Duglas Oger had led along the Lake Road. Such materials, made with silk and gold thread, could not be woven in the Northern Territories and had to be carted all the way from the Far South. Their value was beyond reckoning in the clanholds. The next sack contained exquisite furs: whole lynx pelts, brushes of blue foxes, mink, vair, ocelot, ermine, miniver, and sable. The platter Bram had carried from the tower held three dozen bear gallbladders, preserved in layers of salt. Another held copper breast-pins, cloak-pins, warrior torcs and wrist guards set with sapphires, moonstones, diamonds and blue topaz. One basket held a suit of armor packed in delicate gauze. Robbie held the breastplate up for the Milk chief's inspection, so she could see the honeycombed metal, the silvering and engraving, and the raised-thistle device that circled the neck.

Wrayan Castlemilk's manner was still cool, but Bram could

see the light of desire in her eyes. That armor had been made for a queen. And not for any queen, but for the great Weeping Moira herself. She had fought in it a thousand years earlier at the Hill of Flies, and clan no longer knew the art of honeycombing metal so that it was light of weight but hard as stone.

But still Robbie wasn't finished. The last basket was long and shallow, so heavy that to move it Bram had been forced to drag it across the Brume Hall floor. Robbie paused before slitting the cloth that covered it, and addressed the seven warriors who protected Wrayan Castlemilk.

"I have offered gifts to your clanwives, your healers, your old men, and your chief. And now I offer the gift of swords to you."

Robbie slit and pulled back the canvas, revealing a stash of twenty swords, unsheathed and laid point-to-hilt. Their edges rippled, throwing off sparks of blue light. Every man in the room grew still. Water steel. Dhoone Kings wielded it, warriors had killed for it, and only one man in the clanholds knew the secret of its forging.

Bram stared at the swords, transfixed. He did not understand how Robbie had managed to lay his hands on so many. No man who owned one would willingly give it up. And then he saw it, close to the top of the pile, the pommel shaped like a rabbit's foot, cast from lattern and blued steel. His father's sword. The one Mabb Cormac had ordered refitted to honor his second wife, Margret. Twin to the blade that Robbie now held in his fist. Bram blinked. That sword was *his*.

"I see the rumors are true, then," Wrayan said to Robbie. "You *did* relieve Skinner of some of his war chests when you fled his camp."

Robbie shrugged. "I prefer to call it taking what's rightfully mine."

Wrayan laughed, but this time her laughter was brittle and quickly done. She glanced at her warriors; their attention was still rapt upon the swords. "You've brought some pleasing trinkets, I'll allow you that much."

"Water steel is no trinket, lady."

"What is easily acquired is easily given."

"Then you refuse them?" Robbie's voice was dangerously light.

"No. I'll accept them. But I want something more."

"Lady, I have no more riches to give. If you would only—"

Wrayan waved a hand to silence him. "Spare me your protests. Another sword means nothing to me."

"Then what would you have?"

As Bram waited for Wrayan to speak, he was taken with the idea that everything had been leading to this. Robbie was clever, but this was his first time at the negotiating table, whilst Wrayan Castlemilk had been striking deals for thirty years. Outside, the moon shone through a thin veil of cloud, making the entire dome glow. Its light was cold and alien, and everyone sitting beneath it looked made of stone. Bram shivered, though instantly he wished he had not, for the Milk chief's gaze fell upon him.

"I'll take your brother, Robbie Dun Dhoone, to foster here at this clan."

TWENTY-NINE

The Robber Chief

I t was strange, the way the snow here seemed to hold no water, just crystals of parched ice. Raif felt it crunch beneath his boots like chalk as he walked the length of rimrock, waiting for midnight to fall.

The Rift Music had started, and hundreds of fires blazed against it, one at the entrance to every inhabited cave in the city. With so many fires burning it should have been light, but it wasn't. The Rift vented darkness like a volcano venting steam. Raif grinned at his own fancy. Mostly he felt old inside, as if the things he'd seen and done had aged him, but tonight he felt strangely light. Mad. Lost. Addie's song had revealed a path for him, and he knew he wasn't fit to take it. But if he didn't, who would?

Raif knew the answer—he could hear in the Rift Music.

No one.

Sobered, he turned away from the rim, and let the dry smoky air cool him until he felt ready to face the Robber Chief, Traggis Mole.

Raif had never been close to the chief's cave before, but he knew where it was. Most Maimed Men chose to live in the upper terraces, closer to the sun and stars, yet Traggis Mole had made his home low. The lower terraces were the oldest part of the city, and the walls and stairs were roughly mined and crumbling. Bird lime had bleached the outcroppings, and some trace of phosphorescence made random edges glow. Raif followed a stairway where the stone steps were so badly deteriorated that oak boards had been laid over the powdery rock. Below, he could see the ten-foot longfire that burned at the mouth of the chief's cave.

No one stood guard by the entrance, and as Raif crossed the ledge toward the fire he wondered what he should do. The longfire was burning fiercely, completely sealing off the mouth of the cave. Glare from the flames prevented him from seeing inside. Just as he was about to call out, a flagstone was thrown over the coals, flattening a section of the flames and creating a narrow bridge through the center of the fire. Raif moved forward. He still couldn't see beyond the flames, but the message was clear. *Enter.*

He stepped onto the flagstone, hearing coals pop beneath him. For a moment his ears roared with heat and he smelled the singeing of his own hair, and then he was safe on the other side. Quickly, he ran a hand over his scalp, checking that he wasn't actually on fire. Out of the corner of his eye he saw a shape move inside the cave.

"It's a true Orrl cloak, then," came Traggis Mole's rough, quiet voice. "The flames touched it, but it didn't char."

Raif was angry at being watched. He made no reply, using the few moments this bought him to take in his surroundings. The chief's cave was narrow and twisting, its gallery sloping downward, boring deep into the cliff. The walls were painted, and Raif could see traces of color peaking through the scale of soot and lichen that coated the rock. Crosscurrents touched his face, and he realized that the chief's cave must lead to other caves and tunnels that he could not see. The living quarters were sparse and orderly. A pallet bed was pushed against a flat stretch of rock wall, its fur coverlet pulled straight. A second fur lay on the floor, close to a cast-iron brazier and two leather camp chairs. A hogbacked chest stood at the foot of the bed, and a weapons stand holding both live and guarded steel stood at its head.

"Step aside," Traggis Mole commanded.

The moment Raif did so, Traggis Mole tugged on a length of rope, dragging the flagstone off the coals. Flames leapt up immediately, blocking the way in. And out.

The Robber Chief moved close to Raif, and sniffed him. The bore holes in his wooden nose made a sharp little piping noise as he inhaled. He was dressed richly but with little regard, like Orwin Shanks at the Dhoone Fair: aware that he must display his wealth, but careless of how he went about it. Raif recognized the finery of several clans on his back. The heavily embroidered tunic was pure Wellhouse, its design picked out in all the colors that heather could be. The double-woven cloak trimmed with swan feathers had once belonged to a Harkness warrior, and the hare-skin pants were the type made by the Hailwives each summer when the hares ran wild in the Wedge. Other items—tooled leather boots, a metalwork sword belt, and a linen undershirt gathered at the neck and cuffs—were city-made and foreign to Raif.

"Not all Orrl cloaks are created equal," Traggis Mole said, his black eyes looking steadily at Raif. "Only a very few are proofed against flames. Cloaks made for chiefs and the sons of chiefs. But then, you know all about that."

Raif held the Robber Chief's gaze and did not speak.

Traggis Mole's finely shaped lips curled, then he was gone. Raif saw him settle down on one of the camp chairs, and wondered how he moved so fast.

"How old are you?" the Robber Chief asked.

"I passed my eighteenth name-day this winter."

"When?"

It was a question Raif didn't want to answer . . . because he'd never be entirely sure. "Recently."

Traggis Mole let the silence lie there until Raif felt compelled to fill it.

"Da always said I was born on Lambing Night, in the last month of winter. But when I was a bairn I remember my mother celebrating my name-day earlier, at Winter Fest."

As soon as Raif spoke he regretted it. Never before had he mentioned this to anyone, not even to Drey. He'd always used the day Tem had given. But even a child of four can remember things, and he distinctly recalled his mother giving him a tiny wooden boat to sail on the Leak. It was at Winter Fest, he knew, for as he watched his toy boat bob along the icy stream, he remembered the clan maids in their winter whites, singing to Ione, pleading with the Stone Goddess to find them a mate before Lambing Night.

Traggis Mole sat perfectly still, watching him. Raif was aware of the man's power, the potential for absolute violence that charged his body like a drawn bow.

"The Vorlanders say that if you lose an eye in battle it is a good thing, for that eye will go ahead of you to heaven and will send you glimpses of other worlds. Me, I lost a nose, and I've come to believe that if I sniff very hard I can scent a lie." The Robber Chief paused, gauging Raif's reaction. "Now I will ask you one question, and if you lie to me I will kill you. Do you understand?"

Raif nodded slowly. He feared this man.

The Robber Chief waited, choosing his moment before speaking. His eyes were black as night, and you could not see his soul through them. "The Orrl cloak. Did you kill the man who owned it?"

The question was so surprising it took Raif a moment to make sense of it. The Orrl cloak? He met Traggis Mole's gaze. "No."

Time passed, how much Raif was unable to tell. Everything was still and quiet, except the breath piping in and out of the Robber Chief's wooden nose. Suddenly he moved, stood and crossed toward the weapon stand. Again there was that quickness, as if Traggis Mole knew a way to shrink space. "So how did you come by it?"

Raif hoped his relief didn't show. "I took it from a dead man's back. I came across five bodies in the wastelands west of Orrl. I needed clothes." He wasn't proud of it, but Traggis Mole had asked for the truth.

"And did you know who they were?"

"No. Orrlsmen, nothing more."

"Then you'd be surprised to learn that one of them was grandson to an old friend of mine, Spynie Orrl?"

Raif shook his head, knowing he'd fallen into a trap.

The Robber Chief selected a sheathed longknife from the weapon stand. "You're not what you claim, are you, Raif Twelve Kill? Not a white-winter warrior, not even an Orrlsman."

"No."

The word stilled the Robber Chief's hand. He looked from the longknife to Raif. "Linden Moodie says you're a Hailsman. Is he right?"

Raif felt sweat prickle along his hairline. "Yes."

Immediately Traggis Mole was there, at his back, the longknife drawn from its sheath, its point touching the apple of Raif's throat. "Who are you protecting, yourself or your clan?"

The pressure of the knife made Raif gag. He didn't understand any of this. What did Traggis Mole want from him? "I— I don't know."

Just as quickly as the knife was raised, it was taken back. The

Robber Chief released him, and Raif stumbled forward, his hand rising to his throat. His fingers slid across wetness, and whatever it was—sweat or blood—he wiped it away without looking at it.

Traggis leaned against the cave wall and studied him. The longknife was sheathed once more, and only its tortoiseshell grip now showed. "Linden Moodie says you endangered the raid party by letting a sheep herder run free."

"He says a lot. Not all of it's true. The sheep herder was gagged and tied. He was in no state to give warning."

The Robber Chief accepted this with a taut nod. "What if he'd been a Hailsman?"

Suddenly Raif needed to sit. Being in Traggis Mole's presence drained him. He felt as if he'd been awake, guarding against monsters, all night. Without waiting for an invitation Raif sat on the closest camp chair. "I can't answer that."

"Well, you're going to have to. Here, for me." Traggis Mole pushed himself off from the cave wall. "This is the Rift, not the clanholds, and you're with the Maimed Men now. The journey is one-way. No one goes back. We can't. We might wish it, might dream about it every night, tasting the warm buttermilk on our tongues and feeling the spring grasses whip our shins. But we know it's just a dream. We're marked, every one of us. And no one's pining our loss."

As Traggis finished speaking a tremor passed through the cave. Rock settled deep in the earth's crust with a long, bass groan. Flames in the longfire and brazier *greened* as gas escaped through fault lines. Dust smoked from the cave walls in the stillness that followed.

The Robber Chief pulled his wooden a nose a fraction away from his face, letting air travel directly into the bridgeless hole beneath. His eyes dared Raif to look away. When the dust thinned he plugged his wooden nose back into place.

"This may be a rotting wormhole, but I'm king of it. That might not mean much to you, with your fancy cloak and clannish honor, but it's everything to me. Men stay here at my sufferance. You're here at my sufferance, and I tell you now, Twelve Kill, I don't like what I see. Oh, I know you're handy with that bow of yours and you've a talent for coming out on top, but to me you're a liability—a man whose loyalty still lies with his clan."

Traggis Mole's small well-shaped hands twitched, as if they wanted something to do. His gaze pinned Raif. "Many men here hate me. Some think they can take my place. That's fine with me—I can watch my back. But not everyone can. There are fools here who still trust men, fools like Addie Gunn and Stillborn and a hundred others like them. And perhaps they should never have come here, perhaps they should have stayed in their roundhouses and cities and taken whatever tyranny came their way. But they didn't, they came here. And that makes them mine.

"And no one harms what is mine, only me."

Raif looked down; his boots were covered in a film of dust. He understood now what the Robber Chief wanted from him, but he didn't know if he could give it.

"There's a choice here," Traggis said quietly. "Either become one of us or leave. I need to know that when I send you on a raid you'll put your Rift Brothers first. They're a mangy ill-bred lot, but they look to me for protection, and that means I have to watch for those who'd do them harm." His black eyes glittered in the firelight. "Will you do them harm?"

"No."

"Would you slay a Hailsman to save a Maimed Man's life?"

Here it was, the question everything had been leading up to . . . and Raif didn't have an answer. Inigar Stoop had cut his heart from the guidestone: Raif Sevrance was no longer clan.

But it was hard not to be clan. How could you turn your back on all you'd known and loved?

Raif ran a hand over his face. He missed Effie. What did she always say to him? *You can hug me, but no kiss.* Gods, he'd been so lucky and he didn't even know it.

But this was his luck now. A Maimed Man. Looking Traggis Mole straight in the eye, he said, "I can slay a Hailsman." *Mace Blackhail. For Effie, and Drey, and Tem.*

The Robber Chief studied him, pulling air through his wooden nose. Minutes passed. Raif felt his face drawing tight like a mask, but he didn't drop his gaze. When Traggis Mole spoke he could barely hear him.

"We shall see."

Raif closed his eyes for a moment, resting them.

"You've been taken lessons in swordcraft from Stillborn?"

"Yes. I practice twice a day."

Traggis Mole seemed to reach a decision. "Follow me," he said, disappearing into the gloom at the back of the cave.

Raif stood. He was glad Traggis wasn't watching him, for his legs wobbled as they took his weight. Forcing them into obedience, he headed deep into the Robber Chief's cave.

The crosscurrents grew stronger as the light dimmed. The soot from the fires hadn't drifted this far back, and Raif could make out the paintings on the walls. Some of the pigments must have been made by grinding down the phosphorescence in the rock, for parts of the design glowed. A landscape was rendered onto the stone. Vast grasslands were shown yellowing in the sun. Elk and aurochs grazed rolling plains, and killhounds and birds bigger than killhounds wheeled above them, sighting prey. A river snaked and bow-curved through the lowlands, a line of silvery luminescence that glinted like real water. When the light faded to black Raif could still see its course.

"Here," Traggis Mole called, striking a spark with a flint and lighting a tallow-smeared torch. Ahead, the gallery forked into two passages, and the Robber Chief waited at the mouth of the west fork for Raif to catch up.

At some point while they'd been without light the painting on the walls had changed. The river still flowed, but the landscape it cut through was laid to waste. Hillsides were brown, their grasses dead or dying. Carcasses rotted on the plains and bird skeletons littered the riverbank like empty baskets.

Raif pulled his cloak around his shoulders, suddenly cold.

Traggis led him through the passage and into a small, star-shaped chamber. The elk tallow in the torch burned red and smoky, throwing jittery shadows across the painted rock. The river was here as well, circling the cave, but now its floodplains were dry and frozen. Bare rock and frost were all that remained.

"Hold this." The Robber Chief handed Raif the torch. Nail-head chests, iron-banded coffers, and chained crates covered most of the cave floor. The chief's stash, Raif guessed, watching as Traggis slid a key from his metalwork sword belt and knelt by a leather-upholstered chest. The lock turned with ease. Dust slid from the chest's lid as it was opened.

The Robber Chief took something out, something the size of a hand-knife, wrapped in brown cloth. Without turning to look at Raif, he asked, "How well do you know your clan?"

"As well as most."

"Have you ever visited the silver mine, Black Hole?"

A spark from the torch touched Raif's wrist like a warning. "I've been there. It's past the Muzzle, where the balds meet the Copper Hills."

Traggis swung round to face him. "Oh, I know where it is." Rising to his feet, he pushed aside the cloth. "What I'd like to know is how long has it been yielding this?"

It was a rod of gold, so bright and yellow it barely seemed

real. Traggis held it out for Raif to take, eyeing him carefully.

Raif had handled little gold before: a ring that had belonged to his mother, and a case for carrying powdered guidestone that Orwin Shank used on feast days. It was heavy, he knew that, and coveted by everyone in the North. He took the rod, and knew immediately by its heft it was gold. Nothing, not even iron, was heavier.

He handed it back to the Robber Chief. "It can't be from Blackhail."

"Really? And yet it was seized from a cart leaving the mine, along with others still warm from the furnace."

"There are no furnaces at Black Hole. The raw ore is carted to the roundhouse."

Traggis Mole raised an eyebrow. "It's an easy business, setting up a furnace. All you need is a pair of bellows and a pit."

Raif shook his head. "Gold's never been found in the clan-holds."

"Well they found it at Black Hole, and they're keeping it to themselves."

The Robber Chief wrapped the rod in its cloth and returned it to the chest. As he turned the lock, Raif glanced at the wall painting above his head. The silver river bow-curved past a lone peak. Something about the shape of the mountain, the way it rose from the ground like a drum of twisted rock, made him pause. Where had he seen it before?

"I've been having Black Hole watched," Traggis said, snapping Raif back to the business at hand. "They pour the gold into rods, then stockpile them. Every other month at the dark of the moon they're carted south."

Raif said, "Why are you telling me this?"

"I want that gold." The Robber Chief's voice was danger-ously soft. "And you're going to help me get it."

"You don't need me for this."

"I think I do. You know the land, the clansmen. And if you're spotted at the mine shanty no one's the wiser."

A slow creeping dread made Raif's fingertips tingle . . . even the one that was no longer there. "Why don't you attack the cart? There's no need to go near the mine."

Traggis threw his hand toward the chest containing the gold rod. "Where do you think I got that? A bungled raid on the cart, that's where. They'll be expecting another strike on the cart. It'll be guarded, possibly by bowmen. Men could get shot."

Raif tried to think of a counter argument, his gaze resting on the lone mountain in the wall painting. How could he return to Blackhail as a thief?

"You've a sword?"

"Stillborn lends me one."

"Good." The Robber Chief crossed to the chamber's entrance. "Bring it with you tomorrow. The raid party heads west at first light."

Raif bowed his head.

Traggis turned to look at him. "I'll be watching you, Twelve Kill. Endanger anything of mine, and you'll live to regret it."

He was gone before Raif could raise his head.

THIRTY

Pursuit

Ash rucked up her skirt and rubbed wolf grease into her saddle sores. The grease stung at first, and you could smell the gamy whiff of it, but then it melted into your skin like butter. Ash groaned with relief. According to Mal Naysayer, wolves well-fed enough to render fat were rare—especially in winter—and they were lucky to have found this one in the Want. *That* made Ash grin. Whenever she'd had cuts and grazes in Mask Fortress her foster father would send Caydis Zerbina to her with a box of myrrh and scented ambergris. She'd come quite a way since then. And she felt about a million years older.

Now all I have to be is wiser.

She glanced over at the camp, where Mal Naysayer and Ark Veinsplitter where sitting close to the smoking fire, quietly breaking their fast. Ark looked tired. He had taken the late watch while she and the Naysayer slept. The Sull were stronger than men, with a greater capacity for endurance, and it worried Ash to see them weary. Slapping down her skirt, she went to join them.

It was a Sull warrior's idea of dawn—dark as night, but with a band of something that could not yet be called light showing gray on the eastern horizon. Any city man waking at such a time would take one look and go straight back to sleep. Ash had felt the same way at first, but slowly she was beginning to change.

She wondered about that sometimes, the changing, wondered if it were just a case of settling into new habits. Or did it go deeper . . . to her blood?

I won't think about that now, she told herself, kneeling by one of the saddlebags and taking out a pouch of stock that had frozen overnight into a ball of yellow ice. Normally they would only drink stock after they'd set camp for the night, once the body heat from the horses had melted it. But looking at the deep lines on Ark's face and the gray circles under his eyes, she wanted to do something to cheer him.

Using a chunk of rock pried from the permafrost, Ash hammered the stock into pieces and then dumped it into the pot. As it spat and sizzled, stubbornly refusing to melt, she sat between the two Sull Far Riders and waited for the dawn to come.

They'd made camp on the edge of the Want—holding its border, as Ark said. Ash had lost count of the days they'd been traveling this strange nowhere land. One day was the same as the next. The land was mostly flat, sometimes rocky or scored by long-retreated glaciers, but always dead. The only thing that changed was the sky. Clouds did peculiar things here, she'd noticed. They massed on the horizon, mimicking mountains, or boiled upwards in vast towers, or settled into elongated tracts, like plow lines. They never shed their moisture, and the days were cold and dry, stirred by sharp winds that smelled of ice.

The Want wore you down. Walking across it was like walking through water. The sameness of the landscape provided no relief for the spirit, and it seemed each step took you nowhere.

The frozen earth punished your body, stealing strength, raising calluses and tearing muscle.

Ash felt bruised and battered. Walking, riding: it was hard to decide which hurt the most. At least *she* got to sleep at night, unlike the Far Riders who took turns standing watch. She'd wanted to do her share. It had taken her several days to work up the courage to ask if she could take her turn standing watch. She'd feared Ark's laughter or, worse, his contempt. But she needn't have. Ark Veinsplitter was no Penthero Iss. His face was serious as he listened to her, and he nodded once or twice. He wouldn't let her do it, of course, but his reasons were ones she could accept: she must first master both her weapons, and learn more about the Way of the Flame.

Mas Rhal. The prefect state of fearlessness. Mal Naysayer had not brought out the silver lamp that burned with a blue flame since that first evening in the mountains, but every day he and Ark set her small tasks toward it. She had learned to visualize the flame, see it burning against a black ground. Mal urged her to picture it glowing in the center of her mind, in the place where her thoughts first seeded. It was hard, though. A single flame seemed too small a thing to burn away the fear.

There had been tests, and she had failed many of them. Five days back they had come across a stone cairn at the head of a barren plain. The two Far Riders dismounted, and she watched as they bared their forearms to let blood. It was a place of loss, Ark explained. Sull had died here many centuries earlier in a fierce battle against the night. Ark and the Naysayer had stood for several minutes, silent and grave, their hearts pumping blood onto the frozen battlefield, paying their toll to the dead. Only later, after they'd set camp for the night, did she realize she should have joined them and breathed a vein.

And that had not been her only failure. On most days the Naysayer rode ahead, blazing the trail. Ark tracked him. One day Ark had pulled back the gray and given the lead to Ash. She had learned much about the path lores—where to look for the Naysayer's marks and how to read them, how to iden- tify Sull markers sunk into the permafrost like stones, how to tell if the path had been recently traveled, and if the surround- ing landscape had been disturbed—and she was confident she could do the task. The morning went well. She developed a headache from leaning over her horse's neck and squinting for long hours at the ground . . . but she didn't lose the trail. Then, about midday, she came across some markings that confused her. The Naysayer's mark indicated that they should bear south out of the Want, yet his own trail continued east. Quickly, she looked to Ark for help, yet he wouldn't meet her eye. It was a test, she realized, and she decided to play it safe and head south out of the Want.

By sunset Ash was free of the Want—and lost. There was no sign of the Naysayer and she drifted east in search of him. When night fell she panicked, increasing her pace and bend- ing back toward the Want. That was when Ark finally broke his silence, commanding her to fall back. He resumed the lead, and she spent the next hour staring at the stiff set of his spine in the starlight, knowing she had failed him.

She had missed markers, stumbled upon a Sull path bear- ing southeast and then drifted away from it. And worse, she had panicked. Ark told her she should have stayed on the Sull path and had faith that the Naysayer would find her. Never, *ever*, was she to head into the Want unguided.

The tone of his voice still stung her. He was a hard man to fail.

Other tests had gone better. One night the Naysayer had taken the blindfold from his saddlebag and bade Ash tie it over her eyes. She was commanded to sit in silence and imagine the flame until he spoke her name. At first she listened to the sounds of Ark and Mal setting up the camp: the hammering of posts and tearing of canvas, and the *snick* of a flint as a spark was struck to start the fire. She smelled roasting ice hare and saliva filled her mouth. Later, she detected the pungent reek of horse stale, and the mineral whiff of tung oil as one of the Far Riders cleaned his weapons. After that she began to lose things: hearing and smell. And time.

The flame burned strong. It was beautiful, perfectly blue with a faint gold corona shimmering at its tip.

When Ash heard her name called she snapped awake. It was dawn. She had been sitting wearing the blindfold all night.

She smiled, remembering. Her joints had been stiff and her hands and feet were cold, but apart from that she felt rested. It was the morning she began to think of herself as Sull.

Noticing the stock had finally melted, she stirred in some dried seedpods and a chunk of hare fat. The sun was rising now, throwing pale orange light onto the clouds and revealing the land surrounding the camp. A breeze had started up, and feathers and uprooted willows rolled across the frozen plains. In the distance, to the southeast, Ash spied a speckling of dark smudges that she could not recall seeing the previous night. Trees, they looked like. Real ones, not phantoms conjured up by the clouds.

"Drink this," she said to Ark, filling his drinking horn with liquid. He looked at her a moment, and then took the horn from her. The stock must have been scalding hot, yet he took a mouthful anyway.

"It is good," he said quietly, and then, after a beat, "daughter."

Ash made herself busy filling a second horn for Mal. She didn't trust herself to meet Ark's eyes.

The Naysayer finished his drink in one gulp. His tongue steamed as he thanked her, pronouncing himself much restored by it. She loved them, she realized as she watched Mal saddle his mount and Ark begin breaking camp. She had become Sull because she was a Reach and there seemed little choice, but she wanted to *stay* Sull because of these two men.

After the Naysayer departed camp to break the trail, Ash helped Ark roll the tent canvas and dig out the posts. They fell into an easy routine, Ash performing the lighter tasks—killing the fire and sorting through the food packs to plan the day's rations—while Ark packed the horses and hefted water. When everything was done, and all obvious traces of the camp were erased, Ash took out her sickle and chain and began weapons practice.

She had a better feel for the weapon now, and she could have the chain up and swinging above her head within seconds. Today Ark made her practice trapping his sword. He wore full furs and armor, and articulated horn-mail gloves. His "sword" was a tent post cut to size. Trapping a horizontal object involved altering the pitch of the chain's spin, and Ash struggled with lowering her arm while the chain was in motion. When the metal teardrop studded with peridots swung within a finger's length of her eye, she panicked and released her grip too soon. Ark made her do it again and again, until she'd lost her fear.

By the time they were done, her arm muscles were aching and her cheeks felt red hot. Ark's lynx cloak was missing chunks of fur, and he frowned as he inspected the bald patches. "You must learn to move back when you are attacked by a swordsman. You allowed me to get too close."

"*Naza Thani?*"

He nodded. "The Nine Safe Steps. We will practice them as we ride."

Ash wondered how he intended to do that. When they were mounted and turning out from the camp he told her. "We will ride in single file, with you taking the rear. At all times you will keep the head of your horse exactly nine paces behind the gray's tail."

Ash sniffed. This was going to be easy.

They set off at trot, the morning sun shining bright in their faces. The land was flat and strewn with limestone boulders, and from time to time they'd encounter the peculiar patches of *vagueness* that she'd come to expect in the Want. Things shimmered in those patches, and from a distance they took the shape of hills or cities or woods, and then you drew close and saw nothing but mist. Ash felt cheated every time.

Once she'd established a distance of nine paces between the gray and her own mount, she was determined to maintain it. When Ark increased the pace to a canter, she realized it wasn't going to be as easy as she'd thought. The gray had longer legs and a more fluid motion than the white, and she had to push the gelding into a gallop every few seconds to keep up. The concentration it took was exhausting, and the white soon grew agitated at all the minute adjustments in pace. When Ark reined the gray abruptly, it sent Ash scrambling to shorten her reins. And just when she'd managed to get everything under control, the Far Rider pulled something new from his hat. The gray had a fifth gait; a showy high-stepping amble that fell between a trot and a canter. The poor white had nothing quite like it in its repertoire, and Ash had to alternate between a trot and a gallop to keep up.

Ark kept up this pace for the better part of an hour. Ash's neck felt stiff as a board, and she began to suspect that the distance of nine paces was now irrevocably seared into her brain. She quite expected to see *Naza Thani* outlined in chalk in her dreams. Which was exactly the point, she realized.

And then she realized something else. *Naza Thani* was the limit of her safety: the distance at which she could remain safe and still strike. Yet if she just wanted to be safe she could fall

496 † J. V. JONES

back further. This was about more than her ability to judge distance, it was a lesson in keeping herself alive.

Immediately Ash reined in the white. A moment or two passed whilst Ark sped ahead of her before he realized what she had done. Twisting in the saddle, he turned to look at her. His expression was hard, and for a moment she thought she'd made a mistake . . . and then he nodded, just once.

She'd passed the test.

She grinned at the back of his head. The sun had long since disappeared behind a thick bank of cloud, but somehow she felt its warmth. She blew kisses at the white's neck, and promised never to treat him so badly again. Then she remembered seeing an old winter-dried carrot in the bottom of one of the packs. Horse treat! Leaning back awkwardly in the saddle, she unbuckled the lid of the nearest pannier.

As Ash thrust her fist past the tent canvas she heard something howl. The sound felt like ice against her skin, cold and hollow and filled with dark craving. For a moment she froze, transfixed. Her fingertips started to prickle as blood left the tips. Quickly she glanced at Ark. He was holding his pace, undisturbed.

She called his name; it came out as a croak. He turned, and his whole being changed when he saw her face.

He spoke a word in Sull, the name of the First God, and asked her only one thing: "How close?"

Ash had to take a breath. With those two words he had acknowledged her as a Reach, and suddenly she didn't want to be one. She wanted to be Sull. Only Sull. Yet there was no choice here; there never had been. With an effort she found her voice. "I heard a call, to the west. It sounded far in the distance."

The Far Rider relaxed imperceptibly. He glanced at the sky, gauging the time of day. "We will make haste," he said, kicking the gray into a canter.

Ash followed, and they fled east. Midday passed, and they began descending from the high plains. The terrain grew rougher, and once or twice Ash spotted glint lakes to the south. Overhead, the clouds were on the move, carrying a newborn storm to the clanholds. Ash watched them, listening all the while for sounds of pursuit. No more calls came, but she *felt* something hunting her, something that wished her harm.

After the night in the ice oasis she had been watchful, but days had passed without incident and she had allowed herself to believe the danger had passed. It was a child's mistake, and she was angry at herself for making it. Ark and the Naysayer had been vigilant as ever: they hadn't forgotten the reason why they were here.

Ash was too tired to sustain her anger at herself for long. Ark set a hard pace, and would not halt to rest the horses. Ahead, she saw the speckled patches of darkness she'd spotted at dawn. They were drawing closer, and now she was sure they were trees. Had they reached the end of the Want? She wasn't sure what lay to the east. Forests, she'd heard, vast bodies of timber that stretched over an entire continent. Her foster-father owned onion-skin scrolls that mapped them; beautifully worked illustrations, keyed in High Hand and gilded like prayer books. Even as a child Ash hadn't believed them. They filled the Racklands with dangers; dragons and molten lava floes, ice sheets and poisoned swamps.

Her foster-father had congratulated her on her skepticism. A strange thing to find pleasing in a child.

Ash turned her thoughts elsewhere. She couldn't afford to think of Iss now. Her mount was showing signs of weariness; his tail had dropped and his neck was badly lathered. She worried about the extra weight he was carrying, and remembered the release strap under his belly. *If we are pursued, pull the strap.* It didn't feel right to do that now, but she called out to Ark to slacken the pace.

Strangely, he heeded her and they slowed to a trot. Ark's stallion was glossy with sweat, but his tail and ears were up and he looked ready for another run. The Far Rider leaned forward and wiped the mucus from the stallion's eyes.

"Is the Naysayer ahead?" Ash asked him.

"He awaits us in the trees."

Ash felt better for hearing that. Weariness had begun to creep over her, and as the sun descended behind the cloud cover she slumped forward in the saddle. Ark passed her a silver flask, and bid her drink. It was the ghostmeal, she recognized it from its scent. The last fluid she'd drunk had been a cup of water before dawn, and she discovered she had a terrible thirst. Even so, she was cautious with the ghostmeal, and took just enough to fill her mouth. It sent bad dreams, she remembered. A fee for giving strength.

As the light faded they reached the first of the trees. They were stunted, their limbs pale and swollen with fistulas. Rusts fed on their needles, and beetles had girdled their trunks. *Deadwoods.* Ash recalled the name from the map. That placed them north of Clan Bludd.

Ark slowed the gray to a walk as the woods grew thicker. The moon hadn't risen yet and there was little light. Mist began to slither around the horses' coffin bones, and Ash smelled damp earth for the first time in many weeks. The ghostmeal had alerted her senses, and she detected complicated layers of decay beneath the damp. Her night vision improved—ghost-meal was better than carrots for helping you see in the dark— and she saw that many trees grew in clusters, nursing their sickly saplings in protective rings.

Ash was the first to spot the Naysayer. He stood on a small rise, watching their approach, his horse tethered to a tree below him. The bulk of his furs made him huge, like a god, and there was live steel in his hands. He did not make himself known until they drew close.

"*Hass.*" The word was many things: a greeting, an expression of relief . . . and a question.

Ark repeated the word back to him, and for a moment Ash was excluded. These two men had ridden side by side for twenty years.

"We are hunted," Ark said.

Mal nodded; he already knew.

When Ash dismounted her knees buckled, and Mal rushed forward to put a hand about her waist until she got her land legs. He smelled familiar, and the absolute certainty of his strength was reassuring. He had picked a small clearing as their campsite, and Ash saw he'd raised a fire but had not lit it. A raccoon carcass lay skinned and quartered close by.

The two Far Riders spoke quietly while Ash found a sheltered spot to inspect her saddle sores and to pee. A decision was made, and Ark knelt to light the fire whilst Mal began unloading the packhorse. By the time the horses had been brushed and watered, and a makeshift camp raised, the raccoon pieces were crisp and golden. Mal and Ash crouched by the fire, drinking boiled water, as Ark circled the clearing, planting wards every few paces. It was something he hadn't done since the first night in the mountains, and it made Ash afraid.

They ate in silence. Ash chewed and swallowed, but did not taste. She wished she could stop herself from *listening*. Sometimes she thought she heard something, a soft inhalation of breath, like a pause. But she couldn't be sure. No more calls came, and eventually she rested her head on her knees and watched the flames. It was a dark night, she realized. No moonlight or starlight could break through the clouds.

Some time later, Ark touched her head. "Sleep."

Even in the firelight she could see the fatigue on his face. "Only if you will."

His smile was so fleeting she almost missed it. "Perhaps I may. The Naysayer stands watch."

He fetched blankets for both of them, and they settled around the fire. The Naysayer crossed over to the horses, detached their feedbags, and resaddled them in readiness for a quick escape.

Ash felt herself becoming drowsy. She watched as Mal took up position on the rise. His sword glowed as blue as the missing stars, and it made her feel safe. Protected. Closing her eyes she passed into sleep, and dreamed of nothing for a while.

Suddenly she came awake. All was still. The midsection of the moon was showing through a break in the clouds. *Something is wrong*, she thought, but felt no alarm, only a tingling sense of alertness. *They have come.*

Slowly, she drew herself up to a sitting position. Ark lay asleep on the opposite side of the fire, his fully armored body wrapped in furs. Ash looked for Mal Naysayer, but could not see him on the rise. She knew that sometimes in the night the Far Riders would walk wide circuits of the camp, as much to keep their muscles from cramping and their minds alert as to guard against intruders. Peering into the darkness, she strove to find him.

Something moved on the edge of the camp. Moonlight caught an edge and ran along the length of a man's arm.

"Mal," she whispered. "Mal?"

A soft crunching noise broke the stillness. A bough of rotted pine snapped with the force of a blow. Behind her back, one of the horses snorted.

Ash found her weapon and rose to her feet. A cool breeze worked her skin as the blankets and furs fell away. *Seek the flame*, the Naysayer had told her, and she imagined it igniting with a gentle *thuc* in her mind.

In the gloom beneath the pines a shadow stirred. She watched it, fascinated, marveling at how it rippled and gleamed, passing in and out of sight.

"*Maeraith.*" Ark's voice gave the shadow a name. Quick as lightning the Sull warrior was at her side, his furs shed, five feet of meteor steel balanced in his hand

"Behind me," he commanded.

Ash found it hard to take her eyes from the shadow, harder still to move on Ark's word. The thing was revealing itself as the shape of a man. Two red eyes glinted to life, burning mist with an electric crackle. Slowly, and with an immovable sense of purpose, the maeraith's gaze sought Ash March. Ash felt the calmness leave her. She'd learned enough of the Sull tongue to know that *maer* meant shadow, but this thing that stood in the trees beyond the camp was no wraith of air and shade. Its mass occupied space, and when it stepped on a prostrate pine the entire tree shattered like glass.

A queer sound reached her ears, a low humming, almost like the sizzle of lightning searing air.

The thing had drawn a sword.

Naza Thani. Remembering her lessons, Ash stepped back. "Do shadows cast shadows?" she had once asked her foster-father, smiling up at him with a child's guile as she spoke, secure in the knowledge she had stumped him. She had been wrong. "Only in nightmares," he had replied.

Ash felt as if she were in a nightmare now. The maeraith's sword was forged from an absence of light. There was a gleaming around the edge, a bending of moonlight before it was sucked into the blade.

Voided steel.

The thing lurched forward. Ash's gaze rose from the black abyss of its blade to the eerie glow of its lifeless eyes . . . and saw that it had found what it sought. Onward it came, crunching branches and pine needles, moving swiftly and heavily, a thing that could no longer be named a man.

Ark Veinsplitter raised his sword. He was speaking in his own tongue, his voice filled with an emotion she could not name. His face was dark and his teeth were bared, and the letting scars on his neck glowed white.

Meteor steel met voided steel with a shrill screech that hurt her ears. Glittering darkness sprayed from the blades like the opposite of sparks. The Far Rider took a hard breath, and Ash saw his sword arm bend. Shifting his grip on the midnight leather hilt, he made space for his second hand. The thing turned its blade, and suddenly Ash could see the edge; a switching, shimmering insubstance like the space between stars. Watching it, she realized she'd lost the image of the flame. The maeraith had snuffed it.

Swords rang as the blows fell. Ark stepped back, forward, back, falling into the rhythm he called *Ahl Halla*, the Great Game. The maeraith met him blow for blow. It was armored in black iron bossed with cabochons of onyx. Massive and untiring, it gave no ground.

A furious rain of blows forced Ark's sword against his chest. The Sull warrior lost his footing, stumbled . . . and suddenly a gash opened up on his wrist. Blood streamed onto the forest floor. Ark spoke a word, "*Hass*," and Ash knew he was calling to his blood brother in the language of maygi and Sull.

Ark regained his footing, but not his strength. The shadow was relentless, never slackening its attack. If Ark had opened its flesh, it did not bleed. If battle had tired it, it did not slow and make it known. As it forced the Sull warrior to his knees, the diseased pines rustled on the edge of the clearing. A figure emerged from the darkness, every bit as terrible as the maeraith itself.

Mal Naysayer, Son of the Sull and chosen Far Rider, drew

his sword. "*Kall'a maer. Rath'a madi ann'ath Xaras*," Mal whispered. "Come for me, shadows, for I stand ready in the light of the moon."

And the maeraith did, turning from Ark Veinsplitter to the man who stood waiting in a patch of silver radiance.

Afterwards Ash would remember many things about the battle—the way Mal's sword arced and circled and never stopped moving, how his face was grim but his eyes blazed with a savage joy, and how the plates of his horn armor snapped like snakes as he cut into the thing's flesh—but for now she could only wonder that Mal had summoned the shadow, and that the shadow had come.

The Naysayer found a heart where she thought none had existed. He pressed the point of his six-foot longsword against armor older than the clanholds, put the weight of his body upon the cross-guards, and slid his blade into the vast, pumping darkness of the creature's heart.

A howl sounded and the maeraith fell, black liquid spraying from the tear in its plate. Ash felt its wetness burn her face. It wasn't blood and it wasn't warm, yet it tasted familiar all the same.

The Naysayer pressed a foot against the corpse to free his sword. The light had left his eyes, and Ash could see that his hands and neck were cut and weeping blood. Behind his back, at the edge of the tree line, she spied a wolf carcass in the loam. Mal had been away defending the camp.

Ash felt a terrible weakness take her, and the sickle and chain fell from her grip. Ark had been in danger and she had made no move to aid him.

The Naysayer spoke her name. He was breathing hard and his face was blistered with sweat. Gobs of smoking darkness clung to his sword. "Fear is the enemy that will destroy us," he said. "You must always seek the flame."

Ash nodded. She thought of things to say, of how flames weren't always enough to snuff out shadows and how the darkest shadows were cast by the brightest light, but she looked into Mal's eyes and saw that she would only be telling him things he knew. Smiling weakly, she said, "I'll try harder next time."

He looked at her for a long, grim moment, and then turned to tend to his *hass*.

THIRTY-ONE
A Storm Building

The Dog Lord crouched on the Queen's Court at Dhoone and tussled with his dogs. The wolf dog was on its back, trying to nip his fingers, its tail wagging madly, while the others ran in circles, hoping to be picked next. They made Vaylo laugh out loud. Their joy and eagerness lightened his heart. Thirty years ago his rivals had sought to insult him by naming him the Dog Lord, but he'd always thought they'd made a mistake. Dogs were loyal, and fierce in defense of what was theirs, and Vaylo couldn't think of another creature he'd rather be named for.

His joints creaked as he rose to standing. Damn, but the wind was strong. Even in the walled enclosure of the Queen's Court, it snapped back his cloak and set his braids clicking. And the sky! Dark as Blackhail and boiling up a storm. The charged air excited the dogs, for there was something primal about a storm building. It made you feel as if you had nothing to lose.

Vaylo called his dogs to heel, and leashed them. One of the bitches pissed against a dormant rose bush, and then all the rest had to do the same. Vaylo frowned at the pruned stump. Not much chance of *that* one flowering come spring.

It was a queer place, the Queen's Court, not really clannish at all. With its paved walkways, limestone statues and rose bushes it looked as if it had been transported, flowers and all, from Spire Vanis. Well . . . almost. For the statues were half-eaten by birdlime and some of their heads had been knocked off, and since no one had tended this place in over half a year, heather and wild oats had begun to seed amidst the cracks. And as for the little man-made stock pond—Vaylo pitied the fish that wintered there, for some poisonous bright green slime floated on the surface like vomit.

Still. It was an interesting place, built for some long-dead queen by the king who had loved her. Dhoone was strange like that. It had romances, legends. Ancient white-haired scholars in Withy and Wellhouse recorded all the details and the names.

Not so with Bludd. Oh, it had its stories, tales of brave chiefs winning battles and reckless ones losing them. But there was no continuity. Entire centuries had been lost. Even the boast— *We are Clan Bludd, chosen by the Stone Gods to guard their borders. Death is our companion. A hard life long lived is our reward*—had lost its meaning. The Dog Lord wondered about those borders sometimes, wondered about their limits. Did the borders end at Clan Bludd, or did they extend farther, to every last corner of the clanholds?

Vaylo let the wind blow away his misgivings. Too often these days his thoughts were turning inward, when by rights they should have been dealing in the here and now. Clan Bludd was divided, its warriors scattered over the eastern clanholds. Quarro and Gangarric were at the Bluddhouse, sitting as uneasily together as vinegar and oil, and nursing their mutual dislike. Both had crews of Bludd warriors at their command. Quarro's numbers were substantial, and he counted many older veterans in his ranks. Vaylo didn't place high odds on ever being welcomed back there again.

Thrago and Hanro were at Withy, feuding over command of the house. The little clanhold was notoriously vulnerable, and with Skinner Dhoone only four days' ride away at Gnash, and Blackhail-held Ganmiddich even closer, Withy was a sitting duck.

Vaylo puffed out a great breath. His other sons were similarly scattered; Otto had taken the oath at Frees, and gods only knew where Morkir was. Only Pengo was at Dhoone. He commanded a mixed crew of hammermen and spearmen, and had been charged with securing the Dhoonehold.

But the Dog Lord didn't feel secure. He had less men under his direct command than at any other time in his thirty-five-year chiefship. His sons had formed factions and split, taking their forces with them. And now there were two extra houses to secure: Withy and Dhoone. Not to mention the Bludd-sworn border clans, who grew nervous of the Mountain Cities and resentful of Vaylo Bludd.

Vaylo's teeth hurt just to think of it all. Sometimes he wished he'd followed his childhood fancy and become a Maimed Man. Ruling a hole in the earth would surely be easier than ruling a clan.

Barking an order to his dogs, he headed for the gate. The clouds had begun to spit, and Nan would have his guts for bowstrings if he ruined the good cloak she'd made him.

Hunching his shoulders against the wind, he took the sandstone path that circled the roundhouse. The dogs whupped with excitement as the rain began to lash down, and he had to shorten their leashes to control them. Lightning forked over Blue Dhoone Lake and they howled like wolves, unafraid. The great rumble of thunder that followed shook the ground beneath Vaylo's feet, and Vaylo grunted and quickened his pace.

Out of the corner of his eye he saw something move by the nearest gate tower. The wolf dog growled. Vaylo put a hand out to calm him. Now he drew closer he saw that the shape was a man, mounted on a horse. Waiting.

Expect me when the wind blows cold and from the North.

Angus Lok.

Vaylo didn't bother asking himself how the ranger had managed to penetrate their defenses. He was canny, and probably knew the Dhoonehold as well as any Dhoone. And whenever stealth failed him there was always his tongue. Angus Lok had spent eight weeks at the Dog Lord's pleasure, and he had used the time wisely, making friends.

Angus Lok raised a hand in greeting. Unlike most men faced with the prospect of meeting Vaylo's dogs for the first time, the ranger looked relaxed. Even the storm didn't throw him, and he managed to sit his horse as calmly as if it were a mild summer day. Vaylo couldn't imagine how he managed to keep that ridiculous otter-trimmed hat from blowing off.

Feeling he'd been caught at a disadvantage, Vaylo let some of his aggression bleed over into his dogs. He wasn't sure how he did this, just that it had served him well through the years. The wolf dog began to growl again, and soon all of them were fighting the leash.

Vaylo was gratified to see a slight adjustment in the ranger's stance.

"Angus Lok," he cried. "I see freedom agrees with you."

The ranger acknowledged the compliment with a measured bow of his head. "It has its uses."

Unhappy with having to shout above the storm, Vaylo said, "You'd better follow me inside. I'll send a boy to tend your horse."

Inside the Dhoonehouse all was calm. Nan and the other Bluddwives did a good job of keeping the key rooms well lit and comfortable. The blue sandstone walls could be cold to the eye, and they had hung them with tapestries and other fancies. Fires roared in every hearth the Dog Lord might happen to pass, and all corridors leading to the chief's chamber were kept clean of cobwebs and dust. Vaylo handed his cloak to a boy at the door and bade him run it straight to Nan for an airing. Another boy was sent in search of food and malt, and commanded to bring it to his chief at the Dhooneseat.

The walk to the chief's chamber was a brief one, involving the climbing of a single flight of stairs. There were grander places in the roundhouse, chambers where great blocks of cyanide quartz formed altars and platforms for kings, but recent chiefs had lost their taste for them and power had reverted to the chief's chamber once more.

Vaylo liked it well enough. It was comfortable and the isin-glass windows let in light, and the primitive lines of the Dhooneseat pleased him. This was a chair made by men who had never heard of kings.

The Dog Lord chose not to sit in it. Instead he crossed to the fire and leashed the dogs to the rat hooks. Lightning flashed through the chamber as he stirred the embers. When he was ready he turned to look at Angus Lok.

The ranger had made himself comfortable on the wooden chair behind the chief's table. He had shrugged off his outer layers of clothing and was now running a hand through his hair. His copper-green eyes were just as Vaylo remembered them: guarded.

"Have you traveled far?" Vaylo asked him.

The ranger nodded. "That is my fate, it seems."

A moment ticked by in silence, and then Vaylo asked, "Why are you here?"

Before Angus Lok could answer a knock came at the door. Nan herself had brought the food and malt, borne on her best pewter tray. The ranger was off his chair before Vaylo had a chance to react. Walking forward, he took the tray from Nan and thanked her. He inquired of her sister, who Vaylo knew to be ill with lung fever, and complimented Nan on the fine embroidery at the hem and neck of her dress. Vaylo was torn between pride and amazement. Was there no end to the ranger's connections?

Nan was gracious, and slipped quickly away. Vaylo could tell she had been pleased.

The ranger deposited the tray on the chief's table. "Shall I?" he asked, indicating the jug of malt and two wooden thumb cups laid there. Vaylo nodded, and watched as Angus Lok poured the sweet golden liquor Dhoone was known for. They struck cups, and downed their measures in one.

Angus smacked his lips in appreciation. "A pity you don't serve that in your holding cells. A prisoner might never want to leave."

"But you did leave," Vaylo said. "At my pleasure and in my debt."

"I know it, Dog Lord. That is why I have come."

Vaylo did not like the strange lightness in the ranger's voice. "What is it? Is Robbie Dhoone about to pound on my door?"

Angus Lok rested his booted feet on the chief's table. "He might be. Though I imagine he's still a few men short of an invading force . . . unless, of course, Castlemilk has been generous with her manpower."

"He's asked the Milk chief for warriors?"

"That's what I'd do if I were him."

The Dog Lord let that sink in. He'd learned to ignore Angus Lok's assessments at his peril. He said, "Do you have any more intelligence on Robbie Dhoone?"

The ranger shrugged. "Skinner's losing men to him. He's moved out of the Milkhouse and into the broken tower, supposedly to accommodate his greater numbers. His men ride as far south as Ille Glaive on raid sorties, and he's developed a fancy for wearing fisher fur like a king."

Something in the ranger's manner disquieted Vaylo. He took a deep breath. "None of this is the reason why you are here."

It was not a question, and Angus Lok didn't bother to nod. He swung his feet down from the table and said, "An army left Spire Vanis two days ago. They're heading north, to the clans."

Thunder boomed through the chamber, making the flames in the hearth shiver and the dogs jump. Vaylo touched the pouch of powdered Bluddstone at his waist. *Oh gods. And to think I imagined I had troubles enough.* Out loud, he said, "What are their numbers?"

"Eleven thousand. They were assembled in haste. Mercenaries. Grangelords. Hideclads. A mixed bunch."

The Dog Lord nodded, his mind engaged. "Who leads them?"

"Marafice Eye, the one they call the Knife."

That gave Vaylo pause. He had met Marafice Eye, looked into his face and seen a hard man capable of hard things. He had been well respected by his men. "What is the purpose of this army?"

The ranger poured himself another measure of malt. The Dog Lord declined a second cup. "Well, that's the unclear thing. Have you ever heard the legend of the Leper King?"

Vaylo shook his head, impatient.

"Well," Angus Lok continued, unruffled. "The Leper King was a great ruler in the Far South, brilliant and greedy for more land. He set out on a campaign to annex the surrounding states, and he was successful for many years. Then one day he learned he'd contracted leprosy. That was when the campaign became something else. He still fought, but his motives had changed. He blamed the opposing armies for his illness and punished them for it. And he feared that his declining health made him vulnerable to members of his family who sought to overthrow him. So he sent his sons and brothers to fight in the vanguard and then ordered a sudden withdrawal to cut them off." The ranger smiled. "They were all killed. Horribly, I believe. And the Leper King went on to rule his empire for many years."

Vaylo thrust a cube of black curd into his mouth as he thought on this. He didn't like legends. They were all warnings in disguise.

Angus Lok stood and moved toward the fire. "What I'm trying to say is that while Penthero Iss may have planned to take control of the clanholds, his priorities have since shifted."

"I know what you're saying, ranger. I'm not a fool."

The ranger turned to look at him. "I never thought you were."

The Dog Lord tried hard to detect signs of mockery in Angus Lok's face, but could not find any. "So," he said after a moment. "Iss is sending his rivals to war."

Angus nodded. "At least three that I can count. Marafice Eye. Garric Hews. Harald Crieff. Not to mention every grangelord's son old enough to know one end of a sword from another. Spire Vanis is a cold-blooded city. Surlords rarely die of old age."

"So Iss is worried?"

"Living in Mask Fortress, surrounded by statues of slain surlords: It's enough to make anyone consider their mortality."

Vaylo crossed over to his dogs. Although he had been in the same room with them, in plain sight all the while, they strained their leashes to greet him. "You're telling me this army might not be well supported?"

"Exactly. They have fair numbers, but they're not a cohesive force. And they have a long trek north in foul weather. My bet is that Iss will wait and see. If things are looking good—a few roundhouses sacked, riverways taken—he'll keep the supply lines open and bask in all the glory. If things turn soft he'll withdraw his support and leave them high and dry—all the while praying to the spirits of the Bastard Lords that his rivals get slain by you clannish fiends."

Vaylo barked a laugh. Angus Lok was nothing if not succinct. He sobered quickly when he thought on what all this would mean to his border clans. Haddo, HalfBludd, Frees and Gray were all vulnerable. Even Withy. The northern giants were safe, at least for the time being, but that could all change if the campaign was a success. Thinking out loud, he said, "They'll strike Ganmiddich first."

"Why do you say that?"

It was gratifying to have Angus Lok ask a question of *him* for a change. "Because Marafice Eye knows its layout and defenses. He's been there. He came to claim the girl, Asarhia March."

Something happened to the ranger's face when the girl's name was spoken. The guard dropped from his eyes, and Vaylo Bludd saw a pain he recognized there. A moment later Angus Lok's guard was back up, and a question asked to redirect Vaylo's attention.

"Do you think it can be taken?"

Vaylo nodded, though he wasn't yet ready to put the subject of Asarhia March aside. "I heard Marafice Eye ran into trouble in the Bitter Hills. All his men died. Do you know what became of the girl?"

Angus Lok shook his head slowly, in a movement that meant *Don't ask me to speak of it.*

Vaylo knew something of the grief he'd glimpsed briefly in the ranger's eyes so he said no more. He poured two more measures of malt, and placed one in the ranger's hand.

"Will you go to Blackhail with this intelligence?"

"I must warn those at the Crabhouse. My nephew is amongst the Hailsmen who defend it."

"Drey Sevrance?" Vaylo didn't bother to hide the venom in

his voice. A Sevrance had slaughtered his grandchildren. That name would always be damned.

The ranger nodded. "You'd do well to warn Haddo and HalfBludd."

"Aye." But there lay trouble of its own. Once word got out that an army was on the move every Bludd warrior in the round-house would be chafing at the bit to ride south and meet them. Vaylo almost smiled. To think he'd wanted to be Lord of the Clans!

Just at that moment voices sounded at the door. A child's voice cried, "Da!" and another one said, "Da's listening at the door!" A male voice *shush*ed them angrily.

The Dog Lord and the ranger exchanged a glance. The ranger inclined his head toward the door. "Company?" he asked, barely able to keep the smile from his lips.

Annoyed, Vaylo crossed to the door and threw it open. His two grandchildren stood there, grinning up at him, while their father slunk away.

"Pengo!" Vaylo roared. "Get back here!" And then, to his grandchildren: "You two. Over to the hearth. And place your-selves in the custody of my dogs." He tried his best to look stern, but Pasha had him figured out and her grin just got wider. Grabbing her younger brother by the wrist, she dragged him toward the hearth. The collective sound of six dogs groaning very nearly made Vaylo laugh out loud.

Then he was faced with his second son. Pengo's cheeks were so red it was a wonder they didn't steam. His eyes were unre-pentant.

"You'd better come in," Vaylo said.

Pengo snarled. Striding past his father he placed himself in the ranger's view. "Is it true? Is Spire Vanis coming to destroy us?"

Angus glanced at the children who were busy attempting to

tie five dogs' tails into one big knot. When he spoke his voice was very low. "An army has left the city. Yes. Is it a danger to this clanhold? I don't believe so, not in the immediate future."

"Immediate future!" Pengo mocked. "Save your fancy phrases for my father—I have no use for them. An army's heading north, and you say it's not a danger. What would you know of dangers, ranger man? You just ride that fancy horse from one clanhold to another, gossiping with our women, and living off our fare. And I tell you something else—"

"Enough!" cried Vaylo, shaking with fury. "You will be civil to my guest or leave this chamber."

Pengo's lip curled. "Civil to my guest! Gods, he's got you speaking his citified tongue. He's no guest. He's a parasite, feeding off the trouble he stirs. And if he thinks I'm going to sit on my arse and do nothing while an army attacks our Bludd-sworn clans then he's a fool. I'll have a force raised and on the move before he can wipe that knowing little smirk off his face. Spire Vanis won't find Bludd absent from this war." Finished, Pengo snapped around angrily, sending his black braids fanning out from his skull, and strode toward the door.

The Dog Lord thought of halting him, but didn't. As the door slammed he closed his eyes. It was a cruel trick the gods had played, reincarnating Gullit Bludd in the bodies of his grandsons.

Vaylo calmed himself. The children were pale and quiet at the hearth, the dogs forgotten. Sitting himself on the Dhoonechair, he called the bairns to him. He could feel their bodies shaking as he crushed them to his chest.

Angus Lok stayed silent through this. He resumed his seat by the chief's table, and after a time he pulled something brightly colored from his buckskin tunic and began to manipulate it. Glass beads and tiny wooden blocks knocked together with little *chinks*.

Pasha and Ewan raised their heads from their grandfather's chest, curious. Angus continued toying with the thing, a puzzle by the look of it, one of those ingenious playthings they made in the Far South. Without looking up, he said, "You can come and take a look at it if you like."

The children looked at their granda, and their granda nodded. Sliding off the Dhoonechair, they went to investigate. Angus was good with them. He showed them how the puzzle worked, informed them there was no possible way to break it, and then told them they could keep it—but only if they agreed to share. Pasha and Ewan nodded fiercely, already half in love with him, and carried the thing toward the hearth with all the ceremony and gravity of high priests bearing a crown. The giggles started not much later, as the dogs pushed their noses in for a sniff.

"Thank you," Vaylo said simply.

Angus shrugged. "It's nothing, just a bit of wood and tat. I got it for my youngest, but I can pick something else up along the way."

"So you're heading home?"

"After I've stopped off at Ganmiddich, yes." The ranger's copper eyes far-focused for a moment. "It's been a long time."

The two men sat in silence and nodded. Outside the storm was passing overhead and rain beat against the isinglass windows. Lightning flashed, and thunder hit straight afterward like a hammer blast. Absorbed with their new plaything, the bairns barely noticed.

"I'll be heading out," Angus said, rising. "I'll come again in late spring."

They clasped hands. "I'm grateful for the warning," Vaylo told him. "I'll have to keep an eye on that damn son of mine, make sure he doesn't march south with half my men."

Again, Angus Lok was succinct. "Do as you must," he said.

THIRTY-TWO

The Game Room

Raina moved around the Great Hearth, making sure that the returning warriors had hot food and ale. Anwyn Bird had arranged for trays of bannock and blood sausages soaked in heavy gravy to be brought upstairs. Hearty food for weary men. Warriors had returned from Ganmiddich and they were exhausted and soaked to their skins. When the heat of the Great Hearth reached them, their cloaks and furs steamed.

Ballic the Red was amongst them, his stout archer's legs bowed from hours in the saddle, his hands busy setting out arrows and bowstrings at a careful distance from the hearth. They must be dried out, but slowly, else the wood warp and the twine stiffen. He accepted a jug of ale from Raina, taking a moment from his task to smile his thanks.

"Did Drey stay at Ganmiddich?" she asked him.

Ballic grunted. His beard was grown so bushy that you could no longer see his lips. "Aye. He must. He defends it for the Crab chief now."

Raina nodded, wanting to ask more but stopping herself. Mace had been informed that warriors had returned and some were wounded. He would be here any minute.

"It's not as bad as you might think," Ballic said, reading her face. "There's a few skirmishes, usually with crews out of Gnash. But we're holding. Drey Sevrance is seeing to that."

"Did he send word to Effie?"

Ballic looked her straight in the eye. "Doesn't he always?"

Raina felt her stomach squeeze tight. A swift courier had arrived from Dregg two days back, bearing messages from Xander Dregg to the Hail chief. Raina had taken the boy aside and questioned him. No cart bearing Effie Sevrance had ever reached the Dregghouse. Raina had tried to rationalize it—the weather had been bad, Druss Ganlow might have taken a detour—but she was struck with the sense that she should never have sent the girl to Dregg. Effie was gone. Lost. *And I'm responsible. Gods help me when I have to tell Drey.*

"Raina," Ballic said, cutting into her thoughts. "You worry too much."

She smiled at him. Ballic the Red had once spent an entire summer protecting her and Dagro as they rode the length of the clanhold, visiting every farm, village and stovehouse in Blackhail. He had earned the right to scold her.

Just as she was about to scold him back, Mace Blackhail entered the room. She stiffened, feeling her smile collapse despite her best efforts to maintain it. Mace had the ability to single her out in a crowd, and his wolf-yellow gaze swept toward her. *Wife*, he mouthed, and she couldn't tell if it was a greeting or a threat. Her instinct was to run, but she forced herself to turn her back and go about the business of serving ale.

Mace had someone with him, a great beast of a Scarpeman with a hammer on his back. He followed at Mace's heels like a trained dog. Some of the Hailsmen greeted him. Turby Flapp hugged him as if he were a long-lost son. Raina strained to catch his name, but between the roar of the fire and the lashing of the storm she could hear little.

It was late afternoon, and the storm was busy shortening the last remaining hour of daylight. Raina had been busy since dawn, moving livestock and clearing space for shelter. Storms brought hundreds of extra people to the roundhouse, and they all needed food and a place to sleep. The work involved was staggering, and the strain on food stores already run low preyed constantly on her mind. In the past she would have gone to Dagro and they would have discussed the best way to cope. Now she had no one to rely on but herself, and some days it seemed as if the entire responsibility for the running of the clan-hold fell on her.

Mace cared only about Mace. He had let Blackhail become overrun with Scarpes, making their feuds his own. He had actually sent out crews to raid Orrl! Dagro Blackhail would no longer have recognized his clan.

So what are you going to do about it? Raina halted for a moment by the fire, and let the tall flames heat her face. It had seemed so simple while Angus Lok was here: the clan must be rid of its chief. Mace had raped and murdered his way into the chiefship, and he was turning Blackhail into a den for Scarpes. Yet he had stolen Ganmiddich from under the Dog Lord's nose, and taken a pledge of loyalty from its chief. And the latest rumor from the south had it that Bannen was set to turn. Dhoone was doing little to keep its war-sworn clans in line, and Mace was ever one to spot a weakness and use it. He had always been a wolf.

Raina sighed heavily. Truth was, Mace Blackhail won things for his clan.

Studying the ale jug in her hand, she decidedly quite suddenly to pour herself a drink. It was warm and good. Anwyn enriched it with egg and other odd things that Raina didn't know about, and it was almost like drinking a meal.

She watched as her husband spoke with the returning

clansmen. One of the provisions of the treaty struck between Blackhail and Ganmiddich gave Blackhail the right to garrison two hundred men in the Crabhouse for Ganmiddich's protection. That meant crews of Hailsmen were constantly traveling to and from the Crabhold. It was a dangerous run that took them close to the Dhoone stronghold at Gnash, and within sight of Bludd-held Withy. Until recently Dhoone had been an ally in kind to Blackhail, but with the stealing of Dhoone-sworn Ganmiddich all had changed.

Hailsmen making the Ganmiddich run were regularly attacked by Skinner's men. The Dhoonesmen were frustrated, Raina supposed, since their leader had yet to make a move to retake Dhoone. Hailsmen had been slain, and Raina could name every one of them. It fell to her to inform their kin.

As she listened, Ballic told Mace that a crew of Bluddsmen out of Withy had given them chase. Young Stiggie Perch had taken an ax blow to his spine and fallen from his horse. They had not gone back to collect the body.

For a long moment everyone in the Great Hearth was silent. Some men touched their measures of powdered guidestone. Mace Blackhail touched his sword. "Inigar will cut his bones from the guidestone," he said.

Men nodded. It was Blackhail's way.

Orwin Shank entered the room, and rushed to where his youngest living son sat propped against the roundwall. A broken-off arrow shaft jutted from the meat of Bev Shank's upper arm. Laida Moon was tending him. The boy had been wearing ring mail when he was hit, and Raina could see where a portion of the metal had been driven into the wound. Laida was all business, sending Rory Cleet to the forge for wire cutters, and Anwyn Bird to the distillery for hard liquor.

Raina went over and put a hand on Orwin's shoulder. The big, aging hammerman had tears in his eyes. He had lost two sons to the Clan Wars: he could not afford to lose more.

"Come away," she said. "Let Laida do her job."

The tiny, dark-skinned surgeon sent Raina a look of gratitude. Worried fathers only hindered her work.

Gently, Raina guided Orwin toward the fire. It was full dark now and the luntman was lighting the last of the torches. Outside, the storm was raging, and the wind wailed as it hit the roundhouse. To take Orwin's mind off Bev she inquired about his other sons.

"Mull's at Ganmiddich, and Grim's waiting to head out. Bitty—" Orwin shook his head. "He's been sent north to protect the mine. Maimed Men were spotted at the shanty."

As Raina nodded, Bev Shank screamed in pain. Laida Moon had taken possession of the wire cutters, and was now trimming the ring mail around the wound. Raina grabbed Orwin's arm. It was time to take the axman for a walk.

They made it as far as the great double doors before Mace caught up with them. "Wife," he said, halting her. "I don't believe you've met the latest addition to our clan. Mansal Stygo. He's given us his oath for a year."

The massive, black-haired Scarpeman stepped forward and bowed at the waist. The hammer cradled at his back was the size of a child. His gaze traced the curve of Raina's hips and breasts as he straightened his spine. "Lady."

Raina was aware that Mace was watching her closely, and she forced her features to calmness. This man standing before her had murdered a chief, and now he was to become one of the clan? Barely managing to stop herself shuddering, she inclined her head. "You've been here before," she told him, "and trained with Naznarri Drac."

"I'm flattered my lady has heard of me."

The slyness in his voice made Raina bristle. She took a breath, meaning to tell him she knew a lot more than that when she felt Orwin's fingers press hard against her arm. Sobered, she smiled stiffly and said nothing.

"Orwin," Mace said. "I believe you two know each other."

"Aye," Orwin said levelly. "You trained at the same time as my eldest."

Mansal Stygo nodded at the aging red-faced clansman, his eyes cold. The two men stared at each other for longer than was proper; Mansal was the first to look away.

Before anything else could be said, Raina stepped in and informed Mace that she had to take Orwin for a walk—surgeon's orders.

He let her go, but she could feel him watching her as she and Orwin passed through the doorway.

The roundhouse was warm and muggy, crowded with tied clansmen who had taken up places on the stairs. One Scarpeman had ripped a torch from the wall and was using it to brown a chunk of meat. It was a wonder he hadn't set the entire roundhouse alight. Raina thought of reprimanding him, then decided against it. Let Mace deal with his own.

As soon as they were out of earshot of the Great Hearth, Orwin said to her, "You nearly made a grave mistake."

Raina absorbed this for a moment, slowly coming to understand its implications. She glanced at Orwin. He had first made himself a fierce warrior, and then a wealthy man. Dagro had relied upon many clansmen for advice, but none more so than Orwin Shank. Yet Orwin had supported Mace's bid for chiefdom . . . and that made Raina cautious.

As they reached the entrance hall she said to him, "What do you know of Mansal Stygo?"

Orwin stopped to rest for a moment. His hands were swollen with arthritis—the bane of all men who trained with hammer and ax from an early age—and he massaged his enlarged knuckles as he spoke. "I'm not a man for intrigue, Raina, and I have turned my back on many dread things. I tell myself I am old and have no business interfering with the ways of clan. I should look to my sons and my land and be content with my lot. Yet I find myself waking in the middle of the night, stirred by the need for change."

Tiny hairs along the back of Raina's neck lifted. *Easy*, she cautioned herself. *You cannot afford to make a mistake.*

Quickly she glanced around. Entire families were camped in the entrance hall, and dogs and chickens were running lose. One woman was milking a goat. A couple of children had pilfered a head of cabbage and were playing a game of throw. It was too crowded—everywhere was teeming this night. She needed a place that would be quiet, yet she could not take him to her chamber or any other women's place. It would arouse too much suspicion. *Little mice with weasels' tails.*

The only place from which tied clansmen and Scarpes were firmly barred was Anwyn's kitchen. It would have to do. Pitching her voice to carry a fraction farther than normal, Raina said, "Orwin. You must eat. Let me warm you a bowl of sotted oats."

He nodded once. "Lead on."

Raina forced a path through the crowd. Her heart was beating hard, and she felt reckless and powerfully excited. If Mace were to spot her now, just one look at her face and he would know all.

The kitchen was an island of calm. Clanwives had just finished laying out tomorrow's bake, and every flat surface in the chamber was covered with trays of rising bread dough. The beer-keg stench of yeast was overpowering. A bank of vast stone ovens shaped like bells ran long the exterior wall, and a stoker with a long-handed shovel was busy raising the heat. At the sight of Orwin Shank, a fully sworn clansman, no less, clanwives dressed in baker's white rushed to clear a space at the nearest table. Whenever a Blackhail warrior was hungry he was fed.

For appearances Raina accepted a bowl of oats and a jug of ale along with Orwin. They ate in silence for a while, giving the kitchen helpers time to fall back into their routines. Pots needed to be scrubbed and sanded, sheep's blood boiled down for puddings, and onions quartered to season everything from sausages to stew. Out of the corner of her eye Raina spotted pretty Lansa Tanna, her cheeks dusted with flour, fussily chopping carrots. Raina smiled a greeting, but Lansa merely pinched in her mouth. She'd given her loyalty to Mace.

Somehow the snub gave Raina strength. In a low voice she said to Orwin, "Mansal Stygo murdered the Orrl chief in cold blood."

He nodded. "Every hatchetman in the clan knows it. It was one thing while he stayed at Scarpe, but now he's given Mace his oath . . ." Orwin shook his head, letting the thought trail off. He was not at ease in the kitchen, and kept glancing from side to side. Raina wondered if she'd made a mistake.

"Raina! Orwin! I've been looking everywhere for you two." Out of nowhere Anwyn Bird came striding towards them, her long gray braid whipping at her neck. "Raina. Have you forgotten you were to help me take stock in the game room? And you, Orwin Shank. You promised to take a look at the hung mutton—tell me whether its spoiled."

Raina and Orwin exchanged a glance. Anwyn stood before them, hands on hips, her brown eyes challenging them to contradict her. They did what everyone in the clan did when faced with Anwyn Bird: they obeyed her.

The night was growing stranger by the moment, Raina thought, as they filed through the kitchen toward the warren of stockrooms, stillrooms, larders and game rooms that constituted Anwyn's domain. The light level dropped and the heat of the kitchens fell away. No one spoke. They didn't need to. They knew their purpose here.

The game room was kept under lock and key. It hadn't always been that way, but since Scarpes had started inhabiting the roundhouse food had developed a habit of disappearing. Anwyn opened the door and bade them mind the steps. The room had been built belowground, hard against the northern wall. Even in high summer it was cold. Raina took the steps carefully, her breath whitening, and her nose pulling in the strong bloodless scent of aged meat.

The chamber was long and low. A thick woodwork lattice was suspended just below the ceiling, and the meat hung there from iron brain-hooks. Whole, gutted animal carcasses swayed in the ventilating breeze. Sides of beef, black as if they had been burned, lined an entire wall. Pheasants and ptarmigans had been hung from their feet like bats, and hams and flitches of bacon—dipped in honey to encourage mold—had been packed into curing cubbies like brood hens.

At first glance it seemed like a wealth of meat, but Raina could recall the time when the entire fifty-foot length of the room had been packed from floor to rafter with fresh kills. Now only the sides of beef reached back that far, and everything else occupied the first fifteen feet.

Anwyn led them past the carcasses to an old table she used for trussing. She lit a mica safe-lamp, and then went back to close the door. Raina sat on a little milk stool, leaving the only proper chair for Orwin. Anwyn didn't need a seat; the clan matron rarely sat.

An awkward moment passed when no one spoke. Orwin clasped and unclasped his hands, working out the painful stiffness. Anwyn frowned at the table. Looking at them Raina suddenly realized they were waiting for *her* to begin.

She took a breath. "Mace Blackhail is no longer my chief. He ordered the murder of Shor Gormalin and Spynie Orrl. He fills this roundhouse with Scarpes, and turns a blind eye when our tied clansmen are dispossessed of their farms. He is waging war with our staunchest ally, Orrl. And I have come to believe that he had foreknowledge of the attack in the badlands where my husband and your two sons, Orwin, met their deaths."

There. She had done it. She was shaking uncontrollably, but she met Orwin's gaze and then Anwyn's, and she was filled with a sense of her own power. To make things happen you just had to *do* them. Why had it taken her thirty-three years to figure that out?

Orwin looked at her hard and long. Signs of strain were showing in his face, and Raina reminded herself that his youngest son lay in the Great Hearth, badly wounded. "What makes you believe Mace had foreknowledge of the badlands attack?"

It was telling that he had not questioned her statement about Shor Gormalin. The subject of the badlands massacre had to be dealt with carefully. Not until this moment had she dared to speak her thoughts on it out loud. "Remember the day Raif and Drey Sevrance rode home, after everyone thought them dead?" Both Orwin and Anwyn nodded. "Well, I think back on that now and I see things we missed. Remember the first thing Raif Sevrance did? He named Mace a traitor."

Orwin shook his head. "That lad's always been trouble, Raina."

"He drew a guide circle for your sons, Orwin. He and Drey took care of the dead."

The axman sighed. "Aye. I know it. He's a decent lad, but headstrong. Impulsive."

Raina was quick to agree. "Yes, Orwin, he *is* decent. No matter what is said about him he stood up in that stovehouse at Duffs and went to fight with his clansmen."

"Many don't see it like that."

"Then many should learn to think for themselves." Realizing

she had strayed too far from her subject, Raina started again. "Orwin. Raif Sevrance said things that day that directly contradicted Mace's version of events. *He* said the attack took place at noon, not dawn as Mace insisted, and that he and Drey saw no sign of Clan Bludd. And remember how Mace gave that touching speech, about finding Dagro's body by the horse posts. Raif Sevrance swore that he and Drey found Dagro by the meat rack, and that Dagro had been butchering a carcass when the raiders came."

Orwin looked unconvinced.

But Raina wasn't done. "Who benefited from that raid, Orwin? Mace Blackhail or Raif Sevrance? Who rode back on a chief's horse and named himself a chief?"

The axman had no answer for that, and Raina let the silence last. You couldn't force a man to believe in something. He had to arrive at it himself.

At last Orwin nodded, slowly, reluctantly, and Raina knew she had wounded him deeply. To lose two sons to Clan Bludd was a terrible thing, but there was honor in it. To lose two sons to some scheme of a would-be chief held no honor at all.

From somewhere Anwyn produced a small glazed jar of her special malt. She had been quiet all this time, but watching her pull three tiny cups from a knitted bag she wore at her waist, Raina wondered if Anwyn Bird hadn't been the instigator all along. Malt and *three* cups? Had she been the one who told Orwin the truth about Shor's death? She was certainly close with Angus Lok; he had brought her a gift, Raina recalled.

Anwyn Bird's twenty-year malt was a thing to be savored. It tasted like summer smoke. Raina raised the cup to her face and inhaled—the fumes alone were enough to make you giddy. The last time she had drunk it had been on the day Mace Blackhail had stood Chief's Watch. The twenty-year malt was always a marker of change.

Raina set down her cup. Small, coin-sized holes had been drilled into the game room's exterior wall for ventilation—you could not age meat without moving air—and she could hear rain trickling outside as the storm used itself up. It was time to get to the point.

"If we make a move who will be with us?"

"This cannot be done quickly, Raina," Orwin said. "It could take many months, even years."

This was not what she wanted to hear. "Will the hammermen follow us?"

"They must be given time. Yes, they have their doubts about Mace—he tried to put a hammerman's sister to the fire—but a war is being fought and hammermen are men of war." Orwin placed his elbows on the table and leant forward. "The moment's not right, Raina. Mace might have many faults, but he's proven himself a warlord. Give him time. Let him fail."

Reluctantly, Raina nodded. Dagro had valued this man's advice, and she was beginning to understand why. He was right. In times of war men were less discriminating about their leaders. They needed someone strong, little more. She let out a deep breath. Was this how they were meant to leave it? With a simple "wait and see"?

Then Anwyn spoke. She was looking at her cup, tracing a finger around its rim. "If we are to be serious about treason we need a chief. Someone we can rally to when the time is right, someone to take Mace's place."

Raina felt a roaring in her ears. She said, "Orwin?"

He was already shaking his head. "Nay, Raina. I'm too old and irresponsible for chiefdom."

She searched her mind. Shor Gormalin should have been chief, but Shor Gormalin was dead. "Corbie Meese? Ballic the Red? Drey?"

"All good men," Orwin agreed. "Fine warriors. In time Drey

Sevrance may grow what it takes to make a chief, but he's too young for now."

Then who?

They were waiting, both of them. And Raina couldn't believe what they wanted. It was madness, total madness. The roaring in her ears was so deafening she could barely think.

But she *could* speak, and she said what she had to. "I will be chief."

THIRTY-THREE

A Walk on the Edge

The storm had slowed them. They were five days out of the Rift, but the last two had been little more than a struggle against driving wind and ice. Raif tried not to look south, tried not to imagine how the exact same storm would play out in the clanholds. How there would be rain instead of ice, and flashes of brilliant lightning instead of the oppressive sameness of a sky the color of lead.

Tempers had flared, and already the small party had fallen into two camps: Linden Moodie's and Stillborn's. Yustaffa was the wild card, moving between the two with all the glee of a matchmaker in reverse. Raif watched him now—a fat man on a little horse—as he pushed past Addie Gunn to get to Moodie. Moodie had assumed the lead—another fight there—and Yustaffa had taken it upon himself to inform the leader of his followers's dissent.

Raif heard the words, ". . . *And you'll never believe what Stillborn said . . .*" quickly followed by, "*Addie Gunn swore you'd have us lost by midday . . .*" before turning his thoughts elsewhere.

They were traveling along the rim of a canyon in single file. The storm had scaled everything with frost, and even the dead bushes on the canyon floor glittered like crystal. The way was slippery, but Raif was used to that, and he kept a short rein on his pony. It was hard to accept he was heading west. In all his mad fantasies about returning to Blackhail, he had never imagined this.

Lowering his head against the wind, Raif thrust the thought aside and rode on. He had chosen a position at the rear, only to have Linden Moodie order him forward. It was almost certain that Traggis Mole had charged Moodie with keeping an eye on Raif Twelve Kill, and just as certain that Moodie was relishing the job.

They were a small party, eleven in all and three extra horses. Raif didn't know all the men. He was glad Addie and Stillborn were along, but he was less sure about the olive-skinned outlander, the one who had revealed the bridge that spanned the Rift. The man didn't look much like a fighter, more like a priest. He kept to himself, and did not eat the meat Stillborn cooked at the campfire each night.

Raif slowed to guide his mount over a bank of scree, making sure that it was stable before giving the pony its head. The wind funneled through the canyon, raising spirals of ice and dust. The storm had died out in the night, but it had left the land ravaged and the air curiously unsettled. Even though they were not at altitude, Raif's ears ached with the changing pressure.

He was focused so intently on guiding the pony across the scree that he didn't notice at first that Moodie had called a halt. Only when the pony's hooves rang out on hard rock did he risk looking up. Linden Moodie and Yustaffa had dismounted farther along the path. Moodie had flung back his heavy scarlet cloak trimmed with fox fur and was crouched on the ground, inspecting something. As Raif drew closer he realized why the two Maimed Men had stopped. A giant gash in the rock blocked the way ahead.

Raif slid off the back of his pony and went to join them. The fissure ran all the way down to the canyon floor forty feet below, and Raif could smell the newness of it; the stench of burned rock and exposed roots. The walls of the fissure were dark and jeweled with minerals, in stark contrast to the surrounding rock that had been weathered to a dull gray.

Yustaffa sighed with barely contained relish. He was dressed in a tunic made up of bands of alternating rodent fur. Raif recognized the pelts of lemmings, meadow voles and giant hispid rats all layered into stripes. Yustaffa had paired this with glazed leather pantaloons bloused into his boots, and a cloak of dyed and shaved shearling. As the rest of the party drew abreast, he tutted and shook his head. "I *knew* we should have turned north at Grass Gorge!"

Everyone ignored him. Air rising from the fissure stirred hair and beards. On the other side of the gash, Raif could clearly see the path rising along the canyon wall and continuing west.

"This was not here last time I took this path," Moodie said stubbornly.

"And when might that have been?" Stillborn asked, coming to stand beside Raif. "Last I heard you prefer staying closer to home."

Moodie flashed Stillborn a dark look. "It wasn't here a month ago, I tell you."

"He's right."

Everyone turned to look at the man who'd spoken. The olive-skinned outlander stepped forward. He was dressed in loose robes of drab green, covered by a plain gray cloak. The cold had turned the skin on his face ashy, and his left eye had blood in it. "It's not Linden's fault," he continued, calmly. "This crack has just opened."

Stillborn raised his eyebrows. "And who made you an expert?"

For some reason the outlander looked at Raif as he replied, "You don't need to be an expert to know that the earth is warping. Something down there is forcing its way out."

The Maimed Men shifted uncomfortably. Addie Gunn took a withered apple from his pack and bit into it. Stillborn wandered back toward the scree bank, looking for an alternate path. The outlander continued to stare at Raif. After a few seconds Raif decided he'd had enough, and went to check his pony's mouth. As he ran a finger between the pony's bit and its gums, feeling for sores, he sensed the outlander still watching him.

A heated argument soon started up about the best way to circumvent the gash. Yustaffa suggested they should try and jump it—with Linden Moodie going first. Moodie's plan was for them to descend to the canyon floor and follow it west. Not many in the party liked that idea. The canyon wall was steep granite mounded with scree. A fall could break a man's leg. Someone else suggested they climb toward the headland, but even Raif could see there was no feasible ascent and the idea was quickly abandoned.

Addie Gunn ate his apple and said nothing. When he was done he fed the core to his pony. Voices had been raised by then, and Linden Moodie's garrote scar had flushed red. "We're going down!" he cried. "And gods damn the lot of you!"

Heated protests followed, and in the middle of it all Addie spoke a word. "Gentlemen."

The Maimed Men turned to look at him, and he waited patiently, his hand on his pony's nose, until they fell silent to a man.

"An hour back we passed a goat trail that led northwest. Follow it and I'd say we'll make the headland afore dark." His hand slid around his pony's nose strap. "Come on, girl. Time we were heading back."

The Maimed Men stared at him, half indignant and half relieved. No one doubted him: Addie Gunn was a cragsman, and canyon country was filled with crags. Stillborn was the first to follow him, leading his stout little pony through the tight circle on the ledge. Seeing the other men in the party ready to abandon him, Linden Moodie hastily ordered a turnabout.

As Raif led his pony back across the scree, he found himself thinking about Addie Gunn. The cragsman had established a place here, amongst these men. They respected him for what he knew. Raif had been on two expeditions with him and both times men had deferred to his judgment. It seemed incredible to think it, but Addie had been treated better by the Maimed Men than he had been by his own clansmen. Raif frowned, not liking what that said about clan.

"I see you've caught the interest of our failed priest," Yustaffa said, breaking into his thoughts. The fat man was back on his horse, riding directly behind Raif. When Raif made no reply he explained himself. "The outlander, Thomas Argola—I saw him watching you before. A tiresome man, but useful, very useful. Of course, the others can't abide him. Can't think why. He hardly eats but two beans a day, and would rather die than pick a fight."

Raif put his foot in the stirrup and mounted his pony. "Why is he here, then?"

"Good question." Yustaffa trotted his pony ahead of Raif's. The entire party was back on the path now, and Addie Gunn was leading the way east. "He does have a few tricks up his sleeve. Confusion to the enemy and all that."

"He's a magic-user?"

"Not a very good one." Yustaffa sniffed. "It half kills him to reveal the bridge. He's not fit to stand in a Mangali shaman's shadow. One of *them* in your party and you can trot right up to a strong room, whip your drawers off and steal everything in sight before anyone knows you're there."

A gust of wind blew out Yustaffa's shearling cloak, and Raif caught sight of the sword breaker strapped to the fat man's thigh. He said, testing, "Why would he be watching me?"

Yustaffa's laughter was high and tinkling. "Raif Twelve Kill, dear boy. He's watching you for the same reason Traggis Mole is watching you. Because things have a nasty habit of happening around you, and someone usually ends up dead." Still laughing Yustaffa rode on.

Raif pulled on his reins, falling back. He'd asked for that . . . but it didn't make hearing it any easier.

Deciding it was better not to think, he hunkered down in the saddle and continued falling back until he reached the rear. Linden Moodie was breathing down Addie's neck, waiting impatiently to resume the lead. He didn't notice that Raif was keeping company with the packhorses.

The day wore on. They found Addie's goat path and followed it up toward the headland. Whatever force had caused the gash in the canyon wall had sent rocks tumbling into unstable piles and opened up hairline cracks in the earth. Addie had an eye for the dangers, and would signal a slowdown from time to time when everyone would dismount and lead their ponies.

By the time they reached the headland it was growing dark. Addie wanted to halt and make camp, but Moodie wouldn't hear of it. "We have to be at the mine by black of the moon — that's when they shift the gold. Now the weather's calmed some we need to make up for lost time."

No one argued with him. A half-moon had risen, but the cloud cover was too thick to let through much light. The headland was flat, swept clean by hard winds, and the ground underfoot was little more than rock. Hairy weeds grew in the leeward shelter of boulders, and every now and then Raif would catch the eyeshine of tundra foxes.

Slowly, the desire to hunt grew in him. It had been half a

year since he'd last tracked game by night, and he found himself searching out targets. Things besides foxes lived here; small creatures with rapidly beating hearts. Mice. Voles. Nothing worth loosing an arrow for, yet he tracked them anyway. Something inside him needed to.

"Unless you plan on flinging that arrow at Linden Moodie, I'd slip it back in your pack." It was Stillborn, riding abreast of him, and it took Raif a moment to understand what he meant.

There *was* an arrow in his fist, but Raif had no recollection of drawing it from his pack. Feeling foolish, he shoved it back in the bow case mounted on his saddle horn.

"Dark night," Stillborn said. "Moodie's taking us pretty close to the edge."

Raif hadn't noticed. He'd been looking north at the flat stretch of tundra, not south at the rim. Following Stillborn's gaze he saw that the goat path had wound back toward the canyon, and they were descending once again. Addie called a slowdown when they hit the first patch of loose stone.

"Shall we?" Stillborn asked Raif, and they both dismounted.

Ahead, Moodie and the cragsman were exchanging words. Addie wanted to raise camp—the going was becoming too dangerous for night travel—but Moodie wouldn't hear of it. Raif didn't agree with Moodie's urgency, but he understood it. Behind Moodie's impatience lay fear of Traggis Mole.

In the end it was decided to continue at a slower pace on foot. Raif and Stillborn kept to the rear, walking side by side. Stillborn produced a silver flask from the tanned elkskin slung over his shoulder and took a swig. "You best be careful when we reach the mine," he said. "You're a Maimed Man now."

So even Stillborn was giving him warnings. Raif found he had nothing to say to him, and they fell into silence.

Gradually the path began to wind down from the headland, and within an hour they were back against the canyon wall with the black drop below them. Loose rocks littered the way, and Raif spent much of his time watching his footing. He could feel the canyon's updrafts on the underside of his chin, and fear kept him alert.

Most of the party had cleared the scree bank when the rocks began to slide. Raif felt a puff of air on his cheek and heard the deep thunder-rumble of grinding earth. The rocks mounded against the canyon wall jerked forward violently, and Raif found himself scrambling for footing amid rolling scree. Directly ahead, the packhorses bucked in terror. They were tethered in line and if one of them went over the drop, it would drag the others along with it.

Raif fought furiously against the momentum of the sliding rocks. A stone struck his spine with the force of a punch, knocking the wind from his lungs. Something pounded his knee, and suddenly he was struggling to stay upright. The pony's halter reeled through his fingers, leaving him clutching air.

A thud sounded from behind as Stillborn was knocked from his feet. Raif thrust out his free hand toward him, but found nothing. Then the force of the slide yanked him down and around and suddenly Stillborn's fingers poked hard against the center of Raif's palm. Raif closed his fist, catching them.

Immediately Raif felt his entire body jerk forward as Stillborn went over the edge. Hot pain sent his vision flashing red and white as his arm wrenched against its socket. The slide was slowing, but the weight of Stillborn's body sent Raif hurtling toward the edge. Desperate, he thrust his heels down into the scree, searching for a foothold. He kicked and kicked. And then his right toe felt a lip of rock that didn't move.

As his arm was sucked over the edge, he dug his heel into the depression in the bedrock. He came to a wrenching halt. His jaw was clamped so tightly he could feel the pressure on the roots of his teeth. His arm was shaking violently, and the muscles in his side and shoulder were popped out and close to tearing. Below him he could just make out the top of Stillborn's head. Swinging in the black.

"Help me up," Stillborn cried.

Raif felt drunk on pain. He had only a few more seconds of this before they both went over. Unclenching his jaw took real effort. "Stillborn. I want my arrow back."

A disbelieving croak came from below.

Raif's right leg—the one that braced both their weights—began to tremble. Absurdly, he found himself filled with a madman's calm. "The arrow—Divining Rod. Do you yield it?"

"I yield," Stillborn screamed. "Now get me out of here."

It was all pain and no calm after that. Linden Moodie and Addie Gunn scrambled over the unstable scree to help hoist Stillborn back onto the ledge. Raif was shaking uncontrollably by the time they finally hauled him to safety. Moodie left Raif where he'd fallen, and that seemed fine to Raif. The clouds had thinned and he could see the moon. When Stillborn had been helped across the scree Moodie came back for him.

He offered Raif his hand. "Come on, lad. You'd better get up." His voice was gruff, but there was something in it that had not been there before. A kind of grudging respect. "You held onto that big bastard for dear life. It's a wonder you didn't split in two."

"It feels like I have." Raif tried for dignity as he came to his legs, but his knees were having none of it and he swayed like a drunken man. Moodie clamped his arm around him, and together they walked across the scree.

A makeshift camp had been raised on the ledge. Torches had been lit and a fire was burning, with meat hung above it. They had no tents; the Maimed Men simply formed a circle of bedrolls around the fire each night. The seal on a keg of mead had been broken, and the Maimed Men cheered and raised their drinking horns as Raif stumbled toward the camp.

Stillborn had already told the tale of the negotiation for the arrow, and somehow that raised Raif's reputation with the Maimed Men. He had saved Stillborn—and struck a bargain to boot! A Rift Brother couldn't hope for a better outcome. They welcomed him into the fire circle and thrust a horn filled with thick black mead into his hands. Dignity failed Raif again when he tried to drink it, and half of the fermented honey ended up running down the front of his tunic. His hands were shaking badly, and he couldn't taste anything but rock dust.

He sat on a pile of horse blankets and concentrated on not passing out. Yustaffa had produced a stringboard from somewhere and was plucking at chords as he experimented with the opening lines of a new song. *"The canyon was black and the night was chill, and when the rocks began to slide so did Twelve Kill."*

Raif didn't think it sounded too bad at all—which was a sure sign he was no longer sane. Blinking, he held the horn on his lap. Addie came and slapped him on his shoulder, told him that even a cragsman could have done no better when it came to riding the rock slide. Others came and said things and went away. Time passed and the celebration went on, and the Maimed Men got roaring drunk.

Most of them. At some point Raif became aware that the outlander Thomas Argola had slid into place next to him. Things had quieted down by then, and men were dozing or eating, or gaming in small groups. Occasionally someone would propose a toast to Raif or Stillborn, and the Maimed Men would rouse themselves to grunt their support. The outlander waited until everyone's attention had strayed from Raif before speaking.

"You know why the rocks slid?" he asked. Raif tentatively tested his neck muscles by a shake of the head. "They're coming out. The Taken. Already some of the strongest have forced themselves through the cracks. Pressure is building . . . and something must give. Soon. The Endlords will send out one of their servants. Shatan Maer, the most powerful creature that ever lived. The Shatan alone have the strength to blast a hole in the Blindwall. And one stirs this night, I can feel it."

Raif floated above his fear. He said, "Are you one of them? The Phage?"

"I have had dealings with them."

It was not a direct answer, but Raif let it pass. He was still floating. "When will this happen?"

"I do not know."

"And you don't know where, either?"

"No. The place where the earth's crust is thinnest."

Raif heard himself make a sound like a hard laugh. "Why tell me, then?"

The outlander shifted his position so that he was looking straight at Raif. His left eye was full of blood. "Because you're the one who can halt it."

"Though a stronghold may fall and darkness ride through the gate/He will forsake."

The outlander shook his head, puzzled at what Raif had said. For some reason this pleased Raif. It meant the Phage didn't know everything. Clan had its sources too.

"So you can offer me no help," he said, hearing the heat in his voice and realizing he was no longer floating. The outlander had brought him to ground.

A moment passed. Someone threw a pile of bird bones on the fire, and the outlander watched the black smoke rise. "Remember the bridge, how it is revealed?" Raif nodded, and the outlander continued speaking in his softly accented voice. "The bridge itself is crude? Yes. Most people who see it for the first time are disappointed. They make the mistake of assuming the secret lies in the bridge itself. It does not. It lies in the strip of space that connects the clanholds to the Rift. Build anything there and it will lapse into unseeing. That is the nature of the Old Ones' power. Things constructed by their mages live on.

"The Want and the Rift are littered with their ruins. Some we can see, and some are concealed. When you search for the place where the Shatan Maer will emerge you must look hard, and then look again."

Raif was suddenly weary. The muscles in his back and shoulder were aching, and it seemed as if the outlander had told him nothing useful at all, just laid another weight upon him. Sorcerers and holy men had a way of doing that to him, he'd noticed.

Massaging his shoulder, he said, "Why tell me about the Old Ones now? It's the breach that needs finding, not some long-forgotten ruin."

All around the camp men were making preparations to sleep. Torches were snuffed, ale dregs emptied from horns, and blankets bunched into pillows. Yustaffa began plucking a lullaby from his strings.

The outlander stood to leave. "The Old Ones were not that different from you and I. They knew terror. We send bodies to the Rift, seeking to block it. They built a city there, hoping to do the same. Look to their ruins to guide you to the place they most feared."

Raif watched him cross the camp, and then laid down on his blanket and slept.

THIRTY-FOUR

At the Sign of the Blind Crow

Crope was hungry and his feet were sore. He'd tried to sell his boots for coin, but the shrill, big-breasted bidwife he'd approached had just pointed at his feet and laughed at him. "I'd have more chance selling milk to a dairymaid than selling boots the size of those." Her sharp gaze had moved a fraction to the left. "But I'll give you two coppers for the dog. I can have it sold to a pie house within the hour."

Town Dog made into pie! It didn't bear thinking about, and it very nearly made Crope never want to eat pie again. That was three days back, though, and right about now the prospect of *any* kind of pie made his mouth water so violently he had to swallow.

Trouble was, there was no foraging to be done in a city. You couldn't steal from any of the street vendors, because the magistrate might catch and 'prison you. Any place where there were scraps to be had was violently defended by men and women who had declared that particular cranny their territory and were prepared to kill for it. Even Town Dog was having trouble with the cats. They were mean here. Skinny as squirrels and not a bit afraid of dogs.

Shuddering with feeling, Crope pulled the chicken cloak over his head and continued his circuit of Mask Fortress. A light drizzle had started, and he worried about his boots shrinking. It was difficult to set his mind to studying the fortress for a while, but he concentrated hard and by the time he'd passed the second gate he'd forgotten everything else.

The light surrounding the fortress was queer and silvery; there was rain but also sun. You could see a lot of details that weren't normally revealed. For the first time Crope spied a guard station set three storeys above the gate. Last time he'd looked he'd just seen a stone grille and had assumed it was some kind of vent. But now, with the late afternoon sun striking the gate tower just so, he could see flashes of movement behind the grille. That meant that although the gate was secured and patrolled by red cloaks at ground level, someone above was on lookout.

It wasn't good news. Days were passing and he still hadn't found a way in.

Mask Fortress was zealously guarded. Every wagon was checked—some of them stripped down to the bare beds—every load of soft goods was spiked with spears, every barrel was tapped to confirm fullness, and every unknown applicant at the gate was subjected to vigorous examination. The lord who ruled here lived in fear.

Crope rested his weight on his birch staff for a moment. He had not imagined his journey to his lord could be so easily halted. He had carefully considered running through the gate when the portcullis was raised to admit wagons. The gate was patrolled by units of four men, one of whom stayed permanently in the guard station to control the movement of the portcullis. That meant three men would likely chase him. Three men with spears and swords. It was worrying and there were risks, but he reckoned he had a fair chance of making it past them. The trouble would come when the alarm was raised. And now, seeing that the gate was watched by a second station, that alarm would come earlier than he'd thought.

Slowly, methodically, Crope ran the movements through his head one more time . . . but nothing new occurred to him. He needed to gain entry without attracting the attention of the guards. Bitterbean would have said it was time for stealth.

Frowning, he headed west toward the pointy tower where his lord was being held. Rainwater sluicing from the fortress walls made the grease shine on the streets. Town Dog halted to drink from a puddle, and Crope paused until she was done. The streets grew quieter as they headed away from the gate. They passed a deserted courtyard ornamented with oversize statues of knights. Pigeons flocked under the knight's stone skirts, sheltering from the rain. Town Dog was up for chasing them, but Crope called her to heel.

Something was happening to his chest. The closer he drew to the pointy tower, the harder his ribcage squeezed. He had come here every day since entering the city, trying to make contact with his lord.

The tower was pale, and so high that the upper storeys disappeared into the rainclouds. Its stonework smoked like frozen meat, as if it were high above the snowline on the mountain, not here at its base. Crope rubbed his palm on his buckskin pants before touching it. As his fingers neared the icy limestone he felt the tower's pull, an attracting force like a magnet. The smoothly polished stone sucked the heat from his skin, and his instinct was to snatch back his hand, but he pressed harder instead, his fingertips slowly whitening. The cold he could live with, but not the silence.

Time passed, and the sun sank below the city walls and a

gray dusk set in. Crope's fingers grew numb, and he pushed harder and harder, trying to force his way in.

Nothing.

Then, just as he pulled his fingertips away, there was a faint stirring, a reaching-out.

. . . *Come to me* . . .

The words sounded within Crope's bones, and they were no longer a command. They were a plea. His lord's voice was powerless, nearly gone. *Chicken-headed fool. Are you going to let him die?* Crope slammed his fist into the tower. Limestone fractured with a puff of dust, and Town Dog hunkered down in fright.

Crope stepped back. There was blood on his knuckles and his fingers were beginning to swell. He needed to think. *Think.* Force would do no good here. He was strong but he could not bring down a tower. This was no way to save his lord. Then how? He was not Bitterbean with his clever tricks or Scurvy Pine with his way of making men do as he wished. He was giant man, good for breaking walls and mending pumps.

And severing chains. *You be ready when I give the word.* Crope blinked as something occurred to him. Perhaps there was someone in the city who could lend a hand. A plan forming in his head, Crope turned his back on the tower.

Soon, he promised his lord silently. *Soon.*

It was full dark by the time he left the wide roads and dressed stone of the Fortress Quarter. Night came quickly to Spire Vanis, bringing with it a shock of cold that caused the rain to thicken into sleet. Crope passed men and women huddled warmly in thick woolens and furs. Some had purchased roasted chestnuts or fat, grill-split sausages from the street vendors, but Crope tried not to think about that. Brazier men had set up their grill irons on every street corner, and the glow of hot coals and the aroma of sizzling fat drew circles of people around them.

Business was being conducted. Crope saw silver coins flash from one man's hand to another's, and then smallgoods returned in exchange. On one busy street a troop of mummers had set up a makeshift stage, and were performing a masque that involved saying the word "bottom" a lot. Swalhabi was not amongst them. Swalhabi would never deign to perform in a street. Crope felt sympathy with the mummers dressed as girls. It was a cold night to be wearing so little.

He was putting it off, he knew, tarrying to watch the mummers, and he scolded himself for his cowardice. What was his fear, compared to the misery of his lord? Nothing, that was what it was, and he set his jaw forward and moved on.

Trouble was, Crope didn't know exactly what he was looking for. Not just any alehouse or inn would do. He needed to find one that looked right, but he was hard pressed to say what that meant. Certainly not the place across from the mummers' stage, for some of the people entering wore silky furs the color of honey and toast and he knew such things only came with wealth. No. He needed a lesser place, somewhere where the patrons didn't stand outside supping clear ale from pewter tankards while young boys bearing torches warmed them.

He headed further north. Town Dog trotted off every so often, drawn by the irresistible scent of rat. Crope had been wandering the city for several days but he had never strayed far from the fortress until now, and this part of the city was unknown to him. The streets grew shabbier, and fewer people set lamps in their windows. The brazier men were still out selling sausages, but when they cut them with their big knives you could see they were nearly all fat. Men gambled beneath makeshift rawhide shelters, and women dressed as scantily as the mummers shivered in doorways and called out to passers-by.

Crope kept an eye on the alehouses, interpreting the signs above their doors. A hammer and block meant that farriers and blacksmiths drank there. Scissors and a spool of thread meant tailors. Crossed swords could mean two things; either weapon makers or mercenaries. He passed establishments for chandlers, mercers, goldsmiths, grocers, and surgeons—the finest sign yet, a man whose leg had been hacked off at the knee with an ax—when he came upon a sign he didn't immediately understand. It was a magpie with a blindfold covering its eyes. The Sign of the Blind Crow.

Crope stopped to study it. He was in a street that was quiet and very dark. The few men that walked here kept their collars up and their heads down. No one lingered. A dead cat was floating in a pool of runoff, its paws and tail burned.

Birds were something Crope knew quite a bit about. He had spent hours watching them in the poorhouse courtyard as a boy, and much later his lord had lent him books filled with wondrous drawings of every living thing. He could name every bird he saw or heard; he knew their habits, their plumage, their calls . . . and he knew magpies loved to steal. They could not pass by anything shiny without thinking *This would look fine in my nest.*

Crope frowned in concentration. A blindfolded man could not see. If the blindfolded magpie was really a thief, then he was a thief who could tell no tales.

Heaving a great sigh of relief that his brain had actually worked for a change, Crope scooped up Town Dog and headed for the inn door. This was exactly the kind of place he'd been looking for.

Inside it was dark and cool, and Crope felt his good humor slide away, to be replaced by the usual fear: How would these people react to him? He shrank himself, and tried not to think about what had happened the last time he'd set foot in a tavern.

The room was quiet, and lit by only two baleen lamps. A fire stood against the far wall, but a heavy iron guard suppressed the light. Half-walls divided the room into small sections, creating private nooks where men sat head-to-head and spoke in low voices. A few people turned their heads at Crope's entrance, but after a brief assessment of him they returned to their business. Relief flooded through Crope as he realized they weren't interested in him one bit. A counter consisting of varnished pine boards topped with hammered copper was set to the side of the fire, and Crope made his way toward it.

As he settled himself in place, Town Dog squirmed free of Crope's tunic and landed with a thump on the floor. She'd got a whiff of another dog behind one of the half-walls and was off to pay her respects.

"Bitter night," said the man standing beside the counter, by way of greeting. Stocky, with a big belly and a thick neck, he looked like a pit fighter gone to seed. Crope saw interest in his eyes, but no fear. "What's your fare?"

Crope shook his head, anxious not to have a drink poured that he could not pay for.

The pit fighter accepted this with a mild shrug, refilling his own tankard of ale from a glazed jug on the counter. "What's your business, then?"

The question was lightly asked, but there was an edge to it that meant *Do not waste my time.* Crope felt his heartbeat quicken. What if he had made a mistake? The pit fighter folded his arms over his chest, making muscles the size of possums spring to life.

Crope bent and slid a hand down the side of his diamond boot. There, in the place where the leather had separated from the lining, was the thing he needed. Straightening up, he placed the object on the counter and said, "Friend of Scurvy Pine."

Tendons in the pit fighter's neck twitched at the mention of Scurvy's name. Watching Crope closely, he reached for the ring. It was made from the white metal that was rarer than silver, and was as fine and delicate as a lock of hair. Words circled the inner band, but Crope had never learned what they said. The pit fighter held it toward the baleen light to inspect it. His lips moved as he read the words.

Abruptly he put it down, and slid it back toward Crope. "Where did you get this? And don't lie to me. I won't take a lie."

Crope was already desperately shaking his head. "No lie. Was given in the diamond mines. Scurvy gave it. Was told to keep it. *Keep it.* Use when I had need."

The pit fighter raised a hand. "Calm down, calm down now, big man. No one's calling you a liar. You've got the scars of a diamond miner, that's for sure." And then, to a man sitting in the shadows at one of the nooks, "Quill. Over here. You need to hear this."

Crope felt close to panic—speaking with strangers always did that to him. But this was getting worse. The man emerging from the shadows looked mean, there were no two ways about it. He had little eyes and a hooked-down mouth, and he commanded the biggest dog Crope had ever seen. The dog followed the man as he walked to the counter, and Town Dog followed the dog.

"Quill, this gentleman here's a friend of Scurvy's. Met him in the mines."

Quill's eyes narrowed to quarter-moons. He smelled of cellars and beeswax and dog. His hair was dark and greasy and his clothes weren't much better than rags, but he wore a gold earpiece and several fine rings.

The pit fighter nodded at Crope. "Show him the ring."

Crope slid the ring toward Quill, and as he inspected it the pit fighter told him what had been said. After an appraisal worthy of a master jeweler, Quill put down the ring and faced Crope.

"So are the rumors true?" he asked sharply. "Did Scurvy Pine escape?"

Crope nodded.

"When?"

This one was harder. To answer, Crope thought back to how the weather had been the day they broke free of the mine. "Midwinter."

"You came straight here?" Crope nodded. "Is Scurvy with you?"

Crope shook his head.

That made Quill pause and think. After a moment his gaze strayed back toward the ring. "Do you know what this is?" he asked, barely waiting for Crope to shake his head. "It's the ring Scurvy took from the finger of his dead child. Katherine, her name was. Used to call her Kat. And the man who raped and killed her never imagined he was signing the death sentence of his entire family and each and every one of his associates. It was the worst bloodbath the city of Trance Vor has ever known, and it was the reason they sent Scurvy to the mines." Quill took up the ring again, and leaned over the counter toward Crope. "So what I'd like to know is: Why would he give it to you?"

Crope looked down at his feet. Shifting his staff between his hands, he said in a soft voice, "I broke the chains."

"Scurvy's chains?"

Crope nodded. "Shared chains for ten years."

Quill and the pit fighter exchanged a glance. "So you're telling me you were in the mines with Scurvy for ten years, and you're the one responsible for his escape?"

"Helped." Crope could not forget about Hadda the Crone. Hadda had sung the song that brought the darkness.

"Broadie," Quill said to the pit fighter. "You'd better bring this man 'ere some food and ale. We'll be sitting at my table for a while."

"Aye, guv." Broadie went swiftly about his business, apparently well satisfied that matters had been settled.

Quill held out his arm to Crope. "I'm Quillan Moxley, and my dog 'ere is Big Mox. Any friend of Scurvy's is a friend of mine."

Crope took the man's arm and clasped it, careful not to grip too hard. Quill didn't smile and he still looked mean, but the meanness was no longer directed toward Crope. And that suited Crope just fine.

Quill led the way back to his table, and they sat in silence as they waited for Broadie to bring the food. Town Dog and Big Mox, having sniffed each others' rears at some length, trotted off to tour the room as Broadie returned with a tray bearing bread, cheese, cured sausage and a jug of ale. Crope tried hard not to stare, but something must have given him away for Quill said, "Go on. Eat your fill. We don't wait on ceremony at the Sign of the Blind Crow."

Crope ate. It was the best, most delicious meal he had ever had. He had forgotten the way cheese clung to your teeth when you bit into it, and the way the crust on fresh bread crunched into flakes. Quill sat back on his hard wooden chair, keeping his counsel until Crope was done. Occasionally the inn door would open and Quill would turn his head a fraction and assess whoever walked in.

When the last of the sausage disappeared down Crope's throat, he said, "So. What can I do for you?"

Those were the very words Crope had hoped to hear when he'd remembered Scurvy's ring, but now that he was face-to-face with a man who could help him he was unable to find the words. He could not speak of his lord.

Quill looked at him thoughtfully, the gold rings on his fingers glittering as he rubbed a hand across his jaw. "I can find you a place to sleep, probably set you up in a tavern or a coarsehouse, keeping order. You'd certainly put a damper on the fights. But I've got a feeling you want something else. Am I right?"

Miserable, Crope nodded. What he wanted was so fantastic that he might as well ask for a flying pig.

"Say it," Quill insisted. "I'm a man of various means."

Crope took a big breath. *Come to me . . .* In all the years Crope had known his lord he had never heard him beg until today. "Need to break into the fortress. Need to save my lord."

Quill's eyebrows lifted, and a light of interest entered his cool gray eyes. "That's a new one. So. If I understand you rightly you need to enter the fortress and rescue your master who is being held there?"

Crope nodded. He was relieved at how quickly Quill understood him.

"This lord of yours. Do you know if he's been held below the Cask or under the quad?"

Puzzled Crope said, "Below the pointy tower, the white one."

"The Splinter." Quill considered this information for a moment. "Someone once told me there was a deep chasm beneath there that housed a chamber lined with iron—I took an ear from him for his perjury. Seems I may have been hasty."

Crope nodded. Hasty he understood.

Quill leant forward. "I can't help you gain entry to the Splinter—that's been locked down and sealed shut for years—but I can help you get inside the fortress."

"How?" Crope's heart was beating very fast in anticipation of a grand scheme. In a way Quill reminded him of his lord; both were clever and capable men.

Yet when Quill spoke Crope was puzzled, not amazed, for Quill said very simply, "You're going to walk right in."

Crope listened as the thief explained.

THIRTY-FIVE

Harlequins

Effie was growing pretty accustomed to the wagon. It was beginning to feel as if she'd lived here her whole life. Dregg had begun to seem like one of those places in bairns' tales: somewhere you dreamed of but never got to go. And the thing was, she wasn't sorry one bit. This life of camping and traveling and waiting for the men who should have picked up the gold half a month back had become her, Effie Sevrance's life. She had things she was responsible for: feeding and brushing down the horses, warming the ale, cooking all food that didn't involve meat—roasting game was Clewis Reed's territory—keeping the wagonbed clean, doctoring any cuts or grazes, and sometimes even acting as lookout for the gold men.

Neither Clewis Reed nor Druss Ganlow had spent much time around children, Effie guessed, for they didn't treat her like adults usually treated a child. She was given no special consideration, not fussed over at all, and that was something she'd grown very much to like. They barked orders at her in the exact same voices they used for each other. She was a member of the crew now.

As she scrubbed the black stuff from the base of the cooking pot, she checked on the positions of Clewis Reed and Druss

Ganlow. Druss was doing man's business behind a bush close to the river cliff—she could just see the top of his head—and Clewis was a quarter-league farther to the north, walking the tree line, keeping watch.

They'd been camping these past few days amongst the slate crags and fire pines of western Ganmiddich, holing up for the storm. The storm had been quite splendid, Effie decided. So much better when you were out in the middle of it, with only the tree canopies and a stretch of canvas to cover you, than in a roundhouse, all protected by stone. She'd been scared at first, but the inside of the wagon was so snug, like a cave, that it had already started to feel like home, and after a while the fear had slipped away of its own accord. As long as she was inside nothing could hurt her.

Lightning had brought down a tree. The shell was still smoking beyond the tree line, sending up a line of black smoke that rose vertically in the calm air. Even though the storm had passed two days earlier, Druss and Clewis had so far judged the going too soft for the wagon. Even now, runoff was still spilling down toward the river, the water stained brown with tannin from the trees.

The river itself was moving swift and high, its waters the color of mud. Somewhere upstream a saturated bank must have collapsed, for huge chunks of earth and whole trees complete with root balls sped by from time to time. The river made Druss and Clewis frown: it was the cause of all their problems and the reason they had to wait here in the borderlands, unable to return home.

Effie had learned the truth of everything pretty soon after she'd discovered the gold. Druss Ganlow had been against telling her at first, but Clewis had pointed out in his slow, rational way that now Effie had seen the gold with her own two eyes they could either murder or enlighten her. And since he, Clewis Reed, could not allow the murdering of a child in circumstances such as these, that meant they might as well tell Effie enough to ease her mind.

Druss Ganlow hadn't liked this one bit. After inventing several new combinations of curse words, he had made Effie swear a dire oath. *I will not mention the gold to any other person, alive or dead, even if tortured with blades and hot coals, and I vow to take this knowledge to my grave. I do swear this on the lives of Drey and Raina, and the souls of Mother and Da.* He had even taken a spoonful of her blood.

The gold, it turned out, had been mined from Blackhail's own Black Hole. Two years earlier the miners had been reworking one of the oldest seams, a full league beneath the balds, at the head of a tunnel called Dark Maiden. For weeks they had been finding crystals of yellow metal fused to the silver in the wall of quartz they were breaking. They were just flakes at first, a scattering of specks, but then the Lode Master ordered a collapse. When the miners reentered Dark Maiden after the water blast they thought they'd stepped into another world. Gold, a reef of it three feet wide, stippled the newly exposed quartz.

The Lode Master had called a meeting. The miners were already operating a stone mill and a furnace without Blackhail's knowledge, and it was a simple thing for them to refine the gold. Clan need never know. As Druss Ganlow had already been in business with the miners, carting contraband silver south to the city holds, he was the man they called upon to turn the excess gold into goods.

Two years later and the reef had still not run its course. All the tied miners had stashes of gold. A few had drifted south to spend it, but most simply hoarded it in cache holes in the shanty. The miners were cautious men, Clewis said, and their faces showed something close to relief whenever he and Druss turned up to unburden them of the newly poured rods.

Druss and Clewis were due back there in twelve days, but it did not look as if they would make it. The city traders who took the gold from them in return for goods and money on account in Ille Glaive had failed to make the appointed meeting, and now Druss and Clewis were stuck. The gold men had not come, and there was little to do but wait and see.

The Wolf River had been running high for fifteen days. Just when it had looked set to fall the storm had hit, and now it was high again. None of the river crossings were open, and the barges were all beached. Bannen's Bridge of Boats, which Effie had learned to her disappointment was little more than a collection of skiffs and punts roped into a line with boards run across them, had not been afloat in a month. The gold men had been unable to make the crossing into the clanholds.

It was all very worrying. Clewis Reed insisted they moved camp every few days for caution's sake, for a wagon bearing nine stone of gold was a sitting duck.

When Effie had first heard Druss mention the weight she had been impressed. Anwyn Bird had weighed Effie last year on her meat scales and had pronounced her just over four stone. That meant there was enough gold in the wagon to make two of her. She'd been disappointed when she'd finally seen it laid out. Just twenty-four rods the thickness of tapered candles and half their length. That was all the gold it took to make two Effie Sevrances.

The other things in the baskets were just lading. There was some raw ore, its lode of silver still entombed in chunks of quartz, a few sacks of powdered antimony used for making hellfire, and a dozen bars of lead. These were mostly diversions, Clewis said. They gave the gold something to hide behind.

Done with scrubbing the breakfast pot, Effie stood. Her knees had gotten stiff after being so long on the damp earth and they made noises like cracked knuckles as they locked into place. Druss was done with his man's business and was now poking the ground with a long stick. Every so often he would squint downriver and then look up at the sky. The day seemed fine to Effie: the grasses and ferns freshly scrubbed by the storm, the sky covered by the kind of high clouds that seldom meant rain, and the grounded ducks clashing noisily. Only the harlequins entered the water. The berserkers of the river birds.

After a time Druss appeared to reach a decision and headed back toward the wagon. Effie heard him give a high-pitched whistle to summon Clewis from the trees.

Quickly, she gathered up the breakfast things and the ground tarp and hauled them to the back of the wagon. Then she returned and set her attention to the fire. Should she put it out or shouldn't she? Would they be traveling downriver or staying put?

Druss told her nothing, but it didn't look good. Fresh mud had splashed over the crown of his boots. "Fed the horses their mash yet?" he snapped.

She nodded. No one was going to catch Effie Sevrance not doing her fair share.

"And the scrape on Boe's heel?"

"Done." It had been a keen disappointment to learn that the two matched ponies who pulled the cart weren't named Killer and Outlaw after all, but rather Jigger and Boe.

Druss Ganlow grunted. He tried to think of some other way to catch her slacking, but couldn't come up with one, and settled on grunting some more. The damp air had turned his hair into pale wisps, and he reminded Effie of a plump and disgruntled baby. His skin was smooth and he had fat-apple cheeks, and if it hadn't been for his sharp green eyes his expression might have been jovial. He hailed Clewis as the Orrlsman approached, and walked forward a few paces to meet him.

"Any trouble?" he asked.

Clewis Reed shook his head. He had his green antler bow in his fist and was wearing the long, narrow Orrl cloak that somehow drew its color from the sky and surrounding landscape. Today it looked a sort of pale dove-gray. Which was funny, because when Effie'd first seen it in Blackhail she could have sworn it was almost white. He said, "Are we off, then?"

"Mud's bad. The rain flushed out the last of the snow."

"We've been here four days. That's too long, especially with a fire burning to mark our place."

Druss nodded reluctantly. He always deferred to the Orrlsman on matters of safety. "We'll give it a go. See how the road lies."

Effie found her hand had gone to her lore as the men spoke. The little chunk of granite had shifted against her chest. It didn't feel like a bad thing, not a warning exactly, more an affirmation of what Clewis said. Best to be on the road. Away. Quickly she looked at the stand of fire pines that marked the forest border, knowing as she did so that a man more experienced than her had just been doing the very same thing and had pronounced it safe. She saw nothing, and forced her mind to other things. The fire needed to be snuffed.

They worked as a team to get the wagon ready and the horses hitched. When Effie had completed her tasks she found she had a few spare minutes outside while Druss secured the load and Clewis Reed stretched a line of damp arrows beneath the canvas to dry. Careful not to stray too far from the wagon, she circled the perimeter of the camp, kicking up mud, squashing down hot ashes and horsepats: concealing signs of their occupation. It was just a precaution, she told herself. Nothing more.

When the wagon finally shuddered into motion an entire flock of wood ducks took off in fright. Watching them through the canvas flap, Effie took their flight as a sign. You knew you'd been somewhere too long when the ducks had mistaken your wagon for a landmark and were shocked when it started to move.

The going was slow. Runoff had turned the road into mud. The wagon would lurch forward, rock to a halt as the mud sucked at the wheels, roll back a bit and then move forward once more as Druss cracked his whip.

Clewis had chosen to sit up front with Druss on the driver's seat, his braced bow lying across both men's laps. He was worried about his arrows, Effie could tell. In stormy weather the damp got into them no matter what you did to protect them, and a damp arrow had to be dried delicately. Clewis said it was better to shoot with a damp arrow than with one that had been warped by too much heat. Damp meant loss of power. Warped meant loss of accuracy. It wasn't a hard choice. The bow was different, he explained: that was waxed and glazed.

Effie had thought about this for a moment, and then asked, "Why don't you wax your arrow shafts, then?"

Clewis had looked at her for a very long time, his old dignified face perfectly still, and then had replied in a pondering voice, "Do you know, I don't believe anyone's thought of that before."

Effie had been stupidly pleased. She grinned now, just thinking about it, letting her imagination spin out a life where she passed from swordsman to hammerman, from woodsman to stone mason, from pig farmer to head cook, making insightful observations on their crafts. Effie the Wise. Effie of the Keen Eye. Deep Horse-Sense Effie. *That* made her giggle out loud, and she had a picture of herself wearing a horse's head and wandering from clan to clan. Perhaps Anwyn could make her one, once she told the clan matron how to vastly improve the texture of her bannock and brown buns.

Once she'd started giggling she couldn't stop. Anwyn would

kill her. The hammerman would kill her. She'd have to be Effie of the Fleet Foot before she even *thought* of being wise.

As she hugged her sore stomach, her lore jumped. It was such a deliberate movement, an actual moving away from her skin and then a dropping back, that it made a knocking sound as it hit her breastbone.

Effie felt her skin tighten all at once. She stood, and then was immediately thrown back into her seat by the wagon lurching to a halt. As she stood a second time she felt the wagon list as its front wheels sank deep into the mud.

"Clewis!" she cried. *"Clewis!"*

He turned to look at her through the break in the canvas behind the driver's seat. "Everything's fine, Effie. We're just stuck in the mud."

She shook her head at him. "No. *No.*"

Druss spun around. "Effie. Stop your jabbering. There's work to be done here." With that, he pushed himself off from the driver's seat and landed in the mud.

Clewis Reed looked at her a long moment, his pale eyes making a judgment. After a few seconds he nodded once, gravely, terribly, and then went to join Druss to inspect the damage.

Effie dashed to the back of the wagon to check the trees. They'd only traveled a few leagues, and the terrain had not changed much. The tree line had crept nearer to the river bank, and the river cliffs were lower and had broken down into flaky banks of slate. She looked hard but could see no movement in the trees.

Unable to bear it any longer, Effie pushed the wagon flap open and stepped out.

Clewis and Druss were standing by the right front wheel. Druss was looking down, hands on hips, shaking his head. The wheel had sunk a full foot and a half into the mud. Clewis was not looking at the wheel. His gaze was on the trees. He held his long, elegant bow in his left hand, his bracing hand, and there was tension in his callused fingers. There was an arrow in his right fist, and his arrow case was mounted high on his back, level with his left shoulder, so that the flights of his arrows brushed against his silvery hair. *Ease of draw.* Effie had grown up around enough bowmen to know that.

Without looking at her, he said, "Effie, we're going to need plenty of rocks to sink into the mud above the wheel. Why don't you head down the cliff to the water's edge and collect some? The best slate's to be had there."

"Water's edge!" Druss exclaimed. "There's rocks enough on top."

"Then fetch them," Clewis replied with absolute calm. "Effie has her task. You have yours."

Druss Ganlow's green eyes looked from Clewis to Effie and back, picking up the thread of tension between them. Effie saw him take in the exact same things as she had done seconds earlier: Clewis's fingers, his arrow, his bow.

Abruptly, he nodded. "We'll be out of here in a quarter. Don't stray too far, girl. I want you back the minute you're called."

Effie held his green-eyed gaze for half a moment, nodded, and then he was gone. She saw him draw his longknife as he walked away.

"Go on, Effie," Clewis said to her when Druss was out of earshot. "Go and pick some slate and watch the harlequins. If you keep your head very low and stay very still they'll come to you. Remember that. Low and still."

Effie's throat began to ache. Both of them: one man she hadn't liked very much and one she suddenly realized she cared for deeply were making sure she was safe. She couldn't speak, knew she didn't dare speak. Clewis Reed was from a different age. His beard, his hair, the style of his cloak were unchanged from the time of the River Wars. He was a man of dignity. And she suddenly knew what she must do.

She bowed to him, inclining her head and neck from a point in her upper spine. Like the maidens of Clan Orrl.

As Clewis watched her a quiet sadness passed over his face. He bowed back to her deeply, from the waist. "Lady."

She turned then. If she had not she would have failed him. And she did not want to fail Clewis Reed. She wanted very much to be worthy of him.

The climb down to the river passed in a blur. Effie's body worked independently of her mind, her feet choosing ledges of their own accord and her hands dutifully following. Even as she reached the water's edge and the first frothy wave lapped across the bridge of her boot, she heard the unmistakable thunder of hooves.

Druss shouted something. One of the wagon horses, either Jigger or Boe, whinnied nervously and pulled against his hitch. Effie strained to hear more, cursing the river for its noise. Her stupid body was shaking uncontrollably. Spray gusted over her in a wet slap, instantly soaking her cloak and dress. The drumming of hooves had altered its pattern, changing from a unified gallop into many separate beats. Effie saw what was happening in her mind's eye: the raiders had broken free of the trees and reached the river strand, and were now spreading wide to flank the wagon. Clewis would be standing there, close to the sunken wheel, his bow drawn, choosing his target.

He is calm, for a bowman must always be calm. His arrows are damp, and this means that he must delay release of the string. He waits for the perfect moment. *Thuc.* One of the raiders down. That makes some of the raiders rein in their mounts. They had not counted on a master bowman. Even as they reevaluate the old man by the wagon, Clewis picks off another member of their company. This angers the head raider, a pale-skinned man with a half-moon ax.

With cold, pale eyes he watches as Clewis picks another target, waits until Clewis's gaze and attention are fully focused upon that one man, before galloping forward with breathtaking speed and chopping off Clewis's head.

Blood, so much blood, pumping more powerfully than the river. The pale man with the half-moon ax smirks, even as he and his horse are sprayed with blood. He makes the mistake of letting his ax rest, for he cannot see behind the wagon where Druss Ganlow waits with his longknife. Just as the pale man had chosen his moment, Druss Ganlow chooses his. The pale man turns his horse to hail his company and accept their accolades—and that is when Druss Ganlow strikes.

Even from here Effie hears his call.

BLACKHAIL!

The pale man reads the danger in the eyes of his companions, but he is too late. The knife slides in, through the ribs, through the left lung, through the diaphragm to the spleen. The pale man twists in the saddle, gasping, surprised. He is a Dhoonesman, Effie realizes quite suddenly. And Druss looks at him and smiles.

"We are Blackhail, first amongst clans. And we will not cower and we will not hide. And we will have our revenge."

Those are Druss's last words, and as the remaining company of Dhoonesmen descend upon him and cut him apart, Effie thinks, *I must live to tell his tale to my clan.*

So she clings to the rocks and bears witness, and the river that should feel cold warms her as the harlequins speed by.

THIRTY-SIX

The Racklands

"Today we enter the Racklands," Ark had said as they broke camp that morning, yet as the day wore on Ash could detect little change in the forest. It was *alive* here, that much she knew, for she'd heard streams bubbling and loons calling, and the deep-belly groans of blue bears. Somehow over the past seven days the Deadwoods had turned into livewoods, and Ash was inclined to believe that their life had a lot to do with their distance from the Want.

Snow was still on the ground here, a crisp white blanket littered with pine needles and cones. When the horses' hooves cracked it, they punched perfect holes that held their edge. Overhead the sky was a brilliant late-winter blue. A horned moon showed low in the south, so pale that you had to look for it. The sun was up and rising, its warmth nearly undetectable by Ash but sufficient to coax the sharp scent of resin from the pines.

It was, Ash thought, the most beautiful day she could remember since passing through the clanholds with Raif.

Raif. She had no sense of him, she realized with a small shock. No sense that he was out there, living any sort of life.

Breathing deeply, she filled her lungs with cold, sparkling

air, held it for a moment, and then let it and Raif go. She was Sull now.

As the morning wore on the forest floor began to rise. Ash spotted a stand of silver firs on a ridgetop, giant trees as tall as thirty men, with their boughs spreading as wide as buildings. Other trees began to appear—blue spruce and lacebark pine and white hemlock—and gradually the colors of the forest changed from browns and greens to cool silvery blues. When a needle creek cut across their path, Ark and Mal dismounted. Both men stripped off their heavy gloves, knelt on the creek bank and splashed water over their faces. *We're here*, Ash thought, sensing some shift in their beings that she could put no name to. *We're in land held by the Sull.*

She jumped from her horse and led it to drink. The earth felt solid beneath her booted feet. The creek carried a little breeze with it, and Ash let it lift the hair from her shoulders and cool the riding blisters on her palms. Below her, the water ran so perfectly clear that she could count the rocks on the creekbed. It was good to be here.

The creek was only a few feet wide, and Ash was suddenly determined to jump it. So she did just that, taking a little run and landing in the hackled snow on the other side. The horses looked at her as if she were mad. Ark Veinsplitter frowned, maintaining his dignity. Mal Naysayer put a foot to the stirrup, mounted the blue and, after trotting the stallion back a few paces, he jumped the creek on horseback. He didn't once crack a smile, but there was crinkling around his ice-blue eyes.

Turning to look at his *hass*, he said, "There is no shame in wading if you are afraid."

Ash pushed her lips together to stop herself from giggling. Ark stood on the far bank and frowned at them. Unhurriedly, he turned to Ash's white and slapped it firmly on the rump, directing the horse across the creek. He did the same with his gray, and then—bunching his great wolverine cloak in his fists until it was raised as high as the tops of his boots—he waded solemnly across the creek.

"My feet are much cooled," was the only thing he said to them before mounting his horse.

He made them ride like fiends to catch up with him.

Ash's jaw ached from grinning by the time they slowed. She was out of breath—and the less she thought about her saddle sores the better—but she was perfectly content. These were her men. And she would ride with them forever if they would let her.

Yet she had made no move to help Ark when he'd been driven to his knees by the maeraith. Ash glanced at Ark's left wrist, and felt her good spirits float away. He had not yet pulled his gloves back on, and the bandage showed. She had wound it herself this morning, boiling strips torn from her linen shift to use as dressing. The strips had been spotless five hours ago, but now there was a dark stain on the cloth over the cut. She worried about that. The Naysayer had taken some gashes, but they were shallow and the skin was already knitting together as it healed. Ark had taken a cut to the head of his ulna where it met his wrist. Bone had been exposed. Ark shrugged it off. His hand was stiff but he used it. If there had been a loss of articulation he covered it. Yet he couldn't cover the dark fluid leaking from the unhealed cut, and Mal Naysayer couldn't cover the fact that he had refused to stitch it. Ash knew of only two reasons why a surgeon would not close a wound—infection, or bone fragments lodged in the flesh—and neither eased her mind.

Yet Ark's spirits seemed good, especially since they had crossed the border into the Racklands. Ash thought of asking him about the wound, but decided to wait until later. She didn't want to break the mood.

Pulling alongside him, she asked, "Will we see Sull settlements soon?"

He shook his head. "We travel the northern forests, and some amongst us make homes along the Greenwater and Innerway to the north, and others still live in remote places we will not pass, but no Sull lives in this land. We claim and defend it, but others who are not wholly Sull make homes here."

Hearing the censure in his voice, she said, "Trenchlanders?"

"It is so." He held his head perfectly level and continued to look straight ahead. She thought he wouldn't say any more, but after a moment he continued. "In a few days we will pass into the lowlands they are named for. The earth is soft there, and the river clan name the Flow has changed its course many times. All the ancient course changes may still be read in the land, and from Hell's Town one may look upon them. Some hold they look like trenches."

Somehow this offended Ark's pride, but Ash wasn't sure why. She made an adjustment to the reins to guide the white around a thick hump of rootwood poking through the snow. "What do *you* think they look like?"

"The Sull named the lowlands *Glor Arakii*, Land of Changing Rivers."

Here it was, the source of his pride. The Sull had named the land one thing, yet the Trenchlanders had moved in and named it something else. "And the Flow?"

Ark sat his horse stiffly. "The Sull named it *Kith Masaeri*, River of Many Ways."

They had names for all the lands they'd passed through between here and the Storm Margin, she realized. It had all been theirs, the entire Northern Territories, and now they had only the Racklands left. She didn't understand how they had lost so much. Everyone in the city holds and clanholds feared them. She had seen with her own eyes how fiercely they fought, how they had knowledge and equipment superior to that of any other people in the North. Their horses, their swords, their very strength and stamina were unmatched. Yet somehow they had been losing ground for centuries—longer, even. Thousands upon thousands of years.

Ash looked up. The sun had fallen below the tree canopy, but the sky was still a deep, cloudless blue. On a rise in the distance she could see a break in the forest, a thick tract of burned stumps and charred tree skeletons that stretched beyond the horizon. She had so many questions for Ark Veinsplitter and Mal Naysayer it was hard to know where to start.

Nodding her head toward the tract of scorched land, she asked, "What happened there?"

Ark did not follow her gaze, but said in a harsh voice, "Trenchlanders burn the forest. It is their way. Their hunters set fires to flush game. If they are lucky the wind aids them, and the animals flee toward their spears. If they are unlucky the wind forms a storm and the fire escapes their control. Tens of thousands of trees and animals are destroyed. Hunters die. Only the cindermen profit, for it is their task to walk the smoking earth and claim carcasses." His nostrils flared in anger. "Often beneath a charred pelt the meat is good."

Ash shuddered. "Why do you put up with them on your land?"

At last Ark turned to look at her, his sable eyes hard. "Because they are Sull, part of them. We share ties of history and blood. And even one drop of Trenchlander blood is worth more than a sea of clan or city blood."

They fell into silence as the low boughs of a silver fir forced them to duck. Ash felt ice-cold needles tickle the back of her neck. Mal had ridden on ahead while they were speaking, drawing his bow from the marten-fur case slung over the blue's rump. He braced it now as Ash watched, and then pulled an arrow from a hard-sided cylinder attached to his gear belt. Turning in the saddle, he raised the arrow in signal to his *hass*. He was off to hunt.

"Are the Trenchlands dangerous?" Ash asked, her eyes following the Naysayer's blue as it effortlessly accelerated to a gallop, its hooves churning up clouds of snow.

"Daughter," Ark Veinsplitter said, cutting into her thoughts. "Every land we walk in is unsafe."

The day cooled quickly as the sun began to set. Ash heard unfamiliar animal calls coming from deep within the forest. The trees creaked, and sometimes vibrations from the horses' hooves made them shed their loads of snow. Ark seemed to be heading for a particular place to camp, for he had ceased following Mal's path and had taken a sharp turn north between two massive paired spruce. After a short climb they crested a ridge and the trees began to thin. Ash caught a glimpse of standing water, and then Ark led the way into a clearing and called a halt.

Lacebark pines, their trunks a patchwork of flaking silver and gray bark, ringed a gently sloping glade. The snow had shrunk back into islands, exposing patches of velvety moss and dark ferns. Tiny plants with leaves like needles had forced their heads through the snow; most were in bud, but a few had opened to reveal violet flowers shaped like stars. Ash's gaze was drawn toward the far side of the clearing where a length of broken wall, not much higher than her waist, rose starkly from the snow.

Ark dismounted, and walked toward the wall. The light was fading quickly now, and the snow was glowing blue. The Sull warrior raised his arm, in readiness to touch the stone. He had his back toward Ash so she couldn't see his face, but for a moment his shoulders were very still. Muscles in his neck moved as he spoke a word. Ash thought he might open a vein, but his silver letting knife remained at his waist, its chain glimmering softly as he breathed.

He turned abruptly and walked back, and soon they were busy stripping branches for the fire and raising the corral for the horses. The Naysayer returned not much later, leading the blue. An eviscerated whitetail-deer fawn was laid over the horse's back. When Ark came forward to help with the quartering, Mal crossed over to the broken wall.

Watching them, Ash made a decision, and before both Far Riders could get their hands bloody with the butchering, she said, "The wards, that night in the Deadwoods. Why did they fail?"

Ark and the Naysayer exchanged a glance. Ash knew her voice had been a bit too loud, but she pressed her lips together and stuck by her question, looking from man to man. They owed her answers. And she was going to get some. Pointedly, she sat on a rug by the fire and waited.

They left the deer carcass in the snow and drew near the fire. Ark crouched on the opposite side of the fire, but the Naysayer chose to stand.

"Ash March," Ark said, reaching beneath his cloak. "No fail-safe exists to ward against the creatures of the Blind. When the maeraith broke the circle I awakened. This Sull gives thanks to the First Gods for that." He pulled out the cloth pouch that held the wards, and handed it above the flames to Ash.

As she took the pouch, Ash caught another glimpse of Ark's bandaged wrist. The stain had spread, separating into rings of color that bled from black to red.

The pouch was made of soft shammy, and was surprisingly heavy. When she emptied the contents onto the rug she was disappointed to see little chips of gray rock run through with white veins. They felt like rock, too, rough and inert. Ark watched her turn them in her hand, hold them to her ear, and rub them together like flints before he finally spoke.

"All the pieces come from the same wellstone. A maygi

shattered it, and when the pieces are separated the memory of their wholeness remains. Yet they are stone and cannot move. Place them at a distance from each other and you may feel their attraction."

Ash took the two biggest pieces and placed one to either side of her, then passed her hand through the space separating them. Something, a faint tingling like the beginning of numbness, traveled across her palm . . . and then was gone. It was so tenuous a sensation that she doubted she'd really felt anything at all, and tried it again. This time, even though she knew what to expect, she barely registered the weak prickle along her skin. She looked at Ark. "Do you feel this, when the space is broken?"

He shook his head. "Only when I complete a circle with the stones."

Ash looked from Ark to the Naysayer as she gathered the fragments and emptied them back into the bag. They had revealed one of their secrets, but she wondered quite suddenly if it had been a distraction, to lure her away from all the others. Abruptly, she let the bag drop. "What happened to the body of the maeraith? It was there when I finally slept, but it had disappeared when I awoke."

Again, the Far Riders exchanged that glance. Ash had seen the stain the thing's body had left on the frost, the outline of itself drawn in mottled black, and the deep trench burned by its sword. Ark said, "The Naysayer dragged the remains away to a place where it would not disturb you. When a creature of shadow is slain its flesh is consumed by flames. Shadowflesh burns cold, one cell at a time, from the inside out. The flames consume the interior, but never the shell, the skin. After *maer dan* is burned the outer shell fades over time. Every sunrise robs substance from it until it becomes nothing more a shadow on the earth."

"And the sword?"

Ark's eyes showed surprise.

"I saw the trench," Ash insisted. "The voided steel burned a foot of earth."

It was the Naysayer who answered her. "Voided steel is forged from an absence of matter and light. Its potency continues after its wielder is slain. It burns through the earth, sinking deep like gold in a furnace. How long it continues sinking before its power fades is something this Sull does not know. I took the sword from the soft earth it had fallen on and set it to rest on a saddle of hard rock. This Sull cannot do more than that."

Ash found she had to look away from Mal Naysayer's ice-blue eyes. There was something she hadn't seen before within them, and it unsettled her. He didn't possess the infallible strength and knowledge her imagination had bestowed upon him. He had limits . . . and he knew it. Both the Far Riders were vulnerable, and she wished with all her heart that they were not.

They had done so much for her. Mal surely hadn't slept that night in the Deadwoods. He had stood watch, slain the maeraith, and then dragged away the body so she wouldn't have to look upon it when she awoke. And Ark. Ark had been the one who had asked Mal to do it. *Take it from this place, hass,* she could hear him say. *Our daughter has been through enough this night.*

Ash looked beyond the Far Riders to the clearing. It was full dark now, and the stars were out, silvering the trees and the edges of the standing wall. A snowy owl was proclaiming its territory with a deep three-note call. *Who-who-who.* She had a choice here, she decided. She could leave the subject of the maeraith, or she could force them to tell her more. There was something about being here, this first night in the Racklands, that had freed the Far Riders from normal constraints. She did not know if this would last, so she hardened herself against her feelings and spoke.

"What killed the maeraith? I saw it take many blows from Ark without slowing . . . and yet . . ."

"The Naysayer put steel through its heart," Ark finished for her. "Only that will halt them."

Oh gods. Raif. Ash could still see him, that night in the Copper Hills. Three Bluddsmen heart-killed. And then there was the day she had first set eyes upon him, outside Vaingate. Four brothers-in-the-watch slain with arrows to their hearts. She felt her own heart racing as she thought on it. How calm he had been, how it seemed as if he had been born for it. Slowly, her understanding of events began to turn, like a great stone wheel grinding on its axle. Raif.

Raif.

Almost she could make sense of it. But the harder she tried to grab hold of it the more it turned away from her, and she was left with little but the certainly that Raif had a part to play in this thing she had started.

Ark and the Naysayer were quiet, watching her. The deer carcass had bled out while they'd been speaking, dyeing the surrounding snow black.

"What is happening?" she asked them. "I need to know more."

Ark nodded, heavily. The time had come. "You are *Mas Rahkar*, the Reach. You were born to break the boundary between worlds. We first heard of your existence from He Who Listens, but we had been expecting you for many years. Every thousand years the shadows rise and the long night descends. Ice caps grow and recede, oceans rise and fall, lands dry to deserts and others sink beneath the sea. All things lie in balance, and all must change. We have lived through ten hundred years of light, and now dusk falls.

"As Sull we know and accept this, and stand ready to fight. But we grow few. Our lands diminish. Four thousand years ago every blade of grass in the Northern Territories was ours. We could ride for months in any direction and see no end to our bounty. And before that we held the Soft Lands to the south, and twenty thousand years before that everything between the Horn of Little Hope and Time's End was ours. Man was young then, and we did not deign to notice him. We let him claim the places we did not need—the deserts and edges and mountains—and let him drink the water we judged unclear and hunt the beasts we held unsound. Some say we should have known better, for we are Sull, the oldest of living races, and nothing is new in our history."

Ark paused for a moment to stir the fire. Five paces behind him stood the Naysayer, proud and unmoving, lit solely by starlight. When Ark's voice came again the pride in it was woven with sadness.

"The First Gods birthed us to fight the darkness. That is our destiny and our curse. The Old Ones in the Time Before had fought and failed, and even as we launched our ships from the Far Shore they lay wasted. As we prospered they grew weak, and we moved into the lands they abandoned and took on their battles as our own.

"Yet we are just one people, and the darkness grows ever stronger. Every new assault is more terrible than the last. More and more souls are added to their reckoning, and the armies of the Endlords swell. They have taken our kings and queens and our greatest warriors, and each morning we pray to the God of Creatures Hunted that today we may not meet our ancestors in battle.

"The maeraith who attacked us the night in the Deadwoods had once been a mighty knight, but he was not Sull, and for that we give thanks."

Ash realized Ark held a small carving in his hands, a chunk of rock crystal with smooth edges that he warmed in his fists as he spoke. It was one of the talismans they laid around the fire each night.

"Ash March," Ark said, looking her straight in the eye. "When we found you in the Storm Margin we knew what you were. We had a choice: Kill or save you. You were not Sull and you were not bound to us, but we knew you searched for the Cavern of Black Ice, and I asked the Naysayer if we should put steel to your throat and he said *Nay. She tries to discharge her power safely. Let us aid her.* And so we did. We feared many things at that time, but we did not think to fear that the worst had already happened. The Blindwall had been cracked prior to our meeting. You had discharged your power earlier. Perhaps it was nothing to you, a simple lashing-out, but it was enough to weaken the substance of the wall.

"Creatures worked upon that flaw and work upon it still. Already what was a hair-thin split has been forced wider. The Taken can force their way through one by one . . . but things are stirring in the Blind, dread creatures who once walked the earth and possess the power to tear it open.

"Not all things in the Blind are men or Sull. The Endlords have existed as long as the gods, and together they have overseen many Ages. Dragons, giants, igols, behemoths, basilsks, krakens, shadowchangers, wralls . . . and the shatan. The shatan when they are unmade become *Shatan Maer.* They lose nothing of their shape or strength, and we fear one moves toward the flaw."

Ash felt her mouth go dry. Had she heard accusation in Ark's voice? She couldn't be sure. "What will happen if one breaks through?"

Ark's smile was sweet and bitter all at once. "Ash March, this Sull believes you ask the wrong question. It is not *if* but *when.*"

"When, then?" She heard the tremor in her voice.

"When they break through, the number of unmade creatures escaping from the Blind will increase. Each successive passing will tear the rent wider until whole armies can march through the breach."

"And the Endlords?"

"There are nine Endlords, and though we know their names we will not speak them. Never, in the history of all our battles, have all nine ever ridden out from the Blind. We believe it would mean the end of the world if they did."

"But—"

"Nay, Ash March," cautioned the Naysayer, the first time he had spoken to her since entering the glade. "Some things are best not said. To speak of the Endlords draws their attention, and that I would not wish upon any here this night."

"Are we not safe here in the Racklands?" Although Ash had asked almost the same question earlier of Ark Veinsplitter, she couldn't help herself. But straightaway, she regretted it, for Mal Naysayer only ever gave one answer to any question ever asked.

"Nay."

She waited, but he said no more.

The night had cooled and deepened, and the stars were turning above them. The little sliver of moon was back, and Ash watched it for awhile. Finally, she looked to Ark Veinsplitter. She had one question left, but she was almost afraid to speak it. "The touch of an Endlord is enough to make a man unmade?" Ark nodded. "Then how do the maeraith unmake one?"

He did not look at his wrist. "If we are killed by voided steel we are unmade."

"And if one is wounded?"

Again came that bittersweet smile. "One fights." Ask stood to quarter the carcass, and the conversation was done.

THIRTY-SEVEN

Chief-in-Exile

Bram sometimes thought he was going mad. He had been bought and sold to Castlemilk, but was now heading west to Gnash—at the head of his own company, no less. It was all Robbie's idea, of course. Who better to send a message to Skinner Dhoone than the Thorn King's own flesh and blood?

The company was a small one, and Bram didn't fool himself that he was anything but its token leader. Guy Morloch and Diddie Daw and two other swift horsemen rode with him, and Bram seriously doubted that they'd listen to him if he shouted *"Bluddsmen on the road!"*—let alone issued an order.

Guy Morloch rode at the fore, his Dhoone-blue cloak spreading wide in the rising wind. They had been on the road for over two days and had just crossed bounds into the Gnashhold. A well-traveled road ran between Castlemilk and Gnash, and once the Milk was forded they'd made good time. The land here was lightly forested with old hardwoods—a good hunting ground for deer and boar—and every so often they caught glimpses of the River Gloze as it ran east to join the Flow. The storm that had shaken the clanholds ten days back had left everything green and moist. New grasses had sprung up overnight and bluebells were in flower around the feet of ancient oaks.

Even the sun was attempting to shine, though truly it was bitterly cold. Bram's cheeks were hot from riding at gallop into the wind. He was glad of the cold and the haste, glad of the long days in the saddle and the dry, six-hour camps, glad because it left him too exhausted to think.

Here. Bram. Take this. I had Old Mother weave it for you.

No. He wouldn't think of Robbie. Yet even as he tried to push the thought of his brother from him, he could still see Robbie's hands on the cloak. Dhoone-blue it was, just like Guy Morloch's, only a little bit shorter and shabbier. No fisher fur, or thistle clasps. Bram had held it to his face and smelled it; it smelled of Old Mother's sweat and Robbie's guilt.

What was the point of giving a Dhoone cloak to someone who had been sold to another clan? *Don't worry*, Robbie had said to him that night after the negotiation with Wrayan Castlemilk had been completed. *I told her she can't have you till Dhoone is won, and who knows what may happen between now and then?* Robbie had cuffed him then, grinned one of his charming grins, and walked away. Two days later there came the cloak.

Bram frowned, trying hard not to give in to weariness. He knew Guy Morloch and the others had not expected him to keep up with them, and had been surprised by his skill in the saddle. Part of Bram had discovered he liked surprising people, and he was determined he wouldn't fall back.

Ahead, Guy raised his arm, signaling a slowdown and a slight change in direction. The Gnashhouse lay half a day's ride directly west, but they were heading to the Old Round, and that lay nearer, along the Gloze. The company turned north until it hit the riverbank and then followed its course due west.

Many songs had been written about the Gloze. It was said

to be the most beautiful river in the clanholds, its water green and clear, and its banks gently sloping and grown over with moss. Old willows tapped into its waters, and it fed countless pools where water lilies bloomed and kingfishers hunted. Bram knew many of the ballads, sad songs where maids and clansmen met and parted, or where pitched battles were fought *"On the rolling banks of the Gloze"*.

Thinking of the songs made Bram wish for his stringboard. It had been lost the night Bludd invaded the Dhoonehold . . . such a small loss amongst so many that he had never mentioned it to anyone. Algis Gillow had taught him how to play, how to find and finger the chords. Old Algis had never tired of telling anyone who listened that in his day it was proper for a Dhoonesmen to play at least one of three things: the strings, the drums, or the pipes. Bram hadn't seen Algis Gillow in half a year, and it wouldn't surprise him if the old man was dead.

"Bram. Where's your new cloak?"

Bram looked over to see Diddie Daw drawing abreast of him. The fierce little swordsman was dark-skinned and golden-eyed, and people said his mother had slept with the forest folk. When Bram didn't immediately answer, he said, "Best draw it on. We're charged to make a good showing at the Round."

Diddie paced ahead, leaving Bram to bring up the rear. Four men ahead of him now, every one of them in fine blue cloaks.

Here, Bram. Take this. I had Old Mother weave it for you.

Bran let out a soft breath. Even Robbie's gifts had thorns. It wasn't just guilt that had given rise to the cloak, there was self-interest too. This was the first company Robbie had ever sent to meet with Skinner Dhoone, and that company must befit a king. Robbie Dun Dhoone couldn't very well send out his brother looking less stately than one of his sworn men. His pride wouldn't allow it.

Turning in the saddle, Bram reached back to pull the thing.

from his gelding's pannier. The cloak was creased, and three days of sitting in damp leather above the horse's rump had done little to improve its smell. Bram grimaced as he shook it out. He used his father's old cloak pin to secure it, and then carefully folded his old cloak away. When the visit was done he'd want it back.

The company was moving at a brisk trot now, and the mid-afternoon sun shone in their faces. The trees had begun to thin, and sheep and cattle were out amongst the grazes. Gnash was a large and wealthy clanhold, with many thousands of acres of rich black soil. Three rivers served them: the Flow, the Gloze and the Tarrel. Bram had been here many times when Maggis Dhoone had been alive and chief, yet he had never seen or visited the Old Round.

It was the old Gnash roundhouse, he knew that much, abandoned a thousand years earlier after Blackhail had torched it. Some violent dispute over Gnash's northwestern reach had resulted in a fire that legend held could be seen from as far away as the Dhoonehouse. Bram didn't believe that, but he did wonder about the fire. Stone buildings were hard to torch: they would often blacken but remain standing. The Scarpehouse had been doused with oil by Orrl marksmen shooting bladder arrows before it was set alight, but by all accounts it had still made a poor fire. The collapse had come two days later when one of the crucial supporting timbers had given way. Somehow the draft created by the collapse made the fire spring back to life, and this time it burned inside as well as out.

Bram wondered about the Old Round. Gnash had not rebuilt it, and instead had chosen to relocate their roundhouse seven leagues to the west, on the southern banks of the Tarrel. It could be a defensive move, he supposed, for three rivers now stood between Blackhail and Gnash.

Often Bram found himself thinking of such things, working

out strategies in his head. He liked to know the reasons behind events, and sometimes wished he had been born in Withy or Wellhouse where the histories and sum of clan knowledge were kept. A little voice inside him said *Too bad Robbie never sold you there*, but its ugliness made him recoil and he pushed it aside.

As the company emerged from a copse of water oaks they were greeted by the sight of nine armed and helmed Dhoonesmen riding at canter toward them. Big men with blond braids whipping clear of their thornhelms and the blue steel drawn but held at rest crossed the length of pitched graze, scattering sheep as they went.

"Easy," commanded Guy Morloch slowing to a walk. "Bram. Trot ahead and give the sign of no contest."

Bram nodded and drew his sword, kicking his stallion forward as the other four men fell back. It was proper in situations like this for the leader of a company to draw fire away from his men by raising his sword above his head—one hand on the grip, the other closed around the point—indicating no contest. But there was more at work here, Bram knew. It was galling for seasoned warriors to appear so vulnerable, especially when three of the four would be yielding to their own clansmen. And Bram knew he was small for his age. Fifteen, and not much taller than a child. Guy Morloch was counting on that smallness to give the Dhoonesmen pause.

The point of Bram's blade had been ground less than five days ago on the swordmill at Castlemilk and he could feel it biting through his boiled-leather gloves. His heart felt big and out of place, and he thanked the Stone Gods that his gelding was easy beneath him and not taking advantage of the slack reins. The head Dhoonesman raised a fist, slowing his men. Bram could not see his eyes through the thornhelm.

Coming to a banking halt a hundred paces away, the head

Dhoonesman cried out, "In the name of the Dhoone chief, who comes here?"

Bram hoped that from this distance the man couldn't see his sword shake. He concentrated on holding it level as he spoke. "Bram Cormac, Robbie Dhoone's brother, come to treat with the chief-in-exile, Skinner Dhoone."

The head warrior pulled off his helm and shook out his braids. His face was flushed with trapped heat and sweat, and his skin was thickly laid with tattoos. Bram watched his gaze travel to Guy Morloch, Diddie Daw, and the other two swordsmen. Bram felt for Jordie Sarson as the man's gaze rested upon him and his lip tightened in contempt. Just six weeks earlier Jordie Sarson had counted himself amongst Skinner's men, but he had defected to Robbie Dhoone on the Milk, and now had returned as a member of Robbie's company. Jordie kept his face impassive, but his skin was the pale kind that showed every change beneath it, and Bram saw spots of color rising on his neck.

"Take me to Skinner Dhoone," Bram was surprised to hear himself say. "My message will not wait upon custom." With that he lowered and sheathed his sword, and stared levelly at the head warrior until he had forced the man to blink.

The head warrior exchanged glances with his men. Most had followed their leader's example and pulled off their helms, and Bram found himself recognizing several faces. Turning his horse, the head warrior addressed his men. "Ransom their weapons, and accompany them at canter to the Round." He kicked spurs into horseflesh and started back at gallop across the graze.

Guy Morloch hissed something under his breath. Diddie Daw muttered, "No sense fighting it, man," and unhooked his scabbard from his sword belt and let it fall upon the earth. Bram did the same, and Jordie and Mangus Eel followed suit. Guy

Morloch relinquished his blade last. No warrior liked to have his weapons ransomed, but only a fool would travel to a warring clan and not expect it. At least the Dhoonesmen didn't further insult them by searching their bodies for hand-knives and other small weapons, and one of their number simply dismounted and collected the swords.

When the formalities were done, the Dhoonesmen arranged themselves in point around the visitors, and led the way back to the Round.

Somehow Bram found himself maintaining his place at the head of the company. The land was rich here, and soon graze gave way to plowed fields. Crofters' stone-built cottages nestled in little valleys, surrounded by hedgerows.

The sun was very low now, beaming straight into Bram's eyes, and he found it difficult to see the Old Round at first. He had expected something broken and charred, but had not counted on the force of nature. Exactly half of the old roundhouse still stood, forming the shape of a half-moon. The part that had collapsed was gone, stone and all, but the outline of its foundation could still be read beneath the gravel court that had replaced it. The standing half had retained its dome, but the roof had ceded to nature. Turf and ground willow grew there in thick mats, and Bram knew enough about their root systems to realize that pulling them up was no longer an option. They would break the stone if forced.

It was an extraordinary sight, the shaggy half-moon dome set on a bank above the Gloze. Newly constructed lean-tos had been set against the flat end-wall, and horses and men trotted back and forth between makeshift stables and the Round.

The Dhoonesmen increased the pace for the short climb, and then brought the visitors to a halt upon the half-circle court. Grooms came out to take their horses, and already Bram could tell that word had spread. Interest was high amongst Skinner

Dhoone's men, and Bram found himself treated with a queer mix of distrust and respect.

Stupidly, he found himself staring at the women. Almost he had forgotten that Dhoone had any, and to see them here, carrying oats for the horses and pails from the well, was a shock. He couldn't stop staring. The older ones stared back, hostile, but the younger ones regarded him with frank interest. He heard one whisper, "That's Robbie's brother, Bram."

Taking quick stock of himself and his four companions, he had to admit that Robbie had been right about the cloaks. They set the five of them apart, and endowed them with something long missing from Dhoone: the courtliness of an older Age. Strangely, Bram felt his confidence growing. If one good thing had come from the meeting with the Milk Chief, it had been the fact that Robbie had been forced to reappraise him. Wrayan Castlemilk was no fool. If she had asked for Bram Cormac it was for good reason.

At least, that was what Robbie reckoned. Bram managed a wiry smile. He suspected the fosterage was just a game to Wrayan Castlemilk, something to throw Robbie Dhoone off guard . . . but he kept that thought to himself.

"Follow me."

Bram and his four companions were bidden to follow a Dhoone warrior through a break in the end-wall, passing from the blaze of a red sunset into the dank shadows of the Old Round. The half-dome had been braced with bloodwood stangs a hundred feet tall and buttressed with rock pylons. The ground underfoot was little more than mud at first, with slabs of slate laid across it like stepping-stones. Deeper into the building greater effort had been made to render the place habitable. Gravel had been scattered to cover the mud, and fragrant woods burned to mask the stagnant-well stench of the stone. Some old corridors were still in place, and Bram could see where the women had been at work, laying down rushes and lime-washing walls. The warrior led them up a partial stair to a chamber that lay ten paces above ground level.

After the dimness of the entrance Bram had to hood his eyes to stop the light from dazzling them. A large seven-sided chamber lay in front of him, and torches spaced at foot-long intervals ringed the walls. There had to be at least two hundred, Bram figured, yet even combined with the fires burning against three of the seven walls they didn't create sufficient light or heat to drive away the atmosphere of decay.

Skinner Dhoone sat on a big ugly chair carved with thistle barbs for armrests. *He has aged*, Bram realized. His braids were lank and graying, and his face had the florid puffed-up look of someone who drank too hard on a weak liver. His eyes were pure Dhoone, and all the arrogance of chiefs and kings lived there. Looking Bram up and down, he said, "I know you. You're Mabb Cormac's boy—you've even less claim to the Thistleblood than your brother Rab."

Bram nodded; he had not been charged to argue with Skinner Dhoone. All around, Dhoonesmen stood in silence and watched him. The chamber was full of them, all armed, many armored. Bram recognized the brothers Mauger and Berold Loy. Mauger acknowledged him with a grim nod.

Skinner had been expecting Bram to be provoked by his statement, and Bram's agreement confounded him. Curling his fingers around the carved wooden barbs, he said, "So you do not deny your brother has no claim on king or chiefship?"

Behind him, Bram heard Guy Morloch hiss something in response.

"What say you?" demanded Skinner, seizing upon this. "Step forward, *Milk*man, and speak your mind."

Guy Morloch laid a hand on Bram's shoulder to push past him, but Bram jerked his head around sharply and said, "Guy.

You speak out of turn. *I* was charged to treat with the chief-in-exile. No one else."

For a wonder, Guy Morloch fell back. Or perhaps Diddie Daw or Mangus Eel grabbed and held him. Bram would never know. He had turned to face Skinner Dhoone once more, his heart racing. This had to be done right.

"Answer the question, rabbit boy."

Bram stilled himself. His mother had trapped many creatures: coaties, and ringtails, and foxes. She had not trapped rabbits alone, though even she would have admitted they were her favorites. A *rabbit is good eating* and *skinning*, she would say. *Try putting a weasel in a pot.*

Feeling calmer, Bram said, "Robbie Dhoone relinquishes the chiefship to you."

Gasps circled the chamber. Dhoonesmen stirred. Mauger Loy crossed to the thistle chair and whispered two words in Skinner's ear. Bram's good eyes saw Mauger's lips move and read them. *Be cautious.*

Skinner Dhoone roused himself from the chair, and stood. His boots were deerskin and very fine, but the mud of the Old Round still clung to them. Approaching Bram, he said, "And what has brought about this change in Rab Cormac nee Dhoone?"

Bram concentrated on looking at the drink-puffed skin on Skinner's nose; the Dhoone blue eyes were too much for him. "It is not a change as Robbie sees it. He has been constant in his wish to see Dhoone united."

Behind him, Diddie Daw, Mangus Eel and the rest grunted their agreement. Even a few of Skinner's own men nodded their heads. They had heard the messages Robbie had sent through Mauger Loy.

Skinner Dhoone rocked back onto the heels of his boots and snorted. "So Robbie's been constant, has he?" Lunging forward suddenly, he locked gazes with Jordie Sarson. "And what would you say to that, Jordie Treason?"

Jordie swallowed. *He's not much older than I am*, Bram realized. Tilting his chin up a fraction, Jordie said, "I'd say Robbie is an honorable man, who loves Dhoone more than his own life."

Bram made his face a mask. Jordie *believed* what he said, that was evident, and there was something about Jordie Sarson — the fairness of his skin and hair, his youth and fine looks and clear blue eyes — that spoke to Dhoonesmen. Any man here would be proud of such a son.

Robbie had calculated well. It had been a risk sending Jordie with the company, and another risk not to let him in on the plan. But both risks had paid off. Jordie's conviction was beyond price.

Skinner's lost a beat of concentration. His blue eyes weren't as clear as Bram had thought; there was water in them. "Am I to hear Rab Cormac's plan?" he challenged.

Bram stepped forward to draw attention away from Jordie and back to himself. "Robbie has a deal to propose."

"Does he, now?" Skinner said quietly, unsurprised. "Go on."

"Robbie has men who are sworn to him, and he will not force them to break their oaths to return to you."

Skinner let out a gasp of foul air. "The arrogance of the bastard! He stole those men in the first place and now refuses to give them back!" The chief-in-exile shook his head, but Bram didn't think it was in genuine amazement, more the show of it for his men. "And what else does Rab propose?"

Bram took a breath to steady himself before speaking. "Robbie is willing to cede Dhoone to you. As long as you agree not to interfere with his taking of Withy, he will not interfere with your reclaiming of Dhoone."

It took a moment for this statement to sink in. Skinner's eyes blanked for a moment, and then focused sharply as all the implications occurred to him. *"Withy?"* he repeated and this time his amazement was unfeigned. "You are telling me Rab Cormac intends to take the Withyhouse?"

Bram nodded. Only one final piece to say; relief gave him confidence. "We have made plans. Robbie believes it can be taken. It's vulnerable, and the Dog Lord's sons fail in their vigilance. Robbie *will* have a clanhold." He looked Skinner Dhoone straight in the eye. "And he's judged Dhoone impossible to retake."

Skinner shook his head, clearly agitated by Bram's words. His lips moved, muttering something, and though he turned before Bram could catch it all, Bram recognized part of the Withy boast.

We are the clan who makes kings.

When Skinner turned back his face was changed, and some of the water had left his eyes. "If I agree to these terms, when will Rab take Withy?"

"Within the month. I can say no more than that."

Skinner nodded, as if he had been expecting just such an answer. Drawing himself up to his full height, he said, "Go now. I must think on this. I will send Rab Cormac my word within the tenday."

They were dismissed, and as Bram made his way from the chamber he was struck by the fact that when cunning showed on the face of a Dhoone they all looked much the same.

THIRTY-EIGHT

Raid on the Shanty

They halted when they saw smoke in the distance. Two bald hills separated them from the shanty; a distance of perhaps five leagues. Raif had led the party this last day, and it was he who called the halt. They were in Blackhail territory now, and he knew how easy it was to spot any sort of movement on the balds. They would make a dry camp until sunset, and then move under cover of dark.

Raif could hardly believe it was happening. Seventeen days west and he was here, where he had never thought to return. Ride five days southwest at a fair pace and he'd be back at the roundhouse, back with Effie and Drey and Corbie and Anwyn, and Bitty and all of the Shanks.

Home, he mouthed, feeling nothing.

He knew these hills, knew how the wind scoured anything that dared grow higher than a stalk of heather, knew where to look to find springs and old mine shafts, and the best place to flush out rabbits. He had taken down his first major kill not far from here: a big lone moose that had strayed south. Abruptly, he turned his mind to the arrangement of the camp. Some instinct involved with preserving his sanity warned him to *do*, not *think*.

They were not far from Dhoone here, but already the Copper Hills had deflated into the humps and bluffs of the balds. Five days earlier they had made the crossing from the badlands into the clanholds. The weather had been with them, and in a way so had the clanwars. They had met no hunters on the road. The stout ponies favored by the Maimed Men were not bred for speed, and once they were past the worst of canyon country the journey had been almost restful. The lengthening days of spring and the clear weather meant they'd easily made up for days lost during the storm. The moon had shrunk a bit every night and now there was nothing of it left.

Tonight would be completely dark.

Raif bandaged his pony's hocks. The poor creature had just missed going over the cliff in the landslide, and its legs had been cut up by rocks. It threw a kick, and Raif dodged it. At least he still *had* a mount. Stillborn's gentle black mare had been lost, along with the three packhorses and the gear they'd been hauling. Now they were eleven men and ten mounts. Few were happy about this, especially Addie and the outlander, Thomas Argola. Having been judged the lightest members of the group, they had been forced to share Yustaffa's powerful garon. Yustaffa in turn had set his sizable rump upon the outlander's mount, and Stillborn had taken Addie's pony. So far no more horses had died—but many tempers had been lost. Raif had made a point of walking part of each day so he could offer Addie use of his mount. Mostly Addie just walked right alongside him, glad to be in full command of his hill legs.

Addie had some knowledge of this part of the clanholds, and Raif didn't doubt that he could have led the raid party to the mine without him. Already the cragsman had located a spring and a tender stretch of saxifrage for the horses.

Raif decided that was something else he didn't want to think about: why Linden Moodie had given him the lead. Quickly, he trimmed the pony's bandages and stood. The sun was hanging above a bank of streaky clouds, still an hour or so from setting. Some of the Rift Brothers were gnawing on ptarmigan bones to fill the time, others were talking in low voices, or seeing to their mounts. Stillborn was oiling his weapons.

The big Maimed Man had lost a considerable portion of his collection in the fall. An assortment of swords, longknives, katars and other more fantastically bladed weapons had gone over the cliff, never to be seen again. All Stillborn had managed to save had been the sword and longknife, the nail hammer he kept permanently hooked to his gear belt, and a number of items stashed in a stiffly tanned elkskin that had been slung across his back at the time of the slide.

Raif had a strange feeling about that. Two of Stillborn's three packs had fallen into the canyon along with his horse, yet the arrow Divining Rod had not been lost. Stillborn had found it wrapped in a stained length of linen, safe and sound in the elkskin pack. When pressed he said he *did* remember placing it there—it being so light and all—but it was the only thing in his daypack that he could claim no practical use for.

Sometimes Raif wondered how many of the Maimed Men— wittingly or unwittingly—conspired to push him toward a certain point. Stillborn, Yustaffa, Addie, the outlander, even Traggis Mole himself seemed to be propelling him forward onto a course he barely understood himself.

Enough. Glancing over at the smoke rising above the hills, Raif forced all unfinished matters from his mind, and went to speak with Stillborn.

"How will it happen?" he heard himself ask.

The Maimed Man was working linseed oil into the Forsworn sword with a bit of rag, and he slowed a fraction as he answered. "Smoothly, if all goes to plan. The cooled gold is kept in a locked room just below the mouth of the mine. It's guarded by one sleepy miner or another, sometimes by the Lode Master. Any hot gold is set to cool near the furnace which is just upwind of the mine. We close in on the shanty after dark, wait until lights out, and then move in and seize the gold. If there's scuffles we'll keep them short and quiet."

Raif nodded. "How do you know so much about the layout of the mine?"

"How d'you think? The Mole had it watched."

"Why isn't the watcher in the raid party?"

Stillborn set down his rag. For good measure he had worked linseed oil into his matched bullhorns too and they now shone black as sin. "Stop asking questions you already know the answer to, Raif. Save us both some time. Watcher's dead, picked off by an arrow from the mine."

Traggis Mole hadn't mentioned that, but it fit in more with what Raif knew about tied miners. They were hard men, and they relied on their clan for little, including defense. If they had endured one attack by the Maimed Men and found another man snooping, then things were hardly going to run as smoothly as Stillborn claimed. Raif looked at Stillborn and Stillborn stared back, his warning still in effect. *No more questions you know the answer to.*

There was nothing for Raif to do but make preparations for the raid.

Camp had been made in the leeward base of the hill. Some old sheep-run had once been dug into the soil and lined with rocks, like a streambed, and now water was trickling along it. Raif jumped down into the trench and scooped up a handful of muddy silt. Scouring it across his face and over the back of his hands, he shrouded himself for the night. The mud tingled as it dried, pulling his skin tight.

From across the camp, Linden Moodie watched him. Something in his deep-set eyes, a certainty that he knew exactly what kind of man Raif Twelve Kill was, gave Raif pause. Moodie had already dismissed what happened on the canyon cliff as a fluke. *I'll be watching you this night,* he mouthed, clearly, precisely, for Raif's eyes alone.

Raif let his expression harden along with the mud. In a voice pitched to carry, he called the Maimed Men to him, and then spent the next quarter digging out handfuls of mud from the old sheep-run and passing them up to each man. Anything that might catch a beam of torchlight was darkened, even the horses' stars and socks. Yustaffa alone refused the mud, claiming that when the Scorpion God made his skin He cast the color just right. "He ran out of dye by the time He got to you lot," Yustaffa explained airily. "And didn't think you were worth the trouble of mixing up a new batch."

Maimed Men grunted at this. Already, tension was mounting. A few men were squatted around their packs, casting blocks. Gambling was normally serious business for the Maimed Men, and disputes and fighting common, but this time the gamblers were subdued, their gazes flicking to the setting sun more often than to the faces of the wooden blocks. Stillborn and Addie were speaking quietly, Addie gesturing northward with his fist. Moodie had folded and stowed his scarlet cloak, and was fixing a plain gray one around his throat. A mine was no place for finery.

"Tonicker?"

Raif looked over his shoulder to see Yustaffa walking toward him, holding out the hollow stopper of a jug. The fat man's eyes were twinkling. The very things that made other men nervous seemed to delight him. Raif shook his head; he wanted no malt.

"Your loss." Yustaffa held the stopper to his lips and drank. "Quite a bite." He sent a hand questing inside his pieced-fur tunic. "How about something to eat instead? I've some bannock—stale as stones, sadly, but you can always nibble around the blue bits—a little pot of sotted oats, and a few wilting leeks."

"Nothing."

The word had a hard edge, and Yustaffa ceased searching his tunic for items they both knew weren't there. Reciting the names of clan foods was just another of the fat man's taunts. Yustaffa smiled, sending cheek fat up to eclipse his eyes. "You'll be hungry later."

"I'll be many things later. Hungry isn't one of them."

Yustaffa beamed at this as he walked away. "Remember, *Azziah riin Raif.* It's the excitement I wish to share, not the danger."

Oh gods. Sometimes Raif felt like a joint of meat on the fire; men kept prodding him to test for doneness.

As the sun sank below the cloud cover he loaded and saddled the pony. It was going to be one of those showy sunsets where the sky turned orange and pink. The wind was picking up, and he stood by his pony's head and let the gusts numb him. Time passed, and the sky flared like a fire, and the Maimed Men gathered in a group to watch it, and as soon as the sun disappeared beneath the horizon they mounted their horses and rode west.

Raif led the way. He knew of a game track here, yet had decided against taking it. All known tracks were a risk, and the guarantee of a smooth ride didn't mean as much when the snow had shrunken back and you could search the ground for yourself.

The wind brought them sounds from the shanty well before they approached it. A hammer striking stone rang clear, and the *snick* of a latch as something was bolted away for the night. Raif could smell the smoke now, a pitchy, mineral scent that did not come from wood. Timber fit for burning did not grow in the balds, and the miners burned fuelstone or turf.

The same wind that brought the scents and smells of the shanty toward the Maimed Men blew signs of their own approach away. When they reached the second hill, Raif decided to hold their course and keep the wind in their faces. He was calm except for a murmur in his heart that sounded between beats. The lack of cover worried him, and with every step he took he expected to hear a warning cry of discovery.

Just before the raid party crested the second hill, Raif slowed them. The shanty lay in the valley beyond and they had to decide how best to approach it. Even in the darkness Raif could see the telltale signs of mining: the sunken, undermined slopes, the heaps of slag, the exposed earth where pumped mud and water had stripped away the grass.

When the last of the Maimed Men had gathered about him, Raif said, "We'll work our way down and around. Cresting the hill's too big a risk. If I was the Lode Master I'd have an archer train his arrow on that ridge." He had expected a fight—he was asking them to travel an extra league out of their way—but the Maimed Men merely nodded their assent, and he wasn't sure how this made him feel. "The Bluey's down there," he continued, nodding toward the mine valley. "We'll skirt its banks and approach the shanty from the west. They won't be expecting anyone from that direction."

"The wind'll no longer be in our favor if we move west," Moodie said.

"Then we'll have to be quiet."

"And not fart," Stillborn added.

Raif threw him a look of gratitude. It might have been a poor joke, but it *was* an endorsement. In a choice between keeping the wind and cresting the hill, or losing it for the chance of taking the miners by surprise Stillborn was with Raif Sevrance.

The roundabout descent took an hour. At the halfway point the shanty and the mine lake became visible below them. The shanty was a collection of squat stone cottages built a short walk east of the mine. Orwin Shank used to say they were so small and ill-constructed they looked like outhouses. Which was strange really, Raif considered, as the miners had to possess considerable skill when it came to stone. They knew how to cut, brace and move it, yet lived in unmortared, poorly chinked shanties.

Some of the cottages were lit, others not. Tracks worn in the soft mud led to and from the entrance to the mine. Black Hole was just that: a hole in the hillside, braced with squared-off timbers. The mouth was about six feet high and the same wide; sufficient for ponies and their muck carts to pass through. Two lamps burned at either side of the mouth, and a third, more diffuse source of light came from a vent shaft located a few feet farther up the hill.

The Bluey was a lake wholly created by pumped mine-water. It was too dark to see its color now, but Raif and Drey and the two youngest Shank brothers used to marvel at its unnatural hue. Its water was the same vivid blue-green as weathered copper. No animal would drink from it, and any birds that landed on its surface soon took off for fairer waters. It was, as far as young boys from Blackhail were concerned, a splendid place to swim.

Raif thought about that now as he led his party around its southern shore. Between drinking Tem's home brew and swimming in the Bluey it was a wonder he and Drey weren't dead.

He killed his smile before it could warm him. Memories of Drey had no place here tonight.

The wind was blowing from behind them now, and they slowed their pace as a precaution. The mud helped, muffling hoofbeats, but bridle fittings could not be jounced. Addie was already on his feet, his shared mount abandoned. The outlander had fallen back about thirty paces, and no one seemed concerned with hurrying him up.

As they neared Black Hole more lights went out in the shanty. Raif slid Tanjo Ten Arrow's Sull bow from its makeshift case of coarse sacking. The varnished wood felt cool and glassy. His gaze swept in a quarter-circle back and forth, from shanty to mine, mine to shanty. When he perceived a heart beating in the darkness he did not hesitate: simply put metal to the riser and released. The arrow sped east like a night hawk, silent and deadly. Even before the rest of the raid party realized what had happened a miner lay dead.

"Raif?" asked Stillborn.

Raif spat to remove the taste of sorcery from his mouth. He could not explain to Stillborn, Addie and the rest that he had perceived a heart, not a man. Nor could he explain that the heart's rhythm had undergone a swift change, accelerating from a steady pulse to a jerky gallop as its owner spied a movement along the lake. Raif's arrow had cut off the miner's cry of warning . . . but he couldn't explain that either. "I saw eye whites," was all he said.

Stillborn delayed his answering nod long enough for Raif to know that the Maimed Man suspected more.

Raif spoke hastily to head off Stillborn's thoughts. "There's a dead man at the mouth of the mine. We'd better get started before he's found."

You could tell the Maimed Men weren't clan, for they accepted this without question and drew weapons. Stillborn released the Forsworn sword from its sheath, its edge glimmering softly. Addie slung a thick eweman's flatbow across his back, leaving his weapon hand free for his longknife. Moodie brandished a bell-bladed ax, the kind meant for throwing. Raif left his borrowed blade were it was, choosing to keep his hand on his bow. Kicking the pony forward, he set his sights on Black Hole.

All was quiet. Mist had begun to peel from the lake and was moving east with the wind. Something about it struck Raif as strange, but he couldn't decide what and he dismissed it from his mind. The murmur was still sounding between his heartbeats, and he was aware of the need to think only in the now. When the cry came he was almost expecting it.

"Raiders! Raiders at the mine!"

As the raid party mounted its charge on Black Hole, Raif loosed another arrow. It occurred to him that Traggis Mole must have known all along that this raid could not be carried out by stealth. The Robber Chief had dealt lives, hoping for a return in gold.

Ahead lights were being struck in the shanty. Shouts sounded. An arrow whistled past Raif's ear. Two miners raced down the mud tract that ran between Black Hole and the cottages. Addie Gunn picked one off with a shot to the thigh; Raif took the other with a shot to the heart.

Stillborn and the other bladesmen in the party bore down on Black Hole, Raif and Addie covering them. Raif slid down from his pony. The mist was rapidly thickening, and he could see Addie squinting into it to close a shot on a miner who was running down the hillside toward the mine. Addie released the string of his flatbow but his vision had failed him and the arrow went wide. *He doesn't know it*, Raif realized with a thrill of fear, as he watched the little cragsman nod to himself and move on to another target.

The mist. Addie couldn't see through he mist—none of them could. Raif couldn't. He couldn't see men or landmarks . . . but he could perceive hearts. He hadn't seen the miner escape Addie's shot, he just knew that the miner's heartbeat had continued on uninterrupted.

Raif took a breath, made a decision. "I'm going into the mine."

He hardly cared if Addie heard him. He simply knew that he couldn't continue to stand here and pick off men through the mist. Three dead so far by his hand. *Miners*, he told himself. *Miners*.

Stillborn and five other Maimed Men were battling to gain entry to the mine. Miners, the skin on their faces rutted with huge pores, the breath wheezing in their throats, had formed a defensive line around the mouth. They wielded pickaxes and hammers and had claimed the high ground of slag that had been heaped against the entrance. Raif slid the Sull bow into the case on his back and drew his sword. *It's time you learned how to kill someone and look them in the eye.*

The Listener's words tumbled crazily in Raif's head as he joined the Maimed Men. The fighting at the mouth was savage and ungainly. Although the miners had the higher ground their weapons were not suited to close-quarter combat. Stillborn was leading the assault, his seamed faced red with fury, the pearly tooth at the base of his neck snapping as if it wanted to bite. The Forsworn sword screeched as it slid along the poll of an ax. Raif thought he saw the curl of iron as the sword shaved the ax blade. Other Maimed Men were following Stillborn's lead, fired by his aggression. Linden Moodie threw his ax and it sank deep into a miner's face, cutting his mouth and nose in two. As he fell he caused disruption in the line as some miners moved to catch him and others shoved him aside to fight.

Raif spotted an opening. Springing forward, he raised his borrowed sword and, guiding it through a space just vacated by a miner's hammer, thrust the point hard into a man's hand. The man had been helping Moodie's victim to the floor, and he dropped the body and shrieked in pain. Seconds of chaos followed as one dying man and one wounded man blocked the miner's line.

The murmur in Raif's heart was deafening now. When a rock hammer swung toward his neck he did not hear it coming, and only Linden Moodie's newly drawn sword stopped him from taking a mortal blow. Moodie's weapon was an old-fashioned broadsword with a single edge, black as iron and heavy as a log. It bent as it absorbed the hammer blow, but did not break.

The miners were losing ground. Not one of them could stand against Stillborn. His fury was relentless, and while his sword was in motion he raged at them. "Come on, pretty boys! Here's your chance to take me, big ugly bastard that I am."

Once he'd started spotting openings, Raif couldn't stop. In a way it was like watching Yelma, waiting to see where she'd swing. The miner's line was crumbling, and there was dead air between the men. Raif moved in and out of it, spiking elbows and knees and necks. Fighting miners wasn't the same as fighting sworn clansmen. The battle fury wasn't there. One wound was enough to discourage them.

Finally the line broke, and the miners began to scatter. Behind him, Raif was aware of Addie picking a few of them off with his bow. Stillborn chased one man down and put a sword through his guts, and the sight of that made the other Maimed Men sober up. Breathing hard, they lowered their weapons, some bending to wipe the blades on the bodies of dead miners. Half a minute passed while they got their wind back. One Rift Brother, a big southerner with a bald head, had a nasty-looking gash in his forearm where the edge of a pickax had fallen. The ragged hole was full of blood.

Raif wiped sweat from his eyes, and his palm came back black with mud. His heart would not calm down. He wondered where the outlander was, for he had not seen him during the fighting. Yustaffa was there, but he had kept to the edge, claiming something about the miners possessing no swords for him to break. Still, there was blood on his curved scimitar, and his chest and belly heaved as he pulled in air.

The mist had turned stringy and was receding. Raif could see all the way back to the shanty now. All was quiet as miners returned home to nurse their wounds.

"Right," Linden Moodie said. "First things first." He held his bent sword blade up to the lamplight. "Anyone got a spare?"

The Maimed Men managed a kind of groaning laugh. Stillborn held out his longknife by the blade for Moodie to take.

"Gully. Kye. Hold the entrance. Rest of us'll take a look inside. If one of those miners as much as looks at you the wrong way, holler like you're on a hot spit. D'you understand?" Moodie paused to let the two Maimed Men nod. Satisfied, he told Addie to fetch one of the lamps hanging from a nail on the upright bracing timbers, and then lead the way into Black Hole.

THIRTY-NINE

Black Hole

The smell of bad eggs was the first thing that got you, not strong exactly but persistent. You couldn't turn your head away from it because it was carried on the up-mine breeze. Raif was aware of it, but not in the same way as the other Maimed Men who were blowing air through their nostrils and grimacing. Something was turning around in his head, and he didn't know what it was.

Something about the moment he entered the mine, something about the light . . . He shook his head, unable to push his mind through the black spot. It was probably nothing.

But it unnerved him.

The entrance tunnel to Black Hole was braced with square-set timbers and its roof was lagged with heavy planks. Sections of the floor were also lagged, and from time to time the Maimed Men's footfalls would ring out, marking a hollow space below. Ladders led down. Wheeled muck-carts had been lined up against one wall, some still heaped with ore. All was cool and still. Addie carried the lamp as steadily as if it were a candle floating in oil.

They had already come thirty feet, and still there was no sign of the locked room where the gold was reportedly held.

No one doubted its presence—miners had lost lives attempting to bar them from this place—but it appeared Traggis Mole's information was slightly off. Once Linden Moodie started grumbling, others followed. The Maimed Men lived in a city facing south and open to the elements: mines made them uneasy.

Stillborn had not sheathed his sword. After another ten feet, he sent Raif to take a look down one of the ladders. Raif had noticed they'd passed an unlit safe-lamp a short way back and ran to fetch it. Addie gave him a light.

The nearest ladder led down through the mine floor and into the first under-level. All looked pretty much the same as above, except the entire surface of the floor was lagged and the tunnel was noticeably narrower. Just as he was about to shout, "Nothing here!" he heard a cry from above. Racing up the ladder, he emerged in time to see Stillborn raise his sword to the chest of a miner. The tunnel branched into a crossroad directly ahead of him, and Stillborn must have flushed the miner out of the shadows.

"Where's the gold, pretty boy?"

The miner shook his head. He was young and dirty, dressed in pieced hides and with thick buckskin gloves tucked under his belt. His fingers were closed around a silver-handled dagger, but no one had bothered to tell him that holding a single-edged knife with its blade down, instead of up, was a mistake.

The same nameless anxiety that had struck Raif upon entering the mine reasserted itself. Something was turning over in his mind. *The lamp shining outside the mine, the halo of amber light it created . . .*

"Don't know about no gold," the miner cried, breaking through Raif's thoughts. "We dig silver here. Silver!"

Stillborn nodded reasonably. The point of the Forsworn sword dropped from the miner's sternum to the little dimple in the man's hide shirt that marked the location of his navel.

Stillborn made a show of thinking. "So if it's only silver you have here, then, you'd better tell me where the rare yellow kind is. You know, the kind that a man like me might kill for."

"Where is it, dirt shoveler?" Moodie hissed, impatient.

Stillborn tutted; it was unclear at whom. "Best tell me where that special yellow silver is, boy."

The miner's eyes darted between Moodie and Stillborn. Black mud streaked both men's faces, crusting in the scar tissue, and bleeding out like the spokes of a wheel around their eyes. The knife wobbled in the miner's grip. He let out a breath and Raif could see his chest deflating. "It's down the north fork, locked in the old stope room, 'bout sixty paces on the left."

Stillborn nodded. "Interesting. Now lead the way."

The Maimed Men followed the miner down an inclined tunnel leading north from the mouth. The walls were hewn rock braced with cross-timbers, and they narrowed sharply after the ten-foot mark. A pale light shone in the distance, and the miner headed toward it. He still held the knife, but loosely, without intent. Raif spied a rough plank door set into the mine wall, fixed with a large shield lock, the kind clan had to trade with city men for.

Stillborn waved a halt. "Anyone in there?" he asked the miner.

The miner shook his head. "I just left."

"Then you'll have the key." Stillborn held out his hand, palm up, fingers twitching. When the miner didn't move, he wagged his head toward Yustaffa and said, "See that fat man over there? He could pick his way out of the nine spiraling hells if he had a mind for it. And he may have to do just that—seems he's currently considering killing a man in cold blood."

Yustaffa obligingly raised his scimitar and smiled.

"So the way I see it, while you're just saving *us* time by handing over the key, you're actually saving *yourself* from a considerable shortness of breath."

The matter-of-fact tone of Stillborn's voice seemed to calm the miner. "You swear you won't kill me?"

Stillborn's gaze was clear and true. "I swear. Now hand over that key."

Raif watched as the miner pulled the key from a slit in his belt, and Stillborn unlocked the plank door. Raif's apprehension was growing, but he hardly knew why. His eyes were developing the same black spots as his thoughts; places where his perception couldn't go, details that his gaze jumped over. *Amber light, spilling across the ground* . . .

He switched back into the present as Stillborn opened the door. A lamp was burning low, outlining the stark lines of the room. It was small, no more than eight paces across, with timber cribbing bracing the walls and a floor of chiseled quartz. Two lead troughs lay against the far wall. The first contained rusted shovel heads, a headless pickax handle, chisels, an ancient windlass missing its rope, a pair of moldy boots, and a safe-lamp with a cracked guard. The second trough was covered with an oiled tarp.

"Gentlemen," Yustaffa said, pushing past Stillborn and Moodie to reach the tarp. "Step aside. I believe a little flourish is called for." Using the point of his scimitar to hook the tarp, he uncovered the contents of the trough. "Gold," he pronounced, beaming. "I could smell it across the room."

The Maimed Men stood speechless. The trough was filled with perfectly shaped rods of gold, lined up like the pipes of a flute, all shining with dazzling brilliance. Addie Gunn swallowed. Moodie's hand rose to his garrote scar and massaged it gently. Stillborn's hand closed around the miner's arm. "You're wi' me, boy, till I decide otherwise."

Moodie shook himself. "Let's get loading it on the ponies."

Yustaffa did a little jig as the Maimed Men began to organize themselves. The big wounded southerner was sent to bring the ponies to the mouth of the mine, while Moodie and Stillborn argued over the best way to carry the gold to the surface. Addie lifted one of the bars and sniffed it. "It's heavy enough," he said to no one in particular.

Raif felt nothing at seeing the gold. The black spot in his mind was like a sinkhole; it was a struggle to pull anything out. His body felt lit by tension, pulled in opposing ways . . . but ready. *Ready.*

When Yustaffa touched his arm, he jumped.

The fat man raised his hands in mock fright. "On my mother's grave I promise not to take more than my fair share."

Raif said nothing. Trading barbs with Yustaffa seemed a feat far beyond his resources. It was all he could do to understand the words.

Yustaffa moved close enough to breathe on him. "Did you enjoy the mist, eh?" Noting Raif's confusion, with a tiny smile of satisfaction, he continued, "Argola's piss-maker. You did know it wasn't real? Conjured it out of the lake, he did. I warned him it might harm as much as help us, but he wouldn't have any of it. Said that there were some amongst us who'd be able to see right through it." A sly glance. "I really can't say what he meant."

"Go away," Raif said to him.

Yustaffa closed his mouth. He waited a moment, perhaps hoping for something more, but when it became obvious that Raif was done speaking, he turned smartly on his heels and walked away. A few seconds passed, and then Raif heard him tutting loudly as he began passing on fictional details of their conversation.

Light on the ground near the entrance to the mine. Something glinting . . .

"Raif."

Raif felt a hard object being thrust into his hands. Stillborn stood before him, holding out one of the rusted shovel blades from the first trough.

"Take this. Load it with gold, then move out the tunnel sharpish. Take the lamp. See what's happened to Jake. Make the outlander get a move on wi' the horses."

Raif nodded. The shovel blade was large and curved; it took two hands to hold it. As he crossed to where Addie was waiting to load him up with gold, Stillborn placed a hand on his arm and said one last thing.

"You did good tonight, lad."

The words were sucked into the black spot.

Gold rods chinked softly as Addie laid them on the flat of the shovel. Light reflecting up from them made the cragsman's face glow like a painting. Addie kept tally of the number; out of habit he said, like with sheep. The shovel grew heavier, and Raif settled it against his chest. When Addie judged the weight sufficient, he hooked the lamp over the shovel's tang. "You're done. Don't be long, now. You're leaving six of us here and one lamp."

The incline leading from the stope room seemed sharper than Raif remembered, and his thigh muscles had to work to support the weight of the gold. The lamp swung loosely with each step, sending crazy flashes of light along the walls. Now that he was alone the black spot was growing strangely fluid, expanding then contracting, allowing glimpses of something, then snatching them back.

As he approached the crossroad the up-mine wind raised hairs on the back of his neck. *Something glinting by the entrance to the mine, a sword fallen from a man's hand . . .*

"So it *is* you," came a familiar voice. "I thought it, but I didn't want to believe my eyes."

Bitty Shank stepped out from the shadows. He was heavily armored in iron plate fitted with chain webbing at the arm and neck holes, and he held a thick-bladed shortsword in his hand.

He had lost the tip of two of his sword fingers to the 'bite, but Orwin Shank bred strong sons, and Raif could see where muscle had grown large on the saddle of his thumb and the rise of his wrist to compensate. He wore no helm, and his fine blond hair was caught in a single knot braid. As his gaze passed over the gold rods in Raif's grip, his mouth twisted in contempt.

Raif felt the shame burn him.

"You killed Darren Cleet, Rory's brother. It was his first time out as a sworn yearman. He'd just taken over my watch when you shot him."

An armored corpse glowing pale in the lamplight, an arrow growing from its chest.

A sworn clansman.

Raif breathed in and out, in and out, keeping his body still. The black spot was still there, warning him not to think.

A sworn clansman.

Bitty Shank watched him, the knuckles on his sword hand softly flexing. He had matured since Raif had seen him last, and carried himself with measured confidence. The blood drying on his sword had to belong to Maimed Men.

"The miners are Hailsmen, too."

Raif closed his eyes, receiving the blow. He knew it, had known it before he'd let the first arrow fly. His eyes had seen their lores, the horns of powdered guidestone at their waists, the black thread woven into their hair. His ears had heard their voices, the same as his own. The miner who Stillborn had gutted had died speaking the name of his clan.

What have I done?

"Set the gold down, Raif. I won't kill an unarmed man."

Raif shook his head. "No, Bitty. Go."

"I can't, Raif. I can't."

He couldn't, Raif knew that. Clansmen had been killed here, and a Shank could not let that go.

Kill an army for me, Raif Sevrance.

Raif bent at the knee and lowered the shovel holding the gold onto the mine floor. The lamp was heavy with oil; it wobbled onto its side, and as a reflex he righted it. Bitty's face was grim and beautiful in the lamplight, and the contempt had gone. Raif would be forever thankful for that.

Bitty Shank moved forward with a clansman's grace. Even if he won here he would die, he accepted that—had waited for Raif to draw his sword knowing it. Raif turned aside his first strike, letting Bitty's blade slide down the flat of his sword. Bitty stepped into Raif's deflection, bringing his weight to bear on his shortsword. The impact jarred Raif, and caused a dangerous bending of his elbow. As he rolled back onto one knee to recenter his weight, Bitty's sword tip drew a line across his knuckles.

Raif sucked in breath through his teeth. Hot wetness trickled down between his fingers and over the grip of his sword. Instead of parrying to nurse the pain, he sprang forward. His blood made a sound like the first drops of a rainfall as it splashed against Bitty's armor. His blade made contact with an expertly rolled glancing edge, and slid away from Bitty's organs with a speed and efficiency that would have made an armorer weep.

Bitty took a breath to pace himself. Quick as lightning he swung to the side, creating a powerful shift in his body weight that he channeled into his sword. Raif raised his own blade vertically in defense, but his feet were still working to find their balance, and he didn't have the rigidity to brace it. He nearly lost his sword. The ball of his foot twisted strangely and he had to pull himself back to upright with his toes. Bitty stepped into his retreat.

Kill ugly and kill fast. Stillborn's words caused a kind of pain in Raif's head. As Bitty stepped toward him, *he* stepped toward Bitty. A moment passed where the sword points slid against each other. An oily squeak sounded as the sword points found their level—heavy on the bottom, light on the top—and then Bitty's sword slid down as Raif's angled up.

The clansman's heart was his.

In the blade went, puncturing the armor with a hiss. A whiffle of air was sucked through the tear as Bitty's heart and lungs contracted. Bitty's blue eyes widened. His sword clattered to the earth. Raif stepped forward to embrace him, yanking his sword free and falling to one knee as he took Bitty's weight.

Raif Sevrance looked Bitty Shank in the eye as he died.

Gently, Raif laid the clansman on the ground. Bitty's sword had many men's blood on it, and Raif placed it back with the body. Bitty's hands were soft, and Raif couldn't get the fingers to close around the grip. He tried, but they kept falling open. After a time he gave up. Bitty Shank had carried his measure of powdered guidestone in the coiled horn of a bighorn sheep. It was heavy, and it took a lot of powder to fill it, and the thin cap of silver that sealed it had to be punched through.

Raif stood and walked the circle for Bitty Shank. He would not name gods he had forsaken, but he would lay his clansman to rest . . . just as he had done for Bitty's brothers another lifetime before. Even as he completed the last quarter and the circle was joined, he was aware of the sound of footsteps coming from the direction of the stope room.

Picking up the lamp he turned to face them. It was Stillborn, of course, it had to be Stillborn. There was a matter of a sword unresolved between them.

Stillborn slowed as he neared the light. His face twitched as he took in the scene; the body, the blood, the gold. When his voice came it was almost soft. "You all right, lad?"

Raif shook his head. Bitty was dead. Rory's brother was dead. Raif Sevrance was all wrong.

He raised the lamp high. "I want my sword, Stillborn."

Stillborn nodded, reading the intent on Raif's face. "Fucking me again, are you, lad?" He spoke with more resignation than anger.

"And the miner," Raif said. "Let him live."

Something like hurt shone in Stillborn's hazel eyes. "You do me a disservice, lad."

"I have to be sure."

Stillborn grunted. Crouching down, he sent the Forsworn sword skittering over the mine floor to Raif.

Without taking his gaze from the Maimed Man, Raif moved forward to claim it. When he had it in his scabbard he set down the lamp. Oil sloshed heavily in the reservoir.

"Will you come back?" Stillborn asked.

Raif had no answer. *Away*, his mind was screaming. *Away.*

Stillborn made a small gesture that took in the lamp and the sword. "This here. This is just between me and you."

Raif nodded—he had to. Stillborn was exercising a clansman's grace. "How do you live with it?" he heard himself ask. "Being clan . . . and . . ."

"You find a way, Raif. You find a way."

Tears sparkled in both men's eyes as Raif turned toward the surface and headed out of Black Hole.

FORTY

Fighting One-Handed

Penthero Iss walked across the quad, followed by two members of his personal guard, Axal Foss and Styven Dalway. Iss had taken to calling them Eye Men, and for more reasons than one. They were Marafice Eye's cohorts, elite members of the Rive Watch charged with their surlord's protection. Their job was to keep Iss alive, but Iss felt less than gratified by their attention. They watched him for Marafice Eye, they shielded him for Marafice Eye: given keys and locks and a bucket for the slops, they really could have passed as jailers.

And that made Mask Fortress a kind of prison. Crossing from the north gallery toward the Cask, Iss contemplated making a detour to the stables. It was a fine day on the mountain, one of those rarities where the cloud had drawn back to reveal the peak, still white with snow, and within an hour he could be beyond the tree line and climbing toward it. He wouldn't reach it, of course, but he might make it as far as the Cloud Shrine before sunset, and then he could turn his horse in the darkness and look down upon the city he owned. Iss took shallow breaths as he contemplated this. The path he and his horse stood on would be another thing entirely. The most easterly of Mount

Slain's passes and the paths leading toward them would soon be in possession of the Knife.

That rankled. The wealth Marafice Eye had married into was mind-boggling. He was a butcher's son now become a landholder and man of means. When he returned from the clanholds all it would take would be the slightest outreaching to make himself a grangelord. Only two men stood between the Knife and his elevation to the nobility and on the day of his wedding the Knife had named them father and brother. Roland Stornoway and his son, also named Roland. Two murders amongst so many were nothing to the Knife. He had slain a surlord—what were the deaths of others after that?

Iss quickened his pace; behind him the two brothers-in-the-watch quickened theirs. The flagstones of the quad were greening as moss sunk its taps into the frost-corroded stone and muck from the horses fed them. The massive chunk of obsidian known as Traitor's Doom that dominated the central court of Mask Fortress stood gleaming and unbroken, save for the nicks cut out of its upper face due to the falling of the executioner's sword. Male jackrabbits were using it as a platform to box with their rivals, and they bounded away as the surlord and his Eye Men drew close. Styven Dalway drew his sword and speared one, and a little jet of blood was flung over the flagstones as Dalway shook the creature from his sword. It was a pastime for brothers-in-the-watch, spearing the rabbits that lived in the quad; a casual test of speed.

"Leave me," Iss commanded Dalway and Foss as they neared the entrance to the Cask. The two men waited for an explanation but he gave none, and they stood uncomfortably for a moment, shifting their weight from foot to foot until Axal Foss conceded with a nod.

Blond and handsome, Dalway leant against the curved wall

of the Cask as if he meant to stay there a while. "We await you, Surlord," he said.

Iss flung back the gate and then pushed the heavy red oak door into motion. "Why don't you run along and clean the rabbit's blood from your sword instead?"

He didn't bother to wait for a response. Dalway had been one of his recruits, and Axal Foss one of his captain's when he'd held the position of Protector General. Iss knew these men. They were loyal solely to the Watch and the man who commanded it. Once that man had been Penthero Iss, now it was Marafice Eye. Iss knew better than to take their insolence personally. He knew, but didn't like it.

Inside the great rotunda of the Cask more of their kind patrolled the entrances to the principal chambers. South lay the way to his private quarters and the Bastard Walk lined with stone statues of the Founding Quarterlords, but for now Iss chose to head toward the Blackvault. A wide flight of stairs led down, each step perfectly graded to be a fraction darker than the last. The Cask was built from light-colored limestone, and rather than shock the senses with an abrupt transition from white to black, the stonemasons had chosen to pave the way with all the shades of gray in between. Iss's soft-soled boots hit dove and slate and charcoal before touching the raven marble the vault was named for. Legend had it that Harlaw Pengaron had burned his brother alive here, and later ordered the charred walls painted. Limewash and then strong lead pigments had been used to mask the burn, yet nothing ever quite succeeded. A month would pass and then the soot would suddenly start to reappear, rising up from the base stone like damp. Harlaw Pengaron had eventually ordered the vault's complete refitting with black marble, but he never lived to see the results.

Someone probably killed him, Iss thought as he entered the Blackvault. It was the way most surlords' stories ended.

The chamber was chilly and dim. Earlier that morning he'd bade Caydis Zerbina light a fire beneath the closest mantle and set candles burning about it, but black marble was ever a challenge to heat and light. The Blackvault stretched long beneath the fortress, its roof braced at its center by a line of arches that ran the entire two-hundred-foot length of the room. The High Examiner was supposed to walk the archways before investing a new surlord with the Killhound Seal, but no one had bothered with that for ninety years.

Iss crossed to the fire. He had expected to feel some kind of relief at being finally alone, but he was strangely agitated. Events had started, a world was turning, and here he was, boxed in by walls and men.

The armies of the Spire were moving north. Last he'd heard, they were raising camp on the east shore of the Spill. His darkcloaks sent birds to mark their progress, loosing a rook from the back of the wagon train each night. The progress had been beset by delays. The storm, the thick muds of spring thaw, and rivers in spate. Only thirteen days out and already there was illness in the ranks. The flux, doubtless brought on by men shitting where they ate. Not an illness likely to take grangelords and commanders, more's the pity. Iss managed a wry smile. He envied none of them, he must remember that. A surlord who valued his life *sent* armies, not led them.

"Master."

Iss turned from the fire to see Caydis Zerbina standing at the chamber's entrance. Caydis had been his personal servant for seventeen years, and Iss had long grown accustomed to the fact that one never heard him approach. Caydis was tall and striking, his skin the color and texture of polished cherrywood. His neck was long enough for two men, and he could do things with it, bend the bones in a certain way, rotate it a degree past normal, that reminded Iss of a gazelle. He wore plain, undyed linens, and sheathed his arms in bone bracelets that announced to all who looked that he worshipped with the priests in the Bone Temple.

"Guest is here," he announced softly.

"Bring him to me. Help him down the steps if he needs it."

The elder Roland Stornoway entered the Blackvault accompanied by a dry tapping of his cane, and a wheeze that conveyed both the level of his exertions and his annoyance. He had refused Caydis's offer of assistance, but Caydis knew a dodderer when he saw one, and stayed close in case of sudden need.

"An ill place for a meet, Surlord," Stornoway barked from the entrance, ever determined to have the first and last word. "You insult me with the setting."

"It *is* marble," Iss said evenly.

"Pah!" Stornoway raised his cane and took a swipe at the air. "I won't play your games, Surlord. Find me a seat and speak."

Iss gestured to Caydis, who brought forth a gilded, rack-backed chair with a red cushion on the seat, and then left. The Lord of the High Granges, Lord of the Highland Passes, and Lord of the Rape Seed Granges looked at the cushion as if it were a serpent, shoved it onto the floor with the butt of his cane, and then sat. "I'll give you no more backing for the war," he said with some spirit, as if Iss had just pleaded with him to do that very thing.

A hard old nutgall, that was what Borhis Horgo had called him. He was massively rich, but never took any joy from it—unless you counted the entertaining he did with scandalously young whores—and just grew more joyless and worse dressed with age.

"I could raise a Battle Levy if I needed to," Iss pointed out.

"Raise all you like—I won't pay it."

Iss accepted this with apparent equanimity. Money *was*

always a problem, but that was not why he had brought the grangelord here today. Guiding the subject toward his objective, he said, "Am I to take it you have no interest in your son-in-law's success?"

"Ha!" Stornoway snapped. "I knew it. The Knife's up your arse and twisting."

Iss hid his distaste. "I'd be more worried if I were you, old man," he said lightly, coldly. "Marafice Eye needs a grange before he can take my place."

Roland Stornoway in no way acknowledged this as a fact, but he had to know it. "My granges go to my son."

"You know I passed an Act of Ascendancy?"

Stornoway nodded harshly. "A more fool thing I have never seen in all my sixty years."

He was right, of course, but Stornoway wasn't the only one who could refuse to yield. "Well, it is done. Watch your back."

"And while I do I'm watching yours as well, eh?" Stornoway's shrunken little eyes were almost gleeful. "You tell me nothing new, Surlord. Do you take me for a complete fool? I know Marafice Eye would like me dead. My own son and half my enemies would like me dead. Yet I'm not dead, I'm here, and I've a fancy to stay."

Iss felt some measure of relief. Marafice Eye had miscalculated here if he thought Roland Stornoway would lie easy under his knife. Iss said, because he was genuinely interested, "It was your choice to marry him to your daughter."

Stornoway actually chuckled, a thin, hiccuping wheeze that sounded as if it might kill him more readily than Marafice Eye. "Well, I'll have the last laugh there."

"What do you mean?"

"The girl's four months gone with child. By the time the Knife's back from the wars she will have presented him with her bastard."

It explained so much. The scandal involving the book-binder's son was damaging but not ruinous. A bastard out of wedlock *was*. "And he doesn't know it?"

"He will when he sees the babbie. The bookbinder and his son both have six fingers on each hand." Stornoway slapped his thigh with the sheer deliciousness of the deceit he had practiced upon the Knife. "Who will they say is the fool then?"

Probably still you, Iss thought, but didn't say it. He wouldn't want to be in the room when the Knife discovered what the old bastard had pulled on him.

"I'll let you go now," Iss said, somehow unsatisfied with the meeting despite the fact it had lifted some fear. He really didn't care for Roland Stornoway; his harshness was arrogance in disguise. All the grangelords had it, that arrogance. Iss had been dealing with it most of his life.

"So I'm dismissed, am I?" Stornoway grumbled, shifting weakly in his chair. "Well, help me up, then."

Iss ignored him and left the chamber.

He passed his servant on the stairs, and bade him fetch some warm honey from the kitchen. Caydis Zerbina looked pointedly toward the Blackvault. "Leave him," Iss said. "Fetch the honey and meet me by the Killdoor."

Passing patrols of brothers-in-the-watch, Iss headed in the direction of his private quarters. As always the Bastard Walk, with its hugely curving walls and grotesquely hewn statues, calmed him. This was his domain, and his alone. Only he and the fortress servants ever walked here. Drawing to a halt by the steel-plated door that led to the unused east gallery, he unhooked one of the three keys he kept in a pouch sewn to the inside of his silk robe.

As he waited for Caydis to arrive with the honey he studied the door. The Killhound standing rampant above the Splinter had been stamped into all eight of its metal plates. It had been some time since he'd last opened it—weeks, perhaps even months. What was the use of entering an empty storeroom? The Bound One was failing, useless. If it hadn't been for the occasional ministrations of Caydis Zerbina he would already be dead.

Still. *Still.* Iss was loath to give him up. A bound sorcerer was not something one disposed of lightly. Their value was high . . . and there were risks.

Iss turned the key. With Sarga Veys gone—the devil knew where—and the Bound One unresponsive, Iss had lost various options. Sorcery wasn't power in itself, but it did provide the means to achieve it. Iss likened it to one of the light and deadly sickle-knives used by Caydis Zerbina's people. The blades were specially constructed to be used in the left hand. You could fight without one, using just your sword, but you lost the ability to surprise your opponent. And why wield one blade when you could wield two?

Sorcery had always been the weapon in Iss's left hand, yet for months now he had been fighting one-handed. Oh, there were the darkcloaks—the surlord's special force, his spies—but they hadn't consciously drawn sorcery in centuries, and though they used the remnants of it they did so without acknowledging the source. They threw birds into the sky, waited in alleyways and listened outside doors, poisoned, bribed, procured, fought with live steel when they had to, and silenced loose tongues with knives: All the while throwing the suggestion of shadows around themselves—a fluttering, an inconsistency of light that could not withstand a hard stare from an onlooker. It was how they got their name: Darkcloaks. They had magic, but it was as insubstantial as the shadows they drew around themselves to enhance their stealth. It was a pretty trick, no more.

Skills such as Sarga Veys and the Bound One possessed were

something else entirely. They had the power to hold back nature. There were a dozen things they could do with mist. They could compel wild animals to spy for them, looking out through the uncomprehending eyes of a rabbit or a fox; they could steal into a man's body and snap his ureter so his urine drained into his pelvic girdle, not his bladder; they could throw a false landscape across hills and plains to confuse a traveler; they could aid or obstruct healing, command shadows, defend themselves with a single thought, and track others of their kind like hounds. Necromancers could hold a man's soul in his corpse while it rotted. Spellbinders could cast a spell on an object that lasted for thousands of years. Archmages could cloak fortresses, men, and armies. And the Sull maygi could stir time.

This was what Iss wanted. All of it. Yet though many men and women were born with traces of the Old Skills—Iss could name at least ten people in the fortress who had them in some small measure, Corwick Mools and Caydis Zerbina amongst them—very few were born with enough to make them sorcerers.

And Iss knew he was not one of them. That was why he'd bound one to him, a chained sorcerer who would do his bidding.

For nearly two decades he had enjoyed the advantages access to such power brought. Nearly fourteen years ago, when the day came to storm the fortress and overthrow the aging and sickly Borhis Horgo, the Bound One had thrown a shadow over the entire city. And later, during the ten bloody days of the Expulsions, it had been the Bound One who had tracked down the Forsworn knights in their lairs so Iss could send red cloaks to slay them. And so it had continued on over the years: compulsions, far-speaking, ensorcellments. Iss was in little doubt that he would have made surlord without the Bound One's aid, but it had hastened his rise, and fortified his position in a hundred different ways.

The Bound One had ever been Iss's sickle-knife, but now the left-handed blade had grown dull.

Iss sighed as he watched Caydis Zerbina approach, holding a cloth tit of honey, a pewter flask and a tiny guarded lamp. "Wrap them for me," Iss commanded, and waited while his servant detached a length of fabric from his linen kilt and fashioned his surlord a makeshift pouch.

Caydis's hands were finely shaped, the fingers elongated and capped with startlingly white nails. When he was done, Iss said, "The Eye Men, the ones who follow me day and night. I would prefer to see less of them."

"Master." Caydis bent his long gazelle neck.

"A little illness in the ranks would be sufficient." Iss considered his options. "The flux, perhaps."

Again, there was another bending of the neck. It would be done.

Iss took the linen pack and the lamp, and passed beyond the steel-plated door and into the unused east gallery. It was dark here, the windows boarded, the torches unlit for over ten years. Pigeons warbled in the roof groins. A fine dust of dried bird droppings and crumbled masonry crackled beneath Iss's feet. Once the air had held a charge that grew stronger as one approached the interior doorway of the Splinter, but it had weakened to almost nothing over the past six months. Now all Iss felt was a sense of settling, of things drawing to a close.

The door to the Splinter was set in a wall carved with stone reliefwork. The Impaled Beasts of Spire Vanis sat with surprising triumph upon poles, and as always Iss was glad to put the sight of them behind him. Once within the Splinter he adjusted the flame on the lamp. He had forgotten how cold and utterly dark the oldest of Mask Fortress's four towers could be. Even now, with spring showing in the city as budding trees and thawed lakes, winter held here. Hoarfrost plated the walls just as surely as steel plated the Killdoor. Seven thousand feet below the snow line on Mount Slain, yet the temperature and conditions were the same. Just as lightning rods drew lightning, so the Splinter drew ice.

Iss shivered and moved quickly to the underspace below the stairway where the entrance to the Inverted Spire could be found.

Speaking a word of command he revealed the portal, its gate rumbling back to display a descending flight of steps. He took them with some haste, not wishing to dwell on the weakness he experienced performing a single small act of sorcery.

The Inverted Spire was calm this day, its winds barely stirring. The small lamp Iss carried lacked the power to illuminate the great chasm at its center. Down the steps wound, past walls ground with lenses of ice and veined with hairline cracks. *Have they been here all this time?* Iss wondered. *These flaws forking through the stone?*

By the time he'd finally descended into the first of the round chambers Iss was weary. The thought of having to climb back up disheartened him, and he wished suddenly he had not come. Steeling himself, he passed through the Inverted Spire's upper two chambers and into the dark well below.

The Bound One stank, not of the foulness of human waste, but of the sharp sourness of old men close to death. He lay in his iron cradle, his arms and feet drawn up close to his belly, his chains wrapped like an umbilical cord around him. He did not move, yet he seemed to for a moment as the lamplight impelled the caul flies crawling upon his body to take flight.

Iss moved closer. The Bound One's skin had a gray-yellow cast to it, the kind that came with a drawing inwards of the blood. The chafe marks on his wrists were no longer red, but black, and that same blackness had spread like welts around his pressure sores. Iss knelt to touch him, his heart aching softly in his chest. There had always been love between them; some deep, needful breed of it born out of dependency and isolation and the terrible act of Binding. For eighteen years the Bound One had drawn toward his master's touch, had sought it like a dog seeks affection from its owner. And Iss had always felt the corresponding pull. He felt it now, as he touched the Bound One gently on his cheek.

Nothing. Not even a tremor of acknowledgment or recognition. Iss let the linen pack containing the water and the honey drop to the floor, out of reach. Great sadness filled him. An end was drawing near, but it was surely better this way, letting the Bound One weaken gradually over many days and weeks. Less dangerous. Only a very great fool would forget who lay here. And only a greater one would attempt to end that life by other means.

Iss leant over and laid a kiss on the Bound One's head. It was over between them. Eighteen years—now this.

With a heavy heart Iss departed the iron chamber, closed the door and drew the bolt.

He waits, waits. Such a small and terrible thing to wait, such a relinquishing of self. Yet wait he must, and he concentrates on moving air in and out of his lungs in small degrees as he listens to the Light Bringer retreat.

He knows he is failing, and sometimes that fills him with such despair that he begs the darkness to take him. Surely he has endured enough. When do you give in and say, *This life is too painful, let me end it?*

Not yet, comes the reply from inside himself, surprising him with its heat. *Not yet, Light Bringer. Not yet.* So he waits and gathers his power about him, and sometimes the moisture in the chamber condenses and rains down upon him and he open his lips and lets its sweetness fall on his swollen tongue.

Not yet.

FORTY-ONE

Desertion

The earth tremor in the night had left the dogs uneasy, and the Dog Lord found himself impatient with their fussiness. They had not eaten the horse liver he'd cut up for them this morning, and they'd fought their leashes as he pulled them outside. Damn-fool dogs. So what if the earth was shaking? Did they think themselves safer in the roundhouse, chained to their rat hooks, than here under the open sky? Briefly, Vaylo wondered why no man had invented a dog whip—they worked passing well for horses, by the gods!

"It's just beyond the basswoods," Hammie Faa said, leading the way from the Dhoonehouse. "You'll see it in just a bit."

Vaylo huffed. Hammie Faa was getting fat. Some people did that, he'd noticed, grew into their names as they matured. Molo Bean had been the same way. His head had started out a normal shape, but somewhere along the way it had developed a certain off-centeredness—a bulbous forehead and a bulbous chin and a concavity in between. Bean-shaped, no doubt about it. The Dog Lord wondered what that meant for him. Quickly deciding it didn't bear worrying about, he kicked some speed from his dogs and followed Hammie Faa through the trees.

The day was a fine one, despite the violent shake-up in the night. There were clouds, but they didn't mean anything, just some puffed-up sheep shapes in the sky. The sun was pale and still rising, and there was a tickler of a wind. The bare branches of the basswoods clicked together as they swayed; a dozen of them had been planted too closely and were now competing for the same space. If Vaylo had his way he'd chop them all down and be done with it. The basswood was a Blackhail tree. They hollowed them out and laid their dead in them—perhaps he'd have them felled and sent there as a gift. As always, thinking of Blackhail made the pressure build in his head. Seventeen grandchildren slain. And Blackhail had not paid for it. Vaylo woke every morning into a world where Blackhail had not paid.

Breathing out heavily, he yanked on his dogs' leashes to bring them into line. Some things a man could not think of and remain sane.

Ahead, Hammie Faa had drawn to a halt by the curiosity he had brought his chief to see. There had been a well at the center of the grove, but Vaylo did not know what it could be called now. The entire bricked well-shaft had popped out of the ground like a cork forced from a bottle.

The Dog Lord felt a chill take him. *We are Clan Bludd, chosen by the Stone Gods to guard their borders.*

Hammie inclined his pink face toward the queer cylinder of stone. "Happened in the night. Tremor did it."

The dogs would not go near it. They were already spooked enough. Aware that Hammie was watching him expectantly, Vaylo kept his expression bluff. "Well, that's one less place to draw water from, eh? We can always use the bricks to build another outhouse—you can never have too many of those."

Hammie had been hoping to astound his chief, and Vaylo could tell he was disappointed. Faa men had never learned to rule their faces; that was partly why Vaylo trusted them. Masgro,

Hammie's father, had been a devil of a man, a gambler, a wencher—and straight to the hilt.

Vaylo made an effort. "It's a sight, Hammie, I'll give you that. Has anyone else seen it?"

"I told Pengo where it was. He said to fetch you first thing to take a look at it."

Something about this statement struck the Dog Lord as odd. An instinct he didn't fully understand made him glance in the direction of the Dhoonehouse. He and Hammie had come about a league east, and the trees and the slight rise in the land prevented him from seeing the domed and gated structure. "I think we'll head back, Hammie," he said, crouching to release the dogs from their tethers. "Go!" he commanded them. "Home!"

The dogs raced off eagerly, and Hammie and his chief followed at a brisk pace. Vaylo noted the presence of a knife and sword slung from Hammie's gear belt. Good. But he'd wished they'd thought to bring horses.

What had been a moderate walk downhill was a climb on the way back, Vaylo swore it. His old Bludd heart was beating harder than it should have, and he felt a weariness that wasn't solely due to lack of sleep. True, he had been woken at midnight along with everyone else in the Dhoonehold—probably the entire North—as the earth shook and the roundhouse ground and rolled above him. But there weren't many times when he slept through the night. His body was accustomed to hard use. No. This was something else. An accumulation of worry. Angus Lok's visit had added to the tally, and now it had reached the point where he could find no restful place in his mind. And when that happened the body suffered.

He saw one of his worries made real as he and Hammie gained the rise. The Horns and the two-storey stable gate had been thrown open and an army of Bluddsmen were assembling there. Grooms and boys were bringing out horses, spears were being thrust into saddle shoes, hammer chains fastened, wagons loaded, plate strapped across chests, barrels rolled over the court, chickens chased, swords oiled, bows braced, helms lowered, and sable greatcloaks fastened at throats. It was a sight to stir a Bluddsman's heart, and Vaylo knew with a certainty he had no power to control it.

A call to arms was mother's milk to Clan Bludd.

Hammie swore, taking the words right from Vaylo's mouth.

Pengo Bludd stood in the center of the field of men, high atop his great gray warhorse, allowing a young boy elevated on a mounting stool to fasten his hammer chains about him as if he were a chief. When he spied his father approaching, he raised a hand in greeting, his eyes triumphant.

He had planned it well, Vaylo had to give him that. Frowning grimly, the Dog Lord approached the Horns.

Pengo had the audacity to ignore him at first, finding himself much occupied with cradling his spiked hammer just so. Men milling around him had the decency to look shamefaced in their defiance, and none had the nerve to ignore their chief. They opened a space for him, nudging back their mounts to give him space.

"Son," Vaylo said quietly. "I see your spine still bends both ways."

Color flushed Pengo's cheeks, and he made his stallion rear to disguise his feelings. "I've raised an army, Dog Lord. Time was when you would have done the same."

Silence spread through the men like a ripple on a pond. At that moment Vaylo would have given his soul for a horse. He shifted his gaze from face to face, taking tally, recalling names. Many here were Pengo's men, but others were not. Cuss Madden, Ranald Weir, the three Grubber boys, Cawdo Salt, Trew Danhro . . . and so the list went on. Even the smith Tiny Croda was geared and mounted.

It was pointless asking how this had been done. Bluddsmen prided themselves on their ability to ride to war at short notice. Jaw depended on swift, decisive action, not meticulous planning. Perhaps Pengo was right: thirty years ago he might have done the same. *But that was a different time and there was less to lose*, he told himself, but he wasn't so sure he was right. Maybe there was always a lot to lose, but the young didn't know it.

"Where do you ride?" he asked.

Pengo looked as if he couldn't quite believe his father wasn't giving him a fight. "South to Withy," he said bullishly.

Vaylo nodded. It was a flexible position. From Withy Pengo could monitor the Spire's armies, move swiftly east to Haddo and HalfBludd, or strike against Blackhail at Ganmiddich. He probably hadn't made up his mind which.

The Dog Lord motioned to the wagons. "I see you're taking a fair cut of my supplies?"

"What would you have us do, Father? Starve?"

You, son, in a minute. "And women, too?"

Pengo shrugged, growing more confident. "A warrior must have other comforts beside food."

Vaylo sprang forward and grabbed his son's booted foot, twisting hard. Pengo rose in his saddle, his eyes widening in shock and indignation. Vaylo thrust up. Somewhere in his son's knee bone cracked.

"Listen to me, boy. Take the men, take the women, take the food. But take my grandchildren and die." Another thrust upward. "Do you understand?"

Pengo winced. One hand had gone to his horse's neck to balance himself and the other had gone to his knee. His gaze flicked nervously from side to side. Men were looking at their feet, their pommels, their fingernails: anywhere but at Pengo Bludd.

"I *said*, do you understand?"

He nodded.

"Good." Vaylo didn't release his hold, though he slackened the upward pressure. "Now I'm going to send Hammie to that cart over there, and he's going to take the bairns back inside. Aren't you, Hammie?"

"Yes, chief."

"And you and I are going to stay here until he's done it."

Hammie moved with the speed of a Stone God, and his task was completed in under two minutes. Vaylo got a good long look at his second son during that time, and decided he very much disliked him. Pengo just got to look ridiculous, and that suited Vaylo well enough. When he was ready he released him.

Pengo swung his weight back into his saddle. He was shaking with rage, and might have charged his horse if it hadn't been for the five dogs moving to circle his father. He settled on sharply jerking its head toward the Dhoonehouse. "I hope you die there," he said to his father.

Vaylo wanted suddenly to be gone. Ignoring his son, he addressed his clan. "Bludd!" he cried. "A hard life long lived to us all!"

Men cheered, and the army began to move out on his call. Pengo sent daggers to his father, and then shoved and bullied his way to the head of the train lest anyone forget who was its leader.

Vaylo stood on the tower court and watched his clansmen trot south along Blue Dhoone Lake. The wagons churned the shore to mud, and a patch of yellow spring flowers Vaylo had admired that very morning was beheaded, crushed and finally driven beneath the dirt. It took Pengo's army the better part of an hour to leave the court, with many warriors and wagons lagging behind. Someone had failed to catch all the chickens, and the stupid creatures flapped and fretted, declining to take advantage of their chance for escape. The dogs wanted at them, but Vaylo wasn't sure yet how badly the Dhoone stores had been raided and he thought he just might need them himself.

Already there had been waste; barrels split and leaking beer—it'd be a boon night for snails—sagging grain sacks discarded, a crock of butter smashed and oozing yellow grease onto the court. As Vaylo looked on a handful of women came forward to begin the clearing-up. They were nervous of him, wary of drawing too close or meeting his eye; Nan had probably sent them. Sighing heavily, he left his dogs to lick up the butter, and crossed into the Dhoonehouse.

Loyal men were awaiting him inside the great blue entrance hall. Hammie and Samlo Faa, Odda Bull, Glen Carvo and more stood in a half-circle and greeted their chief with silent, telling nods. Most were warriors past their prime. *Like me*, Vaylo thought with a stab of black humor. *I've been left in charge of an army of old men.*

Nothing for it but to send the young ones to do the legwork. "Hammie. Do the rounds and take a head count. I want every green boy and maid reckoned for, and weapons found for all of them. Samlo. I need you to ride out to the guard posts along the borders. There should be at least twenty swordsmen between here and the Flow. Bring them in."

Hammie and his younger, bigger brother nodded. Already some of the tension in their faces had eased: the Dog Lord would not fail them.

As they rushed off to do his bidding, Vaylo sent Odda Bull to inspect the Dhoonehouse's defenses and report back to him that night. Odda was graying but still hard. He'd been cousin to Ockish, and could play the pipes; a good man to have around.

"Glen," Vaylo said to Strom Carvo's brother when he was done with setting tasks. "You're with me."

They went to see Nan first. The Dhoonehouse was quiet

and strangely echoing. Torches had gone out and no one had thought to relight them. In the tunnel leading down toward the kitchens Vaylo saw boot prints stamped in something sticky like honey. Flies were just getting interested.

The Dhoone kitchens were a series of high-ceilinged chambers clustered together on the west wall of the roundhouse. "Kitchens" was perhaps too simple a name for them, for some of the chambers contained granaries and butteries, game rooms and brewhouses, a mews for poultry and stock tanks for fish. The kitchens were a lot grander here than in Bludd, and Vaylo found himself wondering where a lad might go to beg scraps and fancies from the cook. He didn't have to wonder long as Nan came out to meet him and guide him and Glen toward the proper part of the kitchens, where things were actually cooked.

Nan's movements were serene, her lovely sea-gray braid smooth as woven corn. "They waited until I'd left to help with the lambing," she said, almost managing to keep the same serenity in her voice.

Vaylo nodded, though he needed no explanation from her. Nan Culldayis's loyalty had never been a question in his mind. She had loved both of them, that was the wondrous thing, first his wife and then him. Nan had been with Angarad the day she died, had held her like a sister as she spoke of the old times when they'd been girls together in Bludd. Nan had been a fair maid in her youth, with long chestnut hair and eyes to match . . . but Vaylo had never thought anything of her. Only Angarad had stirred his heart. Now, nearly forty years later, things had changed between them. Nan's husband had been killed during a raid on Croser the year following Angarad's death. Shared grief had brought some comfort and healing.

The proper kitchen, as Vaylo decided to call it, was in the process of being cleared up. At some point Nan had run out of women to command, and had set a stable boy and the two bairns to cleaning. A lot of sweeping was being done, but Vaylo doubted its effectiveness. The stable boy would sweep one way, and Pasha and Ewan would sweep the dirt right back at him. Vaylo had a half a mind to pick up a broom and show them how it was done—he'd swept out his share of stables and yards over the years—but he suspected cleanliness wasn't the point here. Nan was doing exactly the same thing with the grand-children as he was doing with his men: keeping them busy.

"So, Nan," he said to her. "What have they left us?"

"Some livestock. A little grain." She grinned at him. "All of the eels."

Vaylo barked a laugh, and instantly felt better than he had all day. His grandchildren were here. Nan was here. His dogs were on the court, making themselves sick. At his side Glen Carvo's face was like stone. Glen and his late brother had been much alike: strong warriors, and loyal but serious men. Vaylo missed Strom every day. He missed every Bluddsman who'd died since he'd made chief.

"Is there enough to make do?" Vaylo asked Nan.

"There'll be enough. I'll see to that."

Vaylo nodded, understanding all she had not said. Nan Culldayis was claiming this worry for her own; she would not let him share in it. "I'll be in the stables if needed," he said to her. And then, to the stable boy: "If you're coming with Glen and me you'd better get a move on, lad."

The stable boy couldn't quite believe his luck. He looked hopefully at Nan, who nodded her consent and told him to leave the broom against the wall.

The small party of three left the kitchens and headed west through the darkening corridors of Dhoone. Hammie hadn't yet returned with a head count, but Vaylo could tell it wasn't going to be good. He was taken with the feeling that he, Glen and the stable boy were rattling around in an abandoned ship. Still. He couldn't blame the clansmen who rode south; they were following their hearts rather than Pengo Bludd. They simply wanted to fight.

I waited too long to punish Blackhail. I held on to Dhoone when I should have been visiting the gods' own vengeance upon every Hailsman in the North. Vaylo puffed out a great quantity of air. Glancing around, he noticed they were passing through the King's Quarter of the Dhoonehouse. He could find little to like in its cavernous halls and meeting chambers long stripped of furnishings and other comforts. Some ancient blue velvet curtains hung on a wall that had neither windows not doors, and that seemed to sum this place up. Faded finery without purpose.

Yet it was his. And he must keep it, else it make a mockery of his life. He had traded part of his soul to gain this place, and if he lost it there was no getting any of that missing soul back.

Last night's tremor had released great quantities of dust, and Vaylo roused clouds of gray powder as he quickened his pace. That was another thing that weighed upon his mind: why the earth had shaken. Vaylo recalled one summer nearly a lifetime ago when he and Ockish Bull had laid a wall. It was punishment for some misdemeanor or other, and Gullit had sent them both to Gamber Hench to do his backwork for a month. Gamber was old, but still the best mason in the clan, and he had taught Vaylo and Ockish some things worth knowing. Vaylo had learned that a dry wall could never be laid quickly; stones needed time to settle. Gamber held the earth they walked on was much the same as one of his walls in progress, still settling. That had made sense to Vaylo, and ever since then, whenever he'd felt a slight shift in the land beneath him, he'd think of Gamber Hench and be satisfied there was no reason for fear. Yet what had happened last night had seemed the opposite of that. An *unsettling*. And Vaylo was unsettled.

Yet what could he do about it? He wasn't a Stone God, just a chief.

By the time he reached the stables his mood had darkened, and it was an effort to keep the blackness hidden from his men. First things first. "How many horses are still boxed?"

The stable master had ridden south, but one of the grooms had already taken the initiative and was busy walking the remaining horses to stalls closer to the doors. "Pengo ordered all the boxes to be cleared," the youth said, gulping. "But the master wouldn't do it."

A *kind of loyalty there*, Vaylo thought, even though the man had deserted him. "And how many did the master leave us?"

"Three dozen, not counting the ponies."

Oh gods.

"They didn't take Dog Horse," the groom added quickly, catching sight of Vaylo's expression.

No one would, unless they fancied a swift kick to the vitals. Seeing the groom still watching him, half anxious and half hopeful, Vaylo made an effort. "You've done well, lad. Just be sure to keep these beasts well tended." The groom nodded. "And for now Glen'll be needing his mount."

As the groom went to fetch and saddle the swordsman's horse, Vaylo turned to Glen Carvo.

"I need you to ride at haste to the Dhoonewall. Cluff Drybannock stands there with a hundred and eighty men. We need them home."

Glen left within the quarter, the only man in Dhoone that day heading north. Vaylo watched him leave. It was going to be a long eight days until he returned.

FORTY-TWO

Into the Want

The frozen earth was weeping. The small white badlands sun had warmed its skin, and now the first half-foot of ice was melting. Water oozed around the pony's hooves, and then sank back when the weight was lifted. Black flies hovered in great clouds above the tundra, and Raif couldn't see anything else for them to feed on but him and his horse.

As best he could figure out he was in the badlands northeast of Blackhail. It was a bleak place, ridged and boiled, seeded with plants that looked as lifeless as dry bones. Ground willow, spike grass and fever thorns grew in treacherous clumps along the elk path. Every stone he passed was crusted with lichen or salt, and sometimes when the pony stepped onto one it crumbled like chalk.

The pony was hurting. Its legs hadn't healed properly from the bashing they'd taken at the rock slide, and some of the cuts were still open. The stout little creature soldiered on, but Raif had noticed a slight hesitancy in her step the past few days and guessed walking was causing her some pain. She ate whatever lay close at hand—thorns, grass, some of the wild sorrel and sage that sprang up overnight on the damp fringes of muskegs—

and wasn't at all fussy about her water. Raif could see why the Maimed Men valued these horses. A clan stallion would have been showing its nerves by now.

They were close to the edge, Raif felt it. Close to the place where the Great Want leaked into the badlands. No clansman would come this far north, for fear of being lost. Raif had looked into himself to find the same fear, but there were some dead spots in his emotions now, and though he retained fear of many things the Want wasn't one of them.

To be lost, to wander forever north into the great white vastness that covered half a continent . . . there were worse things. Raif Sevrance could name them.

His lips stretched into something. It couldn't have been a smile because it hurt. The skin on his face was absolutely dry, covered with winter scale. His knuckles ached deeply where Bitty's sword had cut. At first the wound had been a straight line, slashing across the highest three bones, but the edges had dried and curled, the scar tissue pulling the joints apart, and now the cut was shaped like an oak leaf. It was not infected; trust Bitty to use a clean blade.

Bitty Shank had fought fairly. The question was, had Raif?

He needed the answer to be *Yes*, but he found his memory wasn't clear. Had he heart-killed Bitty? Or had he simply placed his sword well? It seemed something he would never resolve. He couldn't go back and tear the moment apart until it gave him what he needed. That would be using Bitty's memory to relieve his guilt.

And he hadn't sunk that low yet.

Tell that to Blackhail, snapped a hard voice inside him, and though it was cold Raif felt the shame-heat burn him. How many days had passed since the raid. Three? Four? Someone with a swift horse and little need for sleep could be at the round-house by now. It was, quite simply, an unbearable thought.

He could not bear it.

What had the Listener said to him? *Grow wide shoulders, Clansman.* He had, but they were not wide enough. Just to imagine Drey's face as he heard the words *Your brother has turned Maimed Man* caused a stab in his heart. This time there were no excuses, no misunderstandings. Raif Sevrance had killed members of his own clan. The blackest of all evils, and he had done it.

Gently, Raif guided the pony up a bluff littered with rocks. Scratching the soft skin behind her ears, he encouraged her to place her feet. Black flies were bothering both of them: there were pinpricks of blood on the pony's neck and corresponding stings on his own. If they were lucky the wind might pick up and drive the pests away; he wished it more for the horse than for himself.

The day was halfway through, and the sky was open but pale. When they reached the crest of the bluff a sea of drowned grass spread wide before them. The top ice had melted for leagues and the water just stood there, unable to drain. Raif grimaced and eased the pony toward it.

He had nearly not brought her. After he'd left Stillborn and emerged from Black Hole he'd had little thought except to get away. Some things had been sharp in his mind, others not. *I have my sword, my bow, and Divining Rod*, he remembered thinking. All three things had been in his possession as he left the tunnel; he could not recall taking stock of any other need. Yet here he was with the pony and a fair portion of supplies.

It had been the outlander's doing, not his own. "Mor Drakka," he had called from the shadows by the lake. "Do not walk into the darkness unprepared."

Raif remembered the voice quite specifically. Something in its pitch had halted him at a time when he had been determined not to be halted. It made his skin crawl even now, that feeling of being gripped.

The outlander's eyes had been strangely bright, and blood was leaking from one of them. Now that the mist had gone the night was clear and the wind raised snake tracks on the water. "Take the pony," the outlander said, pulling the reins and making the little horse trot out in front of Raif. "It's a hard journey north."

Raif had not questioned him. In a night full of terrors it had seemed such a minor one: that anticipation of his purpose. Now Raif knew it for the cold-blooded horror that it was. The outlander had loaded the pony with fresh water, blankets, a flint and striker, hoof grease, a quarter-weight of oiled grain, and the sum of his own food rations for the past fifteen days. The raid party had consumed the last of the cheese during the storm, yet there was cheese. They'd run out of honey by the fifth day, yet there was a pouch of it wrapped in greased hide in Raif's pack. Lardcake, raw pheasants' eggs, even dried and roasted chestnuts: these were all things the raid party had eaten with haste and to hell with planning—there was always hardtack and dried meat for the journey back. Yet someone had planned ahead. Someone had set his rations aside for another purpose.

The outlander had known all along where Raif was headed.

Laying his aching hand on the pony's neck, Raif took comfort in her living, breathing warmth. Had the slaying of Raif's own clansman been part of the outlander's plan? Had the outlander raised the mist, hoping to add to Raif's confusion? And if so, what did it change?

Nothing, was the answer, and Raif tried to push the subject aside. The outlander was just like Heritas Cant in Ille Glaive: not interested in people for what they were, just in how they fitted into long-laid plans. Cant had been Phage, too.

Having reached the shallow sea of standing water, Raif

dismounted. Water oozed over the top of his boots as he led the pony forward. Ahead, the land ran flat and uninterrupted for leagues. It would take them hours to cross this place. Raif took some lardcake from his pack and split a portion between himself and the pony. The pony lipped against Raif's palm to get at the last of the goodness. More black flies were hatching from the water, rising up in a buzzing mist. The pony swiped them with her tail, and Raif batted them away with the back of his hand. His toes were beginning to tingle. The top ice might have melted, but the water temperature was only a beat above freezing.

What was he doing here? Only a part deep within him knew. He'd had to flee the mine, he'd been sure of that, and it had seemed his only option was to head north. Raif shook his head a bit, scorning the hollowness of that last excuse. It took too much effort to lie to yourself in this place. He had come north because he *chose* to. He was here because from the moment Ash March had left him his life had been leading toward this moment and place.

Raif slid the Listener's arrow from the pouch rigged atop his bow case. *Take this arrow named Divining Rod that has been fletched with the Old Ones' hair, take it and use it to find what you must.* The arrow always surprised Raif with its lightness, the sense that the slightest draft of air could carry it for leagues. Raif believed now it had been inevitable that he would win it back from Stillborn. Perhaps even Stillborn's claiming of it had been inevitable. A delay, until Raif was ready to do what he must. The same with the Forsworn sword; Raif had not been prepared to wield it until now.

The sword's weight felt good, lying in its sealskin scabbard against his thigh. Right. Natural in a way it had not felt before. The chunk of rock crystal set in its pommel flickered with brilliant light. For a moment, Raif wondered what had become of its brother-sword, the one held by the head knight. Its edge had been blackened and warped, he remembered, as if something stronger than acid had burned it. He hoped no one had dared enter the knights' redoubt and take it. A man could lose his soul by such an act.

We search, the knight had said. *For the city of the Old Ones. The Fortress of Grey Ice.*

Raif returned the arrow to its case. Suddenly it seemed there were too many things he didn't fully understand. The answers were like objects balancing on the edge of his thoughts; the slightest turning of his mind toward them was enough to send them plummeting into an abyss. If he could just sneak up on them, that was the thing. Sneak up on his own thoughts.

That was why the gods had invented dreaming, he supposed.

Glancing over his shoulder, Raif calculated how far he'd come across the shallow sea. Farther than he'd imagined, for he could no longer see the lip of rock marking the bluff. His trail had gone, of course, sucked away by the standing water. The sky and sea stretched endlessly in all directions.

A chill went through Raif, and he pulled the Orrl cloak tight across his chest. Tem Sevrance had been the best tracker and huntsman in the clan; he had taught his sons and daughter to navigate through grasslands, forests and high country, how to follow and blaze trails, how to read winds and the moss on trees, and how to watch the sun and stars for bearing. Yet for the first time in fifteen years Raif was no longer sure where true north lay. It had to be ahead, for the sun lay behind him, but there were many ways ahead, many subtle degrees of difference. And now he found it impossible to gauge the movement of the sun. It hung there, cool and lifeless, a silver disk in a silver sky. Raif stood and watched it, guarding his eyes with his hand. Its light scorched ghost rings into his retinas that he saw even when he blinked.

The thing didn't move. Raif grinned insanely at that. Of

course it moved . . . it just wasn't letting him know it. Turning his back, he took careful note of the alignment of his pony's head. She hadn't moved all the time he'd been standing here, working things out, and now she was the sole indicator of the direction in which he'd been traveling.

"Good girl," he said softly, leading her forward. "This means you'll get chestnuts tonight."

It was getting colder, he realized. For the first time that day his breath whitened as it left his body. After an hour or so had passed he noticed the shallow sea was quickening, its water growing turbid and losing its ability to mirror light. Almost as a reflex action, Raif bent at the knee and ran his hands along the surface. Its temperature was shocking. When he brought his fingers to his lips and licked them, he tasted the brackishness of dissolved salts.

On he walked, with the sun like a fixed point behind him. When he calculated it was close to the time when light began to fail he monitored the sun's reflection in the sea. The disk skimmed over the freezing surface, and then suddenly the water clouded and the image was gone. Light dimmed. Raif slowed but did not halt. He wasn't sure he wanted to look over his shoulder again. Curiosity got the better of him after a while and he stole a glance. Gray clouds now covered a third of the sky, masking the sun and any path it cared to take toward the horizon.

Not wholly satisfied, Raif turned back . . . and saw the way ahead had subtly changed. Confused, he swept his gaze in a half-circle. Something about the shallow sea was different, and even as he tried to discern exactly what had changed, the pony's hooves made a cracking noise as they hit the first of the ice. The water had frozen. Thin blades of spike grass jutted through the hard surface, trapped.

"Easy now," Raif said to the pony, wondering if the words were wholly for the horse.

Quite suddenly, he realized that the black flies had gone and he couldn't recall when he'd last been aware of them. Now the only thing hatching was mist. Threads of it rose delicately from the ice, grazing the pony's hooves and sliding along the salt stains on Raif's boots. Watching it, he decided it was best to keep moving forward and not think too much.

Some measure of light still held, and he and the pony struck a fair pace. It was easier now the water had gone.

Time passed, and the new moon appeared in a quarter of the sky he would not have expected. The light stretched on. A handful of stars winked into existence, and Raif was relieved to see he recognized their formation. He fed a handful of chestnuts to the pony, and by the time she'd swallowed them the light had gone. To reassure himself Raif looked again for the known stars, the formation known as the Hammer. Something else now shone in its place.

He couldn't say he was surprised. He had realized some time back that he'd entered the Great Want.

No going back, he told himself. Tem had once told him that the way you entered the Want was never the same as the way you left it. You either found another way out or died trying.

A strangled laugh escaped Raif's throat. He was in the hands of the Old Ones now.

In a way night was less challenging than day. Losing your way in darkness was to be expected. It was easier to relinquish control. Raif found he wasn't so particular about the pony's heading any more, and let her wander where she chose. Sometimes she stopped to sniff the frozen grass. Once she tried eating it, but found it little to her liking and let it fall from her mouth in chewed tafts. When she increased her pace with no prompting from Raif, he guessed she'd caught a whiff of something worth investigating.

It was an island in the ice. A hummock of earth about forty

paces across and crowned with clusters of ground willow rose above the frozen sea. The pony slowed as they neared it, letting out a low whiffle that Raif took to mean *Here. This is where we'll spend the night.*

He followed her as she found a path up the shore. It was a good place: bitterly cold and exposed to the wind, but mercifully above the mist. Some of the ground willow had died on the root, and it made fine wood for a fire. Salts crusted on the bark fired colors into the flames as it kindled. Raif brushed down the pony and emptied out a careful measure of oiled grain on the hard earth before settling down to rest and eat. He doubled up his blanket to make a rug, and then sat and stared into the fire.

Bitty Shank had been with him and Drey that day on the Bluddroad. They'd all been scared together, but no one had shown it. Funny how it seemed a lifetime ago now. They had all been so young and not even known it.

Raif laid his head on the blanket and fell into a fitful sleep.

When he awoke the world was pearl gray, and there was nothing but mist below him and the pony. They could have been on the top of a mountain or on a rock in the middle of the sea. The wound across Raif's knuckles was throbbing, and he felt stiff and ill-rested. Terrible things had happened in his dreams.

The fire had gone out, and he quickly decided against relighting it. He drank some water from the skin, and then poured some into the cook pot for the pony. As she drank her fill, he removed her blanket and rubbed down her legs. One of the cuts on her heel looked in a bad way, and he greased and bandaged it. Worrying about the pony stopped him worrying about his dreams. Bitty Shank had been alive in them, walking with Raif's sword through his heart.

Raif broke camp and set off through the mist. All bearings

had been lost in the night and it was impossible to say in which direction he was heading. For all he knew it might not even have been dawn.

The mist moved like ice on a lake, subject to currents other than the wind. It lingered for hours after true daylight had come, and then drained away in the space of a quarter. Raif had been walking beside the pony ever since they'd left the island, but the sudden clearing of the air made him eager to ride. The pony seemed willing enough, and set her own pace at a trot.

The landscape was stark, like the face of the moon. The ice underfoot had turned rocky, and they had to be careful of narrow draws and sudden drops in the tundra floor. The sky was white and filled with clouds, and there was no sign of the sun. They crossed a great trench at what Raif judged to be mid-morning, and then a second one later in the day. As they climbed from the second basin, something the Listener had said came back to Raif. *In ages past the Great Want was green with trees, and blue water flowed there along riverbeds so broad and deep that entire villages could be tossed into their centers and sink without a trace.*

Raif glanced back at the trench. Could a river have run here? Abruptly, he turned the pony and headed down again. This time he saw things he had not noticed before. Stones with rounded edges, flow ripples on the walls of the trench. It was a dry riverbed, and he had crossed it at two points. Raif jumped down from the pony, stirred but unsure why. Something mattered here. Crouching, he grabbed a handful of small stones and litter from the riverbed and let them sift through his fingers as he thought. A river . . . and he had cut through its path twice. One thing was certain: It was the river's path that had bow-curved, not his own. He might no longer know in what direction he was headed, but he still knew how to hold a course.

A bow-curved river. A memory was balancing on the edge

of his thoughts . . . a silver line on a cave wall. As the image plummeted into the abyss he caught a glimpse of Traggis Mole's face.

Raif stood. The Robber Chief's cave. The wall painting. A river flowing through a land that started out green and finished dead. A lone mountain upon its banks . . .

We search.

Raif took a quick breath as all the answers that had eluded him fell into place. The Forsworn knights had been searching for the same thing he was searching for now: the fault in the earth's crust most likely to give. That was why they'd a built a redoubt in the badlands on the edge of the Want: because this was where they needed to be. They had known much more than he did, had possessed a book to guide them. Raif could still see its yellow pages laid open to show a massive spire of rock.

The mountain in the cave and the one in the book were the same.

Clicking his tongue to call the pony, Raif headed upstream along the trench. The river would show him the way.

FORTY-THREE

A Severed Head

Iago Sake was laid to rest in accordance with the ancient
death rites of Clan Dhoone. Robbie Dhoone had asked
for and received a special dispensation from the Milk chief,
allowing him to name this twenty-foot stretch of the Milkshore
as the Dhoonehold in absentia. Three guide circles had been
drawn around the pit: the first using Iago Sake's own portion,
the second using powder from the Dhoone king's horn, and
the third using earth from the Dhoonehold. Iago Sake's body
had been stripped and cleaned, and the great axman lay naked
on the grass.

Bram found it difficult to look at the body. Iago Sake had
been pale in life, but in death strange colors had invaded his
skin. The undersides of his thighs and buttocks had turned a
deep wine-red, while his hands and feet had yellowed, and his
face and chest had taken on the chalky blue color of veins. The
wound that had killed him seemed such a small thing, not even
visible now the death crew had laid Iago on his back. A single
puncture through the ribs was all it had taken to claim Iago
Sake's life. One well-placed stab with a knife.

Robbie had wept when the small raid party had returned with
the body. They had borne it north on a stripped wagon drawn

by two matched ponies. The men were ragged with lack of sleep, their cloaks stiff with dried mud. One had swayed in his saddle, and Diddie Daw had rushed forward to steady him. Bram had just returned from his meeting with Skinner Dhoone, and Robbie had been questioning him closely on how it had gone. When the commotion broke out beyond the walls of the broken tower, Bram had just told Robbie that Skinner had promised to give his answer within ten days. Robbie had smiled, well pleased.

Darkness had fallen quickly after that. Robbie had rushed out to the river shore, Bram following. You could read death on someone's face, Bram realized that evening, as he watched Ranald Vey sit weary on his horse, his gaze finding and holding only one man: Robbie Dun Dhoone, his king and chief.

Robbie had taken swift and silent count of the raid party, and then said two words: "The Nail?"

Ranald Vey had dipped his head in defeat. He was the eldest warrior in Robbie's camp, one of the first to disavow Skinner and declare himself for Dun Dhoone. His skills at horse were unmatched in the clan. "A Hailsman took him," he said.

Robbie's face tightened. "And the others?"

"Taken by an Orrl bowman."

It hadn't made much sense at the time. Bram didn't think it made much more now. Two men defending a wagon, showing no colors or ornaments of clan, had somehow managed to slay three Dhoone warriors. The raid party had mistaken them for Glaivish traders and had attacked without due caution. Dhoonesmen had died in the charge, and later Iago Sake had been taken by surprise. Bram had listened to Ranald Vey tell the story several times, and it seemed to him that Iago had been at fault. He should have made it his business to learn the nature and number of men in the wagon before launching an attack. No one said that, not out loud. When a great warrior like Iago Sake died he was to be honored, not censured.

His death had brought wealth to the clan. Gold, twenty-four rods of it, found in the back of the wagon along with a heap of old stones. Everyone in the broken tower had been curious about it. Copper was Dhoone's metal, the tawny ore that striped the northern hills, but copper had lost its worth over the centuries, overtaken by hard steel. Gold was worth — Bram struggled for a suitable reckoning — its weight in gold. Robbie had ordered it removed from the wagon and taken to a secret place of his choosing. Bram did not know where.

"Lower the body," commanded the Castlemilk guide, his voice breaking through Bram's thoughts. Dhoone's own guide was at the Old Round, ministering to Skinner and his men, and Robbie had asked the Castlemilk guide to summon the gods in his place.

Robbie, Mangus Eel, Diddie Daw and Ranald Vey crouched by the body to lift it. Their faces were grave, and their shoulders shook as they performed the awkward task of transfering Iago Sake's body into the three-foot-deep pit. Ropes should have been used, Bram realized, but this rite had not been performed for many decades and practicalities had been lost. In the end Ranald Vey actually jumped down into the pit and raised his arms to accept Iago's head and chest. Wet mud oozing from the pit walls brushed as high as Ranald's waist as he slid the body to the floor.

Already the river water was seeping in. The pit had been dug on a level bank twenty paces from the shore. A shallow sluice running between the two was blocked with a plug of loose stones. The Milk's waters ran along the sluice and then swirled idly as they encountered the plug. Beneath the surface trickles spilled through.

The clan guide was dressed in a pigskin mantle that had been polished with pumice and white lead in the Castlemilk way, but to honor Dhoone he had drawn a collar of blue wool across his shoulders and closed copper bands around his wrists. When he lifted Iago Sake's half-moon ax from the warrior pile containing Iago's belongings all present fell silent. There was not a man in the Castlehold who did not know that ax.

Bram glanced around the watchers as the guide knelt over the pit and laid the ax on Iago's chest. Hundreds of Castlemen and Dhoonesmen had gathered on the shore. As soon as Robbie had announced he would "Float the Oil" for Iago's death word had spread quickly between the clans. Withy and Wellhouse kept the histories, but some things were remembered by all clansmen, and the death rites of Dhoone warriors in the time before the River Wars were known and held in awe throughout the North. Bram did not think it chance that Robbie had decided to go ahead with such a spectacle this day.

The morning light was hazy on the Milk. The sun was still low in the east, rising over the pine forests of Castlemilk, as the clan guide bade Iago's clansmen each to pick a stone from the sluice. Bram joined the line. He had reverted to wearing his old brown cloak, and was one of the few Dhoonesmen not clad in dress blue. As he crouched by the head of the sluice to take a stone from the plug, the point of his sword scraped in the mud. Everyone here today was armed and clad in field armor, including Bram. He didn't possess mail or plate but had donned a boiled-leather chestguard and heavy gloves.

Even as Bram picked a stone he could see the sluice had started to run. The Dhoonesmen who'd gone before him had cleared a passage for the river's course, and the body in the pit had begun to rise. Bram backed away, the stone like a chip of ice in his fist. He didn't want to watch Iago Sake's corpse slowly float to the top of the pit, but he couldn't seem to look away.

Weapon hooks jangled and metal plate chinked as the gathered clansmen breathed heavily and shifted their weight. The guide stood at the head of the pit, naming the Stone Gods in a voice hard and terrible, as a clan guide's must be. *Ganolith, Hammada, Ione, Loss, Uthred, Oban, Larannyde, Malweg, Behathmus.*

The sky darkened and a wind picked up along the riverway. The guide knelt again, and this time his apprentice rolled a great black churn toward him. As Iago Sake's body rose, the guide floated shale oil on the water's surface. The clear oil lapped over Iago's chest, closing around the eye of his ax, and spilling like heavy syrup down along his ribcage to the water that buoyed him. The two liquids stirred uneasily at the meet level, oil swirling down and bubbles of water rising up, but the guide had a steady hand and the oiled settled as he continued to pour.

The guide's timing was good, for the river water in the pit found its level and ceased rising as the last drops of oil slid from the churn. The guide rolled the container across the muddy grass and his apprentice carried it away. All was silent on the shore. Iago's body hung pale and ghostly in the pit, trapped between water and shale oil.

The clan guide rose to his feet and took several steps back. "Behathmus!" he shouted, flinging his arms wide. "Dark Brother and Bringer of Death. This warrior died in your service. He has earned his place in the Stone Halls, and we command that you take him there."

Something happened then, a spark, and Bram couldn't say where it came from. The oil ignited with a low roar, and the air was sucked from Bram's chest. The front of his ribcage was pinned against his spine, and he had to suck hard to inflate his lungs. The pit was an oblong of white fire, the air above it shimmering with heat. Bram felt his eyeballs dry. The heat drew the wind off the river and sent it rolling over the shore, and the cloaks of the Dhoonesmen and Castlemen snapped in the hot gusts.

No one moved. Minutes passed, and then the water in the

pit began to boil. The mud walls buckled, turning liquid. A soft gulp sounded as mud collapsed, and the pit water flooded into the sluice. Iago Sake's body was borne on the rush, sliding toward the river, a nightmare of flames.

Bram looked away then. He heard the terrible hiss of heat hitting cold water, felt the steam puff through his hair. For a moment he didn't breathe; the smell of burning was too much. Dhoonesmen had gone to their gods this way for centuries, their bodies burning like wreckage as they floated along the Flow. Sometimes the pit didn't give and the walls collapsed inward and buried the corpse. It was said Behathmus was sleeping on such a day.

Slowly, men's gazes shifted from the hollow burned-out shell of the pit to Robbie Dun Dhoone who stood at the head of the bank. He was dressed with all the trappings of a king, with fisher fur and steel plate on his back, and a bronze torc set with blue topaz protecting the vulnerable hollow of his throat. His shoulder-length golden hair was braided with copper wire, and Bram could see redness on his left cheekbone where his latest blue tattoo had not yet healed.

"Men," he said quietly, knowing there was no need to raise his voice. "Prepare yourselves. We ride to war within the hour."

He turned and left them, walking to the broken tower alone. None dared follow him for a while.

Bram couldn't seem to move. He hardly knew what he felt. Sometimes he didn't know if he would ever make a Dhoonesman.

"Are you the boy?"

Looking up, Bram saw the Castlemilk guide watching him from across the pit. Two large patches of mud stained his cloak where he had knelt on the ground. Seeing Bram's puzzlement, he spoke again. "I said, are you the boy, Bram Cormac? The one who's coming to us?"

Bram felt his face tingle with shock. How could he have forgotten? Robbie had sold him to Castlemilk. Stupid. *Stupid*. Why had he thought that riding to the Old Round and meeting with Skinner Dhoone would change things? *Because I felt like a Dhoonesman that day.*

"You're a quiet one, Wrayan said as much," the guide said, eyeing Bram carefully. He was a small man, but powerfully built, with dense black hair that stood upright from his skull. "Thought I might be able to teach you some things. Thought I might find a place for you at my hearth."

"You have an apprentice."

The guide lifted a thick black eyebrow. "So you do have a tongue. That's good to know."

Bram colored.

"And adequate circulation." The guide started back in the direction of the Milkhouse. "When your brother wins back Dhoone come and see me. The future might not be as dire as you think."

Bram watched him go. It was hard not to think about what he said.

The river shore was clearing now, as men headed off to collect their horses and supplies. The ground around the pit had sunk and was steaming slightly. The smell of cooked turf rose from it. Bram glanced up at the sun. Time was passing, and there were things to do.

Activity around the broken tower was intense, and as Bram approached he could see Robbie in the center of it, war-dressed and mounted. An ax and a longsword were cross-holstered across his back, making an X. When he noticed Bram he called out for him to hurry and saddle his horse. Old Mother was at Robbie's left, sitting astride her mean white mule. Someone had brought her an antlered helm which she wore with a self-satisfied air. Once Bram had saddled and mounted his gelding, she trotted forward to take a look at him.

"Brambles need thorns," she said firmly, after inspecting him at some length. "Else the birds'll pick off the berries afore they're ripe."

Bram just looked at her. One of them was mad, he was pretty sure of that.

"Riders! From the west!" came a call, instantly galvanising the war party. Relieved at having an excuse to ignore Old Mother, Bram turned his horse west, along with eight hundred other men. Two mounted figures were riding at speed from the direction of the Milkhouse and the Milkroad that lay beyond. Bram recognized the giant red warhorse of Duglas Oger. The axman and a small crew had been absent from the broken tower for twenty days. Bram had assumed he was raiding; Duglas excelled at that.

"Make way!" cried the second rider, another Dhoone axman, as the two approached the tower at full gallop. "Urgent message for the king!"

Bram glanced at his brother. Robbie's expression remained unchanged. He kicked his honey stallion forward a few paces so he was free of the press of men.

"Rab!" called Duglas Oger, as he brought his horse to a hard halt. "I brought you a wee gift." His tone was light, but his breath was labored and the neck of tunic was black with sweat. His horse was so badly lathered its coat was scummed in rings around its withers.

"Duglas," Robbie said in greeting, and then, to the second man: "Gill."

Now he had stopped, Duglas Oger took a moment to absorb the sight of hundreds of men assembled on the hard standing of the broken tower. "Got here in time to claim my place, then," he said, his chest pumping.

Robbie waited a beat before replying. "What have you for me, Duglas?"

Something in Duglas Oger's big flushed face fell, but he recovered himself quickly. A coarse brown sack hung from his saddle horn, and he thrust his hand down to the bottom of it. "Something to keep you warm at night—a Bluddsman's head."

He pulled out something small and waxy, with sunken eyes and white lips, and shockingly glossy hair. With a grin, Duglas threw it toward Robbie. Robbie caught it in both hands, and turned it to face him.

"Who is it?"

Duglas and his companion shared a glance. "Messenger. Found him one day north of Dhoone. Sent to bring Cluff Drybannock's forces back from the Dhoonewall."

Robbie glanced swiftly at Duglas. "How do you know this?"

Duglas made a shrugging gesture, causing the head of his great war-ax to rise above his shoulder. "Who used to skin all your kills, Rab?" he asked gently.

Bram shivered. They had tortured the Bluddsman.

Robbie relaxed a fraction, turning the head's face away from him and resting it against the head of his horse. "So the Dog Lord is getting worried."

"Better than that." Again, Duglas shared a glance with his companion. "His men have deserted him, and headed south."

A murmur of disbelief rippled through the war party. "How so?" Robbie asked. "Skinner couldn't have mounted an attack so soon."

"Oh, it's not Skinner who's drawing men away from the Dhoonehouse. It's the armies of Spire Vanis."

Robbie looked to Douglas's companion. "Gill?"

The man nodded. "He's right. Spire armies are heading for the border, and the Bluddsmen are riding south, first to Withy and then on to the Wolf to meet them."

Robbie tilted back his head and laughed. "The Bludd forces

have gone to Withy. *Withy!* Now we know for certain the Stone Gods are with us."

Mangus Eel started to laugh, and soon Guy Morloch and others joined in.

"I pity Skinner when he turns up there looking for an easy fight," Diddie Daw said. "He'll be cursing us all to his grave."

Diddie's words seemed to sober Robbie. "Let's not forget he commands Dhoonesmen."

Men were quick to nod and the laughing stopped. *Send word*, Bram thought, but didn't speak it. *If you want to save Dhoonesmen's lives, send a message to Skinner, and admit that the deal you offered him was a ruse designed to make him attack Withy.* A strike upon Withy would force the Dog Lord to send an army to defend it, leaving the Bluddhouse vulnerable to an attack from Robbie Dun Dhoone. That was the plan, and it looked as if Skinner had taken the bait. His chief's pride would not allow for the possibility that Robbie might win a round-house for his own, especially one with the boast *We are the clan who makes kings.* Now there would be a massacre at Withy if Skinner attacked.

Robbie knew that. All the fine words he'd spoken to Mauger Loy that night in the broken tower were hollow, Bram realized. It would take nothing to send a boy east with a message, but Robbie chose to do nothing.

"Duglas," he said, throwing the head back at the axman. "Get yourself clean and kitted. And find a place for the head."

As Duglas and Gill trotted toward the tower, Robbie stood in his stirrups and addressed the war party. "Dhoonesmen. Castlemen. Today we ride north to Dhoone. Home for some of us, and for others a place to find glory. We are one now, joined in purpose, and the Stone Gods have blessed us with good fortune. *We are Dhoone, Clan Kings and clan warriors alike. War is our mother. Steel is our father. And peace is but a thorn in our side.*"

Hearing the Dhoone boast, men started to rap the butts of their spears against the earth. One man started up the chant, "Dun Dhoone! Dun Dhoone! Dun Dhoone!" and others quickly joined him, and soon the noise was deafening.

Bram sat in his saddle and listened to the roar. One of the Castlemilk warlords looked to Robbie, and then ordered his troops to turn out. Hundreds of men began to move toward the Milkroad on his say. Robbie waited in the center for the Castlemen to clear the area east of the broken tower, allowing the warlord the honor of leading out the army.

When he was ready Robbie drew Mabb Cormac's sword and cried, "North to Dhoone!"

Bram watched him, and when the time came he kicked his horse into a trot. He was no longer sure what he'd be fighting for, but that didn't change the fact that he must fight.

FORTY-FOUR

To Catch a Fish

ish, Effie decided, were stupid. Which was just as well, really, as she wasn't that clever herself and it wouldn't have taken much to better her. A pig could have done it easily. Pigs were smart. Jebb Onnacre had once taught her a song about a pig. A pig and a twig. When she'd told it to Letty Shank, Letty had gone and repeated it to everyone—and it had been Effie who'd got the beating for it. She was still mad about that.

Even so. It *had* been a good song.

Suddenly disheartened and not a bit sure why, Effie rocked her bottom back onto the bank and took her hands from the pool. They were a strange color, like ham. They were a bit numb, too. The water was cold. There were still some fish floating in the pool, but she decided three was enough. She could always come back for more.

Rubbing her hands against her cloak, Effie stood. The noise from the waterfall was deafening, and its spray spattered her face. All sorts of interesting rocks lay around, battered into round shapes by the force of the fall. It had been a long while since she'd had time to consider rocks, and she was a bit rusty. Granite over there, even though it was red and looked like sandstone.

Or was it trap rock? The fact that she didn't know upset her. Effie Sevrance wasn't good for much but she'd always known her rocks.

Noticing her hands were still tingling a bit, Effie crossed her arms high and thrust them into her armpits. The spray wasn't helping, making her feel goose-pimply all over, but now she'd found this place she didn't want to leave it. It was a little rocky draw, like an inlet, set deep into the cliffs and back from the river. A stream overhead dropped in a sheer fall, crashing into the pool before running down through the rocks to the Wolf. It was sheltered on all sides, and that seemed good enough reason to stay. Up there, on the headland, nowhere was sheltered. When someone attacked there was no place to hide.

The harlequins had led her here. After . . . the *thing* happened, she had clung to the cliff for hours, not daring to move. The raiders had taken a long time with the wagon, and it had been dark before they'd left. Even after she'd heard the wagon creaking into motion she'd waited. Just because the raiders hadn't shown any caution didn't mean Effie Sevrance needn't. Da always said that ability to wait was what set the best hunters apart from the rest. Never think of it as *waiting*, he'd told her. Think of it as *learning*.

So Effie learned in the darkness. No sound came for the longest while after the raiders had ridden off, and then much later the howl of a wolf scenting blood had reached her. The wolf's howl told Effie all she needed to know: no live men around. Wolves were particular about that.

The climb up was the worst part. Effie's legs were all shaky and she couldn't feel one of her feet. When she made it to the top of the cliff she had to grab the hem of her dress and wring it out like washing. Letty Shank once told her that moss grew on anything left damp overnight, and Effie definitely didn't want that.

It was funny how your brain was scared of things that it shouldn't really be scared of at all, and then not afraid of others that it should fear a lot. The bodies were in pieces. A wolf was trotting away in the direction of the trees with a man's hand in its jaw. Effie saw this and wasn't afraid. It was the wagon that bothered her, the fact it had gone. There was no longer any place to be inside.

The raiders had hacked off the wagon's canvas and the ribbing, and big hoops of wood lay on the ground like dragon bones. Other things lay there too: baskets filled with ore, empty chicken crates, a smashed lamp, the string of arrows Clewis Reed had hung from the ribbing to dry. Bits of body were littered amongst them. Effie swallowed. She'd watched Da butcher kills for as long as she could remember—she wouldn't allow herself to be squeamish now.

Thinking of Da helped. Da was a hunter. Da would take what he needed and move away from this place. *Blood draws predators*, he'd always said. *Both kinds: Man and beast.* So she had run to the wagon site, loaded one of the baskets with whatever she could find that might prove useful, and then run back to the cliffs where she felt safe. The bodies she wouldn't think about. Clewis Reed and Druss Ganlow had ceased to exist. Clewis was too big a man to be reduced to such small parts.

The basket had a leather strap attached so Effie could carry it slung across her back. That was important during the climb down the cliffs. She chose a different place to make the descent, a little upriver where it looked more . . . lumpy. The cliff wasn't as sheer, and there were places for a girl to rest. She found a small space between two big rocks, curled up with the wagon canvas around her and slept.

The next morning she had known she wouldn't climb up to the headland again. It was better here, between the river and the cliffs. More like inside. She hadn't found much food during her forage of the wagon site—Clewis usually shot fresh game for them each day—but she scavenged some grain and a few other things. The barley meant for the horses nearly broke her teeth until she figured out you had to soak it. It was pretty tasteless too, but she was now in possession of Clewis Reed's small but effective spice collection, and she'd found an interesting red powder that made everything taste better. It caused heartburn of the tongue later, but Da said everything good came at a price.

Later that day she'd set off upriver along the cliffside. It was much like mountaineering, Effie supposed. Or caving. The rocks were slick and there wasn't always an obvious path, but if you stopped for a bit and waited—*learned*—you could usually see a way to carry on. After a while trees started invading her territory, dry old water oaks growing right out of the cliff. Their roots were slowly pulverizing the stone, and other plants had taken advantage of the gray, powdery scree they had created. Bushy things mostly, and some spectacularly thorny-looking weeds. It made things harder, but it was still better than the alternative: up there, with no place to hide.

A day had passed and then another, and Effie hadn't got very far at all. The barley was running low, and she was contemplating living on spice alone. At some point the trees had begun to choke the way ahead, and now all she could see in front of her were tree canopies and swirling river water. The Wolf had widened and it was suddenly difficult to perceive it as a whole. Below her a rocky shore curved inward and then was lost in a dense coppice of bushes. It was midday so she stopped to eat the last of the barley. Some of it was sprouting where the damp from the river had wetted it; you didn't have to soak those bits for as long.

Effie watched the river as she ate. Its level had dropped in the past few days, and its water was clearer and more settled.

Great currents moved across it, creating crosshatched ripples and powerful tows. Close to its middle, water was turning in a huge spiral; Effie couldn't understand why. She *could* wait and learn, though, and she sat and studied the kingfishers who dove down through its cold surface and emerged with wriggling fish; the treader flies who skimmed over the slack water at the shore; and the pair of fat-tailed beavers who were constructing a dam across a small channel separated from the main body of the river by a wall of rocks.

Then she spied the harlequins, a mated pair. They had emerged from beneath the coppice, swimming on a channel that passed beneath the ash bushes. Effie looked hard at the coppice. She hadn't even noticed the water running there.

The harlequins swam the rapids for a bit, the big handsome male performing all sorts of cross-current hopping to impress his mate. The dun hen followed him effortlessly, her tail feathers moving like a tiller. When she'd had enough of her mate's posturing she made her way across the eddies and swam under the channel cloaked by bushes. Effie waited but they didn't come out. After a time she looked at the sky. Perhaps an hour or more had passed. It was time to follow the ducks.

The way down was treacherous, and the thorny-weeds tore holes in her skirt. By the time she'd reached the coppice she just *knew* bruises were forming. Crawling through the shallow channel under the bushes was positively, absolutely the worst thing ever. Every part of her got soaked—and not a caught-in-the-rain sort of soaked either. No. A genuine fallen-in-the-river sort of soaked. Her teeth were chattering like a whole lot of crickets when she finally pushed her way through to the other side.

The first thing she heard was the territorial honking of the male harlequin, and then she became aware of the crashing of water. Quite suddenly she realized the noise had been there all along, running alongside the roar of the river. She had entered a kind of draw in the cliffs, a little pocket screened from the river by bushes and rock walls. A waterfall streamed from the cliffs above, and the force of its drop had hollowed out a plunge pool in the rocks. The harlequins had made their nest there, beneath a birch brush.

It was the perfect place to hide. Straightaway she had stripped down to her small linens and laid her clothes over the rocks to dry. The ducks watched her warily, the male charging her if she drew too close to the nest. *Must have eggs*, she thought.

The idea of eggs made her mouth water—the red spice would taste most delicious on raw duck eggs—but her gaze had already been drawn to a second, if slightly less appealing, food source.

Fish. They came over the waterfall, dropping right along with the water, and landing so hard when they hit the pool that they were temporarily stunned. Watching them was as good as watching a puppet show at the Dhoone Fair. The noise they made when the slapped into the standing water was like . . . like the sound of a wet fish. Effie didn't know the names of many fish, but she reckoned these were mostly shiners. Their scales were quite glinty, and they were silver and pink. When she got one and crushed it with a rock, its insides were full of bones. She tried a piece raw. Tried another, this time with the application of a great deal of the red spice. Her eyes watered as she swallowed. It was definitely time to build a fire.

The woody bushes provided good burning timber, but between the waterfall and the river everything was a bit wet. She broke off the most likely-looking branches, using her foot to stamp them free, and hauled them to the driest place she could find. Even here, on a flattish rock in the middle of the clearing, the drift from the waterfall still sprinkled them. Effie frowned as big wet blobs fell on her tinder pile. There was exactly nothing she could do about that.

Kindling, that was what she needed. Turning a critical gaze around the inlet she searched for something dry and crackly. Raif could start a fire with almost anything, that was what Da always said. Pity he wasn't here now. Him and Drey.

No. No. No, Effie warned herself. *Absolutely no feeling sorry for yourself.* Sevrances had never been cowards or complainers.

Warmed a little by her anger, she ran over the rocks and around the pool for no good reason at all. Letty Shank and Florrie Horn would be scandalized. Running around in her smallclothes! Did she think she was a child, not a maid of nearly nine?

Her running scared the ducks and sent them fleeing from the nest to the safety of the water. Effie slowed to a halt and watched them. *Good time to steal eggs,* said a little voice inside her. No. They were berserkers; it wouldn't be right. At least not until she got *really* sick of fish.

Still. Something beneath the birch bush drew her eye, and she crossed over and knelt beside it. The nest was perched on a platform of pebbles that kept it high and dry above the river water. It was protected from the waterfall by the canopy of the bush. Seven pale green eggs lay in a thick matting of straw, down, twigs and moss. Kindling. Effie reached in, carefully nudged the eggs to one side, and then tore off a big chunk of the nest.

She giggled on the way back. It was probably the first time ever in the history of nest-raiding that someone had taken the nest, not the eggs. As she stuffed the kindling around the fire-wood, the male harlequin returned to the bush to investigate. Effie tried not to move too much as he poked nervously around the nest. She'd caused him enough anxiety for one day.

The fire was not nearly so easy to light as she'd imagined. She had taken possession of Clewis Reed's flint and its iron striker, and it made good sparks, but catching them on the kindling was difficult. They were fickle things, and sometimes the wind helped and sometimes it didn't. It took at least three hundred goes to start the kindling burning, and it had grown dark by then and the knuckles on her striking hand were bleeding.

Once the flames had gotten started on the wood, Effie went to fetch her clothes and basket. Her skirt and cloak were still pretty damp, and she tried to work out a way to dry them. The whole fire business had left her exhausted, and she couldn't think of anything cleverer than putting on her dress and using herself as a drying rack. It was a horrible thing, to pull on something wet, and it started her teeth chattering all over again. Steeling herself, she settled down to cook fish.

Ten days had passed since then. Every morning Effie awoke and thought, *Perhaps I might get going today*. But she didn't. Here, in the inlet, she was safe and protected. Cliff walls surrounded her on three sides. The space was small and contained, about the size of the guidehouse, only rocky and a lot wetter. There were fish and water, and the fire didn't go out *every* day. True, her clothes were never entirely dry, and sometimes she felt a bit lonely at night, but it had to be better than being in the wide-open spaces of the headland. Just thinking of them made her shiver.

No. She'd stay here for a while longer. Her lore would warn her of any danger, and there hadn't been a peep out of it in days.

Besides, the harlequin eggs might hatch at any moment. The ducks were fat and glossy now—Effie supposed she wasn't the only one to benefit from the stunned fish—and one of them attended the nest at all times. They'd grown quite accustomed to Effie, and only honked when she was especially close. She even talked to them sometimes, not that they listened, of course. It was more about hearing the sound of a human voice . . . even if it was just her own.

Feeling the sensation returning to her fingers, Effie pulled her hands from her armpits and wondered what to do next. Firewood, she supposed. *Not much fun but it has to be done,* that was what Jebb Onnacre used to say about clearing the stables of horseshit. Effie grinned as she walked toward the bushes. Collecting firewood *had* to be better than that.

The waterfall made it feel as if it were raining every day. It was pretty, she had to give it that, but rainy and noisy counted a lot more than looks, and she fervently believed the inlet would be much improved without it. Water droplets spattered her back as she yanked off ash and birch branches.

Effie's hands began to return to a more normal color as she worked, and it made her wonder what the rest of her must look like. Absently she ran her fingers through her hair. She knew she wasn't supposed to be vain about it, but Raif, Drey, Da and Raina had all said they loved her hair. Even Letty Shank had once admitted it was pretty enough, if you liked things the color of tree bark. It was, Effie thought rather disdainfully, a stupid thing to say. Tree bark came in all sorts of different colors, depending on the type of tree. Letty Shank wouldn't know that because Letty Shank couldn't tell a turnip from a pinecone.

Effie grimaced. Her hair felt like straw and there were *things* in it. Leaving the firewood where it was, she crossed to the fire and sat on the pallet of wagon canvas and heaped twigs she'd made to keep her bottom off the cold rocks when she ate. Using her fingers like the teeth of a comb, she worked on her hair, pulling out feathers and burrs and rubbing dried on mud until it disintegrated. It took a long time; Effie Sevrance had a lot of hair.

When she noticed the fire was burning perilously low she took a rest and went to fetch some of the firewood. It was getting dark, and she hadn't cooked her three fish yet. As she bent to pick up a heavy branch of white birch she heard a shout from the east. Stilling herself, she listened. After a few seconds the shout came again, only this time it sounded south of her. Carefully, Effie laid the branch on the ground, and then brought her hand to her lore. The little ear-shaped chunk of granite was vibrating but with little force.

She held it, thinking. A shout to the east and then the south. Men were calling each other from across the river. The gold men! She stood. Perhaps the city traders who had been meant to take the gold from Druss and Clewis were finally making their crossing. Perhaps they'd arranged for a bargeman on this side of the river to bring them across.

Effie paced, agitated, unsure what to do. What did she owe the gold men? Nothing. What had she to give them? Only the information about Druss's and Clewis's deaths. The manner in which they had died was worthy of telling, but would city men value the knowledge in the same way clansmen would? What was her responsibility here? She owed nothing to the gold men, but what did she owe to Druss Ganlow and Clewis Reed?

Glancing at the bushes, she made her decision. She owed Druss and Clewis her life. The least she could do for them was go and take a look at the river and see who was crossing. Perhaps when she saw whoever it was she'd know what to do.

Quickly, she grabbed her basket and cloak. Already her skin was breaking out in gooseflesh at the mere thought of entering the channel again. Uncle Angus had once told her that the men who lived beyond the Topaz Sea used water as a means of torture. *Boiling?* she'd asked him. *No*, he'd said. *Cold. One drop at a time.*

Effie snorted. They must have very delicate constitutions beyond the Topaz Sea, for her body was about to take a whole lot of cold droplets—and without her even speaking a word.

Not much fun but it has to be done. Gritting her teeth, she knelt by the bushes and entered the water. By keeping her head low and pushing forward with her toes she managed to avoid the overhanging branches. She could feel the icy water seizing her chest, but thoughts of the Topaz Sea men kept her going. Ragged stones along the channel bottom scraped her knees as she cleared the coppice.

Effie could see nothing at first, just blackness where the river flowed. It was a dark night, the sky thick with clouds. Even when her eyes grew accustomed to the light level she still couldn't make out much. The river glinted, a little bit, and she followed the glint east to see if she could determine the source of the first call.

Nothing. But then, farther in the distance than she'd imagined, she saw the pale red glow of a turned-down lamp. A thrill of fear made hairs rise on Effie's neck—even the wet ones. She'd been right; someone was making a crossing. Two ferrymen were pulling one of the large flat barges used for transporting cattle and horses. The barge was rigged to thick guide-ropes that traversed the river, and both men were working cranks mounted to either side of the vessel. After a time the noise of the cranks drifted downriver and Effie could hear the swift *whir* of well-oiled wheels.

A crossing at night. Instinct made Effie keep very still. The gold men were likely to make a crossing at night, true, but surely a few city traders wouldn't need so big a barge?

Her gaze tracked the barge as it labored across the river. As it neared the south bank she spied a movement on the shore. Yet it didn't make any sense; it was kind of rippling, like a wheatfield in a wind . . . or thousands of ants moving on a hill.

Effie felt a blade of cold fear enter her heart as she realized what she was seeing. Not gold men, not smugglers. An entire army waiting to gain passage to the clanholds.

It would take them from now until dawn to cross the river.

The barge beached with a violent jolt and one of the ferry-men rushed to anchor it while the other removed the lamp from its post. Effie felt the world tilt on its axis as the lamp passed close to the man's face.

She knew him.

It was one of the Scarpemen who had been in the forge the night Old Scratch went to the fire. What was his name? Uriah Scarpe. The Scarpes' chief's son.

Even before she could let out a breath of disbelief, Effie felt a cold hand clamp across her nose and mouth. A powerful arm yanked her back and down. She smelled horses and a sharp green fragrance she couldn't place. Her hands flew out to find a hold beneath the water, but the owner of the arm jerked her violently back.

"Keep your silence, girl," came a low, shrewd voice. "I've come to take you to your future. This war's not for you."

As he dragged her back through the bushes she wondered why her lore had failed her.

FORTY-FIVE

Fixing Things

Town Dog wasn't happy at all. She was squirming in her little cloth pouch beneath Crope's new wool cloak. The pouch was slung crosswise over Crope's shoulder, and Town Dog was housed just below his left armpit. He squeezed down gently with his arm, hoping he was calming, not smothering her.

Truth was, he didn't feel too good himself, but Quill's words circled in his thoughts, black as vultures. *Unease kills thieves.* So he had to pretend that he was calm, like the mummers pretended they were ladies when they were actually boys.

His new clothes helped. Quill had chosen the fabric and style himself. Crope had always nursed a liking for the color orange, but Quill said no, that wouldn't do. "You need to be forgettable, overlookable, and harmless." He'd glanced critically at Crope. "We're going to need a lot of help."

The tailor Quill brought in was tiny and fierce. If you so much as looked at him while he was measuring you up, he stuck you with his pins. He and Quill had consulted at some length. Drab-looking fabrics were held up to the light, a calendar was reviewed. Coin changed hands. A different fabric was held to the light, still drab, but odd-looking. More coin changed hands, and the tailor left, satisfied. Five days later a cloak, a pair of leggings, a tunic and an undershirt arrived at the Sign of the Blind Crow. There had been no time for boots. According to the tailor, no cobbler in the city had lasts the size of Crope's feet. Special ones would have to be carved, and "special" meant money and time.

Crope had taken a bath before he donned his new clothes; his second in under five days. Baths felt unbelievably good to him, warm and floaty, and he stayed there until the water cooled and the soap scummed-up around the rim. Quill thought it funny when he caught Crope scrubbing out the bath when he was done. The thief said that was what servants were for, and Crope agreed and carried on scrubbing.

His new clothes fitted very well, and they were only a bit scratchy around his neck. Quill brought a glass for Crope to look at himself, but Crope declined. He did not like to see himself. Besides, if Quill said he looked 'ceptable that was good enough for him.

Quill had made him wear the clothes every day since then, "To work up some creases and a shade of dirt." Crope was mortified at the thought of soiling such riches and wasn't properly happy about it even when Quill had explained. "Anything too old or too new draws the eye. If your aim is to be forgettable your clothes must fall between the two."

It was a lot to think about. And there was something to remember, too. The cloak was the special kind that you could wear turned inside out. Double-faced, the tailor called it. Quill was most insistent that Crope remember this. "Gray for day," he had recited. "Brown for sundown."

Crope mouthed the words now as he waited in line at the fortress gate. A queue of close to two hundred men and women had formed, and Crope was about midway in line. It was early morning, crisp and bright, with a breeze snapping the red-and-silver pennants standing out from the fortress wall.

Quill had wanted him to carry a knife concealed in his boot, but Crope had shaken his head with quiet determination. No blades. His staff would do. Strangely enough, Quill had accepted this. "A man's weapon is a particular thing," he had said. "By the time he's developed a preference it's usually too late to change it." Quill's own preference was a knuckle knife: a band that fitted around your knuckles with a long spike protruding between the second and third fingers. Crope knew this because he'd seen Quill wield it in the back of the Blind Crow. No blood had been shed, but coin had changed hands. Crope knew how such things worked from his time in the mine. Bitterbean used to do it for extra food.

Thinking about the diamond mine made Crope sad. He missed Mannie Dun and Will. If Will were here he'd probably be taking a nap; he was the only man Crope had ever met who could sleep standing up.

Crope thought of some of Mannie's songs for a while and was soothed. Even Town Dog settled down a bit, and when the portcullis finally clunked and shivered into motion both of them were a little surprised.

"All here for the Surlord's Justice say 'Aye'!" shouted a big, gruff red cloak, coming to stand in the center of the gate, placing one booted foot to either side of the gate trench.

A loud chorus of "Aye!" sounded as nearly everyone at the gate replied.

Just as Quill had told him, Crope nodded but didn't speak.

The red cloak's gaze passed over the crowd, not much interested. A second man came out, this one wearing a fancy long mantle with glittery bands around the edges. The glittery man said something to the red cloak and the red cloak nodded, and then the glittery man walked away.

"Right!" shouted the red cloak, addressing the crowd. "The surlord will see a hundred count today."

A murmur of dissatisfaction stirred the crowd. One man behind Crope told the guard exactly what he thought of the surlord, and two red cloaks came and escorted him away. The crowd was quiet after that. Crope tried to keep calm as the head red cloak walked the line, choosing the hundred he would allow through the gate.

"Surlord's Justice, it's called," Quill had explained. "Every tenday the fortress is opened to any man or woman in the city with a grievance. It's a tradition from way back, when Spire Vanis was little more than a fort and you could count all the people in it on thirty hands. Surlords were different then. Less high and mighty. They didn't just pass laws, they *enforced* them. Land, coin, titles: they dealt it all. Now they just pass out a few coins and listen to fishwives complain about their rivals, and bakers accuse millers of gritting the chaff. Still. It's custom and they're bound to do it. They may take a scalding hot bath afterwards but they know better than to shun it. The Spire's a vicious city, and no surlord fancies a vicious end."

Crope had been quietly amazed at these facts. Not disbelieving, for he trusted Quill completely, but taken aback by the thought that a powerful man might make himself so vulnerable. He'd said as much to Quill.

"Red cloaks search anyone entering the fortress," Quill had replied. "And they watch 'em like hawks once they're in."

"You. Go ahead," the red cloak said to an old woman ten paces ahead of Crope. "Report to the brother by the watch station. Do as he says." The woman nodded and then made a dash for the gate, not giving the red cloak any time to change his mind.

Crope slipped the coin from his gear belt. "Silver," Quill had decided. "Gold will just make you memorable." Crope hoped very much not to be memorable as the red cloak approached him. The urge to shrink himself was great and he had to fight the desire to bend his knees and curve his spine. *Unease kills thieves*, he told himself. *Unease kills thieves.*

As the red cloak's gaze passed over him, Crope raised his hand away from his body, just as Quill had shown him; fingers open to reveal the coin. The red cloak didn't appear to see the coin, and Crope felt the first stirrings of panic. Quill had said the red cloak would take the coin. Just as Crope was about to swing his arm wider, the red cloak passed him and Crope felt hard fingers delve into his palm. And—just like that—the coin was gone.

"You," the red cloak said to him. "Inside."

Crope was so relieved he forgot Quill's instructions to stay calm and bolted for the gate just like the old woman before him. Heart thudding against Town Dog's head like a hammer, he entered Mask Fortress.

His master was here, he could feel it. The flagstones beneath his feet rang as if there were hollow spaces below. The men and women chosen to petition for Surlord's Justice waited in a huddle by the watch station that contained the mechanism for the raising and lowering of the gate. Four red cloaks had them under guard. One of them approached Crope, his eyes narrowing. "Big bastard, eh?" he said, as he drew the point of his spear along Crope's side and over his ribs, prodding every few seconds to test for the hardness of a concealed weapon. He prodded Town Dog, but the little white mutt kept her silence, and since she didn't feel like steel or iron the red cloak passed over her. When he was done he looked critically at Crope's staff. "I'm going to have to take that."

"Need it to walk," Crope said.

The red cloak's gaze passed over the bulge in Crope's cloak were Town Dog was concealed. "Deformity?" he asked.

Crope nodded. This hadn't been amongst the contingencies Quill had planned for, but Crope figured it was covered by the general rule: *Don't rile the red cloaks.*

The red cloak seemed satisfied with Crope's nod and moved on to the next petitioner. Crope watched him, turning the word "deformity" around in his head. Yes, he was deformed.

When the portcullis was lowered and the gate closed, the four red cloaks marched the petitioners along a high-walled alleyway and into an open space as long and wide as a tourney field. "Form a line by Traitor's Doom," one of the guard's ordered. "And keep yourselves well ordered."

Crope moved along with everyone else, careful not to drift too far behind. It was colder here than outside, and the wind hardly moved. Quill had explained that Traitor's Doom was a stone block where people lost their heads. Crope worried about that. Even before the line was fully formed people started to grumble. The old woman who'd been allowed in before Crope turned to him and complained. "We'll be here for hours. 'Is lordship won't be out afore noon."

Crope nodded solemnly; it was just as Quill had said.

They waited. The sun rose, disappeared behind the mountain, and then rose again. Crope's feet began to ache, and he wished he had some lasts. He wasn't sure what they were, but he knew you needed them for new boots. Occasionally some grand-looking man or lady crossed the quad, and the crowd ogled them. At the far end, close to the pointy tower, some mounted red cloaks were playing a game of charge. Crope watched the stables. It was a large stone building covering almost an entire wing of the fortress, with big double doors flung open onto the quad. Grooms trotted out horses for exercise and grooming. When they were done they brought their mounts to a great lead-lined trough and pumped fresh water for the beasts to drink.

After what Crope judged to be nearly three hours of waiting, liveried servants entered the quad, carrying rolled carpets and a big chair. More servants raised a canopy constructed of red silk and gilded poles. When the flurry of activity was finished the big chair sat atop plush patterned carpets, shielded from sun and rain by a silk roof.

The petitioners pushed forward a little, their hopes high. Another hour passed. Everyone except the red cloaks stared at the empty chair. Crope was growing anxious, and he drew up the hood on his cloak. Surely Quill's plan should have gone into action by now? He glanced at the stables. Nothing.

Suddenly there was a blast of horns from the fat tower shaped like a beer barrel. The red cloaks stood to attention. Another surge forward amongst the petitioners forced Crope to push back gently. *Mustn't get too close to the chair. Must be forgettable.*

The pale-eyed man who'd taken Crope's lord strode out from the fat tower, flanked by two big men, one fair, one dark. He was dressed more plainly than the other grand people they'd seen that day, but he was wearing a thick chain of office across his shoulders and he walked in the measured, unhurried way of a man certain of his power. Crope looked down. *Unease kills thieves.*

And then, even as the surlord approached the big chair, it happened. The pump in the stables started to creak. The hand crank jerked up violently, and water began to gush from around the seal. Almost immediately the lead trough filled to over-flowing and fluid spilled in sheets to the floor of the quad. Everyone, including the surlord, turned to look. The groom nearest the trough tried to force the handle back down, but he just created more pressure and the water spurted higher. A horse by the stable door shied. Another one tried to buck its rider. Someone called for the stablemaster. The stablemaster, a big man wearing a leather apron, rushed out to take a look. Water was rushing over toward Traitor's Doom now, and the fancy patterned carpets placed nearby.

The stablemaster shook his head, took a nervous look at the surlord who was nearly at his chair. "Anyone here know pumps?" he shouted, slightly hysterically, to the crowd.

It was Crope's cue. Stepping out from the line of petitioners he said in a soft voice, "Master, I know the pumps."

The stablemaster looked him up and down. Crope could tell he didn't like what he saw, but his pump seal had broken and the surlord was watching and he didn't have much of a choice. Beckoning Crope impatiently, he said, "Well, come forward then. See to it."

Crope did just that, and for an instant, as he left the other petitioners behind, he felt the pressure of the surlord's attention on his back. It chilled him down through his new clothes to his skin.

When he arrived at the flooding pump he began to feel better. Pumps he knew. Kneeling, he set his big hands on the pump shaft and twisted, pulling the entire cranking mechanism from the ground. Straightaway the pressure abated, and once he'd drawn the seven-foot plunger shaft from the well-hole, the flow fell off to a manageable run.

The stablemaster sighed in relief. Horses calmed. One of the grooms standing close to the trough winked once at Crope and then was gone. Quill's man in the fortress.

Crope was soaked, but so intent on saying his next line properly that he barely noticed. "Needs tow and clay—for the seal."

The stablemaster looked at his grooms. None moved. "Well, go and fetch what the man needs," he ordered them. "And you. Get him a towel."

The excitement was over. Grooms drifted away, walking their horses into the stables and fetching brooms to manage the water spill. Over by Traitor's Doom, Surlord's Justice was called into session, and the first petitioner moved forward to kneel on the patterned—and only very slightly dampened—carpets.

Crope reached inside his cloak and scratched Town Dog's ears, hunkering down for a long wait. By the time the groom came back with a pot of tow and a hunk of clay wrapped in a wet cloth, the surlord had seen over two dozen petitioners. The man was quick, Crope had to give him that.

Accepting the tow, Crope made a point of squinting hard at the clay just as Quill had advised. "If they bring red clay ask for gray," he'd said. "If they bring gray ask for red. That'll keep 'em busy for awhile."

"Needs red," Crope said gently.

The groom, a stick of a boy with big lips and a big nose, sneered at him. "'S no difference."

"Needs red," Crope insisted.

The groom rolled his eyes.

"He wants red," ordered the stablemaster, coming to stand at the head of the trough. "*Get* him red."

The groom huffed and went off in search of more clay. The stablemaster watched Crope for a moment, shook his head with feeling, and then walked away.

Crope waited again. The line of petitioners was dwindling now, as the red cloaks guarding the surlord ordered a limit on the length of all applications. Every so often, the surlord would turn to his Master-of-Purse and command coin to be dispensed to a petitioner. Gradually, the quad began to darken. Braziers were brought out to illuminate Traitor's Doom, and safe-lamps were lit within the stables.

Still the groom didn't return. Crope's stomach rumbled as the surlord heard the final petition. Checking that no one was paying attention either to him or to the pump, Crope quickly reversed his cloak, raised the hood, and leant back into the shadows behind the trough. *Gray for day. Brown for sundown.* This side of the cloak was a bit strange, shimmery like water, and Crope decided he liked the other side much better.

Finally, the Surlord Justice was done and the surlord stood and made his way back to the fat tower. As the servants came to disassemble the canopy and roll carpets, the groom returned with a square of red clay. He appeared to have some difficulty seeing Crope at first, and when he finally spotted him he was not pleased. "Had to go all the way to Potters Walk for it," he complained, letting the clay drop at Crope's feet. "You best be done soon, else you'll be locked in for the night."

Crope took the clay and began to knead it. Kneading was soothing. It made time pass. When the stable's double doors rolled closed he kept kneading. When the stablemaster came out, peered into the shadows by the trough, and said to himself, "He's upped and gone," Crope kept kneading. *Unease kills thieves.*

The fortress fell into quiet and darkness around him. When Crope judged it safe he stood. Muscles in his legs that hadn't moved for hours threw cramps, and he had to rest his weight on his staff for a moment.

Come to me, his lord had commanded. And now at last he could.

Crossing the quad, he headed for the boarded-up gallery that ran opposite to the stables and bordered the pointy tower. Quill had warned him that he was on his own once darkness came. "Thieves may help other thieves," he had said. "But the act of thievery must be committed alone." Crope understood that. A man could only rely on himself past a certain point.

A boarded-up window at cellar level collapsed inward as he kicked it hard with his foot. Wood splintered and there was a sharp crack as the board hit the floor, but Crope couldn't say he much cared. His lord was very close and very weak, and Crope had waited patiently long enough.

The drop down wasn't as bad as he feared, and he rolled out of it without harm. Releasing Town Dog from her pouch, he went in search of a stairway.

His eyes had already grown accustomed to darkness in the quad and he found his bearings quickly. The chamber ran the length of the gallery with stairs at either end. Crope headed in the direction of the tower and climbed. By the time he emerged at ground level his heart was racing in strange and painful ways. A great sense of urgency filled him, and when he saw the wooden door to the pointy tower he ran toward it with all his might.

Crack! The door jumped in its frame but did not give. He went at it again, and again, ramming his shoulders into the wood. On the fourth assault it gave, and the noise it made as it crashed open was deafening.

Crope and Town Dog stepped into the cold darkness of the Splinter. A chill mist curled up around them, and for the first time in eighteen years Crope could feel the living, breathing essence of his lord. It nearly drove him insane.

As he moved toward the stairway a soft click sounded, and a section of wall began to swing inward.

Come to me.

Shivers passed along Crope's spine as he descended into the underworld. He could not see, Town Dog could not see, but somehow they were guided. Down they went, the chasm below them roaring with wind, the first sounds of alert echoing from above.

By the time they reached the first chamber, Crope was taking four stairs at a time. Wildly, he swung his head in great half-circles, searching for his lord.

Farther down.

Crope could not take the final stairs fast enough. A door bolted from the outside halted him. The horror of that one little thing, what it said about the man who'd taken his lord, made the white rage fork behind his eyes. Wedging his fingers behind the bolt he tore off the entire plate. *Locked up and never let out.* Crope knew all about that.

And then, quite suddenly, he was in the presence of his lord. Tears sprang to Crope's eyes as he knelt by the hideous iron cradle and touched the man who was his life. Gently, carefully, he lifted him, trying hard not to think about the terrible lightness, the *diminishment* of his lord. Chains tugged against him so he broke them like twigs. He wished for more. Suddenly there were not enough things in the world to break.

His lord weighed so little it was like carrying a young child. Almost he could not bear it, the thought of what his lord had borne. As he carried Baralis up through the large chamber and into the chasm he heard Town Dog growl.

A figure with a lamp standing halfway down the great spiraling flight of steps froze. The surlord. The pale-eyed man.

Something for Crope to break.

"Come to me!" he roared, charging toward him. "COME TO ME!"

The figure turned and began to head back up the steps. White rage filled Crope, gushing through his body like water from the pump. His eyesight sharpened, his muscles engorged, and he was filled with the strength of ten men. Cradling his lord with one arm, he hoisted his staff over his shoulder with his left hand and let it fly.

The staff punctured the surlord's chest like a sword, impaling him from behind and knocking him forward onto the steps. Crope was upon him in a matter of seconds, not caring if the surlord were alive or dead, and heaved his jerking, bleeding body into the abyss.

That was when the first rumble started—a deep bellowing of rock followed by a high-pitched creak. The tower shook. Stone facings popped from the walls. Crope hurried to carry his lord to the surface.

A great black crack opened up, running forking splits along the curtain wall. Something gave with the force of snapped rock. The tower heaved. Masonry flew past Crope's head. Dust bloomed, thick and acrid, and when Crope rubbed it from his eyes he saw two figures barring the way out.

Red cloaks, the ones who had accompanied the surlord to and from the fat tower. One fair, one dark.

Without a staff he had no weapon . . . and they were big men. Crope had no choice but to meet them. The red cloaks drew swords and waited.

The stairway was buckling now, and capstones and risers were flying from it with small explosions. Crope climbed the final stairs. Hunching his shoulders to protect his lord, he received the red cloaks' blows. They were wary, surprised. One of them looked ill. Sticking him with their swords, they opened deep cuts on his arms and shoulders. Pain came, but it wasn't much really. It would not stop him. He was calm now, the white rage gone. The cuts of the red cloaks' swords stung and he could feel his own blood, running slow and unnaturally hot over his skin.

When the tower lurched violently to the side, one of the red cloaks lost his footing and went screaming into the chasm. Crope pushed past the remaining man, the dark-haired one, receiving stabs to the liver and buttocks. At some point the man ceased stabbing, perhaps to save himself. Crope continued to climb. He and his lord could feel the breeze now. A new beginning was in sight.

The tallest tower in the North collapsed, sending debris across quarter of the city, as Crope carried his lord to safety.

FORTY-SIX

A Fortress of Grey Ice

The hour before dawn was a strange time on the dry riverbed. Noises echoed softly across the trench. Raif heard the sound of water splashing and the low moan of a great blue heron as he lay bunched within his blanket, emerging from sleep. When he opened his eyes the sounds fled, and it was easy to believe he'd never heard anything at all. The mist was different. Just before dawn it filled the trench and began flowing like a river, moving with muscular force. The first time it had happened Raif and the pony had been sleeping in the center of the riverbed and the mist river had rolled over them. It had been the only time the little pony had abandoned him, her ears down and her eyes wide in panic as she fled the trench. He made sure neither of them slept there again.

For the past few days they had climbed from the riverbed each night, and had made camp on the raised bank. The Want was full of ghosts. Sometimes when Raif looked up at the misplaced stars, he wondered if he wasn't seeing them as they had once appeared in a different Age.

Whole days had passed when Raif believed the Want was leading him in circles, where every bend of the river and outcropping of rock looked familiar. One morning he had scratched his mark on a flat slab of granite embedded in the river wall, imagining that here was a way to know if he passed this point again. Raif sucked in his breath, half smiling at his own lack of insight. Nothing was that straightforward in the Want. Within an hour he had passed a second slab of granite so similar to the first one that he began to wonder if some man or ghost had purposely erased his mark. Within two hours he began to doubt that he'd actually *made* a mark, imagining that perhaps he had intended to, or dreamt he had but never actually gone ahead with scribing a raven's likeness in the stone.

That was the secret of the Want, Raif had discovered. It made you doubt yourself. It was better not to worry that the river trench was taking you nowhere. Even if that were true there was exactly nothing you could do about it. The Want took you wherever it chose to.

Raif did the things he could: kept the pony's wounds greased and her coat well tended, rationed his food, watched for clean ice that could be melted for water. The rest he could not control.

Even the days themselves were hard to track. Raif thought he had spent perhaps seven nights here, but he could not be certain. The food stash was down to hardtack, dry meat, the last few lardcakes, and the oiled grain for the pony. That seemed as good a gauge of time as anything else here; how much food you ate on the journey.

The earth moved every day, he knew that much. Small tremors that set the river debris bouncing and sent loose stones rolling down the banks. The middle of the trench was the best place to be then. Two days ago there had been a sustained shaking that had opened cracks in the riverbed. Raif had dropped to his knees while rocks crashed from the trench walls and a storm of dust whirled around him. When the dust settled, he saw that boulders the size of haystacks had moved, and the riverbed's crust had split for leagues. *Shatan Maer*, Raif thought with a shiver. *Time grows short.*

Shrugging off his blanket, he rose to his feet. The mist river had passed, and dawn was showing pink on two opposite horizons. He ignored them both and went to rub down the pony.

The cut on her heel looked a little better, drier and scabbed, and she didn't shy when he greased it. She knew the routine now—greasing, brushing, bandaging her hocks, and then a treat—and took it all with stout resignation. Every day Raif sent silent thanks to the outlander for forcing her upon him. She made the journey bearable. They were *two*, not one. And Raif found it frighteningly easy to imagine what would become of one man alone in the Want.

As they broke camp and set back down the slope toward the river trench, Raif decided it was time the pony had a name. He thought for a moment, and then a band of muscle began to tighten slowly around his chest. Every part of his mind held traps and this was one of them. Moose, that was the name of his last horse, given to him by Orwin Shank. Bitty's Da.

Raif dragged a hand across his face, pressing hard against his eyes and teeth. That was the thing with clan; all those connections. You injured one, you injured them all.

What have I turned into? But he knew the answers, they were all in his names. Twelve Kill. Watcher of the Dead. Mor Drakka.

There was nothing to do but carry on down the course of the river, not knowing if he was heading east or west. After a time he rested his hand on the pony's neck, and some time after that it all became bearable again. That was when the pony's name came to him. Bear: with all its connections, just like clan.

It wasn't an especially feminine name, but it suited her, and that's what counted. Raif called her it a few times and she flicked her ears and seemed to take to it. She was walking better now, not resting her injured leg as much. It was a good day for a name.

Bear. Raif breathed in deeply, feeling his lungs push against the last traces of tightness in his chest. He'd always wanted the bear lore, like Drey and Da; now he had the bear horse instead.

Morning passed, or perhaps it didn't. The light changed, turning the sky a shade of blue he'd only ever seen before in deep, algae-covered water. Clouds were in their usual place, around the sun. A day moon showed for a while, and then was snuffed. The problem with walking in a trench was that there was little to look at but the sky. During the day Raif barely caught a glimpse of the headland. Sometimes he saw the needle peaks of basalt spires, or long barrows of mounded rocks. Once he'd seen a fully petrified tree, its main branches all preserved. Mostly, he looked at the river walls.

The trench varied in width and depth, but even at its narrowest point Raif judged it to be a third of a league wide. Its landscape of rock, calcified debris, tumbled stones and frozen earth changed as he walked. Seams of fossils were exposed in some places, revealing the forms of creatures Raif did not know. In other sections he saw where the force of the river had worn hard granite smooth, and elsewhere noticed that softer rock had been broken into sand. At midday he spotted something that made the hairs rise on his neck. Steps, a flight of them cut into the bank. He slowed Bear and they went to investigate.

The steps ended at a point partway down the river terrace, and to reach them they had to climb a wall of trap rock. Bear was sure-footed, but Raif found himself making mistakes and stumbling. This was the first sign of a civilization he had seen since entering the Want. Someone had cut these steps, perhaps so they could wash clothes in the river or bathe. Steps meant a settlement. Close.

As Raif reached the first square-cut ledge, a reflex action

made him check the sky—it was how he'd come to measure the Want, to gauge its temper. All changes in the Great Want were foreshadowed by the sky.

Clouds were on the move, rolling toward him in waves, and the colors in the sky were changing. The Gods Lights had begun to burn.

It was time.

Bear sniffed the step at some length before she put a hoof upon it. Raif knew exactly how she felt. After so many days of walking on rough rock, the hewn stone felt strange beneath his feet. The steps were low but wide, each one about ten paces in length. People could have sat upon them, talking whilst they cooled their feet in the river. Raif tried to imagine what the Old Ones had looked like, but his mind was strangely blank. The Listener had told him so little about them, and Heritas Cant even less. Their Age had long passed, he knew that. In a way, these steps were like the fossils he'd seen earlier: a sign of life lost.

Raif counted thirty-five steps in all, and by the time he reached the seventeenth he could see the peak in the distance. The mountain of rock he'd come for. The one painted on the cave wall in the Rift, and drawn in the book of the Forsworn. The fault most likely to give.

Raif rushed up the last steps to see it better. Its shape, the way the rock was twisted and buckled, as if by some terrible calamity, was just how he'd imagined it would be. Two things surprised him, though. He had not been prepared for its size— its massive, towering bulk. Valleys, ridges, and cliffs circled its base, and dry rivers flowed from its peak. Thousands of feet high and thousands wide: it was a monstrous wasteland of stone.

And he had not expected it to be sheathed in ice. As he and Bear took their first steps on the headland toward it, the wind brought its coldness to them. The temperature dropped, and the scent of dry ice, of glaciers turned gray with age and compression, and of frost smoking off freezing lakes made Raif want to turn back. He had not bargained on this. It was another trick thrown up by the Want.

"Bear," he said. "What are we doing here?"

No more questions you know the answer to, warned Stillborn in his head.

Managing something like a shrug, Raif continued walking.

The land surrounding the mountain was deeply flawed, but it wasn't until he reached higher ground that Raif realized there was a pattern to the canyons, fault lines and dry riverbeds: they radiated outward from the mountain like the spokes of a wheel. The mountain formed the absolute center of devastation, and even as he thought this the earth shuddered.

Bear shied, biting at her reins in fright. Tiny stones jumped around Raif's feet. The mountain shivered, and deep within its folds the ice fields ground and squealed. It was over in a handful of seconds. Disturbed ice crystals floated upward, forming a sparkling mist that ringed the peak. Some drifted on the breeze toward Raif and Bear, landing on their shoulders and backs like a fine snow. When one landed on Raif's lips he put out his tongue and tasted it. Nothing. He couldn't decide if that was good or bad.

The wind was picking up now, gusting back and forth with no consistent direction. Overhead the clouds had rolled in, almost covering the sky. The Gods Lights lit them from behind, sending out red flares that glowed like embers. Inigar Stoop had once said that whenever a sky turned red somewhere a Stone God was bleeding. Raif found he didn't care. *Let them bleed.*

Guiding the pony into a shallow canyon, he set a straight course for the mountain. As they drew closer, he began to doubt himself. The mountain was huge; it would take days just to circle its base. And what was he looking for? A fault line? Hundreds of them cracked the earth here: he and Bear stood in one now. Did it mean they'd have to search every one of them, looking for the deepest? The Rift was the deepest fault in the North, Addie said. But it didn't mean it would be the first to give. So how could he be sure of picking the right one?

Raif glanced up at the mountain. The ice was gray and old, weathered over centuries so that it reflected no light. From here he could see that its surface was brittle and crevassed. Surely he and Bear didn't have to climb it? One misplaced step and they'd be dead.

Nothing seemed certain or right. Raif drew on his gloves, wincing as the goat hide tugged against his wounded knuckles. It was getting colder. He took Bear's blanket from the saddlebag and laid it over her back. Ahead the land began to rise, and he knew it was time to climb out of the canyon before the walls grew too deep and trapped them.

Another tremor shook the earth as they emerged on the raised plain of the mountain. As he braced himself against the rolling motion, Raif thought of what the outlander had said about the Shatan Maer. *One stirs this night—I can feel it.*

Grimly, Raif waited for stillness and marched on. It wasn't long before the ground turned to hard granite beneath them, as the mountain showed its roots. Slowly, they were ascending, and the path began to grow rocky and uneven. Raif scanned the lower slopes, looking for . . . *something.* He didn't know what.

The light held as they climbed, the wind funneling along the fault lines toward the mountain. After a few hours they arrived at its base, and Raif stopped to rest the pony and eat. They split the last lardcake and drank melted ice that tasted faintly of salt. Raif restowed the pack for a heavy climb, choosing to leave the cook pot and the pony's saddle beside a rock. When he was finished he sat on the rock and looked up. Now he was here he wasn't sure what to do next.

We search. What would the Forsworn knights have done

here? Had they known something he didn't? He tried to recall exactly what the dying knight had said. Had he mentioned the Old Ones? A cold thrill prickled the skin on his arms as a memory returned to him.

We search.

For what?

The city of the Old Ones. The Fortress of Grey Ice.

Raif stood. Understanding lay there on the edge of his thoughts. Think. *Think.*

Fortress. One was mentioned in Addie's verse. *Though a fortress may fall and darkness ride through the gate.* Raif frowned. Did it mean that the darkness would emerge in the fortress first? What had the outlander said? *Look to their ruins to guide you to the place they most feared.* The Old Ones had feared the Rift and built a city there. Had they built a city on this mountain as well? If so, there was no sign of it now—just ice and frozen rock.

Raif let out a long breath, his head aching. People *had* lived here, he knew that much. Someone had carved those steps. Yet how could he hope to find a city on the mountain? A search could take weeks, even months. And then there was the danger of the ice . . .

The Fortress of Grey Ice. What did the name mean? Was the fortress *beneath* the ice?

Raif crossed over to the pony and began scratching her ears. The Listener, the knight, Addie, and the outlander had all told him fragments of things, scraps that didn't add up. He wasn't a mage or a wiseman. He wasn't anything any more.

This was all he had, this search, the hope that he might hinder the darkness. It wasn't much, but it was more than Bitty Shank had.

Steeled by that thought, Raif began to walk the length of the slope, watching the mountain and running through everything again in his head. The answer was here; he just had to dig for it.

His breath whitened in the freezing air as the temperature continued to drop. Something about the ice on the mountain bothered him. It had been so unexpected. The Want was arid. Frozen but dry. Surely that much ice would have melted and evaporated over the years? What held it there? A second thrill goose-pimpled his skin as something suddenly occurred to him.

The bridge over the Rift. The Old Ones had created a force spanning the Rift that still held to this day. The outlander had said as much. *Things constructed by their mages live on.* Could the ice itself be a construction? Raif raised his hand to his throat and closed his gloved fingers around the hard piece of raven ivory that was his lore. If the ice *was* a construction, then how to blast it away?

We search.

It seeks.

Raif opened his fist and let his lore drop. Suddenly he knew what he must do.

He walked to the pony and took two things off her back. The Sull bow, and the arrow Divining Rod.

Take this arrow named Divining Rod that has been fletched with the Old Ones' hair, take it and use it to find what you must. It seeks, what I cannot tell you, for the echoes from things so old are weak.

The Listener was right; the echoes *were* weak, but he had finally heard them. Stupidly he had imagined he would need the arrow to slay the thing that came through the breach— even though the Listener had warned him it would be wasted if he used it to kill. Raif stripped off his gloves and ran a hand down the arrowshaft. The workmanship humbled him. The skeleton ferrule that bound the head to the shaft must have taken someone days, even weeks, to forge. Each band of metal had to have been painstakingly fired and hammered, and constant adjustments made for fit. The fletchings, bound and glued in spiral form to make the arrow spin in flight, represented further days of work. Someone had spent as much time and effort making this arrow as it took to make a sword.

And they had named it Divining Rod.

Raif braced the Sull bow and drew the arrow to the plate. As he set his sights on the mountain he let all conscious thoughts fall away. The mountain was a dark form, dead and immense: a tower of icy rock. No heart pumped within it for him to find; it did not matter. The Sull, the Old Ones and Clan stood here. A bow, an arrow, and a man. It was enough. Being here with these things was enough.

Raif picked a target, drew his bow, and waited for the wind.

When the time came he released the string, and the arrow shot from the bow. A sweet humming reached his ears as the arrow began to spin. The Old Ones' hair channeled the wind, using it to propel the arrow high and true to the center of the ice.

He didn't hear the impact. The humming filled his thoughts, pulling at memories and things beyond memories that no clansman should ever have. Suddenly he knew the age of the arrow, and the age of the mountain, and then the age of the earth itself. Seconds passed where knowledge was revealed to him; ancient histories and battles, the pain of birth and loss. He looked into faces that were neither human nor Sull . . . and he found beauty and understanding there. He strained to see more, to know more, but the humming ceased abruptly. A moment of absolute stillness followed, when the wind died and the Gods Lights raged like a fire in sky.

And then the mountain began to move. The ground trembled. Rock sawed against rock. Snow so ancient and dry it had become a substance beyond ice shook free from the highest slopes. As the first cold glitters landed in Raif's hair, the ice itself began to crack. Like lightning, a flaw flashed into existence and forked into many more. The fissures split and split again, until the entire face of the mountain was a web of darkly glowing flaws. Raif had long lost sight of his arrow, but he knew it was there, in the heart of the ice, still spinning, drilling deep, destroying all it touched. He felt no wonder, only a sense of a task completed. He and Bear had come here; now there was one less thing for them to do.

The crack of sundered worlds split the air. Raif's eardrums pulsed, and he felt a sharp, sickening pain. His grip tightened on the bow as the ice face shattered and began sliding toward the earth.

The pale ghost of a city emerged from the chaos. Massive slabs of ice fell away like rotting tiles, revealing rock shaped by a living hand. Vast bulwarks of gray granite were hewn from the mountain wall, rising as sheer as any cliff to support the fortress that stood above.

Kahl Barranon—he knew its name now. The City of the Old Ones. A Fortress of Grey Ice.

Raif's breath cooled in his lungs. Almost he could taste the rock the fortress was built on. It was cold and raw and bitter as the winter itself. The ice face might have fallen away but another kind of ice lived beneath. Spires of gray quartz reached for the sky, slender and transparent as icicles. Great halls lay below them, their high arching roofs clad in frost-colored lead. And below them lay the curtain wall, where quartz fused with granite to form the ramparts. Everything shone gray and silver, and Raif imagined that if a city could be carved from the heart of a glacier then it would look much like the Fortress of Grey Ice.

What did they fear? Raif wondered, and then: *How could the race who built this be lost?*

He had no answers. He wasn't sure he wanted them.

Calling softly to the pony, Raif began the climb. He'd already seen a path.

FORTY-SEVEN

A Bolt-Hole

At sundown the Dog Lord gave up his watch. Glen Carvo had not arrived back. Not today. As Vaylo turned Dog Horse on the great northern graze of Dhoone, he kept his jaw and shoulders high. Behind him stood a small company of men, and he could not let them know his fear. Cluff Drybannock, his fostered son and the best longswordsman in the clanholds, had not returned with his hundred and eighty men.

"Back to Dhoone!" Vaylo hailed his company, kicking a starting gallop from his old, ornery stallion. "First man to the Horns wins a keg of Dhooneshine!"

Vaylo heard them whoop and holler as he left them in the dust. Gods! But it was good to run! The wind in his face, the black soil of Dhoone beneath his horse's hooves, and the sky as clear as a lake above him: What chief could want for more? At full gallop Dog Horse gave just about the worst ride a man could endure, but that troubled Vaylo not at all. It was a *winning* gallop, that's what counted.

Behind him, he heard his company gaining, as men bent low over the horses' necks and hooves dug divots from the turf. They were shouting back and forth to each other, goading their comrades on with good humor and placing their own bets. Hammie Faa waged one of his mother's highly dubious love potions against Nevel Drango's city-embroidered smallclothes.

Vaylo listened and felt joy. In a way, being here in the Dhoonehold with only forty warriors at his command was like being young again, at Bludd. It was few against many, and to hell with the odds. Oddo Bull felt it, too. He was the only one of the forty who had ridden with Vaylo that day, nearly thirty-six years ago now, when he'd stolen the Dhoonestone from Dhoone. Oddo knew what it was to ride in a small company and love every man within it like a brother. Armies were good for many things, but you could not know the strengths and weaknesses of every warrior, and you could not be brother to them all.

Hearing someone gaining on him, Vaylo swerved into the rider's path and beat some more speed from Dog Horse. He would win this race, dammit. He might be old and a fool, but he could still outride anyone in the clan.

Nearing the northern wall of the roundhouse, Vaylo cut west, knowing the others would take the easier eastern path. The west way had jumps—ditches and dog cotes and water pumps—but it was shorter. The others would have to ride clear of the stable block. Dog Horse hadn't jumped in a while and was nasty about it, but was too proud an animal to refuse. He battered Vaylo's bones . . . but he jumped.

By the time they rounded the final quarter of the round-house and caught sight of the Horns, Vaylo was aching in all the places a man hated most to ache. He could barely breathe, either, but the Horns were his. Reaching them an instant before Nevel Drango, he laughed at the sheer bloody-minded exhila-ration of it all. Once he started, everyone joined in, and soon there were eight men at the gate, all sitting tenderly in their saddles and laughing like fools.

Nan Culldayis brought them to order. "Clansmen," she said, striding toward them. "Much though I hate to break up your sewing circle, Samlo's waiting to seal the gate."

They sobered after that. It was full dark now and the moon hadn't risen. Blue Dhoone Lake was black, and the wind made it slap against the shore. "Who watches this night?" Vaylo asked Nevel Drango.

Nevel commanded the twenty swordsmen Cluff Drybannock had stationed at the Dhoonehouse. He had some of the wild blood of Clan Gray in him, and he fought with an executioner's blade. Nevel named seven men, and Vaylo nodded. "Put one on the roof."

It has come to this, Vaylo thought as he dismounted. Forty men were not enough to secure a roundhouse, let alone an entire hold. None could be spared for border patrols. All must be at the house.

Resting an arm around Nan's waist, he walked inside. When a girl came to take away his riding cloak, he bade her send a keg of Dhooneshine to those at the gate. He doubted they would drink it, but that wasn't really the point.

Nan had supper waiting for him in the chief's chamber, and they sat by the hearth and shared a simple meal of bread and melted cheese. Afterwards, Nan blew out the candles and came to him by the fire. She knew he was worried—he could not hide such things from her—and laid kisses on his neck and temples as she gently kneaded his shoulders. Her long, silky braid tickled him where it brushed against his arm, and he pulled out its ties and worked the hair loose with his fingers. She laughed then, a gently throaty laugh that he had come to love. When he kissed her she tasted of honey, and her need was the same as his own. It was a blessing, this love come so late, and Vaylo thanked the Stone Gods every day for it.

Later, when they were finished, Nan sat up and combed her

hair and Vaylo watched her, content. She was beautiful in the firelight, proud and serene, her hair falling down to her buttocks.

The alarm sounded as he was pulling on the last of his clothes. Two great blasts of the warhorn. *Dudaaaa! Dudaaaa!* Vaylo fastened his swordbelt around him and looked to Nan. "Get the bairns. Bring them here and bar the door. Open to no one but me."

She nodded. He loved that she showed no fear.

They'd said all they needed to by the fire, and Vaylo left her knowing she would take good care of herself and his grandchildren. It was enough to settle his mind.

Dudaaaa! Dudaaaa! The horn sounded again as he rushed toward the gate. Hammie and Samlo Faa, Odda Bull, Nevel Drango and others were already gathered in the entrance hall, strapping on their armor and weapons chains. Vaylo beckoned a boy to fasten his back and chest plates about him as he drew on armored gloves with leather palms. Already he could hear them.

Dun Dhoone! Dun Dhoone! DUN DHOONE!

"How many?" he asked a spearman running down from the East Horn.

"Hundreds. They're swarming around the lake."

"I've three men out there," Nevel Drango said. "And one on the roof."

Vaylo nodded, grim. They could not raise the gate. "They gave us warning," he said.

An explosion rocked the gate. An eerie white light flashed in the hall and then was gone. Hellfire. Vaylo hadn't seen it used in forty years. Naphtha, lead and antimony: it burned hot and long, and only sand could snuff it. He turned to Samlo. "Will the gate hold?"

Samlo was a Faa man: he didn't know how to lie. "I can't say, chief. It's armored. It'll take more than fire to break it."

Vaylo looked to the spearmen and bowmen. "To me." He took the stairs to the East Horn three at a time, his heart drumming against his plate.

At five storeys high the Horns were the tallest structures in the clanhold. The East Horn boasted archers' roosts and lookout slits, and Vaylo commanded his warriors to man them and fire at will. Taking the topmost embrasure for himself, he put an eye to the slit and looked out upon the army massing on the northern shore of Blue Dhoone Lake.

Dun Dhoone! Dun Dhoone! DUN DHOONE!

Hundreds of Dhoonesmen and Castlemen, war-dressed and mounted, were forming themselves at the gate. Their mantles rose in the wind, and the torches they held trailed white flames. A war drum was leading the chant, and as Vaylo looked on a standard was raised: the Bloody Blue Thistle of Dhoone. Vaylo searched for a leader, but could not discern any particular warrior to whom the others deferred. That worried him. The Dhoonehouse was huge and sprawling and he did not know all its ways. Quickly, he gauged their numbers, and then made his way back to the entrance hall.

Another explosion rocked the gate as he took the last stair. The sharp stench of smelted lead made his eyes burn. "Oddo. Where are the weaknesses?"

Oddo Bull stood ready by the gate, his red hammer chained and in his hand. On the Dog Lord's orders he had taken count of the Dhoonehouse's defenses and if anyone amongst them knew this place it was him. "Stables and kitchens. Both have doors leading in. I've sent crews to cover them."

Vaylo nodded. He didn't want to ask the next question, and he breathed deep for a second or two to put the moment off. "Did the grooms have time to pull in the horses?"

Oddo Bull shook his head.

Dog Horse. "Did they bar the doors?"

"Aye."

Vaylo left it at that. They both knew the external stable doors were great flimsy wooden things that wouldn't withstand an assault. Horses were brought into the roundhouse's fold during a strike, and all stables abandoned as indefensible. You needed adequate warning for such a strategy, and without manpower to watch your borders you were undone. Vaylo ran a hand through his braids. *It is my failing.*

Out loud he said, "I won't have them burn the horses, Oddo."

"Aye, chief." Oddo understood what this meant; they had to unseal the internal door and bring them inside.

Vaylo accepted his war hammer from the same boy who'd fastened his plate. "Fetch the dogs," he bade him. "They're in the kitchen chained to the hearth. Bring them to me at the stable door." Vaylo looked at the boy a moment. No more than eleven or twelve, he was wearing a motley of unmatched armored pieces and carrying a kitchen knife as a weapon. "What's your name, lad?"

"Brandin."

"Here," the Dog Lord said, pulling his four-foot longsword free from its hound's-tail scabbard. "Take this for the journey."

The boy hesitated, his eyes wide.

Vaylo glowered at him; sometimes it was better to scare the young ones. "It's a swap, lad. I take the knife, you take the sword. Now quick about it."

For some reason the idea of a swap made sense to the boy, and he came forward and took the sword. His mouth fell open as he inspected the patterned steel edge.

"Go," Vaylo commanded him, claiming the kitchen knife.

The boy ran. He knew how to hold a sword; that was something.

Vaylo turned to the company of men in the hall. "Oddo. Nevel. You're with me."

As they made their way to the stable run, a great thud sounded from behind. Vaylo and Oddo exchanged a glance: the Dhoones were ramming the gate. Vaylo quickened the pace.

The eastern quarter of the roundhouse was little used and poorly lit. Leagues of tunnels were accessed by ramps, not stairs. *Probably for the horses*, Vaylo concluded. The place felt like a tomb. He didn't like the way his footsteps echoed. There was too much empty space here. And not enough men.

Seven swordsmen stood watch by the stable door; more of Cluff Drybannock's twenty by the look of them. Their faces were tense, their weapons drawn. Vaylo felt for them. Waiting was always worse than fighting. It gave a man's fear time to come to the boil.

The door linking the roundhouse to the stables was tall and strangely shaped, narrow with a bulb-shaped top like a keyhole. Three iron bars guarded it, held in place by iron cuplets bolted into the stone walls. Vaylo motioned toward the door with his head. "Any word?" he asked the swordsmen.

"Banging a few minutes back," one of them replied.

"We've been smelling smoke a while," said another.

Vaylo looked long and carefully at his men. Ten here, including himself. Eight swordsmen and two hammermen. By rights he shouldn't be even *considering* opening this door. But being Clan Bludd meant something. It had to, and perhaps he'd forgotten that these pasts few months, sitting as cozy as a king at Dhoone. Perhaps he'd thought too much and done too little, and perhaps Pengo was right: he should have moved to raise an army before now.

Taking a deep breath to steady himself, the Dog Lord made his decision. "Unbar the door. We're going in to fetch the horses."

Every one of them, from the oldest—Oddo Bull—to the youngest, a slip of a swordsman not much older than seventeen, nodded without hesitation. Vaylo felt the pain and beauty of it deep inside his heart. As Nevel Drango drew back the bars, Vaylo spoke the boast. *"We are Clan Bludd, chosen by the Stone Gods to guard their borders. Death is our companion. A hard life long lived is our reward."*

"Bludd! Bludd! BLUDD!" the nine shouted in response, raising their weapons. And then the door was opened and the chaos began.

Air was sucked through the door with such force that Vaylo felt it lift his braids. All was darkness. Black smoke churned in noxious clouds, making it impossible to see. A few safe-lamps were lit, glowing yellow like cats' eyes, doing nothing to illuminate the murk. Vaylo took a breath, his lungs filling with hot foulness. Acid tears sprang to his eyes.

The horses were screaming, kicking at their boxes, mad with fear. Wood splintered with a deafening crack as one of them broke free. Vaylo moved forward with his men, his sense of resignation growing. The horses would not come into the house in such a state. Their terror was too great. These were Bludd horses: None had passed through the internal door before. They did not know it, and when a horse was panicked it needed the comfort of things it knew.

Vaylo squinted into the darkness, trying to discover the source of the smoke. He couldn't see any flames, and decided that either the roof or the front of the double doors was afire. Possibly both.

"Unbolt the boxes," he ordered, keeping his position close to the door. The younger ones had better eyes than him, and that was a fact he could do nothing about. "Give the horses plenty of space. Stay close to the walls."

The sharp retorts of swiftly drawn bolts followed, like the firing of quarrels. Men coughed and hacked. Horses sprang out, bucking and rearing, blinded by fear and black smoke. One swordsman screamed as a panicked horse kicked out at him.

Vaylo damned Dhoone. They had turned the stables into a hot, choking hell.

"Nevel. Oddo," he commanded, the moment the bolts ceased firing. "To the double doors, one a side. Everyone else, behind me."

Madness, that's what this was. *Then I am mad and my clan is mad . . .* and that seemed just about right. As seven swordsmen formed up at the internal door behind him, Vaylo gave the word for Nevel and Oddo to lift away the bar on the great double stable doors of Dhoone.

Wind howled through the stables as the two Bludd warriors set the doors in motion. Smoke funneled around itself, forming a vortex that was sucked through the opening. Flames sprang to life, spilling along the edges of the doors, dripping onto the hay-strewn floor and shooting out fountains of sparks. As Oddo and Nevel ran back, the horses of Clan Bludd charged through the double doors. In the crush of horses, Vaylo made out the hard black form of Dog Horse, his head low and his ears pinned back: he'd trample some Dhoonesmen along the way. When Oddo and Nevel were behind him, Vaylo called the retreat. The horses were on their own now. Stone Gods save their souls.

Almost they made it to the internal door before the first Dhoonesmen rode in. Five there were, with the thornhelms turning their heads into grotesque shapes and the blue axes of Dhoone in their grips. Vaylo set his three-stone hammer in motion, and stepped forward to meet them.

"BLUDD!"

Horse blood sprayed in Vaylo's face as his hammer blasted into the first Dhoonesman's mount, making contact deep in its chest. The horse reared and fell back, and the Dhoonesman lost his saddle and was unseated. Vaylo whipped his hammer back, circled it once to gain momentum, and then sent it flying into the Dhoonesman's guarded face. The thornhelm crumpled inward, and the man fell to his knees, vomit spewing from the helmet's mouth hole. Vaylo swung his hammer back into motion and picked another target. His men were fanning out around him, forming a protective wedge around the door. The advantage was theirs, Vaylo realized, at least until the Dhoonesmen's eyes grew accustomed to the dimness and the smoke.

At his left Oddo Bull was matching his hammer against a Dhoonesman's sickle-bladed ax. No weapon could match the hammer for strength, but it had a short reach and needed space to be properly swung. The Dhoonesman knew this, and was forcing Oddo back. Vaylo was torn between aiding Oddo and saving himself from a newly arrived Dhoonesman bearing a longsword of blue steel. Swinging his hammer above his head, Vaylo loosened his grip on the hammer loop and let the weapon fly. It smashed into the longswordsman's chest with the force of a battering ram, sending the man flying backward in the saddle. As he fell into the line of Dhoonesmen behind him, Vaylo took the kitchen knife from his belt.

"To the door!" he screamed, springing toward the axman engaging Oddo. Sometimes a small knife was best, he thought, as he rammed the blade into the axman's kneecap. "Oddo. Back," he commanded, as he yanked the knife free of bone. Ahead of him the seventeen-year-old had fallen, his shoulder cleaved off by another blue ax. Vaylo shuddered, stepped back.

Seeing his chief no longer had his warhammer, Nevel Drango stepped forward to cover him on the retreat. Nevel's sword was an ugly bastard, no doubt about it. Black and curved, with six separate fullers running like plowlines down the blade. It had one purpose—chopping off heads—and Vaylo saw the Dhoonesmen shy away from meeting it. Covered, Vaylo risked a backward glance at the door. All but he and Nevel were through.

"On my word, Nevel," he cried, his voice hoarse. "*Now!*"

They stepped backward together in a strange sort of dance. An ax was loosed and *chunk*ed into the door frame. Nevel swept his executioner's sword in a half circle as Vaylo edged toward the opening. Shooting out a hand, Vaylo grabbed Nevel's gear-belt and dragged the swordsman through the door.

Then, mercifully, the door was closed, six men throwing their weight against it as the bolts were shot. It would not hold. Vaylo knew it would not hold, but it would give them precious minutes to rally and reform.

Turning to his men, he wiped the film of sweat and blood from his face. Two of them were gone; forever lost on the other side of the door. Oddo had taken an ax slice to the side of his jaw, and his earlobe was hanging off. Another man's face was deathly pale, and Vaylo looked down to see the man's fist digging into a hole in his armor. Blood pooled around his fingers. Sweet Gods, he'd taken a longsword to the gut. Vaylo put his arm out for him, and the man came to him. "You're a brave lad," Vaylo said as he drove the kitchen knife through the man's armor and into his heart.

The six remaining warriors stood in silence, their breath coming hard, sweat dripping from their chins and noses. They knew all about the different ways to die, knew that wounds to the gut were amongst the worst of them.

There was no time to think or grieve. The assault on the stable door had begun.

Vaylo glanced around. Surely there was some way to seal this section off? A wooden door standing between you and your enemies didn't rank highly on anyone's list of defenses. He noticed he was pressing the flat of his hand against his chest, and stopped himself. Some pain there. Probably indigestion. Even before he could decide the next course of action, a cry came from west of him.

"Dhoonesmen in the roundhouse!"

The Dog Lord looked to his men. This night was turning from one kind of hell into another. He could ask no man to stay here and guard this door—it was certain death for little reward—but it turned out he didn't have to. Oddo Bull and a small, fair-haired swordsman stepped forward.

Vaylo suddenly felt old and damned, but he could not let them know it. In silence, he clasped both men's arms. Oddo Bull wished him a life long lived, but Vaylo could not say it back to him. Their fingers held for a moment. Vaylo found his voice. "Tell the bastards we sunk their guidestone."

Oddo smiled. It was enough, it had to be.

Vaylo turned and made his way west through the round-house, a crew of four swordsmen flanking him.

The main gate still held but fighting was under way in the entrance hall. Hammie Faa ran to meet them. A door in the kitchen had been breached. Dhoonesmen were forcing their way in by the dozen. Bluddsmen were dead. Samlo was dead, Vaylo could see that for himself. Hammie's younger, bigger brother lay in a bloody pool by the stairs to the East Horn.

"He stopped a Dhoonesman from raising the gate," Hammie said.

"He was a strong fighter," Vaylo murmured, touching his pouch of powdered guidestone. "Just like his father before him."

Hammie's shoulders began to shake. Vaylo vowed then to kill his second son. Pengo would die for this; it was as simple as that.

"Hammie," he commanded. "You're with me. Nevel. Lead the crew to the kitchen, see if it can be sealed. Protect the women. You know what to do if it comes to it."

Nevel Drango nodded: Kill the women rather than let the Dhoonesmen despoil them first and kill them later at their leisure. "Chief."

The word was a farewell. Vaylo knew in his heart he would never see Nevel or the other three men again. *We have been routed.* Vaylo put his arm around Hammie's shoulder, and headed north to the chief's chamber.

They met only one invader along the way; a Castleman who looked like he didn't know where he was going or where he'd come from. Hammie was armed with a nine-foot spear, and saw him off with a vicious blow to the lower gut. The spearhead smelled of shit when Hammie yanked it free.

Vaylo pounded on the chief's door when they reached it. "Nan! Let me in."

Nan Culldayis opened the door, holding a two-foot maiden's helper in her hand. It made Vaylo proud to see it.

"Nan. Get the bairns. Quick now."

She moved swiftly, asking no questions of him. Tension lines drawn in her forehead made her look older than her forty-eight years, but to Vaylo she had never seemed more beautiful. She would have killed herself and his grandchildren rather than let the Dhoonesmen have their way with them. *This* was a woman worth loving.

The two bairns clung to her skirts, and Vaylo crouched down for a moment to talk to them. "We must all be quiet and swift. Like foxes. Can you do that, for your old Granda? Be quiet and swift?"

Pasha nodded, pale and frightened. The youngest made no reply.

Vaylo had no time for more. He stood. "Hammie. You're in the lead. I'll bring up the rear."

"Where we going, chief?"

It was a good question. "To the Tomb of the Dhoone Princes."

Hammie accepted this as if it were perfectly sane and logical; Vaylo loved him for that. "Lead on."

The entrance to the tomb lay further north of them, in the great barrel-vaulted guidehouse. It was a short walk, but Vaylo knew luck wasn't with him this night. When two helmed Dhoonesmen appeared on the path in front of him, blocking the entrance to the guidehouse, he couldn't say he was surprised.

"Bludd Lord," came a voice through the thornhelm. "All your men lie dead and dying. I'd say it was time you yielded this house."

Vaylo scanned the man's weapons and battle dress. Fisher fur, a fine blued longsword, plate bossed with copper: it was the Thorn King himself, Robbie Dun Dhoone.

"Yes," Robbie said, reading the knowledge on Vaylo's face. "The king has returned."

Vaylo heard something then that quickened his blood and gave him hope. "Hammie," he murmured. "Forward on my say." To Nan he sent a look that said, *Easy*. To the Dhoone King, he said, "You got my name wrong, Robbie Dun Dhoone, I'm not the Bludd Lord, I'm the *Dog* Lord."

And then his dogs rushed in. "Nan! To the tomb," Vaylo screamed, as five hounds, part wolf, part dog, streaked past him in a single body of bunched snouts, bared teeth and flattened ears to get at the men who threatened their master. Straightaway they brought the Dhoone King's companion to ground, one bitch springing as high as the man's neck, sinking her teeth into his carotid arteries, whilst another fastened its mighty jaw around his ankle. Robbie Dun Dhoone stepped away, his expression hidden by the thornhelm, his blue sword sweeping in a protective circle around him.

Hammie rushed up to him, pinning him at a distance with his nine-foot spear whilst Nan, Vaylo and the grandchildren moved through. Hammie and the dogs held the Dhoone King there while Vaylo rushed into the guidehouse and pulled on the great iron ring attached to the flagstone that formed the entrance to the tomb.

Cold, still air rose to meet him as the flagstone fell back. "Down!" he commanded Nan and the bairns. "Hammie. To me!"

Two of the dogs were tearing the Dhoone King's companion limb from limb, and the other three were snapping at the king's heels, feinting and snarling, their eyes shrunken to dots. Hammie lowered his spear and ran for the tunnel. Vaylo heaved the great flagstone on its end, so the face with the ring was now facing down, lowered himself into place, and then called for his dogs. The dogs, hearing a tone in their master's voice they had never heard before, obeyed instantly, breaking contact and hurling themselves toward the tomb. Vaylo felt their dog heat as they passed him.

Grabbing hold of the ring, he heaved the flagstone back into place, plunging them all into darkness. "Hammie. Your spear." Vaylo could hear the Dhoone King rushing forward, his feet pounding against the stone. Feeling his way in the blackness, Vaylo thrust Hammie's spear through the ring, securing the entrance. It would hold for now—it was awkward enough to lift a sunken flag of stone without a handle, let alone one that was jammed in place with a spear—but it would not hold for long.

For a period of perhaps six seconds, Vaylo did nothing but sit on the step and breathe. He was worn out. Now that his eyes had grown accustomed to the darkness he could see moonlight spilling in ahead. The tunnel passed under the roundhouse's walls, leading north to the tomb, and blocks of quartz in the ceiling let in light.

"Come on," he said, his voice weary. "Down we go to pay our respects to the dead kings."

Everyone, including the dogs, rose at once. Vaylo felt Nan's hand gently touch his arm. He had to push it away. His grief was too raw.

The dogs understood what his lady did not, and followed him at a careful distance, their tails down. The wolf dog whimpered softly. Little Ewan began to sob. Vaylo had no comfort to give, not yet, and led the way to the tomb in silence.

The Tomb of the Dhoone Princes was much as he remembered it: stale and haunted by memories of past glories. The standing tombs glowed pale in the moonlight, sentinels guarding the underworld. Vaylo shivered, and realized quite suddenly he was terribly cold.

"Hammie. Nan. Pasha. Ewan," he addressed his small party. "If we're ever to get out of here we have to think. Last time I was here the ranger Angus Lok told me there was a tunnel leading north from this very chamber. Said it was so old that even Dhoone had forgotten it. Right now that tunnel's our only hope. So what I need all of you to do is push, prod, knock and shove every bit of stone in this place to find the opening mechanism." It sounded insane even as he said it, but all four of them accepted it calmly and began to spread out around the tomb.

Vaylo frowned for a minute, trying to recall the little rhyme Angus Lok had said. How did it go now? *In the Tomb of the Dhoone Princes there be, a Bolthole for those who canna look nor see.*

Everyone turned to look at him. "Is that the clue, Granda?" Pasha whispered excitedly.

"Aye. It's the clue," he told her, not wanting to disappoint. The rhyme said as good as nothing, and the black thoughts circling his mind settled into place. First Ewan, then Pasha, Hammie, Nan, and then himself. The order seemed important, and he asked the Stone Gods for the courage to see it through. The Dhoone King had talked of yielding, but Vaylo had seen the truth of it in the pale blue eyes beneath the thornhelm. Robbie Dun Dhoone was not a man to be held to his word.

And time was running out.

"Granda! Why does this man have no eyes?" came Ewan's high voice. The boy was too young to be afraid of death and all its trappings, and was swinging from the effigy of the Dark King, Burnie Dhoone.

Vaylo shrugged. "The masons never got around to it."

Pasha was kneeling by one of the fallen tombs. Coming to her feet, she said matter-of-factly, "That means he canna look nor see."

Vaylo felt the gooseflesh prickle along his arms. Quick glances to Nan and Hammie told him they'd both felt it too. *From the mouths of babes . . .*

All three of them walked toward the stone likeness of Burnie Dhoone. Pasha joined them, smug as could be. "It has to be the eyes, Granda. That's why the masons never finished them." With that she hiked up onto Burnie Dhoone's feet, and pressed both fingers into the rough globes of stone that were his eyes.

Something deep inside the chamber rumbled. Damp, fetid air wafted in as an entire section of wall swung inward. The dogs shrank back on their haunches, frightened. Ewan ran across to the opening, delighted. Pasha stepped down from Burnie Dhoone's feet and said, "Well, I think we'd better hurry, then."

Vaylo stared at the opening on the opposite wall. It was black and lifeless, entirely unwelcoming, but to him it looked like hope.

Calling his dogs about him, Vaylo led the way north out of Dhoone.

FORTY-EIGHT

The Stand At Floating Bridge

"Here," Ark Veinsplitter said to Ash. "This is the last ice-spur of winter." The Sull Far Rider handed her a delicate white flower as large as her fist. The petals shimmered with silver veins, and in the center its feather-like anthers glowed deep, midnight blue. "You crush them," Ark explained. "And they will give you their scent."

Ash pressed the anthers between her fingers, smelled nothing at first and then a moment later the scent of winter—fresh snow, cinnamon, evergreens, apples, and woodsmoke: all of them rendered sweeter, fairer—possessed her completely. It made her remember things: falling in the snow as a child, so thickly wrapped up that she could not right herself; getting tipsy on mulled cider with Katia, both of them hiccuping and feeling a bit sick; running across the Quad, eager to see the Winter Candles that were lit each year in the great circular dancing hall in the Bight. Ash breathed deeply. She hadn't thought about those candles for years.

Ark was watching her carefully, his dark brown eyes searching her own. "This Sull believes that sometimes when you look back you may see things you have missed."

Ash nodded slowly, her understanding growing. He was right. She *had* missed things. Her life at Mask Fortress had been terrible in many ways, but there had been moments of real joy, silliness, anticipation—times when she had lived the carefree existence of a child. The ice-spur had showed them to her.

"You are daughter to us now," Ark said. "You have nothing to fear from the past."

Ash looked down at the flower, unable to hold his gaze. How did he know so much about her?

"The Daughters of the Sull wear ice-spurs in their hair when they ride into battle." He thought for a moment. "Also when they choose a mate. Sometimes this confuses the Sons."

Ash grinned, feeling big tears well up in her eyes.

"Eventually the Sons learn, though. We know much about our Daughters' hearts."

Tears plinked into the snow.

"Come. We must ride long hours this day."

Ash looked up as the Far Rider moved away. "Thank you," she murmured. "For the flower."

He bowed in acknowledgment and went to tend to his horse. Ash watched him crouch down by the gray's forelegs and rub grease into the hooves. The bandage that she had wrapped around his hand only an hour earlier was already spotted with dark blood. Fixing the ice-spur in her hair, Ash went to help him break camp.

They were in the Trenchlands now, a day's ride east of the Bludd border, camped in a dense forest of towering trees. Five-hundred-year old cedars circled the clearing, giant trees with drooping branches, their needles blue as smoke. Somewhere close by, water was splashing over rocks, and the raucous calls of ravens at a kill disturbed the quiet. Yesterday they had ridden through a tract of burned forest that had taken them from noon to sundown to cross. Once or twice Ash had spied log cabins and hide tents raised at the edge of the burn-line. She had smelled smoke and heard dogs bark, but had seen no men. Ark Veinsplitter and Mal Naysayer had set a hard pace, choosing to ride through the burned forests to save time. They had no love of the Trenchlanders, and would ride on swiftly whenever they encountered signs of settlement. The Naysayer had not hunted in two days, and contented himself with bringing down ice hares and rabbits from the saddle with his bola. It seemed there was no weapon invented he could not use.

The weather had held so far, but glancing up at the sky as she headed for the stream, Ash thought they might not be so lucky today. White clouds meant snow. It was just the right temperature for it, too—cold, but not icy.

She shivered as she passed through the cedars. The stream followed the course of the land, falling in tiers as the forest floor dropped into a hollow. Pine needles had dammed it in places, sending water sheeting wide over rocks. The water tasted of resin. Ash cupped it to her face and scrubbed. As she rubbed it from her eyes she spied a movement between the trees on the far bank. Ever since the night in the Deadwoods Ash carried her sickle and chain with her at all times, and she pulled it from the squirrel-fur pouch she had fashioned for it. Light was dim amongst the cedars. "Who goes there?" she challenged, settling the sickle's weight in her hand.

A tree rustled, and a figure sprinted away, heading deep into the forest. Trenchlander.

Ash found she had to sit down for a minute, her legs shaking. The sickle glinted, its wickedly hooked blade looking starkly alien when set upon a mat of cedar needles. The Trenchlander had been afraid—of *her*. She didn't know what to make of that. After a time she decided it was good. Very good. Nodding to herself, she filled the water-skins and headed back to the camp.

"I saw a Trenchlander," she said to the Naysayer as she dumped the heavy skins at his feet. "I scared him off."

The Naysayer raised an eyebrow; Ash had never seen him do that before. "A settlement stands close."

"Is that why you were away this morning, scouting it?" It seemed the confidence had gone to her head, for she'd never had the nerve to question the Naysayer's movements before. The Naysayer did whatever he chose to, and not even his *hass* forestalled him.

"Nay, Ash March. This Sull scouted no Trenchland settlement this day." His ice-blue eyes regarded her levelly, but there was no invitation for further questions in them.

Ash nodded in response to what he didn't need to say. Some things she could not question. Not yet. Determined to take no offense, she went to brush and pack her horse.

Snow began falling as she strapped the last of the saddlebags in place. Whilst she'd been gathering tent canvas and poles, the two Sull Far Riders had walked off to the far edge of the clearing. They spoke quietly at some length, and Ash couldn't stop herself from glancing at them from time to time. At some point the Naysayer brought a package from his furs, something wrapped in faded red silk. Ark stripped off the bandage from around his hand, and held out his wounded wrist toward the Naysayer. The Naysayer unwrapped the silk and took out a small bulb-shaped container. He unstoppered it, and then poured a few drops of its contents straight into Ark's wound. Ark stiffened, grasping his forearm. His lips whitened as he held a grimace, and then slowly regained their color as he relaxed. Mal rested one of his huge ice-tanned hands on his *hass*'s shoulder for a moment, and then went into the trees to open a vein. Ash knew that was his intention: she saw him reach for his silver letting knife before the cedars hid him.

Suddenly cold, Ash thrust her hands into her lynx fur.

Medicine. The Naysayer had gone off this morning in search of medicine for his *hass*.

She had a bad feeling about the day after that. Once the snow had begun it grew rapidly thicker. No wind stirred, and the flakes fell heavy and straight as Ash and the Far Riders left the clearing. Visibility was poor. The path between the cedars was narrow and twisting, and icy boughs slapped against Ash's legs. The Naysayer did not ride ahead as usual, taking instead the lead on the blue. No one spoke. The breadth of the Naysayer's back as he sat his saddle seemed as wide as two men to Ash.

At midday they halted briefly to feed and water the horses. The forested ridge they stood upon looked down over the valley they would cross later that day. Leaving her horse to its snuffle-bag, Ash hiked to the edge to take a look. A vast river flowed below, its surface the color of rust. Spring thaw had caused it to burst its banks, and its waters had spilled over into the surrounding forests and fields, creating leagues of shallow lakes. Above it stood a city the likes of which Ash had never seen before. It was made of timber and mud. Squat, unlovely log cabins, shanties and lean-tos were crowded upon a hump above the river, clinging to it like barnacles on a rock. An entire section of the city looked to be nothing more than felt-and-skin tents, and Ash could see that the river had already begun swallowing up some of them. Roofs and animal hides floated like rafts nearby.

"Hell's Town," Ark said, coming to stand beside her. "It is the time of the flood. All the trenches are filled."

She risked a quick glance at him. The Far Rider's skin looked pale and dry. "This is the Easterly Flow?"

He nodded. "It swells. Many rivers drain into it."

"*Kith Masaeri.*"

Ark seemed pleased that she had remembered its Sull name. "The River of Many Ways, that is what we named it."

Ash felt stupidly glad to have pleased him. Scanning the bloated length of the river, she asked, "How do we cross it?"

"The Floating Bridge."

Something in his voice made her turn toward him.

"Once we cross it we are home."

Ash thought of the Naysayer's hand resting upon Ark's shoulders, and suddenly she wanted to do the same. Just rest her hand there for a while. But she didn't. She heard the longing and weariness in his voice, brought her hand up to touch him and then let it drop. She'd lost her nerve.

"Let us go," Ark said. "If we make good time we will arrive at the bridge before dark."

They didn't make good time. The snow turned slushy in the river valley, and the ground underfoot became a bog of freezing mud. The Naysayer chose a path that lead them west of Hell's Town, but even so they soon began passing people on the road. Filthy children and tired-looking women gave the Sull Far Riders a wide berth, often stepping off the path while they rode past. One man abandoned his cart in the middle of the road, and only returned to reclaim it once the Far Riders had passed by. Ark and Mal seemed indifferent to the stir they caused, and rode with their heads high, looking straight ahead. Ash wished she could have done the same. She felt the Trenchlanders' gazes upon her, and found herself flicking her hair back and making unnecessary adjustments to the reins. Did she look like Sull to them? Or did they know her for the impostor she was?

It was a question she couldn't answer. She saw heads turn to track her silver-blond hair and appraise the golden richness of her lynx fur, but she couldn't tell what they were thinking.

As the day wore on they passed Trenchlander settlements set amongst the trees: muddy villages of log cabins wreathed in woodsmoke, surrounded by barrels for the curing of hides. They even passed an inn. But the Far Riders did not halt. Ash felt their anxiousness, their desire to be upon land they named wholly their own.

By sunset they had still not reached the river. It grew dark early amid the tall trees, and the road began to empty. The snow became firmer underfoot as the temperature dropped, and it showed no sign of getting any warmer. Ash huddled in her furs, watching her breath whiten as she exhaled. The smell of cedar and woodsmoke made her drowsy, and she found herself slumping forward in the saddle. She'd just fallen into a sleepy daze when she heard a wolf howl. Blinking, she turned her head and listened. Nothing. Probably a dream.

It was an effort to keep her eyes open. The road was passing through thick forest now, the trees forming a wall around the road. Stars were out, and there was a faint red tinge to the sky. Gods Lights. When the road made a sharp turn, Ash saw the glimmering waters of the river ahead of her . . . and then heard the wolf howl again.

Straightaway she snapped awake. It was a wolf—she had heard them often enough on Mount Slain—but it was something other as well. Cold tingles passed up her spine, making her shoulders jerk. Another call came, this one pitched higher. Wolves. And they were Unmade.

"Ark!" she cried, and he turned in the saddle to look at her. "They have come."

"To the bridge!" he called, falling into place behind her, waiting for her to start galloping before doing so himself. "*To the bridge!*"

Ash's mount sprang to life beneath her, and suddenly cold air and snowflakes were rushing into her face. Cedars shivered as she passed, dropping their loads of snow. All she could hear was the drumming of hooves and the beat of her own heart. Ahead, Mal Naysayer led the way to the bridge. Ash saw the river draw closer, saw the ripples of currents on the surface, and then she saw Floating Bridge.

Sull have made this, she knew with absolute certainty. It had to be made of wood, but it was blue and lustrous, and it came from no tree she knew. The fixed span at the shoreline swept down toward the surface in a series of reducing arches, while the movable spans floated like a ribbon of silver on the water, buoyed by pontoons shaped like great whales. The entire bridge seemed to breathe, rising and falling with the river's swells. It was beautiful, but Ash didn't see how it could save them from the Unmade.

The howls were becoming louder, hungrier. Ash could hear the saliva snorting in the wolves' throats as they breathed. She fell low in the saddle, digging her heels into the packhorse's ribs. A mad desire to know seized her: she turned her head— and saw three wolves transformed into nightmares break from the trees.

Gasping, she faced ahead, knowing she had lost a crucial beat of speed by the simple act of turning. Directly behind her, the tent poles rattled in their casings, and the saddlebags squeaked and sawed as they bounced against the horse's rump. It occurred to her that Ark and the Naysayer should be pulling ahead—the two Sull stallions could not be matched for speed at full gallop—but they were keeping pace with her.

If we are pursued, pull the strap. How could she have forgotten?

Tugging her fingers from the reins took an effort; they just didn't want to let go. The cold had made them numb, and when she thrust her hand along the horse's belly she couldn't feel a thing. Where was it? She found the trace and slid her fingers along it, working more by pressure than touch. There. Something sticking out. Grabbing onto it, she pulled down hard. A series of snaps sounded, like the cracking of whips, and then everything fell away except the horse's saddle and harness.

Ash heard tent poles and cook pots tumble onto the road behind her, heard Ark's stallion jumping them so lightly he never lost his pace.

Her own horse suddenly found new speed and sprinted forward, passing Mal's blue. The Floating Bridge was so close now she could see the spillway in its center. Kicking her mount frantically, Ash headed straight for it.

The two Sull Far Riders had stopped keeping pace with her, she realized as she reached the boarded ramp at the shore. Turning in the saddle, she called to Ark.

"*Go on!*" he cried. Behind him she could see a wolf shape closing distance, see the fluid ripple of shadowflesh as muscles bunched and unbunched around its neck. Its eyes burned red like coals, and its teeth were black ivory set in wholly black gums. Howling eerily high, it sprang upon Ark's horse.

The Sull stallion reared its back legs, trying to buck the wolf off its rump, but the creature's fangs had sunk deep and its jaw was locked. Ark Veinsplitter drew his sword. Meteor steel slid into shadowflesh with the sizzle of hot metal entering cold water. The wolf's jaw sprang open and, just like the packhorse's saddlebags, the beast fell away.

Ash breathed, realized she hadn't done that in minutes. Her horse had led her onto the fixed span of the bridge and was now trotting forward. Hollow wood rang out beneath its hooves. Ash could feel river breezes working her skin. More wolves were breaking from the trees. Two. Three. Five. *Oh god.*

"*GO ON!*" screamed Ark, motioning at the bridge with his sword. The gray's rump was washed in blood, but it held its head high and showed no fear.

The Naysayer gained the ramp to the bridge, drew his mighty six-foot sword, and turned to face the Unmade.

Feeling a fluid buoyancy beneath her, Ash realized she had passed onto the floating span of the bridge. She reined in her horse and reached within her furs for her sickle blade. She'd run long enough. It was time for this Daughter of the Sull to make a stand.

She quested for the flame, sucking air between her teeth as if somehow that would ignite it. Quite suddenly it was there. Tiny as a baby's tooth. But there. Sliding from her horse's back Ash March searched for a wolf to kill.

A battle was raging at the ramp. Mal Naysayer stood there like the gatekeeper to hell, a fearsome sword in constant motion in his hands. As Ash stepped forward, Ark rode past Mal and onto the bridge. A thrill of fear made her shiver as he reined in his horse and dismounted. Ark and the Naysayer weren't like her: they didn't need to dismount to wield their weapons. Perhaps in time *she* wouldn't need to . . . but she hadn't learned that lesson yet. Suddenly Ark crouched down by the edge of the fixed span, his hands reaching for something. Had he dropped his sword? No. It was there, laid across his knees.

Ash took the chain in her hands and began to spin the weight. She could not count the wolves now, and still more were tearing from the trees. They bayed and howled, snapping at Mal Naysayer with breathtaking speed. As he plunged his sword into one creature's chest, another streaked past him and onto the bridge. Ash thought, *This one will do*. The chain and its weight were *thrumm*ing over her head, moving so quickly nothing but the green halo scribed by the peridots could be seen.

Her wolf was leaping toward Ark's throat. Ash saw the flame, blue and cool. *I cannot miss here*. Adjusting the chain's torque, she waited a tiny fraction of a second, and then released it. The chain flew forward, reeling through her fist like a fishing line, and snaked around the throat of the wolf. Ash yanked with all her might, heaving back and out, and whipped the Unmade creature into the water. As it crashed through the surface, she twisted sideways with her wrist, unreeling the chain to reclaim it. The weight shot back toward her like an arrow, and she lost the flame for a moment when she thought it was going to hit her. A hasty bit of sidestepping was called for.

When Ash recovered her footing, she saw Ark Veinsplitter watching her, his eyes shining. "Daughter," he said. "You make this Sull proud."

She wished with all her might she had laid her hand on his shoulder then . . . for she never got the chance to do so again. Not in this world.

Ark had something in his hand, something he had pulled from the board of the bridge. A lynchpin, long and large, and even as Ash realized what it was she began to float away from him. Ark Veinsplitter had set the Floating Bridge adrift.

There was a moment when she might have jumped the distance between them. That was something she would hold with her for the rest of her life. That moment, its passing. And then the distance was too great and the swift black water opened up between them, and Ark Veinsplitter rose to fight. His *hass* battled alone, and he must join him.

If there was a nightmare so terrible as watching the people you love battle for their lives, unable to help them, Ash March never heard of it. She had to watch, it was the only currency she had to pay with: watch and bear witness to the Stand at Floating Bridge. The night was long and the battle dread, and when it was over no wolves and only one man was left standing. And still the horrors weren't done, for the Naysayer knelt by his *hass* and took him in his arms and screamed terrible words to his gods. When his anger was gone he kissed Ark's eyes and took a knife to Ark's throat and performed *Dras Morthu*.

The Last Cut.

Ark Veinsplitter went to the Far Shores that night. Ash March knew this because she watched his soul depart.

FORTY-NINE

The Gates To Hell

The fortress glowed red beneath the Gods Lights, like something built from frozen blood. Raif led Bear toward it, feeling a strange sense of calm. It should have been dark in the Want by now, yet light persisted. The clouds had withdrawn and the sky was clear, and the stars turning within it were clustered into giant constellations shaped like wolves. Raif did not know these stars; he wasn't even sure what world he was walking on any more.

Ahead lay the curtain wall, rising sheer from the mountain's face. It towered before them, casting a shadow so absolutely black that it looked like a hole in the earth. The path leading toward it had been hewn from live rock, the granite expertly finished to be smooth yet still provide traction for travelers. A series of tiered steps raised the path every hundred paces or so. The climb was not difficult, but Raif took it slowly. He was in no hurry to reach the fortress. The light would hold, he was sure of that. Light did whatever it chose to in this place.

Massive plates of ice lay strewn across the valleys like wreckage from a hurricane. One piece was as big as a roundhouse, and it took them minutes to pass it. Chunks of granite were suspended in the ice like flies in amber. Raif was glad he had enough water with him to last a day or two. The last thing he wanted to do was melt and drink this ice.

As they rounded a curve in the path Raif saw the gates to the city. Rising as tall as ten men and wrought from silvered iron, they commanded a break in the curtain wall. Iron dragons stood rampant to either side of them like sentinels, protecting the entrance to the city with hooked talons and razor jaws. *The Gates to Hell.*

Raif shivered, looked back. The mist had risen along with him, and he could no longer see the path leading down. The Want was playing tricks, reminding him that he could not leave the way he had come in. Shaking his head gently, he continued on. He had to think of Bitty, that was the thing. Even this kind of life was better than no life at all.

Bear grew uncharacteristically reluctant the nearer they drew to the gates, slowing her pace and then tugging against the reins. Raif halted to look at her. The little dun pony lowered her head, and regarded him with wariness. It was time to go on alone. They were passing through a field of smashed ice and granite boulders, and he led her a little way off the path to where an outcropping of rock offered some protection from the wind. Pouring out a portion of oiled grain on the rock face, he told her not to worry. He'd be back to fetch her in a while.

It was hard to leave her there. Not wanting to see her disappear into the mist, he did not look back.

The curtain wall stretched ahead of him, a rampart of unscalable stone studded with deadly reefs of quartz. Nothing moved upon it. This city was dead. Drawing the Forsworn sword from its sheath, Raif headed for the gates.

The earth shook as he approached them, a single violent rolling motion that made the iron posts grind together with a piercing squeal. Something deep within the city smashed with the force of an explosion. Raif flinched. As he waited for silence to fall again, he glanced down at his sword. It seemed too small a thing to protect him here. The Gods Lights burned green as he put his hand on the gate within the gate. The smaller gate was inset into the larger one, mimicking its dragon design precisely. It wasn't secured in any way, and swung back when Raif pushed it. It didn't even creak.

Raif swallowed, his earlier calmness gone. If he had been Sull he would have opened a vein before entering this place. If he had been clan he'd have drawn a guide circle and called upon the Stone Gods. He didn't know what a Maimed Man would have done, so he did nothing at all. Holding his sword in one hand and his raven lore in the other, Raif Sevrance entered the Fortress of Grey Ice.

It smelled of Ages long past and glaciers, and it was like no other place Raif had ever seen. It looked spun from molten glass. Translucent spires, hundreds of them, reached skyward, no two the exact same height. Bridges as delicate as ropes of pearls spanned the summits, creating a spider's web of passageways and stairs. Lower down, arched and domed roofs capped vast, windowless halls, and lower still the mountain thrust its bedrock through the ground in vast primitive humps that formed the base of all buildings. It was as if the city had been savagely fused onto the face of the mountain.

Raif found himself in the gateyard, a vast circular space paved with flagstones of darkly glimmering schist. Mountain rock broke through in places, forming graceless saddles of stone. Raif's footsteps echoed sharply, and some caution he didn't understand made him place his feet with care. The Forsworn sword felt heavy and lifeless, and he couldn't find its balance. Looking ahead he saw many paths he could take; stairways and arches, doorways and passages. Choosing one at random, he headed inward.

The light was shifting, favoring blue and gray tones, and dimming slightly. Raif watched his shadow circle his body and then come to rest behind him. Nothing seemed fixed here. His sword's weight felt in flux, and the tones of his footfalls lengthened and shortened. Who had lived here? It didn't merely feel abandoned, it felt . . . lost. He walked past an empty arena circled with stone benches that showed no wear. A fountain hewn from speckled limestone held no water, nor did it have any moss stains around its bowl. What had the Listener said? This was the final fortress built by the Old Ones. They might have built it but they couldn't have lived here. Not long.

Raif picked a building to enter, a great hall with arched columns of stone. A floor tiled in black and white marble stretched away across empty space. The walls were bare except for one, at the opposite end of the hall, that had been painted. He walked over to inspect it. It was a rendering of the mountain and the surrounding landscape done in miniature. Water flowed through the river, and green plains stretched wide in all directions. Raif couldn't see the fortress depicted on the mountain, so he leaned in for a closer look. Then froze. The artist had pained a vast gap in the mountain, right at the point where the fortress now stood. And something was coming out of it.

Raif turned away. The outlander had been right: the Old Ones had built this fortress out of fear, fusing it to the mountain's core as if by doing so they could seal the gap. Perhaps they had sealed it . . . but all seals were meant to be broken.

As Raif moved to leave, the entire building shuddered. The floor warped, sending mortar dust spewing upward. Raif ran. A stone headpiece from the ceiling fell as he passed beneath it, crashing onto the tile right behind him. This city had been preserved in sorcerer's ice for thousand of years, and now it was ready to come down.

Raif ran until he was winded, not caring what route he took. His lungs felt itchy with dust, and no amount of coughing could clean them. Crouching on his haunches he caught his breath.

One of the quartz spires must have fallen here, for the ground was littered with shards of crystal. Looking up, he decided he needed to be somewhere else. He didn't fancy being impaled if another spire went. It was time to find the center of the city. He was done with looking around.

A wide avenue led him past open arcades and a series of lead-domed buildings. The stonework was becoming more ornate, mounted with relief-work dragons and other, stranger beasts. Stone columns had been shaped into tightly coiled serpents' tails and likenesses of creatures changing from one form into another. Raif felt the temperature dropping. The fortress was in continual motion now, swaying and jittering. His sword, which had seemed heavy ever since he passed through the gate, suddenly felt too light.

When he came to a circular building, intricately wrought with statues set deep into stone niches, he knew he'd found the heart of the fortress. The statues were half shadow, half man: they were in process of being unmade.

Raif took a breath, waited to see if his body would stop shaking. It didn't. For some reason he thought of Addie Gunn as he entered the temple. *We can be more.*

The *shifting* in things that had begun outside was accelerated in this place. The air was unstill, blooming patches of darkness like blood dropped in water. Raif's sword became fluid in his hands, its weight running from one end to another as he lifted it. And something else was stirring, something he had no name for. He went to take a step and as he took it, it felt sharply familiar, as if the step had already been taken. *Time*, he supposed. *Time is stirring.*

The temple had no windows, yet some kind of light drifted in. The circular walls were fused onto a crater of mountain rock. The violence of their binding could be read in the scorch lines that blazed along the join. Great force had come to bear here. Someone had wanted to make sure nothing got out. A central altar dominated the space, and Raif moved slowly toward it. He could already see the dark space beneath the capstone and knew it could be lifted off.

The altar was hewn from black quartz threaded with gold, and touching it was like touching ice. Raif felt his skin cleave to it, felt the chill of it travel inward to his heart. He waited for the moment to lift as he had waited for the wind to rise before loosing Divining Rod. Just as wind shifted on the mountain, weight shifted in this place. When he felt his sword lighten he set it down, positioned both hands on the lower edge of the capstone and pushed up with all his might. The stone cracked in two as it slid to the floor. Raif heard himself make a sound, something halfway between a laugh and a sob. No going back now.

There never had been.

A narrow flight of steps led down through the altar and Raif picked up his sword and descended. He could smell the inside of the mountain now, the iron and sulfur and dampness. As he reached the final steps the earth began to shake once more. A low and terrible howling sounded. Raif's fingers tightened around the hilt of his sword. The chamber before him was rolling like a ship in uncalm seas. Patches of darkness deepened, holes within the black. A shadow form came into view, faded.

Raif felt his mouth go dry. *Shatan Maer*, the outlander had named it. The most powerful creature that had ever lived. Strange how you could be told something, listen to what was said, and still not hear it. But wasn't that exactly what the outlander had counted on? Who would come here with full knowledge of what was to be found? No one. One glimpse, and it was enough to know all. One sword wasn't enough. One man wasn't enough. The outlander should have sent an army . . . but the outlander didn't have an army to send.

So he'd sent a fool instead.

Raif found he was baring his teeth, like a wolf. The madness was there below him, just another hole in the black. *Kill an army for me, Raif Sevrance.* Wasn't that exactly what he was doing—one Hailsman at a time?

He laughed then, bitterly, as he imagined his life stretching on. More deaths. More friends betrayed. Three people in this world he loved, yet he'd never get to see them again. *Drey. Effie. Ash.* What good was life without those you loved? It was a shadow, and perhaps the outlander had seen this in him, and had sent one shadow to battle another.

Raif took the final step into the chamber, and immediately felt as if he'd taken it seconds earlier. All things were in flux here. The chamber itself was strangely ill-defined, its walls fluid. Part of the floor was tiled in intricate mosaics depicting beasts changing into other beasts, dragons becoming shadows, and serpents lapsing into unseeing, but most was bare rock. This was where the fortress ended and the mountain began, and as Raif moved across the floor he heard the ring of unspeakable hollowness beneath him. The mountain had been cleaved in two here. Raif Sevrance now stood upon the fault most likely to give.

The patches of darkness were quickening. Something dread thrashed in the shadows, howled and then faded away. The chamber was a blur of movement and shifting time now, the floor buckling like wet wood. Dimly, Raif was aware of great crashing sounds filtering down from above as the spires of the fortress fell.

Taking a two-handed grip on the Forsworn sword, he began to chant.

> *"Though walls may crumble and earth may break*
> *He will forsake."*

The Shatan Maer rippled into existence, held, and then melted to black. Deep within the mountain, rock began to tear.

> *"Though night may fall and shadows rise*
> *He will be wise."*

Time echoed the word *wise* back to Raif. A crack opened up in the floor, and the smell of another world came through it. All the shadows and patches of blackness in the chamber began to coalesce on a single point.

> *"Though seals may shatter and evil grow*
> *He will draw his bow."*

The crack widened and Raif felt the cold breezes of hell. The single point of darkness was swelling, shaping itself into a portal. The Shatan Maer stood behind it, thrashing and flailing, a monstrous beast beating against its chains. *Imagine your worst nightmare, then reckon it tenfold.* Who would have thought a cragsman would be so good with words? Teeth bared, Raif moved into position.

> *"Though a fortress may fall and darkness ride through*
> *the gate*
> *He will lie in wait."*

A violent wrench shook the chamber. Something integral to the nature of time and being snapped, and in that instant Raif saw things that no man should ever see. A hundredfold of nightmares, a thousand lifetimes' worth of horrors: all moving forward, *pushing* to get out. And riding amongst them were the nine horsemen. The Endlords on their black stallions, their swords forged from an absence of all things, the substance of souls ground to hold an edge. They felt Raif's attention upon them, and turned slowly to meet his gaze. Their eyes were holes leading to a place beyond hell, and they pulled their lips back and smiled at him.

Soon, they promised. *Soon.*

In that instant the Shatan Maer stepped through the breach. A monster from another Age, born in shadow form. Raif adjusted his sword, searched the black void of the creature's body for some semblance of a heart . . . and found one. An immense primitive pump that moved the shadowblood around its body, keeping it Unmade. Raif felt its powerful suction pull him in, and fought against it. He could not afford to lose himself in this muscular blackness. It was the second gate to hell, lying in wait.

> "And when the Demon emerges and all hopes depart
> He must take its heart."

Raif lunged forward, touched shadowflesh with the point of his sword, heard it *hiss*. A deep roar sounded. The Shatan Maer moved. Raif did not see the blow that felled him. He lost time. Blinking awake he saw a faint shadow of himself being felled. He reached for his sword. *Where was the sword?* As his hand scrambled over rocks, searching desperately, the Shatan Maer turned toward him. Its eyes were forked with black veins, and they were filled with hateful yearning. Raif pushed himself back with his heels. Suddenly he wanted very much to live.

As he regained his feet, he saw another faint glimmering of himself finding the sword, and just as his glimmer self raised it, the Shatan Maer fell upon him. Raif saw his own death there, saw his leg torn off like a twig. He grinned insanely. At least he knew where his sword was now.

Probably not a good time to fetch it, either. He still had the Sull bow and some arrows on his back and he slid them off as he walked backwards, away from the Shatan Maer. For some reason the sight of the bow agitated the creature and it sprang straight forward. Raif rolled back, cracked his head on a rock. Rolled back, cracked his head on a rock again. Time was splitting. As he came to his feet he drew the bow, released the string. The arrow bounced off the monster's thick, flaking hide.

The Shatan Maer howled in rage. Raif caught sight of his sword, waited a beat to see if time was warping around it. No shadow selves claimed it and were killed. That was good. As he lunged toward it, the Shatan Maer struck. Raif felt claws puncture his jaw and rake down his neck. Blood filled his mouth. The terrible cold odor of the monster filled his nostrils, like a small taste of death. Before he could move, another blow struck. His head snapped back, and he swallowed his own blood. Time spooled, showing him many outcomes—too many to track. The Shatan Maer struck again. Raif scrambled back, felt icy claws pierce deep into the meat of his shoulder. Pain bloomed, but he was too confused to translate it properly and he thought it felt pleasantly hot.

The sword was his. The last blow had propelled him toward it, and as the Shatan Maer sprang forward for its final strike his hand closed around the hilt.

The heart was his.

"*For Bitty!*" Raif screamed, as he drove the sword up through the Shatan Maer's ribcage to the heart.

Nooooooooooo . . .

Deep down, in the place where worlds met, creatures howled. An Endlord rode up to the shrinking portal and laughed without making a sound. A rushing noise filled the chamber as the darkness was sucked out. The portal collapsed into nothing, leaving only a memory scorched in thin air.

Raif lost time. Shadow selves piled on top of him, slowly sinking in. The Shatan Maer lay collapsed across his chest, and

Raif didn't know if he possessed the strength to move it. Each time he exhaled, the weight of the beast robbed a fraction more space from his lungs. Shadowblood soaked into his shirt, burning like acid. All things considered, he felt pretty good.

We can be more, Addie had said, and Addie had been right. Pity he wasn't here right now; he could have helped lift this great monstrosity off Raif's chest.

More time lost. He really needed to get going now. Experimentally, he tried shifting his weight to the side. Straightaway, things began hurting that hadn't hurt before. Grimacing, he made an effort. Sometimes the pain was worth it. The pain meant you were alive, and right now that seemed precious to him.

With a mighty heave, Raif rolled the Shatan Maer off his chest.

It was time to fetch Bear, and find himself a better sort of life.

Outside the sun was shining, of course. You had to give it to the Want: it had no end of tricks. Bear came running up to greet Raif as he reached the gate, and together they headed east. Or was it south? With the Want you could never be sure.

EPILOGUE

A Trail of Flowers

Angus Lok stopped off at the Three Villages to purchase some spring flowers. He knew it was a fool thing to do, what with Darra having a whole garden's worth of flowers at her disposal, but he felt in a courting mood. The sun was high and it might even have been a bit warm—it was difficult to tell with all his layers on. Lambs were in the fields, and the sight of them darting under their mothers' fleecy skirts as he cantered past on the bay made him smile. *We were all so young and frightened once.*

His smile vanished when he thought of Darra and the girls alone for the lambing. They were good girls, hard-working, but lambing was a man's job. Too many things could go wrong, and though he knew for a certainty his wife was a more able person than he would ever be, he wished he could spare her the distress of it. He wished a lot of things recently, none of them for himself.

The little market held every tenday in the village square was winding down as he approached. All the sorry-looking vegetables were left: green beans with black spots, loose cabbage heads, and some remarkably slimy leeks. Anyone venturing into the Ewe's Feet for a noonday meal had a good chance of seeing those leeks again. The vegetables concerned might even be able to walk there on their own.

Spying a young girl holding a big basket of snowdrops and sweet peas, Angus reined in his horse and hailed her. "How much?" he asked her as she came running toward him.

"A copper a bunch."

"No. For the lot."

Her eyes widened. Angus guessed she was younger than Cassy but a bit older than Beth. A pretty lass. But not as pretty as his girls. His request had sent her into a confusion of risky mental calculations and uncertainty, so he solved it by handing her a gold piece. "Tie the basket to the saddle bags with some fancy ribbon and we'll call it done."

She had the sense not to argue. Her hands, he noticed, were rough and callused, the skin toughened by farm work. "What's your name?" he asked when she'd finished securing the basket.

"Bronnie."

"Split the gold piece before you go home, Bronnie," he told her. "Take half home to your Da, and buy yourself some fancies with the rest. No one but me and you need ever know the price you got for the basket." He rode away, knowing from the worry in her face that she wouldn't do it.

Shrugging gently, Angus kicked the bay into motion. Home. He could smell it, he was quite sure of that. Smell rabbit in Darra's cook pot, and some sticky honey monstrosity cooked up by Beth on the hearth. Gods, but you knew a man was a fool and in love when he ate his women's burned cooking!

He couldn't get there soon enough. Caution demanded that he work his way around the oldgrowths and the stream, but caution could go to the nine spiraling hells. He'd been cautious for too long. It was time to get to his family by the quickest, shortest route.

Some of the flowers were lost in the gallop and he grinned,

imagining the trail he left. Some poor fool might follow it, believing there must be a princess at the end of such a scattering of blooms. He'd get an ugly middle-aged bordeman instead. Angus slapped his thigh. He hoped there wouldn't be kissing.

His grin fell a bit as he left the main path and took the little horse-trail that led to the Lok farm. No smoke. Darra must be cleaning out the hearth. A shiver of anxiety passed down through his shoulders into his spine. This trail hadn't been walked on for months. The grass was thick and untrodden. And the apple trees in the east orchard—they hadn't been cut back since before winter. Darra usually tended them like babies.

Angus Lok's mouth went dry.

As the trail wound around a low mound of blackberry bushes, he caught his first sight of the house. Burned. The walls were black and the roof had partially collapsed. Even before the horror of it hit him, there was a part of his brain that took in the details. This had not been recently done. There was no odor of char in the air, and the blackening on the walls had been crazily streaked by many rains.

"They got away," he said out loud, hardly knowing that he did it. "They must have got away."

But he'd been a member of the Phage too long to fool himself with false hope. For twenty years he'd been trained for the worst.

And now it was finally here.

The Sull horse knew, he *knew*, and he slowed to let his rider dismount. Angus's feet touched earth, and he made a bargain with his gods. "Take me now," he murmured. "Bring them back and take me instead."

The gods didn't answer. The gods were dead.

Angus took a breath to steady himself, and then walked into his house.